Chapter 1

The sun was high in the sky now and dust. From our vantage point on the out on the plain below could be se⟨ dust were being kicked up all a⟩ legionaries, which stood as a rock, against which waves of horse archers unleashed swarms of arrows against the leather-clad Roman shields. The Roman legion, now immobile and alone, was slowly being ground down, ground down on the rock-hard earth of Mesopotamia. We had caught them early, just before dawn, my father's bodyguard smashing into their auxiliary cavalry at the head of a thousand cataphracts. The lightly armed enemy cavalry had been swept aside with ease, as the heavy spears of our fully armoured horsemen impaled their targets, cutting through wooden shields and mail shirts to skewer enemy riders. Within minutes dozens were dead and the rest were fleeing across the plain.

The Roman legionaries, their officers screaming orders, had formed an all-round defensive formation after their cavalry had disappeared, the front ranks kneeling and locking their shields before them while those behind also knelt and hoisted their shields above their heads. The legion thus formed a giant hollow square, edged with red as five thousand shields were locked outwards to face us.

As our heavy cavalry finished off the remnants of the Roman horsemen with their swords in a series of violent but brief mêlées, our horse archers took up position on all four sides of the legion, constantly lapping round the enemy and pouring volley after volley into their densely packed ranks. Our arrows, fired from powerful Scythian bows, made of layers of wood, sinew and bone, pierced their shields and armour to slice into flesh and bone. Gradually, as the time passed, dead legionaries could be seen along all four sides of the square. The dead were left where they fell, their place immediately taken by a new legionnaire. The wounded were dragged back into the relative safety of the square, to be placed under wagons or makeshift shelters roofed with canvas. But all the time the hail of arrows was taking a steady toll of the defenders. The Romans had only one defence against our horse archers: to maintain their discipline and cohesion long enough in the hope that they would run out of arrows.

Like the rest of our army, the horse archers were organised into thousand-man units called dragons, each one commanded by a general. Each dragon was further divided into hundred-man companies for ease of command in battle. The dragons had their own six-foot square banners, upon which were emblazoned boars, eagles, lions, tigers, gazelles, and elephants. Mythical beasts such as the Simurgh, a kindly creature with the head of a dog and the body of a peacock, and fire-breathing dragons could also be seen.

The horse archers would approach the enemy at a slow trot, always being careful to remain out of range of the Romans' own arrows and javelins. This was not hard, as our bows had a range of at least five hundred feet, whereas Roman bows were effective at under half that distance. Then the horsemen would move into a canter, stringing their bows with arrows as they approached the enemy, before breaking into a gallop as they got within firing range. Then they would suddenly wheel left or right, loosing their arrows as their mounts guided them away from the enemy line. The most proficient archer would be able to string and loose a second arrow as his horse retraced its steps back to our own lines, the man twisting round in the saddle and almost firing over the horse's hind quarters.

'This lot are professionals; it's going to be a long day.' Bozan pulled another chunk of bread from the loaf he was holding and stuffed it into his mouth as he stared intently at the scene being played out below. Squat, barrel chested and crop-haired, he had been my father's second-in-command for over twenty years, and my tutor for the last ten. I stood next to him under the large sunshade that had been erected by our servants on the hill, but he was not speaking to me. His words were directed at my father, King Varaz of Hatra, who was watching the battle with as keen an interest.

My father waved forward one of his officers. 'Pass a message on to the dragon commanders that they are to conserve their men's arrows.'

The man saluted. 'Yes, majesty.'

My father turned to Bozan. 'The camels should be here soon, and then we can turn up the pressure. I want this over before nightfall, otherwise they'll get away.'

'That's why they're standing still,' replied Bozan. 'Trading casualties for time. Clever bastards, these Romans. What do you think, Pacorus?'

Pride swelled up inside me. Bozan, who had taken part in countless battles, was asking my advice. I decided that now was not the time for timidity. 'We should attack with the cataphracts immediately. Smash straight through them. Show them no mercy.'

Bozan threw back his head and roared with laughter, while my father eyed me, frowned and shook his head slightly. As I felt my cheeks burn as I blushed, I shot glances left and right towards the officers of my father's bodyguard standing nearby – all attired in scale armour made from overlapping plates of bronze sewn onto an undergarment of leather. Several were smiling, though not in mockery, at least I hoped not, but at my youthful enthusiasm.

'That should get us all killed, sure enough.' Bozan strode past me and patted me on the shoulder. 'Come on. Let's get something to eat.'

My father took my arm as we walked towards the long table that was being prepared with meats, bread, fruits and flagons of wine.

'We must be sure that the enemy has been sufficiently weakened before we send in our heavy cavalry, otherwise the result will be a lot of Parthian dead for nothing.'

'But father,' I said, 'surely they have been weakened enough? We have been pelting them with arrows for nearly two hours now; and under this sun they must be tired and ready to run.'

We sat down at the table, my father in the middle flanked by Bozan and myself. He held up his silver goblet, which was filled with wine by a servant. He took a sip and ran his fingers over the gleaming vessel.

'The Romans are among the finest soldiers in the world. It takes them about five years to train a legion, and the end result is five thousand men who can march all day, fight a battle at the end of it and then build a wood and earth stockade before they lay down their heads to sleep. Every man knows his place, what his duty is, and how to die if necessary.' He paused as the rumble of battle filled the air. 'Their drills are bloodless battles and their battles are bloody drills. We had one piece of luck when we surprised and routed their light cavalry, but that's the only luck we'll have. From now on we'll have to use better tactics against the best tacticians on earth. So we wait.'

I was chafing at the bit though, eager to prove myself in the cauldron of combat. All my life had been in preparation for this day, when I could prove myself in battle. Here I was, with my father facing the Parthian Empire's greatest enemy, the Romans. My father had brought three thousand horse archers and a thousand cataphracts to this place; a barren, arid stretch of land thirty miles from the city of Zeugma. It was a professional standing army paid for by the wealth of the Kingdom of Hatra, my home, the land between the Tigris and Euphrates rivers. In times of emergency the army's ranks could be swelled by thousands more horsemen raised from the kingdom's lords and landowners and their servants who paid homage to my father, their king, but this meant nothing to me.

All knew that he had, for the first time, brought me on campaign with him, for only one purpose: to fight beside him. But today all I had done was stand around like a servant boy. I had been elated when he had brought me with him on this campaign, which came about when we received intelligence that a Roman legion was marching from Syria to the city of Zeugma. We always paid spies to give us information about what was happening beyond our kingdom's borders, which often turned out to be money wasted. But this time the intelligence was correct, and we were waiting for the Romans when they marched though Hatran territory on their way to Zeugma.

How I envied my mentor, Bozan, the man who had taught me to fight with a sword, to wield a lance from horseback, and to command heavy cavalry. The large scar he had down his right cheek was, to me, a mark of honour, the badge of a warrior, and I wanted one. I had no appetite for the sumptuous meal that was laid before me.

As my mind mulled over the possibilities of what might happen, I hardly noticed an officer race up to where my father sat, kneel and convey a message. At once my father stood and addressed his officers seated at the table. 'Gentlemen, the camels have arrived. It is time to put these Romans to the test.'

As one the officers stood, saluted and scattered to join their commands. Bozan turned to me. 'You'd better get your armour on; you will have need of it.'

Where before there had been calm and polite conversation, suddenly there was bustle and excitement as companies of cataphracts began to form up. I was nervous, but tried not to let it show. Bozan, ever vigilant, recognised the change in me.

He slapped me on the shoulder. 'Go and get your horse ready. The two hundred camels have finally got here, each carrying dozens of fresh arrows. I reckon it'll take about an hour to get them distributed, another to soften up the Romans, and then your father will launch his heavies, so you've got plenty of time. Report to me when you're mounted up.'

In the next valley to where the battle was taking place, hundreds of horsemen were preparing their mounts and equipment. Each man was carefully checking his horse's armour and saddle straps, before moving on to his personal weapons and armour. Servants fussed round, helping when instructed, but it was a Parthian tradition that each soldier checked his own equipment. No one placed his life in the hands of another. As I checked my horse over, Bozan's words, drilled into me countless times, filled my head.

'Never trust anyone else with your own life. In some armies slaves or servants prepare a man's arms and armour, but not in Parthia and certainly not in Hatra's army. Would you trust someone who might despise you, might wish you dead, with sharpening your sword or saddling your horse? When preparing to fight do even the most menial things yourself, so in battle you can think about killing the enemy and not worrying if your saddle straps are tight enough, or have been cut through by a resentful servant.'

My horse, a white mare of six summers, was called Sura, meaning 'strong'. She nuzzled her head in my chest as I strapped on the reins and bridle. Then came the saddle, built around a wooden frame with four horns, two at the front and two at the back, each wrapped with bronze plates and padded, they and the rest of the saddle covered in leather. The horns held the rider firmly in place once mounted. I checked Sura's horseshoes, before covering her head and body with armour. The latter comprised rawhide covered with small, overlapping steel scales, and was able to withstand powerful blows. Even her eyes were protected by small steel grills, although these did limit her vision somewhat.

Each cataphract had two squires to pack his equipment and tend to his horse, but the royal bodyguard was more lavishly provided for. My weapons and armour had been laid on a wooden table beside the temporary canvas and wood stable that had been erected for Sura. To one side stood a rack holding twelve-foot lances, each one tipped with a long, iron blade.

I picked up my suit of scale armour and put it on. The hide was covered with square-shaped segments of steel, which covered my chest, back, shoulders, arms and the front of my thighs. It was heavy and I began to sweat, though whether from the heat and armour or from fear I did not know. I picked up my helmet and examined it. It was steel with cheek and neck guards and a single strand of steel that covered the nose. A long white plume, worn by all of my father's heavy cavalry, tipped it.

'Prince Pacorus.'

Startled, I turned to see Vistaspa standing before me. Tall, slim, with cold, dark eyes, the commander of my father's bodyguard expressed no emotion as he examined my appearance. He had yet to don his armour, being dressed in a simple white silk tunic with loose-fitting leggings.

'Lord Vistaspa,' I answered.

'So, your first battle. Let us hope that all the time and effort invested in your military education has not been wasted.'

I sensed a slight note of disdain in his voice. I confess I had very little affection for Vistaspa, finding him cool and aloof at the best of times. This coolness served him well in battle, and twenty years ago he had saved my father's life in a battle with the Armenians. Vistaspa had been a prince in his own land then, in a city called Silvan on the Armenian border, but the Armenians had destroyed the city and killed his family when his father, the king, had entered into an alliance with Parthia. My father had been part of the army sent to strengthen Silvan's forces, but had ended up being worsted in battle, along with the Silvan host. So Vistaspa had come to Hatra, a man without a home or a family. His dedication to my father had been rewarded by him being made commander of my father's bodyguard – five hundred of the best warriors in the army. My father adored the man, at fifty being five years his senior, and would not have a word said against him. In response, Vistaspa gave unqualified loyalty to my father. But it was like the adoration of a vicious dog towards his master. Everyone else was viewed with suspicion. Whereas Bozan was feared by his enemies but loved by his friends, Vistaspa was feared, or at the very least disliked, by all. I doubted he had any friends, which also seemed to suit him. This made him all the more cold and remote in my eyes.

He walked past me and grabbed my sword in its scabbard. He drew the blade and cut the air with it. It was a beautiful, double-edged weapon, with an elaborate cross-guard and a silver pommel fashioned into a horse's head.

'I hope to do my father honour.'

Vistaspa cut the air again with the blade. 'Mmm,' he placed the sword back into its scabbard and passed it to me. 'A fine sword. Hopefully, it will taste some Roman blood today.'

With that he nodded his head curtly and strode away.

An hour later I was in full armour sitting on Sura, beside my father, along with a thousand other heavy cavalry. We were hidden behind one of the rolling hills that skirted the battlefield, but the noise of men and horses getting wounded and being killed was carried to us by a gentle wind. My father, his helmet resting on his saddle, turned to me.

'Pacorus, you will lead this charge.'

Bozan, on my right, turned in surprise. 'Sire?'

'It is time, Bozan. Time for the boy to become a man. One day, he will rule in my place. Men will not follow a king who has not led them in battle.'

My stomach tightened. I had expected to ride into battle beside my father, but now I would lead his cavalry alone, with all eyes upon me to see if I would pass the test of manhood.

I swallowed. 'It will be an honour, father.'

'I would request to ride beside your son, sire,' said Bozan.

My father smiled. 'Of course, Bozan, I would not entrust the safe keeping of my son to anyone else.'

With that my father rammed his helmet on his head and wheeled his horse away, followed by Vistaspa and his bodyguard; they would form a reserve. The large scarlet banner, emblazoned with my father's symbol of the white horse's head, fluttered as the royal party made its way to the brow of the hill, from where they would watch the charge. Bozan reached over and grasped my shoulder. 'Remember everything that you have been taught. Focus on the task at hand, and remember that you are not alone.'

He fastened his helmet's cheek guards together to make his face disappear behind two large steel plates, then turned and gave a signal to his captains. Horns sounded and the entire formation moved as one. Each man had a white plume on his helmet and rode a white horse, though only the beasts' legs were visible as each one was protected, like Sura, by scale armour.

We were formed up in two lines, each of two hundred and fifty men, with a hundred yards separating each line. We started out at a walking pace to ascend the hill's gentle slope, my heart pounding so hard that I thought it would burst out of my chest. The sounds of battle grew louder as we topped the brow of the hill, and I gasped as I saw the scene below. The legion, still in its hollow-square formation, was being assaulted on all four sides by swarms of horse archers, but the main effort was being made against the two corners at each end of the side we would be assaulting. Although it was high in the sky, we would be riding with the sun in our faces, which alarmed me greatly.

'Why do we ride against the sun and not with it at our backs?' I shouted to Bozan.

'Have faith in your father,' was all the reply I received.

I could see Parthian foot soldiers running to get into line at the foot of our hill, to our right and left, each one carrying a shield with what appeared to be a silver facing. For what purpose I knew not.

The two hundred camels that had brought fresh arrows were now proving their worth. Each horse archer could fire around ten arrows a minute, which meant his thirty-arrow quiver would be exhausted after three minutes, but now dozens of servants were ferrying bundles of arrows from the camels to where companies of horse archers were reforming after expending their arrows.

We moved forward down the hill at a trot, about half a mile from the Romans. I had done this so many times before that I nudged Sura forward without thinking, my eyes fixed on the wall of enemy shields before me. They suddenly looked very large. My lance was still over my right shoulder as we moved into a gentle gallop. On our flanks light horsemen thundered towards the Romans, each one carrying an earthen pot holding naphtha on the end of a length of rope, a lighted rag secured in each pot. Each one approached the Romans, swinging his earthen pot over his head and then releasing it to smash into the wall of shields. As soon as it hit, each pot shattered, spilling its black liquid content, which immediately ignited. Naphtha not only burns fiercely, it sticks to what it's spilled on. Individual Romans, their shields, arms or helmets aflame, tried frantically to put out the fire, breaking their unbroken shield wall. Some clutched burning flesh and writhed in pain, others tried to flee to the rear.

At around four hundred paces we broke into a gallop and levelled our lances, holding the long shafts with both hands on our right sides. At the same time our foot soldiers slanted their shields towards the Roman line, the burnished surfaces reflecting sunlight into the enemy's faces, blinding them as we closed the gap. In front of us stood a ragged line of legionaries. I screamed my war cry as Sura raced forward, the air filled with the shrieks of frightened horses and men gripped with bloodlust. When we hit the Romans, the sound was like a loud crack of thunder as our first line drove into the disorientated enemy. Time seemed to slow as I aimed my lance at the centre of a Roman shield. The momentum of horse and rider was enough to drive the iron-tipped lanced through the shield, into the legionary and then out through his back to spear another man standing behind him. The shaft broke and I let it go, reaching across with my right hand to draw my sword from its scabbard.

Then I was in the midst of a herd of Romans, and I slashed left and right with my sword. A spear jabbed at Sura's chest, but failed to penetrate her armour. I slashed at the man's helmet as I rode forward. To my left, Bozan was screaming his war cry as he brought his sword down with all his might, splitting a Roman helmet and the skull beneath. For the first time I experienced battle, that and the sensation that my armour and sword were as light as feathers. I seemed to be able to see everything that was happening around with matchless clarity, somehow detached from events, yet at the same time an intimate part of them. So this was combat; this was the supreme test of manhood. I felt like a god: invincible, immortal, the bringer of death to my enemies. These thoughts filled my mind for what seemed like hours, but were probably no more than a few seconds. A spear flew through the air and glanced harmlessly off my armoured left forearm.

'Reform, reform,' Bozan's shouts and the blasts of horns brought me back to reality. I glanced behind me and saw our second line pouring through the gaps that had been made in the Roman line. The legion's square had lost one of its sides.

'They're finished,' I shouted.

'Not yet, boy.' He gestured to our front with his sword. 'See that eagle. Capture that, and then they're finished.'

Our second line of cataphracts came up and we formed into one body. These men still had lances, and they moved through us and towards the Romans who were trying to form a defence around the legion's eagle and senior officers in front of their wagons and wounded. Then we launched our second attack, not as disciplined as the first as some were wounded and many horses were blown. But it was enough. The Romans closed around their officers and their standard – a silver eagle mounted on a long pole – but within seconds we had them encircled and were jabbing at the legionaries with our lances. There was no charge, just violent thrusting with the lances. Horse archers came up to join the cataphracts, pouring a withering fire of arrows into the thinning ranks of the enemy. The latter, surrounded and hemmed into an ever-decreasing circle, could do little except wait to die. Occasionally a rider would be felled by a Roman javelin, but most of the legionaries now only had their swords, which were useless, as they could not get close enough to the horses to stab them or their riders. As our cavalry formed an iron ring around the enemy, I could see the eagle in their midst, held by a soldier whose armour and helmet were covered in a lion skin and who carried a small circular shield. I felt as though I could reach out and touch it. I don't know what madness gripped me, but I decided that I wanted that eagle.

My father's white horse banner was being held by a rider behind me now, signalling to all that a royal son of Hatra was in battle. Cataphracts pulled back and gathered about me, around fifty or so, forming into a single line. I held up my sword and ripped off my helmet. I shouted as loud as I could: 'Aim for the eagle, take the eagle.'

I put my helmet back on and nudged Sura forward with my thighs. The other riders closed up tight either side of me, their lances levelled one more time. Thirty seconds later we hit the Roman shield wall, and as before legionaries were speared on our lances, their pierced bodies trampled under iron-shod hooves. A Roman ran up and tried to stab me in the leg, but I brought down my sword to knock his weapon out of the way. The blow shattered the hand gripping his sword, knocking the weapon to the ground and severing several fingers. He screamed in pain and collapsed onto his knees. I moved past him, Sura barging a legionary to the ground as a rider behind me speared him with his lance. Then, suddenly, the legion's eagle was before me. I lifted my sword to bring it down on its holder, but this man was experienced and he moved expertly aside so I cut only air. My left hand was gripping Sura's reins as I swung wildly at the standard bearer with my sword. But then he rammed the eagle into the ground, drew his sword and sprang at me, smacking his round shield into my side. It was enough to send me sprawling from the saddle and crashing to the ground. Sura bolted away. Bozan's words came flooding into my mind. 'If you're on the ground you are already half-dead. Get to your feet as quickly as possible, otherwise you're finished.'

I sprang to my feet and faced the standard bearer. I was at a disadvantage as he had a sword and shield whereas I had only my sword. He lunged at me and I parried his blow. I could see that he was sweating. So was I. He charged forward, his shield in front of him, and crashed into me. The blow caught me on my left arm and a pain shot through my shoulder. He tried to thrust his sword into my neck but I caught the blade with my sword's cross-guard and pushed it aside. I suddenly felt tired and was breathing heavily. He came at me again and once more I parried his blows.

Then I attacked, gripping my sword with both hands and raising it above my head. I brought the blade down to split my opponent's shield and shatter the bone in his arm. He screamed in pain but still managed to swing his sword, which hit one of my helmet's cheek guards. He stumbled in pain. I swung my sword above my head and brought it down again, screaming as I did so. The blade was a blur as it found my enemy's exposed neck. The blade cut down at an angle, slicing through the flesh and spine to send the head spinning onto the earth.

I stepped over the headless corpse and wrenched the eagle standard out of the ground, holding it aloft for all to see. The battle that had been raging all around seemed to cease instantly as I waved the silver eagle in the air. It was as if it was a magic charm, which to the Romans, I suppose, it was. With their senior officers dead, individual legionaries began to ram their swords into the ground, discarding their shields and kneeling as a sign of submission. Our men, most of them having fought all day under a merciless sun, gladly accepted their surrender. Soon, whole groups of Romans were giving up, the loss of their legionary eagle having shattered their morale.

Bozan, his armour missing many steel plates from the blows he had received in the fight, walked over and embraced me.

'I knew you wouldn't fail me, Pacorus. Well done.'

He winced as he let go of me, blood showing around his armpit.

'You're wounded.'

'It's nothing,' he replied.

Around me cataphracts were dismounting and walking over to me, offering their congratulations. Among them was Vata, the son of Bozan and my best friend. Like his father he was squat and stocky, a barrel of muscles, and like his father he had a carefree attitude to life. But, like me, he wore his hair long, his black locks falling to his shoulders. He embraced his father then grinned as he gripped me in a bear hug.

'You're not saying much.'

'That's because you're crushing me,' I managed to say. He burst into laughter as he released me.

He slapped me on my left arm as he stared at the eagle.

'So, this is what we've been bleeding for. Haven't seen many of them in my travels. I reckon the Romans will be mightily aggrieved when they discover we've got it.'

'Let them come and get it,' I said, trying to sound impressive.

'Yes,' spat Vata. 'We'll beat them a second time.

Then I felt a curious sensation in my arms and legs, as they began to shake. I suddenly felt afraid. Was I dying; had I been wounded? I sank onto all fours and looked at Bozan in despair. He knelt beside me.

'Easy, boy. It's just the shakes.'

'The shakes?'

He grinned and handed me his water skin. 'Drink. A lot of men get the shakes after battle. When you fight the muscles get tense, like tightly wrapped rope, and when it's over they unwind, so to speak. You'll be fine in a few minutes.'

He was right. After a while the shaking stopped and my limbs became my own once more. As groups of disarmed Romans were escorted to a main holding area, the squires and servants were brought forward to tend to their masters. Water wagons began arriving, too, their drivers filling buckets for our exhausted cataphracts and their mounts, while the squires pulled off the horses' armour.

My squire, Gafarn, rode up on his horse. Dressed in his simple white linen tunic and baggy trousers, he helped me off with my armour then attended to Sura, who had been retrieved and returned to me. Gentle mare as she was, she waited patiently as the head guard and armour coat were removed. He then threw a silk coat over her as she was sweating profusely and the sun was beginning to set, its colour changing from gold to a light red. The heat of the day was abating.

'Your cloak is in the saddlebag, highness.' He pointed to the eagle that I was holding. 'What's that, highness?'

'It's a Roman eagle, Gafarn.'

'Looks expensive. It should fetch a nice tidy sum at market.'

I was aghast. 'It's not for selling; this is a great treasure.'

'If it's a great treasure, then you're a fool for not selling it.'

'And you're a servant who talks too much. How is she?'

Gafarn stroked Sura's head gently. 'She's beautiful, highness, that's what she is, and she's fine. Next time you should try to stay on her.' He held a bucket of water to her mouth so she could drink.

I walked over to my horse and patted her neck. 'She is that. No warrior could find a better horse.'

The army's horse surgeons had now arrived on the field, attending to those mounts that had been wounded. Some, too badly injured to be treated, were mercifully dispatched to join the immortal wild herd of horses that belonged to Shamash, the Sun God whom we worshipped and whose victory this was. Ahead of me I saw a large group of Roman soldiers seated on the ground in front of their wagon park. Many were staring at the eagle I was holding. I walked over to Vata.

'Take this,' I handed him the eagle.

'Where are you going?'

I pointed at the Romans. 'To talk to them.'

'Be careful,' he said. 'One of them might have a weapon concealed.'

But my curiosity was too great. I had been taught Latin and Greek as a child and I wanted to speak with these men of the Tiber that I had heard so much about but, until today, I had never met. As I got near, one got to his feet and squared up to me. Two guards levelled their lances at him but I waved them away. He was shorter than me by about six inches, but stockier with broad shoulders. His short-cropped hair was encrusted with dirt and blood from a wound to his forehead. The blood had already congealed to form a black patch above his right eye. Though he wore no armour or weapons he was still an imposing figure. He looked straight at me.

'You're the one who took our eagle,' his words were laced with venom.

'Took?' I rose to the challenge. 'I found it lying in the dirt.'

'You speak passable Latin, foreigner.'

'I was taught it as a child,' I replied. 'I find it a vulgar language.'

'It is good that you have learned it.'

'Why is that?' I enquired.

'Because when we have conquered your land you will be able to understand what your masters are saying.'

I could feel my temper rise within me. 'This is Parthian land, Roman, not some weak province.'

He laughed. 'The whole world is a Roman province, Parthian. You have beaten one legion, but it will be different when many cross your border. And that day is coming, and sooner than you think.'

I decided that it was futile to indulge him further. 'We will be waiting, Roman.'

With that I turned away from him and walked back to where Vata and his father were standing. The prisoners were being sorted into groups, each one being tethered with rope. The Romans fought with helmets on their heads and mail shirts over their tunics, which ended just above their knees, and curved oblong shields that protected their entire torsos and thighs. Their weapons and armour were now being loaded onto carts.

Bozan was chewing on a piece of bread. 'That lot will fetch a tidy price in the slave markets. They'll end up in the eastern part of the empire somewhere, well away from here so it won't be worth them making any trouble.'

'Will they ever see Rome again?' I asked.

Bozan shrugged. 'I doubt it. It's the fate of beaten soldiers never to see their homes again. Still, better them than us.'

At that moment the air was filled with the blaring of horns, and I turned to see my father riding towards us escorted by Vistaspa and his bodyguard. The cavalrymen looked resplendent in their brightly polished armour, white-plumed helmets and lances flying white pennants. Behind my father fluttered his scarlet banner sporting a white horse's head, the cloth edged with silver braid. My father wore a silver, open-faced helmet topped with a gold crown. His horse was draped with a richly adorned white coat edged with silver, with the mounts of the other riders protected by scale armour. On his right rode Vistaspa, glancing right and left like a hawk searching for prey. The group halted a few feet from where I

stood and my father immediately jumped down and marched over to me. The others and I knelt before him with heads bowed, but he clasped my shoulders, picked me up and embraced me. There were tears in his eyes as he stepped back to look at me.
'My son, you have proved yourself a worthy son of Hatra. This day will be remembered by future generations of our people.'
I felt ten feet tall. I stretched out my arm and clicked my fingers. Vata gave the eagle to Gafarn, who rushed up and passed it to me.
'My gift to you, father.'
He took the standard and admired it, then addressed all those kneeling around him. 'Rise, rise all of you, and bear witness to this great victory and the man, my son, who made it possible.'
The assembly rose and broke into applause. Bozan and Vata walked over to my father, and after they had both bowed, Bozan grinned broadly at my father and the two embraced. My father congratulated Vata, for he too had covered himself in glory this day.
'This will send a message to Rome, father.'
'The loss of a legion will be a great dishonour to them, the more so because we, or rather you, have taken its precious eagle.' He paused for a moment and a momentary look of concern spread over his face. Then he turned to me. 'They will be back, Pacorus, rest assured.'
Flushed with victory, I actually welcomed the opportunity to smash more Roman legions. 'Let them come,' I boasted. 'We will beat them once more.'
My father smiled. 'Perhaps we will. Though let us hope it is not for many years.'
But I didn't want to hear of peace. I had become a man and had taken a Roman eagle. My thoughts were filled with more military glory, which would spread my name far and wide. I was so preoccupied that I did not hear the commotion behind me. I barely noticed the guards screaming as I turned slowly to see one of the prisoners running towards me with a spear in his hand. Then I saw that it was the man I had been talking to. Transfixed and rooted to the spot, I saw him bring the spear up to his shoulder, ready to throw it. Like a hare caught in the cold stare of a cobra, I could do nothing except watch and wait for the spear to slam into me. The Roman, wild-eyed, had a triumphant look on his face in the second before he threw his weapon, which suddenly turned to an expression of surprise, then disappointment and finally acute pain. The arrow had hit him squarely in the chest, stopping him in his tracks. He slowed and then fell to his knees, then keeled over to

collapse onto the ground. I snapped out of my daze and marched over to where the Roman lay. I knelt over him, the arrow sticking out of his back and blood oozing from his mouth. As life ebbed from him, he tried to look up at me but his strength was draining away fast. I leaned closer to hear his words, which were faint, barely audible. He coughed, causing more blood to pump from his mouth. The only words I heard were: 'We will return, Parthian.' Then he died.

I stood and saw Vistaspa astride his horse with a bow in his left hand. He was the one who had saved me. I nodded at him in acknowledgement; his only response was a thin smile, which I swore turned into a sneer.

'Keep those prisoners under control,' screamed Bozan to the guards.

Vistaspa rode up. 'Never turn your back on your enemies, even if you think they are unarmed. Next time I might not be around to save you.'

He kicked his horse and rode away to attend my father, who was shaking his head at me.

The next day we burned the dead, as is our custom. It took most of the morning for the prisoners to dig two pits, one for our men the other for the Romans. The one for the latter was far bigger for they had lost over a thousand dead. Normally we would have left the enemy dead to rot, but my father did not want their carcasses to pollute the soil of Hatra. We piled the wooden shields in first, all five thousand of them, coated the top layer with naphtha and then tipped the dead legionaries on top. Our own dead numbered less than four hundred, though an equal number had been wounded, along with three hundred horses killed. Most of the horse archers and foot, plus the Roman prisoners, servants and supply camels, headed south back to Hatra. Most of the cataphracts also headed for Hatra, accompanied by Bozan and Vata, who also took a rich haul with them: the twelve chests of legionary gold. The prisoners would be sold at Hatra, probably to another Parthian king, though we would only sell them to a king who ruled in the eastern part of the empire. This would make it very difficult for any to escape back to Roman territory, having to cross hundreds of miles of barren desert. This being the case, they would more readily accept their new position in life. Better a slave than dead.

I escorted my father on the journey to the city of Zeugma, along with his bodyguard and two hundred horse archers. Though I was loathe to let it out of my sight, the eagle was also sent to Hatra. We had won a great victory, and already riders were being dispatched to the four corners of the empire to announce the good tidings. And yet my father was troubled. The morning we set off for Zeugma he hardly spoke at all. Behind us two long columns of black smoke spiralled into the blue sky – the funeral pyres of our own soldiers and those of our enemies. Zeugma lay thirty miles to the north, and we made our way leisurely along the road, which was nothing more than a dirt track. We had scouts riding ahead and covering our flanks, but for hours we saw no other signs of life.

'Strange, Vistaspa, don't you think?' asked my father.

Like most of us, Vistaspa had been lulled into a relaxed state by the heat and the gentle ride. 'My liege?'

'Only a day's hard ride from Zeugma and not a scout in site. Where is the garrison? I would have though that a Roman legion marching towards the city would have prompted some response.'

'I have no answers, my lord,' replied Vistaspa, unconcerned. 'Not all kingdoms in the empire have our eyes and ears.'

He was right. The Parthian Empire was made up of eighteen separate but aligned kingdoms. These were Gordyene, Hatra, Atropaiene, Babylon, Susiana, Hyrcania, Carmania, Sakastan, Drangiana, Aria, Anauon, Yueh-Chih, Margiana, Elymais, Mesene, Persis, Zeugma and the oldest kingdom of all, Parthia. The empire stretched from the Indus in the east, north to the Caspian Sea and the border with the Uzbeks, and west to the frontiers of Pontus and Syria and south to the clear blue waters of the Persian Gulf and Arabian Sea. All of these lands were ruled by the 'king of kings', Sinatruces, who sat in the ancient city of Ctesiphon. Hatra was, I liked to think, the strongest of the kingdoms. Sandwiched between the Euphrates and Tigris rivers, its western side extended all the way to the border with the Roman province of Syria, though Sinatruces controlled a thin strip of land on the western bank of the Euphrates that was administered by the frontier city of Dura Europus. Hatra was rich and getting richer, and as such was looked on jealously by outside enemies and even other Parthian kings. So my father had created and maintained a large army and garrisons throughout his kingdom, especially the towns to the north of Hatra – Singara and Nisibus – and Batnae in the northwest. But he had also raised a large contingent of scouts who covered every inch of our kingdom, ever vigilant for threats. It was the scouts who had ridden hard to alert my father that the Roman legion had crossed the border. The city of Zeugma had its own garrison, but we had not heard nor seen anything of it since we had ridden north.

'Perhaps not all kingdoms still want to be a part of the empire.'

'Father?' I admit that I had no idea what he was suggesting.

'Nothing,' he mused. 'We will know more presently.'

The next day we reached Zeugma. Two hours after dawn we were approached by a patrol of cavalry, their commander's lack of surprise about our presence explained by the courier my father had sent to the city immediately after our battle. The twenty riders were all light horseman wearing no armour and carrying swords and shields. They had a passable appearance, though I noted that their shields were battered and their uniforms scruffy. We wore no armour, which was packed and carried on the camel train that accompanied us. My father, his bodyguard and I wore white silk tunics, baggy leggings and loosely fitting cotton caps. Swords hung in scabbards from our leather belts and our shields, which we didn't carry when wearing scale armour, were slung on our backs. Fastened to our saddles were our bows in their leather cases, with a quiver full of arrows attached to a leather strap that ran over our right shoulders and across our chests, with the quiver itself sitting at our left hips. Our horse archers formed a mounted phalanx behind the king's bodyguard, followed by the supply camels and a rearguard of more horse archers. Our lances were similarly strapped to the camels, which spent each day spitting, belching and breaking wind. They were truly disgusting creatures, but absolutely essential to the Parthian war machine.

The commander of the Zeugma cavalry saluted my father. 'Greetings, highness. King Darius is eagerly awaiting your presence at his palace. Already news of your victory is spreading throughout the empire.'

My father said nothing but merely nodded at the young officer, while Vistaspa also fixed him with a cool stare. The silence was most oppressive and if I was feeling uncomfortable then the officer must have been feeling worse, as sweat began to trickle down his face.

My father nudged his horse forward, past the young officer. 'Give my greetings to my friend, King Darius. Tell him we will pay our respects at his palace this afternoon.'

With that my father's horse idled past the static riders, as did Vistaspa and I. Their commander, unsure what to do, eventually gave the signal to his men, who turned around and galloped back to the city, their horses kicking up a cloud of dust as they did so.

'You are angry, father?'

'You saw the state of them,' he replied. 'Darius sends a bunch of beggars to escort us into his city. We're lucky they didn't try to rob us.' This prompted a rare smile from Vistaspa. 'I'm not having my soldiers sullied by having to ride with them. I'd rather ride a camel.'

'We are now in Darius' territory, my liege,' said Vistaspa. 'He may not take kindly to being treated as an unequal.'

Normally the commander of a king's bodyguard would not dare to address his lord thus, but Vistaspa himself had once been a prince and he and my father had a close relationship, almost like brothers, which was another thing that annoyed me about him.

My father bristled at the suggestion. 'We've saved his lazy fat arse from being roasted over a Roman fire, and he can't even be bothered to ride out himself to thank me. He doesn't deserve to be a king. Little toad.'

'A rich toad,' remarked Vistaspa.

We reached the city of Zeugma two hours later. Lying on the west bank of the River Euphrates, the city hugged the river for four miles either side of the bridge of boats that spanned the waterway. Surrounded by rocky outcrops, Zeugma was like a golden egg in a stone nest. As we approached the bridge we encountered heavy traffic on the road, mostly camel caravans going east or heading for Roman Syria. Soon we were covered with a fine dust kicked up by the dozens of camels, donkeys and human feet on the highway. In the distance, on a gently rising hill that swept up from the river, perched a host of large villas, where I assumed the city's aristocrats lived. And on the top of that summit, standing alone but proud, sat a building more magnificent than the rest, with brightly coloured flags flying from every tower.

'Vistaspa, find a place to pitch our camp for tonight. My son and I will visit our host and convey our greetings. Find a place upstream, where the water is fresh. Come Pacorus,' my father urged his horse forward. Vistaspa motioned for a troop of horse to escort us, and then went in search of the garrison commander.

As we moved across the wooden bridge and into the city, we passed through one of the gates in the city's walls. Guards stood on the ramparts both inside and outside of the wooden gates. Each gate hanging on large iron hinges. The guards watched us as we passed but made no effort to stop us. Clearly we were expected. Once inside the city we were met by a richly adorned officer on a shiny black stallion flanked by two of his men, who also rode immaculate black horses. He wore a red headband, a yellow tunic with silver edging at the neck and yellow trousers. His only weapon was a sword at his left hip, which was encased in a red scabbard adorned with jewels. He placed his right hand on his chest and bowed his head.

'King Varaz, my liege King Darius welcomes you to his city and asks that you partake of his hospitality.'

'I and my son would be honoured,' my father replied. 'Please lead the way.'

Our escorts rode before us as we headed away from the city's wide main thoroughfare onto a side road that was obviously reserved for nobles and the king, as it was empty of all traffic. Guards in yellow tunics and trousers, armed with spears and wicker shields, stood on each side of the road every ten paces or so.

After about twenty minutes of climbing gently we came to the royal palace. The palace's main gate was a single arch flanked by two towers, the whole structure covered with yellow enamelled tiles. The palace itself was set in the middle of verdant gardens filled with palm trees, fountains and carefully manicured lawns. Servants rushed forward and placed wooden stools beside our horses to aid our dismounting. Our escort also dismounted and bowed again to my father.

'Your horses will be fed, water and groomed. My master awaits your pleasure, King Varaz.'

My father acknowledged him and bade him lead the way. I followed, while our cavalry troop led their horses towards the stables. The palace was of pure white stone fronted with white marble columns with gold-covered volutes. We ascended the marble steps and entered the portico, which had a marble floor. We were led through the portico and into the throne room, the centrepiece of which was a golden throne, upon which was sitting a middle-aged plump man with a bulbous nose, piggy eyes and a somewhat leering expression. As soon as he saw us he jumped out of his throne and ambled towards my father, arms outstretched.

'Hail King Varaz, conqueror of our foes. Slayer of our enemies,' his voice was slightly effeminate.

'Hail, King Darius,' replied my father, as they embraced each other as brother kings and equals.

My father turned to me. 'May I present my son, Prince Pacorus, whose courage brought victory against the invaders.'

Darius observed me slyly for an instant with his piggy eyes, then forced a smile as I bowed to him. 'Of course, of course. How grateful we are that you have saved us from a dreadful fate, Prince Pacorus. Splendid. Now we must eat. You must be hungry. I certainly am.'

He gestured towards a small ante chamber, into which he scurried, followed by a host of slaves, most teenage boys and girls, all of whom were young, attractive and immaculately groomed, and all of whom were naked from the waist up. In the antechamber Darius flopped down on a luxurious red couch. He invited me and my father to sit on other couches that were arranged in a circle around his. The walls were covered with paintings of wild animals and naked nymphs. Guards in yellow tunics and trousers stood at each corner, each armed with a spear with a highly polished blade. Darius clapped, and within seconds more semi-naked slaves brought in silver platters piled high with food – bread, fruit, roasted lamb, fowl and fish – while others carried flagons of wine. A small table was laid in front of us, upon which was soon piled dishes of food. A young girl, no older than sixteen, poured wine into a silver goblet held by another young slave, a pale-skinned boy who bowed and passed it to me once it was full. The wine was exquisite.

'They will come again,' said my father, 'you must look to your defences. How many troops do you have?'

Darius was being fed honey-coated lamb by a young boy, who pushed the meat into the king's mouth with his fingers. I looked aghast as Darius then licked the meat's juices off the boy's fingers. My father looked disgusted at the spectacle. 'Alas, King Varaz, my army is small,' Darius pointed to a bunch of grapes on the table. A slave plucked one and daintily pushed it into his mouth. 'Solders cost money, and my treasury is bare.'

This was not the answer my father wanted. 'Yes, I can see that times are hard. You must strengthen your city's defences.'

'But brother,' protested Darius. 'The Romans have been defeated. With warriors such as you and your son, I'm sure we have nothing to fear.'

'We have everything to fear, King Darius. This time they sent only one legion, next time they will send an army.'

Darius pointed at me. 'Then they will be as stubble to your son's sword. Is that not so, Prince Pacorus?'

I pushed another piece of freshly baked almond cake into my mouth. It melted on my tongue. 'Yes, sire.'

In truth I was loving the feast and taking almost no notice of the conversation, but I could see that my father was annoyed. When we had finished eating Darius clapped his hands and the food was taken away. More slaves appeared carrying bowls of warm water and towels for us to wash our hands. Afterwards two female slaves each took one of my hands and began massaging the fingers with oils. They were both in their late teens, gorgeous, bare-breasted with gold bracelets on their arms. They had dark complexions and teeth of pure white, with thick eyeliner to accentuate their large brown eyes. They smelt and looked divine. Another, a beautiful

Persian woman with a gold headband and oiled black hair, motioned to me to lie back on the couch. I did so and she began to massage my temples with her fingers. Her touch was sublime, and soon I was drifting into a trance-like state as she massaged my head. The conversation between my father and Darius was becoming fainter as I surrendered to the angelic caresses of three female slaves. This was heaven, and I wanted to experience it forever.

I was rudely awakened from my bliss by my father, who shook me out of my dream.

'We are leaving, Pacorus.'

'Father?'

'We have imposed on King Darius' hospitality enough,' he bowed to Darius. 'We thank you, lord king, but we must be on our way.'

Darius had been lying back with his eyes closed, listening to a young harpist who was playing at his feet. He now looked at us in surprise.

'Leaving? But surely you will stay for the night. Your son, does he like boys or girls? Such a hero should be rewarded with at least one night of abandon.'

'Alas, no,' replied my father. 'We must get back to Hatra.'

'Such a shame. Very well, very well.' Darius beckoned to one of the guards and instructed him to see that our horses were brought to the palace steps. We thanked Darius and left him to his harpist and young boys and girls.

Our horses had been groomed, fed and watered and the troop of my father's bodyguard had been similarly revitalised. The men were happy, as was I, but as we trotted from the palace and through the bustling city, my father's mood darkened. At the bridge across the Euphrates we met with Gafarn, who had been sent by Vistaspa to inform us where he had made camp.

'Five miles upstream. Did you have a nice time, master?'

'Very,' I replied. 'King Darius is a generous host.'

'King Darius is a snake,' snapped my father.

'How so, father?' I asked, surprised.

'He wants to leave the empire and become a client king of Rome.'

I was astounded at the idea that anyone would want to leave Parthia. 'Surely not. Why?'

My father halted his horse to face me. 'Because, my son, it is easier to be a servant of Rome than a Parthian king. As long as Darius is prepared to lick the boots of some Roman governor then he can live in his gilded palace forever without having to worry about keeping his kingdom.'

'Why would he do so?'

My father smiled, the first time he had done so that day. 'Because it is easier, especially for a fat king whose only ambition is to surround himself with pretty catamites and teenage girls. And I'll warrant that the Romans have used honeyed words and the promise of much wealth if he should do so. Zeugma stands on the western edge of the empire, and if it becomes Roman it will point like a dagger at Hatra. A Roman army at Zeugma could strike south into my kingdom with ease.'

We finished the journey to camp in silence. I could not understand why a Parthian would want to be under Roman rule, but I was young then and naïve about the avarice of men. We moved through rocky terrain until we came upon our camp, a collection of canvas tents arranged in lines beside a fast-flowing stream. Soldiers and servants groomed horses and fed camels, while other soldiers sharpened sword blades. Vistaspa had posted guards around the camp and had scouts out patrolling as well. My father dismounted and immediately marched off with his commander, deep in conversation. The light was fading now, the sun disappearing behind a snow-capped mountain in the western sky.

Gafarn took Sura away to the makeshift stable area of stalls constructed from wooden poles and canvas sheets as I sat on the ground beside a small fire. I checked my sword in its scabbard, the straps on my shield and ensured my bowstring was taught and my quiver full. Looking round, I was beginning to wish that we had stayed in the palace of King Darius. A night sleeping on the ground, with a breakfast of salted pork and hard biscuit washed down with water, did not fill me with relish. The darkness was encroaching quickly now, and as I glanced at a guard standing not twenty paces away I saw movement out of the corner of my eye. The next instant there was a dull hiss followed by a groan, and then a clatter as the guard fell to the ground. I saw an arrow protruding from his back, and then suddenly other arrows were cutting through the air. I grabbed my shield and drew my sword as other arrows found their targets. Horses squealed in panic and camels bellowed as animals were pierced by arrows.

'Rally, rally.' I felt as though I was alone as I sprinted away from the fire to throw myself behind the relative safety of a tree. Then the air was filled with shouts and cries as our unseen assailants attacked – black-clad figures armed with swords and spears. Had they been assailing a civilian caravan they would have achieved an easy victory, but they were fighting the cream of Parthia's warriors, and though we had been surprised it did not take us long to find our discipline. Vistaspa was a hard taskmaster, and now his hard work paid dividends.

Horns blared as he and my father formed a solid block of the royal bodyguard, fifty across who locked shields to defeat the volley of arrows launched before our enemies attacked. Our assailants then hurled themselves into a charge, screaming wildly as they did so. There was a loud crack as the two groups came together and started the killing at close quarters. Man for man we were fitter, stronger and more skilled, our blades reaping a deadly harvest of the enemy. I saw my father and ran to get beside him. The enemy was between him and me and so I slashed and hacked at black-clad figures in front of me. I felt the same calm determination as I did when I fought the Romans, only this time I was in a hurry to kill. An enemy ran at me with a spear levelled at my belly. I caught the blow with my shield, feinted right and plunged my sword into the man's shoulder. Withdrawing the blade, I saw another figure about to swing his sword at my unguarded right side. I dropped onto my left knee and ducked so his blow cut only air. I swung my sword and the blade cut deep into his right leg just below the knee. He uttered a high-pitched scream and collapsed to the ground.

I reached my father's side, the king briefly acknowledging me as Vistaspa bellowed an order. 'Archers, ready. First line, kneel.' As one our ragged shield wall knelt to allow the archers who had formed up behind them to fire. As they loosed their first volley the archers immediately strung and fired a second. Then my father screamed the charge and we raced forward, over a line of arrow-pierced bodies to get to grips with what remained of the enemy. They were losing heart now. They had expected an easy victory, these assassins of the night, but had instead met with determined resistance. I ran at one of them, who was armed with a sword and a wicker shield. He tried to aim a blow at my chest, but the impetus of my charge meant my shield barged his sword out of the way and, screaming, I thrust my sword through his shield and into his throat. He made a gurgling sound and died still skewered on my blade. I yanked the sword from him and saw a figure try to run to safety. I raced after him, tripped him and sent him sprawling to the ground. Before he could get up I brought the edge of my shield down hard on the back of his neck, the loud snap signalling the spinal cord had been broken.

I look around. Vistaspa was supervising the reduction of the last pockets of resistance. My father, bareheaded, was leaning on his sword, Gafarn dressing a wound to his neck. I sheathed my sword and went over to him. We met and embraced.

'Are you hurt, father?'

'It's nothing, I was lucky,' he replied.

'That's why we have helmets,' said Gafarn. 'If you don't wear one, what do expect?' He was expertly stitching the two sides of the cut together, oblivious to my fathers' wincing as he did so.

'Be quiet and do your job,' my father barked.

'Of course, majesty,' replied Gafarn. 'And then I'll get your helmet so you can put it on.'

'I sometimes wonder if you know that you are a slave.'

Gafarn had been a slave in the royal household since he was five. He was found wandering among the dead and dying when my father's father, King Sames, had attacked and routed a Bedouin tribe who had been raiding Hatra's borders. My father had taken the young boy back to the city and had given him to me as a playmate. The same age, we grew up together and Gafarn, a low-born slave, became like a brother to me, the more so when my mother and father had no more boys of their own. He was brave and quick-witted, and became well liked in the palace. My father had him tutored in reading and writing, and although he was forbidden to train as a cataphract, he and I learned archery together, a skill at which he excelled.

Vistaspa marched up and one of his men threw an injured, black-clad figure to the ground. 'We've killed most of them. A few got away. They slit the throats of our guards on the perimeter. That's how they got so close. The only prisoner we've got so far is this one.'

'Our losses?' asked my father.

'Twenty dead, about the same wounded. A few camels slain.'

My father brushed Gafarn away as my servant finished his medical duties. My father stood before the prisoner.

'Who sent you?'

The prisoner, a scruffy looking individual with dirty, unkempt hair, chuckled at my father, to reveal a row of black teeth and rotting gums. Vistaspa picked up a broken spear shaft and hit the man hard on the side of his face, sending him sprawling to the ground. He was yanked back onto his knees, his mouth bloody from the blow.

'I ask you again. Who sent you?' The prisoner spat at my father, prompting another blow to the side of the face from Vistaspa, who then drew his dagger, grabbed the man's right arm and cut off his thumb. The prisoner screamed, and Vistaspa again clubbed him to the ground. The loss of another thumb and all of his teeth failed to yield any information from the hapless man. Perhaps he didn't know anything, perhaps he was just one of a ragged band of raiders who attacked us, but my father was convinced that he and his comrades had been sent to attack and kill us. When dawn broke the next morning the man was still alive, so we nailed him to a tree, then broke camp to head south. We were tired, cold and hungry, having been standing to arms all through the night in case we were attacked again. But no assault came, so we tended to our wounded, consigned our dead to a funeral pyre and rode south back to Hatra. We left the enemy dead where they fell, fifty of them, though my father ordered all the bodies to be decapitated. The heads were impaled on the enemy's spears that had been stuck in the ground, to form a grisly forest. I pulled my cloak around me as we rode away from the scene of slaughter. Our pace was slow as my father ordered all of us to wear our full armour in case we were attacked again. No attack came, and as the day wore on the sun rose in the sky to warm our bodies and raise our spirits. We were going home.

Chapter 2

It took us seven days to reach Hatra. After the first two days we relaxed our guard when it became apparent that no one was trailing us. My father's mood began to lighten as we neared home, the more so when scouts rode in to inform us that the army had reached Hatra safely and the city was excited about our victory. Hatra, how that name filled me with pride. Sandwiched between the Tigris and Euphrates, the Kingdom of Hatra was the eastern shield of the Parthian Empire. As well as being a mighty fortress, it was also a flourishing trading centre through which caravans travelling both east and west passed. From the Orient the caravans brought furs, ceramics, jade, bronze objects, lacquer and iron. Caravans heading towards the east carried gold and other valuable metals, ivory, precious stones, and glass. Many of these goods were bartered for others along the way, and objects often changed hands several times. Yet the most precious commodity of all was silk, the expensive material that was said to have come to earth as a gift from the Goddess of Silk to Lady Hsi-Ling-Shih, wife of the Yellow Emperor, who was said to have ruled the Orient three thousand years before our time.

There were many routes from Africa, Syria and the Roman Empire to the East, but the most important ones passed through the Kingdom of Hatra. The rulers of Hatra had grown rich on the caravans that travelled through their territory, each one paying a toll to secure safe passage. At first this toll paid for a troop of horsemen to escort the caravan from one end of the kingdom to the other, to provide protection against the many gangs of bandits that infested the desert regions. But this was deemed a waste of money, as there was always a multitude of caravans, which required a huge army to guard. So the kings, my ancestors, organised massive sweeps of the kingdom to destroy the bandits. A combination of bribery, fire and sword eradicated their threat, and since those times the severest penalties had been in place for banditry and theft. The bandits and their families were hunted down and slaughtered without mercy, the bodies being staked out in the desert or impaled on stakes beside the road as a warning to others. It worked. Now, few bandits dared to show their face in the Kingdom of Hatra, its example being followed by the other rulers in the empire, for without trade the Parthian Empire would quickly wither and die.

Now the caravans, glad to have safe passage, paid their tolls and we grew rich. Some kings, such as King Darius, spent their wealth on an indolent way of life, but others, like my father, built strong defences and large armies to protect what they had. For the Romans in the west and the Asiatics in the east were like hungry wolves when they turned their gaze towards Parthia. My father had once told me, as his father had told him, 'if you want peace, my son, prepare for war'. And so it was. Throughout the kingdom stone forts protected the trade routes and deterred aggressors. These forts were simple stone structures, with a garrison of twenty-five horse archers, a quarter of a company. They had one entrance, four watch towers at each corner and were austere at the least. But they served their purpose and made it all but impossible for bandits or enemy troops to operate within the kingdom with impunity.

'It will be good to see your mother again,' mused my father as I rode beside him on our way south. It was the first time he had mentioned her name since we had left home.

'Yes, father.'

'A man without a good woman beside him is an empty shell.' He looked at me. 'We will have to find you a wife soon, my son.'

'Yes, father,' I replied with little enthusiasm. Royal marriages were used to cement alliances and secure kingdoms; the wishes of those getting married were often of little or no concern.

'Perhaps the Princess Axsen of Babylon. That would make a good alliance, though if she's as fat as her father you'll need a good cook to keep her happy.'

My spirits sank. 'Yes, father.'

Our conversation was interrupted by Vistaspa galloping up and halting before my father. He saluted. 'Message from the city, sire.'

He handed my father a scroll. He read it, glanced at me and smiled. 'Good,' he said. 'Give the order that we will camp here tonight and enter the city tomorrow.'

'We are close to the city, father,' I said. 'Are we not entering it tonight?'

'No, Pacorus. We have a surprise for you.' Vistaspa eyed me and his thin lips creased into a smile. Please Shamash, I prayed, do not let it be the Princess Axsen.

We pitched camp later that afternoon, and two hours afterwards a large camel train appeared from the south, led by an escort commanded by Bozan. He jumped down from his horse, bowed to my father and embraced me.

'Heard you nearly got yourself killed by some wild bandits. That bastard Darius paid them, no doubt. Probably thought a few thieves could do what a Roman legion couldn't.'

'We don't know that, Bozan,' said my father.

'Course we do. You're just too polite to say so. He's a greedy little bastard, and he thought that if he killed you, then he could invite the Romans back and present your two heads on a platter to them,' he nodded at myself and father.
'Welcome them back?' I queried.
'A Roman legion doesn't wander around in the desert, lost, boy. It was on its way to Zeugma.'
'Enough,' spoke my father. 'These matters are for the council chamber and not for idle gossip.'
Bozan nodded his head and winked at me. 'In any case, all that matters now is that Pacorus has a great triumph tomorrow.'
I was shocked. 'Triumph?'
My father smiled. 'You brought us victory against the Romans, my son. It is only right that the city should acknowledge your achievement.'
Gafarn stumbled out of the dusk carrying a suit of scale armour, the light from our campfires glinting off the scales.
'Is this made of lead,' asked Gafarn, 'because it feels like it?'
'Iron and silver, you cheeky little bastard,' replied Bozan.
'The Suit of Victory,' said my father. 'It has been worn only a few times. My father wore it after his defeat of the Palmyrians. Now you will wear it tomorrow.'
I hardly slept that night, but kept looking at the suit of armour that was hanging in my tent on a wooden frame. When the dawn came I kicked Gafarn awake and began to dress. Gafarn brought me a breakfast of bread and warm milk, and then went to make sure Sura had been watered and fed. He returned a few minutes later. As I sat on a stool outside my tent finishing my meal, the camp around was bustling with activity. Officers barked orders to men, while grooms attended to horses. As the sun rose in the eastern sky, signalling another glorious summer day, I began the process of turning myself into a cataphract. First came the silk vest, worn next to the skin. My father equipped all his horsemen with these items of clothing. Horse masters from the east had told him that the riders of the steppes wore these garments as protection against arrows. Apparently, if you were struck by an arrow while wearing a silk vest then the arrow would wrap itself around the material as it drove into flesh. This made extracting the arrow easier, though I was unconvinced. Nevertheless, the vest was pleasant to wear and let sweat pass through its fine fibres. Then came white cotton trousers and tunic, both loose fitting for extra ventilation. Gafarn had to assist me putting on the armour, standing on a stool and lifting it over my head to allow me to slip it on. It was beautiful,

with long hems and broad sleeves. Every second armour plate was made of silver, which meant the suit shimmered with any movement. Gafarn put on my leather boots and passed me the gloves, which were covered with thin silver scales. The helmet was steel with a decorative gold band around the skull.

'You look like a mighty warrior, highness,' said Gafarn, who was beaming broadly.

'I feel like I'm carrying a mighty weight. But I thank you for your help.'

I stepped outside my tent, to be cheered by my father's waiting bodyguard, mounted and at attention. White pennants on their lance shafts fluttered in the light breeze, and white horses chomped at bits and kicked at the ground in impatience. In the royal bodyguard all horses were white, and their highly groomed tails swished from side to side. The bodyguard wore white plumes in their helmets and white cloaks around their shoulders. They looked truly magnificent, none more so than my father, who wore his golden crown atop his open-faced helmet. On this occasion, as befitting his position as the commander of my father's bodyguard, Vistaspa carried his banner – a white horse on a scarlet background. I saluted my father and then mounted Sura, who wore her body armour though none on her head, as it was restrictive and not needed today.

Trumpets sounded the advance and our column left camp and headed south, to Hatra. It was still morning when we sighted the city, a massive citadel of stone in the middle of a desert called Al Jazirah. There were four roads into the city, from the north, south, east and west. We were on the northern road, which today was lined with the troops of my father's army. Ranks of cataphracts and horse archers lined each side of the dirt road for a mile up to the main gate. There must have been five thousand horsemen, while on the city walls I could see spearmen standing to attention. As we entered the final leg of our journey we were met by Bozan and his son, Vata. They were in the road mounted, and before them was a foot soldier holding the Roman eagle that I had taken. Bozan and Vata drew their swords, saluted my father and me, and then took their place in the procession immediately behind my father and Vistaspa. The soldier with the eagle marched at the head of our column directly in front of me. As we passed each group of horsemen on the road, the lances of the cataphracts were dipped in salute, as were the drawn swords of the horse archers.

Hatra was a city of one hundred thousand people, and as such occupied a large area. The whole of the city was encompassed by an outer stone wall fifty feet high, made of large square blocks of brown limestone, with defensive towers at intervals of every hundred feet. Access to the city was via four gates at each of the four points of the compass. In front of the city walls was a deep, wide ditch, with wooden causeways spanning it at every gate. At the gates were drawbridges, wooden platforms with one hinged side fixed to the wall and the other side raised by chains. These bridges were pulled up at night to seal the city. For added security, each gate had two portcullises – heavy grilled gates suspended from the gatehouse ceiling. They could be rapidly dropped down if the city came under attack. They were made of oak bars and had iron spikes at the bottom. Held in place by ropes, they could be released quickly by slashing those ropes.

Inside the city, in its northern sector, stood an area surrounded by a second stone wall. This was the palace quarter, which also housed the imperial barracks block, the city's temples and the houses of the aristocracy. This inner city also had four gates, which were more like small citadels than mere gatehouses.

Hundreds of years ago the area now occupied by Hatra was an oasis, fed by freshwater springs that pumped water from deep within the earth. It was these springs that filled the city's massive moat, watered its citizens and kept the gardens green and fountains working. But the area around the city was deliberately deprived of water to keep it desert. My father said that this was because, should an enemy army besiege the city, it would have no supplies of water for its troops or animals.

We rode across the causeway that led to the outer wall's northern gate, then under the wall and across the wooden bridge that led to the inner wall's northern gate. Spearmen stood to attention on each side of the bridge and trumpeters sounded the salute as we entered the environs of the palace quarter. Once over the bridge and through the gate, we rode into the great square. On normal days the square was quiet as no stallholders were allowed to ply their trade on its sacred stones. Sandwiched between the royal palace and the Great Temple, the square was reserved for august occasions only. Today was such a day. It was a massive rectangle, and on its south side was the royal barracks housing the king's bodyguard and their horses. These comprised a sprawling mass of stone billets, stables and offices. Beyond the barracks were situated the houses of Hatra's nobles and prosperous citizens. Anyone could purchase a spacious house in the inner city, if they had the wealth. Today, Hatra's finest citizens were gathered in the square to pay homage to the king and his army, and to me also, I surmised.

On the steps of the royal palace, surrounded by courtiers and priests, stood my mother, Queen Mihri. Every son will say that his mother is beautiful, but I believed that my mother was the most striking of all, and her appearance today only reinforced my opinion. Two years older than my father and nearly as tall, she was dressed in a pure white gown with a delicate gold belt around her waist. The gown covered her arms and legs, while on her head she wore a gold crown engraved with the image of Shamash at the front. Her long, black hair was naturally curly, though today it had been oiled, swept back behind her neck and fastened by a gold hair clip. A slave held a large sunshade over her as protection against the sun that was now high in a clear blue sky. Either side of my mother stood my two teenage sisters, Adeleh and Aliyeh. Like myself and my parents, they were both tall and olive skinned. Adeleh, the younger of the two at sixteen, had a round face and was always smiling. She had a carefree nature unlike her sister, Aliyeh, who was thinner and far more serious. Too serious, I always thought, for a girl of only eighteen. Immediately behind my mother and sisters stood the high priest of the Sun Temple, Assur. Now over sixty years old, his long hair and bushy beard were white. Thin as a lance, with a long, bony almost serpent-like face, his black eyes fixed me with a steely gaze as I dismounted at the foot of the palace steps. As a young boy he had always terrified me; indeed, I thought he was Shamash himself come to earth. Truth was he still unnerved me, though today I hoped he was pleased that I had brought a great gift for his temple.

My father, also dismounted, to stand beside me and then walk to my mother. She bowed and he stepped forward and embraced her, to the light applause of the nobles and their families standing in the square. He embraced my sisters and then turned and nodded to Assur. The priest held out his hands and looked to the sky.

'Let us pray to the Sun God,' as one we all knelt and bowed our heads. Assur's voice was loud and strong as he made his dedication. 'O, Great Shamash, O light of the great gods, light of the earth, illuminator of the world's regions, exalted judge, the honoured one of the upper and lower regions. Thou dost look into all the lands with thy light. As one who does not cease from revelation, daily thou dost determine the decisions of heaven and earth. Thy rising is a flaming fire; all the stars in heaven are covered over. Thou art uniquely brilliant; no one among the gods is equal with thee. Great Shamash, bless those here assembled to honour you. And bless in particular King Varaz and Queen Mihri, who by your infinite wisdom have produced their son and your servant, Prince Pacorus, who now returns safely to worship you, having smitten his enemies.'

I was bursting with pride as his words resounded across the square. He bade us rise, then strode over to the soldier holding the eagle, took the Roman standard from him and then marched across the square towards the Great Temple. Because Shamash was the Sun God, the main entrance to the temple, a large porch flanked by two wings that jutted into the square, faced east. Shamash can see everything on earth, and is the god of justice. Shamash and his wife, Aya, have two children. Kittu represents justice, and Misharu the law. Every morning, the gates of Heaven in the east open, and Shamash appears. He travels across the sky and enters Heaven in the west. He travels through the Underworld at night in order to begin in the east the next day.

Assur wore a golden sun symbol on the back of his white priestly robe, as did his priests who served him, and who now followed him up the steps of the Great Temple. At the entrance to the temple Assur turned and faced the crowd, his priests filing past him into the building.

'This offering to Shamash will now be placed in His temple, so He may know that the city of Hatra loves and fears Him. Praise be to Shamash, and may He bestow great fortune on those who devote their lives to His service. Amen.' The crowd shouted 'amen' and then began to file into the place of worship. The Great Temple was the earthly home of Shamash, and once inside we were treated to a rather tedious sermon from Assur. Once it was over and we had filed outside, many nobles and their families came to me to offer their congratulations. These men and their sons and grandsons were the backbone of my father's bodyguard, the cream of Hatra's society: men of courage and honour whom I was proud to serve with. Any man could offer his services to my father's army, but only those born and bred in Hatra could enter his bodyguard.

That night there was a lavish banquet in the palace and I got very drunk. I didn't intend to, but the celebratory atmosphere, seeing my mother again and being acclaimed a hero by some of the most beautiful young women in the city got the better of me. Why not enjoy myself, I thought? I was, after all, the conqueror returned home, the vanquisher of the might of Rome and still only twenty-two years old. So I drank and drank until I collapsed face-first onto the floor. In truth I only remembered the start of the evening; the rest was a blur. But I do remember the stony stare of my parents and the look of horror on the face of Assur as I made an idiot of myself. The rest was darkness.

I was rudely awakened by someone throwing cold water over me in the darkness. I coughed and gasped at the same time and tried to catch my breath.

'What is the meaning of this?' I moaned weakly, astounded that someone had the audacity to do such a thing.

'Get up. You are required to attend morning exercise,' I recognised Vistaspa's emotionless voice.

'Lord Vistaspa, I ...'

'Get up. Now! You think our enemies will wait until a spoilt boy recovers from his hangover after making a fool of himself?' He grabbed me by the hair, yanked me out of bed and threw me to the floor. The first shards of daylight were lancing through the shutters of my room. Vistaspa's face was a stone mask in the half-light.

'The company is already assembled, lord prince,' he spat the last words in sarcasm. 'Get yourself dressed and be in the square in five minutes. Full armour. Shield, helmet and spear.' Then he marched from the room, leaving me soaking and groggy.

'Gafarn, Gafarn,' I half-shouted. My mouth was dry and I felt sick.

'Highness?' a weak voice murmured from under the window. Gafarn had obviously slept a few feet from me and had barely stirred as Vistaspa had stormed in.

'What are you doing here?'

'Too much to drink, highness,' he replied.

'Fetch my armour and spear'. There was no reply. He had obviously gone back to sleep. I walked over to where he lay and kicked him.

'Get up and get my armour and spear.'

He rose unsteadily. 'Yes, highness.'

After gulping down some water, I left the palace and made my way into the square. The dawn had broken now, though the morning was still cool. I wrapped my cloak around me, with my shield on my left arm, a spear in my right and a helmet perched atop my head. I didn't have time to strap it on, an omission I was soon to regret. When I arrived in the square a company of the king's bodyguard was standing to attention, a column of two files fifty ranks deep. Vistaspa stood at its head, looking more stern than usual, which was saying something.

'The noble Prince Pacorus has finally arrived, gentlemen. But what's this?' He strode over to me and knocked my helmet off my head. 'Is that the way you wear your helmet?'

'No,' I replied. My stomach felt worse than ever, and all I wanted to do was lie down.

'No, lord,' he bellowed. 'Address me properly when you speak to me, boy.'

'Yes, lord. Sorry, lord, I…'

'Silence,' he snapped. 'Pick up your helmet and get in line. There, at the head of the column. Move!'

I put my helmet on and trotted to stand beside Vata, who acknowledged me.

'Watch yourself, Pacorus,' he said quietly, 'he's in a foul mood. I think he wants to take out his frustration on us.'

'Why's he frustrated?' I asked.

'Some slave girl must have turned him down last night. Plumped for his horse instead.'

I laughed, which in the circumstances was the worst thing I could have done. Vistaspa was in front of me in an instant, his face inches from mine.

'So, little shit, found something to laugh about, have we? Would you like to share it with us all.'

'No, lord. It was nothing.' Vata stood like a statue, staring directly ahead.

'Prince Pacorus thinks he is a great war hero, don't you, boy.'

'No, lord.'

'Didn't tell anyone that he was nearly skewered by a Roman prisoner because he wasn't looking, or that if I hadn't put an arrow in the man the crows would be picking at his bones right now. We've wasted enough time. Column will advance in quick time. March'

We marched out of the square at a fast pace, a hundred men in full war gear, moving through the inner city, over the moat and then through the northern gate into the desert. Vistaspa kept a cruel pace, and after thirty minutes I was struggling. My mouth was parched and the sun's rays were roasting my helmet, increasing the throbbing in my head. All around me the men's breathing became heavy as we marched through the barren landscape.

'Increase pace.' Vistaspa moved into a light run and we followed, my thighs aching more with each mile we travelled. The previous evening's indulgence was catching up with me fast. I began to cough and breath heavily. I gulped in hot air, which tortured my lungs.

'Run, you dogs.' I was convinced Vistaspa was trying to kill me as we ran across the shimmering desert. The sun was high in the sky and pummelling us with a murderous heat. My mouth was parched and my lungs felt as though they were going to burst through my chest. My shield and spear felt like heavy weights, the burden of carrying them engulfing my arms in a searing pain. Those behind me were struggling as well, though Vata seemed to be coping well. We had been marching for two hours now under a vicious sun, and I knew I couldn't go on for much longer. Sweat was pouring off my forehead into my eyes and the helmet's cheek guards were rubbing against my face.

'Halt!' Vistaspa suddenly stopped and I and Vata nearly clattered into him. 'Two ranks. Move!'

Behind me the men raced to left and right to form into two lines of fifty soldiers, one behind the other. We had reached an area of low-lying hills, and from behind one emerged a camel train. I estimated that it was a least a mile away, maybe less.

'Level spears,' ordered Vistaspa. 'that train is our target.' He drew his sword. 'When I give the command, you will charge and capture it.'

I was astounded. We were nearly spent, and yet he wanted us to charge across open ground for a mile.

'For Hatra,' Vistaspa sprang forward and we followed, shields to our front and spears levelled. We yelled our war cry as we raced towards our target. I was amazed at Vistaspa's stamina, a man of fifty who was out-running us all. After about half a mile our lines were ragged as men stumbled as their legs began to give way. Yet they pushed themselves beyond endurance. A piercing pain shot through my right side, causing me to wince in pain. Sweat poured into my eyes and my vision became blurred.

'Come on, Pacorus, straight on. Don't give up.' I hardly recognised the strained cries of Vata beside me, but his encouragement did force me on. On we went, our pace having slowed into a trot.

'Move, you lazy bastards,' bellowed Vistaspa, as he widened the gap between himself and us. Where did he get his energy from? I was having difficulty breathing now as the caravan loomed large in front of us. I heard men groan around me and the sound of clatter as some fell to the ground, no doubt to be yanked back up by their equally exhausted comrades. It felt as though my chest was in a vice that was being closed shut. I couldn't breath, my vision went black and I couldn't feel my legs. I saw a group of camels ahead and figures scurrying around them, and then all was black.

I was awakened by water being poured over my face. I opened my eyes and saw Vistaspa holding the leather water sack from which the fluid poured. Beside him stood my father. I tried to get up but my limbs refused to move.

'Will you excuse us, Vistaspa,' said my father.

'Of course, sire.'

Vistaspa walked away as my father knelt beside me.

'Give your body time to recover. Compose yourself. While you are doing so, you might reflect on your behaviour last night. You embarrassed your mother and me but, far worse, you embarrassed yourself. You must be an example, my son, not a figure of derision. If you want to be a peacock, go back to Zeugma and live with Darius and his young boys. You are a son of Hatra and are expected to act as such. Remember that, above all.'

I felt crestfallen. After a few seconds of awkward silence he handed me another canteen. I drank greedily and gradually feeling returned to my arms and legs. I was helmetless but still wore my scale armour. Vata helped me up, a wide grin on his big, round face.

'How do you feel?'

'Terrible,' I replied. 'How long was I unconscious?'

'Not long, and you weren't the only one, so don't worry.'

I looked around and saw the company sitting on the ground, eating rations that had been brought from the city. They looked dirty and exhausted, a stark comparison to the impeccably attired other soldiers of my father's bodyguard who were sitting at tables beneath a large canvas awning that had been erected to shelter them from the sun. My father was at the top table, with Vistaspa beside him, dressed in a fresh uniform. Servants prepared and served a light meal of roasted lamb and rice, washed down by water. We ate hard biscuits, but at least we had water. After thirty minutes Vistaspa ordered us into two columns once again. It was now an hour past midday and the sun was at its most brutal. The march back to the city was hard in the searing heat, though at least we had been watered and fed, of sorts. There were no mad charges, though, just a steady march back to the city. I slept like the dead that night.

The next few weeks were spent undergoing the perennial training routines that I had grown up with: rise before dawn, route march on foot in full war gear for two hours; breakfast; archery practice for two hours; wrestling and other unarmed combat for one hour; a two-hour break for lunch and to let the daytime heat subside; then mounted manoeuvres in the late afternoon. The latter could last for up to three or four hours, depending on where they took place. Usually we rode out of the city into the northern desert where the terrain was mostly flat and free of wadis. The surface was hard-baked earth rather than sand, and was thus ideal for cavalry training. All Parthian nobles were taught to ride a horse in childhood. As the years passed we learned all the skills needed to fight war on horseback: how to jump obstacles, gallop over uneven terrain, and to execute circles, turns and stops. Once I had reached adulthood I became a cataphract and learned heavy cavalry skills. These included opening and closing ranks, charging, pursuing, turning and wheeling. Sometimes we went into more hilly terrain to learn how to charge uphill and downhill. It was an unending cycle of practice followed by yet more practice. Once finished for the day we would ride back to the stables where each of us would groom and feed our mounts. The stables themselves were cleaned by the young stable hands. The royal stables block in the palace quarter was spacious and luxurious, as befitting the home of the most highly prized horses in the kingdom, but in truth all the army's stables were well appointed. Parthians loved their horses, for it was their discipline and courage that won battles; and in disaster carried their masters to safety. Geldings or mares were preferred for cavalry mounts, as stallions, though more feisty and faster, were almost uncontrollable when mares were in season.

This, then, was my life. Six days of constant training and drills followed by a day of rest, though even on my day off I liked to hone my sword skills. Occasionally I sparred with my father, who invariably humiliated me. 'You must always move, Pacorus,' he would tell me. 'Stay light on your feet. A man who keeps still is already dead.'

It was two months after I had taken the eagle that an invitation for my father and me came from Sinatruces, the King of Kings, to attend him at the city of Ctesiphon, the capital of the Parthian Empire. Ctesiphon was located on the left bank of the Tigris and at the mouth of the Diyala River. This was something of a surprise, as Sinatruces was nearly eighty years old and something of a recluse. The last time my father had seen him was five years earlier, and then only briefly. Two days after the summons, my father convened a meeting of the city's royal council.

The council met once a month to discuss matters relating to the city and the kingdom. This meeting was special in two ways. Firstly, because it was extraordinary; secondly, because it was the first one that I attended. As the son of the king I would, one day, head the council, but until now I had been forbidden to attend. However, as I had proved myself in battle I was accorded the honour of formally being admitted to the council. In truth there was nothing grand about the location where the council met, a small, comfortable room behind the palace's throne room. There was a large wooden table, comfortable chairs and a large leather map of the Parthian Empire covering the whole of one wall.

Attending were my father, Vistaspa, Bozan, Assur, Addu, the royal treasurer, and the commander of the city's garrison, Kogan. The garrison numbered two thousand men who were housed in four barracks in the city itself. They were the soldiers who policed the city and kept the peace. His was an onerous task with one hundred thousand inhabitants, plus thousands of foreigners who came and went with the caravans passing through the city every day. Peace meant trade and trade meant wealth. It was Kogan's responsibility to maintain the peace, which was relatively easy as long as any trouble was quickly stamped on. My father left the policing of the city to him, knowing that this dour, studious individual who was the same age as my father would never let the king down. Like most efficient administrators, Kogan also had a cruel streak, though to be fair he kept this side of his nature under strict control, mostly.

After Assur offered prayers to Shamash, the meeting got under way. The mood was relaxed. Bozan sprawled in his chair, Vistaspa sat bolt upright, while Kogan watched everyone like a hawk. Assur fussed over his parchments.

'I have called you all here for two reasons,' began my father. 'The first is to welcome my son to the council. He has proved himself in battle and I thought it proper that he acquaint himself with the administration of the city, which in time he will be responsible for.'

'Not for many years, I hope,' said a stern Assur.

'With Shamash's blessing,' retorted my father. 'The second reason is that I and my son have been commanded to attend the High King Sinatruces at Ctesiphon.'

'I thought he was a recluse,' said Bozan.

'He is,' replied my father.

'Obviously our little spat with the Romans has aroused his interest,' continued Bozan. 'No doubt he wants his cut of the spoils.'

'As King of Kings he has a right to such rewards,' added Assur.

'He's only the King of Kings because of our spears,' sneered Bozan.

'Thank you, Bozan', said my father. 'Hatra will make a donation to his coffers should he request one, though I see no reason for it to be generous.'

'Maybe the Romans have made a formal complaint to him,' said Vistaspa. 'Maybe he wants you both there to explain yourselves. You're a fool to go.'

I was amazed at the way Vistaspa addressed my father, but then reminded myself that in such meetings all those who attended were free to express their views regardless of rank. My father told me that there was no point in having a gathering if those present were not allowed to give their views.

'Were you commanded to attend?' asked Assur.

'We were requested,' replied my father.

'Then you are free to refuse, though I would judge such an action imprudent,' said the priest.

Vistaspa shrugged and looked out of the window. Bozan placed his elbows on the table and rested his head in his hands.

'They want their eagle back,' he said.

'What?' I uttered, somewhat in surprise. It was the first time I had spoken and I felt myself blushing.

'That's right, Pacorus,' said Bozan, looking directly at me. 'You stole their eagle and they want it back. I reckon that they sent an embassy to Sinatruces, grovelling at his feet and spinning a tale of how we entered their territory and massacred their men.'

'That's a lie,' I said.

Bozan laughed. 'Indeed it is. But the Romans are lying bastards as well as greedy ones.'

'They can't have the eagle,' I said. 'It's mine.'

There was a ripple of laughter around the table; even Kogan smiled.

'You took it, boy,' said Vistaspa, 'but can you keep hold of it?'

'Enough,' said my father, clearly irritated by such trivia. 'We will go to Ctesiphon and see what Sinatruces has to say for himself. Meanwhile, I intend to enlarge the army.'

'Good idea,' said Bozan.

'That will be expensive.' It was the first time that Addu, a gaunt man in his fifties with thinning brown hair, had spoken. His voice was slightly high-pitched, giving the impression that he was in distress.

'But the treasury is full, is it not?' queried my father.

'Indeed, your majesty,' replied Assur, 'but military spending drains it like water running out of a broken cup.'

'Those chests of Roman gold should be used to pay for more heavy cavalry,' remarked Vistaspa.

'Or more troops for the garrison,' offered Kogan.

'Why does the garrison need more troops?' asked my father.

'There are Romans in the city, majesty,' replied Kogan. 'They may be fomenting rebellion.'

Kogan was right, but then there were many nationalities in Hatra. Indeed, there were the offices of many foreign trading companies in the city, all organising the commerce between the east and their home countries, including Rome. As long as they paid their taxes and caused no trouble they were left alone, as were the many temples that had been established throughout the city. A host of different gods were worshipped in Hatra, including Al Lat, Mithras, Maran, Shiu and Saqaya. Again, as long as they paid their taxes and incited no trouble, the temples were tolerated. Assur and his priests were vociferous in their opposition to the city allowing alien religions within its walls, but were partially soothed by the generous donations made to their temple courtesy of the foreigners' places of worship. An offshoot of this religious tolerance was that Hatra was known as Bet Alaha, the 'House of God'. This in turn resulted in a healthy traffic in pilgrims, who in turn brought more wealth to the treasury.

'You are our eyes and ears in the city, Kogan,' said my father, 'and I have every faith in you to maintain security. However, only an army of horsemen can defend the kingdom from outside enemies. Pacorus and I will go to Ctesiphon. Bozan, you will organise the raising of an additional five hundred heavy cavalry and a thousand horse archers. We will leave in three days.'

In the interim, Vata and I took the opportunity to pay a visit to the city. Though we lived in Hatra, our duties rarely allowed us to wander through its bustling streets. Seeing a myriad of nationalities and different races was always a curiosity, though, along with the temples that were clustered around the east and west gates, through which human traffic and trade flowed all year round. Inside the city were parks where animals could be fed and housed for the night, which were supplied with watercourses for man and beast, and which were guarded by troops of the garrison, though many caravans also had their own guards. The air around the markets was filled with the strange aromas of exotic spices brought from the Orient, while other traders hawked silk and other expensive materials. By chance, Vata and I came across a Roman merchant house whose agents traded in the Parthian Empire, mainly in silk of which Rome had an insatiable appetite for. We entered the whitewashed two-storey building through its large porch. Inside the spacious reception area men were sitting at desks conducting business with travellers and natives of the city. The interior was functional if a little spartan.

'I wonder if they make it look like the insides of the buildings in Rome?' said Vata.

Before I could answer a short man, about thirtyish and dressed in a simple beige linen tunic, approached us, his hair cropped short as was the Roman fashion.

'Can I help you?'

'We are just looking,' I said.

'At what?' he snapped. 'Are you businessmen?'

Our appearances – gold-edged white tunics and leggings, leather boots, ornate leather belts from which hung silver-decorated scabbards – suggested we weren't. I saw no reason to hide our identities.

'I am Prince Pacorus and this is my friend, Vata.'

The Roman looked directly at me. 'So, you are the one who took the eagle.'

I detected a mocking tone in his voice.

'It was easy enough,' I replied, 'I found it lying in the dirt.'

He bristled at this. 'Rome never forgets its enemies.'

'Parthia always looks for new victories.' I was enjoying our verbal duel.

He moved closer to me, our faces inches apart. His audacity, considering he was in my city, was astounding, but I was to become all too familiar with Roman arrogance. 'We have many more legions, Parthian,' he spat, his bad breath reeking in my nostrils.

I clutched the hilt of my sword with my right hand. 'Then go and get them.'

'Enough, Pacorus,' said Vata, laying a hand on my arm. 'Pick on someone your own size. It's unfair to start a quarrel with a dwarf.'

We both laughed, causing the Roman's cheeks to turn red with rage, his fists clenched. We left the building and went back into the street.

'Cocky little bastard, wasn't he,' remarked Vata.

'I think we'll be fighting Romans again very soon.'

'How many legions do you think they have?'

'No idea,' I replied. 'Who cares?'

Vata shrugged. 'Still, at least they're shorter than we are. It's always easier to kill someone who's smaller. I wouldn't like to fight a race of giants.'

My father and I left for Ctesiphon three days later. Vistaspa came with us, of course, along with a hundred of my father's bodyguard, a hundred horse archers and our tents, food and spare weapons loaded onto forty camels. Ctesiphon was two hundred miles from Hatra, a journey we made at a leisurely pace.

The journey through the kingdom allowed my father to inspect part of his domain. He always told me that it was important for the people to see their rulers, and to offer an opportunity for them to speak to him. Many kings viewed their subjects with distaste and suspicion, believing themselves to be appointed by gods to rule on earth.

That is a very dangerous way of thinking, to my mind,' he said as we rode past a group of workers repairing an irrigation ditch in a field. 'Some of them, and I have met them, believe that they are semi-divine themselves. That's all very well until some common soldier in an opponent's army shoots them with an arrow or runs them through with a sword. They don't look so god-like when their guts are spewing all over the place.

It is true, for example, that you were born into a royal household and thus were a prince from birth, but the kingdom you will eventually inherit will grow rich only if you ensure the welfare of your subjects.'

All of them?' I asked.

We can do nothing about plagues and famine. These things are sent by Shamash. But we can ensure that the kingdom is safe. And a safe kingdom is a prosperous kingdom. If this land,' he waved his hand to indicate all around,'was infested with bandits there would be no trade passing through, no well-tended fields to harvest and no functioning irrigation ditches to water the fields. The people would flee and we would live as paupers. Our swords and lances keep the peace and allow the people to prosper. Always remember that, for when you forget it the kingdom is doomed.'

Yes, father.'

And he was right. The land, our land, was rich and prosperous. The distance between the Euphrates and Tigris is two hundred miles at its widest point, and in the area along their banks extending inland, grains and vegetables and dates were cultivated. A complex system of irrigation dykes and ditches drained water from the rivers and kept the land fertile. Oxen were used to pull ploughs, and cows, sheep and goats provided dairy products and meat. There was also a thriving textile industry producing wool for cloth and flax for linen.

The land itself was owned by nobles but worked by farmers, each of whom paid rent to their vassal lord. The aristocrats who lived in Hatra owned vast estates, but those who lived in their villas in the countryside owned much smaller tracts of land. It was the duty of each farmer to own a horse and a bow and practice his horsemanship and archery skills on a regular basis. In this way Hatra had a ready reserve of soldiers that could be called on.

Inevitably there were some who neglected their military duties for farm work, but in general the system worked well enough. And when a general muster was issued, the lords were the first to ride to war. Parthian kings and nobles always led from the front.

The heat of the summer was receding now and the days were sunny but not stifling. The harvests were being gathered, which meant every road was filled with carts pulled by donkeys. When our column neared them, the carts and any human traffic on the road would move aside to let us pass. They bowed to my father and then carried on with their tasks.

'You see, Pacorus,' remarked my father, 'they do not feel threatened by the appearance of soldiers.'

'That's because they are lazy and stupid,' remarked Vistaspa, who had drawn level with us after leading a scouting party.

'That's because they feel safe,' said my father.

'They've become too accustomed to peace,' growled Vistaspa.

'But our army is the finest in the Parthian Empire, is it not?' I added.

'The army is, yes,' said Vistaspa, 'but if we have to issue a general call-up we'll be in trouble.'

'Not every man can be a warrior,' remarked my father.

'More's the pity,' said his bodyguard's commander. Vistaspa then muttered something under his breath and rode towards the rear of the column, no doubt to take out whatever was irritating him on some poor trooper.

My father smiled. 'He's a good man, Vistaspa,' I remained silent, 'but he is too intolerant, I fear. But there is no man I would rather have beside me in battle.'

Ctesiphon was something of a disappointment. It was undoubtedly large and sprawling, but its squat brick buildings were dirty and its walls were also brick and coloured a dark yellow. It was also poor, or at least its inhabitants were. The people eked out an existence from agriculture, but the Silk Road did not pass through Ctesiphon, and therefore it could not tap its wealth. But it did not have to, for all kingdoms in the empire paid tribute to the King of Kings, thus there was a constant flow of money to the capital, though it obviously was not spent on its defences.

We were met outside the city by a detachment of cavalry led by the son of Sinatruces, Phraates. They carried the eagle standard of the King of Kings and were well appointed, with bright steel helmets, whetted lances and burnished shields. They wore mail vests and red cloaks on their backs. Phraates himself, bare headed, rode at the head of the column and greeted my father as an equal, as he was a king in his own right.

'Greetings, King Varaz,' he bowed his head. My father reciprocated. Phraates then looked at me. 'And this must be your son, Prince Pacorus, whom we have heard so much of.'

I bowed my head. 'Highness.'

Phraates was a studious-looking individual, his hair cropped just above his shoulders with a neatly trimmed, short beard flecked with grey. He had a broad face and a rather bulbous nose. I guessed he was nearing sixty years of age.

During the ride to the palace Phraates rode beside my father, with myself and Vistaspa immediately behind.

'You are to be congratulated, Prince Pacorus,' he said. 'Your valour is the talk of the empire.'

'You honour me, majesty,' I replied.

'You are a worthy son of Hatra, the home of the empire's finest warriors.'

His flattery seemed genuine, and I for one could not help but smile as we rode through the royal gates and came to a halt before the steps of the palace. It was a large, tall building with an ornate white stone façade. Guards stood on the steps, spearmen with large wicker shields and red felt caps on their heads. Our horses were taken from us and Phraates led us up the steps, through the reception area and into the throne room. This was a cavernous area some three storeys high, with a white and black marble floor, thick stone columns on either side and a golden throne on a dais surmounted by a griffin at the far end. Courtiers were clustered in groups around the throne while a guard stood in front of each column. As we were led into the room the various hushed conversations died away. All eyes were on us as we approached the dais. We halted a few paces from the figure seated on the throne, an old man with white hair and a wispy beard, which was platted to resemble a serpent's tongue protruding from his chin. On his head he wore a golden crown encrusted with gemstones, while his black tunic was adorned with golden stars. His face was thin and bony, his cheeks slightly sunken. But his dark brown eyes were alert and piercing, and had fixed on us as soon as we had entered the room.

Phraates nodded to a tall, thin man with a staff who stood beside the throne, some sort of chancellor I assumed.

'Majesty, may I present King Varaz and his son, Prince Pacorus,' we went down on one knee and bowed our heads.

'Arise, arise,' said the king, to polite applause from the courtiers. The king's voice was deep and powerful, which came as something of a shock to me considering his frail body.

'You are most welcome, King Varaz, and we congratulate you and your son,' he nodded at me, 'on your victory over the Roman invaders.'

'Thank you, majesty,' said my father.

Sinatruces held out his right hand, into which the chancellor placed a rolled scroll. The room was silent as he carefully unrolled it.

'This document is the reason I invited you here, King Varaz, for it is a demand from the Senate of Rome. A demand that I return their legion's eagle, which they say has been stolen, and furthermore that I pay them reparations for the destruction of said legion.'

There were angry mutterings around the room, which were silenced by Sinatruces holding up his left hand.

'It would appear to me,' he continued, 'that the Romans think that the Parthian Empire is a vassal state, which must pay homage to them. This they must be disabused of. I have therefore replied that it is they who should be paying reparations to us for their gross violation of our sovereignty, and that any future incursions will be countered by great force.' Again, applause filled the room.

'A most wise reply, father,' said Phraates.

I kept my eyes fixed on the floor as Sinatruces spoke, as befitting his rank, though my father looked directly at him. After the preliminary niceties were out of the way, Sinatruces spoke into the ear of his chancellor, who announced that everyone was to leave the room except for myself, my father and Phraates. Once the courtiers had filed out, the two large wooden doors were shut. Guards still stood around the room and I had no doubt that they would be listening intently to what was about to be said, to be later disseminated as idle gossip among their comrades.

Guards placed chairs in front of the dais for us to sit in, while a slave came forward with a tray holding silver goblets. I took one and drank, slightly surprised to discover it was cool water, not wine. Sinatruces sighed and then began to speak again.

'King Varaz, your kingdom is the shield that protects our western border, and I fear that in the months ahead that shield will be battered by Roman spears. Rome is not threatening war, but there is a large Roman garrison in Syria and I'm sure the commander there will be ordered to test your defences and will do so. Hatra is strong and will defend itself with honour, I doubt not.'

'Majesty,' replied my father. 'Hatra is strong but would be stronger with reinforcements.'

'Ah,' sighed Sinatruces. 'I thought we would come to that. I have to tell you that the empire is threatened from the north by the Alans and by the Sakas in the east. I cannot ask for troops from the kings who are facing those threats, for to do so would risk leaving our borders vulnerable.'

'Rome is a bigger threat than tribes of nomads, majesty,' said my father.

'You are right, King Varaz, but Hatra's army is the strongest in the empire. We are not unmindful of your dilemma, and thus are prepared to grant you aid.'

'Troops?' my father asked.

'Alas, no, but we will give you ten cartloads of gold to allow you to sustain your war effort.'

I cast a glance at my father and saw his eyes light up. Hatra's treasury was already full, and such an amount would allow my father to strengthen the army.

'A most generous offer, majesty.'

Sinatruces clapped his hands. 'Excellent! You will both stay for the banquet tonight. A most satisfactory meeting, I think.'

We were shown to our luxurious quarters in the palace where we were waited on by a host of slaves. I bathed and afterwards had a massage at the hands of a lithe Armenian girl, whose fingers erased the aches from my neck and shoulders and sent me into a dream-like state. It was a most excellent life being royalty, I had to admit.

The evening banquet was a sumptuous affair. Parthians believe that consuming red meat and fats create evil thoughts, and is in any case the food of barbarians. Thus the trays were piled high with fruits, vegetables, fish, fowl and lamb. Delicacies included oranges, pistachios, spinach, saffron, sweet and sour sauces, kabobs and almond pastries, all washed down with the finest wines. My father was seated on the left side of Sinatruces, with Phraates on his right side. I sat next to my father, while behind us were guards. The chancellor and a number of other officials sat down at another table, one of some twenty that were arranged around the feasting hall. In the centre a troupe of jugglers was entertaining the guests as a small army of servants ferried trays to and from the kitchens. Sinatruces, I noted, ate sparingly and drank little, speaking the occasional word to my father, who smiled and nodded dutifully.

I also noticed that an old woman had suddenly appeared in the room and was shuffling towards the top table. I was somewhat surprised, not least because no one seemed to be taking the slightest notice of her. She was dressed in rags and had a stooped appearance. She was constantly looking right and left and seemed to be muttering insults at all and sundry. Her stooped posture, misshapen nose and sore-covered face was in stark contrast to the beautifully attired and attractive guests that filled the room. She continued to shuffle towards us, and a feeling of horror came over me as I realised that she was heading directly for me. I stared in disbelief as she stopped opposite me on the other side of the table. She cackled in a most disconcerting way to reveal a row of brown teeth. Her breath, even from a distance, was repellent. She pointed at me.

'Give me your hand, little lamb,' she spat.

Who was this foul old crone who dared to speak to me thus? I felt my anger mount, and was about to rise and order her out of the room when Sinatruces spoke.

'You had better do what she asks, Prince Pacorus.'

I was stunned. 'Majesty?'

'This is Dobbai, a Scythian from the mountains of the Indus. She is a sage, some say a sorceress, and has been a member of my court for many years now. She has a gift. She can see the future. That is why we tolerate her.'

'That is why you fear me, Sinatruces.' She pointed a bony finger at the king. 'Let me speak to the lamb, otherwise I will turn you into a warthog.'

To utter such words to the High King was to invite immediate execution, but Sinatruces merely smiled and gestured to me to hold out my hand.

I have to confess that I was hesitant to extend my arm. She not only looked revolting, but her sunken cheeks and emaciated frame suggested that she had not eaten for a while. Perhaps she wanted to eat my hand! Suddenly confronting an army of Romans seemed less daunting. However, aware that all of those sitting at the top table were observing me, along with others on nearby tables, I held out my right arm.

The old hag grabbed it with her right hand with a grip that was surprising strong. Her clutch was bony and cold. I shivered. She looked at my upturned palm and then spat into it. I felt a wave of nausea wash over me. Filthy old crone, how dare she treat me like this.

She then drew her left forefinger across my palm, mumbled some nonsense to herself and then looked me directly in the eyes. This made me feel even more uncomfortable. I felt my cheeks colour. For what seemed like an eternity, but was actually only a few seconds, she stood motionless.

'Portents,' she spat the word at me, 'portents of doom. You will slither like a serpent into the belly of your enemies, and there eat away at their innards.'

She was clearly mad, but she still held my hand fast. She looked at the palm a second time after drawing circular motions with her forefinger in her spittle.

'The eagle will scream in pain but will thirst for revenge. Many eagles will pursue you, but under the desert sun you will pick at their bones. A pale goddess with fire in her eyes will be your companion, son of Hatra.'

Then she let go of my hand, reached over and grabbed some pork ribs from my plate, and shuffled away. As she passed Sinatruces she turned to him.

'Merv burns while you stuff your face, old man.'

Sinatruces looked alarmed as the old hag walked away, chewing on a rib as she did so. He beckoned to his chancellor who scurried over. Sinatruces spoke to him in a somewhat agitated manner, and then the chancellor hurried off.

'Merv is a city on our eastern frontier,' whispered my father.

'Do we listen to the ramblings of an insane, stinking witch?' I replied, wiping my hand with a napkin.

'I don't know, Pacorus,' he said, staring at me. 'Do we?'

I could barely hide my annoyance. 'No, we do not.'

I called for a servant to refill my goblet with wine. The hag had disappeared now, along with my appetite. I dismissed what she had said from my mind. Eagles, serpents? I shook my head. Out of the corner of my eye I saw Vistaspa looking at me, but not with his usual mocking stare. Instead, he nodded and toasted me with his goblet. This discomfited me even more.

The next day we departed Ctesiphon for Hatra, taking the cartloads of gold with us. Our audience with Sinatruces and Phraates that morning had been brief, and the old king had seemed very distracted. Phraates offered us extra guards for the journey but my father declined his offer. Vistaspa's men were more than adequate, though for additional security he sent riders ahead to order that more of Hatra's cavalry meet us on the road.

'This gold should pay for the additional troops you want to enlist,' said Vistaspa as we rode at the head of the column.

My father nodded thoughtfully. 'An unexpected bonus, that's for sure. I was worried Sinatruces was after a portion of the Roman gold we took. Still, what with that and his gift, we should have enough spears to keep the border secure.'

'You think the Romans will attack us, father?'

'For certain,' he replied.

'Raids, most probably,' said Vistaspa. 'A few villages burned, maybe a town, if we don't keep our guard up.'

'We'll have to watch the north especially,' said my father, 'since I doubt our old friend Darius will give us any support.'

Vistaspa nodded. 'He might pay a few more tribesmen to cause us problems.'

'Two can play at that game,' said my father.

But thoughts of Roman raids soon passed as we travelled along dusty roads baked hard under blue skies. The pace was leisurely, and for long periods we walked beside our horses, resting under canvas shades two hours either side of midday, when the heat was most fierce. Four days from Hatra, a detachment of the city's cavalry led by Vata met us during the late afternoon. Vata pulled up his horse in front of my father, bowed his head then reached inside a saddlebag to hand him a scroll. My father read it, frowned and passed it to Vistaspa.

Vistaspa, as was his wont, read it without expression. 'It's begun, then.'

'Sooner than I thought.'

'What is it, father?' I asked.

'A message from Bozan. A week ago Roman cavalry attacked and plundered Sirhi. They must have crossed the Arabian Desert from Syria. They have taken many captives, no doubt to be sold as slaves.' Sirhi was a town on the banks of the Euphrates, in the north of the kingdom.

'I have to get back to Hatra. Vata, you will escort the gold to the city. I, Vistaspa and Pacorus will ride to the city tonight.'

After a light meal we left in the early evening, riding hard. We covered the fifty miles in a day, arriving at the palace late at night. Bozan was waiting for us in the council chamber. After going to see my mother, I and my father went to the chamber where Bozan was deep in conversation with Vistaspa.

'Well?' enquired my father, 'how bad is it?'

'Not as bad as we first feared, my lord,' replied Bozan. 'The town remains intact, though the outlying villages have been mostly reduced to ashes and their inhabitants carried off into slavery. The garrison commander panicked and exaggerated the size of the Roman force and the damage they did.'

'Doesn't mean there aren't more Roman troops in the area,' added Vistaspa.

'There is a legion at Damascus, but to march it across the desert just for a raid seems too big a risk,' mused my father.

Bozan was in a bullish mood. 'Strike back at them, my lord. They cannot be allowed to get away with this outrage.'

'A wise course of action, I agree,' added Vistaspa, 'but the question is, where to strike?'

While my father deliberated, servants brought us wine, fruit and bread. We were tired and covered in dust, while our eyes were ringed with black through lack of sleep.

'I can't decide tonight,' said my father at last. 'We will reconvene in the morning.'

Chapter 3

After a night's rest I had breakfast with my mother in the small palace garden that she tended as a hobby. The plants and flowerbeds were immaculate, and the gentle sound of the fountain in the middle of the shallow pond filled with goldfish gave a sense of calm. My mother was dressed in a simple white dress, with a gold chain at her waist. Her shoulder-length black hair was loose, showing its natural waves. She wore little make-up or jewellery and wore simple leather sandals on her feet

Servants served us fruit and bread. Queen Mihri was in a happy mood.

'How did you find King Sinatruces, Pacorus?'

'He's old,' I replied.

She laughed. 'He certainly is, but also wise and astute. You don't rule a collection of kingdoms for nearly fifty years without ability.'

'I suppose not,' I said, watching a shapely servant girl walk from the table carrying an empty food tray.

'Your father tells me that you had a private audience with the king's sorceress.'

I shuddered. 'She was a disgusting old hag. It was humiliating.'

My mother laughed. 'I'm sure she was, but the fact that she picked you out is of note. Some would consider it a great honour to hear her words. The prophecies of Dobbai are famous throughout the empire.'

'Meaningless drivel, mother. She is clearly insane and no one should pay any attention to her.'

'You speak with the certainty of youth.' Her big round brown eyes hinted at gentle mockery. I shrugged. 'But do not dismiss her words too lightly. I for one believe that she can see the future.'

She could tell by my expression that I had no interest in discussing the old crone any further, so she moved on to another subject.

'Your father and I think it is time to think of a bride for you.'

'What?' my heart sank.

'You are now a famous warrior, and in any case a prince of Hatra cannot remain single for ever.'

'I'm too young,' I protested.

'Nonsense, you are twenty-two, which is old enough to be betrothed. I hear that Princess Axsen of Babylon is available.' I suddenly lost my appetite. 'Perhaps we will arrange for you to see her. The daughter of the Kingdom of Babylon would strengthen the position of Hatra.'

'I would prefer to marry someone whom I loved.'

'You are not a farmer, Pacorus. Princes must marry to cement alliances and ensure the safety of their kingdoms,' she rebuked me. 'Besides, is there someone who has stolen your heart?'
'Of course not.'
She smiled. 'Then surely you have no objection to meeting Princess Axsen, at the very least? I hear that she is a great beauty. I'm sure love could grow from such a match.'
I was about to protest but thought better of it. My mother had the appearance of a softly spoken, acquiescent woman, but she had a will of iron and was not to be crossed lightly. I therefore just nodded my agreement and began thinking of how I could avoid meeting Princess Water Buffalo.
She clapped her hands for the servants to take the food away. 'Excellent.'
I rose and kissed her on the cheek. 'Thank you, mother.'
Feeling somewhat aggrieved I left her and made my way to the council chamber. The day was hot and airless, but the marble-tiled palace was cool and quiet. I took my place next to my father, who looked refreshed and in a good mood as he chatted with Assur. In fact, everyone was in attendance – Assur, Addu, Bozan, Kogan and Vistaspa.
The doors were closed and my father spoke, his tone stern. 'We have now been attacked twice by Rome and it is time for us to retaliate. There can be no peace until Rome has understood that Parthia, and especially Hatra, is not a lamb but a lion. To this end I intend to launch an assault across the desert against Syria. I will lead this expedition. Our strength lies in speed and stealth, therefore I will take no heavy cavalry, light horsemen only. To aid us in our little adventure, we will hire some Agraci to accompany us.'
'But, my lord,' protested Bozan, 'the Agraci are scum who would slit your throat in the same breath that they would offer their hand in greetings.'
'I know that, Bozan, and I have no doubt that they helped the Romans attack Sirhi, but they can be bought easily enough. Offer enough gold and they will sell their own mothers and daughters.'
'I would rather have their camels,' said Bozan.
The Agraci were a tribe of nomads who inhabited the Arabian Peninsula. Like all of the tribes in that region, they consisted mostly of thieves and beggars who preyed on the unwary. We spent considerable resources on keeping them away from the trade routes, frequently having to launch punitive raids into the desert. Being wanderers, they were often difficult to find. Occasionally we

got lucky and were able to slaughter a lot of them, leaving their bones to bleach in the sun. But, like flies, they seemed to be eternal, and just as irritable. Their only redeeming feature was that their services could easily be hired if you had enough gold.

'Just make sure you keep upwind of them on the journey,' added Vistaspa.

'This raid is only one part of our response,' added my father. He got up and stood beside the large map of the Parthian Empire that hung on the wall. He pulled the dagger from the scabbard that hung from his belt and used it as a pointer.

'We will launch a second, smaller raid here, against Cappadocia. Five hundred men mounted on swift horses should be enough to give the Romans a taste of their own medicine. Bozan, you will lead this expedition.'

Bozan grinned and ran his hands across his shaved head. 'A pleasure, my lord.'

'Remember,' continued my father, 'it's only a raid. Go in fast, hit them hard and then get out. And to continue his military education, Pacorus will ride along with you.'

I looked at Bozan and grinned, who nodded his approval. This was an excellent development. The chance of fighting again filled me with joy, the more so since it would get me out of the city and away from my mother's schemes to get me married. Addu cleared his throated rather noisily.

'You have something to say, Lord Addu?' asked my father.

'Er, merely this, majesty,' Addu replied, gingerly rising from his seat. My father indicated for him to remain seated. 'Though I am sure that these expeditions will add more glory to your name, they may damage trade. May I remind you that Palmyra, Petra and Baalbek, all towns in the area you intend to assault, are of importance to Hatra. If they are destroyed then our revenues will suffer.'

'I am aware of the importance of trade to the city,' said my father. 'Rest assured that we will not be attacking caravans or trading centres. We will be striking military outposts. There are a number of forts along the desert frontier. It is my hope to surprise one or two and put them to the torch.'

'But what if the Romans retaliate by halting their trade?' asked Addu.

My father, who I could tell was losing patience with his treasurer, sat down and stared at him. 'I can assure you, Lord Addu that the last thing the Romans want is to stop trading with the east.'

'That's true,' added Bozan, 'the bastards have an insatiable demand for lions and tigers to slaughter in their arenas, and they can't get enough silk.'

Assur winced at Bozan's course language, but nodded in agreement. 'Lord Bozan is correct in what he says, even if the words he uses to express his opinion are somewhat vulgar. We cannot allow Roman outrages to go unpunished.'

'But, your majesty,' said Addu.

'Enough,' snapped my father. 'The decision has been made, we will leave in seven days.'

A crestfallen Addu stared at the table in silence.

'There are Romans in the city, majesty.' It was first time that Kogan had spoken. 'If they hear of any expeditions they will surely send word back to their masters.'

There were nods around the table.

'You are right, Lord Kogan,' said my father. 'No one is to speak of this matter outside of this room. As far as the city is concerned, we are merely carrying out training manoeuvres. When we have left the city I will send riders to the Agraci to see if they want to earn some gold. Hopefully, I will be able to get a lot of them killed in battle before I have to pay them anything. That is all.'

Everyone stood, bowed and then left the room. My father called me over.

'Pacorus, say nothing of what you have heard to Gafarn or Vata. Is that understood.'

'Yes, father.'

'The Romans have spies everywhere. We cannot be too careful.'

'Will there be war between us and the Romans?' I asked.

My father sighed and considered before giving his reply. 'What we have now is an armed peace. The Romans are testing us, seeking to discover our strength.'

'We have a strong army,' I said, proudly.

'It is not just a question of spears and horses. It is also one of will. The Romans are strong because they never give up. Their army is like a machine that chews up everything in its path. Many kingdoms lack the will to fight the Romans. They are not unbeatable, we have proved that, but to fight them year in, year out, takes an iron will. Few possess that quality. There are many like King Darius who want to live a life of luxury. But here's the clever thing about the Romans. They offer individuals like Darius the opportunity to be a client king. Be our friend, they say, and you can rule your kingdom in peace, unmolested as long as you pay your dues to Rome. But a client kingdom is a slave kingdom, which eventually will be filled with Roman soldiers and civilians, who build garrisons, towns, roads and ports that bring in yet more Romans. And then Rome annexes that kingdom and it is swallowed up, to become just one more province in the Roman Empire.'

'Parthia is strong, father,' I said, though partly to reassure myself as well as him, for the image of an all-powerful Rome did little to fortify my courage.

He slapped me on the shoulders. 'If we keep it that way, then the Romans will think twice before they try to conquer us. But always remember, Pacorus, the old saying, "it is better to die on your feet than live on your knees". For even the richest ally of Rome is in reality no more than a slave dressed in fine clothes.'

We left the city at dawn on the seventh day. Two columns of horsemen, one heading west into the Arabian desert, the other going north back towards Zeugma, though we would swing sharply west before we reached Darius' kingdom. I wondered if the bodies of those we had slain were still lying where they fell. I dismissed such trivia from my mind. Before we left I had gone to see my friend Vata. I found him in the royal stables. He grinned when he saw me. He was always smiling, that was one of the reasons I liked him, that and his loyalty to his friends. He would be riding with my father into Syria.

'Why can't we take our own horses?' he asked.

I knew the reason, of course: heavy cavalry horses were too valuable to be risked on raiding parties. That was the reason I could not take Sura with me. I felt bad about lying to Vata.

'I know not, my friend.' I walked over to him as Gafarn entered the stables.

'We are ready to ride, highness.'

'Thank you, Gafarn. Meet me outside.'

I walked over to Vata and embraced him. 'Keep safe, my friend.'

'You mean try not to fall off my horse.'

'No, I mean. It doesn't matter. Just return safely.' This could be the last time I saw him, and I wanted to tell him so but could not.

'You're getting too soft, my friend,' he said, slapping me on the back. 'That's what happens when you spend too long in the palace dreaming about Babylonian princesses.'

I left him and walked to the waiting Gafarn, who was mounted on a horse and held the reins of mine. We trotted from the stables.

'Do you feel bad, highness?'

'What?'

'About lying to your friend, I could see it in your face.'

'Shut up. What do you know?'

'I know nothing, highness, he said, 'except that you were not telling the truth to him and it must have hurt lying to your friend.'

'Be quiet.'

'To lie to a friend can be unpleasant, I agree.'

I drew up my horse sharply. 'I could have you flogged.'

He was unconcerned. 'You could, but that would not make you feel any less remorseful.'

I kicked at my horse and he sprang forward. Gafarn was right, as usual, which made it even more irritating.

Three days out from Hatra we reached the town of Nisibus where we picked up extra provisions. These along with our spears, enough to sustain us for a month, were loaded onto mules that would accompany us on our expedition. Each of us carried a sword, shield, bow and fifty arrows, while for protection we wore helmets only, no body armour. In Nisibus we also picked up a guide who said he knew Cappadocia intimately, though by the look of him I suspected he was more intimate with the town's whores. He had a sullen look, with dark, brooding eyes and lank black hair. He was unclean, unshaven and dressed in what appeared to be rags.

'Are we to trust this man?' I asked Bozan.

'The garrison commander says he was once a soldier in the army of Mithridates when he was a teenager, who fought the Romans in Cappadocia. If that's true then he could be useful. Says he knows which roads the Romans use to send their supplies to Pontus. It could all be true.'

'And if it isn't?' I asked.

Bozan shrugged. 'Then I'll slit his throat personally.'

'He could be leading us into a trap.'

'Listen, Pacorus,' he said, 'war is always a gamble. You never really know what the enemy is doing, what's on the other side of the hill. But nothing ventured, nothing gained, as my old dad used to say.'

'What happened to him?'

'An Armenian skewered him with a lance in an ambush, poor bastard.'

I was filled with doubt, but then again the guide could be telling the truth. King Mithridates had been fighting the Romans for years. The ruler of Pontus, he had been gradually pushed back through Greece to his kingdom in the north. He was still fighting Rome, but now there were Roman legions on his borders. It was possible that this man had fought for him. Whatever the truth was, he led us north from Nisibus into the wild country that was Cappadocia. A barren, arid region, it was bordered to the north by the peaks of the Black Sea mountain range and in the south by the Taurus Mountains. We rode through gorges and canyons with steep sides, passed through valleys criss-crossed by streams and gazed at dazzling rock formations fashioned by wind and water. We saw few people, and I was beginning to think that the whole area was uninhabited when our guide suddenly pulled up his horse. I was riding beside Bozan when he galloped up to us.

'We camp here tonight, lord,' he said. 'Fresh water nearby, lots of cover. Very safe.'

'What about the Romans?' I asked.

'No Romani, lord.'

He rode away to show our scouts where we could camp for the night. I had to confess that the spot he chose was a good one: near fresh water and high in the hills, giving us excellent views of the surrounding terrain. If we were attacked there were also avenues of escape through the rock formations. So as not to advertise our presence, Bozan forbade the lighting of any fires that night. As the sun went down the temperature fell, but fortunately the wind that had been blowing all day disappeared as well. Gafarn and I fed and watered our horses before we ate our own meal. While we were attending to our mounts our guide ambled up to observe us, accompanied by two guards (it appeared Bozan didn't trust him, either). Yet he appeared unconcerned by being almost a prisoner, no doubt content to have the first payment of gold in his saddlebag. He would get the rest at the end of our mission.

'You Parthians love your horses,' he said, smiling.

'A Parthian without a horse is like a man without a right arm,' replied Gafarn. I glowered at him, but he continued to engage the man in conversation. 'We are busy,' I snapped.

The man bowed. 'Of course, lord. Did not mean to cause offence.'

I laid my horse's saddle and saddlecloth on the ground, Gafarn watching me all the time. 'What?' I asked.

'You do not like him?'

'I do not trust him. There is a difference.'

'Why, because he does not wear fine clothes?'

'No, because he takes gold.'

Gafarn laughed. 'Why shouldn't he? He has to put food in his belly. He does not have a fine palace to live in and servants to do his bidding.'

'He could also be taking Roman gold, have you thought of that? He might be leading us into a trap.'

'Or he might hate the Romans and want revenge on them for murdering his family.'
'How do you know that?' I asked.
'I spent some time talking to him. You should try it sometime.'
'I don't have time for idle gossip, that's for servants.'
'Then you won't be interested to hear about Merv.'
'What about Merv?'
'Burnt to the ground, I hear,' he said, nonchalantly examining his scabbard.
'You're lying.'
He looked hurt. 'Why should I lie?'
'To annoy me,' I replied.
'There are easier ways of doing that, believe me.'
'Enough! Tell me what you know.'
'When we were in Nisibus I was idly talking to a dispatch rider, who told me that a horde of Scythians had attacked the city and set fire to it. Didn't that old woman at Ctesiphon say something about a burning city?'
'I can't remember,' I lied.
'Oh, I think you can. Makes you think, though.'
'Enough, Gafarn. My ears are aching.'
'Yes, highness,' he said, smiling mischievously.
I hardly slept that night, thinking about what Gafarn had told me. He must have been mistaken. Towns and outposts were always being attacked along the empire's eastern frontier, especially from the north, the land of the nomads of the steppes. But still...
The next day we were led across a wide, grass-covered plain, with the northern mountains capped with snow on our flank. The guide led us into a small wood, where we tethered the mules and left guards to watch over them, while the others checked their weapons, saddles and mounts. The guide, Bozan and I then made our way on foot to the other side of the wood, which looked out onto another, smaller plain bordered on the far side by a low-lying rock plateau. A dirt track ran across the plain. The sun was now at the midpoint in the sky, which was dotted with white puffy clouds. The air in the wood was still and humid; sweat formed on my brow and ran down my face. Bozan peered at the flat terrain in front of us.
'You're sure this is the way they come?'
'Sure, lord,' replied the guide, whose name Gafarn told me, was Byrd.
'When?'
'Two hours.'

Bozan turned to me. 'Pacorus, he says there will be a Roman supply column coming through here, on its way to Pontus, so I intend to stop it here. Being so far from the fighting there should be only a light escort. Nevertheless, we hit them hard and then get away fast. No looting.'

'Yes, lord,' I replied. The thought of battle made my pulse race with excitement.

We made our back to the men, which was a ten-minute walk through widely separated poplar trees. The passage through the trees would be easy enough for horsemen, but if we placed our cavalry too close to the edge of the wood, the enemy would see them. Bozan organised us into companies of just under a hundred men each, with a few men left behind at the camp to look after the food, spare weapons and the mules. I would lead one company, he another and the other three by appointed officers. The guide remained at the camp. He wanted to fight with us but Bozan said no. If he had betrayed us, the thought of having to fight hundreds of Roman infantry and cavalry cooled my passion somewhat. I told Gafarn to stay at the camp, though he wanted to ride beside me. He may have been a servant, but he was as skilled as I in the use of a bow, perhaps more so, and could also handle a sword if need be. Despite his protests I insisted that he remain behind. We were making our last equipment checks when a soldier ran up to Bozan with the news that the enemy had been spotted.

Bozan gave the signal that the cavalry were to mount up, then he pointed at me and indicated that I should follow him as he and the guide ran towards the edge of the wood. Minutes later I was kneeling beside Bozan peering across the plain towards black shapes that had appeared in the distance. Bozan must have heard my heavy breathing.

'Calm yourself, Pacorus, there's plenty of time.'

As the minutes passed the shapes began to take on recognisable forms. Ahead and on the flanks of the column were horsemen, I estimated around a hundred, though there was probably more at the rear of the column. Then came a phalanx of infantry with their red rectangular shields, steel helmets and mail shirts, though some were carrying long spears and green, round shields – auxiliaries. At their head marched a figure with a transverse crest and a legionary carrying a red, square-shaped standard mounted atop a long pole. Then came the four-wheeled wagons, each one pulled by a pair of oxen. The pace of the column was slow, both men and beasts maintaining a leisurely pace. I estimated that they would be level with us in around twenty minutes, maybe less. It took us half that time to get back to our troops, issue orders to the columns and make our way back to the far side of wood. Byrd stayed with Gafarn and the reserve.

I, Bozan and three other officers were at the head of our respective companies, all eyes on Bozan. The Roman flank horsemen were getting close now, though their riders were not really scouting, merely maintaining the regulation distance from the wagons. Bozan plucked an arrow from his quiver and placed the feathered end on the bowstring; everyone else did the same. Each of us held the bow with our left hand and the drawstring with our right. My heart was like a hammer pounding against my rib cage, waiting for the sign. Waiting, waiting. The silence was deafening, broken only by the occasional snort of a horse. Bozan's gaze was fixed on the enemy. Then we charged.

Bozan gave a shout and kicked his horse into the attack; nearly five hundred horsemen followed. In any assault the first two or three minutes are crucial. The enemy is temporarily stunned, and even the best-trained soldiers in the world cannot react in the blink of an eye. But these were not the best-trained troops; they were a mixture of legionaries and auxiliaries, and they were strung out in a long line. Our five columns of horse archers lapped round the column like waves crashing against a spit of land. As my horse raced towards the rear of the column I saw one of the drivers stand up on his cart with a spear in his hand. I released my bow as I neared him, the arrow slicing through the air and hitting him in the stomach. He collapsed back into the cart as I galloped past him. The enemy outriders were already dead, pierced by arrows before they had a chance to react.

The air was filled with screams, curses and shouts as my company reached the end of the column, which consisted of two overloaded carts. Some of my men put arrows into the oxen as others fired at the auxiliaries protecting them. These men tried to form a shield wall, but their shields were round not oblong like those of the legionaries, and it was easy for us to shoot at exposed heads and torsos. Within seconds the line had broken. I fired an arrow that slammed into a man's throat, sending him spinning backwards onto the ground. We kept moving around the column, for a man on a horse presents a large target to a spearman when he is stationary. I strung another arrow as I turned to make another pass at the column. Within minutes the ground was littered with dead and dying men and oxen. I could see no enemy cavalry at all; the survivors must have fled.

I wheeled to make another pass at the enemy and strung another arrow. Some archers had taken up position next to a cart in the middle of the column and were returning fire at our horsemen. But their bows had less range compared to ours and their arrows were falling short. I decided we had to destroy this threat.

'Follow me,' I shouted at the riders behind me.

We rode hard along the column, ignoring and staying out of the range of enemy spears that were flung in our direction. The archers were shooting in a haphazard fashion, each man trying to identify and hit a target instead of firing a concentrated volley. I urged my horse into an even quicker pace as I approached the group of archers. My aim was instinctive, honed by years of intensive training in the saddle with a bow. Before I drew level with the archers I wheeled my horse sharply to the right and away from the enemy, at the same time loosing an arrow in a high arch towards them. The riders following did likewise, and in a matter of seconds nearly one hundred arrows were peppering the enemy formation. As we regrouped to make another attack I could see lifeless figures on the ground where our arrows had found their mark. I estimated that we had dropped around a third of them, maybe more.

Bozan rode up. He was sweating and had removed his helmet.

'It's almost over. Leave those archers. They'll run away if given the chance. Up ahead we've got about fifty Romans who are sheltering under a wall and roof of shields. We need to break them fast.' With that he rode away.

The Romans had taken up position in the open away from the line of carts, locking their shields outwards while those inside the small square hoisted theirs over the front ranks to give overhead cover from our arrows. A lull now descended over the scene as officers gave the order for around half our men to dismount and rest. The others were formed into troops of fifty horsemen who were positioned all around the Romans but stood off at a safe distance – the enemy had javelins and knew how to use them. I dismounted, took a swig from my water skin and strode over to where Bozan was standing alone, looking at the Roman formation. There was a frown across his scarred face.

'We might have to leave these bastards,' he spat on the ground. 'They aren't going anywhere and I don't want to hang around.'

Bozan loved a fight, but he was also a commander and he knew that it was not worth wasting time and lives over an insignificant number of the enemy. Even so, I knew that the fact that the enemy stood defiant in good order must be rankling him. Behind us smoke drifted into the sky as the carts and their contents, minus the food that we had removed, were burned. Some of our men armed with daggers were putting the enemy wounded out of their misery, while Bozan had sent another fifty riders to hunt down and kill those of the enemy who had fled when we first attacked.

'Have you demanded their surrender, lord?' I asked.

'Of course. They declined to accept my invitation. Arrogant bastards. It doesn't matter. We've caused them some damage, and by tonight we will be well away from here.'

'I would like to try something, lord,' I said.

'I'm not wasting any men, or horses, just to prove a point.'

'What I have in mind won't cost us anything.'

He looked at me and glanced at the Romans. He nodded. 'Very well, you have one chance. Don't waste it.'

I ordered a dozen of our dismounted soldiers to cut the straps of the two dead oxen that were still lashed to one of the carts. The corpses were hauled aside and the carts were pushed towards the Roman formation, halting about two hundred feet from it. We piled enemy shields, broken spear shafts and any other dry wood we could find onto the front of the cart and set the lot on fire. Soon the front of the cart was ablaze. We now had a race against time.

'Heave,' I shouted, as ten of us gripped the rear of the cart and pushed it forward with all our strength. Around the cart dozens of horsemen readied their bows. Pain shot through my legs as I helped to haul the burning cart forward. We were now less than a hundred feet away and gaining momentum. The cart was burning fiercely and the heat was searing my face. The Romans now broke ranks to avoid the blazing hulk that was bearing down on them. Ahead I saw legionaries readying their javelins to launch at us. A few managed to throw them, a couple spearing men who were pushing the cart.

'Back,' I yelled.

We let go of the cart as it rumbled forward and then came to a halt. The Romans, realising that they were not going to be crushed by a burning cart after all, tried to reform, but they were too late. The air was filled with arrows as our bowmen found their targets. Arrows slammed into chests, arms, legs and faces, filling the air with piercing screams and yelps as iron tips lacerated flesh and shattered bone. The Roman formation was broken. Our horsemen were among them now, hacking away with their swords. Some Romans fought back, slashing horses with their swords or stabbing them with javelins, and bringing riders down and killing them. But for every one of our men who was killed four or five Romans were felled. The enemy group dwindled in number, until there was just a handful left. I saw that the figure with the transverse crest on his helmet was one of them. He also saw me as I unsheathed my sword and hoisted my shield to guard my left side. He came at me at a steady trot, his short sword in his right hand. He was obviously some sort of leader, and I wanted to kill him to seal our victory.

I was supremely confident as we closed and hacked at each other with our swords. My confidence soon started to disappear as I realised that I was in a life-and-death struggle with a man who was an expert fighter. His grizzled visage glared at me from under his brightly polished steel helmet. I charged at him, shield against shield and tried to hack down with my sword to split his helmet, but he anticipated the move, parried the blow with his sword and then slashed with his blade aiming for my neck. Only my reflexes saved me, as I instinctively jumped back to avoid the blow. He attacked again and again, forcing me back and battering my shield with heavy hacking blows that splintered the wood. His speed was amazing as he tried to deliver a killer blow with his sword. I caught one blow with the cross-guard of my sword and tried to press one end of it into his neck, but in a trial of strength he was the stronger, and he pushed my right arm down. While our swords were still locked he smashed the edge of his shield into the side of my face. A searing pain went through my skull as he jumped back and began circling me. I thought I was strong, but this man seemed superhuman. I was sweating profusely and panting hard. Then he came at me again.

He must have decided that he was going to die and so he was going to sell his life dearly, because he screamed and attacked me with scything strokes of his sword. I parried as best I could, but one blow cut my right forearm before I could get it out of the way, the blood soon covering my arm. I lunged at him with all my weight using my shield, but it was like hitting a rock. He stopped my attack and then tried to rip open my stomach with an underhand stabbing attack, though I was able to parry the blow with my shield at the last moment. But my legs had got tangled around his and he gave a low grunt as he pushed me back over his right leg, sending me crashing to the ground. I was finished, I knew that as I saw him draw back his sword to deliver the final blow. Then I heard several whooshing sounds and then saw two arrows slam into his side. He groaned but remained standing. Incredible; was he a god? Then another arrow hit him, then another and another. Finally, after what seemed like an eternity, he collapsed sideways onto the ground.

Shaken and bloody, I staggered to me feet. He was dead and I was alive. My mouth was dry and I called for some water. A soldier ran up and gave me his water skin as I raised my sword in thanks at the archers who had saved me. Then I saw Bozan marching towards me, with a face like thunder.

'You stupid little idiot. The next time you fancy being a hero don't do it under my command.'

'Lord?'

He stood before me and pointed at the dead Roman at my feet. 'You know what that is, boy?'

'A Roman,' I said, somewhat smugly.

Bozan grabbed my hair and forced me to look at the dead Roman. 'Insolent brat. That is a Roman centurion, boy. They are among the best soldiers in the world. You'll need to be a lot better if you want to kill one face to face. Stick to firing arrows. I didn't bring you along to play gods and heroes. Grow up, Pacorus. This is war, not some game.' He let go of my hair. 'Get your servant to patch up your arm.'

I hung my head in shame. I was crestfallen, but I knew Bozan was right. But for those archers I would be dead by now. I was angry with myself, but was determined that I would not make the same mistake again.

We made a funeral pyre for our own dead, who numbered nineteen, and left the Roman dead to rot. Bozan was eager for us to be away from the ambush site as quickly as possible, and so as the sun was sinking in the western sky we rode hard towards the east. The guide led us for three hours along winding paths through rocky terrain, across stone-strewn plains and finally into an area of curious, minaret-shaped rock formations that resembled cones with hats on top. It was dark when we made camp in a small valley among the strange rocky shapes. Bozan allowed us to light fires as the night grew cold, posting guards a half mile in each direction, though Byrd assured us that we were far from any dwellings.

After we had eaten a warm meal of plundered Roman broth, which I had to admit was extremely tasty, Gafarn stitched the wound in my arm. The pain was bearable, more so than his irksome comments that I was forced to endure.

'I heard a Roman nearly killed you.'

'Did you?'

'I can just imagine your mother's face as your corpse was taken back to Hatra. Poor woman.'

'Just get on with stitching,' I said, wincing as he pushed he needle through my flesh again.

'And your poor sisters, weeping uncontrollably at your funeral.'

'You may have noticed, Gafarn that I am not, in fact, dead.'

He tied off the last stitch with a knot and then bit through the thread with his teeth. 'Not yet.'

We stayed at the camp for a few days, dressing our wounds, mending our weapons and attending to the horses. There was a small lake nearby, and we all took the opportunity to bathe in its ice-cool waters. On the third day I was called to an officers' meeting under a canvas shade that had been erected in the lee of a rocky outcrop. The guide, Byrd, was also present, looking as shabby and untrustworthy as ever. Bozan was in a relaxed mood, obviously pleased by what he had been told by the guide. As we sat on the ground in a semi-circle around him, Bozan outlined our plan of campaign.

'We've made a good start. Our guide, here,' he nodded towards Byrd, 'tells me that there is a town called Sebastia to the north of us that contains a Roman garrison. It's two days' ride from here. So that is our next target. Byrd assures me that the Romans have a camp that has wooden walls, so it should burn nicely.'

'How many troops?' I asked.

'Not more than one hundred,' said Byrd, smiling at me and nodding his head. 'Easy target.'

'We cannot attack stockades,' said one of the officers.

'I know that,' replied Bozan, 'but they don't know we are here, so I'm counting on surprise aiding us.'

'They might know raiders are in the area after the attack on the supply column,' I said, concerned. 'They might be out looking for us.'

Byrd shrugged, as if unconcerned. Bozan noticed his gesture.

'We will scout the area thoroughly beforehand,' he said. 'If their guard appears to be down, we will ride in, kill as many as we can and burn their camp. Then we are gone. Any more questions?'

There was silence. 'Very well,' said Bozan. 'We leave in two days.'

The raid was a success. Bozan and I went forward alone to scout out the target the day before the attack. The town garrison in fact consisted of local recruits, not Romans, and their discipline was poor. Guards stood hunched at the camp gates and those on watch in sentry towers appeared to be more interested in gossip than on observation. We could have walked into the camp through the gates there and then; in fact, that's what we did when we attacked: galloping into the stockade and shooting down everyone in sight. The camp was positioned just outside the town, so we approached from the north and left the town alone. Within minutes the camp was ablaze, is wooden huts and walls burning brightly, the ground littered with bodies. We lost ten killed and eight wounded.

Over the next two weeks we attacked a number of enemy outposts, most of them staffed by local auxiliary units. In the second week we clashed with a detachment of Roman cavalry that had obviously been sent to find us. They numbered around two hundred men, all dressed in mail shirts and armed with red painted shields, spears and swords. They looked impressive enough, and when they deployed on a wide, grassy plain a neutral observer might have assumed that they were going to slaughter us. We offered them battle, fanning out into three long lines to overlaps their flanks. They levelled their spears and trotted forward; we did the same. Bozan was in the centre of our line, while I was on the right flank. We carried no spears and had our shields strapped to our backs to offer protection from sword thrusts. The Romans increased their pace and we strung our bows. The two lines closed and the Romans broke into a canter. I kicked my horse into a gallop and veered to the right, heading beyond the Romans' flank. Our horsemen on the left flank did the same, while those in the centre also broke left and right. This meant that the Romans were charging into an empty space as our horsemen formed into two columns that passed by the Roman left and right flanks. A Roman horseman at the extreme edge of their line attempted to turn his mount to face me as I thundered past, but I released my bowstring and put an arrow into his chest. The man behind me also loosed an arrow, as did those following as they passed by the Roman line. Now I wheeled my horse hard to the left and then turned him left again, so that I was now in the rear of the Roman line and following the enemy formation. Our cavalry on the opposite flank were doing the same. I strung another arrow and shot it into the back of a Roman trooper who had halted his horse. He fell to the ground, dead. We had charged, swept around their flanks and were now in their rear, firing arrows at an enemy who was completely dumbfounded by our tactics. Some Romans in their first line had continued their charge, but those in the second line had halted in an attempt to turn and face us. They were too late: we killed over half of them and then wheeled away. The survivors tried to mount a ragged charge but there was nothing to charge at. We simply moved to the flanks once again and swept past them. Meanwhile, their first line had halted and turned about face, just in time to receive our arrows as we swept into the wide gap between their first and second lines. I loosed an arrow at a standard bearer, who looked shocked as the point went through his neck; I strung another arrow and bent over my horse's hind quarters as I galloped past another Roman horseman, and shot him in the back.

If we had outnumbered the Romans at the beginning of the encounter, after our volleys of arrows we dwarfed them in numbers, and the survivors had decided that they had had enough. Small groups started to gallop from the battle. Bozan stood waving his sword in the air, shouting as he did so,

'Let them go. Let them go. Rally to me.' Horns blasted to signal recall.

I was elated. It was the first time I had fought Roman cavalry and we had won an easy victory. These were not local auxiliaries but sons of Rome, and we had bested them. We had enjoyed victory after victory, and I was beginning to believe that I was becoming a worthy son of Parthia. I felt as though I was unbeatable; perhaps the old crone at Sinatruces' court was right. I was still dreaming of glory when tragedy struck.

In the flush of victory, when the bloodletting has ceased, those who are left alive are filled with relief, relief that they are still alive. Some men cry and shake, others fall to their knees and give thanks to whatever gods they worship. I always felt as though my body had been freed of a great weight, though for a while my arms and legs shook uncontrollably. But in the afterglow of battle even the best soldiers relax and let down their guard. And so it was, as the last dregs of the Roman cavalry were fleeing for their lives, Bozan was struck down. I did not see it happen, but I was told later that an enemy horseman who had been knocked from his saddle, and who must have been rendered unconscious, recovered and thrust a spear into him, driving the blade deep into his chest. Bozan, who already had his sword in his hand, managed to split the spear shaft in two with a blow, before the Roman was hacked to pieces by officers who had been attending our commander. But the damage had been done. Bozan sat up in his saddle, before collapsing forward and slumping to the ground. He was dead before his head hit the grass.

The first I knew of his death was when an officer galloped up to me and beckoned me to come in haste. When I arrived there was a crowd gathered around him. I leapt from my saddle to reach his body. I knelt beside the lifeless corpse and stared in disbelief at the man who had been a second father to me. It was Bozan who had taught me to use a sword, a bow and how to fight on horseback. His was the voice that had encouraged, cajoled, threatened and berated me since I was a child. And now, here he was; dead. Gafarn also appeared at my side, observed Bozan's body and started to weep unashamedly. He never hid his feelings. Why should he? He was a servant. But in the next few moments I would have gladly swapped places with him as I tried to stem the flood of tears that were welling up inside me. I wiped my eyes, aware that all eyes were now on me as well as Bozan. I stood up. My legs were shaking and as I spoke my voice was faltering.

'We shall burn his body here, and the arms and armour of his enemies shall be laid upon his pyre in honour. Go!'

The officers and others left to build a funeral pyre, leaving Gafarn and me alone. He was sobbing now.

'Why do you blubber so?' I snapped

'I weep for both of us, so you don't have to. Though I know how heavy this loss is to you.'

I looked away from him as tears streaked down my cheeks. How right he was. A hatred of Romans and all things to do with Rome gripped me. I vowed to avenge Bozan's death a thousand fold. I posted guards around his body and ordered that the Roman dead be stripped and their heads cut off. The headless corpses were dumped in a heap at the edge of where the battle had taken place – the crows could feast on them. A company – one hundred men – was detailed to build a funeral pyre, scouring the area for any wood they could find. After two hours a large mound of wooden logs and branches, twice the height of a man, had been erected. The Roman shields were stacked around its side and their tunics and capes were laid on top. Bozan's body was then carried to the top of the pyre and laid there. At his feet were placed the Romans standards we had taken, while his sword was laid along his body, the pommel resting just under his chin and the end pointing at his feet.

As the sun started its descent in the western sky, we gathered round the pyre to bid our farewells. As a lighted torch was passed to me the men knelt in respect. I lit the foot of the pyre, which after a while began to burn, the wood spitting and crackling as the flames took hold, gradually eating their way up the mound as the heat increased in intensity. Then the mound became a hissing, seething red and yellow fireball as Bozan's body was consumed and his spirit made its way up into heaven to sit at Shamash's right hand.

We kept a vigil all night as the pyre burned into nothing but a pile of ashes. In the morning, cold and bleary eyed, I ordered the severed heads of the enemy dead to be placed on captured spear shafts, which were thrust into the ground. The poles with their leering heads were placed in a circle around the ashes in salute to their conqueror. Then we made our way from that place of dead flesh, walking our horses in silence, led by Byrd. He had maintained a deferential silence throughout our vigil. At last, as he walked beside me at the head of the column, he spoke.

'We go to safe place, lord. No Romani near. You go back to Parthia now?'

I trudged along, my mind indifferent to the direction we were heading. I kept going over in my mind Bozan's death, and how my father would receive the news. Would he blame me for his friend's death? Was I to blame? I had no answers. I certainly wasn't paying any attention to the guide, whose cheerful demeanour was beginning to annoy me.

'What?'

'I find a safe place, lord. No Romani.'

Gafarn was walking behind me, and I could feel his eyes on me.

'He wants to know if we are going back to Parthia, lord,' he said.

'I haven't decided.'

'Have we not done as your father asked?'

'Have we?' I replied. 'And here was I thinking that you were a servant, not a military strategist.'

Gafarn did not reply and we continued to silence. But in truth I had no idea what course of action to take. The idea of slinking back to Hatra did not appeal, but what else could we do?

That night we camped in a desolate rock- and screed-littered gorge that had little vegetation. I sat at a small fire as the darkness descended. The temperament of the men was like my own: subdued. I was in no mood for company so sent Gafarn away to amuse himself. As the cold encroached I remained sitting on the ground with my cloak wrapped around me, a felt hat on my head. I didn't notice Byrd approach and sit himself beside me. I ignored him, hoping he would go away. I could have ordered him to go, but was not disposed to speak to anyone. For a long time he said nothing, but then uttered one word.

'Caesarea.'

'What?'

'Caesarea, lord.'

I sighed loudly. 'Am I supposed to make any sense of what you say?'

'You wish to avenge your friend and master, lord. Caesarea gives you that opportunity. Small town, no walls, tiny garrison. Many Romani, mostly traders and their families. It will burn nicely.'

I looked at him, interested. 'Go on.'

He told me that Caesarea was a trading centre before the Romans had conquered Cappadocia, and afterwards they had expelled many of the locals and brought in their own people. The town had still prospered, though, and Byrd painted a picture of a ripe fruit waiting to be plucked.

'How do you know there is no garrison?'

'Not certain, lord, but the legions are in the north, fighting Mithridates in Pontus.'

That I knew was true. Valiant Mithridates was battling the might of Rome to keep his people free. And we had encountered few enough legionaries during our present expedition.

'How far is Caesarea from here?'

'Three days' ride, lord.'

'How do you know of this place,' I asked.

His expression changed suddenly, a look of utter sadness on his face. ' I used to have a life there once, lord. Before Romani came.'

He looked away and stared into the fire. Nothing more was said between us. After a while he rose to his feet and walked away. I mulled over what he had said in my mind, but the possibility of revenge was too strong. I reached a decision: we would attack Caesarea and make a truly worthy sacrifice to Bozan.

We stayed in camp for two days. As far as I could tell, morale was still good despite the death of Bozan. The evening before we left for Caesarea, I assembled the officers. They were seated on the ground around my fire, their faces full of confidence. Byrd was also present.

'Tomorrow we ride to Caesarea. Byrd tells me that it has no walls and no garrison. Regardless, we ride in quick, cause as much damage as possible and then get out as fast as we can.'

'Do we then return to Hatra, lord?' asked one of the company commanders.

'Yes,' I replied, 'after we have burnt Caesarea to the ground we will have avenged Bozan and fulfilled our orders.'

They seemed pleased by this, and I was glad that they appeared to have accepted me as their commander. I was the son of their king, but I liked to think that they were riding with me out of respect and not begrudging duty. At least that was what I hoped.

We left just after dawn, four hundred horsemen, spare mounts and mules riding hard through a stark landscape. Cappadocia suited our mood – rocky, windswept and barren. Dotted with woods and grassy plains, the mountains and plateaus appeared to be never ending. Byrd told me that he had kept us away from the few towns out of security, and informed me that many people lived in dwellings carved out of the rocks, eking out a miserable existence.

'And Rome wants this land?'

He shrugged. 'Rome wants all lands, lord.'

After three days we reached our target – Caesarea. I observed the town from the top of a nearby hill. Caesarea lay in the middle of a wide plain flanked by low-lying hills. A single road ran through it from the south, running parallel to a small river that also flowed through the town. There was no cover to hide our approach, so we would have to cross at least a mile of open ground before we reached it. There was traffic dotted along the road, passing both ways, mule trains, carts and travellers on foot, going about their everyday business. I could see no soldiers, no camp, no walls and no watchtowers. Byrd was beside me, lying on the ground watching the town. The afternoon was sunny, with a fresh northerly wind.

'You were right, I can't see any troops.'

'No soldiers, lord.'

We made our final checks – weapons, saddles, straps and horses – before we moved out to attack the town. Our tactics were simple: we would advance in one long line and gallop through the town firing flaming arrows. This necessitated halting before we attacked, as the arrows had rags that had been dipped in pitch wrapped around the shaft, just below the point. They would have to be lit before they could be fired. Each of us had only one such arrow, because once buildings were set on fire the flames would soon spread to other dwellings. So we trotted across the plain until we were around five hundred paces from the outskirts. As we halted, I heard screams and shouts being carried on the wind. We had been spotted. Soldiers dismounted and lit torches, and then went from horse to horse so the riders could light their arrows. I cast a glance at Byrd, who sat stony faced in his saddle; Gafarn was beside him. I strung the arrow in my bowstring and shouted 'For Bozan!' at the top of my voice, then kicked my horse forward. My men cheered and followed. In less than a minute we were flooding through Caesarea's streets. Men, women and children fled before us as we fired their town. Soon buildings were burning as our flaming arrows set alight wood and other flammable materials. I packed my bow into its leather case tied to my saddle and drew my sword. A man, wild-eyed, ran at me with a pitchfork. He died as my sword came down with full force and hacked half his face away. As the flames took hold, people forget about the mounted soldiers in their midst and tried to save themselves and their families from the inferno that was engulfing their world.

My men were now out of control. All discipline had gone as they cut down any who offered resistance and killed others who simply got in their way. Horses trampled screaming women and children, and I watched in horror as a man, his clothes burning on his back, ran from a house clutching a small child in his arms. Flames leapt into the sky and the sickening smell of burning flesh filled my nostrils. Gafarn rode up and halted in front of me.

'This is slaughter, highness. You have to stop it.'

I stared at him, unsure of what to say. Behind me a multi-storey building collapsed, which spooked my horse. It reared up on its back legs and almost threw me.

'Highness!' shouted Gafarn.

But it was too late. Men possessed by a blood lust had been unleashed and were now visiting death and destruction on Caesarea. They were scattered throughout the town, and in the confusion and terror no one man could stop it. Gafarn saw this in my eyes, spat on the ground in front of me and rode off. The killing continued for what seemed like an eternity, but then suddenly ceased abruptly, for the simple reason that there was no one left to kill. Those who could had escaped from our swords and arrows, but many had been killed or had perished in the flames. The heat was so fierce in some streets that it was impossible to ride them down, and many horses refused to go near the flames. I eventually found two officers and we moved in a group down the main road that ran through the centre of the town, shouting 'rally, rally,' to gather our horsemen. Small groups of riders, their faces blackened by soot, their horses streaked with sweat, appeared and dropped into line behind us. I ordered them to muster on the plain from where we had launched our attack and there to await orders.

It took a long time to gather all the men. By now the blood lust had subsided and exhausted men lay on the ground beside their equally tired horses. Men gulped from their water skins as their officers moved among them to determine who had failed to return. They reported to me half an hour later. We had lost twenty dead and thirty wounded. More than fifty horses had also died and a further twenty had to be put out of their misery due to their severe burns. The town formed a glowing red backdrop as the evening approached and we led our horses from the horror. The town of Caesarea no longer existed.

I felt no elation or sense of victory after our attack. All we had done was assault an undefended town and massacre its inhabitants. A morose Byrd led us south, to Cilicia, the region that lay on Cappadocia's southern border, from where we would cut east cross-country to the north of the city of Antioch, and then back to Hatra. He hardly spoke to anyone during the journey. He had led us to the town where he had lived before Cappadocia had been conquered by the Romans, and his reward was to witness its destruction. He must hate us now more than he did the Romans, I mused. At least my men's spirits were rising with the promise of seeing their homes and families again. Gafarn, I noticed, attended to his duties diligently but rarely engaged in conversation and averted his eyes. No doubt he was still sickened by what he had witnessed at Caesarea. No matter, he would get over it. My own mood lightened as we travelled south. The death of Bozan had been a blow, of course, but, I reasoned, he had been a soldier and soldiers get killed in battle. But we had defeated a detachment of Roman cavalry and had rampaged at will through Cappadocia. We were returning to Hatra as victors. Hopefully Rome would now think twice about raiding Parthian territory, for to do so would invite retaliation. It never occurred to me that the Roman cavalry we had defeated had been but one of the groups sent out to find us. It thus came as a nasty shock when we were pounced upon by Roman legionaries and cavalry on the Cilician border.

Chapter 4

It would have been convenient for me to report that I had decided to engage the Roman horse and foot, that I took a command decision after weighing up all the possible outcomes. But the reality was that I was caught totally unawares. Roman scouts had obviously been tracking us for a while, though our own scouts had failed to detect them. Worse, whoever led them had a more intimate knowledge of the country we were travelling through than we did. And so it was that as we were journeying through Cilicia, moving in column between two widely separated woods through a field of lush grass, that we were confronted by a line of Roman cavalry blocking our route. They looked the same as the ones we had defeated in Cappadocia. I gave orders to form a wedge, as the woods protected their flanks and we would be unable to sweep around them. No matter. We had beaten them once and we would beat them again.

So I gave the order that we would adopt a wedge formation with four ranks. We would be outflanked but would simply punch right through them. In each rank every other man was armed with a spear and shield to match the weapons of the Roman cavalrymen, but the others were horse archers who would unleash at least one volley of arrows before the two forces clashed. In this way the enemy would be disordered at the moment we hit them. We moved rapidly into formation and I gave the signal to advance. I was at the tip of the wedge, spear in my right hand and shield in the other. As we moved forward I noticed that the Roman cavalry remained where they were, not moving an inch. I found this slightly odd, but saw no reason to interrupt our advance as we trotted forward. As we gathered pace I suddenly heard loud 'hurrahs' coming from my right and left, and looked to see Roman legionaries pouring out of the woods to the right and left. My horsemen saw this too, and several pulled up their mounts in surprise. In no time at all our ranks were disordered and we had to halt to redress our lines. Still the Roman cavalry remained rooted in position. I understood now that they were the bait, and we had taken it. My instinct was to charge forward regardless, but as I looked ahead I saw that the enemy cavalry was moving towards us. On the flanks the Roman soldiers were not halting to address their lines, but were closing on us fast – two blocks of iron and steel closing to crush us.

'Forward!' I yelled, and kneed my horse towards the Roman cavalry.

My men followed, but we had no time to build up any momentum before we smashed into the enemy, horses rearing in terror as arrows and spears found their mark. A horseman charged at me on my left side, his spear levelled at my chest. His thrust was ill aimed and I glanced away the blow with my shield and aimed my spear at his shield. A wooden shield offers protection against blows, but not the combined weight of a horse and its rider hitting it square on. I gripped the shaft tightly as the point went through his shield and into his body. I let go of the shaft, pulled my sword from its scabbard and slashed at another Roman rider that passed me on my right, the blade hitting the flesh of the neck between his mail shirt and helmet. He dropped from his saddle as I clashed with a horseman in their second line. He tried to jab me with his spear but I easily deflected the blow with my shield and lunged with my sword. His shield was held high to protect his chest and face, so I aimed a blow that pierced his thigh; he screamed in pain and dropped his spear. He tried to pull his horse away from me, but the beast whinnied in terror and reared up on its hind legs. Its rider lost his balance and crashed to the ground, managing to limp away from me.

I looked around and saw Roman legionaries closing in from both flanks. The first ranks had already thrown their javelins and had drawn their short swords to hack and slash at our horses. My men could not manoeuvre as they were trapped in the middle of a Roman vice, so they tried to shoot down as many of the enemy as they could. It was a savage battle; the Romans tightly packed and jabbing at our horses with underhand sword blows as they held their shields high; our men trying to control their horses as they searched for targets with their bows. Horses, maddened by sword cuts, reared and kicked out with their hooves. Roman soldiers had their helmets crushed by an iron-shod hoof or were trampled underfoot as their comrades in the rear ranks shoved them forward to get at us. I sheathed my sword and began to shoot my bow. A Parthian is an expert with a bow even at long ranges; at short distances he cannot miss. Gafarn was next to me as we put arrow after arrow into the enemy. After a while no Roman horsemen would come near us, and we were free to shoot at the legionaries. I thought we might yet save ourselves, but more infantry were assembling to our front and many of our men had fallen. Then I reached into my quiver to string another arrow and felt that it was empty. As the air was filled with less and less arrows I realised that others, too, had exhausted their ammunition. We were beaten. Then a javelin slammed into my horse's left shoulder and he went down, throwing me to the ground. I tried to get up but received a blow to the side of my helmet. Then all was night.

When I came to the fighting had ended. When I regained consciousness I was next to Gafarn, who was sitting on the ground beside me. He had his knees drawn up to his chin looking at the earth.

I tried to rise, but the pain in my head forced me to abandon the idea.

'Gafarn?' I muttered, weakly.

He turned and looked at me, his face full of misery.

'Try to rest, highness. We are captives of the Romans.'

I didn't take in what he was saying at first. I was only interested in the battle's outcome, which, had I considered my position more closely, would have seemed obvious. Gafarn helped me to sit up, and glancing round I realised that I was on the edge of a large group of my men, who were all sitting on the ground. We were guarded by legionaries, who stood facing us with their javelins levelled. My wrists hurt and as I looked down I saw why – I had been manacled. My sense of outrage expelled all feelings of pain. That I, a prince of Hatra, had been shackled like a common criminal was an insult to all I held dear. The anger began to well up inside me. A hundred paces away, the Romans were hurling our bows, quivers and shields onto a raging fire. Gafarn was watching me.

'They put the shackles on while you were unconscious.'

'And you didn't protest?' I said, naively.

'Oh yes, highness. I insisted that they should not wrap me in chains, but then they held a sword to my throat and a spear at my belly, so I changed my mind.'

'All right, all right.' I was thoroughly dejected, as were those of my men who still lived, though for how long I did not know. After a few minutes a small group of what I assumed were officers came towards us. I noticed that one had a transverse crest on his steel helmet, in the same style as the man who had nearly killed me before Bozan had saved me. I tried not to think of Bozan, for it would only serve to increase my despondency. The group of Romans halted a few paces in front of us and observed our motley band. The leader, a senior officer of some sort I assumed, began to speak. He was of average height, dressed in a white tunic that ended just above his knees, with a highly polished steel cuirass and a rich white cloak edged with purple hanging from his shoulders. He was bare headed and bald, aside from two thinning bands of grey hair above his ears. I put his age at around fifty. He turned to the soldier wearing the transverse crest on his helmet.

'So, centurion, how many have we taken?'

'Two hundred and fifty, sir, though some are wounded and may not survive.'

So the man with the crest was a centurion, who must command one hundred men. They obviously thought none of us understood what they were saying. The older man continued.

'Well, they will have to do. Add them to the others and send them south.'

The centurion was shaking his head. 'We should crucify a few, sir, to set an example.'

His superior got annoyed at this suggestion, which I was grateful for. The older man, his skin pale and his body running to fat, shook his head, which wobbled his flabby chin. 'No, no, no, centurion.' He looked directly at the Roman soldier, whose lean, scarred face was in stark contrast to the chubby visage of his commander, who started to wag his finger at the centurion.

'You see, what you don't understand is that I have to think about the wider picture.'

'The wider picture, sir?'

'Indeed, centurion. How long have been in the army?'

'Twenty years, sir.'

'You see, twenty years killing barbarians and all and sundry with a sword has blinkered you. I, on the other hand, have responsibilities, both to myself and to Rome. I have considerable estates in southern Italy: estates that have to be worked to produce a profit. And who is going to work my estates, for they don't work themselves?' He gestured towards us. 'Slaves, centurion. Slaves are the key. These are valuable chattels that I intend to put to good use on my land. You want to nail them to crosses, whereas I want them to produce a healthy profit before they leave this life. Have I explained myself clearly enough?'

The centurion looked bored and resentful. 'Yes, sir,' he replied curtly.

The elderly Roman turned to his other companions, who had been eagerly listening to his little lecture. By the look of them, all appeared to be in their early twenties, clean-shaven and well dressed, I surmised that they too were officers of some sort.

'Gentlemen,' he said, 'after our victory I think we deserve a celebratory banquet.' He waved over another soldier who was standing a few feet behind the group. The soldier presented himself before the man and snapped to attention.

'Legate.'

So the old man was a legate, though I knew not what this was, but of some importance for certain as he was the centre of attention.

'Arrange a banquet for this evening in my tent.'

'Yes, sir.' The soldier turned and marched away. The legate and his group followed in the same direction. The legate then stopped and looked back at the centurion.

'And feed them something,' he nodded at our group. 'I don't want any of them dying before they even reach Italy.'

'Yes, sir,' said the centurion. Then the legate was gone. The centurion scowled at his back. 'The sooner you're back in Rome, playing with your boy slaves, the better.' He spat the words with bitterness.

He turned to look at us. His sword was sheathed, and in his right hand he carried some sort of cane, which he was tapping lightly against his thigh. He walked slowly up to us and halted in front of me. We were still all seated on the ground, with all eyes on the centurion. As I looked at him he placed the tip of his cane under my chin.

'You long-haired little bastard. If I had my way, you and all your bandit friends would be nailed to crosses by now. That's the penalty for killing Romans where I come from. But the barrel of fat who commands this legion has decided that you are going on a little journey.' He then drew back his cane and hit me across the face with it. The blow had a vicious sting that sent me reeling. Gafarn made as though he was going to spring at the Roman, but I shook my head at him.

'Who's this, then,' the Roman said, looking at Gafarn, daring him to attack, 'your lover?'

He spat on me and then squatted down so his face was near mine. 'There's a long way between here and Italy, and I guarantee that the route will be littered with your corpses. Savages. You don't even understand what I'm saying, do you?'

He stood and marched away. I was somewhat demoralised, but tried to hide my despondency.

'Are you hurt, highness?' asked Gafarn.

'No,' I said, feeling the side of my face, which was throbbing with pain.

'What was he saying?'

'He's annoyed that he can't execute us.'

'What are they going to do with us, highness?'

'We are going to Italy, apparently, to do some sort of work.'

'Where is that?' asked Gafarn.

'A long way from Parthia.'

Surprisingly, the Romans fed us that night. The food was a sort of thick porridge, and I passed orders that everyone was to eat as much as they gave us, as I didn't know when we would get fed again. They also gave us copious amounts of water, which I was glad about as I had had nothing to drink since early that morning. Then the Romans threw us loaves of bread, which were hard and stale. Again, I ordered that we should eat as much as we could. The centurion was stalking around like a wolf, delivering the occasional kick to one of my men but generally keeping away. I could see that he was an individual who was full of anger. Later that evening, as we were preparing to get some rest, he stomped over and squatted before me. For some reason, he had picked me out as a target of his wrath, which unnerved me I had to admit. For a few moments he just glared at me, and I was aware of Gafarn fidgeting next to me, which made me even more nervous. I sat up and tried to match his stare, though I was in a position of helplessness and he had supreme power over me. He reeked of ale.

'So, pretty boy, you and your band of thieves will be making a journey to the sea tomorrow.' Did he realise that I could understand him? Surely he must. And yet, perhaps he was just giving voice to his thoughts. 'It is my misfortune that I have been ordered to take you back to Italy. My misfortune and yours.'

He stood up and whipped the end of his cane under my chin. He then forced me to stand. He grabbed my hair with his left hand, twisting it painfully as he pulled my face toward his, until we were only inches apart.

'You'd better pray to whatever miserable god you worship that my temper improves, otherwise I guarantee that the road will be littered with your carcasses.'

He then threw me to the ground and marched away.

'More bad news, highness?' queried Gafarn.

'Yes. But it appears that our centurion friend is going to be our escort from tomorrow. Pass the word that we should be wary of him. We must do everything to avoid any conflict with the guards.'

I saw the forlorn look on Gafarn's face. 'Don't worry, an opportunity will arise for us to make a bid for freedom, but for the moment we must bide our time.'

I was lying, of course, but better to offer a glimmer of hope than none at all.

The next day we were disturbed early by a host of legionaries, who used their feet to waken us from our slumbers. As we stood bleary eyed and with aching limbs, we were ordered to form into a column, four abreast. I was in the front rank. Then each of us was chained to the man in front and behind, so that not only did we have manacles on our wrists, but also one on our left ankles.

'Be strong, soldiers of Parthia,' I shouted, 'Shamash will protect us.' As soon as the words had left my mouth a cane was lashed across my face, causing a shooting pain that made me feel sick. The centurion's face was contorted with rage.

'Silence, you sons of whores. The next one who says anything gets a flogging.'

Satisfied that his example had done the trick, we were then shoved forward by the flanking guards and began our march. The pace was slow, though we had had no breakfast and I wondered when our first rest period would be. After two hours our column was joined by another group of slaves, who included women and children. They too were formed into a long column, in front of us, and ordered to march. I estimated their numbers to be around fifty. And so we trudged for another two hours, along a dirt track through an arid landscape dotted with trees and bushes. The sun was up and the heat was increasing, which made my mouth dry, though as I observed the column of captives ahead I wondered how long it would be before one of them got into difficulties. We were soldiers and in our prime, but they appeared to be civilians, at least the women and children were.

It must have been around noon, with the sun burning our faces, when a woman who was at the rear of her column suddenly dropped like a stone. The man who was shackled in front of her stopped as he felt the dead weight on his ankle, and within seconds the whole group had shuffled to a halt. A guard went over to the prostrate figure on the ground and examined her roughly, grabbing her hair and bellowing at her to stand up. As she was a local, I doubted whether she understood what he was saying, though if she were still conscious she would have got the gist of what he was shouting. He yanked her to her feet, but as soon as he let go she fell to the ground again. She was clearly totally exhausted. The centurion, who had been marching at the head of the column, arrived to see what the hold-up was. He looked at the woman and ordered her to be unshackled. Perhaps he was not a monster after all. Another Roman ran up with a small hammer and chisel and released her from her chains, taking them away. The centurion then whipped out a dagger from a scabbard on his belt, bent down and slit the woman's neck. She made a faint gurgling sound as the red liquid oozed from the wound onto the ground. I stared in horror as he looked up at me and grinned. He then barked an order to his men who shoved the other captives forward, leaving the body in the road. Soon the air was filled with the wails of frightened people who had witnessed the murder. The guards, annoyed at the commotion, began using their shields to shove and push individuals forward. We Parthians walked along grim faced, passing the corpse whose lifeblood was seeping into the earth.

The next few days saw more horror as we were marched under a merciless sun towards the sea. The centurion maintained a cruel pace, which caused many captives to collapse from exhaustion, starvation and dehydration. We were given little to eat and not enough water. My limbs began to ache and blisters broke out on my feet. But at least we still had our boots; those who trudged in front were barefoot, and I could see that the manacles on their ankles were chafing flesh and their feet were bruised and bloody. Some were hobbling now, while others were limping badly and had to be helped by their neighbour.

At night we lay exhausted on the ground, trying to keep our spirits up through hushed conversations. One of my officers, Nergal, a man in his mid-twenties who had a thick black mane of hair, a round face and a long nose, was a great help. He had been with the army when we took the Roman eagle and had fought well during our raid into Cappadocia. His ability to always see something positive in adversity was infectious. He had tramped for four days beside Gafarn without complaining, though he was badly sunburned on his neck. I think he was slightly in awe of me, mainly due to my capture of the Roman eagle. He appeared to have forgotten that it was my poor leadership that had contributed to our capture, for which I was grateful.

'I saw it, highness,' he said as I was trying to find the paradise of slumber.

'Mmm?'

'The eagle you took. I saw it in the temple after it was laid there. I prayed to Shamash that he would also grant me the privilege of one day taking an enemy standard.'

'It could have been anyone,' I replied. 'I was in the right place at the right time, that's all.'

He was indignant. 'Oh no, highness, it was your destiny. You are destined for greatness, and that is why I am untroubled by our present circumstances.'

'Really?' I was taken aback somewhat by his confidence.

'The gods protect those whom they love, highness.'

'You think the gods love me, Nergal?'

'Yes, highness.'

'Why?' I asked.

'Because they gave you the eagle, no one else. I have heard that to the Romans each eagle is sacred. So only a god could grant you the power to steal it from under their noses.'

'And what of our present situation?' I asked him.

'The gods are saving you for great things, highness, of that I am sure.'

'Get some sleep, Nergal. It's going to be hot tomorrow.'

The night was cool and during the hours of darkness we lost five of our men. They had been wounded in the battle with the Romans and their injuries, plus the hard usage they had been subjected to, was more than their bodies could endure. The first rays of the sun revealed their ashen faces. We said a prayer to Shamash and tried to bury them, but the guards hurried us along after a sparse meal of hard biscuit and a mouthful of water. They left our comrades beside the road, carrion for crows and wild animals. The nights were always the worst, not only out of fear that we would lose more comrades, but also because at night the Romans raped the women prisoners. We heard their screams and could do nothing. Some of my men wept tears of rage at their impotence. All we could do was hold our hands over our ears to try to shut out the cries of pain and misery.

In the morning we were given a meagre meal and a few mouthfuls of water and then we were on the road again. This day was different, though. Four of my men had decided that they had had enough. As they shuffled along in their chains, they passed a group of legionaries who were laughing and joking with each other. They didn't give my men a second glance as they passed by, but then my men lunged at the guards, wrapping their wrist chains around necks while other made a grab for spears and swords. One Parthian, a large man with long arms and legs, choked a guard with his right forearm and with his left hand pulled the Roman's sword from his scabbard and rammed it through his back, the point bursting out of his chest. A notable feat given that his wrists were chained. We stopped and hollered encouragement, but within seconds other guards stood around us, brandishing spears at our bellies and sword points at our throats. Those who had attacked the guards were swiftly killed as more Romans rushed up, the big man going down only after being literally hacked to pieces by four Romans, their swords and arms wet with his blood. But five Romans were also dead.

The centurion was beside himself with rage, and would have killed us all there and then had it not have been for another soldier, who must have been of the same rank, reminding him that he was responsible for delivering us to the legate's estates. At first denied his revenge, he nevertheless ordered that the dead Parthians be beheaded; their severed heads were then hung around the necks of the front rank, which included me. Thus we marched, it taking all my efforts not to throw up in disgust at the gore that was dangling from my neck. The centurion decided to amuse himself by trying to goad me, though I had to smile internally at the fact that, as far as I knew, he still did not know that I understood Latin.

'Do you like your new necklace, pretty boy?'

I stared ahead with a stony gaze.

'You son of a whore,' he hit me hard on the arm with his vine stick, the blow made me grimace and I looked down to see that he had cut my flesh. He saw that I was looking at the wound.

'Your flesh cuts easy, little girl. You won't last long in the fields. Your girly locks and baby flesh will be food for crows before the year is out. My only regret is that I will not be there to see it.'

He wacked me again with his cane, this time across the back, but the one-way conversation was clearly boring him and he took himself off, bellowing at the guards to move us along at a faster pace. The first column of civilian captives was clearly incapable of doing so, and the plethora of blows and insults delivered at them resulted only in several men and women collapsing. In the end, the centurion had to order a halt to allow his beaten, half-starved victims time to recuperate. Even his tiny brain must have realised that if he continued his thuggery, all his captives would be dead before they reached the sea.

As we rested beside the road I tore off a piece of my tunic to fashion a makeshift bandage. By now all our trousers and tunics were frayed, cut and dirty. We were not allowed to leave the column to relieve ourselves, so had to perform our bodily functions where we stood or lay. This meant that we stank to high heaven, though as we all emitted a foetid odour I suspect that our guards were more repulsed than we were. I had to remind myself that I was a prince of Parthia, for our filthy, stinking, unshaven column barely resembled humanity. I certainly didn't feel like a prince, or even a man.

On the sixth night of our nightmare journey we received more rations than we had since we had been captured, and the guards then came and took the rotting heads that we had been forced to wear away. We were also given ample quantities of water to drink.

'What's happening, highness?' asked Gafarn, between great gulps of water.

'I do not know,' I replied, though I suspected it was all part of the centurion's cruelty. I rubbed my shin, which was bruised and bloody as a result of the constant chafing of the manacle.
'Are you in pain, highness?' asked Gafarn, with concern.
I smiled. 'No more than you, Gafarn.'
'How much longer do you think we will walking on this accursed road?'
'I do not know. But I suspect it won't be for much longer.' He seemed happy at this prospect. 'But remember, when our journey ends we will begin another, by sea, which will take us further from Parthia.'
In fact, it was the next day that our long walk ended, for after we had travelled through a mountain pass we joined a highway that was thronged with traffic of every kind. Camels, horse-drawn carts and donkeys laden with goods jostled for position on the road, going in both directions. The centurion halted our two columns before we reached the road and bunched us all up. The guards were deployed at the front, on each flank and behind – clearly he feared some making an escape attempt, though in truth we were so weary that we barely had the strength to walk, let alone run. As we trudged forward the air was filled with a refreshing cool breeze and after an hour we crested a hill and entered a plain that swept down to a deep blue Mediterranean. Though we were in chains, our spirits rose as we temporarily forgot we were captives and looked upon a calm sea and a port whose harbour was filled with ships. Our guards were more interested in keeping other travellers away from us than they were in tormenting us, so the final leg of our journey was not that arduous. The pace was slow – the traffic was heavy as we neared the port – and we had to halt frequently along the road.
When we reached the port we were marched through the streets and straight to the harbour area. The docks were filled with pallets of goods being loaded and offloaded onto ships. On a long stone cob that stretched out of the harbour were moored a dozen or so biremes: wooden-hulled vessels with a single square-rigged sail positioned amidships, with two tiers of oars for rowers along each side of the hull. These vessels were, I supposed, designed for war, as I could see what looked like a ram at the bow of each. Other warships moored in the harbour were triremes, masterful vessels of war that had three rows of oars each side. The ship's staggered seating permitted three benches for oarsmen per vertical section. The outrigger above the gunwale, which projected laterally beyond it, kept the third row of oars on the deck, out of the way of the first

two rows that were below decks. The triremes also had a mast amidships.

By comparison, the merchant boats that crowded the dock area were squat and ugly, designed to carry goods and not sailors or marines. They were sailing ships and had no rowers, as they required the greatest possible amount of space for their cargo. They were broad-beamed and had large square linen sails, off-white in colour. Their hulls were lined with tarred wood, and over that had been secured lead sheeting. With this protection, the water could not penetrate into the hold and the merchandise was kept safe and dry. Burly dockers adorned with black tattoos, operated ropes and pulleys attached to crossbeams that swung loads of oil, wine, fruit, grain and cattle onto and off the boats. The activity was frenetic. We were herded into one of the wooden warehouses that lined the docks. It was large, cavernous and empty, and so could accommodate us with ease. It smelt of freshly cut corn. A well-dressed Roman in a toga attended by three clerks waited for us. The centurion barked orders to the guards, who shoved us into ranks and files, after which the clerks began to count us. As they did so I saw the toga-clad Roman screw up his face as our stench reached his nostrils. The clerks finished their tally and scurried to their master. The Roman listened to what they reported, frowned and gestured to the centurion for him to attend him.

As I was in the front rank I could hear the conversation that followed. The well-dressed Roman's mood quickly turned sour. As he surmised that none of us could understand Latin, he made little attempt to subdue his voice.

'Centurion Cookus, I was informed by dispatch that you started out with three hundred captives.' The centurion shrugged nonchalantly, but made no attempt to answer, so his superior continued. 'And yet, I find myself confronted with only two hundred and fifty, which means fifty are missing. Do you know where they are?'

'Dead, sir,' replied Cookus, flatly.

'Dead? How did they die?'

Cookus was clearly bored by the proceedings, but indulged his questioner. 'Some died of exhaustion, others were killed because they rebelled.' He cast me a hateful glance.

'Legate Tremelius entrusted you with the safe conduct of these captives to this port, from where they are to be transported to his estates in southern Italy. And yet you present me with these miserable creatures, half of whom I doubt will survive the sea voyage. And, to add insult to injury, you have managed to lose fifty dead.'

'They're only slaves,' replied Cookus.

'No!' snapped the other Roman. 'They are valuable property of the legate, you idiot. I've a good mind to report you for dereliction of duty.'

Cookus marched up to him and glared at the somewhat flabby civilian, who involuntarily shrank back from the grizzled veteran soldier with the big sword hanging from his belt.

'Captives, die, sir,' Cookus said slowly and loudly. 'And my job is to kill Rome's enemies not play nursemaid to slaves. So, here they are and my duty is done.'

'Not quite, centurion,' smiled the Roman, who held out his pink right hand, into which one of the clerks placed a scroll. 'These are your orders from the legate. You are to personally escort the captives to his estate at Capua, there to hand them over to his chief bailiff.'

Cookus went red with rage. 'In the name of Jupiter, this cannot be!'

'Indeed it can, centurion. So I would advise you to take better care of your charges from now on. So rest them, get them fed and then see to it that they are shipped to Italy tomorrow. I have already paid the Cilicians to escort the three ships, so you have no fear of being boarded by pirates.'

'The Cilicians are pirates,' said Cookus, indignantly.

The Roman official raised an eyebrow as he pondered the statement. 'Technically, you are correct, but at the moment it is convenient for Rome to pay the Cilicians dues so that they do not interfere with our ships. The spoils of the war taken from Mithridates are considerable, and Rome presently sees no need to create difficulties for what is a very lucrative agreement, albeit temporary. Rome will deal with them in time, but for the moment they are tolerated. You see, centurion, it's all about strategy, something I don't expect you to understand. It is better to fight one war at a time. Once we have destroyed Mithridates, then we will rid the sea lanes of pirates. Quite simple.'

'The Cilicians are no better than this lot of bandits,' he jerked a finger at us Parthians.

'That may be, but just concern yourself with getting your cargo to its destination. Now I must have a bath and a massage, the aroma coming from them,' he indicated us captives, 'is really quite distasteful.'

With that he turned and strode from the warehouse, followed by his clerks. Cookus was left alone with us, and his thoughts. He called over two of his men and spoke to them quietly for a couple of minutes, then marched from the warehouse. We were ordered to take our ease on the floor, and we grabbed the opportunity to lie down. I stretched out my aching and bruised limbs and closed my eyes. What a nightmare we were living, with little prospect of matters getting any better. But for the moment at least we were allowed to rest. I drifted into a deep sleep, only to be wakened by what seemed seconds later by a loud whistle being blown. I raised myself up, though my arms felt like lead weights, and saw other slaves carrying buckets of water walking among us, while others handed out bread. A slave stood before me and offered me water from a wooden ladle. I hesitated, then pointed at Gafarn, who eagerly accepted the gesture and drank greedily. After he had finished I also slated my thirst. The liquid was the sweetest I had ever tasted, and the bread was like the eating the finest feast I had ever attended. Ludicrous of course, but when you are thirsty and hungry even the simplest fare seems like the food of the gods. Cookus, sitting on a bench and leaning against the far wall, observed us with his cold, black eyes.

I had come to change my mind about Byrd over the past few weeks. At first all I saw was a mercenary, a man who would sell his soul for gold, but as he guided and accompanied us during our expedition in Cappadocia I saw that he was a man whose life had been destroyed, and who lived only for an opportunity to get revenge on the Romans. One evening, in the black, humid prison that was the ship's hold, I spoke to him as we both lent against the hull while other men slept fitfully at our feet.

'I am sorry, Byrd,' I said.

'For what, lord?'

'For being responsible for getting you enslaved.'

He didn't speak for a few moments, then sighed. 'It does not matter, lord. My life was empty when Lord Bozan hired me to act as your guide. I was glad to be given a chance to strike back at the Romani.'

'Even though you are now their slave?'

I could barely see his face in the half-light, the hold dimly illuminated by moonlight streaming through the iron grating above us, which was located in the centre of the deck. Without that, we would surely die of suffocation.

'Romani killed my family when they attacked Caesarea. I was a trader in pots, and so travelled far and wide in my land. I was away when they killed them, and since then I have wished that I too had died that day.'

'And yet you live,' I said, flatly.

'Yes, lord. Perhaps I too will get to kill Romans. Like you.'

I feared that my Roman-killing days were over but remained silent. The Romans were the least of my worries, for as the days passed several of my men became weaker and weaker. On the seventh day what I feared happened: two died. They had never recovered from the wounds they had received in the battle with the Romans, and the ill usage they had received since killed them. In the dawn their bodies were unchained and taken up to the deck, and then unceremoniously thrown overboard. We were then ordered onto the deck, the guards using their spear shafts to beat us as we climbed the wooden steps, which proved difficult to manoeuvre with the manacles on our wrists and the chains on our ankles. But it was pleasant to stand in the sun again and feel a light sea breeze on our faces. The day was cloudless, and we squinted in the bright sun, our eyes unused to the light. Centurion Cookus, standing on the raised aft deck, was chewing on a piece of bread, and watching us intently. Beside him stood a burly, bearded man with a large scarlet cloth wrapped around his head; the captain I assumed. Unfortunately, Cookus did not choke on his food and after he had finished his meal he descended the steps to the main deck and walked up to me, his usual evil grin on his face.

'So, pretty boy, how do you like your quarters aboard this fine ship?'

I looked at him quizzically, making out that I did not understand him. He had his cane in his right hand, and he brought it up as if to strike me across the face. But the blow was lazy, probably made to impress the captain, and despite my manacles I was able to block the strike and grab the cane from his hand, which I hurled overboard into the sea. Why did I do it? Perhaps it was the hopelessness of my situation that made even a small victory all the more appealing, or maybe a part of me wanted to die and end the unbearable humiliation of enslavement. Not the physical pain of chains on my wrists and ankles, but the mental anguish of being treated like an animal. So I grabbed that damned stick and threw it into the sea.

For a moment Cookus looked stunned, amazed that I, a slave, would have the audacity to do such a thing. I could swear he also looked hurt that his beloved cane, the instrument with which he inflicted so much pain on all and sundry, had been taken from him. And in those few seconds I realised that I had made a terrible mistake. I remembered my father's words – better to die on your feet than live on your knees – but the fear I felt in the pit of my stomach made me think that I was certainly about to die on my feet. But Cookus was not only a bully and a thug, he was also an accomplished sadist. I expected to be beaten to a pulp and then thrown into the sea, but instead, with all eyes on him, Cookus merely smiled and walked calmly back to the aft deck, where he had a few brief words with the captain. The captain then signalled to two of his men, who grabbed me and hurled me against the rigging. My arms were then forced above my head and lashed to the rigging and my tattered tunic was ripped from my back. My fellow Parthians, who were murmuring in anger, were speedily herded back into the hold, some being thrown down the steps, which pulled down others they were chained to. Then the iron grilles were shut and locked, leaving me alone with my captors. I looked at where Cookus stood, his arms crossed in front of him. The captain lent forward and whispered something in his ear. Cookus threw back his head and roared with laughter. How I hated that man.

Suddenly there was a searing pain across my back as the first blow of the whip struck my flesh. The pain resembled a severe sting, which was followed by another strike, this time slightly lower on my back, just below the shoulder blades. I flinched involuntarily as the leather thongs bit deep into my back, this time near the base of my spine. The pain was unbearable and I screamed as the cords lashed my flesh. Each strike wracked my body and sapped my strength, and my body sagged as I hung limply on the rigging. My back felt as though it was on fire as waves of nausea swept through me. I lost count of how many times I was lashed. Then, mercifully, the flogging ceased. I could feel liquid running down my back – my own blood. I was aware only of the gentle rolling of the boat, everything else was silence. Then I was aware of the voice of Cookus in my right ear, his words calm and methodical.

'Well, pretty boy. That was for stealing my cane. But we don't want you too damaged otherwise you won't be much use when I deliver you to your new master, who no doubt will want to assault your arsehole every night until you are all used up.' He patted my face. 'Don't worry, we'll make sure you won't die on this boat.'

He snapped his fingers and a sailor passed him a bucket. He stepped back and threw its contents on my wounds, which caused me to arch my back and scream. The other sailors repeated Cookus' actions and sprayed me with salt water. My groans of agony made them laugh out loud until Cookus told them to stop. I was almost unconscious now, noises seemed distant and muffled and I could feel nothing. Out of the corner of my eye I saw Cookus, standing on a wooden box. He lifted his tunic and pissed over me. I barely heard the bouts of laughter as I drifted into unconsciousness.

They left me there for what seemed like hours, my back throbbing with pain, my mouth dry and my arms numb from being lashed tightly to the rigging. Eventually, as the sun was dropping on the western horizon, they released me from my bonds and hurled me back into the hold. Nergal and Gafarn tried to make me comfortable, but I was so weakened that I was barely aware of them or anything else, and drifted in and out of unconsciousness. I probably would have died on that stinking hulk had it not have been for the fact that two days later we docked in Italy. I did not know it at the time, but in the previous forty-eight hours dead bodies had been thrown off each boat into the sea as captives succumbed to their wounds or died from heat, exhaustion and lack of food. The women and children were the main victims, and as we were unloaded onto the quay in a fierce heat and under a vivid blue sky, our Roman guards suddenly seemed concerned. Not out of consideration for us, but rather from the realisation that our numbers had dropped substantially. Cookus was berating his men.

'Get them off the boats as quickly as possible. Don't let any more die.' He barked his orders to his soldiers, who scurried about, cajoling us and making threats, though I noticed that they did not actually beat us. I was finding it hard to breathe, my body weakened by the flogging I had received. My back hurt like fury, causing me to wince each time the course cloth of the stinking tunic I had been given rubbed against a weeping sore.

'Are you all right, highness?' asked Gafarn.

'I'll live,' I replied, unconvincingly.

Gafarn supported me on one side and Nergal on the other.

'How many did we lose?'

I saw the look of pain in Nergal's eyes. 'Thirty have died, highness.'

'And the civilian captives?' I asked.

He shrugged. 'I do not know, highness, but there are hardly any children left.'

I could have wept at that moment, wept for those we had lost and for what lay ahead. It seemed so long ago when we had left Hatra, all of us proud warriors of the Parthian Empire. Now, what was left of us stood chained on a quay in a Roman port. Our clothes were in rags, our faces unshaved and our hair matted and filthy. Our legs and arms were covered in welts and sores, out feet bare and bruised because we had been stripped of our footwear when we had boarded the boats. We were all mostly in our early twenties, but anyone who cast us a glance would have thought we were twice that age.

As we waited I looked around at the harbour at which we had been offloaded. It was massive, being hexagonal shaped and enclosed within two breakwaters. The waterfront comprised a long row of warehouses, which teemed with workers loading and unloading carts of varying sizes. Sacks, livestock and pallets holding clay jars were being offloaded from huge ships moored along the docks. Clerks were tallying lists and merchants were supervising the shipment of their goods. The level of activity was amazing and dwarfed anything I had previously seen. As we waited, we were given no food or water.

Eventually a chariot arrived, pulled by a pair of black horses and driven by a slight young man dressed in a pure white tunic. Beside him stood a portly middle-aged man, also in white, wearing a wide-brimmed hat. He was sweating profusely. The chariot stopped a few feet in front of us and the rotund man stepped off and walked over to Cookus, who saluted stiffly. The elder man spoke to Cookus, who nodded and then pointed at us. The older man then strode over to where we were being guarded. The day was getting hotter and I was getting weaker, having to rely increasingly on Gafarn and Nergal to stop myself from collapsing onto the ground. The man pulled up a couple of yards from us as our stench reached his nostrils. He put a handkerchief to his nose.

'They smell disgusting, centurion.'

'Yes, sir,' replied Cookus. 'You know what these eastern types are like, sir. Never wash, live in filth most of the time.'

'It never ceases to amaze me how disreputable these barbarians are. They look as disgusting as they smell.' His gaze fell on me as I stared at him from black-rimmed eyes. 'What happened to that one?'

'Trouble-maker, sir,' Cookus replied. 'We had to give him a flogging.'

The elder man nodded his approval. 'Good. Slaves need to be reminded that they exist for one purpose, to serve their masters. If you have any more trouble from him, I would advise nailing him to a cross.'

Cookus smiled. 'Of course, sir. You want them shipped to Capua.'

'Mmm, er no. They are to be transported to the legate's estate outside Nola. The eastern war has been very rewarding with regard to slaves. His estates around Capua have enough slaves. The one at Nola has need of them. The legate owns that warehouse,' he pointed to a large wooden structure that fronted the docks. 'Put them in there for the night and start out early in the morning. I've arranged food and water to be delivered, it should be here within the hour. Also some wine for you and your men.'

'That's very kind, sir.'

'Well, I must be away. The legate is a very important man and I have to be in Herculaneum this afternoon. Hopefully the rest of my journey will be uneventful.'

With that he turned and went back to his chariot, gesturing with his right hand to the driver, who shouted to the two immaculately groomed horses, who walked forward at his command. Then they were gone and we were herded into the warehouse. I was glad to be out of the sun and even more relieved when we were allowed to lie on the floor. I rested on my side as it was too painful to lie on my back. I wanted to sleep, but Nergal and Gafarn wanted to know if I knew anything.

'We are going to be transported to a place called Nola.'

'Where's that?' asked Nergal.

'I've no idea.'

'How long will it take?' asked Gafarn.

'I don't know.'

'What will happen to us there?' enquired Nergal.

'Enough,' I snapped. 'Enough of your questions. Get some rest. Food and water are on the way. Now let me sleep.'

I knew what lay ahead: more chains and whips, and being worked like animals on the land. I did not want to demoralise them, but they must have known that we were slaves with little hope of escape. Escape. We had talked in hushed tones about how we would escape, but in truth the further away we got from Parthia the likelihood of a successful escape diminished. The Romans were not fools. Each of us had manacles on our wrists and was chained to at least one other person via our ankles. The guards watched us like hawks and checked our iron bonds every day. And we were weak, with all our efforts aimed at staying alive rather than dreaming up complex escape plans. Any spare moment was devoted to rest and, most precious of all, sleep. Merciful sleep, where one could escape from the nightmare we were living.

The next morning we were woken early, Cookus kicking me awake and forcing me to my feet with his cane: his new cane, which he had obviously acquired while we were resting. He gave me a sharp whack across the face that sent me spinning to the floor. Gafarn and Nergal helped me back up.

'You like my new stick, pretty boy?' Cookus grinned maliciously at me. He reeked of ale; obviously he had been drinking heavily last night. He spat in my face then turned around and started barking orders to his men.

'Get these bastards moving. It's a long march to Nola and I want to be back here within the week.'

We were roughly organised into a long column, three abreast, and then our guards used their shields to shove us out of the warehouse and onto the road. Dawn was just breaking, but already the port was bustling with activity. After half an hour we had left the city and were on the road. Roman roads were a marvel to behold, and even in my debilitated state I could appreciate the engineering that had gone into them. The road itself was made up of flagstones laid side by side, with well-tended verges on either side that were flanked by ditches, for drainage I assumed. The road itself was around thirty feet wide, the verges ten feet wide or thereabouts. Curiously, only people were walking on the road, donkeys and their carts were travelling on the verges. I had no idea why this was, but I was thankful that the road, arrow straight, was at least not taxing to walk on and also that the day was still cool. I, Nergal and Gafarn trudged at the front of our ragged column, while ahead of us strode Cookus and half a dozen of his men. Guards were positioned on each flank of the column.

To our right was the sea, while on our left rose a massive hump-backed mountain the like of which I had never seen before. It was like a huge green tent with a flat top, and I could not but help stare at it. We had left the port and were tramping on a road in a lush green landscape. There were large fields on our left that were filled with workers, slaves no doubt. The chains that held our ankles dragged on the flagstones, producing a metallic shuffling sound. The sound was melodic, almost trance-inducing. But then I was awakened from my daydream by the sound of screams. At first they were muffled, but as we continued on our journey they became louder, and then I saw why. Ahead, about a quarter of a mile, a cross had been erected by the side of the road, upon which an individual was writhing in agony. As we got closer I could see that a soldier was frantically nailing the man's feet to a block of wood that was attached to the vertical part of the cross. The impaled man screamed in agony with each blow of the hammer, as the nail was driven deeper into the block of wood. When the soldier had finished we were only a hundred yards or so from the scene, and I could see that another man was lying on the ground, his arms held in place against a wooden crosspiece by two more soldiers. The Roman in charge wore the same type of helmet as Cookus. He halted the proceedings as his fellow centurion greeted him.

'Salve, friend. Centurion Cookus delivering this bunch of rogues to the estate of Legate Tremelius at Nola. What's this, a bit of sport?'

The other centurion ambled over and the two men clasped arms in greeting.

'Centurion Sextus. Runaways from Capua. We found them yesterday and were ordered to plant them here'

'Capua?' said Cookus 'That's a long way from here.'

'There's a whole band of them camped on Vesuvius up there,' Sextus pointed to the flat-topped mountain. 'I'm here with Praetor Caius Glaber to wipe them out.'

The crucified man was moaning in pain, which seemed to annoy Sextus. He pointed at the soldier holding the hammer.

'Put another one in his feet if he wants to annoy us with his voice.'

Clearly sadism was inherent in all centurions. The soldier reached into a bag that hung from his belt and fished out a long nail that had a mushroom-type head, then held it against the bloody foot of the victim and hit it hard with the hammer. The air was filled with an ear-piercing shriek as the iron was driven through the man's foot into the wood. The man screamed again and again as the grinning soldier hit the nail on the head, the iron being driven expertly into the foot until the head was compressed against the bloody pulp. Convulsions gripped the victim and he shook violently, which only increased the pain in his pierced feet and arms. Blood streamed down the cross from his feet. I was revolted but transfixed by the horror that was unfolding before me. Sextus looked at the other man who was being held on the ground.

'Gag him first, I've got a headache and I don't want his screams making it any worse. Where are you camping tonight, Cookus?'

'By the road, looks like.'

'Why don't you camp with us?' asked Sextus. 'There are six cohorts below the summit, so there's enough food and wine for you and your men. The garrison of Rome eats well, I can assure you.'

'Six cohorts of the garrison of Rome?' Cookus was clearly surprised. 'For a bunch of runaways?'

'Not ordinary runaways.' They had begun to nail the other man to his crosspiece, his screams of pain being clearly audible despite his gag. 'This lot are gladiators and they know how to fight. They've already killed the Capua police sent to fetch them back, and a few citizens unlucky enough to cross them.'

The new victim was hoisted into place beside his unfortunate comrade by means of ropes, the cross slamming down into a hole dug into the roadside verge. Thus it was that as we were marched away, two forlorn figures played out a grisly dance of death beneath a merciless Roman sun. Most of us Parthians had seen crucifixion before; indeed, it had been invented in the east, and were not unduly troubled by its proximity. No doubt the thought had flashed through everyone's mind that they would suffer the same fate – it had certainly gone through mine. After another hour's walking we came to a dirt track that led off the road to the left, up towards the large mountain that dominated the landscape. We followed this track for another two miles or so, the sun now beating down on us and causing us to sweat. Our pace slackened, though the guards did not use their fists or spear shafts to quicken the pace. They and Cookus seemed in good spirits, and as we crested a small hillock I understood why.

In front of us was a Roman camp, containing line upon line of neatly arranged tents. It had been laid out with precision beside the track and there must have been hundreds of tents, most small, some large and ornate, covering dozens of acres. The whole camp was surrounded by a freshly dug earth rampart about a man's height, with a ditch on the outer slope of the rampart from where the earth had been dug. Guards stood on the rampart every ten paces or so, their red shields resting on the earth with the men facing outwards. A gap in the rampart indicated the camp's entrance, which was flanked by more guards. I had to admit it was an impressive sight, and had I been in better physical shape I might have appreciated it more. As it was, I just wanted to collapse on the ground and rest.

We were herded off the track and made to sit in a field just outside the camp – obviously no one wanted us inside. After talking and laughing with Sextus, Cookus came over to where we were sitting. We had no shade, water or food. My mouth felt parched. As usual, the centurion singled me out, shoving his cane under my chin and painfully dragging me to my feet.

'This, pretty boy,' he said, pointing with his cane at the camp, 'is the might of Rome. While your mother was whelping you in a stinking mud hut, Rome's legions were conquering bastard heathens such as you. And now, son of a whore, you will live out your miserable life serving her. You and all the rest of you. Tonight I intend to get very drunk with my comrades of the garrison of Rome, and tomorrow I will deliver your stinking hide to your new master.'

He whipped the cane across the side of my face, splitting my nose and sending blood shooting over my face. The pain made me feel as though I was going to throw up. My knees buckled, but before I collapsed he grabbed my hair and yanked my bloody face to face him. 'Or perhaps I will crucify you tomorrow. Over there, on the rampart, where everyone can see.' He grinned and let me go. I collapsed in a heap at his feet. He delivered a sharp kick to my back before he turned and marched off. I lay on my side and felt blood trickle down my face. I was so very weak.

'Try to rest, highness.' Gafarn looked at me with some concern.

'It's all right, Gafarn,' I said. 'I'll live.' But I no longer believed that.

My men and the rest of the captives were lying or sitting on the ground, a sad, miserable collection of humanity wrapped in chains. I heard crying and turned my head to see two guards prodding a lifeless body with the butts of their spears shafts. A woman was weeping over the obviously dead individual: a friend, a relative, a husband? The Romans unchained the corpse and hauled it away – just another dead slave. In stark contrast, the sounds of merriment and laughter coming from the camp filled the air. The Romans were obviously enjoying their slave hunting. I was totally drained of energy, made worse by the fact that I had had nothing to eat or drink since early morning. The blood had stopped running down my face now. That was my last thought as I drifted into sleep.

I was woken by Nergal and Gafarn shaking me roughly.

'Wake up, highness.' As I regained consciousness I was aware of the alarm in his voice. It was dark – I must have been asleep for a long while – and my arms and legs felt heavy. My back ached, but then my heart started to pound as I heard the familiar sounds of combat: the sharp smack of metal against metal, the shrieks and yelps of men being cut down, and the whinnying of frightened horses and the smell of leather, sweat and blood in the air.

'Get me up,' I said, and Nergal and Gafarn hauled me to my feet.

My men were also on their feet, along with the rest of the captives, though they were scared and some were wailing in alarm. I tried to understand what was going on. In the darkness it was difficult, but it was obvious that the camp was not being assaulted; rather, the battle seemed to be taking place within its confines. Some of the tents were on fire, producing a red glow that shone on our faces and cast a supernatural pall over everything. Then the first runaways appeared, legionaries fleeing from inside the camp

through the gap in the earth rampart. Frightened men, without weapons or mail shirts, were stumbling and falling as they fled the source of their terror. One soldier, obviously wounded, staggered towards us, a sword held in his right hand.
''Over here, soldier,' I shouted.
'Highness?' said Nergal.
'When he gets close, use your manacles to beat him to the ground.'
'I hope your trick works,' remarked Gafarn.
'So do I,' I replied.
The legionary wove a haphazard path towards me. He was obviously disorientated and scared.
'It's fine, I said, 'just come to us. Everything will be fine.'
The sword was still by his side as he reached me, his eyes bulging with terror.
'They just came out of the dark, we didn't stand a chance, I…'
He said no more as Gafarn, Nergal and Byrd swung their chains in his face, smashing him off his feet. I lunged at him and snatched the sword from his grasp. He was probably unconscious as I plunged the tip of the blade down hard into his throat, causing blood to shoot upwards. We took the dead soldier's knife attached to his belt and tried to free ourselves from our bonds using it and the sword. The ends of the iron bars through our wrist and ankle shackles had been hammered flat on an anvil, though, which meant they would have to be cut with a chisel on an anvil to break them. We were trapped still. By now the sounds of slaughter filled the air as men were being cut down. Individuals began to appear on the ramparts, not soldiers but men dressed in rags and cloaks and wielding axes, spears and swords. One jumped down and caught a legionary with a vicious swing of his axe that took the man's head clean off. Then a legionary, his clothes aflame, careered past us waving his arms wildly as the heat peeled off his flesh. This night was filled with horror, which transfixed us all. A figure ran up to me, his face blackened with soot and his eyes wild. He carried a huge sword, which he swung around expertly with his right arm. He stopped and saw our chains.
'Have no fear brothers, we will be back for you.'
Then he went back to killing Romans. The sounds of battle, which had begun at the far end of the camp as muffled noises, now increased in volume and swept around us as the attackers made it to the camp entrance near where we were standing. Individuals were cutting down Romans, wielding their weapons with dexterity and ease, each of them seemingly an expert at close-quarter combat. We were cheering wildly by now, cheering every time a

Roman skull was cleaved in two or a legionary's stomach was ripped open. It was as if the gods had descended from heaven and were wreaking vengeance. Then I saw him: Cookus, my tormentor during the past few weeks. Cookus, bare headed and wearing only a tunic and sandals, staggering around in confusion. Was he drunk or suffering from the effects of a wound? I could not tell.

'Centurion Cookus,' I shouted. He turned and looked in my direction, unsure as to who was hailing him.

'Centurion Cookus, you miserable piece of filth.' He was in no doubt who was shouting at him now. His eyes narrowed to slits as his gaze locked on me.

'What's the matter, Roman dog, frightened of a slave now you haven't got your guards to back you up?'

He spat and strode towards me and I saw that he had a sword in his right hand. 'So, you speak our language, pretty boy. I was going to kill you anyway, but it might as well be tonight rather than tomorrow.'

'It is the language of the sewer, the place where you and all your kind were born.' I was relishing insulting him. I felt ten feet tall because of it. Was I mad? Probably.

He was totally oblivious to the slaughter that was going on around him, as was I to a certain extent. This was between him and me. Like all bullies he had an unshakeable belief in his own superiority, and like all bullies he was to prove a paper tiger when someone faced up to him on an equal basis. Equal? In his eyes I was a beaten, broken and chained slave, so he could not lose. It was unthinkable that a Roman, the masters of the world, could be humbled by a slave.

As he neared me he raised his sword above his head. He was going to swing it and slice my skull in two. One swing and that would be the end of me. But in his rage and arrogance he had failed to spot that I too had a sword, a short Roman sword like his, which I had in my right hand but which I had kept tight to my right leg. Before he cut me down I lunged with as much effort as I could muster and thrust the sword forward. I used both hands because my wrists were chained to each other.

It was not the expression of pain that was etched across Cookus' face when the blade went effortlessly into his stomach to the hilt, more surprise, with perhaps a hint of disappointment. For an instant I thought that he was still going to bring his blade down onto my head, but he just seemed to sigh, then cough. He tried to speak, but though his mouth opened a little nothing came out. My men behind me were silent. Cookus looked down to where my hands clasped the grip of the sword, which were now being covered by his blood that was pumping out of his stomach. I yanked the blade from his body and he still stood there, though his hand released the sword and his arm fell limp by his side. I could feel my heart pounding in my chest as I took deep gulps of air. I screamed and swung the sword low at his legs, cutting into his left thigh. He collapsed on the ground. Then I was on him, thrashing wildly at his head and torso with my sword, hacking chunks of flesh out of his face, neck and shoulders. He was dead but it didn't matter. I wanted to cut him into little pieces to erase all memory of him from the earth. As I slashed at his corpse I also shouted at it.

'I am Prince Pacorus, son of King Varaz of Hatra, a lord of the Parthian Empire and a son of the Arsacid dynasty. We are masters of the east, conquerors of the steppes and horse lords. And you are Roman filth not fit to lace our boots. You miserable vermin, I will kill a thousand of you before I have washed your filth from my body and can go back to my land. We are Parthians, Roman, and no Roman army will ever conquer us. Hatra will stand for a thousand years and more, and she will see Rome ground into the dust.'

I swung with fury, aware only of the bloody pulp that lay before me. But I was also aware of Nergal's voice, which seemed faint as though far away.

'Highness, highness,' he was saying.

I stopped my thrashing and saw that I was covered in blood, though it wasn't my own. I turned to look at Nergal.

'What?' I snapped.

But he and Gafarn were staring ahead, as were all of my men. I turned to see what they were looking at. In front of us, arranged in a loose semi-circle, was a large group of warriors, all looking at me. I raised myself up and stood before them, the sword still in my hand. Others were joining the group, some armed with swords, others with spears and axes. A few carried torches to illuminate the scene. I suddenly noticed that there was almost no sound now. The battle, if it was ever a battle, was over. The odd scream and moan pierced the night air, but quickly disappeared as a soldier was killed or a wounded man was put out of his misery. Parts of the camps were still on fire, which produced a red backdrop to the figures that stood before us. My eyes were drawn to one man in particular, who stood in the centre of the group, a few paces in front of the others. Tall, bare headed, his expression was one of unyielding determination. His eyes were fixed on me. His chiselled face had a strong jaw line and he had broad shoulders under his mail shirt. His arms were thick and muscular, which made the Roman short sword he was holding seem small, like a toy. His tunic reached to just above his knees, and his shins were protected by silver greaves. I felt that he was studying me, weighing me up to determine his next course of action. His hair was cropped short, like all Romans. But was he a Roman? His dark eyes were boring into me, like a cobra does with a rabbit before it strikes. I glanced left and right and saw that others were also looking at him, waiting for his orders. They were a fearsome lot, with blood on their weapons and bloodlust in their faces. But their leader held them in check by. By what? For he had not spoken. By his will, I guessed, the same will that was now looking into my soul.

My heart was still pounding in my chest. The silence was excruciating. I decided to break it, even though it might cost me my life. I looked at their leader, this fearsome man of stone who stood before me.

'Who are you? What do you want?'

He took a few steps forward until he was but a few paces from me, his piercing eyes looking momentarily away from mine to glance at my sword that I held at my side. Then he fixed me with his iron stare.

'I am Spartacus.'

Then I passed out.

Chapter 5

I spent five days lying in a cot in a Roman tent, a tent made of oiled calfskin. It smelt pleasant enough, and the cot I lay in was low but had a mattress admirably stuffed with hay. I liked the aroma of the dried grass as it reminded me of a stable, and my thoughts turned to home. The first four days I spent drifting in and out of unconsciousness. On the fifth day a doctor, or at least I assumed he was a doctor, visited me and tended to my wounds. He reassured me that the injury to my nose was only superficial and that it would heal without leaving any scars or being misshapen. I have to confess that my vanity was relieved by his assurance.

'I can't say the same about your back, though,' he said after examining the whip marks. His voice was slightly high-pitched and he appeared agitated. 'I have given your slave, er, your friend, some ointments which must be applied every four hours. The wounds will heal, but you will have some permanent marks on your back. Nothing too gruesome. Well, if that is all I will take my leave of you. Good day.'

He was obviously keen to be away.

'Thank you,' I said. 'I am in your debt.'

The doctor cleared his throat. 'All debts have been settled. Goodbye.'

Then he was gone. Gafarn entered the tent, the front flaps of which were open to provide some ventilation. He was carrying a tray of bottles.

'Medicine, highness, for your wounds. This lot must have cost a lot of money. What is the currency in these parts?'

'I have no money.'

'I know that,' he said, putting down the tray on the small table beside the cot. 'So does he, but the big man fetched him and gave him gold.' He sat down in a small chair the other side of the table and stretched out his legs.

'I've got some porridge cooking outside, should be ready in a few minutes. Got to get your strength back up. Now,' he picked out a bottle and uncorked it, 'this is to be rubbed into your back every four hours, apparently. Smells nice.'

He started to apply the ointment, which had a sweet smell but felt cool on my skin.

'Who's the big man?' I asked. 'You know, their leader. What's his name?'

'Spartacus. Why do you call him the big man?'

'Well, he's bigger than you for a start, and for another he's seems to be the head man of this little group.'

'Slaves, or most of them are.'

'What?' for some reason I was outraged.

'Nothing wrong with slaves. After all, you have been tended by one for years, and you yourself were one, for a while at least.' I went to raise myself up but he forced me back down. 'Lie still. Actually, they are gladiators.'

'Gladiators?'

'Yes,' he applied more ointment to my shoulders. 'Apparently they fight to the death in an arena.'

'I know what a gladiator is.'

'Of course you do,' he said. 'Anyway, turns out that they escaped from their school and ended up here, luckily for you, and me.'

I was finding it hard to stay awake, so after I had eaten a dish of porridge I slept again. Over the next few days I at last began to recover my strength. I shaved the beard off my face and Gafarn brought me a change of clothes – light brown trousers, red linen tunic and leather boots.

'They're Roman,' he said as I fastened a fine leather belt around my waist. 'Thought you might want to keep this.' He hand me a dagger in a beautiful silver sheath. It looked familiar but I didn't know why.

'It belonged to that bastard centurion who gave you a hard time.'

'Cookus,' I said involuntarily. I pulled the blade from its sheath. The brass handle and steel blade were of the highest quality. 'I'll keep it,' I said as I slammed the blade back in place and attached the sheath to my belt.

I walked outside and was greeted by my men, who gave a cheer and closed around me. It was good to see them and in truth I found it difficult to hold back the tears. They looked well, having lost their chains and having been groomed and fed. They did look odd, though – they were all dressed in Roman uniforms and could have been Romans had it not have been for their long hair. After I had embraced each one I suddenly realised that I did not recognise my surroundings. As I looked beyond our group I saw that we were in a vast rock bowl, with sheer sides all the way round, the ground we stood on was carpeted by grass and the rock face covered in foliage, though what kind I could not tell. I saw there was but one gap in the tall rock wall, a V-shaped ingress through which a steady stream of individuals was coming and going.

'It is called Mount Vesuvius, highness,' said Nergal, anticipating my question.

'Vesuvius?'

'The mountain we saw when we were captives, just before we were rescued.'

'After you passed out the gladiators stripped the Roman camp bare and brought everything here,' said Gafarn. 'They released us from our chains and invited us to accompany them to this place. They said it would be safer. We carried you and others of our party who were too weak to walk. And I've picked up a few words of Latin.

At that moment one of the gladiators sauntered up. He was dressed in the uniform of a Roman soldier, but was bare headed and had a spear and shield only, no sword. He looked at me for a few seconds; I assumed he was weighing me up in his mind. His arms were bare and I could see that he carried scars on both. He saw that I had spotted them.

'Mementos of my time in the arena.' His accent was strange, guttural and vulgar. 'Spartacus will see you now. Follow me.'

Without waiting for my reply he turned and strode off. Nergal shrugged. I nodded to him and Gafarn, and I followed my guide. I caught up with him and walked beside him as he maintained a steely gaze ahead. He obviously felt no compunction to say anything and I had little interest in engaging him in conversation. All around were tents similar to the one I had been recovering in. I noticed that they were all arranged in neat lines and rows. To my right I could see groups of men being drilled, with figures shouting and barking orders at the recruits. I would have liked to see more but my guide walked briskly, passing pens full of pigs and goats, forges with white-hot fires where burly leather-aproned men were hammering red-hot iron bars on anvils, and passing stables where men were grooming horses. We eventually arrived at a tent that was larger than the others, and which was positioned, as far as I could tell, in the middle of the camp. It was taller than the height of a man and the two front flaps were tied back to reveal the interior, which comprised a large-rectangular space. On the right-hand side was a large table where three figures were sitting. The entrance was flanked by two guards dressed as Roman soldiers, each one armed with a spear and shield. My guide gestured for me to enter and then left. I stepped inside the tent, the roof of which was supported by three thick poles arranged in a line down the middle. I recognised the man who sat in the centre. It was the one they called Spartacus. He wore a simple mail shirt over a red tunic. His gaze was as I remembered it – piercing, alert. He was obviously a man of some intelligence, not given to rashness but more calculating. I estimated his age to be around thirty, maybe older. He extended his right arm and invited me to sit in a leather chair that was on the other side of the table. I eased myself into the chair and stretched out my legs. My limbs still ached, and I was glad to be able to take the weight off them. I looked at the two men who flanked Spartacus. On his right side was a man with a long face, brown eyes and a full head of brown hair, cut to just above his neck. His beard was neatly trimmed and his eyes were staring at me intently. He wore a simple blue tunic, his hands folded across his chest. I put his age at about twenty-five. The one to the left of Spartacus was a bear of a man, a wild-looking individual of the same age or thereabouts with an untidy mass of long, red hair. On each side of his face were long plaits that rested on his huge chest. He had no beard, but rather a long, thick moustache that had plaited ends. His head was massive, as were his arms that were bare and shot out from either side of his green tunic. At his throat he wore a thick silver torque, with smaller silver bands around his wrists. His blue eyes regarded me with disdain, no doubt weighing me up as he did an opponent in the arena.

Spartacus spoke first. 'Welcome, Pacorus. I am glad to see you on your feet again.'

'Thank you,' I replied, 'and thank you for releasing me and my men from our bonds.'

'Your servant speaks Latin well,' continued Spartacus, 'and he has been telling me a little about how you came to be in Italy. But perhaps you could enlighten us further.'

'If I can, lord.'

'Ha, he's no lord, boy,' the big man had a voice as big as his frame. He slapped Spartacus hard on the shoulder. 'He's a killer, trained by the Romans to entertain them on special occasions. He's a Thracian, which in the order of things is below a Gaul but,' he leaned forward and smiled at the man with the long face, 'above a German. Isn't that right, Castus?'

'I've been remiss,' said Spartacus, ignoring the interruption. 'I must introduce you to everyone.' He turned to the big man. 'This is Crixus, a brawler from Gaul who was rescued from his life of tending pigs by the Romans, who introduced him to the art of killing men with a sword. One day he might be good at it.' Crixus sniffed in mockery. Spartacus turned to the other man. 'This is Castus, who the Romans took when they raided his village and found him sleeping off a hangover.'

'Bastard Romans, we signed a treaty with them and they agreed not to cross over the river into our territory,' there was a genuine look of indignation on Castus' face. 'We are a people who respect treaties, but the Romans just broke it like a shot.'

'Imagine that,' said Crixus, mockingly.
'What is your story, Pacorus?' asked Spartacus.
So I told them, of how we were raiding into Cappadocia, of how Bozan had been killed and we had been captured. I told them about Hatra and the Parthian Empire, and how my father had led another raid into Syria. I must confess I was slightly nervous concerning their intentions towards me, and was reluctant to tell them all about me. Spartacus looked down at the table and occasionally nodded as I related my tale. He abruptly looked up at me.
'And who is your father?'
'His name is Varaz,' I replied.
Spartacus leaned forward and fixed me with his hawk-like eyes. 'That would be King Varaz, would it not, Prince Pacorus?'
'Son of a king, eh. He should fetch a nice ransom,' quipped Crixus.
'Much gold to equip our army,' mused Castus.
I was indignant. It appeared that I had escaped one lot of gaolers only to land in the midst of a set of cutthroats. I leaned forward and tried to look purposeful, staring directly at Spartacus.
'I will not be treated like an animal. You saw fit to free me from my chains. I have to tell you that you will not be putting any back on me. I am just one man, but I will fight each and any of you. Give me a sword and I will show you how a Parthian fights.'
It was, I thought, a brave speech, though in my weakened state I wouldn't have lasted long fighting any of them, let alone all three. I prayed for a quick death at least. Spartacus looked at first Crixus and then Castus. Spartacus and Castus burst into laughter. Crixus sat stony faced.
'We don't want spoilt, royal bastards who have slaves to wipe their arses,' he spat.
'We need all the good soldiers we can get our hands on,' said Spartacus.
'He can't be that good if the Romans captured him,' replied Crixus.
'They captured you too, didn't they?' I said. 'What does that say of you?'
Crixus jumped up and glared at me. 'Why don't we see who is the best; here and now.'
'Sit down, Crixus.' Spartacus' words were stern.
Crixus did as he was told, fixing me with a hateful stare as he did so.
'We want you and your men to join us, Pacorus.'
'Not all of us,' mumbled Crixus.
'Join you?' I was somewhat taken aback. They were hardly my idea

of a disciplined army.

'We will not sway you either way,' said Spartacus. 'But we might be your best hope of getting home. You are, after all, in Italy, and a long way from Parthia. Fight with us and you might see your family again.'

'And what do you fight for?' I asked.

Spartacus smiled. 'The same thing that you used to take for granted, my young prince - freedom. The freedom from a life of bondage and cruelty. The same cruelty that you yourself have experienced, if only for a while. Am I not flesh and blood like you? Am I not a man that deserves to live his life free from the whip and branding iron?

'Do your men follow you because they are loyal or because they fear you? Will you let them decide their own fate or will you be as a tyrant to them? You think we are base because we were slaves, I can see it in your eyes. But do not slaves have thoughts, dreams, fears and the capacity to love? Few of us were born slaves, Pacorus, and yet Rome saw fit to condemn us to a life of servitude. You have killed Romans to defend your home; why shouldn't we be allowed the same privilege?

'Our plan is to organise ourselves here, around Vesuvius, and then march north to the Alps. Once there we will cross over the mountains and then head for our homes. I have no doubt that the Romans will try to stop us, but we will fight them every inch of the way if necessary. All we wish is to be out of Italy and never to see any Roman again.'

'My people lived in peace until the Romans butchered most of my village and forced the survivors into slavery,' added Castus, the pain clear in his voice.

'I can still see the corpses of my friends with Roman spears stuck in them,' spat Crixus.

'Whatever your decision,' continued Spartacus. 'We will respect it. Do not decide now. Think on it; discuss it with your men.'

The conversation was at an end, so I nodded, rose from the chair and made to leave.

'One more thing,' said Spartacus. 'Your slave.'

'Gafarn?' I replied.

'Yes. He too is free. He is your slave no longer. He may follow you of his own volition, but you have no sway over him. There are no slaves in this camp.'

I never thought of Gafarn as being a slave, though of course he was. We had been companions for so long that I thought of him as, as what? A friend? I knew not, because I had never had to think about it. I assumed he would always be with me.

'Yes, lord,' I replied.

'Oh, and Pacorus,' said Spartacus.

'Lord?'

'You don't have to call me lord.'

When I returned I gathered my men and we sat on the ground. The afternoon sun was beginning its decline in the west to disappear behind Vesuvius' crater, as I explained to them the offer made by the slave leader. They, like me, wished to return home, but we were faced by a host of difficulties. We had been brought to Italy by boat and were in the south of the country. It would be almost impossible to return home by the same method of transport, as we had no boats. That meant we would have to go across land, land that was the enemy's heartland. From what little I could remember from the maps I had seen, and which I doubted were accurate, Italy was a long land that ran north to south, and we were in the south. They listened intently as I explained that the slaves were marching north to some mountains called the Alps, after which they would disperse to their homelands. I told them that each of them was free to make their own decision as to their course of action, for I was no longer their lord and commander but just a man like them, intent on seeing Hatra again. I looked at Byrd, who was not one of us and who had lost his family and his home. What would his decision be? Most of them were of a similar age to me, though whether they had wives and children I knew not. In fact, the more I thought of it the more I realised that I had never known anything of the men I had led into battle. They were just soldiers, men on horses carrying spears or bows who obeyed orders, who sometimes died carrying out those orders. But here, in this volcanic crater in an alien land, they suddenly were not faceless individuals. They were fellow Parthians, comrades in arms. Dare I think a sort of family?

Afterwards we dispersed and went about our duties. We may each have a decision to make, but we still had to maintain discipline to make life in camp bearable. Latrines had to be dug and then filled in, water had to be fetched from nearby streams and food had to be prepared. I was still in a weakened state so after I had instructed Nergal to take the men out on a long route march the next day, I retired to my bed. Gafarn rubbed more ointment into my back, which was healing nicely, or so he told me.

'You're free, Gafarn,' I said casually as I lay on my front in the cot.

'Free, highness?'

'The slave leader, Spartacus, has told me that you are now free.'
'That's very kind of him,' said Gafarn, nonchalantly. 'What does that mean?'
'It means that you can do want you want, go where want and follow your conscience.'
Gafarn re-sealed the ointment bottle and carefully placed it back in the wooden tray on the table beside my cot.
'We are in Italy, are we not?'
'We are,' I replied.
'And we have no gold or horses.'
'That is correct.'
'And the Romans will be sending more soldiers to try to either kill or enslave us once more.'
'That seems likely.'
'To sum up, then,' said Gafarn. 'I am free but am in the land of my enemies, with no gold, no horse and little prospect of seeing Hatra alive.'
I said nothing. He sighed.
'The next time I see Spartacus, I must thank him personally for this great privilege he has bestowed on me. I hardly know how to contain my excitement. Good night, highness.'
With that he was gone.
Two days later a mounted Spartacus arrived at our tents with a spare horse. He wore a mail shirt over his tunic and a shield slung over his back. We had just finished our breakfast and I was preparing to take the men out on a march. Though we had no armour or weapons we still drilled in the morning and afternoon, both to build up our strength and to keep boredom at bay. I also sent groups off to the stables to help with the care of the horses. Our assistance was gladly received, for Parthians know more about the care and breeding of horses than any other peoples.
'Are you fit enough to ride, Pacorus?'
I was delighted by his offer. It had been many weeks since I had been in the saddle, and the chance to ride again was an offer I would not pass up.
'Indeed, lord,' I replied.
Spartacus pulled on the reins of the spare horse and brought her forward. She was a healthy chestnut brown Arabian mare with an arched neck and high-carried black tail that she used to brush away the flies. I took the reins and stroked the side of her head. Her eyes were bright and her coat shone in the morning sun.
'My stable hands are indebted to you and your men for their help with our horses.'

'No thanks are necessary,' I said, stroking the mare's neck. 'We love horses and love being around them.' I grasped one of the horns of the saddle and heaved myself onto the mare's back. I felt a surge of elation sweep through me as I felt a horse beneath me once again. Strange to say, I also had to choke back tears – I never thought I would ride again.

'Shall we ride?' asked Spartacus as he nudged the flanks of his horse with his knees and trotted forward. I followed, catching up with him and riding by his side. As we rode through the camp towards the giant gash in the rock face that was the entry and exit point, I discerned that it had increased in size. There were dozens of brown tents, and other makeshift shelters made from canvas sheets with wooden supports. But all were arranged in neat rows either side of us. I saw that we were riding down what seemed to be a main thoroughfare through the camp, while leading off it right and left were smaller avenues between the tent blocks. The whole resembled the layout of a town or city.

'Your camp is neatly arranged, lord.'

'Laid out exactly as Roman camps are when they are on campaign.'

'You have studied the Roman army, lord?'

'I was in the Roman army,' he replied.

I looked at him in surprise. He saw the expression on my face and laughed.

'That's right, Pacorus. I was once an auxiliary in one of their legions. I served for five years hauling a shield and spear around Germany and other parts.'

'You were conscripted?'

'In a way. I was young – eighteen – and after the Romans had conquered my homeland their recruiters came looking for men to serve in their army. I could ride, wield a sword and spear and I thought, why not? Thrace, the place where I come from, is poor and I could see myself spending the rest of my life looking after goats and living a miserable existence. The thought of loot and glory had some appeal. My mother had died giving birth to me and my father died of the plague when I was young. I had no ties. So off I went.

'It was I have to confess, a great adventure at first. The food was passable, the pay was regular and I got to be very good with a sword.'

'So what path led you to this place?' I asked. We had passed through the camp and had reached the slope that led to the gap in the rock face, through which a steady stream of people were coming and going on foot. Most looked as though they were poor farm hands. We trotted up it and out of the great rock bowl.

'Rome is a hard taskmaster. I soon discovered that there was very little loot to be had sitting in a wooden fort by the side of a German river. So I got bored. As an auxiliary you sign up for twenty-five years of service, and at a third of the pay of a legionary, so I decided to leave, me and a few others. We earned a living of sorts as bandits, living in the woods and robbing travellers, sometimes hiring ourselves out as mercenaries to tribal leaders. But the Romans never forget and certainly never forgive, and it was only a matter of time before we were caught. We were stupid, you see. We should have kept moving but we stayed in one place and eventually they trapped us.'

'Why didn't they kill you all?' I queried.

'Oh, they nailed a few to crosses as an example, but the Romans are a practical people. We could still be of use to them, and as we were good with weapons they sold us to be gladiators. And that's how I ended up in these parts.'

I had more questions but decided they could wait. Now we were on the grass-covered slopes of the mountain and could see for miles around. In the distance was the sea beyond a massive plain that stretched from the slopes of the mountain to our left and right. The land we rode across was an ocean of lush grass, while in the distance I could make out large, square fields. The sky was cloudless as we rode down the slope. All around us were groups of individuals making their way towards the slave camp. In fact, the more I looked I could see that the entire landscape was dotted with figures making their way towards the crater. Two riders came galloping up and halted before us. One I recognised as Castus, the German with the long face and trimmed beard. He wore a mail shirt and carried a shield and spear, as did his companion. He acknowledged me with a nod.

'A good day, Spartacus. More recruits are coming in by the hundred. My scouts tell me that most of the estates around Nola have been abandoned.'

'Good,' replied Spartacus. He cast me a glance and then looked back at Castus. 'Are they still there?'

Castus nodded. 'Excellent. Then we will go and see them.'

'Just the two of you?' asked Castus. 'There might be Romans patrols out.'

'I doubt it. We haven't had any reports since we gave them a bloody nose. A few escaped but they would have scurried back to Naples. But if we see any, we'll get back to Vesuvius.'

'Even so,' protested Castus.

'We can out-run any Romans, Castus. Isn't that so, Pacorus.'

'If you say so, lord,' I answered him.

With that he kicked his horse forward and I followed. We cantered across a wide expanse of grass until we came to a track, along which we rode for about a mile or so. The terrain gradually became more organised, with fields of olive trees right and left, though I saw no one tending them. The sun was high in the sky now and the air was hot. I was glad when we came to a larger expanse of trees on the side of a low hill, through which we rode. The air was still and warm as we directed our horses slowly through the trees. After a few minutes we came to the edge of the wood and Spartacus halted his horse. Ahead was a small valley, through which ran a stream. And around the watercourse were groups of horses, some drinking and others munching on the grass. None wore bridles, saddles or harnesses.

'Whose horses are they?' I asked.

'Yours, if you can tame them.'

I felt a tingle of excitement ripple through me. I saw that there was a collection of greys, tans, one or two blacks and others that were chestnut, dun and piebald.

'Wild horses, Pacorus. If you and your men can tame them then they are yours.' Spartacus cast me a sideways glance. 'When do you make your decision whether to stay or go?'

'Tomorrow, lord. Each man will be free to make up his own mind, as you requested.'

The horse is a sensitive creature, and those on the fringe of the group suddenly became aware of our presence. Their ears flickered, indicating that they were attentive. Others looked up from their grazing and drinking, while some began to move away, their senses telling them danger was present. Though we were hidden from view among the trees, the group was clearly getting agitated. It was time to leave. We rode back to Vesuvius along deserted tracks. When we arrived back at camp we dismounted and walked the horses back to the makeshift stables. People came up to Spartacus and either saluted or embraced him; for his part, he responded to their greetings in kind, always happy to stop and talk. I had to admit that I was warming to him. He may have been a bandit and a slave, but he was clearly a leader who held a motley band together through his personality. That said, the band was getting larger by the day. When we had dismounted another group of young men trooped into the camp, being directed by the guards to a section that had been earmarked for new arrivals. They looked weather-beaten but fit. Spartacus explained that they were herdsmen.

'Herdsmen?' I said.

'Yes, slaves who are sent by their masters to tend flocks of sheep and goats in the hills.'

'Are they not guarded?' I asked.

'Who can guard those who guard their masters' animals? No one. Roman vanity does not consider that these men might spend the lonely nights thinking of freedom instead of ensuring their flocks are not attacked by wild animals or stolen by thieves. So they send fit, young men into the hills armed with knives and sticks to look after their investments, certain that they will be good and obedient slaves. All of southern Italy is full of such men.'

'And now they join you.'

'And now they join me. Wiping out six Roman cohorts made an impression on everyone, it seems, not just the Romans.'

We reached the stables and handed over our horses to the grooms, some of whom were my men lending a hand.

'I have to attend to matters of organisation, Pacorus, so I will bid you good day.'

'Tell, me, I said. 'Why did you show me that group of wild horses?'

'I thought you might appreciate the sight, seeing as you Parthians are horse lords.'

'So it wasn't an attempt to sway me to stay.'

He laughed. 'Of course it was. We will have much infantry and no cavalry. Besides, any commander would want a man in his army who has taken a Roman eagle. Your former slave told me, despite his poor Latin, he is very proud of the fact. If you decide to stay with us, you shall be my general of horse.'

I admit I was flattered, and I liked the idea of being a general. But then I remembered that this was not an army but a collection, albeit growing, of runaway slaves. He could see that I was churning over thoughts in my mind.

He offered me his hand to shake. I took it.

'Until tomorrow, then, Pacorus.'

'Until tomorrow, lord.'

He walked away and then turned. 'And Pacorus,'

'Lord?'

'You don't have to call me lord.'

I made my way back to my men slowly, wondering if he knew that I would abide by their decision. That was the least I could do for them. I was their leader when we were captured, and I owed it to them to respect their wishes. All around me men were being drilled and lectured in the use of arms. Some practised stabbing and slashing at thick wooden posts that had been sunk in the ground. They used wooden swords to thrust and slash, while their instructors barked and shouted orders at them. Their shields appeared to be crude wicker affairs, like the ones our foot used in Parthia, and I wondered if there were real shields enough to go round. I walked on, and made way for a column of recruits being drilled. Either side of the column were instructors who used canes to keep individuals in line and in step. I shuddered – it brought back unpleasant memories. I also thought of my own time spent being drilled and practising with weapons. Bozan had believed in the doctrine of train hard, fight easy. So I and others of my age spent endless hours learning how to fight under a hot Mesopotamian sun with a sword, lance, spear, and above all, a bow. The training was repetitive, so much so that the weapons became extensions of our limbs, and wielding them became second nature to us. My military training started at the age of five. Before that I had been in the company of my mother and other women of the court; afterwards I became a student of Bozan and Hatra's army instructors. It seemed like yesterday.

I ambled past another group of men, around my age I guessed, throwing javelins. They were dressed in rags most of them, but they had enthusiasm and their sinewy arms and frames indicated years of manual labour. They hurled their shafts hard into the air, cheering as they landed among a host of posts driven into the ground with straw wrapped around them to resemble enemy soldiers. Except that these soldiers didn't fight back.

The next day I woke early, the sun still making its way into the eastern sky as I pulled back the tent flaps, to find the men waiting for me. They certainly looked better now after a few days of food and rest. There were still red marks around their wrists and ankles where the Romans had manacled them, but they looked like soldiers again. They stood in silence, each of them looking at me. Gafarn, Nergal and Byrd stood in the front row of the semi-circle, waiting for me to say something.

'Sit, all of you, please,' I said, as each one found a space on the ground. 'I told you all that each of you was free to follow his conscience to decide his own course of action. I have told the slave leader Spartacus that we will give him our decision today, but I have to tell you that I will abide by the decision that you make. I am the one responsible for getting you into this mess.' There were murmurs of disagreement but I held up a hand to still them.

'Therefore I leave the decision of our course of action to you.' With that I sat on the grass and waited.

Nergal looked nervously at men either side of him and behind, who urged him to speak. He rose to his feet.

'Highness, we have talked among ourselves and we thank you for having faith in our sense to make the right decision. But our decision is that you are our commander and we stay with you.'

Gafarn clapped his hands. 'That is excellent. Prince Pacorus says it is up to you and you say it is up to him. So in effect no one has to make a decision.' He jabbed a finger at me. 'You must decide, otherwise we might as well put our chains back on. At least the Romans seem to be able to make decisions.' His freedom had made him more impertinent than ever. Nevertheless, his words stung me into action. I rose to my feet.

'Very well. We are in southern Italy and have no means by which to leave this land by the sea. It appears that our best chance is to head north with Spartacus to leave Italy after crossing the Alps. Thereafter we can head east into lands not ruled by the Romans, and then to the Black Sea and Pontus, and thence home. But before we can do that, doubtless we will have to fight the Romans. But that is what we do: fight Romans. They are the enemy and we are soldiers, and it is the duty of every soldier to fight his enemy. This Spartacus wants cavalry, and we are the best cavalry in the world. So we stay and we fight. That is my decision.'

There was a brief moment of silence, then they rose and began cheering and embracing each other. I was happy enough, for now I would have a chance to avenge Bozan and perhaps wipe out the shame of my capture. Shamash forgive me, but I also craved glory for myself. That was hopefully in the future, but for now my ambition was to kill Romans and lay their land to waste. Was that evil? I did not think so. They were my enemy and here I was, in their heartland. The Romans wanted to put me in chains and treat me like a dog. Well, this dog was going to bite back.

We ate breakfast in silence, though some of the men smiled at me when I caught their eye. I smiled back. We were a band of brothers in an alien land and I was glad to be in their company. I hoped that they were glad of mine. I still had their trust and respect, I knew that now. I was determined to retain them. I must confess that I was growing fond of the Roman food that was available to us. The former slaves had plentiful supplies of milk from their herds of goats that thronged the slopes of Vesuvius outside of the camp, and Gafarn had spent many an hour while I was lying in my tent recuperating talking to all and sundry about everyday matters. He came back each afternoon with a wealth of information. The country we were in was bountiful in foodstuffs, unlike the barren wastes of much of Hatra, aside from the fertile valleys of the Euphrates and Tigris. Spartacus was generous with his rations. I quickly regained my strength on a diet of broad beans, lentils and chickpeas, lettuces, cabbages and leeks, and fruits such as apples, pears, wild cherries, plums, grapes, walnuts, almonds and chestnuts. Gafarn told me that some of the best wines of Italy came from the region where we were located, which was called Campania, and one evening we were treated to a drink of wine mixed with honey, which the Romans called mulsum. It was wondrous to taste. Aside from porridge, which certainly provided good ballast for the stomach, my favourite dish was named dulca domestica, a delicious concoction of pitted dates stuffed with dried fruit, nuts, cake crumbs and spices, the whole soaked in fruit juice.

I went to see Spartacus after breakfast.

I found him watching what must have been at least a hundred men being instructed in the use of the sword and shield, each of them paired, jabbing and parrying with wooden swords and Roman shields. The instructors who were watching lambasted any that tried an overhead stabbing motion. Each Instructor carried an accursed cane, and wasn't afraid to use it. They screamed over and over at their charges. 'Keep your shield close by your side, never over-extend your sword arm, stab your sword forward, never slash, better to stick an enemy with the point than cut him with the side of the blade, you only need to stick two or three inches of steel into him to put him down.' Spartacus stood like a rock, arms folded, watching the scene. He wore no expression on his iron-hard face, though as I neared him I saw that his eyes were darting to and fro, observing the pairs closely. The instructors shouted encouragement, urging individuals to speed up their movements to find an opening in the opponent's defence. The spring day was growing hot and I could see great sweat patches on the backs of the men's tunics. The dull thud of wood striking wood echoed across the flat ground; with the occasional shout as a stick found a fleshy target. I walked up and stood next to him, both of us watching the mock combats spread out before us. His grey eyes were fixed on the practice being carried out.

'You have reached a decision.'

'We have decided to stay, lord,' I said.

I thought I saw a flicker of a smile on his face, but it was quickly replaced by a stony stare. 'If they catch you again, they will crucify you. There will be no mercy the second time around.'

'I've seen Roman mercy, such as it is,' I replied. 'I have no desire to stay in this country, and I believe you are our best chance of my men seeing Hatra again.'

He turned to look at me, and then offered me his hand. 'There will be much hard fighting before you do. But I am glad that you are with us.'

I clasped his rock-hard forearm in salute, and then he gestured for me to follow him as he walked away from the training.

'We're fortunate that most of those coming in are herdsmen and shepherds, men used to hard living in the hills. This lot,' Spartacus gestured towards the men practising with swords and shields, 'will be ready in two or three months. But we need many more if we are to fight our way north.'

As we walked, he told me of how the gladiators had taken refuge in the crater of Vesuvius, and how they had raided local farms for food and weapons. They had gained some recruits, but both slaves and citizens had shied away from what they assumed was just another group of bandits whom the authorities would soon deal with. The arrival of three thousand legionaries from the garrison of Rome seemed to confirm their imminent destruction. But the Romans had underestimated their foe and though they had erected a palisade they had failed to build a wooden wall on top of it. Moreover the gladiators had attacked first, which caught the Romans by surprise. The result was slaughter and the capture of three thousand sets of arms and armour, plus all their camp equipment, food, cattle, horses and wagons. But an even greater boon was the boost the victory gave to recruitment. Suddenly hundreds of former slaves thronged to Vesuvius, and more were coming in each day. Spartacus now had some four thousand men.

'How many cavalry?' I asked.

'How many men have you got?' he asked.

'Just over two hundred.'

'Then we have two hundred horsemen.'

This was the size of two Parthian companies, which was totally inadequate for anything more than a contingent of scouts.

'We will need more,' I said. 'How many horses do you possess?'

'Fifty, plus four hundred mules. Though I can't give you all the horses, as I promised Crixus and Castus that they would have horses for them and their officers. Which leaves thirty horses for your cavalry.' He could see the disappointment in my face. 'Do not worry. There are plenty of horses in these parts.'

I was unconvinced but hoped he was right. I had seen one wild herd myself and assumed there would be others, but I knew that

Roman armies were composed mainly of infantry, and as Spartacus had been trained by the Romans then his lack of cavalry did not concern him unduly.

'I must leave you now. Tonight we will slaughter a bull and have a feast to celebrate your decision. My wife is keen to meet you.'

I looked at him in surprise. 'Your wife?'

'Till tonight, my friend.' With that he was gone.

When I got back to camp Gafarn was sorting through a package of clothing that had been delivered. He held up a rather smart long-sleeved white tunic fringed with blue.

'What's that?' I asked.

'A present from Spartacus, it would appear. There are leggings and boots as well.'

'For the feast tonight.'

Before I left I gathered together my men and told them that in the morning twenty of us would leave to scour the country for horses. Capturing wild horses would not be a problem, but saddles, bridles and harnesses would be. I had no idea how that problem would be solved.

The feast laid on by Spartacus was lavish. There were half a dozen fires, over which roasted pigs, lambs and two huge sides of beef. In front of and around the fires were long tables, at which were seated warriors eating and drinking. They were shouting, singing and laughing as women served them from trays heaped high with meats and bread, while others carried jars full of wine. Spartacus sat at the top table flanked by ten men I assumed were his commanders. I recognised the fierce and wild Crixus, his red hair like a fireball around his head; the serious Castus and his long, somewhat sad visage. The others I did not know. Spartacus, talking intently to a lieutenant beside him, spotted me, beckoned me over and pointed at a spare place at the end of his table. Crixus and Castus ignored me as I sat down beside a man who had hair plaited in a similar style to Crixus. I assumed they were of the same people.

A woman offered me a wooden platter and another meat from a tray. I did not usually eat red meat, but tonight I would be adventurous. I grabbed a chunk of beef oozing blood and took a bite. It tasted delicious. A young girl, a teenager, gave me a cup and poured wine into it, which tasted remarkably good. Clearly local vineyards had been thoroughly plundered. An attractive woman, her hair black as night and olive-skinned, refilled the silver goblet of Spartacus. She laughed as he slipped an arm round her waist and pulled her close. She had a narrow face, with high cheekbones and full lips. For some reason she reminded me of a mountain lion, all feline grace yet deadly to tangle with. Spartacus said something to her and her eyes flashed at me. She fixed me with a cobra-like stare and then smiled. Spartacus gestured me over with his free arm. I emptied my cup, rose from my bench and walked over to where the slave general and his woman were.

'Pacorus, this is my wife Claudia,' Spartacus exuded pride as he flashed a smile at me and then gazed lovingly at his wife. She was dressed in a simple white stola, with a wide black belt fastened just under her breasts, which accentuated her shapely figure. Her arms were bare, and around each wrist she wore large silver bangles. She was a beautiful woman; that was my first impression, that and a sense that she possessed great inner strength. All conversation died down as everyone watched me. I bowed my head to her.

'An honour to meet you, lady.'

From behind me Crixus let out a loud guffaw. 'He thinks he's back in a Parthian court.'

Laughter erupted from all those present, especially the men sitting around Crixus. I must admit that I was finding him rather boorish. He might be a fearsome sight but he was clearly a brute. Claudia flashed her black eyes at the big Gaul, who sneered and went back to drinking greedily from his cup.

'You are most welcome, Pacorus.' Her voice was feminine yet strong and assured. Her eyes were not in fact black but dark brown and they seemed to be examining me, determining whether I was worthy to be an associate of her husband. 'Spartacus tells me that you are a prince in Parthia and that you and your men have put your swords at his service.'

She may have been the wife of a slave but she carried herself with elegance, betraying a certain education, perhaps.

'We hope to be a valuable part of his army, lady.'

'I thank you on his behalf. I hope you, and all of us, will see your homeland again.'

Spartacus let go of his wife and reached behind him. He stood and held out a sword in a scabbard. 'And to help you achieve that aim take this gift, with thanks. It is called a spatha, a Roman cavalry sword. Use it well.'

I took the scabbard and drew the sword. It was a superb weapon, with a long, straight blade pointed at the tip, and was beautifully balanced. The blade length was about two feet while the hilt was an all-wood construction, with a reinforcing guard plate of bronze inlaid into the forward end of the guard. The grip itself had an eight-sided cross-section with finger grooves that gave a surprisingly firm grip. I have to confess that it was as good as any Parthian sword I had seen.

'A most generous gift, lord,' I said, bowing my head to him.

'He's like a little dog, nodding his head to all and sundry.' The oafish voice of Crixus rang out once again.

I turned to face him. 'Have you something to say to me?'

He jumped up and marched around the table to face me in the rectangular space in front of the tables. Aside from the crackling of the fires there was silence as all eyes were upon us. Crixus, bare-chested and angry, held a sword in his right hand. He was about six foot five, I guessed, with a massive, broad chest and arms that seemed stuffed with muscles.

'I want you to yap like a little dog, boy.' He grinned at me, clearly hoping to provoke me. I took the bait and threw the scabbard aside.

'Why don't you let me cut off some of those filthy locks instead?'

Crixus roared in anger and made to attack me, but in an instant Spartacus leapt over the table and stood between us, sword in hand.

'Put your swords down, both of you. There will be no violence tonight. Have you forgotten that our enemies are the Romans, Crixus? Would you rather kill your comrades?'

Crixus stood still for a moment, then shrugged, spat on the ground and returned to his seat. I retrieved the scabbard from the earth and sheathed my gift. Spartacus stood like a rock as I too took my seat, Crixus glaring at me. Castus heaved the man sitting next to me out of his seat and plonked himself beside me.

'I hope you can use that sword,' he said, as he tore a chunk of meat from a breast of chicken, 'Crixus is a mean-spirited bastard who kills just for the sake of it. And you have just made yourself his enemy.'

I looked as the big Gaul finished yet another cup of wine and demanded that it be refilled, bellowing his order at a young girl who jumped at his roar. His eyes were bulging fit to burst and grease and blood from the meat he had been eating matted his moustache. He was just like Cookus, I decided, a loud-mouthed bully. He was surrounded by his fellow Gauls, who looked just as ugly and who were just as loud as he was. They cut a fearsome spectacle sure enough, but the fact that they had been slaves reminded me that they had once been bested by Roman soldiers. Talk was cheap. I would reserve judgment on Crixus and his Gauls.

Castus was in a talkative mood, and in truth I found his conversation interesting and his company agreeable. He didn't drink as much as Crixus, but then I doubted if anyone did, and though merry from the drink his mind was still clear. Castus told me about Roman gladiators, men who were trained to kill each other in the arena.

'It didn't start out like that,' he said, picking a morsel of food from his teeth and flicking it on the ground, 'but the Romans are a practical people, that and ruthless.'

At first gladiators, invariably prisoners of war, fought each other at the funerals of important Romans. But the contests grew in popularity and in time gladiatorial schools called ludi were established, each one run by a businessman called a lanista who had agents that purchased suitable slaves on his behalf. At the ludus the prospective gladiators were trained and then hired out. I found it strange when Castus told me that the pupils included not only condemned criminals – 'like myself and Spartacus, bandits who had slit Roman throats' – but also a small number of volunteers, men attracted by the lure of violence or adventure, or the prospect of bedding wealthy Roman women. Gladiators were great athletes, fed on a good diet (they sounded like our warhorses at Hatra), trained hard and given the best medical treatment. But the instructors and the lanista never forgot that they were highly trained killers. So the ludus was not only a barracks but also a prison, with bolted doors, guards, iron bars and manacles. Each gladiator had his own cell where he was locked in for the night. Training areas were sectioned off by tall iron railings, and even the dining areas were fenced off and guarded. Gladiators could make a lanista rich, but they were also dangerous animals who could slit his throat if he was careless. Gladiators were never allowed to forget that they were social outcasts, beneath the law and therefore not respectable.

The lanista who ruled Castus' ludus was a man called Cornelius Lentulus. 'A greedy little bastard,' as Castus colourfully described him.

'Thin as a pole he was, with a small, bony face and two tufts just above his ears either side of his head.' Castus took another swig from his cup and laughed. 'He could size up a man in an instant. Know what weapons he would be good with in the arena, how many fights he would win and even when he would get killed, more or less. To be fair to him, may his spirit be the plaything of demons in the underworld, he always made sure that we had enough to eat and the instructors didn't beat us too much – just enough to keep us on our toes.'

Around us the revellers were enjoying the skills of a troupe of jugglers who were performing amazing feats with a collection of

Roman swords, throwing them to each other in a blur of movement. I noticed that Crixus and his companions were shouting that the jugglers should aim better and throw their swords into each other. Castus resumed his tale.

'We fought for Lentulus for three years, and I have to say that his school got a good reputation in Capua and throughout southern Italy for producing fine gladiators. The crowds love a spectacle, you see. Simple butchery isn't sufficient. That's why we spent hours each day practising with weapons, so in the arena, as Lentulus put it, we would "fight with finesse". Spartacus, he was the one. Had over forty kills under his belt by the end. The crowd loved him. Fights with his brain, you see, whereas Crixus is all brute strength and Gallic fury.' Castus spat out a piece of meat and wiped his mouth on the sleeve of his tunic.

'Lentulus was becoming seriously rich renting out his fighters to those putting on displays. If they wanted Crixus and Spartacus, he could just about name his price. He was happy, we were happy; everyone was happy.'

'How could you be happy living like an animal, trained to fight?'

He looked at me in puzzlement, I think trying to work out whether I was stupid or genuinely ignorant of how these things worked. He gave me the benefit of the doubt. He smiled as a juggler missed his timing and the point of a blade embedded itself in his arm. Crixus spat out a mouthful of wine and bellowed his approval as the man collapsed onto the ground in pain.

'It's not like that, at least not for Spartacus. Look, a lot of gladiators are killed during their first few fights, either because they are unlucky or, more likely, because they are no good. But a good fighter, and Spartacus is one of the best, wins his early fights. He gets more confident in the arena, he wins more fights and soon he has prestige, which increases with every contest. That way many of the contests are as good as over before the fight begins, because the other man knows he can't beat who he's up against. And also, a champion has a lot of supporters, and they make sure that they shout the loudest if he has a bad day, and they sway the officials and save his skin. Simple, really.'

I was confused. 'If life was so good, then why did you break out?'

He smiled to himself. 'Same reason that men have been fighting since the beginning of time. A woman.'

'I don't understand.'

He looked up and sighed loudly, then shook his head. 'Like I said, Lentulus was becoming rich, and like all rich men he wanted some trophies around him to show how wealthy he was. So he starts dressing in the finest clothes and buys expensive slaves. Young boys from Numidia, learned Greeks to read to him and young girls to play with at night. But one day he comes back from the slave market all excited. Turns out he had bought a Gallic woman, twenty years old, he said. Same race as Crixus. He asked Claudia if she would instruct this girl in how to conduct herself as his wife, saying he won't touch her until she is his wife. Remember, Claudia is Spartacus' wife and wasn't a slave.'

I looked at him in more confusion.

'I'll explain another time. Anyway, this girl arrives and her and Claudia become friends. But this girl doesn't want to be the slave of Lentulus, much less his wife and she tells him so. I remember that day. We were all in the mess hall eating our midday meal when he comes in with her beside him to show her off to his gladiators. But she starts to argue with him and so he slaps her hard. So Claudia steps between them and tells him to stop. Lentulus slaps Claudia, which was a bad mistake, for it was the last thing he did before Spartacus split his skull on a stone column. Then he killed a couple of instructors, Crixus killed two more just for the hell of it, and the next thing we are hot-footing it out of Capua as fast as we could. Like I said, all over a woman.'

'Who was she?' I asked, not sure if he was making it all up.

'Who, Gallia? See for yourself, she's over there.'

I looked to where Castus was peering and saw a vision of beauty that made everyone and everything else disappear. I've often thought of the first moment I saw Gallia and have often wondered if all men experience the same emotions when they cast their eyes on 'the one'. She was wearing a simple blue stola, with a black belt around her waist. She embraced Claudia and then Spartacus, laughing and obviously at ease with her friends. Her long, thick blonde hair cascaded down over her breasts and framed her flawless, oval face with its high cheekbones and narrow nose. She was beautiful, yes, but aside from the perfect features nature had gifted her she also gave the impression of strength and pride. She was tall, around six foot, and her dress highlighted the contours of her lithe body. She held herself erect and strong, undaunted by the coarse gathering of gladiators around her. I noticed that she glanced at the now ragingly drunk Crixus and frowned. Claudia whispered something in her ear and she cast me a quick glance. My heart leapt but she quickly returned to conversing with her two friends. I noticed she wore no jewellery; she didn't have to. No amount of gold could improve upon her natural beauty. Perhaps I had had too much wine, but this woman called Gallia had burst into my world like a flaming comet crashing to earth from the heavens. I wanted to know more about her, at the very least talk to her, but she never looked at me again that evening. I yearned to be near her, but she sat next to Claudia and Spartacus and ignored me. Later another woman, with brown hair and a kind if unremarkable face, sat next to Gallia. It was apparent that the two were friends, and Castus informed me that her name was Diana and that she had been a kitchen slave at the ludus.

The days after the feast were filled with the task of creating a force of cavalry from nothing. Spartacus gave me the thirty horses he had promised, which had been captured from the Roman force he had destroyed on the slopes of Vesuvius. They were adequate beasts, but did not compare to the specially bred Arabians of Hatra, which were noted for their depth of chest, masculine power and size. They were also intelligent, especially my Sura, on whom I had fought my first battle. The most common colours in Hatra were grey and chestnut, though the royal stables of my father had always specialised in breeding pure whites. His whites were famed throughout the Parthian Empire, and were highly sought after. This being the case, Hatra attracted its fair share of horse thieves; if caught, which they invariably were, they were usually impaled on stakes outside the gates of the city as a warning to others.

The horses we now rode on were certainly not Arabians, yet they were hardy enough and were responsive to our commands, being military horses. The Roman saddles we rode on were similar to Parthian ones, being built around a wooden frame with four horns reinforced with bronze plates at each corner to hold the rider in place, the front horns supporting the inner thigh and the two back horns supporting the hips. The whole saddle was padded and covered in leather. I led the party of horsemen that included Nergal and Gafarn. We rode to the valley where Spartacus had showed me the herd of wild horses. They were still there when we arrived, around fifty of them, maybe more. We tethered our own horses in trees out of sight of the herd and then approached them on foot. Taming wild horses requires time and patience, but first they have to be captured. We Parthians were horse masters and we knew all the tricks. First of all, each of us peeled off the top layer of the chestnuts from our own horses and rubbed them on our hands. The chestnuts were the small, horny calluses on the inner surface of a horse's leg, and they gave our hands the reassuring smell of a fellow horse. We all had ropes as we gently approached a wild horse, making sure we were all upwind of our targets.

The air was warm as I slowly approached a grey stallion, which turned to look at me when I was five or so paces from him, approaching from his right side. I stopped, being careful not to look directly into his eyes, which was the action of a predator. I spoke to him quietly as I inched my way sideways towards him, thereby presenting no threat. He turned away and resumed his chewing at the grass. I stopped and watched him for a few minutes. There was no rush; it could take us all day, but our patience would be rewarded. I inched closer until I was near enough to touch him. I stopped again and did nothing for several minutes, looking away from him but talking in a quiet voice, reassuring him that I was his friend and would not hurt him. He could not understand, of course, but he would understand the calm tone of my voice. I extended my hand with my fingers closed – spread fingers would give the impression that I was a wild animal – and gently touched his neck. He drew back so I withdrew my hand. It was some minutes more before he resumed his grazing, and once more I extended my hand and gently touched his neck. This time he did not draw back, so I continued to stroke his neck, talking to him soothingly and calmly.

I do not know how long I stood there talking to this stallion, perhaps an hour, but in the end I was able to put the rope halter over his head and lead him away towards where my own horse was tethered in the shade. By late afternoon we had tamed many horses and were leading them back to camp. Being a herd, once the head stallion had been tamed, by Nergal, which flushed him with pride, all the other horses were soon haltered. While we were away the rest of my men were building wooden pens to hold our new charges. The sun was on our backs and sinking into the west as we trotted back into camp with our four-legged captives. They were then led to the pens and safely secured, after which they were fed and watered. A count revealed that we had captured fifty-five horses. We went out again the next day to bring in the rest, which numbered another forty.

The following days were spent taming our new mounts. Spartacus visited us to observe our progress. He seemed pleased by what he saw. Each horse had been allotted to one of my men, who would be its sole master when it was fully tamed.

'How long will it take?'

'Two or three weeks, maybe a month,' I replied.

'That long?' he seemed surprised.

'It takes time, lord.' He obviously knew very little about horses, so I decided to educate him. 'The first step with a wild horse is to establish trust. You have to gain his trust before you can do

anything with him. You cannot work with any horse if that horse does not trust you. You have to visit him every day. You feed him, water him and talk to him in a mild, reassuring manner. Eventually, the horse will start to trust you, and will know that you are not there to hurt him. Once this happens, you can go inside the pen and give him a massage or body rub. This helps strengthen the bond that you are now starting to build with the horse. When you are confident that the horse no longer sees you as a threat, you can start showing him objects that he will be using in the future. The rope and the halter must be the first items you should introduce to him. Let him smell it, rub it against his back and neck, so he will get used to it. Let him wear the halter for a few hours every day, but take it off when you leave. And when you have acquainted the horse with objects around him like fences, ropes, the halter, the saddle, and everything else, he becomes more trusting. He looks to you as a leader. This makes training be easier. Horses are intelligent creatures, lord, and it takes time to earn their trust.'
'When will you have your men ready?'
'One month, lord. But I will need more horses and more recruits. I have only two hundred men. You will need more cavalry than that.'
He stared into the distance, saying nothing for a while. 'Nola.'
'Lord?'
He turned to face me. 'We will attack Nola, a town about thirty miles away. That should provide us with more weapons and supplies, and horses for your cavalry.'
'Does it have walls, lord?'
'Yes, strong stone walls with a ditch in front of them.'
'Have you any siege engines? I asked, somewhat surprised that he was thinking of assaulting a walled town.
'None.'
'Then how are you going to take it?'
He looked at me and smiled wolfishly. 'You are you going to take it, Pacorus, you and your cavalry. Come to a council of war in two hours and I will explain.'
With that he marched away, leaving me more than a little bewildered.
I took Nergal with me to the council. As my newly appointed second-in-command it was only proper that he should be privy to the decisions that would affect us. He was delighted with his new rank and though he was a year older than me, he was like a child with a new toy. He was taller than me and slightly lanky, with long arms and even longer legs. He looked awkward when he was

walking, being all limbs, but in the saddle he was a superb horseman, far better than I. Parthians loved their horses, but Nergal, I think, loved them the most and they loved him. When he was riding he and horse seemed to become one, man and beast fused together. He perhaps wasn't the brightest person in the world, but he was loyal and had an infectious spirit.

The council meeting was held in a large leather tent that was supported by two centre poles that held up the roof and numerous ropes that gave tension to the walls. The flaps at each end were open to allow air inside, for it had been a hot day. We went inside and I saw that stools had been placed around a large oblong table in the middle. Wine and water jugs had been placed on tables either side of the entrance. I filled a cup with water and handed it to Nergal, then filled another for myself. Spartacus was already seated and called for us all to take our places. I recognised Crixus, who ignored me, and Castus who nodded as he sat beside another dark-haired warrior who was dressed in a similar fashion to him. Crixus finished his cup (no doubt wine) and shoved his companion beside him off his stool and ordered him to fetch a jug. Spartacus frowned and stood up.

'I have decided we are going to attack and capture Nola. We cannot remain idle forever, and the longer we are passive the more the likelihood that the Romans will attack us again. Besides, we are eating up all our supplies and emptying the countryside of food. We need fresh supplies.'

'Nola has walls,' said Castus.

'There are plenty of rich villas further afield,' growled Crixus. 'Why waste time battering our heads against walls we can't take.'

'We are not going to batter the walls, Crixus,' replied Spartacus, 'we are going to walk up to the gates and they will let us in.'

Crixus burst into laughter. 'You've been in the sun too long. Have some water and lie down for a while.'

Spartacus waited a few minutes until Crixus had finished making his noise. He fixed the Gaul with an iron stare until the silence was oppressive. Castus said nothing. Nergal, who had never seen Spartacus up close, looked upon the Thracian with awe. Spartacus certainly had an imposing presence. Crixus snorted in disgust and played with a giant two-bladed axe that he had rested on the ground beside him. His new toy.

'As I said,' continued Spartacus, 'we are going to take Nola. Pacorus and some of his men will ride up to one of the gates dressed in Roman cavalry uniforms,' he nodded at me. 'Once he is inside his men will seize the gatehouse and keep the gates open long enough for a following force of foot to get inside. Simple and effective.'

I looked at Nergal, who was shaking his head enthusiastically. Spartacus had obviously won him over. I have to confess that his plan struck a balance between audacity and foolishness. It might just work. Crixus glared at me.

'We don't know if he,' he jabbed a finger in my direction, 'and his bunch of riders can fight, let alone take a town. What if messes up? The men following him will be caught in the open. I don't trust him.'

I rose from my stool, but Spartacus waved his hand for me to remain seated. 'I can understand your reticence, Crixus. I will therefore ride with Pacorus and his men, to make sure nothing goes awry. You will stay here with your men. Castus and his Germans will support us.'

Castus smiled, but Crixus jumped up. 'Me and my Gauls should be the ones to burn Nola.' Crixus' companion nodded his agreement, though I noticed he stayed seated. Nergal looked at them both with narrowed eyes. Clearly he had formed the same impression of Crixus as I had.

Spartacus walked towards Crixus until their faces were inches apart. 'We're not going to burn Nola, that's why your Gauls will stay here. We're going to empty it of anything useful. Besides,' he grinned at Crixus, 'if I'm killed, you will then be the leader of the army.'

I could see that Crixus was weighing up the options in his over-sized head and he clearly liked the idea of being a general, for he sat back down and grunted. 'Don't say I didn't warn you. If you're killed I will burn Nola in any case.'

Spartacus smiled. 'I've no doubt. We leave tomorrow. Castus, you and your Germans will be the foot. You will march tonight along the road that leads to Nola's western entrance and stay hidden tomorrow. We will link up with you a few miles from Nola, and then you and your men will follow us. As soon as you get within sight of the town, you will attack through the open gates.'

'And if the gates are not open?' asked Castus.

'Then head back to Vesuvius and put yourself under the command of Crixus.'

Afterwards Crixus stomped off to his section of the camp, while I talked with Castus and his lieutenant, whose name was Cannicus.

'How many men do you have?' I asked.

'Around two thousand. More are coming in every day, but the majority are Gauls and they are swelling Crixus' ranks. He was bragging that he has four thousand men. If Spartacus falls I will be leading my people out of here. I won't serve under Crixus. Think the plan will work?'

'It might,' I said, 'it just might.'

We clasped each other's forearms. 'Until tomorrow, then,' he said.

'Until tomorrow.' I was starting to like Castus. He wasn't a boaster and I believed he had a cool head on his shoulders.

That night Castus led his men out of the camp, hundreds of black-haired Germans marching in column and carrying shields, spears, swords and axes. Mail shirts were few, with most dressed in threadbare tunics and nothing on their feet. Those in the rear ranks carried only wooden shafts whose ends had been sharpened to a point and then held in a fire to harden the end. Spartacus was right – we needed more weapons and equipment. Spartacus had the Roman cavalry weapons and armour delivered to our camp that afternoon: mail shirts, red cloaks, open-faced helmets decorated with bronze, and oval wooden shields, each one covered with hide and having a central steel boss with a wooden grip behind it. The swords were similar to the one Spartacus had given me, though their quality was not as good, a fact commented on sarcastically by Gafarn. Finally, we would each carry an eight-foot-long lance tipped with a steel head, as thick as a man's wrist.

The next day we groomed and fed the horses after dawn had broken and kitted ourselves out in our new arms and armour. Spartacus joined us after breakfast.

'Make sure you and your men tuck your long hair into your helmets. Roman cavalry don't have flowing locks.' His attention to detail was excellent.

I had selected a magnificent steel helmet that had silver cheek guards, a brass visor and a large red crest. It was clearly an officer's helmet and its thick leather lining meant it was comfortable to wear. I insisted Spartacus wore a similar design, since he and I were going to ride at the head of the column and we had to look the part.

We left early in the morning, riding west by the side of well-maintained, stone-paved roads through lush green countryside interlaced with fields. There wasn't a soul in sight. The slaves who had worked the fields had either joined Spartacus or fled, to where I did not know. There was an odd silence around us, as though the land itself was waiting to see what would happen. As we rode in silence, twenty red-cloaked warriors disguised as the enemy, we passed burnt-out houses set back some distance from the road, no doubt the slaves of the estate had taken their revenge on their masters before they had left.

Two hours later, on the orders of Spartacus, we halted beside a large wood that sprawled across a hillside and waited. We dismounted and led our horses into the shade of the trees and rested. Spartacus walked away into the wood and reappeared a few minutes later with Castus by his side. The two of them walked over to me and squatted beside me. Castus nodded at me and smiled. Spartacus' face was hard and expressionless. His briefing was short and to the point.

'Nola is five or so miles down this road. The town sits in a plain, so anything that approaches it from any direction can be seen by the guards on the walls. Castus, you and your men will follow Pacorus and me down this road. If we have succeeded you will see that the gates are open. If they are, get your men down the road and into the town as soon as possible. If the gates are closed then we've failed, in which case get yourself back to Vesuvius. Good luck, Castus.'

Spartacus rose and embraced Castus, then mounted his horse. I too embraced the German and vaulted onto my horse, the same chestnut mare that I had first ridden in this army. Then we rode towards Nola, two abreast, keeping off the road. We did not want to appear out of the ordinary. Roman horses were not shod, though we had fitted the horses we rode with shoes, as was the custom in Parthia. We crested a small rise and entered a wide plain dotted with fields and copses, in the centre of which stood Nola. It was encompassed on all sides by a wall, and from our slight vantage point I caught a glimpse of red roofs and white-faced buildings. We maintained an even pace as the road led us straight towards one of the town's gatehouses. I was sweating as we rode up to the gatehouse, which comprised two square, two-storey towers with red-tiled roofs, either side of an arch that was barred by two wooden gates. Guards stood on the rampart above the gates, in front of which we halted.

As we approached the gates we slowed to a gentle trot. My mouth was dry as I viewed the gatehouse with trepidation, saw guards on the wall above the gates themselves, and windows in the two towers with closed wooden shutters, which no doubt could be opened to make effective ports from which to fire arrows. Spartacus' plan suddenly seemed a very bad idea.

'Stay silent,' he snapped, 'leave the talking to me.'

We halted about twenty paces from the gates as a soldier wearing the distinctive helmet of a centurion peered at us from atop the wall.

'State your business.'

Spartacus, his face enclosed by his helmet and its cheek guards, raised his hand in salute.

'Decurion Batiatus to see the garrison commander.' 'On what business?' replied the centurion.

'On military business, centurion.'

The centurion placed both hands on the wall and leaned over to look at Spartacus more closely.

'Who is your commander?'

'The Praetor Varinius Glaber.' 'I thought he had been killed by the gladiators.'

'You thought wrong. He is camped twenty miles from here, with two ala of horse and half a legion.' Spartacus pulled a scroll from a saddlebag. 'Here are his orders for the garrison commander. I am to deliver them in person.'

The centurion said nothing as he gazed at Spartacus. I could feel rivulets of sweat run down the sides of my face as I purposely stared directly ahead at the gates. The centurion pulled away from the wall and shouted down.

'Open the gates.'

There was a scraping sound as some sort of barrier that held the gates closed was removed, and then they both opened. Spartacus turned to me.

'You take the right-hand tower, I'll take the left.' He jabbed his knees into the horse's flank and moved forward, as did I and those who were following. Then we were through the gates and inside the town. Spartacus halted his horse and dismounted. I did likewise.

'Centurion,' shouted Spartacus, looking up at the Roman on the wall, 'I have something here that will be of interest to you.'

I could see three other guards on the wall, but doubted not that others were in the two towers. There were shops and red-tiled houses either side of the road, though there were few people milling around. No doubt the garrison commander had imposed rationing until the emergency of the slave rebellion had passed. The centurion came down the stone steps from the ramparts and ambled over to where Spartacus was standing. There were two other soldiers standing a short distance from my horse, leaning on their shields and idly watching us.

'What is it? I have to report back...'

Spartacus' right arm flashed as he plunged a dagger through the centurion's throat. He left it there, drew his sword and then raced up the steps and onto the ramparts. His agility was astounding as he cut down two other soldiers before they had time to draw their swords. The other Romans stood open-mouthed at what had taken place, while the centurion, a fountain of blood gushing from his throat, collapsed in a heap on the ground, dead. I drew my sword, leapt from my saddle and plunged it into one of the soldiers standing to my right.

'Clear the towers!' I bellowed at my men as a Roman came towards me with his spear levelled and shield protecting his body. Seconds later my men were running up the steps and into the stone towers. Mercifully, they contained only a handful of men. The Roman came at me but I parried his clumsy spear thrust with my sword, drew Cookus' dagger from its sheath on my belt with my left hand and slashed his right calf as he went past. He screamed in pain and turned to face me again.

'You don't have to die,' I said to him. 'Lay down your weapons and your life will be spared.'

He seemed to relax a little, but then tensed as the spear slammed into his back, thrown by Spartacus, who had reappeared on the ramparts. He pointed at me as the Roman breathed his last. 'Get up here and stop pissing around.'

Along the street people were fleeing in terror, women sweeping young children into their arms and running fit to burst. I raced up the steps and stood beside Spartacus. The gatehouse was secure, but it would only be a matter of minutes before the garrison was alerted.

We stood on the rampart above the open gates and peered down the arrow-straight road. Roman roads were a marvel, I had to confess, always straight and topped with perfectly trimmed flagstones, and this one was especially dear to me because at that moment I saw a column of men pour over the crest of the hill, heading towards the town. Then I heard horns being blown and knew that the garrison had been alerted to our presence. I looked behind me and saw, at the far end of the street, Roman soldiers forming up, perhaps thirty or more. Spartacus saw them too.

'Scatter them, don't let them form otherwise they'll shut the gates in Castus' face.'

I cast a glance back up the road to see Castus and his Germans running towards us, still a mile away. I bounded down the steps and vaulted onto my horse, my men following.

'Mount!' I shouted to them. They likewise reclaimed their lances and saddles. Ahead a centurion was organising his troops into a block in order to retake the gates. The street was about twenty feet wide, so we couldn't form into a line. I levelled my lance.

'Straight at them. They'll break before we reach them.'

I jabbed my horse in the flanks with my knees and she bolted forward. My men followed. We discarded our shields and used the Parthian way to hold our lances, grasping the shaft with both hands and holding it on the right side of the horse. A horse won't charge at a solid object, but will either attempt to go around it or rear up at the last moment. If the Romans held firm then we would fail and end up as a tangled heap of men and horseflesh. But they didn't hold. The sight of twenty horsemen charging towards them, screaming and carrying lances created panic among them. Perhaps they were ill-trained levies, but whatever they were in seconds those in the front had turned and were trying to get out of our way. But they ran into those behind and in the blink of an eye what had been a group of soldiers became a rabble. Some were running back down the street as my lance went through the back of a legionary, through his body and into the chest of the man in front of him. I let go of the shaft and drew my sword as my horse careered through one of the gaps now appearing in the dissolving Roman line. I slashed right and left at fleeing figures as the rest of my men thundered past.

'Don't let them reform,' I shouted. But in truth the engagement was over. The Romans had melted away. I reformed my men into a column and led them forward at a gentle pace. We had suffered no casualties, but I told everyone to be on the lookout for archers on the rooftops. We were still very exposed to enemy missiles should the Romans want to launch some at us. I heard muffled shouts coming from behind me and turned in the saddle. All of us instinctively halted as dozens of men, Castus' soldiers came racing through the gates and into the town. I ordered my men to dismount, lead their mounts to the side of the street and take off their helmets and cloaks, lest the Germans thought we were Romans. Castus was leading his men, a Roman short sword in his right hand held aloft. He ran past us and on into the town. Several minute passed before all the Germans were inside the town. After they had swept into Nola I ordered my men to stay alert and went to speak with Spartacus. He was still on the ramparts, but when I reached him he had taken off his helmet and was sitting on a bench beside the wall. As I approached he looked up and grinned.

'Well that worked out well. Never thought it would, actually, but glad it did.' 'Lord?'

'The main thing is we're in. Should be plenty of supplies for the army.'

'Not if the Germans burn the town,' I said.

'Don't worry about that. Castus has strict orders to keep his men in check.'

'And he will obey?'

Spartacus looked at me with an intense stare. 'We are an army not a bunch of bandits. Only through discipline and organisation can we hope to defeat the Romans.' Then he flashed a smile. 'That and a bit of luck.'

Thus did Nola fall into our laps like a ripened fruit.

Chapter 6

Nola was systematically emptied of anything and everything that was of value. This included weapons, gold, silver, food, sandals, boots, tents and tools. Castus and Spartacus had obviously spent much time thinking about the hoard that the town might yield, for the Germans quickly organised themselves into search parties to scour it from one end to the other for things the army needed, while other groups guarded the captured garrison – three hundred downcast men. And the Germans were very thorough. Their task was made easier by the layout of Nola, which was essentially a large rectangle divided up into a network of streets around square blocks of buildings. I later discovered that there were thirty-two such blocks, each one the same size. The Romans were certainly precise when it came to their town planning. Four gates gave access to the town, one at each point of the compass, and Castus placed guards at all of them to ensure no one escaped. Unfortunately, the garrison commander and several of the town's leading citizens had managed to flee on horseback via the eastern gate before it had been sealed.

The town's population was roughly herded into the centre of Nola, to a place called the forum. Castus informed me that all Roman towns and cities had such a place, and they were always located in the centre. It was a large, open square surrounded by temples, government buildings and shops. The town's residents were divided into three groups: men, women and children, and its slave population. As the day wore on the forum became increasingly crowded as Castus' men entered houses and dragged out their occupants. A few resisted and were killed, but most trudged sullenly into the forum. I also noticed, strangely, that the slaves also looked unhappy.

Castus had brought two thousand men to Nola, a thousand of them now stood guard over the population. The garrison had been disarmed and locked in the town's jail. I had sent my men on foot with a party of Germans to look for horses, and was delighted when they reported back that they had acquired two hundred and a corresponding amount of riding equipment. Around midday Spartacus went over to the group of town slaves and talked to them. He was there a long time, and as I stood beside Castus on the steps of the temple to a god called Saturn I asked him how many would join us.

He shook his head. 'A handful, if any.'

'Surely not?'

'Town slaves have it good. Nice clothes, light duties, even a chance of freedom and Roman citizenship if they are lucky. You might be unlucky and get a bastard of a master who keeps you cleaning the latrines, but generally slaves who live in the towns are well looked after. They have to be. If you're a Roman, you don't want to go to sleep at night knowing there's a slave in your house that hates you. That being the case, why would you want to throw in your lot with a load of country slaves? Besides, town slaves are soft. Mainly Greeks and pretty young boys from Africa who are dressed in nice clothes and taught to recite poetry. Can't train them to use a sword.' He spat on the steps. 'Next to useless.'

Castus was right. Spartacus returned to dejectedly. He sat down on the steps.

'A grand total of twenty. Well, the others will be joining their masters on the road.' He jerked a finger at the few volunteers who were being separated from the rest, while the great mass of people was being moved from the forum down one of the town's main streets.

'One of them belongs to your people, Pacorus, said he could ride.'

My ears pricked up at this, and without saying a word I walked briskly over to the group of freed slaves. Around me wailing women and weeping children were being forcibly removed from the forum. Their men folk had started to protest, but a few cracked skulls courtesy of German spear shafts disabused them of the notion that they had any say in the matter. One middle-aged man in a richly decorated toga refused to move, standing rock-like at the front of the crowd. All eyes were upon him as a burly, hairy German strolled over to him and pointed at the road along which his kinsmen were trudging. He did not move, but glared at the German with ill-disguised disgust then spat on him. I blinked in disbelief as the German grasped his spear with both hands, thrust it clean through the man, and then lifted him off the ground with his muscled arms. The Roman writhed like a stuck pig for a few seconds, and then expired. The corpse was thrown to the ground and the German withdrew his bloody spear, then stood and smiled at any Roman that caught his eye. There were no more protests after that.

I stood in front of the slightly nervous freed slaves.

'Which one of you is a Parthian?' I asked in my mother tongue.

A tall, lean man in his late forties stepped forward. He had short-cropped hair, olive skin and brown eyes. He was dressed in a light grey tunic with a brown leather belt at his waist and good-quality leather sandals on his feet. He looked strong and well fed; perhaps Castus was right about city slaves. He stood in front of me, eyeing me as much as I was studying him.

'I knew you were Parthians the moment I clasped eyes on you. The long hair, the way you sat in the saddle. Though my Parthian is a little rusty after so long being a guest of the Romans.' He extended his hand. 'My name is Godarz and many years ago I was once in the Silvan army under Prince Vistaspa, though doubtless he is dead and his name means nothing to you.'

I felt a surge of emotion course through my body. To hear another talk of someone I knew from my homeland made my heart soar. I grabbed him with both arms and embraced him warmly, which surprised him somewhat.

'I am Pacorus, son of King Varaz of Hatra and the man you speak of is my father's friend and the commander of his bodyguard. He not only lives, but thrives and is reckoned one the finest warriors in the Parthian Empire.'

There were tears in his eyes as I explained to him how fate had brought me to Italy to fight by the side of Spartacus, and how I hoped to get back to Hatra. One day. He laughed.

'We all have that hope, highness, but for most of us it remains only a distant dream.'

I pulled him aside. 'You don't have to call me highness, Godarz.' I nodded towards the figure of Spartacus sitting on the temple steps. 'He doesn't approve of titles.'

'So I've heard,' he replied. 'So that's Spartacus, is it? Well, he looks fearsome enough.'

'And he has a brain, too,' I said. 'It was his plan that captured this town.'

Godarz contemplated for a moment. 'Then the Romans have a problem, for they have difficulties conceiving of a slave who can think for himself. I knew he must have some ability when the town wasn't burnt.'

It took three hours before the citizens and their slaves were ejected from Nola, a long, sad line of humanity making their way out of the east gates towards...? I knew not.

'Who cares?' remarked Castus as we stood on the wall watching them go.

I must admit I felt pangs of guilt about the plight of the women and children, some of whom might perish if their journey was long and arduous. That night we shut the gates, posted guards on the walls and made ourselves at home in Nola's finest houses. We Parthians slept at the house that had been the property of Godarz's master. It was a beautiful abode in the wealthy northern area of the town. The house was built around an inner courtyard that was open to the sky, with more rooms at the back arranged around a garden that was surrounded by a covered walkway. The garden itself was well tended (no doubt by slaves) where herbs and fruit trees were growing, plus flowers and shrubs. The rooms of the house had pictures painted on the walls that depicted mythical beasts with wings and bodies of lions. In some rooms there were scenes of horses, and Godarz informed me that his master had bred horses for a hobby.

'That's how I came to be here. In truth he was good to me,' said Godarz, eating a grape as we relaxed on plush couches in the dining room. 'And he loved his horses. I'll show you them tomorrow, the stables back onto the house.'

That was the first time in weeks that I slept in a bed, and when I awoke the next morning I thought at first that I was back in Hatra. But the grunts and shouts of Germans brought me back to reality. I dressed and joined my men in the kitchen, where twenty Parthians were eagerly feasting on porridge, bread, cheese and fruit. Godarz had risen early in preparation for our departure.

'I'm afraid you'll be sleeping on the ground from now on,' I said, breaking off a piece of cheese.

'At least I will be free,' he replied cheerfully.

We had tethered our horses in the courtyard for the night, and they had used the opportunity to eat many of the flowers and plants. Godarz asked me to follow him into the street, which was filled with dirty looking Germans driving heavily laden carts towards the forum. The two- and four-wheeled carts were piled high with anything that might be of use to us: cooking utensils, garden tools, kitchen implements, anything and everything. The carts were pulled by pairs of mules, some of which were proving reluctant to obey their new masters. Ill-tempered Germans beat the beasts and cursed them as Godarz led me to the rear of his master's walled house and into another walled area, through high iron gates and across a wide courtyard. On the other side was a large white-walled stable block with red roof tiles. I followed him into the stables and was amazed at their luxurious layout. They would not have been out of place in Hatra's royal stables. Each of the stables had half-doors leading onto the central alley and grills between stalls to allow the horses the feeling of space. And inside every stall was a hayrack and water tub. The stables were clean and airy and had a wonderful smell of horseflesh that reminded me of home.

'You tend these stables on your own?' I asked him.

'No, highness,' he turned away from me. 'You can come out now.'

From the far end of the block five figures emerged, all dressed like Godarz, though all were younger than he, men in their late teens or early twenties.

'They have been hiding here. They were fearful of the Germans and expected to be captured, but your arrival saved them.' He cast me a glance. 'At least for the time being.'

'It's quite safe,' I shouted at them. 'You will not be harmed.'

They shuffled towards us with heads bowed.

'Thank you, highness,' said Godarz. 'Let me show you the horses.'

The horses were immaculate and were a credit to their carers. The last stall held a beast of rare beauty, a white stallion with blue eyes. I stared in wonder at him, admiring his muscular shoulders, thick neck and erect head. He stood proud and looked directly into my eyes.

'He's of Carthaginian stock. My master called him Remus,' said Godarz.

'An odd name,' I replied.

'Remus was one of the twins who founded Rome many centuries ago, or so I was told. He should be yours, highness, for he has a haughty and stubborn nature and he requires a true horse lord to tame him.'

I extended my hand slowly to Remus and stroked the side of his head. He seemed to like it.

'We must leave this place,' I said. 'You told Spartacus that you would join him?'

'Yes, highness.'

'What about these other men?' I asked Godarz.

'I speak for them also.'

'Very well,' I said. 'We will take these horses with us. We leave at once.'

I looked at Remus. 'And you, my fine friend, will be my horse from now on.'

Godarz and the stable hands rode behind us, leading the spare horses as we made our way back to the forum, which was now choked with wagons and carts of every description, each waiting to join the main road west out of Nola. I saw a flustered Castus standing with Cannicus at the head of a logjam of vehicles, all trying to get onto the road. I rode over to him. Before we left the rich house we had plundered it of anything of value. I had found a silk vest and an expensive white tunic edged with red and gold. I took both items and put them on, plus a pair of riding boots and a white cloak. I got rid of the red plume on my helmet and replaced it with a long white plume of goose feathers. I was a Parthian not a

Roman, and wanted to look like one. I also took time to comb my hair and shave, instructing my men to do likewise.

Castus looked up at me. 'Nice horse.'

'How long have the wagons been leaving?' I asked.

'Since dawn. At last count we had nearly four hundred piled high. The town armoury yielded a thousand spears and shields, plus a couple of hundred mail shirts.'

I looked at the German warriors on the carts and others standing guard around the forum. They seemed as ill dressed and armed as yesterday.

'Have you re-equipped others of your men?' I asked.

He shook his head. 'Everything goes back to Vesuvius, to be distributed according to need. Spartacus is insistent on that.'

'Where is he?'

'At the amphitheatre. Cannicus will show you the way.'

Cannicus was glad to be away from the in the forum, and led my men and me into the western suburbs of Nola, to a large wooden stadium. We dismounted and I ordered my men to remain outside as Cannicus guided me through one of the open gates. Inside was an elongated, sand-covered space surrounded on all four sides by wooden stands filled with benches. There was no protection from the elements, aside from the stand at the far end which did have a roof supported by wooden pillars, under which were placed elaborate chairs. Spartacus sat on the edge of the covered stand, his legs dangling over the side of the high wooden sides that enclosed the arena. I thanked Cannicus and made my way to him along the rows of benches. He didn't look up as I sat down beside him. He was silent for a long time, looking at the sand surface below.

'I fought here a few times,' he said at last. 'It was always full and always hot. They kill the criminals first, in the morning, and then they like to have animal fights. By the time the gladiators fight each other it was the afternoon and the place stank of blood, piss, vomit and shit. The used to cover the blood with more sand but the stink always got in my nostrils. That's the thing I remember most, not the killing, or the shouts of the crowd, but the disgusting smell. No matter how grand or ragged the arena, the smell was always the same.'

He stood up and looked skywards. 'I had thought of burning Nola, but seeing as it's been most generous to our cause I think I will be merciful. Do you think I should have killed the inhabitants?'

I was shocked. 'Lord?'

'The Romans respect strength. They see mercy as weakness.' He looked at me, his eyes wild. 'But most of all they like blood, lots of blood. Why else would they watch men butcher each other for sport? I promise to give them what they desire most.'

'It was right to let the inhabitants leave, lord.'

He shrugged and walked away. 'We leave today. Time to get back to Vesuvius. This will have stung the Romans into action, and they will be sending another army to wipe us out soon enough.'

It was late afternoon before I and my men left the town, walking our mounts along the western road out of Nola. Ahead was a long line of carts as far as the eye could see, intermingled with Castus' warriors. We too had commandeered some carts, which we had filed with all the equipment from the stables that Godarz had tended, plus others we had plundered. He was happy to be with us, and even happier when I mounted Remus and asked him to attend me as I went to find Spartacus, leaving my men to guard the wagons. We found him two miles ahead, sitting on his horse atop the crest of a hill that overlooked the plain in which Nola was sited. He saw us and nodded, then peered past us. I turned and saw a large plume of black smoke rising from the town into the cloudless sky.

'You are burning the town, lord?' I asked.

'Just the amphitheatre, together with the garrison.'

'Lord?'

'I had them taken there, chained to the benches, covered in pitch and set alight.' He looked directly into my eyes. 'There are limits to my mercy, Pacorus.'

He then looked at Remus and for a moment I thought that I saw a look of alarm in his eyes.

'A man from the east riding a white horse.'

'Lord?'

'Nothing,' he snapped. 'One more thing. We share everything that is taken from the Romans. I will give you the benefit of the doubt and assume that you did not know of my policy, but see to it that it doesn't happen again.'

It took the rest of the day and most of the next to get the booty back to Vesuvius. There was excitement in the by now very large camp when we returned. My Parthians were pleased to see that the cavalry had returned with no losses, and were delighted to welcome Godarz among us. Though he had been a prisoner of the Romans for many years, his presence was a reminder of home and his easy manner meant he fitted in straight away. We now had enough horses to mount all my Parthians, though parties were sent out each day to collect more wild horses and any more we could 'liberate' from the Romans. The news of the capture of Nola must have spread far and wide, for every day more recruits arrived to swell the army. Field hands and shepherds for the most part, with a smattering of better-dressed town slaves who fancied themselves as warriors, but who had no idea of the hardships that would be required of them. The majority were Gauls and Germans, the former being jealously acquired by Crixus, whose contingent was by far the largest. But there were also Dacians who were skilled horsemen trained to fight as heavy cavalry in armour, but who also used bows similar to ours. Thracians also flocked to the banner of Spartacus, most for no other reason than he was a fellow countryman. His infamy was spreading. So many were coming in that Spartacus convened a council of war to deal with the overcrowding. The meeting was held in his large general's tent, a gift from he garrison of Rome, in the centre of the sprawling camp, over which hung a constant pall of smoke from hundreds of cooking fires that were lit every day. I took Nergal and Godarz with me, Nergal because he was my deputy and Godarz because he was familiar with the locality. I had made him the quartermaster of the cavalry, a position he undertook with relish. In no time he had located a number of villas that we had requisitioned as temporary stables. They had belonged to rich Pompeians, but their owners had long since vanished, either to Naples or Pompeii or to the north.

We arrived just as the afternoon sun was beginning its descent into the west. The day had been hot and the jugs of water were indeed welcome as we filled cups and slumped in leather-backed chairs with ornate arm rests: from Nola no doubt. There were no women present. As usual the chairs were arranged around the table. When all had arrived Spartacus rose and asked each of us to provide details on our contingents. Crixus, as large and odious as ever, belched loudly and rose first. Surprisingly he did not have a total lack of manners, introducing the two Gauls with him, whose hair was similarly unkempt and who also wore torques at their necks and had blue tattoos on their faces. The one who sat on the left of Crixus was named Dumnorix, a gaunt-looking man with deep-set green eyes and lank brown hair. The other individual was Oenomaus, a barrel-chested oaf who seemed less intelligent than Crixus, if that was possible. Crixus announced that he had four thousand Gauls ready to kill Romans, and he wanted the chance to prove it, berating Spartacus for not taking him and his men to Nola. Spartacus brushed aside his protests.

'We have talked already about that,' he said, 'and the matter is closed.'

I smiled at Crixus who glared at me and sat back in his chair, breaking wind loudly after he had done so. Castus rose next, smiling at me as he did so, and stated that his Germans numbered three thousand, though half of them had no weapons or armour save wooden clubs and spears. Spartacus promised that the next batch of weapons would be allocated to the Germans, but he emphasised that the whole army lacked weapons and that only half of it was adequately armed. He nodded at me to give my report.

'I have two hundred cavalry,' I said proudly.

Crixus and his two companions burst into loud laughter.

'Two hundred?' thundered Crixus, 'what use is that when we are faced by ten thousand Romans?' He then pointed at Spartacus. 'I warned you about this, said it was a waste of time. But you wouldn't listen, and here's the result.'

'It's quality, not quantity that counts in battle' I said. 'An ill-armed mob can be scattered easily enough by a handful of horse.'

Crixus rose from his chair, his cheeks flushed red, his axe in his right hand. 'Careful boy, I just might lop your head off and use it as a piss-pot. It's obviously wasted on your shoulders.'

My right hand went to the hilt of my sword hanging from the belt on my hip, just as Spartacus rose and drew his Roman short sword, called a gladius. His words came slowly but were reinforced by steel.

'Do not draw that sword, Pacorus. Crixus, take your seat. There will be no fighting here. Since none of you has fought in a legion I will provide a short lesson. A legion consists of five thousand men.'

'I know that,' grumbled Crixus.

'But did you know, Crixus, that every legion has around a hundred and twenty cavalry attached to it, to do scouting, patrols, guarding the flanks and pursuing and cutting down a fleeing enemy? Cavalry are useful to the Romans and will be useful to us. Two hundred is an excellent start.'

'Lord,' I said, 'it would be most helpful if an appeal could be made for all those who can ride to join the cavalry. Horses are not a problem in these parts,' I nodded to Godarz in appreciation, 'but riders are.'

'No Gaul will ride with you,' snapped Dumnorix, prompting a guffaw from Crixus.

'Can Gauls ride?' I quipped.

'Enough,' shouted Spartacus. 'Sit down, Pacorus. Your request is granted.'

I took my seat and stared in contempt at Crixus, who returned my disdain. As we engaged in our childish game Spartacus informed us that he had two thousand Thracians plus an assortment of Greeks, Jews, Spaniards and Africans who made up a further five hundred.

'In two or three months' time,' he said, 'we will be ready to move.' The next day with Nergal and Godarz, in a tent with flaps, I interviewed those who had come forth to serve in the cavalry. True to his word, none of Crixus' Gauls was present. The majority were Germans dressed in ragged tunics with nothing on their feet. But I liked them. They were a straightforward people whose men folk seemed to like fighting. Obviously Castus had encouraged those within his ranks who could ride to volunteer themselves. I would thank him later. There were also Dacians, a few Greeks and Spaniards, and even a few men who had fought for Mithridates of Pontus. They burned with hatred against Rome and I was pleased to accept them. When we had finished it was late in the day and Nergal and I were very pleased with ourselves. Godarz sitting on a stool with a pencil and parchment, had been keeping count of our new recruits.

'Three hundred and two, highness,' he said, beaming.

'Excellent. If they all get through the training that will make five companies in all.' I stretched back in my chair and closed my eyes. 'A good day's work, gentlemen.'

'Are you still looking for recruits, Parthian?'

I opened my eyes and saw a vision of a goddess before me. It was Gallia, the one who had made my heart soar at the feast, who now stood proudly before me, her piercing blue eyes looking down at me. Up close she was even more perfect than I remembered. Her light skin was flawless, her full lips clamped shut and her blonde hair tied behind her in a long plait. She wore a blue tunic edged with white, with tan knee-length breeches and laced leather boots. At her waist was a black leather belt decorated with bronze stiffeners and studded with fasteners to allow the attachment of personal equipment. One such item was a dagger that hung on her right side. Her posture conveyed strength and determination, while her exquisite face had the look of the huntress. I was at first lost for words. I just wanted to look at her for eternity. Nergal brought me back to reality.

'Highness?'

I cleared my throat and stood up. I must appear calm and collected, I told myself, even though my insides were turning to mush. I bowed my head.

'Your servant, lady.'

'We wish to join your cavalry.'

At that moment I noticed that she had brought a companion, another woman of similar age though slightly smaller in stature, and of a more fragile build. She had light brown hair, a round face and brown eyes, with an altogether more vulnerable appearance. She too wore knee-length breeches beneath a light brown tunic. I recognised her, it was Diana. She was attractive, I suppose, though next to the fierce and untamed beauty of Gallia she diminished greatly. I told Nergal what she had said, as he as yet understood only a few words of Latin.

'Join the cavalry?' he laughed. 'You have more chance of sprouting wings.'

Gallia did not understand what he said, but she understood his mocking tone well enough.

'What did he say?'

'He thinks it would be inappropriate for you to join the cavalry.'

'I was told that Prince Pacorus was the leader of the cavalry,' she said. 'Perhaps I was misinformed.'

'I can assure you that I command here,' I replied.

She jerked her hand towards Nergal.

'Then shouldn't he be shovelling dung or doing something else useful?'

I put my hands up in a conciliatory manner. 'He meant no offence, lady.'

'He should engage his brain before he opens his mouth,' Gallia's blood was obviously stirred. Nergal jumped up.

'What did she say, highness?' I told him.

'I do not take insults from a woman.'

I could see that neither would back down, which made me admire her even more. Clearly she had no fear. She was some creature, that's for sure, this woman from Gaul.

'Leave us, Nergal,' I said.

'Women do not fight. Women cannot fight,' he sneered, before saluting me and stomping off.

'I apologise for Nergal,' I said to Gallia. 'He's a little hot-headed.'

'Clearly,' she purred. She looked at me with her blue pools for eyes. Her anger disappeared as her manner became conciliatory, almost seductive. 'Spartacus says that you are a great warrior, so I thank you for being at his side. He is my friend and I count as friends all those he holds dear.' Her voice was soft and inviting, and I was a willing victim. 'So I ask you, Prince Pacorus, son of Hatra, to let me fight by your side so I too can serve Spartacus. What is your answer?'

I knew that I would not, could not, refuse her; knew that had she asked me I would have given her anything in that moment.

'I would be honoured, lady.' I heard myself saying the words, yet it was as if something had taken control of me.

She nodded. 'And this is my friend, Diana, and she's joining too. We will await your instructions.'

With that Gallia turned and marched from the tent, Diana trailing in her wake.

'I would say that is a victory for the fairer sex,' remarked Godarz, who had been sitting in silence throughout the exchange.

'Probably just a show to try and impress me,' I shrugged.

'Really? From where I was I could have sworn that it was the other way round.'

'Nonsense,' I said.

'I think she is serious about fighting.'

I shrugged. 'I doubt she can even ride.'

Godarz looked at the disappearing figure of Gallia. 'I think that one has many talents, young prince, and she certainly knows her own mind and how to use her charms to get what she wants.'

And so it was that two women became the first females to enter the hallowed ranks of the Parthian cavalry, in the land of my enemies, in an army of slaves.

I told my men of my decision that night and most of them thought it was a joke. Nergal was furious, Gafarn amused, Godarz confused and Byrd unconcerned.

'In any case,' I told them when we were eating cooked lamb around a blazing fire.

'She is obviously trying to impress Spartacus and will drop out soon enough.' I looked at a still fuming Nergal.

'What woman can ride like a Parthian warrior?' he spat.

But in my heart I hoped she would stay with us.

It was high summer now and the recruitment and equipping of the cavalry increased apace. We all knew that the Romans would soon be sending an army to crush us; for all we knew it was already marching south from Rome. I had scouts riding as far north as Capua, as far south as Salurnum and west to Beneventum, and thus far no signs of enemy activity had been seen. The scouts were organised by Byrd who was advised by Godarz, who told me that he had ridden far and wide scouting for horses for his master's stables, so he was well acquainted with the region.

'You were under guard during those trips?' I asked him.

'Of course not,' he replied, somewhat surprised. 'My master trusted me.'

'What stopped you escaping, then?'

'Nothing. But where would I go?' he said. 'My master could not conceive of me running away. He fed me, didn't beat me and let me care for his horses, which he knew I loved. So you see, I was a loyal dog to him. That's what he regarded me as, you understand, not a real person, only a slave.'

It was now time for us to make our Scythian bows for which we were famous throughout the known world. Parthian bows are double-curved, with recurve tips at the end of the upper and lower limbs, and a set-back centre section that was grasped by the left hand. The limbs themselves are thick in proportion to their width. We selected yew for the wood, which is the best for bows, having excellent tension and is also able to withstand the compressive forces when the bow is in use. Thus the base of each bow is yew, with sinew on the outside of the limbs and greyish horn on their inner side. These parts were mated to each other with a glue made from bitumen, bark pitch and animal grease, and the whole bow was then wrapped in fibres – derived from the tendons of slaughtered animals. We would have liked to have used lacquer to have made the bows waterproof, but lacquer came from China and was very expensive. We would have to make do without. Each bow was just over four feet in length.

It took two months to make a thousand bows, which were kept under cover in the rooms of the villas we occupied. The large, empty villas of Campania with their many rooms and voluminous outbuildings were ideal workshops for our bow-making industry. We guarded them fiercely, for these were the weapons that would give us victory in battle.

While we Parthians constructed the bows, Godarz set about making thousands of arrows. The shafts consisted of two-foot lengths of pine with three-bladed bronze arrowheads. Each day he set off early in the morning with two hundred men to cut down saplings to make the arrow shafts. Only the straightest saplings were selected. It could take up to six months to dry the wood, but the heat of the Italian summer meant we could do it quicker. The cut saplings were tied together in bunches and left for two to three weeks, after which they were unwrapped and any remaining bark was peeled, then they were wrapped again for a further two weeks until they had dried.

Once cut to the required length, each arrow was fitted with three feathers that guided it in flight. I told Godarz not to make the feathers too large, big feathers caught more air and shortened the range. We used goose feathers, not the tail feathers but ones from the wings. Tom feathers are preferred because they are heavier and last longer. When glued to the shaft they were positioned at even intervals from each other. After two months Godarz was sick of cutting wood, but I knew his endeavours would reap dividends in the months ahead.

Our quivers were made from cowhide and were large enough to hold thirty arrows, with a hide flap that could be drawn over the top to protect the contents from rain. When mounted we carried the quiver on our left side, held in place by a strap over our right shoulder. In this way a rider could pull an arrow from his quiver with his right hand and string his bow in the same movement. The cases for our bows were also made from cowhide, and when riding were attached to the left side of the saddle.

We had our horses and their riders, but there was still the question of whether horses and riders could be turned into cavalry capable of taking the fight to the enemy.

'Impossible to say, highness.' Nergal had regained his positive attitude since the outburst over women joining the cavalry. He sat with a leg draped over the arm of a chair in the voluminous dining room. It was part of a large villa ten miles from Vesuvius that I had requisitioned as my headquarters. It had obviously belonged to a rich Roman, having many rooms, a courtyard, garden and colonnaded porticos on all sides. He was obviously enjoying his position of rank and in truth he had assumed his responsibilities with vigour.

'Well,' I said, 'the first thing we must do is see if they can ride, then we'll move on to weapons handling and drills.'

'Does that include archery?' asked Nergal.

'We'll have to see how they shape up. There's a big difference between fighting on horseback with a sword and spear and shooting a bow from the saddle.'

'What about the women?' he asked casually.

'What about them?' I really didn't want to discuss Gallia and her friend, if truth be told. I was, I had to admit, slightly embarrassed. 'They probably can't even ride, so they will drop out at the first stage. They are friends of Spartacus, though, so there's no point in alienating him.'

'You didn't consider that when you and Crixus were squaring up to each other.' Gafarn could always be relied on to say the most awkward things. 'But then he doesn't have a body and a face like a goddess.'

Godarz smiled and Nergal laughed.

'Shut up,' I snapped.

The truth unpalatable? Besides, now I am free I can say what I like.'

'Your tongue,' I said, 'has always been free with advice and comments. It appears that the rest of you has caught up with it.'

'What does it matter,' chipped in Byrd, 'if they want to kill Romani that should be enough.'

Nergal shrugged and the matter was closed, for the time being. I had grown to like Byrd. He said little and he must have been lonely, being the only one of his people among us and being able to speak only a little Latin, but he never grumbled and was becoming a valuable member of my horsemen. I had told him that he could come and live in Hatra when we got home, if we got home.

The next day all the volunteers were assembled on a broad plain half a mile from the main camp at Vesuvius. It was early morning, as I didn't want the horses to be tired unnecessarily. The Dacians I had no concerns about. Their cavalry was similar to that of Parthia, and they used a bow like ours. There were over a hundred of them and I was going to form them into a company under the leadership of a fierce black-haired warrior called Burebista. Actually all the Dacians appeared fierce, and Burebista had told me that they believed that death in battle would earn them a place in heaven with their god, Zalmoxis. As they were horsemen, they knew all there was to know about caring for their mounts, and I had already allocated them a bow each.

Rome had an insatiable appetite for foreign conquests, and her armies had reaped a rich harvest in former enemies turned into slaves. Fortunately for Spartacus and me, ex-soldiers can easily be turned into soldiers once again, and so it was with the slaves who were now flocking to his standard, and so it was with the Dacians who were now riding under my command. I had given them the wild horses that we had tamed, and they rode them that morning as if they had been riding them for years. The Thracians were also good horsemen, though they bred their horses for racing and their horsemen were light cavalry. They mustered two hundred men under a dour fellow called Rhesus, though I learned that Thracians did not actually use saddles but rode on saddlecloths only. As such they used spears and javelins on horseback and wore no armour. Rhesus assured me that this did not prevent them from being good fighters, since they killed their enemies before they could get within striking distance. However, I told him that he and his men would be using saddles from now on. Like us, he and his men had been captured during a battle against the Romans, and had spent the last year being forced to work as field hands, chained up every night in stinking pens, woken every day before dawn before enduring endless hours under a hot sun. They burned with a desire to water the soil with Roman blood. They evidently had no problem serving under a young foreigner, as Spartacus had informed them that I had captured a Roman eagle and that I had obviously been sent by Dionysus himself.

'Who's Dionysus?' I asked.

'He's the god of the here and now, lord,' explained Rhesus, 'the god who holds life and death together. He is the bringer of liberation who will strike madness, wildness and terror into the Romans. Raised by Zeus himself, he was. Spartacus' lady is one of his trusted servants on earth.'

'Claudia,' I said.

'Yes, that's her. She's a priestess of Dionysus. She can tell the future.'

I was sceptical. 'Really?'

'Told us you would be coming.'

Now I was curious. 'How so?'

'Said that a rider from the east would come, one who would spit metal, one who would be mounted on a white horse. The son of the wild boar.'

My blood ran cold, for Varaz, my father's name, meant 'wild boar'. I dismissed it as a coincidence.

I had given Gallia the chestnut horse that Spartacus had presented to me, and to her friend I had given a grey mare. They were both reliable, calm mounts, though I still had my doubts about the women's riding ability. That morning I was disabused of my opinion. They were both fine riders, at one with their mounts and just as good as the men, at least when it came to horsemanship.

After the riders had been put through their paces, the horses were rested and their riders dismounted to sit in groups on the ground. The day was getting hotter and I wanted all the horses back under cover, so I told Nergal to instruct the company commanders to return to their abandoned Roman homes that now constituted their bases. I took the opportunity to ride Remus over to where Gallia and Diana were walking their mounts back to Vesuvius. I caught up with them and dismounted.

'A fine day, ladies,' I said.

They stopped and both looked at me. Gallia was as radiant as ever, even after two hours of riding, and she smiled, though not at me.

'He's beautiful,' she purred, extending her free left hand at Remus, who moved his head towards her hand and put his ears forward.

Sure signs that he liked her. Why wouldn't he? She was gorgeous.
'His name is Remus,' I said.
'You have a good eye for a horse, Prince Pacorus,' said Gallia, rather coolly. 'So have we passed the test for your cavalry?'
'The riding part, yes,' I replied. 'But there is more to fighting on horseback than being able to ride.'
'Of course,' she said. She stopped and looked at me, her eyes the clearest blue.
'Would you like to eat with us tonight? A small gathering: Spartacus, his wife, and we two.'
I thought my heart would burst out of my chest with delight. I smiled uncontrollably at her. Diana laughed and Remus, obviously picking up on my emotions, snorted. Gallia gently stroked the side of his head.
'You can bring Remus, too. Claudia would love to see him.'
The early evening was warm as I rode him into the camp at Vesuvius. I could see that the crater was far fuller than it had been when I had first arrived. There were the tidy lines of Roman tents, plus other camps with rough earth shelters with foliage on top for makeshift roofs. Though these too were arranged in lines in a grid pattern, their building materials gave them a scruffy appearance. There also appeared to be more women than before, and even some children. The hundreds of cattle, chickens, sheep, pigs and goats had been segregated into pens that littered the fringes of the camp and also the slopes of Vesuvius. It appeared that the shepherds had brought their flocks with them. I had moved all the horses outside the camp and deployed them in the surrounding countryside. It was not healthy for so much livestock to be crowded into one place; sickness could wipe them all out. The old Roman camp, the one that Spartacus had attacked when I had been freed, had been strengthened with a wooden palisade with watchtowers at regular intervals. Spartacus had placed a garrison in the fort under the command of a fellow Thracian named Akmon, a squat, dark-haired individual who had a deep scar down the right side of his face, a souvenir of a particularly hard fight in the arena, or so Spartacus told me. He reminded me of a devilish imp that my mother had told me about when I was a child, and as I passed the camp I saw him on the palisade. I raised my hand in salute but he just stared at me with his black eyes. Spartacus had told me that he was a good fighter and loyal. It took a long time before I earned his trust.
I rode down the central avenue and came to the general's tent. Two guards stood outside and they snapped to attention as I passed them, while an attendant took Remus from me. I had to admit that

Spartacus was moulding the disparate elements of his followers into a credible force, though whether they would be able to stand up to the Romans in battle was another matter. As I entered, Claudia embraced me.

'Welcome, Pacorus. Spartacus has been telling me how impressed he is with your cavalry.'

'Thank you, lady,' I said.

'You can call me Claudia, we are all friends here. Isn't that right, Gallia?'

I turned to see the owner of my heart standing beside the long table that ran along the far side of the voluminous tent. Her blonde hair was free and cascaded over her shoulders, which were covered by a blue sleeveless stola. Diana was dressed in white and her hair was gathered at the back of her head. I must admit that she too was attractive, though she came a poor second to Gallia. I bowed, Claudia laughed.

'So formal, Pacorus,' she took my arm in hers. 'Come, let us eat.'

Spartacus entered at that moment, carrying a large plate piled high with meats. He wore no weapons, no armour and was dressed in a simple tunic. At that moment he looked like a house slave not a general.

'Ah, Pacorus, good to see you. Sit yourself down. I hope you have a good appetite.'

Claudia led me to my seat, sat down on my right side and invited Gallia to sit on my left. I was as happy as an eagle that had caught a lamb when Gallia sat beside me. Then Spartacus served us wine from an expensive silver jug, into equally fine silver goblets. The meal was a happy occasion and for a while I could forget that I was in the enemy's heartland and far from home. Spartacus, laughing and at ease, was far removed from the assassin of the arena and the calculating commander I had witnessed at Nola. As the evening wore on and the wine took hold, he told us stories of his homeland and his boyhood. How he had been a poor shepherd tending sheep in the harsh landscape of Thrace. Tears came to his eyes as he recounted how his mother had died of the plague when he was a boy, and his father's death from a broken heart shortly after.

'But one day we will return to Thrace and live in peace, far away from Rome and Romans.' He looked into Claudia's eyes. 'That is our dream.'

'It is the dream of all of us,' said Diana.

'Not all of us,' muttered Gallia.

'You do not want to go home, lady?' I asked.

She looked at me with those eyes of piercing blue. 'There are some who have no desire to leave Italy, but would rather stay and rob and kill.'

'I do not follow,' I said.

'Gallia is talking of Crixus,' said Claudia. 'I believe you know him.'

'I know him,' I said.

'Gallia,' interrupted Spartacus, 'thinks that I should send Crixus away. But in truth he draws men to our cause and his Gauls would be a welcome addition to any army. We need men like Crixus if we are to defeat the Romans and leave this wretched place.'

'He draws men like a moth to a flame, it is true,' said Claudia, the oil lamps hanging from the centre poles highlighting her feline grace and beauty, 'but it is not the flame of freedom that burns within you, my love. Gallia is right in her opinion of Crixus, he is dangerous.'

'Of course he is,' remarked Spartacus, 'he's been trained to kill, as have I.'

'You kill because you have to, he kills because he enjoys it. There is a difference. You should not trust him.'

'Enough of Crixus,' said Spartacus, 'he is part of this army and that's final. You see, Pacorus, how I am assaulted on all sides by women.'

I glanced at Gallia. 'You are indeed fortunate to be thus assailed, lord.'

Claudia saw my glance and smiled. 'What woman would you have besieging you, Pacorus?'

I could feel myself blushing and cleared my throat in embarrassment. Spartacus came to my rescue.

'Leave him alone. He is here to enjoy himself, not to be interrogated.'

I stayed the night as the guest of Spartacus, and early the next morning rose and fed and watered Remus before I washed and ate a breakfast of warm porridge that Claudia had cooked. I liked her. At first she had seemed remote and aloof, but the previous evening had revealed her softer side, and I found her intelligent and forthright. After I had finished eating I took her to see Remus. She too fell in love with him and he returned the sentiment. He was a show-off and obviously liked attractive women; he flicked his long white tail as she stroked his neck.

'You like her, don't you?' she asked, innocently.

'Who?'

'Gallia, who else?'

'Well, I, that is…'

'I hope you are not so indecisive in battle,' she said. 'It's nothing to be ashamed of. But she has a fierce, independent will, and will not yield easily to any man. You know she's a princess, don't you?'

I looked at her in amazement.

'It's true, she is of the Senones tribe of the Gallic people, and her father is a king who decided that he could become a greater king if he formed an alliance with a rival chief. So he tried to force Gallia to marry this chief, who was three times her age. But she refused to marry the fat old man, whereupon her father bound her and took her to the nearest Roman town and sold her into slavery for defying him. She burns with anger, Pacorus.' Claudia fixed me with her narrow brown eyes. 'But I think that the one thing she wants most is to be able to trust again.'

It was high summer now, though even the hottest days were not as fierce as Hatra's climate at this time of year. Spartacus increased the tempo of the army's training, and every day the plains around Vesuvius were filled with large bodies of troops learning the drills of the Roman army. Our bows were now ready to use, but before they were issued I called all the cavalry to my headquarters. They had done well, for in addition to forming a bond with their horse, each man had to learn to handle a sword and lance on horseback. I was fortunate to have a cadre of Parthians who could impart their skills to the rest. Even those who could ride and perhaps had been trained in horsemanship had to re-learn rusty skills. In addition, Godarz had organised a unit of veterinaries, grooms and farriers, for unlike the Romans our horses had iron shoes on their feet. The cavalry now numbered eight hundred men, with a trickle of new recruits coming in each day.

With the bows now ready I was keen to turn them into horse archers. Each rider had learnt how to mount and dismount quickly, how to jump obstacles, ride over uneven terrain, and perform circles, turns and fast halts. Then they had moved on to operate as part of a larger formation of a hundred-man company, how to move from column into line without tangling with each other, how to wheel in formation and double back, to turn in a circle, and to press home the charge. It had taken three hard months of daily training to turn a group of freed slaves, albeit some with riding skills, into a disciplined body of cavalry. Now it was time for them to learn how to shoot a bow from the saddle.

It was good to feel a bow in my hand at long last. The assembled included Gallia and Diana, for they too had become part of our brotherhood. Even Nergal had stopped his protests at their presence. In truth I was surprised at how they had both worked hard, drilling constantly, learning basic horse care and tending to their mounts assiduously. I had formed a personal unit of twenty Parthians, which Gafarn rather annoyingly called my royal bodyguard. Into this unit I drafted Gallia and Diana, and for his impertinence I ordered Gafarn to be their personal bodyguard. He might be an insolent pest, but he could ride as well as any of us and he reckoned that he was the best archer in the Parthian Empire; a boast that I reluctantly had to admit had some merit in it. Now he stood with the rest of my cavalry, hundreds of them gathered in a large field in Campania. I glanced at Gallia and smiled and she returned the gesture. My chest heaved with delight. I held my bow aloft for all those assembled to see.

'This is what makes Parthia strong. This is what keeps Parthia free. Our horse archers are the finest in the world and this bow, descended from the ones used by the great horsemen of the northern steppes many generations ago, will out-range and out-shoot any other bow in the world. Some of you are already acquainted with shooting arrows from the saddle, but aside from those from Hatra, none of you has used a Parthian bow. You will be taught how to shoot this bow from a standing position and then from the saddle. There's no secret to being a good archer, it just takes practice, lots and lots of practice. We may be few in number compared to the rest of the army, but in battle we can make the difference between victory and defeat.

'Godarz will issue each one of you with a bow. Treasure it, treat it like your best friend, for in combat it will be the thing that will save your life. With the help of your bows we can defeat the Romans, and if we defeat the Romans then we can all go home.'

Afterwards each man was issued with a bow, its case, two bowstrings, a quiver and thirty arrows. Thus equipped, the companies rode back to their quarters. Gallia and Diana took their place in the queue and accepted their bows from Godarz. I noticed that none of the men objected to them being included. The next day archery practice began. I built a target in the grounds of the villa, a simple circle of packed straw nailed to a post. I asked Gallia and Diana to come to the villa to demonstrate their archery skills, while the rest of the men were divided into groups of five, each of them having a Parthian as an instructor. The groups practised in the fields around the villa. The day was warm and the garden was filled with the sweet scent of oleanders, violets, crocus and narcissus. The Romans, the rich ones in any case, loved their flowers and herbs, and we had found separate alcoves where mint, savoury, celery seed, basil, bay and hyssop grew. Both women were dressed in their tunics and knee-length breeches, with their hair in a single plait. Godarz sat on stool and munched an apple, while I attended Gallia and Gafarn tutored Diana.

I took my bow and faced the two women. 'Archery is very simple and with practice most people can become a reasonable shot.'

'Even a woman?' teased Gallia.

'Even a woman,' I replied.

'Especially a woman, for they have a more cunning eye,' said Gafarn, who winked at Diana.

'Thank you, Gafarn,' I said, sternly. 'First of all, remember to adopt a comfortable stance, one foot in front of the other. Don't tense, let your body become one with the bow.' I took an arrow from my quiver resting on the ground and strung it. 'The arrow should be placed so that two flight feathers are towards you and the third is pointing away from you. Put three fingers to the string. The index finger should be above the arrow and the second and third finger should be under it. Form a deep hook with your fingers; they should be bent in both first and second joint. Place the string in the first joint.

'Now, place your bow hand in the grip and let your knuckles form a line forty-five degrees against the bow. The pressure point should be on the thick part of the thumb muscle so that the pressure from the grip should go as straight as possible into the arm. Then straighten your bow arm, lift it and at the same time lift your draw arm and pull the string from almost nothing to around a third of the draw length. Keep the draw hand at the same height as the bow hand, at the level of your eye.

'Your draw-arm shoulder should be in a natural position, not lifted up or pushed back, just lift the bow as naturally as you can. You can stretch your bow hand, your left hand, against the target at this point and you will automatically get your shoulder in the correct position close to the string. You are ready to shoot, but remember to relax your draw arm and only use the muscles of your back to hold the string. Your bow arm should hold a pressure against the target corresponding to the force that works backwards so the body and bow are in balance. The holding phase is very short, it should not take more than half of a second, enough to relax the arm muscles and transfer the holding weight to the back muscles. Now you aim, drawing back the string a fraction. Don't lean forward or back; keep your body in balance. Don't worry too much about aiming, concentrate on your back muscles, for they are the secret to being a good archer. Your subconscious will take care of the target.

You have seen it, you know where it is, but to hit it you must have a good release.

'The correct way is to simply relax your fingers on your draw hand and let the force from the string move the fingers out of the way. You should not use your muscles in the hand to open the fingers curled around the string as this will disturb the string and cause inconsistent arrow flight. So let your fingers open so the string gets a clear release with a minimum of disturbance. Your bow arm should not move when you take the shot, since you have a tension backwards in the draw arm, and your hand will move smoothly backwards when the string is released. Keep your eyes at the target until the arrow hits it.'

The arrow flew straight and true and slammed into the middle of the target.

'Good shot,' said Godarz, taking another bite of his apple.

'Excellent shot, highness,' said Gafarn, who strung an arrow himself and let it fly, also hitting the centre of the target and splitting my arrow in two. Diana squealed in delight and gave Gafarn a kiss, while Gallia looked at me, grinned and shrugged.

'A lucky shot,' I mumbled.

'Do you want me to do it again, highness?' asked Gafarn, innocently, though with a wide grin across his face.

'No, we are here to instruct not compete.'

'Just as well,' said Gafarn, smiling at a clearly impressed Diana, 'I always beat him.'

It was a marvellous afternoon, and both Gallia and Diana showed some promise with a bow. It was a good start, and the day was rounded off with all of us sharing a meal of bread, olives and fruit, washed down by wine. Afterwards, as usual, I rode with Gallia back to the main camp. Gafarn had taken Diana off to see some wild stallions that the men had just brought in. It was the first time that I had been alone with Gallia. She was happy, I think, and I hoped that being with me made her so, but perhaps it was just because it had been an enjoyable day.

'My arms will ache tomorrow.'

'They will get used to it. Keep practising and your body will become accustomed to shooting.'

We were riding side by side and she turned to look at me. 'Gafarn is very free with his tongue in your company. Is it normal for a servant to speak to a prince so?'

I laughed. 'Gafarn is, well, he has always been with me since I was a child. I put up with him because he has always been the same irritating rascal he is now. But he is loyal, both to me and to my

parents. So much so that I put up with him.'
'And he's a good archer,' she said, smiling.
I grimaced. 'Indeed.'
'Do you miss your home, Pacorus?'
The question surprised me somewhat. 'Yes.'
'What do you miss most about it?'
'My father and mother, I suppose, and my friend, Vata.'
'No one else? No wife?'
I laughed. 'No wife, though my parents would like me to marry, I think. They were engineering a marriage between me and Princess Axsen of Babylon. A marriage that would strengthen my father's kingdom. But she's very fat.'
'You do not like fat women?'
I felt her questions were part of an intricate game, some sort of test. What was her purpose in asking me such queries?
'I think I would like to get to know someone first before I marry them, be they fat or thin. And I would prefer to marry someone that I love rather than be a pawn in a game of strategy.'
She said nothing for a few minutes as our horses slowly ambled towards the hundreds of small fires that dotted the camp at evening time. 'I think that too,' she mused as we passed the crude wooden watchtowers that guarded the entrance. I said goodnight to her at Spartacus' tent. I glanced behind once as Remus trotted down the central avenue, to see her standing arrow straight observing me. This woman was coursing through my heart and head with the force of a desert wind. Gallia was the first thing I thought of when I woke up and the last thing on my mind when I drifted off to sleep at night.
The last weeks of summer were a happy time as eight hundred men and two women were turned into horse archers. There were a fair share of cracked ribs and bruised prides as individuals learnt to shoot a bow from a horse, and often fell from the saddle when turning to the left to loose an arrow or shoot at a target directly ahead. But all of them wanted to learn, wanted to be part of the decisive component of the army. And as the time passed I almost forgot that we were in the land of the enemy and would have to fight for our freedom. But the Romans had not forgotten about us, and as autumn came upon us news reached camp that a Roman force was marching south to destroy the slave general Spartacus and his army.

Chapter 7

It was Byrd who rode to my headquarters and reported the news that the Romans were approaching. His horse was lathered in sweat and he was covered in dust as he gave his intelligence.

'Romani, more than five thousand, most foot, also horse.'

'Where?' I asked.

He drained a cup of water offered to him by Godarz. 'North of Capua.'

'That's only thirty miles away,' remarked Godarz. 'They could be here in two days if they got a move on.'

I rode to Vesuvius with Godarz, Nergal and Byrd, who had been given a fresh horse. We galloped down the central avenue and halted before Spartacus' tent. Guards took our horses as we went inside to find Spartacus and Crixus sitting at the table eating a meal. It was the first time I had seen the Gaul in weeks, and he sneered when he saw me and spat a piece of meat from the bone he was gnawing on the floor. He looked as big and disgusting as ever. Spartacus nodded as I marched over to him and saluted, being careful to ignore Crixus. Nergal, Godarz and Byrd followed me.

'Romans, lord, approaching from the north.'

Spartacus put down his cup and leaned back in his chair. 'Where?'

I pointed at Byrd. 'This man has seen them with his own eyes. Tell him. Byrd.'

'Five thousand foot, thereabouts, five score cavalry. North of Capua yesterday. Closer now, I think.'

'Ha,' bellowed Crixus, jumping up and knocking the chair to the floor, 'we outnumber them. Let me and my men handle them.' He looked at me. 'Your horse boys have done their job, you won't be needed any longer.'

I could not resist the challenge. 'Without my horsemen you would still be feeding your face while the Romans approached unseen. Without my men you are blind.'

'Enough!' snapped Spartacus. 'If you two want a fight there are a few thousand Romans to contend with.'

'Lord Spartacus,' interrupted Godarz, 'if I may. The quickest way to get here is down the Via Annia.'

'What's that?' asked Crixus, picking up his chair and sitting back down in it.

'The main road to the south of Italy,' replied Godarz. 'If they march down that they will reach Nola in a day, then they can head west.'

'And pin us against the sea,' said Spartacus.

'Yes, lord,' replied Godarz.

'Five thousand Gauls say they won't make it to Vesuvius,' boasted Crixus, tearing off a huge piece of bread from a loaf and stuffing it into his equally huge mouth. Did this man never stop shovelling food into his belly?

'How many of your men have weapons, Crixus?' asked Spartacus.

Crixus shrugged. 'About half. But don't worry, we can get the rest when we kill these Romans who are coming. My boys are itching for a fight.'

'Or just itching, from fleas, no doubt,' I said.

'What was that, boy?'

'Nothing,' I smiled. Crixus glared at me. I knew he hated me, but his dislike seemed to have grown markedly since the last time we had seen each other.

'No,' said Spartacus in a stern voice, 'we cannot risk a battle with the Romans yet. We need more weapons and more men. The Romans can afford a defeat or two, we cannot. If we are beaten our army will dissolve. Our first battle has to be a success, for only victory can cement this army together and make it strong for the hardships that are to come. We will reconvene tonight, at dusk. Pacorus, inform Castus to join us.'

'Yes, lord,' I saluted and turned to go.

'And Pacorus,' said Spartacus.'

'Lord?'

'Well done, your men are proving the asset I hoped they would be.'

'Thank you, lord,' I said, flashing a disdainful glance at Crixus, who again spat some food on the floor.

I ordered Nergal to inform the company commanders to assemble their men in the morning and wait for orders; Godarz was instructed to take an inventory of all our spare arrows, weapons, food stocks, fodder for the horses and to gather the carts and wagons that belonged to the cavalry. Castus had moved his men out of the crater of Vesuvius to a camp two miles to the south. One of the reasons he did so being the regular fights that broke out between the Gauls and Germans, some resulting in deaths. I wondered if the different nationalities that made up the army could ever learn to work together; if not, then we were surely doomed. I found Castus on the training ground, stripped to the waist and showing a group of recruits how to throw a javelin. I dismounted and embraced him; he had become a firm friend these past weeks and I enjoyed his company, and that of his pale-skinned, dark-haired warriors. I told him the news about the Romans.

'It's started, then. One thing's for sure, there will be a lot of blood spilt before it's over.'

All the captains of the various contingents of the army were present that night in Spartacus' cavernous tent. Crixus was dressed in his war gear, a mail shirt, large round shield and his two-bladed axe. His two lieutenants, Dumnorix and Oenomaus, were similarly attired, though they wore swords at their waists. Castus and Cannicus wore captured Roman mail shirts and carried swords and daggers for weapons; they had no helmets. I brought Nergal and Burebista, who were both dressed in simple tunics and carried spathas in scabbards at their waist. I wore my white tunic and carried my helmet with its goose feathers. Spartacus was seated behind his long table and did not invite us to sit, but merely examined us all in silence as we faced him across the table. Beside him stood his fellow Thracian Akmon, who eyed us like a raven examines a dead carcass. At last Spartacus spoke.

'We are leaving Vesuvius, it has served its purpose. As you know, a Roman army is marching south towards us. We cannot be trapped here, and not enough of our men are adequately armed, so I intend to march south into Lucania. It's a rich country and there are plenty of men there who will join us. When we have drawn the Romans to a place of our choosing, we will turn and destroy them.'

There were murmurs of disagreement from the Gauls.

'Silence!' ordered Spartacus, who rose to his feet. 'Any man who disagrees with me can leave now. This is not open to debate. You will obey my orders.'

He stood, rock like, challenging anyone to defy him. None did.

'It will take us two days to break camp, therefore we need to buy some time.' He looked at me. 'Pacorus.'

'Yes, lord,' I answered.

'You will take half your cavalry and delay the Romans. Use whatever tactics you deem appropriate, but you have to slow them down.'

'You can rely on me, lord.'

'Good. Crixus,' Spartacus continued, 'your men will form the rearguard as we march. If Pacorus fails and the Romans arrive earlier than expected, you will have to hold them off to let the rest of us get away.'

Crixus looked at me. 'We Gauls will not fail, even if others do,' he snarled.

We were dismissed. I shook hands with Castus and Cannicus as Crixus and his men barged past us. Outside the tent Spartacus accosted me.

'I'm relying on you, Pacorus. Our fate lies in your hands. You must delay them.'

I was immensely proud of having been given this responsibility.

'Have no fear, lord,' I said, gravely, 'we will buy you some time.'

We left at dawn, four hundred riders carrying bows, swords and wearing tunics only, no mail shirts. We were going to harry the Romans, not engage them in battle. Already the air was filled the noise of thousands of individuals taking down tents, packing carts and herding animals for the start of the journey. We skirted Vesuvius and rode northeast, across fields and along dirt tracks, the horses kicking up clouds of dust on a parched earth. Godarz rode by my side, as he knew this country better than any of us. After four hours we halted beside a stream running beside a wood and rested the horses. We took them into the trees and removed their saddles. We would rest out of the sun until the mid-afternoon, and then ride north again, towards Capua. After checking our weapons and examining the horses for any injuries, we posted guards and snatched some sleep. I thought about Gallia. I had not seen her since the news had reached us about the Roman army, but I hoped that I would be able to see her again, Shamash willing.

We each carried full quivers. I had selected fifty Parthians and the best archers from the rest, who were mostly Dacians under the redoubtable Burebista, who was bristling with the chance to exact some revenge on the Romans.

'Forced us to surrender,' he said to me as we relaxed under the trees. 'All because our general was stupid and didn't post scouts as we withdrew, so they sneaked up on us and the next thing I knew he had given up.'

His words were a painful reminder of my own stupidity when we had been captured.

'Well,' I said, 'make sure you don't get captured again. Hit and run, Burebista, that's what we're here for.'

'Yes, lord. I'll make sure I hit them all right.'

The heat of the day was abating as we reached the hills to the east of Capua. These tree-covered slopes afforded us some shelter, for there was a distinct lack of hills or cover on the broad plain on which the city stood. Indeed, as Godarz, Nergal and I viewed Capua from the high vantage point we could see that there was no cover for miles around. The city nestled in the broad bend of a meandering river, like a giant snake, that ran from east to west, with the walled Capua being sited on its southern bank. There were houses and villages dotted around it, and a straight road that came from the north, cut through the city and then continued south. Like

every major Roman road, it was as straight as an arrow.
'That's the road they'll go down tomorrow,' remarked Godarz.
I could see a mass of men and livestock about five miles from our position, with figures scurrying around as the Romans constructed their camp for the night. I had to admit that it was an amazing thing to see. A camp with an earthen rampart and wooden palisade created from nothing at the end of each day. A safe place for an army to rest each night, and a place of refuge in the face of an enemy attack. And in the morning it would be disassembled as the army moved on – truly a remarkable feat of military engineering and planning. From what Spartacus had told me, a Roman army marched an average of around fifteen miles a day, which meant that they could reach the outskirts of Naples tomorrow and be ready to attack our forces around Vesuvius the day after. So we had to do something tomorrow or it would be too late.

We ate an evening meal in a site I had selected to be our camp, a glade by the side of a dirt track that wound up the hillside and through the woods. We lit no fires lest the glow of the flames would alert the Romans in the plain below of our presence. Guards were posted in all directions in case a shepherd or other civilian stumbled upon us, though I hoped that all the shepherds hereabouts had joined Spartacus. Before the darkness descended I told the men of the plan for tomorrow. They formed a semi-circle on the ground, their faces full of enthusiasm. We would attack the Romans tomorrow when they were on the march. I gambled that because they were in Italy, their vigilance would not be as high as it would be if they were marching through enemy territory. They would post a vanguard, that was standard procedure, but we could force the army to stop and hopefully deploy in battle array. In that way we would win our army valuable time, half a day at least.

'Remember,' I emphasised, 'our bows out-range any missile weapons they may have, including any slingers they might possess, so shoot from a distance. Don't worry about accuracy, there are plenty of them and chances are that any arrows you shoot will find a target.'

I didn't sleep that night, but paced around the camp and checked and re-checked my weapons. The dawn came soon enough, and the men fed and watered the horses and then ate a sparse breakfast of biscuit and water. There was no bravado, just four hundred cavalrymen checking their saddles, bows, helmets and bridles. I left Godarz behind with fifty men. I intended to draw away any Roman cavalry into the hills where they could be ambushed. If things went against us, then Godarz's force would act as a rearguard if we were overwhelmed on the plain.

As the first rays of the sun appeared in the east, three hundred and fifty riders made their way down the dirt track that led onto the plain around Capua. Already the Romans would be taking down their camp and preparing to march south towards Vesuvius. As we left the cover of the wooded slope we formed into one long line. I was at the head and the other riders following me in single file. As we advanced at a canter I could already see that the Roman vanguard, made up of lightly armed foot and archers, had left the camp and was marching south on the road. The Romans had posted no outriders; why should they? They were in their home country and were here to quell a slave rebellion and not face an equal opponent in battle. Following the vanguard was a detachment of horse and legionaries, and then engineers followed by the rest of the Roman cavalry. The bulk of the legionaries were still inside the camp, dismantling the wooden palisade and packing their personal equipment.

I estimated that the van of their army was strung out on the road for half a mile or so as we galloped across the plain to get to within five hundred feet, when we would wheel sharply right, which would take us towards the Roman camp. The moment before I turned Remus sharply right I shot my arrow at the head of the Roman column, each rider following me doing likewise. In this way the Roman light troops and archers were peppered with missiles. As I rode along the column I quickly strung and loosed a succession of arrows. The Romans, having experienced an uneventful march through familiar terrain, were temporarily stunned by our presence. The air was filled with curses and squeals of pain as arrows pierced mail and flesh. I saw a centurion beside the road frantically trying to organise his men to form a wall of shields. He had his back to me as Remus galloped past him and my arrow slammed into his lower back. Individual Romans hurled their javelins at us as we drew level to them, but we were out of range and the projectiles fell short. Our arrows, though, were like a metal rain that showered their disorganised ranks, and many a bronze raindrop found a soft, fleshy landing place. In an effort to get closer to us, some legionaries ran a short distance towards us before launching their javelins, but this served only to separate them from their comrades and made them choice targets for the riders following. Many were felled in this fashion, some falling dead, others staggering back to their comrades with wounds gushing blood.

More Romans were now pouring from the camp and onto the ground each side of the road, as the vanguard and those following attempted to get into some sort of formation. But the result was a seething mass of panicking soldiers. I halted my riders about three hundred yards from the camp's entrance and ordered them to fire arrows at the desperately scrambling figures. Out of the corner of my eye I saw enemy cavalry moving towards us from our left. Scores of horsemen in no discernible formation, but nevertheless riding hard in our direction.

'Retreat!' I yelled at the top of my voice. 'Parthians to cover the rear.'

I pointed at Burebista who was beside me. 'Go now. Ride back to the trees. We will cover you.'

He nodded and wheeled his horse away, as did the other riders. As they galloped towards from whence we had come, around fifty others and I delayed slightly before we followed them. We formed a ragged, widely spaced line of horsemen as the Romans, led by a figure wielding a sword, a red cloak billowing behind him and sporting a helmet similar to mine but with a large red plume, closed on us. The gap between Burebista and my Parthians was increasing at the same time as that between us and the Roman horse was decreasing. The Romans, green-coloured shields on their left side, spears in their right hands and riding in close formation, must have sensed an easy kill as they lowered their lances and prepared to ram them into our backs. But these Romans had obviously never encountered Parthians before, much less our fighting techniques, for as one we pulled arrows from our quivers, strung them, twisted our torsos to bring our bows to bear over our mounts' hind quarters, and let fly a volley of arrows. If the Romans had been in an open formation the effect of the volley would have been reduced, as it was the shafts flew into a compact mass of horses and riders. Several horses and their riders in the front rank were hit, men falling from saddles and horses collapsing to the ground. Those following careered into the falling and stumbling beasts, while others attempted to avoid the obstacles in front of them but merely succeeded in crashing into other riders. Within seconds the Roman cavalry was a mass of disorganised riders and frightened and rearing horses. Their leader was frantically trying to reform them as I halted the line and ordered another volley to be let loose. I took aim at the officer and released the arrow, but it missed and went into a rider behind him. In the distance I could see a square of legionaries running to reinforce their cavalry, so I shouted for us to retreat once more.

We galloped hard to the tree line, where I found a waiting Burebista and Godarz, both mounted, as my rearguard filed onto the narrow track that wound its way through the trees to the spot that had been our makeshift camp.

'My men are posted either side of the track, hiding among the trees,' said Godarz, who had obviously not forgotten his training as a soldier.

'Good,' I replied, observing the Roman cavalry now riding hard towards our position. Their leader was clearly determined to get at us. 'Ride ahead of me. Let them onto the track, then kill as many as you can before their foot arrives. No heroics. We've achieved what we came here to do.'

Burebista and Godarz rode ahead as I followed the rearmost rider, glancing back down the track. Then the Roman officer appeared, urging his horse forward and shouting back to his men as he saw me. I nudged Remus forward as the Roman closed on me. As far as he was concerned I was alone and was only moments away from death or capture. His men were following two abreast, their lances held upright.

Either side of the narrow track was a green jumble of fallen branches, long grass and dense brush, from where suddenly erupted the hiss of arrows cutting through the air. The forest was filled with the sound of dull thuds as they hit their targets, lancing through mail shirts to embed themselves in flesh. Riders groaned and either slumped in their saddles or fell to the ground as my bowmen fired arrow after arrow into the line of Roman cavalry. My men were firing from short range – probably no more than fifty feet – and at that distance each missile was finding its mark with deadly effect. Some of the Romans were panicking and attempting to wheel about and flee, but the track was too narrow and congested and their efforts were in vain. Horses, their eyes wild with terror, bolted hither and thither into the trees, knocking over those Romans who had dismounted in an attempt to avoid the hail of arrows. Their officer was frantically trying to rally what was left of his command, but despair had gripped his men and they were not listening to his orders and threats. He saw me standing on Remus, observing his men getting cut own and charged forward, only to crash to the ground when an arrow pierced his horse's shoulder, sending the animal and rider to the floor. He sprang up, his sword in his hand, and walked towards me.

'Today you die, scum,' he spat as he pointed the point of his blade at me. He was brave, I gave him that.

I took off my quiver and hooked its strap on a horn of my saddle, then holstered my bow in its case that was fastened to my saddle. I jumped down and drew my spatha. The Roman attacked me with great slashing movements. He had some skill, I had to admit, and there was strength behind his blows, but his attack was predictable and I parried his sword with ease. He drew back and then launched another attack with a flurry of sword strokes.

'What's the matter, vermin,' he shouted, 'afraid to fight?'

There is no point in wasting energy on shouting abuse at your opponent – better to concentrate on killing him and shutting him up for good. His blows were getting weaker, only slightly but weaker nevertheless. He screamed with rage and swung his sword again in an attempt to bring it down on my helmet and split my skull, but I saw it coming and leapt aside to his right. As his right arm came down I slashed at it with my sword and cut the flesh of his upper arm. He yelped in pain and dropped his blade. He went to retrieve it but the point of my spatha was at his throat in an instant.

I eased the point into the nape of his neck, but he just stood there.

'Take off your helmet, Roman.'

As the blood pumped from the deep gash on his right arm he slowly removed his gleaming helmet with his left hand, to reveal a man in his early thirties with a large face, high forehead, hooked nose and short, curly blond hair. His eyes burned with hate as he stood in silence, while behind him his men were dying and the sounds of battle echoed through the trees. I entertained the thought of ramming the blade through his throat, but then decided to toy with him instead.

'Your men are being slaughtered, Roman,' I said. 'Perhaps you would like to join them?'

'Romans die but Rome always wins, scum,' he was shaking with rage, or was it fear? I knew not.

'Your manners are as poor as your sword skills,' I replied, still holding the point of my blade against his flesh. 'You should come to Parthia if you want to be a swordsman, or a cavalryman for that matter.'

'Parthia?'

'Yes, Roman, for I am a Parthian. Did you not know that by the way we have cut you to pieces?' I was boasting and enjoying every minute and had completely forgotten about what was happening around me. Fortunately Godarz had not, and he suddenly appeared on his horse beside me.

'Roman foot, highness, moving fast towards us. Time to go.'

I broke off the battle of stares with the Roman as Godarz blew his horn. Moments later horsemen appeared from the trees, making their way through the foliage onto the track. I looked ahead and could see the track littered with dead and wounded men, riderless horses standing or walking around, and beyond them a column of legionaries marching at double time towards us.

'Highness!' shouted Godarz, holding Remus' reins in his hand.

I glanced at the Roman, sheathed my sword, turned and leapt into the saddle on Remus' back. As we rode away the Roman, standing amidst the wreckage of his command, shouted after us.

'I am Tribune Lucius Furius, Parthian, and we will meet again. You hear me, Parthian. We shall meet again!'

We followed the rest of my men along the track, which skirted the top of the tree-covered mountain and brought us down the other side. We rendezvoused at the tree line in front of a large, empty field and Godarz organised a roll call. We had suffered only five men wounded, two with broken bones and three with minor cuts. None of the horses had suffered serious injuries. Afterwards we rode hard through green countryside, passing villas and villages but seeing hardly anyone. Those we did see ran in panic away from the column of dust-covered riders. After two hours the horses were blown, so we found a small wood with a stream not far away and rested them in the shade. I posted guards as saddles were unstrapped and harnesses removed. Groups of horses were led to the stream to be watered, and afterwards each man checked and groomed his mount. Only after the horses' welfare had been attended to did we ourselves rest and eat a light meal of biscuit and cheese, which had sweated somewhat during the journey. Godarz organised guard rotas as I lay down beside a tree, Remus munching grain from a leather nosebag. When Godarz had finished he came over and sat beside me. Around us men slept as others paced up and down and kept watch.

'My congratulations, highness. A perfectly executed plan.'

'Thank you.' I had to admit that I too was pleased with myself.

'But you should have killed that Roman.'

In truth I had forgotten about him. 'I wouldn't worry about him, they've probably executed him for incompetence.'

'You're wrong,' he said sternly. 'He said he was a tribune and that means he is a powerful man, or has powerful friends. He will not forget you.'

'Really?' I was unconcerned. He was the last thing on my mind as tiredness swept over me, and I dismissed Godarz so I could get some sleep. All in all it had been a good day, and I said a prayer of thanks to Shamash for protecting me, and hoped Bozan sitting beside him would be pleased at the Roman souls I had offered to him.

We stayed the night there, and in the morning rode south to link up with the main army. We gave Vesuvius a wide berth lest the Romans had sent more cavalry ahead, but in truth we saw no enemy force of any kind, or indeed anyone. The countryside seemed deserted, as it probably was thanks to the spectre of Spartacus.

We picked up the trail of the army easily enough, a vast swathe of trampled grass and churned-up dirt where thousands of feet and hooves had tramped over it. We dismounted and walked beside our horses, having first posted outriders to ensure we weren't surprised by any Roman patrols. The day was sunny and warm, our mood relaxed. The men were flushed with victory and their spirits high. Though my Parthians could speak only a smattering of Latin and many of the Dacians and Thracians among us had only a meagre knowledge of the language, there was nevertheless a lively chatter of sorts among the ranks. This was accompanied by wild and exaggerated hand signals. I sent Nergal ahead with five men to inform Spartacus of our success. Burebista, Rhesus and Godarz walked with me at the head of the column. Godarz was still unhappy.

'You should have killed him,' was all he kept saying. Eventually I had had enough.

'So you keep telling me, Godarz, but it really doesn't matter. I'm sure there will be other opportunities.'

'You can be sure of that,' he said. 'Roman pride is not a thing to be dented lightly. He won't rest until he's avenged his humiliation.'

'I wish I had killed him,' I said. 'That at least would have shut you up. Take five men and ride ahead, Godarz. Find us a good spot for tonight's camp.'

He saluted stiffly, mounted his horse and rode off. Burebista laughed.

'He's like an old woman.'

'Godarz is a good man,' I said, 'but he worries too much. Not like you, Burebista.'

He spat on the ground. 'Worry is for women. What is there to worry about? I have a horse, a brave captain to follow,' he grinned at me, 'a sword in my hand and an unlimited amount of Romans to kill. To a Dacian, this is heaven.'

We camped that night on a hill overlooking a valley dotted with trees and fields. One of my men brought down a deer with his bow so we skinned and cooked it over a fire. After eating little more than biscuits and sweating cheese washed down with water, we ate the meat with relish. Godarz had found the spot and was, I was happy to discover, in a better mood.

'Spartacus took the bridge over the Silarus River two days ago,' he told me while chewing meat from a cooked rib. 'The army is already in Lucania so we're safe for the time being. Crixus and his Gauls are holding the bridge. As soon as we're over, Spartacus is going to tear it down.'

I wondered if Crixus was tempted to destroy the bridge before we got across the river. Perhaps not.

'Any sign of the Romans?' I asked.

'None,' replied Godarz. He went on to tell me that the people of the town of Eburum, only a couple of miles from the river, had shut the gates and cowered behind their walls. Spartacus had no interest in assaulting the place, though predictably Crixus had wanted to unleash his Gauls against it. Nevertheless, Spartacus had sent parties of men into the countryside to plunder all the crops and livestock they could find. It was a rich haul, as Campania in the autumn was a bountiful place. And new recruits were coming in all the time, herdsmen from the hills and valleys, slaves who worked on Campania's vast estates, and even slaves who had escaped from the towns and had made their way to Spartacus, for our general's fame, or infamy depending on one's point of view, had spread. He had gone from being a minor irritant, a runaway slave who would be taken with ease, to the leader of a rebellion that was threatening to engulf the whole of southern Italy.

We rode to the bridge to find it guarded by dozens of wild-looking Gauls armed with Roman shields and an assortment of weapons ranging from wooden clubs to javelins and swords. Tramping across the bridge was a steady stream of men who mainly had no weapons and who were obviously not soldiers. I dismounted and gave the reins of Remus to Nergal, then strode over to where a large Gaul (they all appeared to be large, even their women. I wondered how the Romans ever managed to defeat them) was berating those crossing the bridge.

'Get a move on, you sons of whores,' he bellowed at no one in particular. 'We can't wait here forever. If you don't speed up we'll leave you here to be nailed to crosses. Now move, or I will do it myself.'

His men were lounging each side of the road, making derogatory comments about the latest recruits to the army. Several of them sprang to their feet and grabbed their weapons when they saw me approach. Obviously Crixus had made his dislike of me well known among his own people.

'Who are these people?' I asked their leader.

He viewed me warily with cold grey eyes, his dark hair hanging lankly around his shoulders. 'Newly freed slaves, or runaways. Come to join Spartacus. Where are the Romans?'

His discourtesy was almost as repellent as the stink coming from his body, but I ignored his curt manner.

'We gave them a bloody nose. They won't be here for a while.' I looked at the long line of men dressed in rags ambling across the river. 'We need to get across and report to Spartacus. Clear these people out of the way.'

He laughed. 'You'll have to wait, either that or swim across.'

The river was wide and obviously deep. The stone bridge across it had five arches that spanned the dark blue and fast-moving water. I walked up to him and faced him.

'What is your name, Gaul?'

He grinned, revealing a row of black teeth. 'Tasgetius, captain under Crixus.'

'You know who I am?'

His smiled disappeared. 'The Parthian,' he sneered.

I reached behind my back and pulled my dagger from its sheath, then whipped it up to his throat.

'Then you know that Parthians never back down, so move these people aside and let us pass. That is an order.'

By now all the Gauls were on their feet and were ready to hack me into small pieces, but the sight of nearly four hundred arrows pointed at them made them hesitate, for my men had divided into two groups and were in front of the Gauls. They were now sitting in their saddles with their bows ready to fire. I looked directly at Tasgetius. He blinked first.

'Of course, Parthian, we have no wish to fight you. We are on the same side, are we not?' He pointed at one of his men. 'Move these bastards aside. Let the horsemen pass.'

I withdrew my dagger and nodded at him. 'My thanks, Tasgetius. I shall inform Spartacus personally of your cooperation.'

I vaulted onto Remus' back and took his reins from Nergal.

'Making new friends?' he said sourly.

'These Gauls are more trouble than they're worth,' I said.

'Isn't Gallia a Gaul, highness?'

'She's different,' I said, moving Remus forward as the Gauls manhandled the others aside – I wondered how many were already regretting fleeing from their masters.

'She certainly is,' he smiled.

We made it over the bridge and rode across country to the camp, a massive, sprawling collection of tents, makeshift canvas shelters and groups of individuals huddled around campfires.

The camp seemed to fill miles of the plain that stopped at the foot of a large mountain chain that ran from east to west. In my absence the number of those following Spartacus had increased markedly, though I wondered how so many new recruits were going to be trained and armed in time to face the Roman army that had been delayed, but only temporarily. Food seemed less of a problem, for the entire plain was filled with thousands of animals – cattle, pigs, sheep, goats, chickens and oxen, some in ramshackle pens, others tied to carts and many more wandering freely over the grass. The whole scene resembled a gigantic market day, which would be a bloody day if any Roman forces happened upon it. I said a prayer to Shamash that they would not. Now I realised the huge responsibility Spartacus had entrusted me with, and was pleased that I had not let him down.

In the middle of the multitude was the Roman camp that had stood on the slopes of Vesuvius, dismantled and rebuilt here. Guards stood at the main entrance, which was flanked by wooden watchtowers. On the top of one stood the impish Akmon, who immediately climbed down the ladder when he saw our column.

He raced out of the entrance waving his arms.

'You can't bring those horses in here, we're too crowded as it is. The rest of your lot is camped about a mile away, due west, close to the river.' He pointed at me. 'Spartacus wants a report off you before you go.'

I told Nergal to take the men and find the rest of the cavalry, while I dismounted and led Remus into the 'Roman' camp. As before, all the tents were arranged in neat lines. Akmon walked beside me along the central avenue towards the command tent. He was clearly unhappy.

'Too many people. We won't be able to stay here long.'

'How many people?' I asked.

'Last count, over thirty thousand and more coming in each day. I heard about your little spat with the Romans, your man filled us in on it. Well done, should give us a bit of time.'

'The camp seems orderly,' I noted.

He laughed. 'Of course, Spartacus only lets Thracians and Germans in. Keeps the rest outside.'

'And Crixus?' I asked.

He spat on the ground. 'He gathers all the Gauls to him. He's chafing at the bit. He wasn't best pleased that you won a bit of glory.'

'I can imagine.'

Spartacus stood at the entrance to his tent, which was around twelve feet in height. He stepped forward and embraced me in an iron grip, slapping me hard on the back as he released me.

'I knew I could rely on you. Godarz told me all about it. Come inside and have a drink to clear the dust from your throat. Thank you, Akmon.'

His second-in-command saluted and stomped off as we stepped inside, to be greeted by Claudia, Diana and Gallia, the beautiful Gallia. They all stood applauding me. I blushed, not because of their applause but because I could once again clasp eyes on the blond-haired beauty, she who filled my thoughts. Spartacus put an arm round my shoulder.

'Leave the boy alone, Claudia, and pour us all some wine.'

Gallia strolled over to me, and jabbed a finger hard into my ribs.

'Don't ever do that again,' she hissed.

I was mortified. 'What?'

'Leave without saying goodbye. Don't they have manners in Parthia?'

'I promise that one day I will take you there and you can judge for yourself.' I gazed into her blue eyes and totally forget all else there. She smiled and tilted her head slightly.

'I will look forward to that, Prince Pacorus.'

'Enough,' barked Spartacus, 'we have a war to win first.'

I stayed with them until dusk, drinking, eating and talking. I liked these people, and wanted nothing more than to be with them always. Though they were technically under my command, Gallia and Diana stayed in the camp and I was glad for that: at least they had some sort of protection if it was attacked, for I doubted that the Romans would be long delayed. As the sun sank slowly like a red ball in the western sky, I walked Remus to the man entrance with Gallia by my side. Spartacus had told me that he was riding into the mountains tomorrow and he wanted me to accompany him, but he would say no more.

'Do you like fighting?' asked Gallia.

'That's a strange question.'

'Nergal and Godarz say that you are good at it, so I assume that you enjoy it.'

'Have my men been gossiping behind my back?'

'Not at all,' she replied. 'I asked them a question and they answered. I can be very persuasive.'

I did not doubt that. I would promise her the world if she but asked.

'Well?' she prompted.

I shrugged. 'I suppose I was bred for war.'

She was outraged, her nostrils flaring. 'Bred!'

'The training of Parthian nobles is arduous. From a baby until I was five my time was spent with my mother and other women of the court, and away from my father. Thereafter I was schooled in running, swimming, horse care, hunting on foot and horseback, fighting with the sword, throwing the spear and javelin, and above all archery. I rode and shot the bow every day for fifteen years. Then, at the age of twenty, I entered the army proper as a member of my father's bodyguard. So, after all that effort, I hope that I am reasonably competent at the military arts.'

'The Romans have farms where they breed slaves,' she said. 'Places where masters oversee the mating of selected pairs, and in the arena Romans watch chosen pairs butcher each other for their entertainment. It's disgusting.'

'Yes it is,' I said.

She turned and faced me, determination etched on her face. 'I will never be a slave again. Promise me that if the worst happens you will kill me rather than let me be taken.'

'What?' I was horrified.

Her face showed steely resolve. 'Promise me!'

'I promise,' I replied, though I also promised myself that I would also kill myself immediately afterwards. Where she went, I would follow. She kissed me lightly on the cheek.

'Thank you.'

Having made such a solemn promise I should have gone to bed with a heavy heart, but all I could think about was her kiss.

The next day I saddled Remus early and waited for Spartacus. He came an hour after dawn accompanied by a man I did not recognise, but whom Spartacus informed me was a local guide who knew the area. I carried a water skin and food in a saddlebag, plus my sword, dagger, bow and a quiver full of arrows. I also took Nergal and twenty other horsemen with us; who knew what we would encounter?

Spartacus was in high spirits as our horses wound their way up the mountain via narrow passes. The lower slopes were covered with shrubs, but as we climbed they gave way to chestnut and strawberry trees. These in turn gave way to magnificent beeches with trunks covered in lichens. I had never seen such lush vegetation, a far cry from the parched deserts of Parthia. Huge grey boulders jutted out from the green and yellow foliage, while through the treetops I saw goshawks flying overhead and heard the tapping of a woodpecker. It took us two hours of threading through wooded ravines and along and across foaming streams before we reached the summit, riding out onto a rock terrace that presented a stunning view of a wide, green valley below, one that extended as far as the eye could see.

It was a vast green plateau flanked by mountains, with white dots that were villas sprinkled across its extent. Below us, nestling on the plateau a few miles from the mountain we were looking down from, was a walled town. We had a perfect view of its layout of equally sized rectangular blocks of buildings, the whole bisected by straight roads. As usual there were four gates, with a main road running up to and through the town and across the plateau, disappearing into the distance. The lower slopes of the mountains were covered in trees, and the plateau itself was studied with olive groves. This was rich country indeed.

'Beautiful, is it not?' sighed Spartacus.

'Yes, lord,' I answered.

'That town is Forum Annii, so my guide tells me. And in two days Crixus and his Gauls are going to take it.'

I was horrified. 'They will burn it to the ground.'

'Unhappily, you are right, but he's been wanting to blood his men for some time now, and I would rather him and his men kill Romans than each other, or other members of my army,' he looked pointedly at me. 'The fact is Pacorus, that your timely triumph gnaws away at Crixus, so I will give him what he wants, a chance to kill Romans.'

'The man is an animal,' I spat.

Spartacus laughed. 'So am I, at least to a Roman, and so are you, my friend.' It was the first time he had called me friend, and I was at that moment immensely proud. Whatever Spartacus was, he certainly knew how to win men over. 'The point is that he is idle and angry and has six thousand Gauls who are likewise unoccupied. Besides, the Roman army will be here soon enough so some battle training will come in useful.'

After a brief rest and food to fill our stomachs we rode back to camp. Spartacus called a council of war in the early evening. Present were myself, Spartacus, Nergal, Burebista, Castus, Cannicus, Akmon, Crixus, Oenomaus and Dumnorix. Crixus ignored me throughout, but was delighted when Spartacus revealed his future plans.

'We need to put some distance between us and Rome, and that

means we have to head south, to the Gulf of Tarentum. There we can build and train the army for the march north next spring. Though Pacorus has delayed the advance of the Roman army,' he nodded towards me, 'there is no doubt that it will resume its march towards us. Therefore, we need to get over the mountain, onto the plateau and then head south. But before we can move we have to take the Roman town, Forum Annii, which stands in our way. Crixus, I want your men to take it.'

It was the first time that I saw the Gaul smile when he heard this, a giant leer with his eyes bulging at the prospect of plunder. 'You can rely on us,' he said, his men slapping him on the back by way of congratulations.

'Now remember,' continued Spartacus to us all, 'the road we travelled down from Vesuvius goes round the mountain and leads to a pass that gives access to the high plateau. It will take two or three days for the army and its animals to get there, but only a few hours for Crixus to get his men up the mountain.'

'What garrison does the town have?' asked Castus.

'Who cares about the garrison?' said Crixus before Spartacus could reply, 'they will die along with the rest.'

I looked at Spartacus but there was no expression on his face.

'Listen,' said Spartacus to Crixus. 'You will need scaling ladders and maybe a battering ram. There are plenty of trees on the slopes, so make use of all the wood and get your men ready. They are to attack Forum Annii the day after tomorrow. Any questions?'

There were none.

The next day Crixus and his men went about cutting down wood with gusto, no doubt rehearsing on trees what they would be doing to people the day after. The Gauls were full of enthusiasm, I gave them that, but their coarse language and dishevelled appearance made me shudder. I went to see Castus during the morning as Godarz and Nergal sent out cavalry patrols to the river and allocated new recruits to companies. We had increased our number of horsemen by a hundred, but there was no time to train them in tactics or the use of the bow, so they were given a spear and told to obey their commanders. They wouldn't be any use in battle, but if they survived the march to the sea they could be turned into cavalrymen.

Castus was in his usual good spirits, the more so because his command had been enlarged markedly by the march through Campania.

'Four thousand Germans now, Pacorus,' he said, proudly, 'though only half have decent weapons. The rest have clubs and wooden spears. Still, it's a start.'

'Indeed it is,' I was pleased for him. He was a good man and his men were under tighter control than Crixus' Gauls.

'There's over thirty thousand in camp,' he said. 'Did you know?'

'So I've heard.'

'Southern Italy is nothing but farms and herds of animals, and who are the people who work in the fields and tend to the herds? Slaves.'

'And gladiators,' I said.

He smiled. 'Them too.'

I rode to the Silarus River that afternoon with Gafarn, Gallia, Godarz and Diana. For some reason I was feeling morose and wanted some pleasant company. Its waters were black and fast flowing, and the sky was heaped with dark clouds. It was still warm, but the days were no longer hot and the nights were getting cooler. The Gauls had done a poor job destroying the bridge (why was I not surprised?) and though the parapets had been knocked into the river only two of the five arches had been wholly demolished.

'It won't take the Romans long to rebuild it,' Godarz must have been reading my mind.

'How long do you think we've got?' I asked.

He shrugged. 'Two days at the most.'

I dismounted and walked over to a group of soldiers guarding the bridge. There were ten of them, all wearing mail shirts, helmets and carrying Roman shields, spears and swords. Thracians, I assumed by their long black hair and lack of hostility towards me.

'Any movement on the far bank?' I asked their commander.

'Not till now,' he said, pointing his spear behind me. I turned to see a group of horsemen galloping down the road towards the bridge. Their green shields indicated that we had met before.

'Gafarn,' I shouted, 'get Gallia and Diana away from here.'

Gallia was indignant. 'Why? They cannot fly across the river.'

'I'll show you why,' I shouted, vaulting into Remus' saddle and pulling my bow from its case. The Romans slowed their mounts when they reached the bridge, the horses walking onto it and then halting. I strung an arrow and let it fly. It hit the foremost rider square in the chest, knocking him out of his saddle. The Thracians cheered wildly, though as I strung another arrow I saw a look of horror on Diana's face and Gallia had gone deathly pale.

I turned to Gafarn. 'Now get them out of here and back to camp.' He grabbed the reins of their horses and led them away. The Romans turned and fled, though not before I had knocked another out of his saddle with a shot that hit the rearmost rider in the middle of his back. I ordered Godarz to ride to Spartacus' headquarters to inform him of the news, and watched as Gallia and Diana rode off, while the Thracians looked decidedly nervous.

'Don't worry,' I told them, 'it's just a scouting party.'

The remaining Romans halted a safe distance from the bridge, where they were soon joined by a score of others riding hard towards them. One was wearing an officer's helmet with a rich red plume and a red cloak that billowed behind him. I nudged Remus onto the bridge and walked him to where the first arch had been knocked into the river. The Romans, stationary now, looked on as I held my bow aloft and then slowly and deliberately placed it back in its case. Then I waited. Remus flicked his white tail nonchalantly. The Roman officer suddenly kicked his heels into his horse's sides and galloped towards me. He halted his mount on the far side of the damaged bridge and took off his helmet. I recognised him instantly.

'Tribune Furius,' I shouted, 'are you intent on getting yourself killed?'

He looked at the two dead soldiers on the ground. 'Enjoy your small victories, Parthian, you will be nailed to a cross soon enough.'

'You conversations are becoming repetitive, Roman.'

'That's a fine horse you have stolen,' he shouted back. 'I promise to take good care of him when you are dead.'

'Thank you,' I hollered, 'but he's coming to Parthia with me.'

'You will never see Parthia, I promise that.'

I was getting bored and thus decided to bring this shouting match to an end. I raised my hand.

'Until the next time, Roman.' I turned Remus away and walked him back to where the Thracians stood. 'How far do you think those other riders are from where we stand?' I asked their commander.

'Hard to tell, sir, about five hundred yards, maybe more.'

I turned Remus around to face the river and drew my bow.

'You'll never hit them from this distance,' he said.

I looked at him, pulled an arrow from my quiver, strung it and took aim. Furius was riding back to his men when I loosed the arrow, which arched into the air and then curved back towards the ground. I don't know if it pierced the mail shirt of the man it hit, but his horse reared up and he fell to the ground, spreading panic among the other rides. The Thracians cheered again.

'Stay here,' I told them. 'Spartacus will send reinforcements.'

But Spartacus came himself, marching on foot at the head of a long column of troops, all well armed. The stubby legs of Akmon marched beside him.

'It's just a scouting party,' I told him.

He shook his head. 'Their army will be here tomorrow morning.' He turned to Akmon. 'We'll break camp and march through the night. Pacorus, I know it may pain you, but ride to Crixus and tell him that he must attack Forum Annii at first light. And tell him he has to take the town. I don't want a garrison in front of me and an army behind me.'

I saluted and galloped away. The Gauls' camp was a sprawling mass of makeshift canvas tents, wicker windbreaks and cooking fires, a far cry from the well-ordered camps of Spartacus and Castus, but it was far larger. As I rode among the shelters I saw men working frantically on constructing scaling ladders from tree branches. I had to admit that there was a real sense of urgency about them. Most ignored me as I rode to find their leader, though some gave me a menacing sideways glance as I passed. I found him stripped to the waist and wielding a large axe against the base of a tree. He was sweating profusely as he swung the weapon and cleaved another chunk of wood from the trunk. He stopped when he saw me. There was a large group of his warriors admiring his handiwork with an axe.

'Well, if it isn't the prince of Parthia. What do you want, boy?'

Gritting my teeth, I dismounted. 'Greetings from Spartacus. The Romans are at the river. He asks that you lead your men up the mountain and attack the town at first light.'

The mention of the Romans aroused his curiosity, as he stopped what he was doing and even forget his animosity towards me. 'How many?'

'Just a cavalry patrol, but their army won't be far behind.'

He called over Oenomaus. 'Get everyone ready. We move this afternoon. Where's that guide Spartacus promised me?'

'He's eating porridge outside your tent,' said Oenomaus.

'Bring him to me, I want to make sure he doesn't run away before he serves his purpose. Go.'

His men dispersed, leaving us alone. The silence was awkward. Crixus, his muscled, bear-like torso covered in swirling blue tattoos, picked up a tunic and put it on.

'It was brave of you to come alone, boy,' he said at last, pouring water over himself from a bucket, 'I hear you usually have to have your archers to back you up before you dare face a Gaul.'

He was obviously commenting on my disagreement with some of his men at the bridge. 'Your men are undisciplined,' I said, matching his stare.

He laughed. 'All will be settled in time, Parthian. Now go and play with your horses.'

He picked up the axe, slung it on his shoulder and walked past me. I did not doubt that we would be settling the animosity between us soon enough, but not today.

It took hours for the army to get on the road leading to Forum Annii, not helped by the descending darkness and the steady rain that began to fall soon after dusk. Camp fires were stoked higher and left to burn to give the impression that we were staying put, but anyone with half a mind would have been able to tell that thousands of people and animals were on the move, the shouts and curses and hordes of individuals trying to get on the road and the bellowing and lowing of cattle. Byrd organised the packing of our equipment into carts that had been taken at Nola. The town, or rather its inhabitants, had been generous in supplying a large quantity of equipment for the cavalry, and now Byrd was stacking large buckets, pitch forks, brooms, wheelbarrows, halters, lead ropes, hoof picks, combs, brushes and saddle clothes onto a long line of carts. Another two carts were stacked high with spare arrows, which were covered with waterproof hides to keep the water off them. Byrd's temper was rising as he became increasingly irritated by the apparent lack of progress a group of new recruits was making in getting the carts loaded. I told him to calm down, not least because the cavalry and its equipment would be the last to leave the camp, as we would form the rearguard.

Godarz, as usual, was taking everything in his stride. Having instructed Byrd to load the carts, he was now stood in front of a fire briefing two of my company commanders on what to pack on the mules that weren't pulling carts.

'Don't overload them or they won't move at all. And there's no use in beating them. That will make them more obstinate. Treat them like your women and use soft words if you want to tease the best out of them.'

'But I always thrash my women,' said one cocky young Parthian in reply.

'Then you're an idiot,' said Godarz, 'and will die childless and alone. Now go.'

He saw me and raised his hand in salute, his face wearing a frown.

'Problems?' I enquired.

'Just the usual, not enough time. Let's hope the Romans don't like marching in the rain.'

'Use the new recruits to guard the carts,' I said. 'They will be useless if we have to fight the Romans while covering the army's retreat, and I don't want to lose valuable horses. And unguarded carts are a temptation for any thieving low-life that this army seems to be full of. Do we have enough weapons to equip each new recruit?'

'Spears, yes,' said Godarz, 'but not swords.'

'Mmm. There's no point in giving them swords anyway, it takes a lot of training to be able use one with competence. I hate this rain.'

'Perhaps the Parthians should guard the carts, lord, and the new recruits can be slaughtered by the Romans. That will save you the trouble of training them,' he mused.

'What?'

'It must be very taxing for a prince to be constantly surrounded by low-life.'

I realised that I had offended him. 'Godarz, I didn't mean...'

'These people have nothing, Pacorus. Nothing. They have joined Spartacus because he has given them a glimmer of hope. The hope that they can live as free men. They do not deserve to be talked of as you have just talked of them. The only things they have are the clothes on their back, some not even that. If you think that they are not fit to ride beside you then tell them, at least have the courtesy for that. And now, if you will excuse me, I have duties to attend to.'

With that he saluted and stomped off, leaving me suitably crestfallen. It started to rain harder, thus increasing my misery. It improved somewhat when I rode to see Spartacus at the bridge, accompanied by Akmon whose gangly arms and awkward gait always made me smile.

All three of us walked onto the bridge and stared into the blackness. I could see no campfires, which was a relief.

'They appear to have gone,' I said, trying to reassure myself.

'They're there all right,' sniffed Akmon. 'Probably a few miles down the road, all nicely tucked up in their tents in their camp.'

'They will be here in the morning,' said Spartacus, 'by which time we will have stolen half a day's march on them, and Crixus will also have hopefully captured Forum Annii. Pacorus, you remember that plateau that the town is situated on?'

'Yes.'

'That's where we will fight the Roman army.'

'You think we can beat them, Spartacus?' asked Akmon.

'We have to, otherwise we'll be running forever. And anyway, the plain is wide and we outnumber them, which means we can outflank them, and we have more cavalry than they do which means we can get behind them.' I could tell that he had thought through his plan carefully.

'Roman armies don't worry about numbers,' said Akmon.

'But we have trained our men to fight like Romans, so we will be using their own tactics against them,' replied Spartacus. 'Is your cavalry ready, Pacorus?'

'Ready, lord,' I said, proudly.

'So are my Thracians and Castus' Germans.'

'And the Gauls?' queried Akmon.

'Crixus is a born fighter,' said Spartacus. 'Wild, certainly, but he and his men want to kill Romans and I want such soldiers in my army.'

As we stood in the darkness with only a few small fires burning beside the road, I wondered if Spartacus was trying to convince himself as well as us. From what I could gather, he and Crixus had never been friends, more like uneasy allies. The Gaul had never challenged Spartacus' authority, but I reckoned it was only a matter of time before the two of them clashed; it was also only a matter of time before Crixus and I clashed. But in the meantime we had a Roman garrison to subdue and a Roman army to destroy.

As the night wore on it became increasingly cooler as the rain turned from a light drizzle into a hard, pelting downpour.

Chapter 8

No one slept that night, and as a grey and damp dawn broke all of us had aching limbs and tired eyes. Even our horses had their heads down and looked sullen. A light breeze added to our discomfort by making the morning cooler. There was also an eerie silence, since the army, together with Spartacus and his Thracians, had left hours ago and the road from the bridge was now devoid of all traffic save a few miserable-looking dogs who were scavenging for food. I ordered everyone to search for anything that would burn, and had it piled into half a dozen huge bonfires, which were set alight and were soon crackling as the flames hungrily ate away at the wood. Nergal found a couple of wagons whose wheels had broken, which we dragged back to the bridge, broke up and also threw on the fires. While sentries kept watch we huddled around the fires and warmed ourselves. Then we rubbed down the horses, fetched water from the river for them and then fed them. Then we ourselves ate a hearty breakfast of hot porridge. By mid-morning we were feeling much livelier, and as the Romans had still not made an appearance I gave the order to break camp and follow the army.

We moved out at noon, just as the advance guard of the Roman army made an appearance on the horizon, a long, dark column of legionaries marching six-abreast down the road towards the bridge. I was the last to leave as from the bridge I watched the enemy approaching. I saw no cavalry, but had no doubt my chief opponent, Lucius Furius, was out there somewhere. I rode Remus away and joined the rest of the column as it trotted to meet the rear of the army.

We rode for an hour and then dismounted and walked the horses to give them a rest. Burebista walked beside me as more grey clouds heaped the sky.

'The Romans will be across the river today, lord,' he said, obviously anticipating the coming battle with relish, 'then we will be able turn and beat them.'

'You sound very certain,' I said.

'This army has good leaders, not like mine, and we have cavalry and the Romans do not.'

'They have some,' I reminded him.

He shook his head. 'Romans are foot soldiers, they see no use in cavalry save for scouting and carrying their fat officers. We Dacians and you Parthians are horsemen and know how to use cavalry on and off the battlefield. That's why we will win.'

He had an infectious enthusiasm, and I decided there and then that I would promote him to a senior command as soon as the cavalry was sufficiently large enough. Men prefer to follow confident leaders.

We caught up with the rear of the army in the late afternoon, to find Akmon sitting by the side of the road eating a piece of bread as his Thracians marched in step past him. I rode over to him as my horsemen dismounted and rested on either side of the road. Of the sun there was still no sign on this overcast day.

'The Romans were approaching the bridge just as we left.'

He nodded. 'They'll get their engineers to rig up a makeshift span and then they'll march across tomorrow. They obviously aren't in a hurry. Because they are fighting slaves, you see, they are taking their time. For a Roman, fighting slaves is akin to cleaning out latrines – a dirty, unpleasant business but necessary. That's why they are so hard on slaves who revolt, because it forces them to undertake dishonourable duties.'

'That is fortunate for us,' I said.

He finished his light meal and stood up. 'We'll have to fight them soon, though. Like Spartacus said, we can't keep running forever.'

'I've beaten Romans before.'

He eyed me. 'Took an eagle, so I've heard. That's impressive for one so young.'

'Truth is, I was lucky,' I said.

He slapped me on the shoulder. 'Let's hope your luck lasts, for all our sakes.'

We walked behind Akmon's Thracians as we followed the road up onto the plateau. As we rose higher the road passed through a narrow ravine that was flanked by high, sheer rock faces. I understood now why Spartacus wanted Forum Annii taken before the army moved. Even a small force would have been able to hold us up easily in such a narrow passage. The road through the ravine was littered with animal dung and stank, forcing us to watch our step as each of us navigated around what the army's livestock had deposited. It took us an hour to pass through the ravine and up onto the high plateau. Ahead of us the road went straight to Forum Annii, over which hung a pall of smoke. It appeared that Crixus and his Gauls had been successful. Beyond the town, in the distance, was a vast dust cloud that filled the horizon, the telltale sign of an army on the march. As it was dry here the plateau had obviously been spared the rain that had chilled us earlier. The army had made good time, being already beyond the town. As the road passed straight through Forum Annii and out the other side, we continued our march ahead. I continually sent back riders to relieve the ones who were making sure no Roman cavalry patrols would surprise us, but there was no sign of the enemy. In fact, there was no sign of anything, no birds or wildlife.

'Very quiet, don't you think?' observed Akmon.

As we approached the town I could see that the gates were open, with smoke and flames pouring from the gatehouse above. As we got nearer I saw two dead bodies lying on the road near the gates. Akmon ordered his men to adopt a close formation and to be on their guard. I passed the word to my horsemen to have their bows ready, in case we met any resistance. Akmon's men went into the town first and we immediately followed with arrows on our bowstrings, ready to provide covering fire if needed. But as we passed through the gates and into the town it became apparent that we would meet no resistance; indeed, I wondered if we would encounter anything alive, for bodies lay everywhere. The corpses of people killed by swords, with their tunics stained with blood where they had been run through and slashed by sharpened blades; bodies that had been bludgeoned by axes or clubs, and bodies that had been skewered by spears, the shafts left in their torsos. Blood was splashed on walls and flowed in rivulets in the streets. Some residents had been nailed to their front doors, though whether they had been alive or dead when this had been done to them I did not know. Dogs and cats had likewise been slaughtered, their carcasses lay strewn on the pavements and streets. I had never witnessed such a scene, and by the stunned silence of my men, neither had they. The stench of excrement and offal made my stomach heave, and Remus began to flick his head in alarm. I tried to calm him down as we made our way though the slaughterhouse that was once a town. We rode past a row of houses, each of which had a first-floor timber balcony supported on stone columns that extended over the pavement. From these balconies hung entire families: men, women, children and babies. Some of the bodies had been stripped naked, the women's breasts having been severed and the men's genitals hacked off. Blood was everywhere: on the balconies, staining the columns and splattering over the walls. So much blood.

As we neared the centre of the town we heard noises ahead. We continued on and came to the forum, as usual a large square surrounded on three sides by rows of shops and covered colonnades. A long, red-tiled building that towered over the surrounding houses occupied its fourth side. A large group of Gauls was gathered on the far side, cheering wildly, though at what I could not see. I dismounted and gave the order for the others to do the same.

Akmon and his Thracians had also filed into the forum and had formed up into two centuries in open order.

'Looks like the Gauls are indulging in their favourite sport,' he said. 'Killing people.'

'I'm going to put a stop to it.'

He eyed me with curiosity. 'Their blood is up, and they won't take kindly to you interfering.'

'It doesn't matter,' I said. 'I cannot allow innocent people to be slaughtered while I stand by and do nothing. It is dishonourable.'

He laughed. 'Very well, then. Me and my boys will lend a hand if your expertise at diplomacy is found wanting.'

'Thank you.'

'Don't thank me yet, young Parthian. You may still end up on the end of a Gaul's spear.'

I marched over to the commotion. I had my bow in my right hand and my quiver slung over my shoulder. Burebista walked a few paces behind me as my men formed a line across the forum and readied their bows. The cheering died away instantly as the Gauls became aware of our presence. Their ranks parted and I could see Oenomaus sitting in a large, ornate chair that had been placed in the square. He had one leg draped over one of its arms and was drinking from a richly decorated cup. He was obviously drunk. I also saw with horror a line of headless corpses lying nearby on the gravel with their severed heads lying next to them. Three grinning Gauls with bloody axes stood over the corpses, while behind Oenomaus, tied together and terrified, was a group of around twenty Romans. Obviously citizens of the town, their apparel seemed to be rich, though it was difficult to tell as they had obviously been beaten severely and their garments were ripped and bloody. The women were naked, no doubt having been raped by their captors.

Oenomaus jumped up when he saw me. He drained his cup and held it out with an outstretched arm. One of his men refilled it. 'You have no business here, Parthian,' he said, menacingly. He had the thick muscular neck and curly moustache and eyebrows of his race, with blue tattoos on his arms. His voice was deep and harsh. His overbearing insolence reminded me of his master, Crixus.

I looked at the headless corpses. 'Have not you seen enough blood, Oenomaus?'

'We are having a competition, to see if Nammeius, Orgetorix and Epasnactus can sever a head with a single blow. So far they have done well and Orgetorix is ahead by miles, so to speak.' There was uproarious laughter.

The Gauls banged their spears against their shields in salute. The clatter made the Roman captives shake and whimper. Akmon made his way over to where I stood facing Oenomaus.

'It is time for the killing to stop,' I said.

Oenomaus began to laugh. 'Do you hear that? The prince has spoken and we must all obey. Do you want me to wipe your royal arse while I'm at it.'

More laughter erupted as the Gauls mocked me.

'Be careful, Pacorus,' said Akmon, 'he's a sly bastard and useful with a sword.'

'So am I,' I said, putting my bow and quiver on the ground and drawing my sword. Talking was obviously futile, so I pointed my sword at Oenomaus.

'Fight me here, now,' I shouted.

He wiped his mouth across his face and drew his sword. His men began cheering loudly for my death, while behind me the Parthians and Thracians responded with shouts of their own. Oenomaus had a Roman gladius and he knew how to use it. He attacked immediately, coming at me with a slightly crouched stance. My spatha was longer but it wasn't a jabbing weapon, being designed to slash at opponents from horseback. Oenomaus believed he had the better of me at close quarters, and in truth he was no mean swordsman, delivering a succession of thrusting attacks that I deflected with difficulty. But I kept circling him so he had to keep moving. I lunged at him and he tried to disembowel me with a scything swing, but my reach was longer and his sword only sliced air. The onlookers were hurling encouragement and insults at the tops of their voices, and Gauls, Parthians and Thracians had formed a large circle around us.

The minutes passed and Oenomaus began sweating heavily. He had probably been killing all morning and drinking for a long time after that. His rapid attacks were obviously sapping his energy. I continued to keep out of his reach, waiting for my moment. He started to curse me now, demanding to know why I wouldn't fight like a man, why I was a woman. He worked himself into a frenzy and slashed at my head repeatedly with his gladius. I caught the last blow with the edge of my blade, held his sword momentarily in place, moved forward and kicked his left knee with my foot. He screamed in pain as I jumped back and his balance faltered. In that instant I thrust the point of the spatha forward into his left thigh. He screamed again and I knew he was beaten. His face was contorted in pain and hate, but he could barely deflect my attacks as I rained down a succession of swings and thrusts. The last one knocked the gladius out of his hand, and before he could retrieve it I had the point of my sword at his throat. The cheers died down instantly.

Oenomaus looked defiantly at me. 'Do it.'

'Why soil this fine blade with your blood?' I replied.

'You're a gutless son of a whore.'

'Release the prisoners to me, now!'

The Gauls began to gather behind their leader, their weapons drawn and ready to use, but my men raised their bows, ready to loose a hail of arrows into their ranks, and the Thracians also stood with my men. This clearly deterred them and made Oenomaus think again. Still looking directly at me and unflinching, he gave the order for the Romans to be released. The ragged band of terrified prisoners was roughly manhandled over to where I stood with my sword at the Gaul's throat and they instinctively huddled behind me. Oenomaus smiled.

'Take them, Parthian, no doubt you will take one of the men to warm your bed.'

Several of the Gauls sniggered and whooped with joy. I was seriously tempted to ram my sword through his throat. I resisted the temptation.

'Go now, Gaul,' I said, calmly, 'back to the cesspool that you crawled from.'

He spat on my boots, turned and limped away. His men followed sullenly. Moments later the forum was devoid of Gauls and I sheathed my sword.

'You should have killed him,' said Akmon, who now stood by my side. 'He'll come for you again, without a doubt. Make sure you sleep with one eye open. The next time it will be a dagger in the dark.' He barked an order for his men to form a column and slapped me hard across the back. 'Nice work with that sword, though. We'll make a gladiator out of you yet.'

As the Thracians marched in step from the forum one of the Romans, an elderly man with white wispy hair and pale skin nervously stepped forward from the group.

'Thank you,' he said in a low voice, his eyes looking at the ground.

'You are welcome.'

I gave the order for clothing or blankets to be found to restore the women's dignity. The elderly Roman, seeing that he and his group were not about to be killed, relaxed a little.

'My name is Quintus Hortonius, and I thank you on behalf of

myself and my family and friends.'

There were ten men of varying ages, six women, two of them of teenage years, two small children and a baby. They were all very pale. It appeared that all the women, young and old, had indeed been raped.

'We were hiding in my house when we were captured,' Hortonius continued. 'They must have thought we were rich for they demanded to know where our treasure was. They took all the gold and silver we had, then marched us to this place and...'

He stopped and stared at the bloody corpses that had been beheaded. Tears welled up in his eyes.

'You must leave this place,' I said.

'And go where?'

'There is a Roman army near. I will give you an escort to ensure you all stay out of danger, but you must leave now.'

I told Burebista to give them food and water for their journey, then detailed six of his men to escort them from the town and back down the road we had earlier travelled along. I told him that he and his men should abandon them if any Roman soldiers came into view. As my men rode from the forum the aged Roman approached me.

'I don't know your name, friend.'

'My name is Pacorus, prince of Hatra.'

He extended his hand for me to take. 'Then I thank you, Prince Pacorus, for sparing our lives.' I took his hand, it seemed churlish not to, and he smiled.

'Perhaps we shall meet again, when I shall be able to return the courtesy.'

'I doubt it,' I said, taking Remus' reins, 'for my destination is Parthia and that's a long way from here.'

'What is a prince doing among such a rabble?'

'It is a long story, sir, and I do not have the time to tell it to you.'

'Romans are brought up to believe that all foreign races are barbarians,' he said. 'And yet today you have shown that there is nobility in Parthia. I bid you a safe journey, young prince.'

'Thank you, sir. My men will ensure that you and your companions are not molested. I bid you farewell.'

The Gauls had started several fires in the town, and by now they were taking hold and spewing dense black smoke into the sky. I watched the survivors being escorted down the road, a sad band of homeless wretches trudging over the flagstones. At least they had their lives and were in their homeland.

We caught up with Akmon and his men about a mile from the

town. There was no sign of the Gauls. Three hours later we found the army, camped around fifteen miles south of Forum Annii and spread across the plain from one side of the tree-covered slopes of the mountains to the other. As usual, and which always made me smile, the Roman camp had been erected in the dead centre, with its neat avenues and blocks of tents. After dismissing the men and instructing them to find our camp, I rode into the Roman camp.

I found Spartacus in his tent, sitting in a chair. He looked tired and drawn, his face showing signs of stubble where he had not shaved and there were dark rings around his eyes. He put up a hand in recognition when he saw me and beckoned me to sit. Claudia appeared from the back of the tent, looking equally exhausted.

'Long journey?' I asked as she poured me cup of wine then sat beside her husband.

'Endless,' he replied.

'Where's Gallia?' I asked

That raised a smile from Claudia. 'Have no fear, little one, your beloved is safe and well protected by your horsemen. She and Diana are with your cavalry.'

I felt myself blushing. 'Well, I meant to say, is Gallia and everyone else safe?'

'Of course you did,' said Claudia, teasingly.

Spartacus was in no mood for levity, though. 'Where are the Romans?'

'No sign of them, lord,' I replied.

He looked at me searchingly with narrowed, bloodshot eyes. 'Word reached me that you passed through Forum Annii.'

I wondered what other words he had heard.

'I did, what was left of it.'

'You disapprove of Crixus' methods?'

'I disapprove of Crixus entirely,' I replied.

'So do I,' added Claudia.

'You may be interested to know that he suffered a nasty head wound when taking the town. Seems the garrison put up more of a fight than was expected. That's why his men went on a rampage when they got inside. They lost nearly four hundred dead before they managed to scale the walls. At this moment Crixus is lying in his tent with a mighty headache.'

'Pity his head wasn't split open,' I said.

Spartacus smiled. 'What would you both have me do with him? Kill him, banish him? If I did that I would lose a quarter of my army. The problem I have is that there is a Roman army approaching and I need every man I can get hold of, especially one that likes killing Romans.'

'He certainly likes that,' I added bitterly.

Spartacus grimaced. 'Needs must, Pacorus. This army is bound together by a fear and loathing of the Romans, but some of those bonds are tenuous. I have to keep this army strong and united or we will lose.' He rose and cupped his wife's face in his hands, kissed her and then looked at me. 'Go and get some food and rest. Embrace Gallia and forget about Crixus.'

I rose and saluted. 'Yes, lord.'

'Oh and Pacorus,' he said.

'Yes, lord?'

'I heard about your little disagreement with Oenomaus. You should have killed him.'

I would have to add him to the list of people who were still alive but, according to others, shouldn't be.

I found the cavalry quartered a mile east of the main camp, near the headwaters of a river called the Aciris. The spot was heavily wooded and thus well shaded, was near to water and away from the stench of human and livestock dung that hung over the army. I found Gallia practising her archery with Diana, watched over by Gafarn and Godarz. It was good to see them all, and I ran over to Gallia and embraced her. I kissed her on the cheek and then greeted the others.

'How's their archery coming along?' I said to Gafarn.

'Good, with practice they could be as good as I,' he replied, 'and they're already better than you, not that's much of a boast.'

'All the carts safe and sound?' I asked Godarz, ignoring Gafarn's jibe.

'Yes, highness.'

'Excellent, it's good to be back. I would speak with the Lady Gallia alone.'

'Same time tomorrow, ladies,' said Gafarn, as he and the others took their leave, leaving me alone with my Gallic princess. She smiled and linked her arm with mine.

'I'm glad you're safe, I was worried,' she said.

'You were?'

'Of course. Just because I'm a Gaul does not mean I don't have emotions. We are not all like Crixus.'

'Of course not,' I stammered. 'I didn't mean to insult you.'

'You are always so formal, Pacorus. You must learn to relax more.'

With my heart beating ten to the dozen that was difficult. I wondered if she knew the extent of my feelings for her? I dared to hope. We walked up into the trees and rested beneath a tall birch. The birds were singing and violence and war seemed a long way away.

'The march here was hard,' she mused.

'Spartacus did well to put some distance between us and the Romans.'

'We bypassed the town that Crixus took. They say that it was frightful afterwards.'

'It was,' I said bitterly. 'Crixus killed just about everyone and everything, and when the Romans discover what he did they will be thirsting for vengeance.'

I turned to look at her. Her thick hair shone like gold in the daylight, her lips full and inviting, and her eyes the purest blue. I could feel my heart pounding in my chest as I leaned towards her. Then our lips touched as we kissed long and tenderly. And in those moments I experienced bliss such as I had never believed was possible.

The next two days were quiet and gave me time to think about organisation. I was pleased that the cavalry was now nearing a thousand strong, though equipment, weapons and horses were constant problems. There was no way that recruits could be trained in horse archery while the army was moving, so any recruits that joined who could ride, but who could not use a bow or any other weapon, were placed under Byrd's command as scouts. Soon he had over two hundred men looking to him for orders, which was beyond him as I had forgotten that he had been a civilian scout when he joined us prior to our expedition into Cappadocia. He came to see me as I was grooming Remus on the morning of the second day.

'I'm not a general, lord. Know nothing about horses or feeding men.'

I could see that he was unhappy. 'No, of course not. I did not think.'

'You general, lord, not I.'

I thought about putting him under Godarz, but then Godarz had his hands full taking care of logistics, so in the end I attached the new recruits to Nergal, who seemed happy that his command had increased. Indeed, he was generally in good spirits as he had taken a wild Spanish girl called Praxima as his woman. In general those who had joined Spartacus were mainly men, either herdsmen, shepherds or field hands, with the odd smattering of runaway town slaves. However, as news of the slave revolt had spread more women had drifted into camp. They were Gauls, mainly, with many of them having a very unsettling resemblance to Crixus. They joined their male brethren, but other females attached themselves to the Thracians or Germans, and a few, a small band, found their way into the cavalry. I did my best to put them off, of course, but Praxima could ride, and ride well, and having sweet-talked Nergal I suddenly had another woman on horseback. He was delighted and she also happy, and as I wanted a happy second-in-command, I acquiesced.

'In any case,' Gallia reminded me, 'you accepted me and Diana into your cavalry, so you can hardly turn her away.'

'That was different.'

'How so?'

'Well, for one thing you could both ride,' I said.

'So can she, actually much better than either of us.'

'Well, you two can shoot a bow,' I replied, irritably.

'Only because you and Gafarn taught us. I'm sure Nergal can teach her.'

'If you say so. Anyway, it's done now.'

'Is my lord prince annoyed by my questions?' she said, mischievously.

'Yes, no. I just don't approve, that's all. I've heard she was a prostitute.'

She glared at me. 'Forced to be a whore by her Roman masters, you mean. Don't be so pompous.'

She was right, of course, as she always seemed to be, which made it worse, but I had to admit that overall things were going well. I had decided that if the number of horsemen kept increasing I was going to make Nergal and Burebista commanders of their own dragons. But perhaps I was living in a fantasy land. Reality rudely interrupted my dreams when our camp was invaded by a large group of Gauls led by Crixus, his head bandaged in a grey cloth. They marched over to where I was standing and surrounded me in a menacing manner. I guessed there were around fifty of them, all carrying swords or spears and all intent on seeing my head split open, it appeared.

'The time has come for you and me to settle affairs,' Crixus said, fondling his two-bladed axe affectionately. He was bare headed and dressed in a tunic, trousers and leather boots. He wore no mail shirt, carried no shield and was obviously supremely confident. His hair was as wild as ever and his moustache hung down to his chest. He really was quite revolting.

'It will be my pleasure,' I said. I too wore no armour and carried only a sword and Cookus' dagger.

By now the camp had stirred into action and dozens of my men were forming up around the Gauls. Nergal angrily pushed his way through them and stood by my side, sword in hand, to be joined seconds later by Burebista. Crixus was totally unconcerned about the threat to him and his men.

'Are you going to fight or don't you want to get your princely little hands dirty?'

I told Nergal and Burebista to step away and drew my sword. 'You boast too much, Gaul.'

The assembled throng widened as Crixus and I began circling each other, and I was hardly aware of the sound of horns and trumpets being blown and the frantic banging of drums in the background. Moment later there were loud shouts as Byrd rode into the mass of men. Individuals jumped aside as he rode his horse into the space occupied by Crixus and me.

'Romani, Romani,' was all he said, his eyes wide with excitement.

The fight between Crixus and me would have to wait, for a bigger fight was going to take place first, for the Romans had arrived.

Men scattered in all directions as they frantically mustered in their companies. Crixus and his Gauls raced headlong for their own camp, while I ran to the fenced-off area where Remus was quartered. Gafarn had already saddled him, and was in the process of saddling his own horse. Gallia and Diana were also present, presumably having been sharpening their archery skills. I embraced Gallia then jumped onto Remus' back.

'Don't let them out of your sight,' I ordered Gafarn, pointing to the two women. 'I'll be back as soon as I can. I'm depending on you.'

I'll take care of them, have no fear,' he replied. 'You take care of yourself.'

Akmon's Roman camp was about a mile away. I steered Remus through groups of Germans, Gauls, Thracians and others, all hurriedly gathering weapons and equipment and falling into line, their appointed officers hurling abuse at them and shoving them into formation. I reached Spartacus' tent and went inside. Crixus was hot on my tail, sweating profusely after his run. I noticed that there was a bloodstain on his bandage – hopefully he was in great pain. Spartacus acknowledged me as I joined him at the table, upon which Akmon had placed small blocks of wood and was arranging them into two separate groups. Castus raced in seconds later and joined us at the table.

'We're all here. Good,' said Spartacus. 'We haven't got much time so here's the plan. These are the Romans.' He pointed to where

Akmon had arranged one group of blocks into a straight line. 'We will attack them with a pig's head through their centre.'

'Pig's head?' I asked.

'It's simple,' said Akmon, 'one section of the army is shaped like a spear point. This is our army,' he pointed at the line of wood blocks opposite those representing the Romans. He took one block and pushed it beyond the others in the line, then placed two blocks immediately behind it. It looked like a pyramid. 'See, a wedge shape that can pierce the enemy line.' He then pushed the pyramid made from three blocks into the Roman blocks and forced it through.

'The Romans won't be expecting us to attack, that's our advantage,' continued Spartacus. 'So we'll split their centre, smash straight through, and after that it will just be a matter of mopping up.'

'Let my Gauls break them,' said Crixus.

'Not this time, Crixus,' replied Spartacus. 'You and your men will be on the left. They will form a line right up to the trees on the slopes of the mountain. Castus, your Germans will do the same on the right. Right up to the slopes – you must not let yourself be outflanked.'

What about me?' I asked.

'What about you?' sneered Crixus. 'It's obvious that Spartacus has no use for you and your dainty little horses.'

Spartacus smiled at me. 'On the contrary, Pacorus and his men will form up behind my Thracians in the centre.'

'Not on the wings?' I was confused.

'If we were on a wide expanse of ground, then yes,' said Spartacus. 'But the end of this plateau is narrow and we can't be outflanked.'

'Neither can the Romans,' said Castus.

'That's right. Which is why we must punch through their centre. Split them in two and then Pacorus' horse can pour through the gap and sweep around behind them. The result will be two groups of surrounded and isolated Romans.' Spartacus swept the Roman blocks off the table and onto the floor. 'Simple.'

It did indeed seem simple, but I could tell that Spartacus had thought it out carefully beforehand. He had chosen this spot on which to fight. Claudia brought a tray of cups and a jug of wine. She smiled at me and poured wine into the cups, then handed one to each of us. Spartacus raised his cup.

'Victory. May whatever gods you follow be with you this day.' We raised our cups and drank to his toast.

'And now, to your posts.'

Crixus drained his cup, belched loudly and left, followed by Akmon. I shook hands with Castus and he too departed, while I nodded at Spartacus as Claudia handed him his mail shirt and helmet. I rode back to the cavalry camp, where Nergal, Burebista, Godarz, Byrd, Gafarn and Rhesus were waiting. I noticed that Gallia, Diana and Praxima were stood a few feet away, checking their bows and daggers. I was determined that they would see no fighting this day. Around them men and horses were being formed up; the activity was hurried but not disorganised. I gathered my officers in a semi-circle and told them of Spartacus' plan for the coming battle.

'Makes sense,' said Godarz. 'There is not enough room for us to attack on the flanks.'

'We will form up in three blocks, one of three hundred at the front and the others each two hundred strong,' I told them. 'I will be in the lead; Nergal will command the middle group and Burebista the third. Godarz, you will command the rest, which will form the reserve. The reserve will be made up of those who have had little training and who do not know how to shoot a bow or use a lance from the saddle.'

'I would prefer to fight,' said Godarz.

'If things turn out differently from Spartacus' plan, my friend,' I told him, 'then you will get your wish.'

After I had dismissed them I went to see the women, bringing Gafarn along.

'I want you to stay with them,' I told him. 'And make sure they stay well away from the fighting.'

'I will do my best, highness, as I told you earlier when you gave me exactly the same command.'

Gallia and Diana were filling their quivers with arrows, while Praxima was buckling on a belt with a sheathed sword attached. Where did she get that from?

'You will all stay with Godarz and Gafarn, with the reserve,' I ordered them.

'I want to kill Romans,' said Praxima, who was slipping a dagger into her right boot.

'So do I,' seconded Gallia, her plaited blond hair running down her back. Diana said nothing.

'Have you considered that the Romans might kill you first?' I asked them. 'Being part of an army means obeying orders, and you will obey mine.'

I pointed at Godarz and Gafarn to emphasise the point and then returned to where my horsemen were forming up, Rhesus marshalling the companies into line. The smell of leather and horses was comforting as the cavalry concentrated in the centre of the line, behind Akmon's Thracians. The army used exactly the same formations and tactics as the Romans. 'Their weapons, training and tactics have conquered half the world,' Spartacus had told me. 'I see no reason not to copy them.' And so it was that in front of me thousands of men formed themselves into units called centuries, which were eight ranks deep and ten files wide, though men were detached from the last rank to carry out other duties: standard bearer, a horn blower, water carriers and medical orderlies. Each century had a centurion, a man who commanded the unit and who led from the front. He stood on the extreme right in the front rank. Six centuries made up what was called a cohort, which was around five hundred strong. In battle, as here in front of me, the centuries of the cohort deployed beside each other in a line. Ten cohorts made up a legion, which thus numbered around five thousand men in total. The normal battlefield deployment for a legion, so Spartacus told me, was four cohorts in the first line, three in the second line and three in the third line. But for this battle Spartacus had his Thracians deployed with one cohort at the front, two cohorts immediately behind in the second line, three behind them and four cohorts in the fourth line. There was little space between the four lines, which in my opinion made the whole arrangement very vulnerable to enemy missiles.

The plateau at this point was around two miles wide between the tree-covered mountain slopes. On the left were the Gauls, drawn up in three lines, and in the centre were the Thracians – one legion drawn up in three lines on the left next to the Gauls, Spartacus with his 'pig's head', then another legion of Thracians deployed in three lines on his right. On the right wing were Castus and his Germans forming another two legions. The army filled the space between the slopes, so there was no chance of being outflanked. I rode forward with Nergal and Burebista to the 'Pig's head'. We left our horses at the rear of the formation and walked through the centuries to the front. The mood among the Thracians was amazingly relaxed considering many might be dead in a few hours. I also noticed that all the Thracians had pila, swords, mail shirts, shields and helmets, while many of the Gauls and Germans had no armour and only clubs for weapons. Clearly Spartacus made sure his own men were the best equipped. But then, as they were his most reliable and loyal troops, this made sense. I found him standing in front of the first cohort with Akmon.

'Decided to fight on foot, Pacorus?'

'No, lord. I was going to ask from where you will direct the battle.'
'From here, of course,' he replied.
I was horrified. He stood a good chance of being cut down in the first clash. 'But lord,' I said, 'if you are killed then the army is lost.'
'I am just one man, Pacorus. If I am killed others will take my place. But I cannot ask men to fight for me if I stand at the rear. You understand? Besides, once the battle starts command and control become largely impossible.'
'And it won't be long before it starts by the look of it,' said Akmon, grimly.
We turned to see the Roman army approaching, a long line of red shields. The sun was glinting off thousands of helmets and pila, while overhead a dust cloud kicked up by hobnailed sandals hung over the entire force. They were about three miles away, maybe less, and their appearance prompted cheers, hoots of derision and catcalls from our army, though I noticed that the Thracians remained silent. Spartacus and Akmon had clearly trained them well. Spartacus laid a hand on my shoulder.
'Remember, when we break their centre you must be hard on our heels. Get behind them and shower them with missiles. Don't get close until they break. And good luck.'
'The same to you, lord,' I said. Then we ran back to our horses and rejoined our men. Remus kicked at the earth with his hooves and other horses, sensing the coming slaughter, reared up in alarm. Their riders tried to calm their nerves by stroking their necks and talking quietly to them, though perhaps they only succeeded in transmitting their own nervousness to their animals.
I signalled for the horse to move forward, to the rear of the 'pig's head'. Eight hundred men and their horses ambled forward as the Romans got closer. I was in the front rank of the first group, Rhesus beside me, in the centre of the line. We were close to the last rank of Thracians, many of whom looked back nervously at the men on horses who were at their backs. Their officers barked at them to look to their front, as the crump, crump of the marching Roman army got closer. Suddenly the sound of trumpets echoed across the valley and the slave army started to move forward. From my vantage point astride Remus I could see the Romans dressing their lines, clearly prior to launching an assault, but instead Spartacus was going to launch his assault first. As the rear ranks moved forward so did we, and I held my bow over my head to signal my men to prepare to fire. I strung an arrow as the Thracian front ranks closed to within around a hundred feet of the enemy. I

shot my arrow high into the sky in a wide arc, as eight hundred others did likewise. The arrows would do little damage to helmeted Romans who were able to hoist their shields over their heads, but while they were concentrating on protecting themselves they would be unable to throw their pila. And so it was, for as the arrows disappeared into the Roman ranks the leading ranks of the Thracians threw their pila, drew their swords and then sprinted forward to stab at their opponents, using their shields as individual battering rams. The Roman shield was an amazing item: three layers of oak or birch glued together with wooden reinforcing strips added to the back and faced with thin leather. In the middle is cut a circle, across which is placed a metal bar for holding the shield. Over the carrying bar, on the side facing the enemy, is a metal plate with a round, bulging boss, which can be used to smash into an opponent in a close-quarters fight.

The following Thracian ranks also charged, and immediately the air was filled with the shouts and screams of men killing and being killed. The air was thick with javelins and arrows, for the Romans had their own archers and though their range was inferior to that of our own bows, some still found their mark, hitting exposed limbs and faces. The Thracian rear ranks move steadily forward, a sure sign that the front ranks were cutting their way through Roman flesh and bone. I glanced to my left and right and saw that the slave line was still edging forward, though not at the rapid rate of the Thracians. Already men were ferrying the wounded to the rear, to be treated by those trained in medical care.

We could not fire any more arrows for fear of hitting our own men, so all we could do was wait. Time to seemed to move slowly and I started to get concerned. If Spartacus did not break the enemy then we would be mere spectators to the slaughter. The sound of thousands of men doing battle was like a deep and constant roar, though occasionally a high-pitched scream could be heard as a sword or spear pierced flesh. Then a great cheer reached us and the Thracians in front of us increased their forward advance. The Roman line had given way! Spartacus was through. As the great wedge of Thracians ground its way forward, a large gap suddenly appeared on its left flank. In the chaos of combat the 'pig's head' had actually veered right, but it was enough.

I turned and yelled at those behind me, 'for Parthia!' Then I dug my knees into Remus' flanks. He sprang forward. My men cheered and followed me as I steered Remus towards the ragged gap that could have been no more than two hundred feet across and was filled with dead and dying men. I galloped past a century of disorganised legionaries which was being assailed from the front. At the same time it was also trying to form a line of shields on its left flank which was now hanging in the air. They were too late. I shot one legionary in the chest as my men poured arrow after arrow as they passed into the densely packed soldiers. Then my three hundred horsemen were behind the Roman lines as the 'pig's head' continued to wheel right and began grinding its way into the side of the Roman army's newly created left flank. Attacked in the front and on the flank, I surmised that it would not be long before that part of the Roman army would break. I wheeled my men right to take them behind the Romans. We totalled only eight hundred cavalry, but caused panic as we thundered along the rear of the Roman formations and peppered them with arrows. Nergal told me afterwards that many Romans had not realised that our horsemen were the enemy and had at first ignored them, only to be shot in the back. Indeed, so easy had been the shooting that many of his men had exhausted their arrows long before the Romans had realised their mistake.

I saw a group of Roman horsemen ahead, some holding banners and others dressed in helmets similar to mine but with red plumes instead of white. They were the general and his staff. I called my men to follow me as I spurred Remus towards them. We attacked in a wedge formation, six ranks deep, fifty men in each rank. The Romans saw us, but instead of deploying to attack, they turned and attempted to flee. Their steeds were swift, no doubt the finest breeds money could buy, but our mounts were just as quick and they could not outrun our bows. Arrows hit speeding riders and horses as we closed on them. Some men were thrown from their mounts when their horses were hit, others slumped in their saddles as one or more arrows pierced their flesh. One or two Romans halted and turned, no doubt intending to fight us with their swords. They were shot and killed before they had a chance to use their blades. I saw one officer, a man with a bright red cloaking around his shoulders, riding furiously away. I screamed at Remus, who galloped as though there was a demon chasing him, his eyes wide and nostrils flared. I closed on the Roman, who glanced back at me and kicked at his horse furiously to speed him up. But I was close enough to him now. He glanced back one last time and must have known that he would not escape. I released the bowstring and he screamed as the arrow went through his cloak, through his armour and into his back. He crashed to the ground, dead.

I signalled for the horns to recall the men, and minutes later we were trotting back towards the battle, except that the battle was coming to us, for in front of us were hundreds of Roman soldiers! I was momentarily gripped by panic, but then realised that many of the Romans had no weapons or shields. They were fleeing as fast as their legs could carry them.

'Halt,' I shouted to my men. 'Stand still and shoot them as they pass. They will not fight; they are running.'

We quickly deployed into one long line and shot at the Romans as they neared us. We must have cut down two or three hundred before those following veered right and left in an effort to avoid us. By now the whole plain was dotted with running Romans, but what caught my eye were more Roman horsemen, a small group who seemed to have retained their discipline. One of them was riding among the fleeing Romans with his drawn sword, shouting and cursing at them. Then I recognised him – Lucius Furius.

'Follow me,' I ordered as I kicked Remus forward. I made straight for Furius. This time he would not escape.

'Stand, stand, you cowards,' he was shouting at the top of his voice, to no effect.

I strung an arrow as I neared him, but before I could release it one of his men shouted a warning to him. He turned, saw me and ducked in the saddle as the arrow shot over him and into one of his men. He turned his horse and headed towards me as his command was shot to pieces. I shoved my bow back into its case and drew my sword – shooting him would be too easy. We charged straight at each other, but instead of attacking me with his sword as we closed he threw himself at me and we both tumbled to the ground in a heap. I was momentarily stunned, the wind was knocked out of me, but I staggered to my feet as he did likewise. He drew his sword and lunged at me. My sword, knocked out of my hand, lay several feet away so I pulled my dagger and tried to parry his blade with it. But our duel was interrupted when an arrow slammed into his right thigh. He screamed and clutched at his leg, dropping his sword as he did so. I walked over to where my sword lay and picked it up. But before I could get close to him and finish him off, more Roman cavalry appeared and closed around him. By now my men were also forming up around me and were shooting Romans from their saddles. But Furius escaped with my arrow sticking out of his leg, his horse led away by a subordinate.

Around us screaming Gauls hurtled past, cutting down any Roman they encountered with glee. I remounted Remus as Nergal and Burebista arrived.

'A great victory, highness,' beamed Nergal. 'The Romans are destroyed.'

'Well done,' I said to them both, and then I saw Praxima ride past us, accompanied by Gallia. I cursed with fury. 'Take the men and help hunt down the Romans,' I told Nergal. 'Remember, those you let escape you will have to fight again.'

'Yes, highness. Where are you going?'

'To hunt down a more troublesome prey,' I replied. 'Now go.'

As my men reformed and galloped off to join the pursuit, I followed two riders who were endeavouring to reach the fleeing Romans. Some groups of legionaries had attempted to halt and form themselves into centuries, but they were hopelessly outnumbered and surrounded, and were soon assailed from all sides and cut down. I shuddered as I saw Gauls hacking the heads off some dead Romans and carry them off as trophies. I caught up with the two women just as Gallia loosed an arrow that hit a running centurion in the back, sending him crashing to the ground. My chest filled with pride at her marksmanship. Then Praxima halted her horse, jumped from the saddle onto a Roman soldier and in one deft movement drew her dagger and slit his throat. I drew Remus up in front of them and removed my helmet.

'Stand still, both of you. What in the name of all that's sacred do you think you are doing?' I bellowed.

'Killing Romans,' came Praxima's calm reply.

Gallia looked away from me, strung another arrow and released the bowstring. I turned to see a Roman, who must have been at least three hundred feet away, spin to the ground as he was hit. Praxima screamed with delight and clapped her hands.

'Like my friend told you,' said Gallia, 'we are killing Romans.'

I pointed at Praxima. 'Get on your horse. Now!'

She shrugged and vaulted onto her horse's back. I then rode Remus over to her horse, gathered its reins, did the same to Gallia's horse, and then led them both back to camp and away from danger.

'No more killing Romans today,' I told them.

'Release us,' said Gallia.

'No.'

'Why not? The Romans are running.'

I halted and turned to face her. She and Praxima wore cavalry helmets with large cheek guards fastened beneath their chins. They both sat proudly in the saddle and Gallia looked as beautiful as ever in her boots, tight-fitting leggings and tunic. If it had been a training exercise I would have been lavishing praise on them both, but it wasn't and I didn't.

'Running men can still stop and kill women,' I hissed. 'And besides, I ordered you to stay with Godarz and Gafarn. That's why.'

'Are you going to beat us, lord, for our insolence?' said Praxima, laughing.

'Are you going to put us over your knee and spank us?' added Gallia.

The latter option was most appealing. I said nothing. By now the slaughter had moved on and we threaded our way through dead and dying men, mostly Romans, where the battle had been fiercely contested for a while as each side stabbed and hacked at their opponents. Then there were the bodies of those who had tried to run, with telltale wounds to their backs. I talked quietly to Remus as he threw up his head nervously when he heard the cries and moans of those who lay on the ground, some with bellies slit open and their entrails lying on the grass, others with gaping head wounds. Some sat up and staring in disbelief at a severed arm or leg lying next to them, oblivious to their lifeblood gushing away from a leg stump or arm socket. The women were silent now; it was undoubtedly the first time that they had seen the gory aftermath of a battle.

I found Godarz and Gafarn sitting on the ground with the other members of the reserve, close by their tethered horses. My anger rose as I thought of what might have happened to Gallia, and then evaporated as the men jumped to their feet and started to cheer me wildly. Gafarn raced over as I handed the women back their reins and then dismounted.

'Victory, highness,' he beamed.

'A great day,' added Godarz, who shook my hand.

Others gathered round me and offered their hands. Their faces were full of admiration and joy, and I had to admit that I was proud to be their leader. Even though they themselves had not fought, they had obeyed their orders and stayed where they were. At least most of them did. When the commotion had died down I pulled Godarz and Gafarn aside and asked them to explain the presence of Praxima and Gallia on the battlefield.

'They must have worked it out beforehand, highness,' said Gafarn. Godarz continued. 'Diana came to us both and said she felt unwell, then promptly fainted. So we attended to her and in the excitement Gallia and Praxima slipped away. It was a while before we even noticed that they had gone. They're a sly pair and no mistake.'

'Indeed,' I said. There was little point in reprimanding them, and in any case it would have been mean-spirited to do so in such propitious circumstances. I thanked them both and then left them to find the truants. I found them, plus Diana by some water troughs, congratulating each other as they were taking the saddles off their horses. Gallia had removed her helmet and unplaited her hair. She looked as alluring as ever.

'I congratulate you, ladies, on your stratagem,' I said, 'though perhaps next time you might like to obey orders like the rest of my horsemen.'

'We are not standing idly by when the Romans are so close,' said Gallia with fire in her eyes.

'We have won a great victory, so let us give thanks for that. As for you two, all I am asking is that you obey orders. You can't have an army without discipline.'

'You are a great leader of horsemen, lord,' said Praxima, out of the blue, 'and we are proud to serve with you.' She then knelt and bowed her head.

Her flattery caught me at a disadvantage and I felt myself blushing. 'Well, I, er. I have to report to Spartacus,' I stammered, beating a hasty retreat. Once again they had outwitted me. Perhaps I ought to make them officers. I dismissed the idea as ridiculous. Remus was blown, so I left him with Godarz and the attendants, along with my helmet, cloak and bow and borrowed his horse to find Spartacus. The adrenalin rush of combat was leaving me now and my limbs began to ache, though they did not shake. I rode through groups of soldiers making their way back towards their tents. It was a mark of the discipline that had been instilled in the army that they were still in their centuries, albeit the ranks looked a little ragged. Some were bandaged, other had cuts to the face and head, but most seemed to be unhurt and all were in good spirits. I found Castus with his Germans and called after him. I caught up with him, dismounted and we embraced. He had a cut over his right eye.

He slapped me hard on the shoulder. 'Not a scratch on you. Did you see any fighting?'

'Not as much as you, obviously,' I said.

'Some bastard Roman tried to shove his sword through my eye but I skewered him first. It was bloody work at the start, then they broke and suddenly I was running as fast as a hare trying to catch the bastards. They dropped their weapons and ran. Amazing.' I think some of my boys are still running after them. I left Cannicus to sort them out and bring them back in. Thought I should report to Spartacus, if he's here that is.'

Behind us I could hear the distinctive growl of Akmon. 'Pick your feet up. Just because you've enjoyed a bit of butchery doesn't mean you can slouch.'

We moved aside as he passed, leading a large column of his Thracians that had been chasing after the fleeing Romans. Behind him, being carried on a litter, was the body of a dead Roman.

'Still alive, then,' he called to us. 'You two might want to have a look at this.'

'Where is Spartacus?' I asked.

'In his tent, being patched up by his woman, I suppose.'

'He is hurt?' asked Castus, in alarm.

'Nothing serious,' replied Akmon.

Later, in camp, we found Claudia stitching Spartacus' left arm with a needle and twine, the big Thracian sat in a chair drinking wine as she did so. He seemed annoyed rather than in pain. He nodded to me and Castus as we entered, then frowned as the litter carrying the dead Roman was brought in and placed on the floor in front of him.

'I don't want dead bodies in my tent,' said Claudia.

'Pardon, lady,' said Akmon, 'but this dead body is important.'

'Who is it?' asked Spartacus.

Akmon handed Spartacus a scroll covered in blood. 'We found him face down with an arrow in his back and this in the saddlebag of his horse. Says his name is Consul Publius Varinius, charged by the people and senate of Rome to destroy the slave rebellion.'

Spartacus got out of his chair and examined the body, which was laid face down on the litter.

'That's my arrow, I think,' I said.

'Well,' smiled Spartacus, 'it would appear that Pacorus has killed a consul.'

'What's a consul?' I said.

'Like a king,' replied Spartacus.

'They'll not take this lightly,' sniffed Akmon.

'No indeed,' said Spartacus, straightening and wincing in pain. 'Cut the head off and stick it on a pole a mile down the road.'

'Can you take it away now,' said Claudia, 'it's disgusting.'

Spartacus signalled for the bearers to haul it away, then sat back down and held his left arm.

'Getting slow in your old age?' said Akmon.

'I'll never be as slow as you, Akmon. There's wine on the table.'

We greeted Claudia and helped ourselves to the drink.

'Castus, pass my thanks on to your men,' said Spartacus, 'they did well today.'

'Thank you, lord.'

'Yours too, Pacorus,' he added, 'though I thought that volley of arrows you fired before we charged was going to land on us. I would have preferred some warning'

'My men know how to shoot, lord,' I said.

'Anyhow, Crixus and his men are still chasing the Romans, I believe. Tomorrow there will be a council of war. There is much to do. Do we have any idea of casualties?'

'Most of my men are still pursuing Romans,' I said, 'but I believe we suffered few losses.'

'Cannicus is taking a count of my men now,' said Castus.

'One thing's for sure' added Akmon, 'the Romans have suffered more than us.'

Indeed they had. Nergal and Burebista came in three hours later, to rapturous applause from the camp. The men's horses were lathered in sweat and some had wounds. I ordered that they be attended to immediately. Nergal's hair was matted with sweat and grime and his face was dirty, but he was beaming with pleasure as he told me of his pursuit of the Romans and the accompanying slaughter. He threw a Roman standard, a pole with a square red flag near the top, at my feet, as did Burebista.

'We found these lying on the ground, highness,' said Nergal.

'You have both done well, this is your victory,' I replied. 'Get your horses seen to and then get some food inside you. Then you can both take these standards to Spartacus, with my compliments.'

Nergal beamed and Burebista reached over and slapped him on the back. There is nothing more infectious than victory.

Our own losses amounted to five dead and thirty wounded, none seriously. All the dead were brought back to camp and cremated that night on a huge pyre, the flames lancing high into the darkness. The entire camp gathered to pay their respects and I said a silent prayer to Shamash for bringing us victory. I stood next to Gallia and watched the bodies of our comrades being consumed by fire. She had combed her hair and changed into a loose-fitting green tunic and brown leggings. Praxima and Diana had likewise changed and no longer looked like women warriors, rather examples of feminine beauty. Diana stood between Gallia and Gafarn, Praxima, her arms around Nergal's waist, next to Gallia.

'That could have been you,' I whispered into Gallia's ear as we watched the flames.

'Or you,' she hissed.

'It's my task to fight, not yours.'

'You are not mine to command,' she said.

'I do not command. I ask.'

The timber crackled as the flames ate away at it, spewing cinders into the sky.

'And I ask you for the right to fight at your side.' She turned to look at me, her eyes pleading and her voice seductive. 'You would not deny me that right, would you? We are friends, are we not?'

I knew I would never win this argument, so I told her that we would discuss it at another time. Despite my aches and pains I could not sleep that night, so in the early hours I dressed and walked out of the camp, beyond where the guards were pacing to where the battle had taken place. There was silence now, for those who had been detailed to collect our wounded and kill any injured Romans they found, had finished their tasks. Better a quick death from a slit throat than being tortured by Crixus' Gauls, I thought. The dead would be stripped tomorrow and the weapons of the Roman army collected. It should be a rich haul, and would go a long way to fully equipping our army.

I don't know how long I walked for, but I suddenly became aware that it was cold. The clouds had departed to leave a clear, moonlit night. I gathered my cloak around me and then saw a solitary figure standing like a statue ahead. I made sure I had attached my sword before I walked towards him. As I drew closer I recognised the strong profile and broad shoulders of Spartacus.

'Lord?'

As fast as lightning he turned and drew his sword to face me, then relaxed as he saw who it was.

'Couldn't sleep either, eh?'

'No, lord. How is your arm?'

'It's just a scratch.'

He replaced his sword in its scabbard, and then turned to stare into the distance once more.

'Hard to believe there was a battle here. It's so quiet.'

I looked at the corpses heaped on the ground as far as the eye could see.

'A grim harvest,' I mused.

He smiled. 'This is nothing compared to what is coming. Until now the Romans thought that they were dealing with a few ill-armed slaves. But after today they know that they have a real war on their hands. From this point on they will be hell-bent on avenging the gross insult we have dealt them. When news reaches Rome of their defeat they will send a new army, and it will be larger and better led.'

'Then we shall need a bigger army,' I said.

'Indeed we shall.' He sighed and turned to walk back to camp. 'Come on, let's have some warm wine. How're Gallia and Diana?'
'Despite my orders, Gallia rode into battle.'
Spartacus laughed out loud. 'She's feisty, that one.'
'She shot a Roman centurion and killed another legionary with her bow.'
'She'll want to fight again, now she's got a taste for it.'
'That is what I'm afraid of,' I said.
'In this war, Pacorus, every man and woman with us is fighting for their life. The Romans will make no distinction between the sexes if we lose. They nail women to crosses as well as men, children too for that matter. So let her fight if she so chooses.'
I remained unconvinced but held my tongue.
'Oh, I meant to tell you,' said Spartacus. 'Oenomaus was killed today, a pilum through his throat. So that's one less Gaul for you to worry about.'
'Good, that only leaves about five thousand. And Crixus?'
'It will take more than a few Romans to kill him. I heard about your little spat. I don't want you two squaring up to each other again. That's an order.'
'Yes, lord, but you had better tell him that.'
'I will.' He looked towards the east. 'Dawn's breaking. Should be a nice day.'

Chapter 9

When it was light parties were sent out to strip the Roman dead of their armour and weapons. Most had thrown away their shields and swords when they had attempted to flee, so it took a considerable amount of time to trawl the plateau for weapons and equipment. I sent Nergal and Burebista with five hundred horse to scout the area up to and beyond Forum Annii for anything that could be of use to the army, while I attended a council of war. I took Godarz with me, as it was fitting that he should be accorded the proper rank due to his age and experience. I told him this on the way to the meeting but it meant little to him. He was a man who was more concerned with the here and now rather than theoretical musings.

The battlefield was a sea of men and some women pulling mail shirts off corpses and piling them onto carts, while on other carts were placed sandals, belts, shields, swords, daggers and pila. The latter was a curious item of weaponry, as it consisted of a long wooden handle onto which was fitted a thin iron shaft. The shaft bends upon impact with a shield and thus cannot be thrown back. Quite extraordinary. Godarz assured me that bent pila could be straightened for re-use, but I didn't see the point.

The atmosphere at the meeting was relaxed and cheerful, and in the afterglow of victory even Crixus was in a good mood, and for the moment seemed to have forgotten about our mutual animosity. His head was still bandaged, but the wound seemed to concern him not and he made a point of slapping everyone on the back as they entered, though not me, merely nodding his head when Godarz and I arrived. I did embrace Claudia, though, as I liked her greatly.

'How are my girls?' she asked me.

'Excellent, lady. Gallia and Diana have a new friend,' I replied.

'So I hear. I also hear that you don't approve of her.'

'Perhaps I was being unkind. She makes Nergal happy so I should be grateful for that, at least.'

'What don't you approve of, that Praxima was a prostitute or that she slit a Roman's throat?'

'Both,' I replied.

'You don't like the idea of women on the battlefield, or just a blonde-haired one in particular?'

'I gave explicit orders that they should remain behind.' I was aware that my cheeks were beginning to colour.

'Gallia doesn't take kindly to orders,'

'I wasn't talking about Gallia.'

'Weren't you?' she teased. 'I understand that you want to protect her, but you can't put her in a cage. Her father made that mistake, as did Cornelius Lentulus, and you know what happened to him.'

I did not want to have this conversation. It was as though Claudia was peering into my soul and I found the experience unsettling. I was saved by Spartacus, who ordered us to be seated. Claudia smiled mischievously at me as I took my seat beside Godarz. Around the table also sat Spartacus, Akmon, Castus, Cannicus, Crixus and Dumnorix.

Spartacus started. 'We have won a great victory. Three Roman legions destroyed and thousands of their soldiers dead, the rest scattered. Once we have finished collecting what weapons and equipment we can use, we will move south into Lucania and Bruttium for the winter.'

'What garrisons are there, lord?' I asked.

'I do not know. We will find out when we get there.'

Godarz rose. 'May I speak, lord?'

'Who are you?' said Crixus, menacingly. Clearly his good mood had its limits.

'My name is Godarz and I was a slave for many years at Nola. But my duties required me to travel throughout southern Italy and so I have a certain knowledge of these parts.'

'Please enlighten us,' said Spartacus.

'There are two large towns that have garrisons, Thurii and Metapontum, and both are walled.'

'How large are the garrisons?' asked Castus.

'I do not know,' replied Godarz. 'But they are garrison troops, second-rate, not like soldiers of the legions.'

'We took Forum Annii,' said Crixus, 'we can take these two places.'

'Metapontum is worth taking, lord,' added Godarz. 'It is a very rich port and the land around it is very fertile, with many farms and more potential recruits for your army.'

'Thank you, Godarz,' said Spartacus. 'We will move in five days' time.'

'To where?' said Crixus.

'Which is closer, Godarz,' asked Spartacus, 'Thurii or Metapontum?'

'Metapontum,' replied Godarz.

'Then we march to Metapontum.'

The next day, Nergal and Burebista returned with carts loaded with the fruits of victory. In their haste to destroy us, the Romans had not built a fortified camp but had just left their baggage and mules under a small guard three miles behind their army. These had been abandoned in the general rout, which meant that my horsemen came across hundreds of mules and a few dozen horses, many wandering free over the plateau, and dozens of carts that a Roman legion used. The carts came in very useful and were loaded with the legions' supplies, which included heavy sacks of grain, entrenching tools and other implements; baskets, cooking utensils and hundreds of leather tents. To these were added cloaks, tunics and even small forges. It was a rich haul, and when the cavalry returned it reminded me of a large caravan that Hatra was used to seeing every day. Three hundred carts winding their way into camp was certainly an impressive sight.

It took three days of hard toil for the captured equipment to be distributed equally among the army. I found it rather bizarre, but Spartacus was insistent that all should benefit from our victory. 'For if we fail, all will share equally in our defeat,' he told me. He did, though, give me most of the horses, which meant I now had over a thousand horses and several hundred carts, plus mules to pull them. I also acquired a large commander's tent similar to the one Spartacus resided in, though it was bulky and large and required several men to put it up. I had it stashed away on a wagon until we found a more permanent camp. Gallia and Diana shared a tent but Nergal had also acquired a Roman officer's tent and had moved in Praxima. All three women trained every day with their bows under the watchful eye of Gafarn, and I had to admit that their archery and riding skills had improved markedly. Gallia still retained a slight aloofness towards me that I found enticing yet frustrating.

On the day the army moved south I asked her and Diana to ride with me as we followed the course of the River Aciris. I left Byrd behind with a party of scouts to make sure that no Romans followed us and attacked our rearguard, but in truth it appeared that, for the moment at least, the Romans had disappeared from the world. We left the high limestone mountains behind and entered a wide verdant plain to follow the course of the river. Winter was approaching now and the air was cooler, and already snow was capping the mountains. The army retained its discipline as it marched south, the Thracians in the van, followed by the Germans and Crixus' Gauls in the rear. The cavalry rode ahead, partly to scout the route and also to avoid the dirt, dust and general unpleasantness of trailing in the wake of a large body of people and beasts. I felt like an eagle that had plucked a mighty fish from the river as I rode next to Gallia. Were it not for her long blond hair she could have passed for one of my horsemen, with her newly acquired mail shirt, boots, leggings, bow, helmet, quiver and sword. She also had a dagger tucked into the top of her right boot, a gift from Praxima no doubt. Despite her warlike garb she still looked gorgeous, but then she would look alluring dressed only in a sack. Behind us rode Diana, Gafarn, Godarz and nine hundred horseman, spare horses and our carts, while Nergal and fifty men were scouting ahead. He had taken Praxima with him. Diana and Gafarn had become close and to be fair her soft features, kind nature and large brown eyes seemed to invite a man to protect her. She did not have the inner steel that Gallia possessed, but I thought that she was amiable and extremely likeable. She did have strength, though I did not see it until the time of adversity. She and Gafarn were laughing, about what I could not tell.

'Why don't you amuse us all, Gafarn,' I said.

'I was merely telling Diana of how you were nearly married off to the Princess Axsen of Babylon.'

Gallia turned and looked at me but said nothing.

'I'm sure Diana doesn't want to know about things that have no bearing on the here and now,' I said, slightly annoyed.

'On the contrary, highness,' said Gafarn, 'taking all things into account, I would reason that getting captured by the Romans saved you from a worse fate.'

'I was not going to marry the Princess of Babylon,' I insisted. I glanced at Gallia. 'The person I marry shall be my choice, and mine alone.'

'Of course, highness,' retorted Gafarn, 'as long as your mother and father say so.'

'Be quiet,' I ordered.

We rode on in silence for a while before Gallia said to me. 'What is she like?'

'Who?'

'The Princess of Babylon.'

I shrugged. 'I do not know. I've never met her.'

'She's fat,' said Gafarn. 'Not beautiful like you, lady.'

'Why should I care what she looks like?' asked Gallia.

'Just to reassure you, lady, that she is no rival to you.'

'Is she a rival?' queried Gallia, mischievously.

'No, lady,' he relied, 'for Prince Pacorus has eyes only for you.'

I halted Remus and turned him to face Gafarn. 'That's enough, Gafarn. I don't want to hear any more about the Princess Axsen.'

Gafarn nodded his head gravely. 'Of course, highness.'

'And you're embarrassing the Lady Gallia,' I added.

'Really? I thought I was embarrassing you.'

The light-hearted mood was interrupted by a rider from Spartacus, who wished to see me. I found him with Claudia sitting on the ground under a beech tree. The army tramped by them, soldiers who looked like Romans marching six abreast, kept in line by slaves turned centurions wielding those wretched vine canes. I had to admit, though, that the army conducted itself in a professional manner, testimony to the leadership of Spartacus.

'Apulia,' he said to me.

'Lord?'

'Apulia, Pacorus. A region rich in olive farms and slaves. A runaway slave was brought to me earlier and he told me that he had been working on a large farm in Apulia and he gave me an idea. I want you to raid into the region and see if you can get us some recruits. We march to Metapontum, but cavalry is no use in a siege. Therefore, take your horse into Apulia and give the Romans a taste of what they have done to the lands of other peoples.'

'You mean fire and sword,' I said.

He smiled. 'Fat Romans make easy prey.'

And so it was that we rode into Apulia, nine hundred horsemen divided into three columns. I led the first, Nergal the second and Burebista the third. I left Godarz, Rhesus and the rest of the new recruits to the cavalry with the army, as I thought his knowledge would be useful to Spartacus, and I wanted to leave a cadre of horse behind because slaves were still coming in, even during our march.

Apulia, located along Italy's eastern coast, was a strange land, very different from Lucania and Campania. It consisted mainly of flat land divided into huge agricultural estates. The towns in the area were few and poor. We bypassed one called Silvium on the Appian Way and struck north. Any villas we came across we burned and we released the slaves from their wretched barracks, which were invariably well away from where their masters lived. These were large, square stone buildings with thatched roofs that had small windows with grills in the walls for ventilation. Men, women and children were kept under lock and key and chained to each other during the hours of darkness, before being released in the morning to work another day under the lashes of the overseers in the fields. The latter, slaves themselves, earned their masters' goodwill by administering brutality towards those in their charge. As their reward they were given their own accommodation, which was little more than a hovel next to the slave barracks. By such methods did a few Romans control the lives of thousands. One morning we came across a long column of slaves being herded to pick olives, the main crop of the region.

The morning was overcast and windless, and the only sounds that could be heard were the curses of the overseers and the crack of their lashes across scarred backs. At first the overseers thought that we were Roman cavalry and started to shove the slaves aside to make way for us, but I halted the column in front of them to block their route. We disabused them of the notion that we were their friends and freed the slaves, and as I was in a charitable mood I let the overseers go, though they were promptly killed on the spot by those they had formally terrorised.

Most of those liberated from the fields were told to head into Lucania, towards the port of Metapontum. I reasoned that even if the port had not fallen to Spartacus there would be thousands of his men in the countryside around it, and the slaves would run into them sooner or later. Most seemed happy to be free, though I noticed that some just stood there after the overseers had been killed, unsure what to do. Gallia told me that they had probably been slaves from childhood and had no concept of freedom. Others formed themselves into bands and declared that they would not be joining the 'gladiator Spartacus', but would take to the hills and live off the land instead. I doubted whether they would survive for more than three months before being hunted down and nailed to crosses. However, they were in the minority and as most slaves who worked the land were captives taken in war, I reckoned that Spartacus would be receiving thousands of valuable reinforcements from those freed by our raids.

Any towns that we neared shut their gates and their inhabitants cowered behind their walls. Though as my column numbered only three hundred riders the fear that we struck into the enemy's hearts was out of all proportion to our size. And thus it was that as we were riding near the town of Rubi, along deserted roads and empty fields, we came across the camp of a slave-hunting gang pitched near a field of giant olive trees, which must have been thirty feet high and had thick trunks. The gang saw us coming but barely acknowledged us, no doubt thinking that we were a Roman patrol. When we got nearer I could see that there were about a dozen gang members, unshaven, dressed in filthy tunics with an assortment of weapons dangling from their belts or in their hands. Their horses were tethered under an olive tree, with a cart and two mules also tied to it off to one side. Dangling from the cart was a collection of shackles and branding irons, the tools of their trade.

We halted and their leader, a fat, ugly man with a bald head, ambled over. Behind me my men sat in silence on their horses. I looked past him to where a naked girl was being held down by four of his associates, each one holding one of her arms and feet. She was struggling fiercely but without success as they forced her legs apart. A fifth man walked over from where the others were sitting around a fire and stood over her. He removed his tunic and stood naked with his back to us.

'Don't see many soldiers in these parts,' said their leader, looking up at me.

'What's going on here?' I asked him, nodding towards where the naked man had now knelt and was about to rape the girl. They had stuffed some sort of rag in her mouth to stop her screams, but she was still writhing frantically in a futile effort to stop her imminent violation.

He looked round at the commotion behind him. 'Oh, her. Runaway slave. Mostly when we catch runaways we brand them and return them to their owners, but this one's pretty so we thought we'd use her for some recreational duties. We're just about to start.'

I heard a hiss and saw an arrow slam into the back of the naked man, who collapsed forward onto the pinioned girl. I turned and saw Gallia with her bow in her hand, who was reaching into her quiver to string another arrow. Everyone was so surprised by what had happened that nobody moved. The men holding the girl just stared in disbelief at their dead comrade with an arrow in his back sprawled in front of them, while their leader's mouth opened and closed like that of a fish out of water as he took in what had happened. Then another of Gallia's arrows hit one of his men and he himself drew his sword. Behind him his men released the girl and grabbed their weapons, while those around the fire sprang to their feet and likewise armed themselves. They were quick, but my men were quicker and Gafarn in particular was one of the fastest archers in Parthia. He had dropped two of the gang before they had a chance to draw their swords. Beside him Diana released her bowstring and saw her arrow go through the mouth of a gang member who was charging at us with a spear. I smiled in admiration then drew my own bow, strung an arrow and pointed it at the gang leader. He stood, frozen to the spot as his men were killed quickly around him. One of the gang members did not try to fight but instead attempted to flee, running away through the olive trees. He ran like the wind and I thought he would escape as Gafarn aimed an arrow at him. I kept my gaze on their leader as Gafarn shot and my men cheered as the arrow found its mark.

Gallia took off her helmet, handed it to the now shaking Diana and ran over to where the naked girl lay curled up on the ground. She gently knelt beside her and covered her with her cloak, all the time talking quietly to her.

'My name is Pacorus, prince of Parthia,' I told the gang leader, 'and I ride with Spartacus. Drop your sword.'

Some of my men had now moved to the left and right behind me and there were around twenty bows aimed at him. He dropped his sword on the ground.

'Where's Parthia, then?'

'Far from here,' I said, replacing my bow in its case.

'Gonna kill me, too?' he sniffed.

'We should, for all the atrocities you and your men have committed.'

'Against slaves?' He was indignant. 'They're not real people, just animals, and most Romans are glad that men like me are prepared to round them up for them.'

At that moment Gallia passed him, her left arm round the shoulders of the young girl. The gang leader saw her pass and spat at her.

'Bitch.'

In a blur Gallia reached for her boot, whipped out the dagger with her right hand and stabbed it into the man's neck. She left the blade in his flesh as blood gushed out from the wound in great red spurts. He didn't scream or shout, just looked surprised as he toppled forward onto the ground, which quickly turned crimson. He made some faint gurgling sounds and then fell silent, then my men cheered loudly as Gallia jumped into her saddle and pulled the girl onto the back of her horse. I retrieved her dagger.

We took the cart, mules and horses and left the dead to rot. The girl rode behind Gallia, holding her tightly around the waist, a sullen, sad-looking creature who said nothing and looked down the whole time. When we stopped to make camp Gallia and Diana cleaned her up and found her a set of leggings and a tunic, then they fed her and cut her matted hair. She clung to Gallia like a frightened child, and always looked down at the ground, never at anyone directly. Later, in the evening, when she had fallen asleep in Gallia's tent, I sat with her, Diana and a few of my men around a campfire, over which was cooking a pair of rabbits we had caught. I asked if she had spoken about her experience.

'That would be very difficult for her to do,' said Gallia, icily.

'Why?'

'Because they had cut her tongue out.'

'What are you going to do with her?' I asked.

'She can stay with us.'

I poured some water into my cup. 'She won't be much use, she looks deranged.'

Gallia knocked the cup out of my hand. 'For someone who is supposedly educated, you can sometimes be an idiot.'

She got up and walked back to her tent. Everyone around the fire looked down and averted my gaze. Suitably chastised, I too walked back to my tent.

We had acquired considerable loot from the country villas we had raided, mostly gold and silver coins. Our rapid appearance had prevented the families from burying their treasure in some hiding place, and in truth they were lucky to escape with their lives at the hands of vengeful slaves. Gallia said little to me in the days following the incident with the slave hunters, though I could detect there was a mighty rage inside her. She called the girl Rubi after the town she was rescued near, though the creature still averted any eye contact. Gallia and Diana chatted to her constantly and soon had her trust. And Gafarn seemed to win her over a little, though even his easy charm and good humour found little enthusiasm with her. No doubt her experiences had left her with an unshakeable distrust of men. We kept watch for any enemy patrols, but from what Godarz had told me I was confident that there were few Roman troops in the area. Apparently most of the legions were in foreign lands, stealing territory from the local inhabitants. Italy itself was largely devoid of soldiers save low-grade garrison troops and veterans who had been given land to farm. The latter might be a problem, but in the south of the country it was slaves who worked on the land, thousands of them. And most of them were now flocking to the banner of Spartacus.

On our way to Metapontum we came across a large and exquisite villa approximately ten miles west of the town of Genusia. The villa stood atop of a large but not high hill and was surrounded by neat rows of olive trees, birch trees and beehives. Slaves were working in the fields among the hives, and they barely gave us a moment's notice as we rode up the tree-lined drive that led to the villa, its white walls contrasting sharply with the green landscape it sat in. We halted on a large expanse of well-tended grass in front of the villa and I dismounted.

'No violence,' I instructed, 'and be watchful. Those field hands seemed unusually unruffled by our appearance.'

'Do you want an escort, highness?' asked Gafarn.

'I'll shout if I need assistance,' I replied.

'It's difficult to shout if someone has slit your throat,' retorted Gallia.

'I'm sure you can avenge my death many fold.' I looked at Rubi who had me fixed with a wild stare. 'You and your cohorts.'

I walked into the courtyard, the atrium as the Romans called it, the floor of which was decorated with mosaics, small rectangular black-and-white stones arranged in geometric patterns. In the centre stood a water fountain on a marble base, the sound of running water filled the courtyard with a calming noise. I took off my helmet and suddenly became aware of a man standing on a marble step between two columns in an open doorway. I assumed that he was in his sixties, with thinning white hair and a wrinkled face. He wore a simple beige tunic and leather sandals, which revealed bony arms. In fact, his face and neck were also lean, which led me to assume that he was a slave.

'Fetch me your master,' I told him.

'Who shall I say is calling?' he replied in a firm voice.

'Pacorus, prince of Parthia, and be quick about it.'

'Well, Prince Pacorus, as I have your name it is only proper that you should know mine, despite the fact that you have arrived at my house uninvited and with armed men at your back.'

'Your house?'

'Of course.' He stepped forward. 'I am Gaius Labienus, one time general of Rome and now a pensioner living quietly in the country.'

I looked around at the marble columns, decorated walls and floor mosaics. 'A rich pensioner, it would seem.'

He shrugged. 'A present from a grateful senate for services rendered,' he said. 'Would you like some wine?'

He clapped his hands and moments later a servant dressed in an immaculate white tunic edged with blue arrived carrying a tray holding two silver goblets. The slave offered me the tray first. I took a goblet and nodded my thanks to Gaius. The wine tasted excellent, being obviously of the finest quality.

'What services?' I asked, for surely such wealth was not given lightly.

'Twenty years fighting Rome's wars overseas, in Macedonia, Phrygia and Syria.' He drained his goblet and the slave took it away.

'Your slaves are well trained,' I said with disdain. He noticed the inflection in my voice.

'They are not slaves but freedmen, slaves that I have freed and thus are part of my family.'

'All of them?' I asked.

'All of them. Those in the fields and the ones in my household. All are free to go anytime should they wish it so. That being the case, young prince, I doubt you will find any recruits here.'

'Am I looking for recruits?' I asked, innocently.

'I may be old but do not take me for a fool. I know that you serve under the outlaw Spartacus and that you have killed a Roman tribune.'

I must admit that I was pleased that he had heard of me, but I resisted the temptation to boast.

'He was killed in battle,' I said, 'and his army was destroyed.'

'I know that, and I also know that the slave army looted Forum Annii and now lays siege to Metapontum, and that horsemen ride hither and thither freeing slaves and robbing innocent people. Is that not why you are here, Prince Pacorus? To rob me, perhaps kill me?'

'I am not a murderer,' I bristled.

He was silent for a while but stared at me unblinking. 'No, I do not think you are. But you fight alongside murderers, and when Rome's vengeance is turned against you, and it will be, it will make no distinction between those who fought with honour and those who fought for vengeance and loot.'

'All I want is to get home,' I said.

'An admirable objective, but many of those who fight with Spartacus have no homes. Some are the children of slaves who were born in Italy. Where is their home?'

'At least they are free now, not chained like animals.'

'Are there slaves in the Parthian Empire, Prince Pacorus?'

'Yes,' I admitted.

'And are the chains that bind them any less cruel than Roman shackles? Perhaps chains in Parthia are made of gold, but even if they are I'll warrant they chafe just as severely.'

'I have never killed a slave,' I said indignantly.

'Neither have I,' he replied. 'And neither do I own any slaves. But you were quite prepared to kill me when you marched into my house, were you not, for the sole reason that I was a Roman? Is that not correct?'

'I am not a murderer, neither are my men. But I am an enemy of Rome.'

'Of that I have no doubt,' he said. 'But you should not hate your enemies, prince of Parthia, for it will surely cloud your judgment. Above all, a general must remain aloof from such emotions. You fight for freedom, but the freedom you talk of is the liberty to rule your kingdom and command armies, the freedom to live like a god in a palace. Freedom to most means back-breaking work and trying to stay alive day-to-day. Do not confuse the freedom of privilege with the freedom to starve. You have little in common with those you fight alongside.'

'Did you have anything in common with your soldiers when you were campaigning with them?' I shot back.

'Of course, the strongest bond of all, the bond of blood, for we were all Romans.'

'That may be, Gaius, but there are thousands, like myself, who were taken fighting Rome and are bound by a burning desire, the wish to return to our homelands.

'And now, sir, I must depart. Have no fear of your person or property being molested. My men are under strict orders.'

He followed me out of the villa to where my men were waiting in their saddles. When he appeared a group of around twenty of his servants armed with wooden clubs and pitchforks ran over from one of the fields. In an instant my men had arrows in their bowstrings ready to fire. Gaius held up a hand to calm his men.

'I am unhurt,' he shouted.

I likewise indicated to my men to lower their bows. The two groups eyed each other resentfully. Gaius walked with me to Remus, whose reins were held by Gafarn.

'The famous Parthian bows. I remember them from my time in Syria, though not with affection,' said Gaius. He stroked Remus' head. 'A beautiful horse.'

'His name is Remus,' I said, vaulting into the saddle.

Gaius laughed. 'Somewhat ironic, is it not?'

'Farewell, Gaius Labienus,' I said.

'Farewell, Prince Pacorus,' he raised his right arm in salute. 'From one soldier to another, I hope you eventually find peace.'

I saluted him and wheeled Remus away. My horsemen followed, leaving an old Roman in front of his lavish villa.

'We are not plundering him, highness?' asked Gafarn with surprise.

'No,' I said. 'We are soldiers, not robbers.'

I decided that we had finished with playing at being brigands. Gaius was right. If we carried on down that route we would be no better than murderers. And I was not a murderer. I was a Parthian prince and better than any Roman. But I had to prove that worth, for actions speak far louder than words. I sent riders to the columns Nergal and Burebista were leading, instructing them to desist their activities and rendezvous with me at the coast, ten miles north of Metapontum on the coast of the Gulf of Tarentum. We made camp in a small, sheltered inlet that had a sandy beach. While we waited for the other cavalry to join us, we exercised the horses in the sea and practised our archery skills in the dunes. I came across Gallia and Diana showing Rubi how to use a bow, and the young girl appeared to be enjoying herself shooting at a tunic stuffed with grass that had been fastened to a post. All three were under the watchful eye of Gafarn. The sea breeze made Gallia's untied locks blow wild and Rubi's eyes were wide with excitement as she shot arrows into the target, all the while making grunting noises as she fired Gallia's bow.

'How's she doing?' I asked Gallia as Gafarn showed Rubi how to hold the bowstring correctly.

'Her progress is slow, but physically she is well. But I fear her mind may be damaged permanently. But I am glad that she is with us.' She eyed me, daring me to contradict her.

'Well, lucky we found her when we did.'

'I suppose,' she mused. She looked at me again with her piercing blue eyes. 'Why did you leave that old Roman at the villa alone.'

'I do not wage war on old men.'

'He would not hesitate to have you nailed to a cross if the roles were reversed.'

'Perhaps,' I said.

'Oh, Pacorus. To you it's just a game, isn't it? But it's not about honour or glory, it's about survival. We are fighting for our lives. What are you fighting for?'

I could have tried to give her a deep, philosophical answer, but I smiled at her and said. 'For you.'

'You're impossible,' she replied, sticking out her tongue at me and going back to Rubi.

Nergal came to us two days later, brimming with excitement and full of tales of how he and his men had laid waste to the land with fire and sword. The flame-haired Praxima was with him, dressed in a mail shirt, helmet and carrying a shield and spear. Nergal also had a column of mules loaded with treasure with him. Praxima nodded to me curtly (doubtless she had heard about my disapproval of her) but embraced Gallia and Diana warmly. That night we slaughtered a bull that had been plundered from a nearby estate and roasted it over a huge fire on the beach. The wind had dropped and the evening was warm as we ate and drank with abandon, though I was careful not to drink too much wine. To my delight Gallia came and sat beside me as Gafarn, who had appointed himself chief cook for the evening, cut slices from the roasting carcass.

'They seem happy,' I said of the men who were laughing and joking in groups on the sand.

'Yes, they do. Are you happy, Pacorus?'

'Always, when I'm with you,' I kissed her on the cheek.

She rested her head on my shoulder. 'I too.'

The both of us stayed on the beach until the dawn broke in the eastern sky, along with dozens of snoring drunk and semi-drunk soldiers who woke with hangovers on a calm and windless day. I felt a surge of joy sweep through me as I became aware of Gallia's head on my chest as she slept. I wanted the moment to last forever as, bleary eyed, I watched the seagulls fly and hover over a calm blue sea. Perhaps this could be our future, just the two of us and no one else, no Romans and no wars. I dreamed of perfection but out of the corner of my eye I saw reality, as one of my men bent over and threw up on the sand. Others held their heads, which were obviously throbbing after a night of heavy drinking. The price of 'liberating' wine from the Romans. Others stripped off and walked naked into the sea in an attempt to refresh themselves. I rested my head back on the sand and looked up at the clear blue sky. Suddenly the panting figure of Rubi was beside us, frantically tugging at Gallia's sleeve, who woke up with a start. Rubi was making grunting noises and pointing behind us. She was almost as tiresome as Praxima.

'What is it, Rubi?' asked Gallia, who rose and brushed the sand from her clothes.

I too rose and turned to see what she was pointing at, and saw on the horizon what looked like a column of horse and foot on a distant crest of a hill, heading towards us. Panic suddenly gripped me as I realised that no sentries had been posted the night before. How could I have so stupid, again? This was just like the day when we had been captured. Had I learned nothing? Perhaps that old Roman at the villa had pursued me with a town garrison? I cursed myself and reached down for my sword, hurriedly buckling it to my belt.

'Enemy! Enemy forces approaching! Rally to me,' I screamed at all who would listen.

For a few seconds nothing happened, apart from a few dazed individuals staring at me with irritation as my shrieking voice added to their headaches. Then their fuddled minds grasped the significance of what I was saying, and suddenly the beach was a scene of chaos. Men waded ashore to grab weapons and clothing and race to where their horses were tethered. Others still asleep were kicked awake, pulled to their feet and told to saddle their horses. Gallia and I ran to where our horses were, Gallia pulling Rubi along with her, who bizarrely seemed to be loving the sense of impending doom that was spreading over us. I threw a cloth and saddle onto Remus' back, buckled the straps and then fitted his bridle. Gafarn and Diana emerged from behind a distant sand dune, both of them running fit to burst. I ran to the top of a nearby dune to see where the enemy was, and spied a solid mass of foot steadily marching towards our position, no more than three miles away, I guessed. The enemy horse was flanking each side of the column of foot, with a small mounted party at the head of the whole force.

Nergal galloped up to us as I fastened my water skin, rations, bow case and rolled-up cloak to the saddle. I threw on my mail shirt, helmet and quiver and mounted Remus.

'There are hundreds of them, highness,' he said.

'We have to get off the beach. Form up inland on firm ground.'

'What about the carts and mules?'

'Leave them here,' I said. 'They will only slow us up. Better to live than die with a saddlebag stuffed full of gold. Go.'

We managed to deploy into a two-rank line a short distance inland from the beach, facing the direction from where the enemy was approaching. The latter had made no effort to increase their pace or deploy into battle formation. Indeed, they seemed oblivious to us. As I sat just forward of the first line beside Nergal, I debated our course of action. Though we had been surprised, the enemy had failed to take advantage of this. As they heavily outnumbered us I decided that the most prudent course of action would be a hasty retreat, though it galled me that we would have to leave the booty we had taken. I was just about to turn about when Nergal spoke.

'They have no shields.'

'What?' I said.

'They have no shields, highness. In fact, those on foot don't have weapons at all, or uniforms.'

I stared at the black mass approaching and he was right. No shields, no spears and they were not wearing helmets. Then one of the horsemen broke from the group at the head of the column and began to gallop towards us.

'Ready!' I shouted. It was obviously some sort of fanatic who wanted to make a name for himself. He would be the first to die.

'It's Burebista,' said Nergal.

'What?'

'It's Burebista.' Nergal kicked his horse forward and rode to greet him, while behind me the two lines erupted in cheers. I too rode forward to meet the commander of my last raiding column. He was beaming like a man who had found a chest of gold.

'We thought you were Romans,' I told him. 'Who are those with you?'

'Recruits, lord,' he replied. 'All these men can ride so I asked them to join us.'

'And they accepted your invitation?' I looked past Burebista to where the column was trudging towards us. They looked a ragged band to say the least.

'I told them that they would be serving under "the Parthian". They have all heard of you, lord, and I told them that they would have a horse, weapons and an unending supply of Romans to kill. They took little convincing.'

I doubted that all of them could ride, but no matter, he had done well. Burebista had an infectious enthusiasm that drew men to him like a moth to a flame.

'How many are there' asked Nergal.

'Seven hundred,' he replied, proudly.

I extended my hand in congratulations. He had done better than any of us and deserved praise. And now he had his dragon.

'Has there been a battle?' he said to me though he was looking past me.

'Battle?'

'There, lord,' he pointed behind me. I turned in the saddle to see a large plume of black smoke ascending into the morning sky. It was many miles away but it could mean only one thing: Metapontum had fallen to Spartacus.

After a rest of two hours, during which we groomed, watered and fed the horses and ate a late breakfast, we moved southwest along the coast towards Metapontum. The terrain was flat and crisscrossed by large fields growing wheat, olives and grapes, though the wheat had already been harvested and only the olives and grapes remained. But there was no one to do so, as the slaves had all fled to join us or make their own bid for freedom. I noticed the absence of cattle and sheep, all of which had no doubt been taken on the orders of Spartacus. I sent out patrols ahead, more to cover our right flank and riders behind us to ensure we were not surprised, but in truth there appeared to be no Roman troops anywhere near us; indeed, there appeared to be few Romans of any type at all. I wondered if those who had lived in villas in the countryside had taken refuge in Metapontum? The thickening large plume of smoke that hung in the sky indicated that they had chosen unwisely.

During the journey I went to see for myself the calibre of Burebista's new recruits. For the most part they were barefoot and dressed in threadbare tunics, their exposed arms and legs weathered and tanned by a harsh Mediterranean sun. I was told that farm slaves owned only one tunic and cloak, which was replaced every two years, by which time many were all but naked. I saw ankles with deep scars where leg irons had been worn for years, and some who had the marks of the lash on their limbs. Others had the letters 'FUG', 'KAL' and 'FUR' branded on their foreheads, abbreviations of Latin words denoting 'runaway', 'liar' or 'thief' respectively. Some of these individuals had misshapen limbs where their bones had been broken as a punishment for their crimes. Slaves who killed their masters were crucified, but the Romans had a curiously ambivalent attitude towards their chattels. Slaves were an expense and as such were an investment. A dead slave was a financial loss, so the Romans were reluctant to kill them outright. Far better to whip them, brand them and then set them back to work under the watchful eye of an overseer. I thought about our own slaves in Hatra and wondered if they too were mistreated. I dismissed the idea, and yet the thought of hundreds of individuals living their lives in servitude for the sole purpose of maintaining the high living standards of my father and his family and court made me uneasy. Gafarn himself had been a slave, of course, and in all the years I had known him I had never asked him if he was satisfied with his lot. Why should I? I was a prince and he was a slave. But now, in a foreign land and fighting for a slave general, my head was filled with strange ideas. I wanted to be free and so did the hundreds of others who now marched with me. Were they so different from me?

I dismounted from Remus and walked alongside a group of Burebista's new recruits. It was around noon now, and the day was warm though not hot, with a light breeze coming from the sea. As I walked along the dirt track I caught the eye of a man walking parallel to me, a thin, lean individual in his fifties whose arms were covered in scratches and small scars and who carried a walking stick in his right hand. He was striding along purposely, his feet bare and his head bald.

'He's a fine horse, sir.'

'Yes, he is,' I said. 'His name is Remus.'

'Are you the one they call "the Parthian", sir?'

'Prince Pacorus, yes.'

'An honour to meet you, sir. My name is Amenius.'

'You are from these parts?'

'Not originally. I was captured in Macedonia over thirty years ago. Have been a slave ever since. Always promised myself that I would end my days in my homeland. Have you been to Macedonia, sir?'

'No, never.'

'Beautiful it is. Mountains and valleys, and the air the purest you've ever breathed. There's not a day goes by when I don't think about it.'

I was humbled by his fortitude. Thirty years a slave and still the dream of freedom burned within him. With such men perhaps Spartacus could indeed defeat Rome.

'I hope you see your homeland again, Amenius,' I said.

It took us all day to reach Metapontum, and as the evening crept upon us our column reached the outer ring of sentries that had been posted to warn of any relief force. I was riding with the advance party when we came across a motley band of Gauls who were preparing a fire for their evening meal. A pony was tethered nearby to speed a rider to warn the army if we had been Romans. Their leader, a young man with bristly fair hair and a large moustache typical of his race, stood up and walked over to me. They must have recognised us, or me at least, for the others ignored us and carried on with their culinary preparations.

'The city fell this morning,' he said.

'Where's Spartacus?' I asked.

He pointed down the track. 'The Thracians are camped behind their wooden palisade to the north of the city. We Gauls took it, on our own.'

'My congratulations,' I said without any enthusiasm, for I knew that the streets would be running with blood by now.

With that I nudged Remus forward and carried on past them. Behind us the rest of the column was appearing, riders walking their mounts and the former slaves shuffling along silently. They made almost no sound, as their feet were bare, unlike Roman soldiers with their hobnailed sandals who could be heard for miles, especially when they marched down a stone-paved road. I rode back and instructed Nergal to pitch camp a mile down the track and wait for me there. I took Gafarn, Gallia, Diana, Praxima and Rubi as well, as I didn't want them out of my sight with thousands of blood-crazed Gauls in the vicinity. Ten minutes later we were at the gates of the camp that Akmon built wherever the army was located, looking exactly as it did on previous occasions with its neat rows of tents and perfectly aligned avenues. Spartacus and Claudia were glad to see us, and there were many embraces before he insisted that we sit with them and share a meal. As usual Claudia was the cook, but Spartacus insisted that we all help. Later, as we sat, ate, joked and drank wine, Spartacus told us how Metapontum fell to Crixus and his Gauls. Like most Roman cities it was enclosed by a wall, in its case four miles in length. Curiously, though it was inland from the coast, it was linked to the sea by a canal around five miles long. On the day the army arrived some of the citizens had tried to escape using the waterway, but the canal was only forty feet wide and Spartacus had ordered his men to line the banks. When the boats loaded down with human cargo came within range they were showered with rocks, stones, flaming torches and pila. Half a dozen boats tried to make a run for the sea but all were stopped and set alight. Most of their passengers were burned alive, some drowned and a few made it to the canal banks, where they were hacked to pieces. No more boats left the city.

I noticed that Spartacus continually drained and refilled his cup with wine as he recounted how he had ordered the city to be surrounded. After a week, during which the garrison and citizens had had enough time to see the strength of the army that lay before their walls, under a flag of truce Spartacus had offered the inhabitants safe passage if they took with them only the clothes they were dressed in.

'But we are only slaves, and after they had opened the gates to allow the envoy to deliver his message they killed him, cut off his head and threw it from the city walls.' Spartacus took another mouthful of wine.

'What followed was a slaughter. I was foolish, you see, because it was a Gaul that was sent as an envoy. And when Crixus saw what had happened he unleashed his men against the walls. At first they took heavy losses, many being cut down by arrows and javelins, but the citizens had forgotten that if boats could leave their city via the canal, then men could easily get in the same way. Crixus had selected those who could swim to jump into the canal and swim into the harbour. I have to admit it was a cunning plan, and while the garrison manned the walls his men swept into the city like a plague of rats. Then the screaming started, and went on for hours. Only when it was over did they throw open the gates and let us in.'

'Who, the Romans?' I asked.

'No,' said Claudia, 'the Gauls.'

'It was Forum Annii all over again, only much worse,' said Spartacus. 'Metapontum has ceased to exist.'

Claudia rested her hand on his arm. 'They brought it upon themselves, my love. There was nothing you could have done.'

Her husband agreed, but he seemed particularly morose. But perhaps that was due to the wine. We slept in his tent that night and in the morning I washed and groomed Remus. Claudia came to me as I was brushing his shoulders.

'Crixus grows ever more bold,' she said, stroking my horse's side. 'That is why Spartacus is unhappy. Romans mean nothing to him, but he thinks that Crixus will challenge him for control of the army.'

'Do you want me to kill Crixus?' I asked, 'for nothing would give me greater pleasure.'

She threw her head back and laughed. 'That would be one solution, but I don't think even you, my brave Parthian prince, can kill ten thousand Gauls single-handed.'

'Ten thousand?' I was surprised at the number.

'His numbers grow large, and with each increase Crixus becomes more powerful. I fear he will split the army apart.'

'But he and Spartacus have the same objective, do they not?'

She shook her head. 'Crixus dreams of being a king, here in southern Italy. He has no interest in returning to Gaul, where he lived in a stone hut in a small village.'

'He does not speak for all the Gauls, surely.'

'As long as he gives them victory they will follow them,' she said. 'But the strategy and the victories are Spartacus', not his. Crixus is very good at killing, little else.'

She was right, and I could see how Spartacus had unwittingly created a monster in his midst.

Metapontum was worse than Forum Annii, if that was possible. Because the Gauls had entered the city via the canal, the citizens had no method of escape. The result was wholesale slaughter, and because his fellow countryman had been beheaded by the townsfolk Crixus ordered that every man, woman and child in Metapontum should suffer the same fate. I rode with Spartacus, Akmon, Nergal and Burebista into the city the next day, when the gates had been finally opened. The streets were filled with the dead, whose heads had been hacked off. The main street into the city was awash with blood, which had also been smeared on the walls of buildings. Blood-smeared Gauls sat on the pavements or rested against walls, exhausted by a day and evening of killing and looting. Smashed pottery, clothes and personal items were strewn everywhere, while from balconies and rooftops hung corpses. Because they had had their heads cut off, the bodies could not be strung up by their necks, so ropes had been tied to their ankles or wrists to facilitate them being hoisted up. The result was a grotesque display of flesh, like a giant butcher's shop where the goods on display were human carcasses. I rode beside Spartacus, who sat stony faced in the saddle and said nothing as we made our way to the forum. The horrors of the streets were as nothing compared to what greeted our eyes when we arrived at the city's central square, where stood a huge pile of severed heads. There must have been thousands of them, a dreadful mound of leering visages with tongues hanging out and eyes closed. Already the stench was overpowering, and Nergal retched in disgust at the sight and the smell.

On the opposite side of the square, sitting in a huge chair that had been placed at the top of wide stone steps leading up to a temple, was Crixus. Around him were dozens of his men, most lolling on the steps or carrying loot from the place of worship. We dismounted and tied the horses to a stone column. The forum was enclosed on three sides by covered colonnades, with the temple filling the fourth side. Nergal and Burebista stayed with them as Spartacus, myself and Akmon walked over to the king of the Gauls. As usual he was drinking wine but barely acknowledged us as we stopped at the foot of the steps. He looked drunk and tired, as did his men. The orgy of violence had obviously exhausted them.

'That'll teach them to cut off the head of one of my men,' said Crixus, who finally stood up and descended the steps. He was stripped to the waist, his chest and arms smeared with some poor soul's blood, his cheeks too.

'We march at dawn tomorrow, with or without you' said Spartacus curtly.

'Where?' queried Crixus.

'South. We have no use for this region now.' Spartacus turned and walked briskly back to his horse, mounted it and rode from the forum. We followed. He said nothing more as we left him to join our comrades. Later that day I met with Castus, who as ever was in good spirits. He told me that Spartacus' plan was to head south into a province called Bruttium, which was a mountainous region considered by the Romans to be a wilderness devoid of decent people and a haven for bandits. We would stay there for the winter and organise the army, then march north in the spring. He told me that the only garrison that might bother us was in a city called Thurii, which would have to be taken.

'Herdsmen who have joined us have said that its defences are strong, with high, thick walls and catapults mounted on its towers.'

'We could starve them out,' I said.

'Maybe,' replied Castus, 'but we need the winter to turn recruits into soldiers, not waste our time laying siege to a place that we can't take.'

The army marched the next morning, thousands of men and

livestock filling the countryside in a huge, dense column that moved slowly south. Spartacus and his Thracians formed the vanguard, marching six abreast, followed by Castus and his Germans and then Crixus and the Gauls. Each contingent had its own mules loaded with food, plus carts filled with spare weapons, shields, mobile forges, kitchen utensils, tents, medicines, clothing and tools. Spartacus had had all the captured gold and silver ornaments and the like melted down and cast into bars, which were loaded onto carts and moved under his personal escort. Gold and silver coins had been put into bags and placed in a separate cart, and the legionary gold that had been captured in the battle on the plateau was likewise under Thracian protection. The army had certainly reaped a rich harvest when it came to the spoils of war. The weapons, armour and shields that had been taken after the battle had been distributed evenly among the army, but I noticed that there were still many men without helmets, shields, javelins and swords. Some still carried wooden spears with their points fire-hardened and little else. Those who had joined us in Lucania and Apulia were armed only with what they had brought with them, perhaps a dagger and a club. They invariably had nothing on their feet. The cavalry was in an even worse state, for with Burebista's new recruits we were sadly deficient in horses, weapons and equine furniture. I had nearly two thousand men who wanted to be horsemen, but only twelve hundred horses. The rest walked with the carts and mules on the march, while I tasked Byrd and his scouts to ride ahead of the army and on its flanks to make sure we weren't surprised. I was still smarting from being caught out by Burebista, and was determined that no enemy would take us unawares.

It was sixty miles from Metapontum to Thurii and it took the army six days to reach its destination. We march along the coastal lowlands, but as we moved south the terrain changed from undulating hills to mountains and a more rugged landscape. We moved through areas rich in vineyards and citrus fruit orchards on the lower slopes of the mountains, while higher up I rode through dense forests of oak, pine, beech and fir trees. These woodlands were thick with game and wolves, while eagles flew overhead. Of people we saw none, though perhaps most had fled on our approach. It was cold on the upper slopes, with snow covering the tops of the mountains.

Finally the army arrived before Thurii, a large port in the coastal plain. Its walls were impressive and must have measured five miles in length, encompassing the whole of the city and the port. There were three gates, one in the northern wall, one in the western wall and one leading to the south. Each gatehouse was protected by two large square towers either side of the two gates, the access to which was across a wooden bridge, as the Romans had dug a deep, wide ditch around the whole city. Spartacus deployed the army around the city on the morning of the seventh day in a show of force, but it elicited no response from the city officials. Troops lined the walls and I could see that catapults were mounted on the towers.

Crixus moved his men up to within a hundred feet of the ditch, and promptly withdrew them when great holes were torn in their ranks by machines mounted on the towers. I was with Spartacus watching the whole sorry episode as what looked like darts shot out from the tops of the towers and into the densely packed Gauls.

Spartacus shook his head. 'They are called Scorpion bolt throwers and they can hurl a three-foot dart over five hundred yards. That's about the range of your bows, isn't it?'

'Yes, lord,' I replied.

'The difference being,' he continued as more Gauls were skewered while pulling back to a safe distance, 'is that the Scorpion is operated by two men and consists of two wooden arms that are pushed through ropes made of animal sinew. The sinew has been twisted, making it a very powerful spring. The arms are then pulled back by levers, which further increases the tension. The bolt is notched into a large bowstring and then placed in a trough cut in the firing block. Then it's released. You can see the result.'

'You have seen these things before?' I asked.

'Many times. Each century in a legion usually has one Scorpion attached to it, and there are similar weapons that a legion also deploys in battle.'

'I saw none on the plateau.'

'No, strange that. Makes me think that those we killed were freshly raised from veterans who were retired then called back to the standards.' The Gauls had pulled back to a distance out of the range of the Scorpions and were now taunting the garrison with obscene gestures and exposing their genitals to those on the walls.

'Those walls look strong,' said Spartacus.

'At least thirty foot high,' replied Akmon, 'Perhaps higher. Storming them will be a bloody affair and we've got no siege engines.'

'Even if we did we have no one to operate them,' said Spartacus, glumly.

'With one side open to the sea we also have little hope of starving them into surrender,' I added to the general despondency.

'The best we can do for now is to dig a rampart to face their walls and put a wooden palisade on top of it,' said Spartacus.

In two days the rampart had been erected. The tree-covered slopes of the nearby Sila Mountains provided the materials for the palisade, which was completed within a week. Thereafter little happened. Ships continued to leave and enter the harbour and we continued to train our army. I established the camp for the cavalry five miles south of Thurii at the base of the Sila Mountains. The many streams that cut through the valleys and gullies provided fresh water for the horses and men and kept both man and beast away from the camps around the city, which soon became overcrowded and disease-ridden. As a result, Spartacus pulled the army back and dispersed it to prevent pestilence doing more damage than the Romans. The various contingents took turns in manning the palisade that surrounded the city, though we were excused as Spartacus informed me that it was well known that Parthians were useless in sieges and in any case we had the responsibility of providing an outer screen for the whole army. To this end Byrd and his scouts worked tirelessly in being our eyes and ears. I think Byrd was happiest when he was riding alone far and wide. He rode on a mangy looking horse and carried no weapons save a long dagger. His clothes were threadbare and his appearance scruffy. He reasoned that if he was spotted or captured the Romans would think that he was just a poor traveller, though just as likely they might execute him as a bandit. He had never been a soldier and he never professed any desire to be one, but he and his scouts were happy in the task they performed and I was delighted that he was so diligent in his work. His years spent travelling far and wide in Cappadocia had taught him to read the landscape and it served us well. He and his fifty scouts answered directly to me and paid no attention to anyone else. It annoyed Nergal and amused Burebista, but the arrangement worked and so I left well alone. He had recruited his scouts personally and they were similarly attired, but to his credit Byrd had taught himself Latin and lived with his men. Like him they were outsiders, and that sense of being outcasts bonded them together.

Despite the fact that it was now winter it was still warm during the day, though at night the temperature did drop markedly. And on one particularly cold evening when the wind was blowing off the snow-caped mountains, Byrd rode into camp on his shaggy beast. I was sitting on the ground warming myself by a large fire set by Godarz and some of his veterinary officers when he thundered up. He was breathless and his horse was sweating heavily, which drew mutterings of disapproval from Godarz as he inspected the animal and calmed it down. He then ordered that its saddle be removed and the beast be watered and fed, totally ignoring the wishes of its owner. But then, Parthians love their horses above all things and can't bear to see what they perceive as mistreatment. Byrd was indignant.

'Horse fine, he no need food. I feed him.'

'Obviously not enough by the look of him,' sneered Godarz as the horse was led away. 'I doubt he has been groomed for a week, it's a disgrace.'

'You no talk to me like that,' said Byrd, squaring up to the older but bigger and stockier Godarz.

'Enough,' I said, getting to my feet. 'What do you want, Byrd?'

He smiled at me. 'Have found Romani silver mine.'

'What? Where?' I asked.

'A few miles away, in the mountains. I ride to tell you. No time to stop and feed horse.'

After he had eaten some stew and bread and drunk some wine I rode with him to the Thracian camp. It was dark but the route was easy to follow as the whole plain around the city was filled with campfires. Akmon had established the Thracian camp directly in front of the city's western entrance, approximately a mile back from the walls, with the palisade in between. I often wondered what the garrison thought of a legionary camp built in their midst, but one full of enemies. We rode through the camp to the tent of Spartacus, who was sitting with Akmon when we entered.

'A silver mine,' he said to Byrd, 'you're sure?'

'Romani only dig mines for gold or silver,' he replied. 'No bother with anything else. One of men tell me. Many soldiers at mine to protect precious ore.'

'Makes sense,' said Akmon, wiping his mouth with the sleeve of his tunic after drinking some wine.

'We could take it easily enough,' I added. 'I could leave in the morning with two or three companies.'

Spartacus leaned back in his chair, his fingers tapping on the table. 'A silver mine explains why the city is so well protected and large, and therefore prosperous. The Romans must ship the silver from Thurii, across the gulf to Tarentum and then up the Appian Way to Rome. How far to the mine?'

'Half a day's ride, lord,' replied Byrd.

Spartacus looked at me. 'You and I will ride there tomorrow. But we'll take some of my Thracians as well as your horse.'

'That will slow us up,' I said.

'True, but if as your man says the garrison at the mine is large, cavalry won't be enough.' He pulled his sword from its scabbard. 'Besides, a bit of fighting will blow the cobwebs away. Akmon, you will command in my absence.'

'What use is more silver if we can't buy anything with it?' said Akmon.

The next morning we left early, two hundred horse and the same number of foot. Claudia embraced her husband who seemed in high spirits, the prospect of adventure clearly preferable to spending another day inspecting the ditch and palisade and talking Crixus out of making a direct assault on the city. The day was sunny and warm and soon we had left the plain and were heading up into the mountains, along a track that lanced through thick woods of beech and gorges cut by fast-flowing streams. The air became cooler as we climbed, and our pace slowed as men dismounted to lead their horses on foot, the Thracians in their mail shirts and helmets hauling shields, swords, food and javelins behind us. We made a lot of noise that seemed to irritate Byrd, who was clearly enjoying our company not at all. The area was alive with different flora, such as silver fir, maple, laurel, oak, holly, water mint and Dog Rose. It was also teeming with wildlife – black squirrel, deer, Red Kites and otters. We once saw an eagle soaring above us through a gap in the trees, which Spartacus reckoned was a good omen. Halting mid-afternoon, Byrd, Spartacus and I continued on foot, leaving the track and moving through the trees.

We followed Byrd through the forest, climbing steadily until we reached the top of a large outcrop, one of several that dotted the immediate area. We crawled to the edge of the cliff and peered down. Below us was a large camp containing wooden huts, a fenced-off area filled with rows of tents, a stable block and big sheds where the silver was processed. The camp had been established next to a rock face, the whole area having been cleared of trees and foliage. There was a track leading from the camp. In the rock face itself were two large entrances to the mine, from which emerged periodically slaves hauling sledges piled with ore. Guards stood at the entrance to the camp, which was surrounded by a wooden fence, and at the entrances to the mine, and also at the entrance to the fenced-off area where the slaves who worked the mine were housed. The site echoed with the sounds of men barking orders, while overhead a pall of smoke hung over the camp.

We crawled away from the edge and then walked back to the men. Spartacus said nothing during the journey, though when we got back he collected the officers around him and announced that we would attack in the morning.

'No fires tonight and we move before dawn,' he told us. 'Pacorus, leave the horses here under guard and put fifty of your men with bows on the cliff edge we were looking down from earlier. They are to kill as many Romans as they can from their vantage point while my men and the rest of your Parthians force the gate and take the camp.'

The plan seemed simple enough, though I wondered why we were bothering to capture a silver mine. He told me later as we sat huddled with our cloaks around us, as I leaned against the trunk of a tall pine. The night was cool and the sky clear, the moon casting a pale glow over the forest through the gaps in the treetops. Most of the men tried to snatch a few hours' sleep, but Spartacus could not sleep and neither could I, though my insomnia was due to the cold and knots of bark digging into my back.

'I thought we had captured large quantities of gold and silver,' I said.

'You can never have enough gold or silver,' he said, grinning.

'So we take the mine because we need more treasure? The army lives off the land, so why do we need the mine?'

'To deprive the Romans of it, of course.'

I was confused. 'To what ends?'

'Deep vein mining they call it,' he replied. 'I remember talking to a gladiator back in Capua, a man who had worked in a similar mine before being sold to the ludus. He told me that the Romans only dig underground for gold and silver. The mine we saw today would have taken a lot of time and money to build and more to maintain. And silver mines don't grow on trees, so to speak. So if we take it and threaten to destroy it then the rich owners, who you can bet live in Thurii, will be more amenable to talks.'

'Talks?' I queried.

'Crixus wants nothing more than to storm the place and kill all the inhabitants, and the longer our desultory siege drags on the greater the clamour for him to try, especially among the Gauls. If he succeeds then he will try to take command from me. However, if I can cut the ground from beneath his feet then his power will wane.'

'I thought he was a friend of yours.'

Spartacus looked directly at me. 'Gladiators have no friends, at least not while they are fighting. The ludus is called a family, but it is really a brotherhood, in which we respect each other and promise that we would give those killed a decent burial, but you cannot be a friend to someone you might one day face in the arena. I respect Crixus because he is a good fighter and also uncomplicated. But he is all brawn and no brains and eventually that will be his undoing.'

'I do not like him,' I said.

'And he dislikes you, but you are in good company. He hates me as well.'

'He does?' I was shocked.

'Of course, for I stand in the way of the one thing he desires?'

'You mean Claudia?'

He laughed. 'No, command of the army. Crixus wants to be a king with his own kingdom. He thinks the Romans can be brushed aside easily, leaving him to rule the whole of southern Italy. That's the real reason he dislike you.'

'Because I want to rule the south of Italy?'

He shook his head. 'The cold has obviously addled your brain. No, because you already have a kingdom, or at least are an heir to one. And Crixus thinks that is most unfair.'

'If he thinks at all,' I added.

'He will never leave Italy,' said Spartacus, solemnly. 'He exists to fight. He could have fought in the Roman Army, but he hates discipline and so he kills Romans instead. I assume all Gauls are like him.'

'Not all, lord.'

'Gallia is unique, I agree. You think to take her back to Parthia with you?'

I flushed with embarrassment. 'I had not thought that far ahead, lord.'

'I wager she has. She's a smart one, beautiful too. And now she's good with a bow. She'll take some taming.'

'I don't want to tame her, lord.'

'Very sensible, for I doubt any man can. Anyhow, that's one Gaul who wants to be with you.'

'Really?'

'Claudia told me, though you are not to say that I told you.'

I felt elated and could have shouted out loud. The cold and discomfort fled from me as I mulled his words in my mind over and over again.

We left the horses and a few guards two hours before dawn and moved slowly through the trees, two hundred Thracians carrying shields and pila and nearly two hundred horse archers with full quivers with swords at their hips. A handful we left behind to guard the horses. We moved slowly so as to make as little noise as possible, but even though our eyes had grown accustomed to the moon-washed night, the shadows cast by the trees meant some tripped over tree roots and dead branches lying on the forest floor. Byrd led us. I noticed Spartacus was very light on his feet and seemed to be weightless as he moved through the trees. I followed him and the rest of the men followed me in a long column behind. It seemed an eternity before we neared the camp, and by then I was both cold and hungry. I knelt beside Spartacus and we waited until the last of our men had arrived. He called the officers to him and we had an impromptu council of war. He talked in a hushed voice as he told us his plan of attack. Fifty archers would provide covering fire from the top of the rock outcrop that we had used to observe the camp. Byrd led these men to their positions.

We stealthily approached the gates to the mine, which were nothing more than crude barriers made from cut-down trees flanked by two wooden platforms, on each of which stood a guard. The gates and the fence were obviously designed to keep people in, not attackers out. But then that was no surprise, being in the heart of Italy. Spartacus and I moved to the edge of the tree line that surrounded the mine.

'Think you and one of your men can kill those guards with the first arrow?' he asked.

Of course,' I replied. 'Do you want them shot through the neck so they don't make a sound.'

'Don't get cocky, just drop them and we'll rush the gate.'

I tapped one of my men on the shoulder and we moved into position, either side of a tree facing the gates. The distance was about two hundred feet, maybe less. In the eastern sky the first hint of dawn was appearing, barely discernible cracks of red and orange. Bozan had always told me that the best time to surprise the enemy was as the dawn was breaking, when men involuntarily eased after seeing through another night. Subconsciously the arrival of a new day made the mind relax after the tension of the darkness, when the black could hide a host of enemies. Day means light, warmth and safety. 'Hit them when dawn breaks,' he once told me, 'and your victory will be swift.' I eased back the bowstring and released the arrow; the other archer did the same. The arrows made little sound as they each struck their targets. My man was leaning against the wooden rail on the platform, wrapped in his cloak with his shield propped up against the same rail. He was rubbing his hands together and peering at the interior of the camp. My arrow struck him in the middle of his back, sending him sprawling onto the platform. The second sentry was standing leaning on his shield looking towards the forest when the arrow hit him in the right shoulder, sending him spinning off the platform and landing on the ground with a crump.

Spartacus tapped me on the shoulder as he ran past me towards the gates, followed by the others. I too rushed forward as he stopped at the gates and pointed at two of his men, who placed their backs against the gates and cupped their hands together. Spartacus ran at one of them, put his right foot in the man's hands and was hoisted onto the top of the gate, then dropped over the other side. I followed him, landing hard on the ground inside the camp. He picked me up and we released the iron bar that had been dropped into brackets fastened to each gate to keep them shut. The guard that had been shot off his platform was moaning and trying to crawl away, but Spartacus pulled his dagger and slit his throat. I opened the gates and the others poured into the camp. The dawn was breaking now and in the half-light figures could be seen coming out of the huts that housed the guards. Morning roll call! Spartacus led his Thracians towards the straw-roofed huts, racing in front of the sheds where the silver ore was separated. In front of the huts, about a hundred yards away, was the slave compound, a fenced enclosure containing tents. Two guards stood at its iron gate. These were quickly felled by arrows. But now an alarm bell was being rung and out of the doors of the huts poured legionaries frantically adjusting helmets, belts and tunics. They formed up at the far end of the compound, two centuries of them being roughly shoved into their ranks by two centurions. Spartacus halted his men and formed them up into two groups eight ranks deep, the men standing ready to advance and hurl their pila. I ordered the majority of my men to deploy behind the Thracians, ready to loose their arrows at the Romans, deploying others to act as flank guards at the ore sheds and in front of the two entrances to the mine, as I did not know if there were any guards in the mine itself.

The Romans started to move forward, but then my archers on the outcrop overlooking the camp began a steady hail of arrows against them, which stopped them in their tracks. I gave the order to fire and arrows flew over the Thracians and into the front ranks of the Romans. The latter, true to form, locked their shields to the front, sides and over their heads, to produce what looked like two large red boxes sitting on the ground. The men on the outcrop continued to shoot at the shield blocks, while Spartacus yelled, 'Swords!' and rushed forward. The Thracians dumped their javelins on the ground and charged the Romans. As they raced forward we fired another volley of arrows, which hit their shields seconds before the Thracians smashed into their ranks. I was told later by those watching from above that this charge buckled the front of the Roman formations, and then broke them as Spartacus and his men stabbed repeatedly at their enemies. Seasoned troops may have stood and fought as their comrades in front of them were disembowelled and lacerated by expertly wielded swords, but these were prison guards and in a few seconds the two formations had fallen apart. I led my men forward in the wake of the Thracians, as the fighting suddenly became a mass of individual fights, and soon only one. Most of the Romans threw down their weapons and begged for mercy, while others who carried on fighting were soon cut down. And so it happened that in the end Spartacus stood alone with sword and shield challenging the Romans to fight him. There was no shortage of takers. We formed a semi-circle around our general as he fought against five Romans who circled him. I must confess I was worried, but his men merely yelped and cheered him on.

He fought with skill and speed, using his shield as a weapon as well as his sword, parrying sword strikes and smashing the shield boss into faces and ribs. He moved quickly, light on his feet and swivelling his body expertly to face his multiple attackers. Spartacus also used his enemies, assuming positions where one Roman blocked the attack of another. He split one adversary's skull with his sword, ducked low and swept his right foot to knock another off his feet. He threw off his helmet and fought bare headed, goading his assailants and deliberately exposing his chest to invite attack. One did so recklessly and died as Spartacus feinted to the man's right, tripped him and then shattered his spine with a sword strike as he lay face-down on the ground. The men were shouting 'Spartacus, Spartacus' as he crouched low and delivered a fatal blow to the groin of the fourth Roman, his high-pitched squeal piercing the morning air. The fifth Roman probably knew he would die, but to his credit he attacked with vigour, but died instantly when Spartacus brushed aside his sword with his shield and then rammed his own blade through the man's throat and out of the back of his neck. He left the gladius in the man's flesh and walked away, the body momentarily remaining upright before collapsing on the ground. Spartacus stood with arms raised, accepting the rapturous applause given him, before retrieving his sword and helmet from the bloody ground.

I joined him as he wiped the blood from his sword and put it back in its scabbard.

'I enjoyed that,' he beamed. 'It was like being back in the arena.'
'You liked being in the arena?' I said with incredulity.

He was shocked. 'Of course, why not? I was good at it and everyone likes doing something that they are good at.'

Those Romans who had surrendered were quickly herded into the slave pen, while the slaves were let out and informed by Spartacus that they were free. Most just stood around looking confused, but one individual pushed his way to the front of the group and spoke to Spartacus. A thickset man with a chiselled face and narrow black eyes, he had manacles on his feet.

'Lucius Domitus at your service. I thought I would die in this place but now, thanks to you, it appears that I shall die elsewhere.'

'You are a Roman?' asked Spartacus.

'Ex-centurion of the Thirteenth Legion and for the last six months resident of this shit-hole.'

'And why are you here?' retorted Spartacus.

Domitus shrugged. 'I had a disagreement with a tribune which resulted in him getting a beating and me being sent here.'

'You were lucky,' remarked Spartacus.

'That's my middle name,' smiled Domitus. He tugged at his chains. 'Any chance of getting these off? At least tell me your name.'

'I am Spartacus, a Thracian,' the name made no impression on the Roman, 'and this is Pacorus, a Parthian.'

Domitus regarded me coolly, obviously assuming that my long hair indicated a lack of discipline and fighting ability. He had, however, noticed the effectiveness of our bows. He nodded. 'Clever trick, that, putting archers up on the rocks.'

Behind us the last of the garrison had been thrown into the slave pen, whose iron gate was shut. The slaves, including Domitus, were being led to the smelting sheds where their fetters were broken on anvils. Spartacus ordered that all the weapons, armour, helmets and shields were to be loaded onto carts to be taken back to camp, while all the chains were likewise to be transported back, there to be forged into weapons. I sent twenty men down the track to fetch the horses, and ordered fifty more to retrieve any usable arrows. The garrison's rations were distributed among the slaves, who sat on the ground and consumed them with frenzy. Spartacus and I wandered over to the entrance to the mine: two large passageways side-by-side cut into the rock face. Each tunnel was illuminated by means of oil lamps set into small recesses in the rock. Spartacus ordered that Domitus be fetched to us, and moments later he appeared, delighted to be no longer chained.

'Who's down there?' said Spartacus.

'Fifty guards and a couple of hundred slaves. They rotate us every five days in groups of fifty, which means most of us are underground most of the time.' He looked at the dead guards strewn about the entrance to the mine. 'They'll know what's happened by now.'

'Any other ways out of the mine apart from here?' said Spartacus.

'No,' replied Domitus.

Spartacus thought for a moment, pacing up and down and kicking at the ground. At length he spoke to Domitus.

'I intend to keep the mine working, at least for the time being. You are free to go, but if you help me then you may join us, if you desire so. If you wish to help, then I ask you to go into the mine and tell all those below to come to the surface. Those who guarded you will henceforth mine the ore. What is your answer?'

Domitus rubbed his chin with his right hand and then scratched his filthy tunic. His arms were sinewy and scarred. 'And if I don't want to help you?'

'It's of no consequence to me,' replied Spartacus. 'I will seal the entrances with wood and set light to it.'

'You'll kill everyone inside, slaves and Romans.'

'Like I said,' remarked Spartacus, 'it's of no consequence to me.'

Domitus laughed. 'I like you, Thracian, and seeing as I am in your debt I will run your errand. Give me a sword and some of your men and I'll fetch them up.'

Spartacus picked up a gladius lying beside a dead Roman and handed it to Domitus, who started to walk down the tunnel. Spartacus ordered a squad of his men to follow him.

'You trust him?' I asked.

'Trust has to be earned, Pacorus. Let's see if he returns.'

'He might have been lying about this being the only way in.'

'Perhaps, but if he betrays us I will still fire the mine.' He nodded towards the Roman prisoners. 'What should I do with them if we have to destroy the mine?'

'Keep them as slaves for the army.'

'I was thinking more of killing them, but I'll bear in mind what you suggest.'

As we waited for Domitus and the soldiers to return we walked around the camp, whose storerooms were filled with the tools required to mine silver ore. There were spiked hammers, mauls, chisels, single- and double-pointed picks, mattocks, shovels and rakes. Other sheds were full of baskets and leather bags for carrying ore, plus ropes, ladders, buckets and windlasses for hauling it up pit shafts. One heavily bolted shed contained neatly stacked bars of silver arranged on wooden shelves, each one weighing two or three pounds. There must have been at least fifty of them, all ready to be shipped to the city. Spartacus walked among the slaves as they ate and drank water, telling them who he was and asking them to join us. Most seemed willing to do so, probably out of gratitude and a desire to leave this dismal place. At last Domitus appeared at the mine entrance, followed by a line of Roman soldiers. I quickly formed two lines of archers either side of them and had them place arrows in their bowstrings, lest they had an idea to fight us. But Domitus merely led them out of the mine to a distance of about a hundred feet, stopped and pointed at the ground, whereupon each Roman unbuckled his sword belt and threw it down, followed by his helmet and mail shirt. I stood beside Spartacus as the guards thus disarmed themselves and were then moved to join their comrades in the slave enclosure. Afterwards came the slaves who had been kept down the mines, emaciated, dirty figures squinting as they tried to get accustomed to the daylight. Some were children, who I was informed were used to drag the wooden sleds containing ore along the mine passages. Many collapsed or sat on the ground as soon as they had left the mine, obviously exhausted, frightened and bewildered by the morning's events.

I rode back to the army with Spartacus and half a dozen others, though most of the cavalry was allocated to escorting the carts loaded with captured supplies and the silver bars. He left all the Thracians behind to guard the Roman prisoners, while Byrd and a group of fifty horsemen accompanied the slaves who followed us on foot, including Domitus, who had told Spartacus he would like to stay with us. When we got back to camp Spartacus told Akmon to send another hundred soldiers to the mine to reinforce the garrison he had left behind. Domitus was astounded by the size of the slave army when he saw its camps that surrounded Thurii, and he was even more impressed when he saw that the soldiers drilled in exactly the same manner as Roman legionaries, were armed and equipped the same and used the same tactics. He asked Spartacus if he could be a centurion in one of the Thracian centuries and was granted his request. Thus did our army gain its first Roman recruit, though he was told in no uncertain terms that thrashing soldiers severely with a vine cane was discouraged in this army. He seemed upset by this, but more than made up for it by his later use of threats, insults and foul language that he hurled at those he was training.

Godarz had the cavalry camp organised and running smoothly and had sent out riders to sweep the land to the south and west for horses. New recruits came to the army on a daily basis, mostly runaway field hands or herdsmen and shepherds, and of those any who could ride were sent to us. As usual, those who were Gauls were immediately recruited by Crixus, whose camp was positioned to the north of Thurii and occupied a vast area of the coastal plain. Castus and his Germans were camped to the south of the city, with the Thracians positioned to the east. Our camp was in the foothills of the mountains, behind the Thracians. Patrols were sent out far to the north and south, as far as the River Siris in Lucania and down to Petelia in Bruttium, groups of horsemen also travelling north and south along the Via Annia, the road that began at Capua and ended at Rhegium in the far south of Italy. Daily we expected reports of Roman soldiers marching south or north to fight us, but our patrols reported an empty country, empty of slaves, empty of civilians and empty of soldiers. It was obvious that the Romans had no legions to send to the relief of Thurii. The city was alone and isolated, and although ships entered and left the harbour with impunity, I wondered how long Spartacus would do nothing with an army at his back and an inviting target before him. Its walls were strong, but was the garrison large enough to defend them in the face of an assault thrown against three sides of the city? Would he launch an attack? It was a month exactly after our arrival in front of Thurii that Spartacus requested me at a council of war, where I had my answer.

Chapter 10

The army's morale soared on hearing the news of the capture of the silver mine, though I did not know why as we took what we wanted from the land anyway and there was no opportunity to spend any of the gold and silver we possessed. I was bemused by the conversations among the soldiery about how wealthy the army was and how they would all go home as rich as lords. Still, anything that raised spirits was to be welcomed, and even Crixus seemed to be in a good mood as the captains of the army gathered in Spartacus' tent and made themselves comfortable in well-appointed chairs around the large oak table, a 'gift' from a local villa. Present were Spartacus, Akmon, Crixus, Dumnorix, now second-in-command of the Gauls, Castus, Cannicus, Godarz and myself. Crixus propped his war axe against his chair's right arm, as usual drinking wine from a large cup.

'It appears,' started Spartacus,' that we are at this present time rich. We have acquired the wealth of Nola, Forum Annii and Metapontum and now have possession of a silver mine. I have instructed Akmon to build a camp within this one where all the gold and silver will be stored. However, I do not intend to keep it for it will be a burden when we begin our march north in the spring. Therefore, I intend to spend it.'

There was a stunned silence. We all looked at each other in confusion, and for once even Crixus was lost for words. Castus frowned, Akmon was bemused and Godarz sat stroking his chin.

'Spend it, lord?' I said.

'That's right. Buy something useful with it, things that can help us in our mission to get out of this Roman-infested land.'

'And where are you going to purchase these items?' said Crixus, burping loudly as he finished his cup.

'From Thurii, of course,' replied Spartacus, straight faced.

'You're joking of course,' said Crixus. 'You've dragged us over here for no other reason than to ridicule us.'

'Not all at,' said Spartacus, 'it makes perfect sense. We will make an offer to the rulers of the city. We will pay handsomely for the things that we require, and in return the city's merchants will grow fat and we will not burn the place to the ground.'

'The plan has merits,' said Godarz.

'Merits!' bawled Crixus. 'It's madness. They will probably cut the head off the poor bastard who has to deliver your message, like they did at Metapontum, and then I had to attack and exact vengeance. That's the only language the Romans understand.'

243

'They also understand the language of wealth and commerce,' replied Spartacus, calmly. 'But I think they will listen to the man I will send to bargain with them.'

'Bargain? I'll wager that his head will end up on a spike on the city walls,' added Crixus. 'Who is the poor wretch?'

Spartacus looked at me. 'I intend to send Pacorus to negotiate our terms.'

Crixus clapped his hands in delight. 'On the other hand, perhaps your plan does have merit.'

All eyes were on me, watching for my reaction. 'What say you, Pacorus?' said Spartacus, 'will you accept this challenge? I do not command, only ask.'

Castus looked alarmed but said nothing, whereas Crixus and Dumnorix looked delighted. Godarz was shaking his head at me and Akmon was admiring the cup he was drinking from and clearly intent on avoiding my stare. I had to accept, of course, for not to do so would be a fatal loss of face. Spartacus knew this, but I don't think he was putting me in this position out of malice. He knew that he had to keep on winning or he and his army would be destroyed. But he also did not become the commander of this army by not being ruthless. I believed that he both liked and respected me, but by placing me in this position he was also showing that he would stop at nothing to achieve victory.

'I will do as you ask, lord,' I replied.

'Thank you, Pacorus. Upon your shoulders rests the hopes of the whole army.'

'And don't worry,' added Crixus, 'when they lop your head off, I promise to find it afterwards and give it a decent burial.'

'If that happens, Crixus,' said Spartacus, 'then you and your Gauls will be the first to assault the city, and we will keep on assaulting the walls until we have battered them down stone by stone. And then we will pull down the buildings brick by brick. This I swear.'

Afterwards Spartacus pulled me aside and spoke to me.

'I hope you do not think that I do not hold your life dear, Pacorus.'

'No, lord.'

'This plan either succeeds or I will be forced to attack the city. If we attack we will lose thousands.'

'I will do my best to bring you success.' I said.

'Remember, the Romans are ruthless but they are also a pragmatic people.'

I doubted that, but I knew that we could not remain idle before this Roman city forever. In the next two days Godarz briefed me on what to expect when I met the city's officials, if I met the city's officials! He told me that each major city was ruled by a municipal council called a curia, which was named after the Roman Senate itself. This council administered the food supply, public services, religious festivities, town finance and local building projects. The silver mine, though, would be owned by the Senate in Rome itself, as its valuable ore was used to pay for the legions fighting in foreign lands. Nevertheless, it would be administered on behalf of Rome's Senate by a powerful local individual, who presumably was resident in the city. I asked whether it was a possibility that the city's élite would have fled the city by boat, but Godarz assured me that Roman civic leaders usually prided themselves on their courage and their responsibility to the citizens they ruled over, and as such they would never want to be seen fleeing the city. Godarz also told me that Roman civic leaders often built public baths and other buildings at their own expense, both as a sign of their wealth to the lower orders and as a display of power to their fellow senators, who were often bitter rivals.

I decided that I would look my best to meet the dignitaries of Thurii; after all, I was a member of the Parthian aristocracy and therefore a representative of the empire, albeit in strange circumstances. Therefore I wore a white tunic edged with blue, a silk vest underneath, leather boots, brown leggings, my Roman helmet with a new goose feather plume and a white cloak. Nergal said I should have refused to be an envoy, as did Burebista, though Godarz, rational as ever, suggested that it was probably the best hope to resolve the situation quickly, and he added that there was no guarantee that an assault would succeed in any case. He said Spartacus probably knew this and that's why he wanted to find another way out of his predicament. And he had no interest in taking a city that he would have to abandon come the spring when we marched north. All things considered, therefore, it seemed perfectly sensible to treat with the city. I just hoped that the city was in a reciprocal mood. The one good thing about my new mission was that Gallia was greatly concerned that I might be killed and became very tactile, linking arms and resting her head on my shoulder as we walked through the cavalry camp in the early evening. I have to confess that I deliberately played on her fears, which served to tighten her grip on my arm and send my spirits soaring.

'It was unfair of Spartacus to ask you to go.'

'The interests of the many outweigh the interests of the few,' I said solemnly.

'The Romans may kill you.'

I shrugged. 'That can happen any time in battle.'

'But you will not be in battle, you will be alone.'

I stopped and faced her. 'If I have your affection, I will never be alone.'

Her eyes filled with tears and I moved closer to her to kiss her, but she instead threw her arms around me and embraced me in a vice-like grip. Failed again!

'Promise me you will be careful,' she whispered.

'Of course,' I replied, finding it difficult to breathe.

That night Spartacus sent a messenger to the city walls, a man on horseback who shouted up at the western gatehouse, announcing that we would be sending an envoy in the morning to open negotiations that would be mutually beneficial. The messenger was not shot by an arrow, which was hopeful at least. But then the Romans could have simply ignored him.

The morning dawned bright and sunny, though because it was winter the air was cool and I felt chilly. I ate breakfast in my tent with those I held dear for company. They included Gallia, Diana, Praxima, whom I had grown to like as she kept Nergal very happy, Byrd, Gafarn, Godarz and Burebista. Rubi sat on a stool behind Gallia, hissing at all the men. The mood was subdued and everyone ate little, but I was glad of their company. Afterwards I told Nergal that he would command the cavalry in the event of my death. I emphasised to him that his over-riding duty was to get those in his charge back to their homelands, and himself and the rest of my Parthians back to Hatra. Gallia sat white-faced at the table as I told her that she would have Remus if I failed to return. There was nothing else to say. I stood and buckled on my sword belt and went outside.

My eyes misted as I saw rank upon rank of horsemen drawn up each side of the main avenue that led from the camp, Rhesus saluting me with his drawn sword. I knew that if I looked at even one in the eye I would blubber like a baby, so I paced stony faced through the middle of them, out of the camp and towards the palisade. I felt cold, but perhaps it was the cool embrace of fear. Behind me walked my breakfast companions, but I did not turn to look at them. Spartacus, Castus, Akmon and Claudia met me at the palisade, though not Crixus. I was glad; I had no desire to see his leering visage on what might be my last day on earth. Spartacus looked troubled as half a dozen of his Thracians removed some of the tree trunks that had been sharpened to a point and made up the palisade, to let me through.

'Are you sure of this, Pacorus? I do not command you to go.'

'Yes, lord,' I knew he was giving me an opportunity to save myself, but by now the whole army would know of my task and what would they think of me if I turned back now? Besides, I was a Parthian and we were not raised to run away from danger. I embraced Claudia and shook the hands of Castus and Akmon. The posts had been removed and my route to the city was open. The distance from the palisade to the western gates of the city was about half a mile, a wide expanse of empty space in which nothing moved, apart from today. I turned to look at the people I classed as my friends and the one who I hoped was far more than that. I took off my helmet and walked up to Gallia, clasped her hands in mine and kissed her on the lips.

'I love you,' I said to her, then turned about, put on my helmet and strode away.

I felt strangely calm as I walked alone towards the walls, which seemed higher and more formidable the nearer I got to them. But I wasn't thinking about the Romans, I was thinking about Gallia, my darling Gallia. I had told her the feelings in my heart and that was all that mattered. If I died today then at the very least she would know how I felt about her, and as I walked along I started to smile to myself. Any guards watching me probably thought that I was mad, and they may have entertained the thought of putting some arrows into me rather than letting me enter their city. I carried on walking. It seemed that I was the only person on the face of the earth as I walked onto the bridge across the ditch and finally reached the western entrance, two huge wooden gates separated by a stone arch, each one studded with iron spikes. The gatehouse itself comprised two large square stone towers topped with tiled roofs, each tower having two high-mounted rows of ports for archers and slingers, which were now covered by wooden shutters. The top of the wall between the towers was deserted, but my sixth sense told me that I was being watched by many eyes.

I went over in my mind what Spartacus had told me, that I was to negotiate on his behalf, and to remember that we might only be freed slaves but we possessed the province's wealth. No wonder the leading citizens of Thurri were rich. The province of Bruttium was prosperous indeed, not only because of its silver mine but also due to its large herds of sheep that produced wool and that were taken into the mountains in the summer to avoid the intense heat of the plains. The province also produced excellent wines from its many vineyards, plus massive quantities of olives from the great estates that littered the coastal plain. All of these were now in our hands, presumably much to the consternation of their owners. We had come across few villas, leading Spartacus to speculate that the owners lived in Thurri itself. The province was also home to a beautiful breed of horse that was characterised by a thin head, strong and well-proportioned neck, high withers, strong back, a slightly inclined rump, powerful joints and broad, solid hooves. Godarz told me that the stock had come about because of cross-breeding between Italian horses and those brought from Africa by a general called Hannibal, who belonged to a people called Carthaginians from Africa. Apparently he had campaigned for twenty years against the Romans in their own homeland before being finally defeated. But his legacy was a superb breed of horse that was raised in Bruttium and then sold throughout the Roman Empire. And now these fine horses were being drafted into my cavalry. I also discovered that they had a patient nature, which made the training of new recruits much easier. Spartacus had given strict instructions that no unwarranted destruction should be inflicted on the province, though the Gauls had unsurprisingly ignored these orders until Spartacus himself had marched over to Crixus' camp and demanded that they desist their activities.

I had halted a few feet from the gates and there I stood, for what seemed like an eternity. I said a silent prayer to Shamash that I might have a quick death at the hand of a skilled archer, but instead one of the gates slowly opened inwards. I remained stationary as the gate was fully opened and a Roman officer, wearing a red-plumed helmet and scarlet cloak, strode onto the wooden bridge across the ditch, halted and shouted 'follow me', before he about-turned and marched back into the city. I swallowed and walked forward at a brisk pace. I was nervous but determined not to show it as I left the bridge and entered the city of Thurii.

I walked under the gatehouse and onto a paved street that was flanked with two-and three-storey buildings, many of which were shops that opened up onto the street. I was immediately surrounded by a group of legionaries, ten of them, with a centurion standing at their head. Their commander patently ignored me as he gave the order to march forward, and so I began my journey through the city. It appeared to follow the usual Roman town layout, with streets bisecting at right angles the one I was walking along. I noticed that many of the buildings were large and well maintained, with ornate, over-hanging balconies. The streets were filled with people and all the shops seemed to be open. Clearly the port area was still bringing in supplies of food and other essentials. Few people bothered to pay me any attention as the legionaries shoved aside any who got in the way. After about fifteen minutes we came to the forum, a massive square enclosed on three sides by colonnaded passages and the fourth fronted by a massive basilica with whitewashed walls and a terracotta-tiled roof. My silent escorts and I marched across the square and up the steps of the basilica, then through its main entrance, which was framed by two enormous marble columns. Godarz had told me that the basilica was both a business centre and law court, but today I had the feeling that it was definitely the latter as my escort halted at the entrance. I was left alone to walk towards the dignitaries assembled at the far end of what was in effect a large rectangular central aisle, flanked by two other aisles, one either side of the main one. The central aisle was taller than the sides and there were windows in its top section, through which poured light. The central aisle was supported by thick stone columns and arches, and in front of every column stood a guard in full war gear. I took off my helmet and walked across the grey marble-tiled floor towards the raised apse at the far end of the basilica, upon which were seated three men in chairs. A fourth chair beside them was empty. When I reached the apse I saw that more guards stood against the wall behind the chairs and clerks sat at tables to one side. I halted a few paces in front of the apse and bowed my head to the three seated men. An awkward silence followed. Finally, the man in the middle, dressed in a white toga, addressed me. He was about fifty years of age, with a long, lean face and dark, receding hair flecked with grey. His voice was slightly effeminate as he looked at me with pale grey eyes.

'I am Gnaeus Musius, the governor of this great city. Your name?'

'I am Prince Pacorus, son of King Varaz of Hatra, and I speak for General Spartacus.'

The governor looked surprised. 'And where is Hatra?'

'In Parthia, lord.' I replied.

The man next to him, who looked twenty years younger and who had curly light brown hair, was clearly agitated by the way he fidgeted in his chair. The governor looked from me to him.

'You have something to say Titus.'

The younger man, dressed in an officer's tunic with a muscled cuirass and a red cloak hanging from his shoulders, leaned forward and looked at me intently.

'I am Titus Sextus, garrison commander. Why is a Parthian in my country?'

I bowed my head to him, too. 'The simple truth is sir, that I was captured in Cappadocia and find myself a guest in Italy, albeit a reluctant one.'

'You mean you are a slave,' he said.
'I was a slave,' I replied. 'Now I am making my way back to my homeland, along with others who have the same desire.'
'We do not treat with slaves, we own them, we command them, and when it suits us, we execute them. That will be your fate, slave. What is to stop me killing you right here, right now?'
'Nothing,' I replied, calmly. 'Though you must also ask yourself what is preventing those camped outside your walls from attacking and putting you all to the sword?'
'So what is preventing them?' said the third man, a rotund figure with a double chin and fat fingers whose large bulk was wrapped in a toga and who had thick, unruly hair.
'This is Marcus Aristius, the leading merchant in the city who represents the business class,' said Gnaeus Musius.
'We have no desire to attack your city.'
'He's clearly a liar,' sneered Sextus. 'They obviously lack the means to take the city and hope that by posturing and threats they can capture Thurii by deception.'
'I can state quite clearly, sir,' I said, beginning to lose patience, 'that if we had intended to take this city we would have done so by now. General Spartacus does not wish it so.'
'General Spartacus?' said Sextus. 'This general is nothing more that a runaway gladiator, a deserter who has gathered around him a band of bandits who murder and rape innocent citizens.' He pointed at me. 'This wretch should be flogged and then nailed to a cross for daring to stand before such an august body.'
'That is your prerogative,' I said. 'But if you kill me General Spartacus will attack the city and will take it.'
Sextus waved his hand at me dismissively. 'Empty words.'
'I do not think that they are.' I turned to see an elderly gentleman walk into the apse and occupy the empty seat. He had grey wispy hair and a kind face. I could tell that he held some authority by the way the others stood as he took his seat, then waited until he nodded at them to sit down again. I thought that I knew him, but how could that be?
He looked at me and smiled. 'You don't remember me, do you? Not really surprising, as the last time we met the situation was very fraught and I looked rather dishevelled, but allow Quintus Hortonius to thank you for saving him and his family at Forum Annii.'
The others sat open mouthed as he stepped forward and offered me his hand, which I shook, and then I recognised him. He had his family were about to be murdered by Oenomaus before I had

interceded on their behalf.'

'You know this man, Quintus?' asked the governor.

'I do,' said Quintus, 'and were it not for his good offices I and my family would have been murdered.'

He took his seat and frowned. 'Have we forsaken basic manners? Has Roman hospitality sunk so low that we have forgotten basic courtesies? Where is a chair for our guest?'

'He is a slave, senator,' snapped Sextus.

'Is he?' replied Senator Quintus. 'I thought I heard him say that he was a prince of Parthia. We can argue about his status later, but does it not offend our Roman morality that we all sit while our guest is left standing?'

Without waiting for a reply he signalled to a clerk, who found a chair and placed it behind me. The senator invited me to sit.

'You speak for those who are camped outside our walls?' he asked me.

'Yes, lord.'

'What are your terms?'

Gnaeus Musius inhaled loudly and Titus Sextus banged his fist on the arm of his chair and stood up. 'I must protest. We debase ourselves by speaking to slaves.'

'Believe me, said Quintus, 'being helpless while a town is destroyed around you and seeing its citizens butchered before your eyes is far more debasing.'

Sextus sat down, his face red with rage and his eyes full of loathing for me.

'I ask again,' said Quintus, calmly, what are your terms?'

It was obvious that he was the senior-ranking person present, which I was thankful for.

'We wish no harm against your city. We merely wish to purchase the things we need.'

'Which are?' enquired Quintus.

'Iron, steel and bronze,' I replied.

'For weapons, no doubt,' spat Sextus.

'Yes,' I replied, seeing no gain in trying to deceive them.

'With which to kill more Romans. This is an outrage, senator, which we should have no part in,' said Sextus.

'Under normal circumstances I would agree with you,' replied Quintus. 'But these are not normal circumstances. Tell me, Prince Pacorus, if we refuse these terms what action will this Spartacus take?'

'He will attack the city, lord.'

'So gentlemen,' reflected Quintus, 'it would seem that we have two choices. To do business with this slave general or defy him. If we choose the latter option then we place our lives in the hands of the gods and Titus Sextus. Can you guarantee that this city will not fall, commander?'

'I am certain that we can resist the feeble attempts of slaves, senator,' gloated Sextus.

'Forgive my interruption,' I said, 'but the garrisons of Forum Annii and Metapontum thought the same thing, as did the commander of the army we wiped out some weeks ago. The fact is that we are here for the winter, whether you like it or not.'

'You dare threaten me?' said Sextus.

'I threaten no one, sir, I merely point out the situation as it exists at this moment in time,' I replied. 'If I may try to assuage you, my general has issued orders that the area we occupy is not to be devastated or unnecessarily molested. This means your vineyards, olive trees and silver mine will all be returned to you once we have left.'

'Words are cheap,' said Sextus.

'Indeed they are, sir,' I said, Sextus smarting at the implied insult. 'And we would pay generously for all supplies.' I added.

'How do you propose to pay for goods?' enquired Marcus Aristius,

'In gold and silver, sir. And the merchants of the city may set the price.' I saw his eyes light up and I knew then that I had won him over. His chubby fingers started to twitch excitedly and I smiled at him.

'If we agree to trade with you, we will want supplies of food to be included in any arrangement,' remarked Gnaeus Musius.

'I'm sure that your request could be accommodated,' I said.

'And rent,' said Quintus.

'Rent, lord?' I replied.

'Of course. The land that you occupy is mine, or most of it, and I would be lacking in business acumen if I did not charge you rent.'

'I would have to liaise with General Spartacus first, but I'm sure he will be conciliatory towards your request.' Their demands were bordering on effrontery, but I said nothing.

'I think we need to discuss your offer among ourselves, Prince Pacorus,' said Quintus. He looked at his Roman companions. 'I think we can give you an answer by tomorrow morning. I will deliver it to you in person at the western gates two hours after dawn. And now I think our meeting is at an end, unless anyone has anything else to say?'

Quintus looked at each of his companions, but he had decided that all discussion was at an end and no one challenged his authority. Quintus stood.

'Thank you, Prince Pacorus. The guards will escort you from the city.' I stood and bowed my head to them, then turned and walked from the basilica, flanked by the same guards who had met me at the gate. I felt a great sense of relief when I walked through the gates and back towards our own lines. I did not know how long I had been gone, but when I arrived back at the gap in the palisade everyone was waiting for me. Gallia ran down the earth rampart and threw herself at me, wrapping her long legs around my waist and holding me tight. I was nearly bundled over as she kissed and hugged me. Our lips parted and I saw tears running down her cheeks.

'I thought I would never see you again,' she said. I did not tell her that I had entertained the same thought.

We walked back to the others where Spartacus and Claudia embraced me. As a group of soldiers fastened the poles back into place, we all walked back to Spartacus' tent, Gallia holding onto to me tightly. On the way I told them about the meeting, about Quintus Hortonius and that I believed they would accept our offer, though it may come at a high price. When I told Spartacus about the demands for rent he burst into laughter. Godarz simply said that pragmatism was an integral part of Roman nature and they were never averse to turning a profit. Spartacus remarked that as long as they supplied what we needed, it mattered little how much gold and silver they wanted as we had taken it from the Romans in the first place. I told him about the garrison commander, Titus Sextus, and how he had wanted to refuse our offer, but Spartacus believed that practicality would triumph over a fool's lust for glory.

The city agreed to our offer. Senator Hortonius told me of their decision the next morning at the appointed hour. He walked out of the western gates, across the bridge and met me halfway between the city and the palisade (a part of which had again been dismembered to allow me through). He came alone and unarmed, a sign of his trust in me I liked to think. He informed me that Sextus had been vehemently opposed to any deal but had been over-ruled by the governor and Marcus Aristius, who had been seduced by the prospect of a handsome profit. The senator told me that no goods would be exchanged via the city gates, but would instead be shipped to a stretch of beach five miles south of the city where the waters were calm and boats could come and go with ease. He and the others must have spent many hours thrashing out the details of the agreement, for at the end of our meeting he handed me a scroll, upon which were listed the days and times when deliveries would be made, the persons who would supervise the offloading of supplies and the payments for the metals we needed. Deliveries were to be made on the second day of every week, at two hours after dawn (a time he seemed to like) and I was to be present at each delivery. He also informed me that the prices for the goods we required were listed on the scroll. Before he left, I told him that I wanted to add a thousand saddles to our list of wants. He smiled and told me he would pass on my request to Marcus Aristius.

A week later the first shipment of iron came ashore at the inlet at the rearranged time. There were four boats, vessels with symmetrical hulls. The sides of their hulls were protected by wales and had wing-like projections that protected the side rudders. They had a cabin at the rear. Also at the stern were the two steering oars, which were controlled by a tiller. Unlike warships, these vessels were powered by means of a single large square sail. Under the terms of the agreement neither side was permitted to have armed soldiers present, so I stood on the beach along with fifty of my men in tunics plus fifty more who waited on a track that ran off the sands with a dozen carts, one of which was loaded with the chests of gold. The day was calm with a slight wind, the sea as smooth as a pond. The vessels came into the shallow waters and their crews heaved anchors over the side. Then they stood still in the water, their crews peering at us. I decided to grasp the bull by the horns and walked into the sea and waded over to the first vessel. The water was shallow and barely came up to my chest. A burly man with a ragged beard and a large grizzled face squinted at me from above. His massive, tattooed forearms rested on the gunwale.

'Are you the Parthian?'

'I am.'

'You'd better bring those carts into the water and alongside each boat. How many have you got?'

'A dozen,' I replied.

'More than enough. What about the payment?'

'Loaded on one of the carts.'

He gestured behind him. 'There's an official from the city on board who's to check everything is in order. We might as well start.'

It took us all morning to load the iron onto the carts and load the four chests of gold bars onto the ships. The captain's eyes lit up as I lifted the lid of the first chest and showed him and the pale, slightly effeminate clerk who had been sent by Marcus Aristius to oversee the exchange of goods. The clerk, no doubt a slave, showed no emotion as he meticulously counted the number of bars in each chest. I was standing beside the captain when the chests were hauled aboard by means of a winch and he saw me looking at the clerk.

'A eunuch, that one,' he sniffed in disgust.

'What?'

'They would have lopped off his crown jewels years ago. They like to do that with slaves. Keeps them docile, you see.'

'That's disgusting,' I said.

He shrugged. 'If they catch you lot they'll do far worse.' He looked at me intently. 'They say you're a prince.'

'That's right,' I replied.

'Then what are you doing with a load of runaways?'

'It's a long story.'

He pulled me to one side. 'I've been a sailor all my life and I know the way the winds blow, and I'm telling you that all of you will end up dead. The Romans are unforgiving bastards and they will want revenge for what you've done.'

'You're not a Roman?'

'No, no,' he protested, 'I'm Cretan. They just hire me and my crew when they need us. If you give me a crate of gold I'll take you where you want to go, no questions asked.'

'I'll bear it in mind,' I said dismissively.

He moved closer so no one could hear. 'Don't dismiss the offer too lightly, it's better than being nailed to a cross. Just get yourself down to the docks in Thurii and ask for Athineos. Everyone knows me.'

'Like I said, I'll bear it mind.'

After the clerk had tallied everything to his satisfaction, I said farewell to Athineos and we headed back to camp. The iron was taken to a vast clearing that had been made in the forest at the base of the mountains. The chopped wood was used to build roofs to shelter the furnaces that would be used to forge the swords, javelins and spearheads. Slaves who had been used to produce agricultural tools could just as easily turn their hands to making weapons, their years of hammering metals on anvils made them experts in creating blades that were neither too brittle or too soft. In the clearing lines of furnaces were established, each one a having a wide, low chimney with an opening at the bottom to supply the fire with air. The furnaces were filled with charcoal (which itself had been made from the cut-down trees), which heated the iron bars until they glowed red. The bars were then removed from the white heat of the fire and hammered into shape on an anvil. Any brittle metal left on the bar would shatter as it was hammered into shape, showering the smith's leather apron and his forearms with red-hot splinters. The blade was then quenched in a barrel of brine, to produce a steel blade that would make a gladius. Spartacus told me, as we were watching teams of smiths heat the iron in the furnaces and others hammering glowing metal on anvils, that some Romans liked to quench a new blade in the body of a living slave to make the steel harder, or so they believed.

Once each blade was had been forged, it was taken to the finishing sheds where it was sharpened with files, hand scrapers and natural stone. Each sword blade was double-edged with a flat diamond cross-section, without grooves or fullers. Then it was sent to another shed where the handle was attached. These were intricate affairs. The hilt itself was made of wood with a thin brass plate set into the bottom of the guard, with a round pommel. While this process was going on other workers made the scabbards, which were two pieces of wood covered with thin leather. I marvelled at the level of activity, which went on day and night as the efforts to arm all our troops intensified. I got talking to one old smith, whose arms were covered with burn scars, who told me that it took about a week to produce a finished sword.

Spartacus made Godarz quartermaster general of the whole army, responsible for distributing weapons and also collecting any surplus gold and silver that we might have. There was a large quantity of the latter, as the spoils of Forum Annii and Metapontum included expensive drinking vessels, jewellery and religious items looted from temples. The Gauls in particular had a vast horde, which Godarz demanded and Crixus refused. It took the personal intervention of Spartacus himself before he relented, but relent he did. The precious metal was melted down and cast into gold and silver ingots, which were placed under heavy guard in Akmon's treasury camp. Crixus had his sense of grievance soothed somewhat when Godarz sent him a thousand new swords for his warriors. There was neither the time nor the resources to produce mail armour, Spartacus remarking that new shirts would have to be taken off dead Romans. The same went for helmets, though wicker shields covered with leather sufficed for those who would not be fighting in the front ranks. We certainly had no shortage of leather, having amassed thousands of cattle during our journey from Mount Vesuvius, plus tens of thousands of sheep and goats. And we certainly had no shortage of milk, meat or honey, for Bruttium was famous for the quality of its honey and multitude of beehives.

During the weeks that followed, each day had the same routine as I moulded the cavalry into a force that could beat the Romans on the battlefield. All my Parthians were assigned to lead and train one-hundred man companies. Nergal and Burebista each had their own dragons now, a thousand men divided into ten companies. I commanded the third dragon, with Rhesus as my second-in-command. Nergal and I commanded horse archers but Burebista led horsemen equipped with spears and shields. Not all those who could ride were able to master the bow, even less when on horseback, so they were trained to fight as Roman cavalry. I ordered the shields, oval shaped and covered in leather, to have a white horse's head painted on them to display Hatra's emblem in the heart of my enemy's kingdom.

Thus did the army's mounted arm number two thousand horse archers and a thousand mounted spearmen. No matter what dragon they were allocated to, each day was the same for all those who rode. Up at dawn for an hour of marching fully equipped on foot, followed by breakfast, three hours of riding drills, an hour grooming and checking our mounts, a light midday meal, and then the afternoon spent practising archery and close-quarter combat with spears, swords and shields. Burebista and his Dacians made a point of keeping their bows, even though the other men of his dragon were not horse archers. Byrd and his men took no part in our daily routine, they were a law unto themselves, being mostly a collection of loners, oddballs and undesirables, but they were excellent scouts who rode far and wide and made sure no Roman army would surprise us in our winter quarters. Nergal grumbled that they set a bad example, but they lived apart from us in a separate camp in the foothills of the mountains and we rarely saw them. Byrd reported to me once a week in his usual curt manner, but I was reassured that he and his men were watching over us, and as long as they did their task properly they were worth their weight in gold. Bozan had told me that the key to success on the battlefield was hard and relentless training, 'train hard, fight easy, that's the secret, boy,' he used to tell me. And so it was. I had to admit that former slaves made excellent recruits. They had known nothing but cruelty and harsh discipline, so it was no great transition at all for them to live each day with hard physical toil. The difference being that with us they were fighting to maintain their newly won freedom, and they took to the task with gusto. There was no grumbling or sedition, just a desire to learn the skills that would enable them to kill Romans and stay free.

It was nearly a month after we had taken delivery of the first shipment of iron from the city of Thurri when Nergal burst into my tent in an agitated state.

'We've got trouble, highness.'

I strapped on my sword and followed him outside into the morning light, expecting to see Crixus and a horde of his Gauls drawn up in battle array over some imagined slight. Instead I was greeted by a frowning Godarz, a smiling Gafarn and a column of horsemen a couple of hundred feet away, all in full war gear. About company strength, they looked smart and were armed with bows and swords. All wore mail shirts and helmets whose cheek guards enclosed their faces.

'Shouldn't they be on the training field?' I said to Nergal.

'Take a closer look, highness,'

I really didn't have time for this but I walked towards the horsemen, Nergal, Gafarn and Godarz falling in behind me.

'Who is your commander,' I shouted at the two men who led the column.

He took off his helmet and a great cascade of blonde hair fell about 'his' shoulders.

'No man commands us,' said Gallia, 'but we are willing to fight alongside you for freedom.'

I was momentarily speechless, but then turned on Nergal.

'Is this sort of joke?'

'No, highness.'

The individual next to Gallia also took off her helmet; it was Praxima and behind her sat Diana.

'We can all ride and fight,' said Gallia, proudly, 'and demand the right to do so.'

'Demand!' I said.

'Feisty lot, aren't they,' mused Gafarn, mischievously.

'Be quiet, Gafarn. Godarz, where did they get their weapons?'

Before he could answer Gallia spoke. 'We took them from the armoury. I told the guards that you had given me permission.'

I looked at Godarz, who shrugged then looked down at the ground. I walked over to Gallia, who had acquired a fine mail shirt, as had Praxima. I stood next to her horse, which I had to admit looked magnificent, its mane and coat shining in the sun. All the woman's horses had red saddlecloths edged with yellow, loot taken from Roman mounts.

'Are you going to get down so we can talk about this?' I asked her, quietly.

'Are you going to let us fight in your cavalry?' she said, defiantly.

'It's not as simple as that.'

'Yes it is,' she replied, 'we can fight as well as any man.' There was now a crowd of sightseers gathering round us, which annoyed me intensely.

'Get these men back to their duties,' I snapped at Nergal, who ordered them away.

'If I can prove that we are as good as any man, will you let us fight?' said Gallia, loudly enough for all those around to hear. She had given me a way out of this predicament.

'Of course,' I replied. 'But how can you prove such a thing?'

I looked at Nergal, who nodded in acknowledgement, though Godarz was frowning and Gafarn was shaking his head.

'An archery contest, to decide the matter, such as you have in Parthia,' said Gallia. 'I will pit my bow against yours.'

I burst into laughter and moved closer to her. 'My love, you know you cannot win such a contest.' She was not amused.

'Well, if I cannot win then you can have no objection to competing against me.'

I accepted her challenge. This was the woman I loved, but I was a Parthian prince, whose blood had inherited the skills of the fabled horse archers of legend from the great Asiatic steppes. I had held a bow since leaving the cradle, but I promised myself that I would not humiliate the woman whom I was going to one day marry.

Our training area was a wide expanse of open land near the foothills of the mountains. It was divided into several archery practice courses, each one the same in length and purpose, and were identical to the ones we used in Parthia. Each course was five hundred feet long, with targets on the left-hand side placed at intervals along its length. The targets were square shaped, just over three feet in diameter and each one was divided into five scoring areas, with the inner bulls-eye being eight inches in diameter. All the targets were placed sixteen feet from the inside of the course rope. At its most basic, a horsemen rode up the course and fired at each target as he passed, though only skilled archers were able to hit the bulls-eye of all five targets. Standing opposite each marker, about thirty feet away, was a scorer, who held a coloured flag aloft after his target had been hit, or not as the case may be. A red flag indicated a strike on the bulls-eye, a green the next three scoring areas out from the bulls-eye, and a yellow flag to mark a hit on the outer scoring area. A white flag indicated a miss. To simulate battle conditions, each attempt at the course had to be performed at the gallop with the archer drawing arrows from his quiver. Easy enough for a Parthian, but I doubted that those unused to shooting from horseback would be able to achieve this, much less a woman. The competition had been arranged to take place in mid-afternoon and I expected that only myself, Gallia and a few others would attend. How wrong I was. Word of the competition between 'the Parthian' and 'his woman' had spread like wildfire through not only the cavalry camp but throughout the army. When I rode Remus over to the training area, a multitude had gathered to watch what was going to take place. All Gallia's women were there, plus Nergal, Godarz, Rhesus, Gafarn and several dozen Parthians who should have been instructing their men, but had decided to bring their charges along to watch an archery competition. Then Spartacus and Claudia arrived, together with a horde of Thracians, and Castus with even more Germans. I rode over to where Spartacus was talking with Nergal and Godarz. I dismounted and embraced Claudia.

'A pleasure to see you, lady,' I said.

'How do you think my Gallic girl will do?' she asked.

'She rides well enough,' I replied, 'but archery is in every Parthian's blood. She will not win, I fear.'

'Would you like a wager on that, Pacorus?' said Spartacus, winking at Claudia.

'I would not want to take your money, lord,' I replied.

At that moment Gafarn walked over from where he had been talking to Gallia. He bowed his head to Spartacus and Claudia, and then looked at me, a stupid grin on his face.

'The Lady Gallia asks if you are ready to start, or whether you would like to concede defeat now.'

Spartacus burst into laughter, as did Castus and others behind them and several of his Germans cheered. I was not amused and felt my face blush. I mounted Remus and took out my bow from its case. I pointed at Gafarn.

'I blame you for this.'

'Of course,' he said, unconcerned. 'The sequence is single shot, fast shoot and serial shoot.'

'I'm well aware of the rules, Gafarn,' I snapped.

'Good. You will shoot first, please begin when you are ready. And good luck.'

'I do not need luck,' I said, irritably.

'Oh, I think you do.'

I rode Remus over to the start line, the course stretching out in front of me straight as an arrow. Behind the markers, all along the course, were gathered the spectators, hundreds of them. It was traditional for a judge to lower a spear to indicate the start of a charge, and sure enough Gafarn had furnished Claudia with a shaft, and she now walked purposely to where Gallia and I waited on our horses. Claudia's black hair shone like a horse's mane in the sun as she stood and lowered the spear, signalling me to begin. I jammed my knees into Remus' sides, causing him to rear up on his hind legs and then to thunder down the course. Single shot entailed striking a target three hundred feet from the start line. Remus ran like the wind as I pulled an arrow from my quiver, strung it and let it loose as the target flashed by me on my left. The moment it left my bow I glanced behind to my right to watch the scorer. Red flag! I patted Remus' neck as I slowed him to a canter as we neared the end of the course. Polite applause greeted my shot as Gallia began her run.

Her horse ran arrow-straight as she galloped towards me, the reins around her right arm as she drew an arrow, strung it and pulled back the bowstring. Her posture in the saddle was perfect, her upper body upright, eyes looking along the arrow and her legs tucked in tight. She let her arrow fly and raced down the course. Wild cheers greeted the scorer as he hoisted his red flag. Gallia halted her mount, turned him around and cantered back to the start line. All her concentration was on the competition; nothing else mattered to her at that moment.

We were back at the start line for the fast shoot. This is where the horseman has to hit two targets, the first one being placed two hundred feet from the start line and angled towards the start, not to the side, making it a forward shot. But the second target, about eighty feet forward from the first target, is angled towards the finish line and thus requires the archer to make a back shot over the rear quarters of his mount. This was a Parthian speciality and I doubted that Gallia would even attempt it. Claudia gave the signal and once more Remus thundered down the course. I loosed the first arrow, pulled another from my quiver quickly, strung it, swung in the saddle to my left and fired it over Remus' rump. I halted him at the finish line and saw two red flags being held aloft. Again, polite applause. Then came Gallia, riding hard and fast, leaning forward in the saddle to take the shot at the forward-facing target. The arrow left her bow and she strung another as her horse galloped up to and then past the second target. She effortlessly twisted her torso to the left and took the shot, the arrow hitting the target. But which part? The crowd erupted into cheering again as two red flags were hoisted aloft. So we were dead level. This girl had been taught well, that much was true, but she also must have spent hours and hours on the training field to reach such proficiency.

But now came the hardest task: the serial shot. This was a five-target run, the first target placed a hundred feet from the start line and the other four targets placed at one hundred feet intervals after that. All targets were side shots but they came fast, one after the other. For the final time Claudia gave the signal and I thrust my knees into Remus' flanks and once more he reared up and then shot forward into a gallop. I shot five arrows and all five hit bull's-eyes, and once again I received polite applause from the crowd. Gallia followed me, unyielding, iron-willed and at one with her mount. I saw Gafarn in the way she rode, her legs seemingly having been bolted onto the horse but her upper body moving rhythmically as she fixed her eyes on each target and fired her arrows, stringing an arrow, aiming and firing it at the target in one seamless movement. First target, red flag; second target, red flag; third target, red flag; fourth target, red flag; the scorer hesitated, then raised a fifth red flag as the crowd erupted in a deafening roar. Praxima and Diana ran over to Gallia when she returned to the start line and grabbed her hands as others thronged around her, offering salutations. I walked Remus back to the start line as the crowd parted to let me through. The noise quietened down to nothing as I halted Remus a few feet from Gallia, who watched me from behind the cheek guards of her helmet. A wide circle had formed around us. I saw Spartacus watching me, as well as Claudia, Gafarn, Nergal and Godarz. There was silence as I dismounted and walked with my bow over to Gallia. She took off her helmet and watched as I unstrung my bow and held it out towards her. This gesture was an old Parthian custom that showed respect for an adversary, usually after a battle.

'I Pacorus, prince of Hatra and a son of the Arsacid Dynasty, do hereby grant you your wish, lady. You and those who ride with you shall fight by our side from henceforth.'

Gallia vaulted from her saddle and threw her arms around me, kissing me on the lips as she did so. Thus it was that the cavalry of the slave army of General Spartacus had in its ranks a company of women warriors under the leadership of a Gallic princess named Gallia, one whom I hoped to make a princess of Parthia if we ever escaped from Italy.

As the weeks passed the tempo of training increased to prepare the army for the hard campaigning it would face in the spring. Fewer recruits came in to us now, as the country had largely been denuded of slaves as far as the Gulf of Scylacium. Spartacus had been right when he told me that few town or city slaves would join us. Their lives were mostly ones of ease and good food, and many were given their freedom by their masters, especially if they served as private secretaries or teachers of their children. Almost no slaves fled Thurri to join us, apart from the odd runaway or slaves who had committed crimes against their masters, or had even killed them. Spartacus had such men (and they were always men) executed, which I found inexplicably harsh. But he told me that for such a crime all of the master's slaves would be put to death, and so a man who murdered his master was responsible for their murders as well. I could not understand the logic, but he was our leader and his decision was final.

The shipments of metals from Thurri took place at the allotted times at the assigned beach. The boats commanded by Athineos were filled with iron plus bronze for my arrowheads. And as per the contract we delivered more chests of gold bars, each one carefully examined by the eunuch. On one occasion, after the last cart had been loaded, I waited for the eunuch to finish tallying his records.

'Everything in order?' I asked him.

'It is,' he sniffed.

'Good. I need you pass on a message to your master that I need to meet with Senator Hortonius.'

'Why?' he asked.

'That is none of your business, woman.' I replied.

He smarted at my remark but said nothing. Athineos laughed.

'He is a very busy man,' said the eunuch.

'In two day's time,' I said, 'two hours after dawn at the western gate.'

The eunuch threw his head back like a woman, sniffed in disgust and walked away from me.

'You want to watch yourself, young Parthian,' Athineos said to me as the last load of iron was placed on one of the carts beside his boat. 'Word is that there is a big price on your head. The Romans want to take you back to Rome and parade you through the streets, before...'

'Before?'

He spat into the sea. 'Before they feed you to the beasts in the area or think up some other fancy death for you. I've heard that they had a bull rape a woman in the arena.'

'What?' I was disgusted.

'Yes, recreating some sort of myth or something. Inventive bastards, I'll say that for them.'

'They are a people with no honour,' I said.
'But buckets of pride,' he replied. 'And they can't stand their precious pride being dented, and that's what you and this slave general have done. They also don't take kindly to their cities being looted.'
'They loot other peoples' cities quick enough.'
'Course they do,' he said, 'because to the Romans all other peoples are barbarians, fit only to be slaves, ruled over and the like. It's their mission, see, to civilise the world.'
'There is nothing noble in the way they conduct their affairs.'
'That's another thing they dislike about you,' he said. 'They got rid of their nobility a few hundreds years ago, and they think kings and princes don't belong in the modern world.'
The carts were being driven off the beach now, back to camp for the contents to be turned into weapons.
'They don't mind taking money from their enemies,' I mused.
Athineos shook his head. 'Totally different. Trade is trade and money has no smell, as the saying goes. They'll take your gold, sure enough, but that will have no bearing on the final reckoning.'
'Time to go,' I said, offering my hand to him. His grip was vice-like as he shook it.
'Remember what I said, look for me at the docks in Thurii when your little adventure turns sour.'
I climbed down the side of his boat and jumped into the cool, chest-deep sea. On the beach I watched as the boats pulled up their anchors and sailed back from whence they had come, then rode on the last cart back to camp. It occurred to me that Athineos was right. The Romans would neither forget nor forgive what we had done to them, and in the spring Rome would send another army to fight us.
'We all have a price on our heads,' said Spartacus, his strong profile highlighted by the oil lamp that hung from one of the posts in his tent. He had called a council of war that same evening, having supervised the unloading of the iron at the forges. He had immense pride that they were working night and day producing weapons for the army.
'It's different for you, Pacorus, for you have a home and a kingdom to go back to.'
'So do you all,' I said to all those assembled.
'What, some shit-hole in a filthy, damp forest?' as usual Crixus was drunk and spoiling for an argument. 'I would rather stay in Italy, at least it's warmer.'

Dumnorix banged the table with the hilt of his dagger in support of his commander's words.

'He has a point, Spartacus,' said Akmon, his long arms folded in front of him as he sat back in his chair. 'Thrace isn't much of a land, all rock and dirt-poor villages.'

'I have no desire to stay in Italy,' said Castus, 'and my Germans feel the same.'

'Of course they do,' pondered Crixus, 'they feel at home in the dark forests, that's because their women are so ugly that they don't like to look at them in daylight.'

'Enough,' interrupted Spartacus as Castus drew his sword and in jest threatened to trim Crixus's beard. 'Have we enough iron from the Romans?'

'Enough, lord,' replied Godarz, 'to equip each man with a sword and javelin.'

'I would like to ask for more silver, lord.' I said.

Spartacus looked at the table in front of him. 'For what?'

'A thousand mail shirts, a thousand helmets and three thousand cloaks for my horsemen.'

'And women,' mocked Crixus. I ignored his provocation as Dumnorix stifled a laugh.

'They will command a high price,' said Spartacus. 'Is the mine still working, Godarz?'

'Yes, lord. But much of the gold has now gone.'

Spartacus stretched back in his chair and placed his hands behind his neck, staring ahead. 'Very well, Pacorus, unless anyone has any objections I will grant your request.' He looked at each man gathered around the table. Castus shook his head, as did Cannicus. Crixus merely belched and shrugged his shoulders, while Dumnorix just played idly with his dagger. Godarz shook his head. I had my silver.

'After we've finished trading with the Romans, we should take the city and take all the gold and silver back,' said Crixus.

'That will cost us a lot of men, Crixus,' remarked Spartacus. 'And to what end?'

'To show the Romans that we aren't dancing to their tune, that's why. For as long as we stay here we are still their slaves.' Suddenly Crixus seemed remarkably sober. 'I look at those walls every day and they remind me of the walls of the arena, and I can see all those Roman bastards looking down at me, laughing and drinking and waging whether I will live or die. And that's what they are doing now, earning a fat profit and waiting to see how long it will be before we are all dead. That's why we should storm the city, to kill them before they kill us.'

'In the spring we will march north, Crixus,' said Spartacus. 'There will be no attack on the city, not unless they provoke us. We will need every man if we are to fight our way out of Italy.'

Crixus drained his cup of wine and stood. 'I respect you Spartacus, but I tell you that none of us will leave Italy, so we might as well take as many of them with us as we can.' Then he marched from the tent. I wondered how prophetic his words would be.

I met Senator Hortonius at the appointed time and place. The guards on the gatehouse no longer bothered to rouse themselves as I approached their position, merely casting me a glance and then returning to their conversations, wrapped in their red cloaks to keep out the chill early morning air. Quintus Hortonius was similarly attired, though his cloak was far more luxurious and was edged with purple. I saluted him as he approached me on the wooden bridge.

'I will be glad when the spring arrives and the weather gets warmer. My old bones do not like the cold.'

'I am sorry to have inconvenienced you, sir,' I said.

'Is there a problem with our arrangement?'

'No, but I would like you to arrange a meeting between myself and Marcus Aristius, the merchant.'

He raised an eyebrow. 'I thought we had agreed the proper procedure for the conduct of trade.'

'We had,' I replied, 'but there are some special items that I require that you will probably not want to be involved with.'

Now he was intrigued. 'How so?'

I saw no reason to try to deceive him as he was bound to find out anyway. 'I need a thousand mail shirts, a thousand cavalry helmets and three thousand cloaks, and I believe that he's the only one that can deliver them, probably from Roman stores somewhere in the east. I suspect you would not want to be involved in such a business.'

'And he would?'

I shrugged. 'He's a rich merchant whose only duty is to his pocket. You're a politician whose duty, presumably, is to Rome.'

'A rather cynical view,' he said. 'In any case Marcus would still run a considerable risk if he acquiesced to your request. And the cost would reflect that risk.'

'I've no doubt,' I added, dryly.

He noticed my tone. 'You would do well to remember your position, young Parthian. We do not have to deal with you.'

'I realise that, sir, I merely make a request.'

He smiled. 'In that case I shall pass on your request to Marcus Aristius. His clerk will give you his answer at the same time tomorrow morning, here at the same hour. I think that concludes our business, so I will wish you good day.'

He nodded at me, turned and walked back into the city, the gates closing after him.

Marcus Aristius agreed to my request.

The meeting took place ten miles south of the city and about half a mile offshore, aboard a well-fitted ship, to which I was rowed on a grey wind-flecked sea in a small boat with the eunuch at the bow, a slave rowing in the middle and myself sitting perched on the stern. The eunuch said nothing during the journey. I had ridden to the spot with a dozen horsemen, who looked after Remus while I carried out the negotiations. When we were almost at the boat it occurred to me that I could be killed by an archer quite easily, or run through with a sword and then dumped overboard. However, I believed the promise of further riches would keep me safe, at least for the moment. Later, standing on the deck, I could see that the ship was a sturdy, broad-beamed vessel with a high stern post, which had been fashioned into a gold-leafed decorative finial. There was a deck cabin at its stern. The boat was powered by a row of oars on each side and had a single square, red and blue sail. I was led to the cabin by two huge black soldiers dressed in white tunics, white sandals, mail shirts and armed with long, curved swords which they carried across their chests. Marcus Aristius sat behind a large ornate table in the middle of the cabin, the walls of which were painted white. Two young black boys stood behind him, each one holding a large feathered fan to cool him. In truth it wasn't particularly warm but Aristius was sweating, his brow being mopped by an even younger black boy. Clearly this merchant had a penchant for black male slaves. The boys themselves were attired in pure white tunics with gold earrings and gold torques around their necks. He motioned for me to sit opposite him in a plush chair that had been placed for my convenience. The two guards stood menacingly behind me, yet the atmosphere was friendly rather than hostile. Yet another black slave brought in a tray of fruit, which Aristius picked at greedily with his podgy, ring-adorned fingers. I was offered the tray next, along with a silver platter and a silver goblet, into which was poured wine. The eunuch walked behind me and sat at a smaller table off to one side, then proceeded to ready a parchment for note taking.

'I believe you wish to do business with me, young Parthian,' said Aristius, holding out his hands to be wiped by one of his slaves.

'I need some specific items that may prove difficult to acquire,' I said.

Aristius waved his slaves away. 'Difficult but not impossible, though of course the price will reflect the effort required to obtain said goods.'

The room smelt of incense, which was sickly to my nostrils but seemed to have a calming effect on Aristius, who lent back in his chair and closed his eyes. He then rested his hands on his fat belly.

'I need a thousand mail shirts for my horsemen, a thousand cavalry helmets of the finest quality, plus three thousand white cloaks.'

'Is that all?' asked Aristius, his eyes still closed.

'Yes.'

He said nothing for a while, the only sound being the scribbling of the eunuch's reed pen as he noted down my request. Aristius took a deep breath, opened his eyes and leaned on the table, placing his thumbs under his chin. He looked at me, his piggy eyes excited by the thought of much profit.

'You have gold?'

I shook my head. 'Only silver.'

'Twenty chests of silver bars, then.'

I drained the goblet of wine. 'That's a lot of silver.'

'My final offer, take it or leave it.'

I had little choice, but it irked me that I was being dictated to by this odious barrel of fat surrounded by his catamites. He disgusted me, but I reasoned that the sooner we concluded our business the quicker I could be off his floating brothel.

'Agreed,' I said.

He beamed with delight and told me that the goods would be delivered at this point on the shore in two month's time.

With the approval of Spartacus, Godarz organised the collection of the silver bars. The mine, now worked by the Roman soldiers who had formerly guarded it, produced ten chests of silver, the rest being from the treasure the army had taken the year before. The army had enough weapons now, and Spartacus was confident that he could capture enough mail shirts and shields to equip those who still lacked them, though he was not unduly worried as he had enough to ensure that in battle all of his front line cohorts would be as well armed as their Romans opponents. It was still cool in the evenings and snow still covered the mountain peaks, but the early signs of spring were everywhere. Suddenly almond trees were covered in white blossom, and then meadows, mountain slopes and the valleys were filled with primroses and violets.

It was on such a spring day, with a slight westerly wind in the air, when I set out at the head of fifty two- and four-wheeled wagons south to rendezvous with the ships that were delivering the weapons and equipment for my cavalry. Each wagon had a driver and guard, while the four wagons loaded with the silver had four guards marching beside each one, armed with spears and shields. This was to deter the Gauls as much as the Romans, for I would not have put it past Crixus to try and steal the silver just to spite me. But as we ambled south, parallel to the coast, we saw no other signs of life, and it appeared that my only worry was whether I had brought enough carts. It did not matter; anything that could not be transported immediately would be left on the beach under guard and fetched back the next day. Nergal and Burebista had wanted to accompany me, but their presence on the training field was far more important. In any case, there would be nothing for them to do. The previous exchanges had gone off without incident, and according to the agreement I was supposed to appear unarmed, though I always wore my spatha and instructed those accompanying me to likewise carry swords. It was foolhardy to travel without any protection at all. But we had no bows, helmets or armour.

It was around midday when the ships appeared on the horizon, twelve of them, all single masted vessels being powered by oars as the wind had almost died away. They were different from the vessels that had delivered the iron and bronze on previous occasions, but I thought nothing of it. The sea was as flat as a table and within an hour the ships were at the shoreline. In fact they ran aground on the beach, their iron-plated rams at the bows cutting a channel through the soft sand. I strode forward to the line of ships as the crews folded their sails and the rowers rested their oars in the water. Gangplanks descended from the bow of each vessel. I saw the haughty, gaunt face of the eunuch standing at the bow of one vessel, who beckoned me over to him.

'Prince Pacorus,' he shouted in a high-pitched voice, 'I trust you have the silver.'

'I have, but I want to see the goods first.'

'Of course, of course, please come aboard.' He pointed a pale, thin hand at the gangplank. I ascended and jumped onto the deck. The vessel was sturdy, broad-beamed and in the centre of the deck sat some sort of cargo, over which had been placed a large canvas cover secured in place by ropes. At the stern was a cabin, the doors to which were shut. The eunuch ordered a group of sailors to remove the canvas cover, to reveal wooden crates filled with mail shirts. I pulled one of the shirts out and held it up. It was a waist-length, armless garment comprising alternating rows of riveted and 'solid' rings (links with no riveted join). It had overlapping shoulder sections to provide two layers of protection for the upper body. Though I could not be precise, by its feel I put its weight at fifty pounds, maybe less. I picked up other shirts and found them to be of the same high quality.

'Is everything in order?' asked the eunuch.

'When we have checked your inventory, I'm sure it will be,' I replied, before waving to my men on the beach to board the other ships and begin checking their cargoes. The wagons containing the silver were driven onto the beach and up to the water's edge. The eunuch scuttled down a gangplank and insisted that the chests be opened, one by one. I signalled my approval and his narrow eyes lit up as he caressed the silver bars, counting them meticulously then counting them again. Two of my men came aboard and we began counting the mail shirts. The eunuch came back on board and scuttled past us, heading towards the stern. I noticed that suddenly I and my two soldiers were the only ones on the deck and instinct told me that something was wrong. The hairs on the back of my neck stood up and so I told the two men to stop what they were doing. The eunuch had also disappeared. Time seemed to slow as the cabin doors at the stern flew open and Roman soldiers burst out, legionaries with short swords in their hands. They wore no helmets and carried no shields, though they were wearing mail shirts. We wore tunics and leggings and carried only our swords. The Romans ran towards us and I screamed to my men to get off the boat. They never made it. One tried to stand and fight but was slashed, stabbed and felled by three legionaries. The other tried to run but tripped on the canvas sheeting, stumbled and had a sword rammed through the back of his neck. I drew my sword, raced down the gangplank and jumped onto the sand. I turned just as the first Roman following caught up with me. I feinted to my left and let his momentum carry him onto my extended blade, which went through his mail shirt into his sternum. I yanked the blade free and swung it at a second Roman behind me, slashing his face with the edge of the spatha. I saw more legionaries jumping from the other ships, surrounding and then killing my men where they stood. We were being slaughtered one by one. There was no time to try to form a line as the Romans were swarming all around us. Within seconds I too was surrounded, three legionaries circling me menacingly.

'He's mine,' came a shout from behind one, and he stepped aside to reveal Titus Sextus, garrison commander at Thurri, advancing towards me, sword in hand. His white face was red with rage and his eyes burned with hate as he charged at me, slashing at my head with his gladius. I deflected his blade and circled him, but he turned, faced me and then thrust straight for my belly. I jumped aside but he slashed sideways with his sword and gashed my left forearm. He then delivered an arcing strike, which I ducked under and stabbed him in his right thigh. He yelped with pain and then launched a frenzied attack despite his wound, aiming blows at my head and neck. I managed to block his strikes but was forced back as I did so. He moved his sword across the front of his body, alternating forehand and backhand strikes with dextcrity, strikes that I was able to block with difficulty. But in doing so I stepped back, lost my footing on the sand and dropped my sword. Then Sextus was standing over me, ready to thrust his blade into my chest. A look of satisfaction, akin to pure joy, briefly flashed across his face. Then the arrow struck him.

The arrowhead went through his mail shirt and into his left pectoral muscle, and within seconds a large red stain appeared around the shaft. He coughed and dropped his sword, looking down in abject misery at the wound that was draining his life blood away. Then he collapsed backwards onto the sand. I pulled my dagger out of my right boot and rammed the point down hard through the left foot of the legionary standing behind me. He screamed and fell to the ground as I drew the dagger out of his foot and thrust it at the groin of the soldier standing to my left, who was gaping at his commander lying in front of him. He didn't make a sound as I drove the blade between his legs, but his face was contorted in agony as I retrieved my sword and, with the dagger still embedded in his genitals, ran him through the stomach. I turned to face my last remaining opponent, but his eyes were glazed and he merely collapsed face down in the sand, an arrow in his back. Horsemen were now flooding onto the beach, firing their bows from the saddle and cutting down legionaries and sailors alike. Nergal rode up to me with Gallia by his side. He looked at my arm covered in blood.

'Are you hurt, highness?'

'Nothing that will not heal. Don't let any get away,' I ordered.

He saluted and rode away to instruct his company commanders. He must have brought his whole dragon, as the beach suddenly seemed a very crowded place. Gallia dismounted and pulled off her helmet, her blonde hair plaited and her expression one of grim determination.

'Nice shooting,' I said, walking over to a dead Roman and retrieving my bloody dagger from his groin. Just a few feet away, his chest covered in blood, but still breathing, lay Titus Sextus. I stood over him, his eyes still full of hate for me.

'And this, my sweet,' I said to Gallia, 'is Titus Sextus, garrison commander at Thurri and a man who violated our trade agreement. What should I do with him?'

Gallia walked over, bow in hand and sword at her hip. 'Kill him.'

The killing all around us seemed to have stopped as Nergal's men rounded up the surviving legionaries and placed them under guard. Some of the sailors had jumped onto the beach and had attempted to push their ships back out to sea, but they had been killed by arrows and so their companions surrendered, shuffling off their boats with their arms raised and sitting in sullen groups on the sand. My men went aboard all twelve ships and searched them thoroughly, but only the vessel I had boarded contained any supplies. The rest had piles of sackcloth's heaped under canvas covers to give the appearance of bulky items. When my men had gone onboard to inspect the goods, they had been killed immediately. So much for the word of a Roman.

I told Nergal to search all of the vessels thoroughly for weapons, clothing and anything else that might be of use to us, including the mail shirts that had been used to deceive me, and then to take all the oars from each ship and stack them on the beach. There would be a funeral pyre for our fallen comrades, so treacherously murdered by the Romans. The oarsmen, legionaries and other crew members were then herded back onto their ships and secured below the decks with chains. Gallia bound my arm while this was going on, while Titus Sextus gurgled bubbles of blood.

'It was worth getting wounded just to have you look after me,' I said to her.

'Someone needs to look after you. If we had arrived a moment later it would you be you lying there instead of him,' she nodded at Sextus.

'One question, though. Why are you here? Not that I am ungrateful.'

She finished tying off the bandage, took the bow from her shoulder and strung an arrow from her quiver.

'Claudia had a dream last night. She saw you on a beach being killed.' She walked forward a couple of paces, drew back her bowstring and fired the arrow, which whistled through the air and hit a wounded Roman soldier who was crawling across the sand, leaving a blood trail behind him. He moved no more. 'So she told me and I told Nergal that you were in danger.' She placed her bow back over her shoulder. 'So here we are.'

'Claudia had a dream!'

'She has the gift of foresight,' she said.

I laughed aloud. She looked daggers at me. 'She was right about today was she not, prince of Parthia. Do not dismiss what you do not understand.'

I was saved by Titus Sextus, who let out a groan. I ordered two men to pick him up and carry him to his ship, and then to put him in the rear cabin and nail the doors shut. All deck hatches were similarly nailed shut. The fifty bodies of our dead comrades were heaped onto the pyre, which was set alight. I ordered the carts to be driven back to camp as groups of horses were led off the beach to save them from the nauseating smell of roasting human flesh that now filled our nostrils. Nergal appeared and threw a figure at my feet.

'He says he knows you, highness.' It was the eunuch.

'Indeed he does, Nergal, and he shall stay with us a while.'

'I was not my idea, lord,' he whimpered. 'Marcus Aristius was the progenitor of the plan.'

I grabbed his throat and pulled him up. 'I've no doubt, but he's not here and you are, which is unfortunate for you.'

'What about the ships, highness?' asked Nergal.

'Burn them.'

He gave the order and soon each vessel was alight as the piles of sackcloth on the decks, soaked in oil, were lit. They were soon ablaze as the flames devoured wood, canvas and sails, the screams of those entombed within their holds competing with the roar of the infernos as the flames took hold. I watched as the boats burned fiercely and as the screams gradually died away until the only sound was the spitting and crackling of the burning hulks. I told Nergal to leave me a score of men and to take the rest back to camp. I embraced Gallia and told her to go back with Nergal.

'What are you going to do?' she asked.

I looked at the eunuch. 'Repay a debt.'

We took the whimpering creature a mile inshore, dragging him behind me on a rope that had bound his wrists together. All the time he was trying to save himself, explaining that he was only doing his master's bidding. He probably was, but I was uninterested. All I could think about was how I had been betrayed and nearly killed, and how many of my men's charred bodies remained on that beach, piled onto a funeral pyre. We halted at a place where two dirt tracks crossed each other. I ordered two of my men to find a young tree and cut it down, then cut the branches off the trunk. We dismounted and I drank some water, for I was suddenly very thirsty. The track had been churned up by the horses and wagons that had passed by earlier. I made no attempt to speak to anyone, for I was still seething over the Roman treachery. I do not know why this was so, for what did I expect from my enemies? Yet the fact that they had broken their word offended me greatly.

After what seemed like an age, the men returned with a trimmed tree trunk about twenty feet in length and four inches in diameter. I ordered one end to be sharpened into a point, then instructed the eunuch to be stripped naked and spread-eagled face down on the ground.

'No, lord, no. I beg you,' he screamed as ropes were tied around his ankles and wrists, four men holding the end of each rope. I was impassive to his cries of mercy as the sharpened end of the pole was rammed into his rectum and then driven further into his body by a hammer wielded by a muscled warrior. His screams rent the air and several of my men winced as each blow of the hammer forced the wood further into his anus. The eunuch repeatedly smashed his forehead into the earth as intense pain shot through his body, but there was no release from his torment, which got worse as the minutes passed and as the pole was forced through his body inch by inch until the point came out of his right shoulder blade. As two men dug a hole I handed the man wielding the hammer, and who was now covered in sweat, a water bottle and told him to rest. The eunuch was still alive, still writhing in pain, but made no sound save for barely audible groans. We hoisted him up and planted the hammered end of the pole in the freshly dug hole, then packed it with earth to keep it upright. Then we rode away, leaving the impaled eunuch to endure a slow and painful death. It would take two or three days for him to die, perhaps longer if he was unlucky, and during that time ravens would come and feast on his body. They would peck out his eyes first, and then tear at his flesh with their beaks. It is a cruel death, but pity is wasted on such treacherous people.

When we reached camp I reported to Spartacus, despite my arm being on fire and the bandage soaked in blood. Nergal had informed him what had taken place.

'Are you surprised?' he said, handing me a cup of wine as I sat in his tent and Claudia pressed herbs onto my wound and then re-bandaged it.

'They broke their word.'

He laughed. 'Of course they did. We are mere slaves and are nothing in their eyes. Did you think that being a prince would entitle you to be treated differently?'

'They have no honour,' I replied.

He sat opposite and looked at me. Claudia finished applying the bandage and kissed me on the cheek. 'Listen, my young friend. For the Romans, honour is for equals. We have wounded their pride by rising up, defeating their soldiers and sacking their towns. And now we have held one of their cities to ransom. Forced it to do our bidding. Their sense of outrage had become intolerable for them to bear. Therefore they tried to kill you. The fact that they failed will only increase their thirst for vengeance, especially when they discover their charred ships full of blackened bones.'

'No mercy for those who break their word,' was all I could say.

'You did the right thing,' said Spartacus.

'How's the arm?' asked Claudia.

'It will heal,' I said. 'I owe you my life, lady. Gallia told me that you had warned her that I was in danger.'

Spartacus rose from his chair, walked over to his wife and cupped her face in his large hands. Then he kissed her.

'Useful thing to have a woman to whom the gods talk.'

'I do not talk to the gods,' she chastened him, 'they reveal things to me, that is all.'

'A wondrous gift,' I said.

'Or a curse,' she replied. 'Not all the visions I have are happy ones. I have no control over what is revealed to me.'

'Crixus was right, we should attack the city,' I said, changing the subject. For in truth the only thing that was in my mind was revenge.

'Were you hit on the head as well?' said Spartacus.

'We should put Thurri to the sword.'

Spartacus poured himself more wine. 'We have no time for you to settle your personal vendetta. The army is almost ready. We are done with this place, and we are marching north.'

'They have offended us!'

'They have offended you.'

'Their treachery should not go unpunished.'

'What is hurt more, Pacorus, your arm or your pride?'

He was right, the army was ready and in truth my horsemen were also ready. Deficiencies in mail shirts and helmets would not hinder our effectiveness greatly. But my desire for vengeance still burned brightly within, and I was determined to settle my affairs before I left.

Chapter 11

The only person who could help me was Lucius Domitus, the ex-centurion who now happily trained recruits to kill his fellow Romans. I was suspicious of him at first, but Akmon told me that he was an excellent instructor, albeit a hard taskmaster. I did not doubt that, as all centurions seemed to have an inbred callous streak. Nevertheless, he was the man I needed and so I paid him a visit on an expanse of ground upon which stood dozens of upright wooden posts, and against these posts recruits equipped with wicker shields and armed with wooden swords were practising their skills. Domitus was obviously enjoying his position immensely, hurling a stream of obscenities against the men in his charge. I strolled over to watch him, cane stick in hand, walking up and down the rows of sweating soldiers stabbing at the posts, keeping their shields tight to their bodies and being careful not to overextend their sword arms. And every once in a while Domitus would hit a man with his cane (so much for not being allowed to strike his recruits), then scream at him the reason for the blow. I had the feeling that he could do this all day and all night, such was his delight. He saw me and walked over.

'Fancy some sword practice, sir?'

'Er, no, thank you. How are they progressing?'

'Good,' he replied, smiling. 'They'll soon be ready for the real thing.'

'You don't mind training them to kill Romans?'

'Why should I?' he shrugged. 'I was condemned to death in the mines and Spartacus freed me. Reckon I owe him for that. He's quite a charismatic character, don't you think?'

'Yes he is.'

He opened his water bottle and took a swig, then offered it to me, before bellowing at the top of his voice for the soldiers to stop slacking.

'I'm guessing that you didn't come over here just to pass the time of day.'

'I need your advice,' I said.

He seemed pleased by this as he wiped his mouth with the back of his hand. 'Of course.'

'I need to get into Thurri.'

'Easy enough,' he replied, 'you will need plenty of coin, though. You can pay a smuggler to get you in by the sea. You give him half of what he wants, he drops you at the docks and then picks you up at the agreed time, after which you pay him the rest of the fare at the end of the return trip.'

'Seems simple enough.'

'Simple but dangerous, especially for you. Chances are that any sailor worth his salt would take your money and then sell you to the authorities for a fat profit.'

'I see,' I must have looked dejected as he then made me an offer.

'I could arrange for your passage, make up a story about me wanting to get into the city to see a relative.'

'So how do I fit into your plan?'

'Oh, you could be my slave. No one would bat an eyelid.'

'A slave!' I was not amused.

'It's the only way, sir,' he said. 'I'm a Roman, so no one is even going to look at you if they think you are my slave. You would be invisible, so to speak.'

'What's to stop you selling me to the authorities?'

He looked hurt. 'Absolutely nothing, apart from the fact that I too have a price on my head once they found out who I was. So it would be death in the arena for you and likely me standing beside you. I told you, I owe Spartacus and I know he esteems you highly, so in a way I am paying him back part of the debt I owe him.'

In truth I could not see the logic of his answer, but he had a raw honesty that made me almost trust him. I could have forgotten the idea there and then, but my thirst for revenge needed to be sated. I decided to put my life in the hands of this former centurion. I told him that I agreed to his plan, and two days later found myself standing behind Domitus on a beach less than three miles north of Thurri.

I had asked Spartacus' permission to go to the city and at first he was reluctant.

'What's done, is done, Pacorus.'

But I was insistent. 'No, lord, not yet.'

'And if I lose my cavalry commander, what then?'

'Then Nergal will take my place. He has ability.'

'But not as much as you. I do not like the idea, I have to tell you. All for the sake of pride.'

'Not pride, lord, my honour has been offended. I cannot let this slight go unpunished.'

He shook his head. 'You are a strange one, Pacorus. Do you think honour will act as a shield against Roman swords and javelins, will honour get you out of Italy?'

'No, lord, but it is important to me. And the idea of that fat merchant sitting in the city laughing at me gnaws away at my very soul.'

He threw up his hands. 'Go, then, but if you are caught you are on your own. You will be alone with your honour.'
'Thank you, lord.'
'I hope it is worth the effort.'
It was quiet in the dark save for the gentle lapping of the waves on the shore. Domitus was dressed in a beige tunic, boots, red cloak and had his gladius in a scabbard at his left hip. He carried his ubiquitous vine cane in his right hand. Lean, with short-cropped hair and muscular arms, he looked every bit the Roman centurion. I, on the other hand, must have looked a sorry figure, with my coarse brown tunic and bleached cloak, called a peanula, with its hood pulled over my head. The only weapon was my dagger that I carried hidden in my tunic. Domitus had a leather pouch tied to his belt, in which was a plentiful supply of silver coins – part of the loot that we had acquired on our travels. It was, to use his own words, 'a tidy sum'. I was worried that we were too close to the Gauls' camp for any boats to approach the shore, but Domitus assured me that there was a brisk trade between our army and the small boat owners of the city, all going on with the full knowledge of the Gauls.
'What does Crixus like, apart from fighting and killing?' he asked me as we waited.
'Drinking,' I replied.
'Exactly, and for gold and silver he is provided with the best wines from Italy and Greece. His men probably use this beach, and in return they get all the gossip about what's going on in Thurri and elsewhere.'
'Does Spartacus know this is going on?' I asked.
'Course, but the thing is that Crixus gets to learn all the gossip, sir.'
'So?' I failed to see what value small talk could be to us.
'So' said Domitus, indicating irritation at my failure to see the obvious, 'if the Romans are assembling a fleet of warships to land an army on this stretch of the coast, then friend Crixus gets to hear of it well in advance. Small price to pay for a few gold coins that weren't his in the first place. Ah, here's the boat.'
The boat was a small, single-masted fishing vessel that reeked of rotting fish and salt. I gave Domitus a piggyback ride to the boat, as he said we had to maintain the pretence of master and slave at all times. He was helped aboard by a reptilian-like man who stank even worse than his boat; the captain I assumed. With Domitus aboard and I was left to haul myself onto the reeking vessel, and then told to sit at the bow while my 'master' sat with the skipper at

the stern. Two crew members sat side-by-side amidships, each holding an oar that they used to get us away from the shore and out to sea. In the gloom I must confess I was nervous, being in a small boat on a large ocean, but the captain chatted away without concern to Domitus, who replied with single-word answers. I stared down at my feet during the journey, which took less time than I thought, for within an hour we were sailing slowly into the harbour at Thurri. The docks were lit up by lines of beacons arranged on two curved breakwaters that protected the harbour, with a tall stone lighthouse standing at the end of one of them. The quays were crammed with vessels of every variety and size moored side-by-side. It may have been a city under siege, but the people of Thurri would not starve, such was the volume of shipping in the harbour. On its landward side stood a series of wharves and porticoes to accommodate traders and their goods while either in storage or transit, though because it was night the level of activity was low.

Our miserable vessel docked at a wharf and Domitus paid the captain half the agreed fee. He showed him the rest of the coins and told him to be waiting for us at exactly the same spot at midday tomorrow.

'We'll be here, dominus,' he replied with the expectation of more easy money, though as I followed Domitus past the warehouses and into the city I wondered if he would go straight to the nearest barracks and inform the centurion on guard. Then again, he had no reason to suspect anything. Domitus was obviously a Roman citizen and I was obviously his slave. We found accommodation for the night in a dirty, lice-ridden inn run by a fat oaf who had three chins but only one front tooth. The inn was near the docks and was full of rough-looking sailors who sat around the tables in the dining area, shoving food into their mouths with their fingers, drinking and generally arguing with anyone at hand. Domitus ordered himself a meal of pork, bread and wine, while I trudged outside to find a place in the courtyard, outside the stable block. There were other slaves already there, grey shapes lying along the wall, most sleeping. I took my place beside them, just another bundle of human misery. Domitus came out into the courtyard a while later with a jug of water and a piece of bread. I drank the water but refused the bread, which was as hard as rock.

'We leave at dawn,' I whispered to him. 'I hope you have eaten and drunk your fill.'

He must have noted the sarcasm in my voice. 'I have, thank you slave.'

I hardly slept at all that night, and as the dawn broke cold and grey I trudged over to wash my face in the horse trough and waited for Domitus, who emerged clean-shaven and smiling from the inn. My fellow sleeping companions were also stirring, and so I pulled the hood over my head to hide my long hair and we left the courtyard. Domitus led as we walked into the street and paced briskly along a narrow pavement.

'The rich houses are in the northern part of the city,' said Domitus. 'Marcus Aristius lives in a villa called the Merchant's House, apparently. But we're not going there.'

'Why not?' I asked.

'Because Abundantia has spread her legs for you today.'

'Have you been drinking?' I said.

'Abundantia is the goddess of luck. Last night I was chatting to one of the sailors and he told me that a batch of African slaves is being auctioned today at the market. Now what I've heard about this Marcus Aristius, I think there's a good chance that he will be there.'

He was right, especially if young boys were being sold, and so we went to the slave market. The smell of human misery and unwashed bodies met our nostrils before our eyes beheld the dozens of men, women and children who were on sale. Hundreds of citizens, ranging from the very wealthy to the decidedly ordinary, were present, observing, bidding for and examining the slaves with sticks. Some slaves, mostly women, stood naked on revolving stands so potential buyers could see exactly what they were purchasing. Others were standing on raised wooden platforms, their heads down and blank expressions on their faces. Some slaves had one foot whitened with chalk, which Domitus told me meant they were new arrivals from abroad. Others had placards hanging from their necks, upon which were written details concerning their nationality, origins, good and bad characteristics and any skills they possessed. A brisk trade was being conducted, with buyers and sellers haggling and arguing over the prices of individual slaves or whole batches. I still had my hood over my head and my cloak tied in front of me to preserve my anonymity, but as I followed Domitus around the market I looked out for Aristius. I was beginning to think our journey was in vain when I caught sight of him, an effeminate fat man dressed in an expensive toga with gold rings on his flabby fingers. As far as I could tell he was alone, though no doubt he had slaves nearby to carry his litter. I saw immediately why he was at this particular spot, for in front of him were arranged half a dozen young black boys, no more than sixteen years old. Each had a whitened foot and wore only a loincloth.

'That's the bastard, there, looking at those boys. So let's get nearer to the fat oaf,' I whispered to Domitus who walked slowly in front of me. He ambled over to stand next to Aristius, who was in the middle of a heated debate with the seller, another fat man who was going bald and who spoke in a curious accent that I could not place.

'Six thousand denarii is an exorbitant price,' said an irritated Aristius.

'Fresh young boys from north Africa don't come cheap, so they don't,' retorted the seller, standing his ground.

Aristius was clearly drooling over the young slaves and could obviously afford the goods on offer, but was determined to drive down the price. A small crowd had gathered around him as he haggled over the slaves, and so I edged closer towards him.

'There might be something wrong with them,' he said, waving a stubby finger at the boys.

'They're nearly naked,' said the seller, 'you can see that they be just about perfect.'

'I need to see them naked,' announced Aristius.

The slave trader sighed and nodded to one of his assistants, who indicated that the boys should remove their loincloths. They did so and Aristius' eyes nearly bulged out of their sockets as the boys stood naked before him. I turned to Domitus.

'Give me some coins.'

He passed me a handful of silver coins as I moved to stand behind Aristius. Others crowded around to see what was going on.

'As you can see, there's nothing wrong with them,' said the slave trader.

'They may have been interfered with on the journey. I know what these sailors are like. Get them to turn round.'

'What?' The slave trader was starting to lose patience.

'If I am satisfied that they have not been violated and are still complete, then you will have the asking price,' said Aristius.

The slave trader sighed again and signalled to his assistant, who placed his stick on the back of the first slave's neck and forced him to bend over. Aristius leaned forward to stare at the boy's backside. At that moment I threw a large handful of silver coins onto the ground in front of him. Instantly there was a mad scramble as all and sundry made an attempt to grab the money, including Aristius. For all his property and wealth he was, in the final analysis, possessed of an insatiable greed for money. However, those around him had a similar idea and he was ignominiously barged aside and shoved face-down on the ground. I stood over him in the commotion, bent down and drew my dagger across his throat, then stood up and walked briskly away without looking back; Domitus followed. It was a few seconds before I heard the screams and shouts as people realised that the rich, fat merchant had had his throat slit. Many think that murderers commit their crimes in the dark and in the shadows, but in truth it is easy enough to kill someone in broad daylight in front of hundreds of potential witnesses and not be noticed. As we left the market I made sure there was no blood on my cloak, and checked that my dagger was safely hidden. The journey back to the docks was uneventful. We were a master and his slave making their way through crowded streets filled with shoppers and traders. When we arrived at the docks, the quays and warehouses were teeming with activity and small boats and larger vessels were exiting and entering the crowded harbour. City life was carrying on as normal and we were just two insignificant individuals going about our business. I resisted the temptation to keep glancing behind me lest I draw attention to us, but I still had a nagging doubt that we would be arrested at any moment. To my great relief we made it back to the fishing boat that had brought us into Thurri, and which remained moored to the jetty awaiting our return. In the light it looked even more disgusting than I had imagined, with fish heads littering the floor and the inside of the boat smeared with fish scales and what looked like blood. As I descended the steps to board the boat, its fetid odour made me recoil.

Once we were settled in the boat the captain demanded his money, only to be told in no uncertain terms by Domitus that he would have it when he had delivered us back to the beach from where we had been picked up. The captain grumbled and screwed up his pock-marked face but duly agreed, and within minutes his crew had unfurled the dirty brown sail and was rowing us out of the harbour, past warships and assorted cargo vessels that were sailing the other way. Looking at the hive of activity, I doubted if our half-hearted siege was having much effect on the citizenry. We did, however, posses the city's silver mine, though I wondered how long we would have that, for with the coming of spring the army would be striking camp and marching north. The day was warm and the sea breeze light and pleasant, and the gentle rocking of the boat as it glided across the calm sea made my eyelids heavy. The lack of sleep the night before and the excitement of sending Marcus Aristius to the underworld suddenly made me feel very tired. I drifted off to sleep, only to be rudely awakened by being drenched in seawater. I awoke with a start and glared at the captain who stood with a leer on his face, holding an empty leather bucket.

'You should get rid of him,' he said to Domitus, 'a slave's no use if he's lazy. Why don't you let me throw him over the side.'

Domitus stood and took the captain's bucket and threw it down. 'I will punish my slave as and when he requires it, no one else.'

The captain sniffed and spat over the side of the boat. 'Suit yourself, but I can see he's a defiant bastard. You should use your vine cane on him more often.'

I debated whether to slit the captain's throat, too, but decided that it was far less trouble to endure his taunts and remain silent. In any case, I could not sail a boat and I doubted if Domitus had any nautical skills. The final part of the journey entailed having to endure the other two crew members throwing fish heads at me to amuse themselves, as the wind had increased and the boat was now under sail power only. I kept my hood up and my face down as they taunted me. Domitus smiled awkwardly while this was going on and just as I thought that I could tolerate no more and that I would have to kill them all, the captain told them to stop their playing and trim the sail, for we were nearing the beach. He dropped the small, rusty anchor a hundred yards or more from the shoreline and said he would go no closer.

'Vast horde of slaves on land,' he said. He had shown no such reluctance the previous evening, and suspected that the real reason was that he wanted to see me discomforted some more, for when I jumped into the water it came up to my shoulders, and I had great difficulty remaining upright as I waded ashore with Domitus, who had paid him his fee, on my shoulders, as befitting my 'master'. I was incandescent with rage when he finally jumped down onto the soft sand and waved farewell to the captain and his miserable vessel.

'Sorry about that, sir,' said Domitus. 'Not worth breaking the pretence over a few words.'

'I was seriously thinking of killing all of them.'

He smiled. 'At least you only had to put up with it for a short time. Imagine having to live the life of slave until you die.'

'I would rather not.'

'Do they have slaves in Parthia?' he asked.

'Yes.'

'Not much difference between Rome and Parthia, then.'

I started walking back to camp, which was some miles away. 'A great deal of difference,' I replied, irritably, but in truth there was not, not if you were a slave. I did not like to be reminded of the fact, or that my father had sold the Roman legionaries we had taken captive at Zeugma all those months ago. What was their life like now? Were they even still alive?

'No offence, sir,' said Domitus.

I raised my hand to acknowledge his apology, but I was still thinking about the slaves in the royal palace at Hatra. Dozens of them, all individuals who presumably had their own hopes and fears. Even Gafarn had been a slave. Well, at least he was now free. The thought cheered me little as Domitus and I walked into camp. I invited Domitus to eat with me that evening and he seemed pleased that I had done so. At my tent I penned a short note to Spartacus and asked Domitus to deliver it. I offered him a horse from the stables that had been built in the middle of the camp but he refused.

'Can't ride, sir. Never fancied being in the cavalry. I prefer to fight on my own two feet.'

'You should learn. Speak to Gafarn and he will give you some lessons. It's a useful skill to have.'

After he had left I saddled Remus and rode out to the archery field. There I found Gallia, her women and Gafarn, all sharpening their skills. They stopped when they saw me and Gallia rushed over and embraced me, but recoiled as she went to kiss me.

'You smell bad, you should go and bathe.'

'Perhaps you would like to bathe together,' I suggested, but she grimaced and pushed me away.

'I'm glad you are safe, but you should burn those clothes.'

Gafarn approached then also recoiled from me. 'Dear me, highness, the conditions in Thurri must be atrocious. I trust your mission was successful.'

'Marcus Aristius has paid for his treachery. I will now take my leave to make myself more presentable.'

I acquired a fresh tunic and trousers and found a fast-flowing stream filled with melt water from the mountains. The water was cold when I jumped in and took my breath away, but it was good to feel the filth of Thurri being washed from my body. I shaved the stubble from my cheeks and combed my hair, which had become matted with fish scales. Afterwards I burned the tunic and cloak that I had worn in the city and rode back to camp. That night it felt good to be back in the company of my close companions. There was Nergal, his arms wrapped around Praxima, joking and cajoling Burebista, who was explaining to everyone how Dacians were better horsemen than Parthians because Dacia had large forests that required riders to weave around individual trees, whereas Parthia was flat and treeless and therefore required no skill at all in the saddle. Gafarn and Diana sat next to each other and held hands all evening, thinking they had concealed this from everyone. Godarz sat next to Domitus, who suggested that we should all have a piggy-back fight though warned everyone that I had an unfair advantage, and then proceeded to recount the journey to and from Thurri. Gallia, my Gallic princess, looking like a golden-haired goddess from the heavens, laughed and teased me, her blue eyes alight as she laughed and joked. She wore a dress the colour of her eyes with gold bracelets on her wrists and a gold leaf headband in her hair. I toasted her beauty and she blushed, and when I whispered in her ear that I loved her she brushed my cheek and said she felt the same about me. I wanted that night to last forever as we ate good food, drank excellent wine and basked in fine company. But only the gods can freeze time and live in a bubble of permanent happiness, and sure enough the dawn came and with it the cold reality of what had to be done. For in the morning I received a messenger from Spartacus summoning me to a council of war. Spring was in full bloom and the coming of the new season meant that our time here was done. We had spent the winter turning raw recruits into soldiers and making weapons with which they could fight. The period of preparation was over; the time for fighting had arrived. We were going to war again.

I took Godarz, Nergal and Burebista with me as befitting their status as my senior officers, though Godarz was also the quartermaster for the whole army and so technically he could attend without my permission. By now the army filled a vast area between the foothills of the Sila Mountains and the Gulf of Tarentum, the coastal plain playing host to thousands of men, women, horses and livestock. Mounted patrols were sent north as far as Siris and south to Paternum, and I established several smaller camps between those two places and the main camp, both to provide a defensive screen for the army and also to save the area around Thurri from being laid waste, for an army is a ravenous beast and can strip a land bare quicker than a plague of locusts. Temporary log stables and workshops had sprung up alongside tents and earth banks surmounted with palisades. Spartacus had insisted that all the main camps should be constructed in the Roman fashion, with blocks of tents arranged in a grid arrangement and protected by an earth rampart, ditch and palisade. Entry and exit was via four gates, each guarded and defended by two tree trunks, each one covered with many long iron spikes that could be thrown across the entrance and which would impale anyone foolish enough to try and climb over them. We lived like Romans, our soldiers were armed and equipped like Romans, drilled like Romans and fought like Romans. At least my cavalry used Parthian tactics.

As we rode into the Thracian camp columns of soldiers were marching out, rank upon rank of men carrying shields, javelins and wearing mail shirts and helmets. Marching out for another day's relentless drill practice. Train hard, fight easy; learn drills and commands until they become second nature, until you can carry them out them without thinking, even do them in your sleep. Warfare is thus reduced to its most basic and simple: long periods of boredom interspersed with shorter periods of organised terror.

The council gathered in Spartacus' tent as usual, though when we entered there was an air of gloom hanging over the gathering. Spartacus sat resting his chin on his right arm, Akmon fidgeted with his cup and Castus was shaking his head. Crixus looked defiant.

Spartacus nodded at me then looked at Crixus. 'Crixus, perhaps you would like to tell Pacorus your news, I'm sure he will be interested.'

'Why?' growled the Gaul. 'I've told everyone who's important.'

'Crixus and his Gauls are leaving the army,' said Spartacus to me. My heart leapt and I struggled to suppress a smile.

'Madness,' added Akmon, 'sheer madness.'

'I speak for my people,' said Crixus, 'and their desire is for us to leave this place.'

'And go where, Crixus?' asked Spartacus. 'We march north to get out of Italy, but where will you march to? Have you forgotten about the Romans, for it is certain that they have not forgotten about you.'

'They, and I, have no desire to go back to Gaul,' said Crixus, angrily. 'It is under the heel of Rome so why should we fight to get back to a place that is full of Roman soldiers?'

'There are other places,' said Castus.

'What, Germany?' retorted Crixus, 'a land of damp, dark forests. I would rather live in the sun. We will stay in Italy.'

Everyone save Crixus and Dumnorix, his ragged-haired second-in-command, were stunned.

'Italy! You are truly insane,' said Spartacus, holding out his arms in a gesture of exasperation.

Crixus jumped up. 'Who are you to say what we can or cannot

do?'

I suspected that we were approaching the real reason for the Gauls' decision. 'You talk a lot about freedom, about every man being free to follow his own conscience. But when it comes to it, we are mere subjects for you to order about. We have been here for months doing nothing when we could have been conquering land and killing Romans. You have become like a king, Spartacus.' He pointed at me. 'You even surround yourself with princes. Well, I say no more, and neither do my people.'

He sat back down and there was an awkward silence. Eventually Spartacus spoke.

'If you stay in Italy you will die, Crixus. That much is certain.'

Crixus laughed. 'All death is certain. That's what I was told at the ludus, and I survived that. We can destroy anything they send against us.'

Clearly there was no telling Crixus anything and so Spartacus gave up. I certainly was not going to attempt to dissuade him.

'Akmon,' said Spartacus. 'Please give us a summary of the army's condition.'

Akmon unrolled a scroll placed on the table in front of him and read it aloud.

'We have fully trained twenty thousand Thracians, ten thousand Germans, four thousand Spaniards, three thousand cavalry and fourteen thousand Gauls, soon to depart from us. Concerning weapons and armour, fully four-fifths of the soldiers have weapons, shields and armour. The rest either have no armour or a helmet only, but all have a weapon of some description.'

'Are all your cavalry fully armed, Pacorus?' asked Spartacus.

'All are armed, lord, but a third are without helmets or mail shirts.'

'Does that include the women?' sneered Crixus, prompting Dumnorix to snigger beside him.

'Mock all you want,' I replied, 'I am glad to have them fighting with me.'

'Enough,' snapped Spartacus. 'Crixus, you and your men will leave in two days. I see no reason for you to stay if you desire to leave.'

Crixus rose from his chair and bowed. 'As your majesty desires,' then walked out of the tent. That was the last time I saw him alive. Dumnorix followed him and when they had left I stretched myself out in the chair and sighed deeply. 'Alas for Crixus.'

'I thought you would be pleased,' said Spartacus.

'We've just lost a quarter of the army,' said Godarz, dejectedly.

'And good fighters,' added Akmon.

'Is there anyone else who wishes to follow Crixus?' Spartacus looked at each of us in turn. No one spoke.

'Very well. We will be departing in two weeks' time. We will burn all we cannot take with us. Akmon, see to it that the mine is destroyed.'

'What about the Romans who are working in it?' asked his subordinate.

Spartacus shrugged. 'Break each man's right arm and then let them go.'

'You're not going to kill them?' Castus looked surprised.

'Have no fear, Castus,' replied Spartacus, 'you'll soon have enough Romans to keep you busy. When we march we will strike east then north, along the east coast of Italy. We will have the Apennine Mountains between us and Rome, which will give us time.'

'What garrisons are we likely to encounter?' said Castus.

'I do not know,' replied Spartacus, 'but town garrisons won't be able to stop us. I'm more worried about the legions that will be sent after us. Some are probably marching south at this moment.'

'I have had scouts out as far as Metapontum, lord,' I said, 'and they have seen no Romans.'

'They'll be coming from Rome, down the west-coast road,' mused Spartacus, 'the same road we used to get here. That's why I want to go east. But keep your scouts out, Pacorus, we don't want any nasty surprises.'

'We've already had one nasty surprise,' grumbled Akmon, 'losing a quarter of the army.'

Spartacus rose from his chair. 'There's no point in worrying over what we cannot change. If Crixus and his men want to get themselves killed, so be it, and while the Romans are busy fighting him we might have a chance to hasten our escape out of this country.'

'You would see him be destroyed?' asked Godarz.

'Why not? By leaving us he would see us destroyed. Let me tell you something, all of you. We can keep on defeating the Romans but they will keep on sending armies against us. If we are defeated once, we are destroyed. And as long as we are in Italy the Romans will dispatch legion after legion until we are exterminated. That is what Crixus does not realise, and that is why he will fail. If we leave Italy we have a chance of staying alive. Tell your men that, all of you.'

The meeting ended on a somewhat sombre note, but I have to confess that I was very happy to be rid of Crixus. What did it matter if there were no Gauls with the army? They were an undisciplined rabble fit only for butchering innocent people. No wonder the Romans had conquered them. Then I thought about Gallia. But obviously she was not like Crixus at all. Clearly not all Gauls were brutes, but even so I was glad to see the back of them. Godarz was somewhat downcast, though both Nergal and Burebista were their usual ebullient selves. I would show Spartacus and the army what properly trained cavalry could do, and would more than recompense him for the loss of a few thousand Gauls. As my mood soared I started to hum to myself, which drew perplexed stares from my fellow riders. That day, in the late afternoon following archery training, I walked with Gallia along a stream that ran through a wood filled with tall birch trees. We led our horses, Remus and Gallia's chestnut mare that she had named Epona, after the Gallic goddess of horses.

'You are pleased Crixus is leaving us?'

'Ecstatic.'

'You dislike him, don't you?'

'I think it is more a case of him disliking me,' I said.

'He can be prickly.'

'That's putting it mildly.'

'I think he's lonely,' she said reflectively.

'Lonely?' I was astounded. 'We are talking about the same Crixus, I assume?'

'He wants a good woman like Claudia.'

'Or you,' I said, mischievously. She slapped my arm.

'Be serious. Because he is a fighter everyone expects him to be cruel and vicious, but he was always good to me in the ludus, and was the first to spring to my defence when I was struck.'

Anger grew within me at the thought of someone striking her. 'I thought it was Spartacus who defended you.'

'It was Spartacus who defended his wife and it was Crixus who stopped me from being hurt.' She sighed. 'It seems another life away.'

'A better life now, I hope,' I said, slipping my hand in hers.

She turned and smiled. 'Yes. But you should not be too hard on Crixus. He was born with nothing and has had to fight all of his life. He was not born a prince like you.'

'Or a princess like you,' I retorted.

'We have no say in the circumstances of our birth, Pacorus, only how we live our lives.'

Crixus and his Gauls left the army and we followed them ten days later. Everything that could not be carried was burned. Log shelters, sheds, cattle and pig pens, foundries, stable blocks, everything. The palisade that had been erected on the earth rampart to surround Thurri was also torched, along with the wooden buildings at the silver mine. The mine itself was allowed to flood, though we had little doubt that the Romans would get it working again as the seams were too rich to be allowed to lie undisturbed. The cattle and oxen would accompany the army on the march, the oxen to pull the heavy carts, the cattle to provide milk, then food, and finally leather. The pigs were slaughtered before the journey, the pork being salted down for rations for the march. The pathetic squeals of the pigs filled the air for days as they were herded together and slaughtered. Spartacus gave orders for everyone to gorge themselves on the abundant food supplies we had, for we could not take fruit or vegetables with us as they would decay very quickly, and once on the march food would be strictly rationed. We would take supplies wherever we found them, but it was better to start out well-fed and thus able to shed a few pounds if conditions got worse. Godarz hardly slept during this period, as it was his task to allocate rations to the various contingents. Working with a score of clerks, he ensured that each century had its allotted portions of grain, olive oil, bacon, lard, salt and cheese. Akmon's camp was dismantled and its wooden palisade distributed among the Thracians and the tents loaded onto carts. We had no shortage of the latter, having defeated a Roman army and looted two cities and one town.

Our plan of campaign was simple enough: a march along the coast to Metapontum and then a journey to northern Italy along its eastern coast, keeping the Apennine Mountains, which ran through the centre of the whole country, between us and Rome and hopefully any Roman armies sent south against us. Having reached the north of the country, we would cross another chain of mountains, the Alps, and then head for our homelands. I had asked Spartacus if the Alps were high and he told me that they were, but that Hannibal had crossed them to bring his army into Italy over a hundred years before. 'If he can do it, so can we.' And so it was that on a warm spring day, the army began its march.

It took most of the morning for the army to form into the column of march we would use to travel through Italy. The first part of the army, who would be far ahead of the main body of troops, were Byrd's scouts, who left their camp before dawn and rode far and wide to be our eyes and ears. Operating in groups of no more than half a dozen, they checked the roads, woodlands and hills for signs of the enemy and possible ambush sites. Next came two companies of horse archers as a covering force, which could either reinforce any scouts that encountered trouble, or fight off an enemy long enough for the army to be alerted and give it time to deploy in battle order. Two more companies of horse archers were also deployed as flank guards for the army's baggage train that consisted of hundreds of wagons carrying everything we needed to exist as a fighting force; its tents, tools, spare weapons, food and other supplies. Behind the baggage train marched Spartacus, Claudia, Akmon and various messengers and Godarz's clerks. Godarz himself walked alongside Spartacus, and I think he liked his position of quartermaster general as it was a role of great importance, and after many years of being a slave the experience of being asked for his opinion as an equal was both novel and invigorating. Behind the general's entourage came the foot soldiers, marching along at a leisurely pace six abreast, preceded by their trumpeters, standards and flags, with each national contingent followed by its own mules carrying personal baggage and tents. Then came my cavalry, those that were not undertaking scouting and flank duties. The men walked beside their horses, usually three abreast, with the carts carrying supplies for both men and horses. The cavalry's supply train included two hundred mules that were loaded with spare arrows, for my father had always impressed upon me the necessity of having an abundant supply of ammunition. The rearguard, made up of two companies of horse archers, was the last part of the army, which stretched out for nearly ten miles and covered around twenty miles a day.

At first I rode with the covering force, but as the days passed and we encountered no resistance I marched alternately with Spartacus and my cavalry. Gallia's unit of women I ordered to march with Spartacus, as it would be company for Claudia and if we were attacked she would be in the best-protected position. Each night the Thracians, Spaniards and Germans erected a huge Roman camp and locked themselves inside, but I deployed my cavalry in dozens of separate camps around these locations. I insisted that Gallia and her company stayed in the main camp each night with Spartacus and Claudia, and on occasion I would also eat with my general.

After nearly a month of marching we had passed through Lucania, Puglia, Samnium and were just entering the province of Picenum. As the spring was reaching its height the weather was getting hotter, and the feet of nearly forty thousand soldiers and an equal number of animals kicked up a fine dust that covered us all and got into our throats. Picenum was a wild place, with silent valleys, wild mountain plains and a coastal plain that hugged the blue waters of the Adriatic. There were many herds of sheep in this region and consequently we gained many new recruits, hardy shepherds who brought their flocks and also their women, so soon the army had a sizeable contingent of females in the army. Claudia and Gallia were delighted, but Akmon did nothing but grumble about it.

'They'll be trouble,' he said as we all walked along behind the baggage train on a warm day under a cloudless sky. 'Women are always trouble.'

'All of us?' enquired Claudia.

Akmon was flustered. 'Not you, lady, but women in an army spells trouble, they cause arguments and create bad blood. Next thing you know, the men are fighting each other instead of the enemy.'

'Perhaps I should banish them,' reflected Spartacus. He flashed a smile at Claudia. 'Or kill them.'

'You will do no such thing,' snapped Claudia. 'Men fight better when they are defending their loved ones, isn't that right Pacorus.'

'I suppose, lady,' I said.

'Of course it is,' interrupted Gafarn, 'Prince Pacorus would become a wild griffin if he thought that the Lady Gallia was in danger.'

'What's a griffin?' sniffed Akmon, clearly annoyed that his sound military advice was being ignored.

'A winged monster with an eagle's head and a lion's body,' replied Gafarn. 'Parthia is full of them.'

'I'm sure no one wants to hear your views Gafarn,' I said.

'You'll see them, lady, 'Gafarn remarked to Gallia, 'when the prince takes you back to Hatra.'

'Is that your plan, Pacorus,' queried Claudia, 'to take my friend to far-off Parthia?'

All eyes were on me. I could feel myself blushing and there was nothing I could do. Gallia looked innocent-eyed at me, while Akmon frowned, Spartacus laughed and Gafarn looked smug, while behind us Praxima and Diana giggled. I was about to give an answer when Byrd suddenly appeared in our midst, his horse lathered in sweat and him covered in dirt. He jumped off his horse and ran up to Spartacus, saluted him and then me.

'Romani have destroyed the Gauls.'

We all stopped in our tracks and gathered round Byrd. Spartacus was laughing no longer. His face went ashen as Byrd informed him of what he had discovered. The Gauls had made their base on a large peninsula called the Gargano, an area in Apulia filled with vast forests of pine and surrounded on three sides by the sea. But a Roman army had engaged Crixus and his men and had destroyed them. Byrd's scouts had not seen the battle but they had witnessed the aftermath, a hillside strewn with thousands of dead Gauls, with a forest of crosses on its summit where the Romans had crucified those they had captured. I saw Spartacus grip the handle of his sword and his knuckles go white as Byrd related how a few survivors had escaped and were making their way north to join us.

'But few in number, lord. No Crixus among them.'

'He may have escaped,' said Claudia.

Spartacus shook his head. 'He is dead. He would never abandon his men.'

'He not one of the crucified,' said Byrd.

'At least he was spared that,' muttered Akmon.

'How far away are the Romans?' asked Spartacus.

'Forty miles, lord,' replied Byrd.

'They'll be here in two or three days,' I said.

'Halt the army,' ordered Spartacus to Akmon. 'Council of war in one hour.'

As Nergal was riding ahead of the army with a company of horse archers, only Burebista accompanied me to the council, which was held at the base of a rounded hill covered in pine trees, with the high peaks of the Apennines in the distance. Around us, the army began the ponderous procedure of mapping out and then erecting a fortified camp. Spartacus' mood was subdued, and I realised that although he and Crixus had had their differences, they had attended the same gladiatorial school and had shared a common bond. It was not friendship, more like a mutual respect and even admiration. Crixus had been one of the small band of men and women that had escaped from the ludus in Capua. Most of them were centurions in the Thracian contingent, some such as Eonemaus were dead, others like Castus had risen to positions of high authority, but all shared a bond of comradeship that I was not part of. To lose one of those companions was a hard blow, and I noticed that Claudia and Gallia were also distressed.

We sat on wooden stools – Spartacus, Akmon, Castus, Cannicus, Godarz, I and Burebista – all looking at Spartacus. He suddenly looked tired and drawn, perhaps unsurprisingly for the death of Crixus had been the first defeat for the army, albeit a detached part of it. And perhaps for too long we had lived under the delusion that Rome would not act against us. But now Rome had sent an army to hunt us down and that army had destroyed Crixus and his Gauls. Though no one said anything, all of us must have wondered if we were going to share the same fate.

'We could continue with our march north,' said Castus.

'I have sent out more patrols, lord,' I added, 'to monitor the Romans' movements more closely.'

Spartacus nodded. 'We can't risk having them on our tail. We don't know what lies ahead, and knowing the Romans they will move fast to hunt us down.'

'Do we know how many there are?' asked Akmon.

'Three legions at least,' I replied, 'though Byrd also reported a number of light troops. And they have about three hundred horse.'

'We have no choice,' said Spartacus, 'we have to face them before they receive reinforcements. To wait longer will only make our task more difficult. We will camp here tonight. Tomorrow we will march south and fight them on a ground of our choosing.'

I said nothing to Spartacus about Crixus after the meeting had ended. I was sure that he wanted to grieve in his own way. But later that day, after I had eaten an evening meal with Gallia, a messenger arrived from Spartacus ordering me to attend him immediately. As the sun was casting long shadows across the plain where the army was located, I rode Remus over to see Spartacus. Predictably, the camp had been laid out in its usual fashion, and as I cantered down the central avenue I thought I was back at Vesuvius, with high peaks behind me and lush vegetation all around. When I entered Spartacus' tent I found him pacing up and down, his large hands clasped behind his back. Claudia, looking pale, managed a thin smile when she saw me, while at the table sat a stern-looking Akmon. Then I saw Nergal, covered in dust and drinking from a cup. He bowed his head at me in salute.

'Tell him,' snapped Spartacus.

'A Roman army, highness, approaching us from the north. Maybe two days' march from here.'

'Another army?' I was shocked. 'How many?'

Nergal took another swig of his drink. By the look of him he had been riding hard. 'I counted three eagles, a few horse plus some light troops, archers, slingers.'

'That's another twenty thousand men, then,' said Akmon. 'We appear to be caught in a trap.'

I took the wine offered me by Claudia and sat in a chair by the table. My spirits sank as we waited for Castus to arrive. When he did and was told the news, he too sat dejectedly next to me, resting his chin in his right hand. There was silence for a while, then Spartacus thumped the table, making us all jump.

'Fighting pairs, back to back, like in the arena. You remember, Castus?'

Castus looked up at Spartacus. 'You protect my back, I protect yours.'

'Exactly. ' Spartacus' eyes were now alight with enthusiasm. 'That's the way to get us out of this mess.'

I looked at Nergal in confusion, who shrugged in puzzlement.

'It's quite simple,' announced Spartacus. 'We strike both enemy forces at the same time rather than face one and risk the other attacking our rear.'

'You will split the army, lord?' I said.

'I have no choice, Pacorus. Hit both of them hard. They won't expect that.'

'And if they beat one half of the army,' mused Akmon, 'then we will be back to where we started and with only half the number of soldiers.'

'Let us consider the possibility that we will not be defeated,' retorted Spartacus. 'Akmon, you and I will engage the Romans coming from the north, together with the Spaniards. Pacorus and Castus will march with their men against the Romans who fought Crixus.'

'You will have no cavalry, lord.' I said, 'and the Romans advancing from the north have horse with them.'

Spartacus sat in his chair, poured himself a cup of wine and drained it. 'You're right, but seeing as you are the commander of the horse there seems little point in leaving some of your command with me. No one would know what to do with it.'

'I could leave Nergal with you,' I suggested.

'No,' he replied. 'That will further weaken you. We don't know how many Romans are coming from the south, but I estimate that you and Castus will be outnumbered from the outset. I see little point in lengthening the odds. And take Gallia and her women with you. I want you concentrating on your own battle, not fretting about other things. Any questions?'

There were none.

'Good. You will both leave at first light. Pacorus, you will command.'

Byrd and a dozen of his scouts were sent ahead as a yellow sun rose into an orange sky at dawn the next day, as nearly three thousand horsemen rode south. Despite his protestations, I insisted that three hundred horsemen remained behind with Spartacus to give his force at least a sprinkling of cavalry. They were all horse archers, and I said that at the very least he could dismount them and use them as archers should he so wish. Hopefully he would employ them to harry and probe the Roman lines. I left them under the command of Godarz, whose advice Spartacus listened to and who as a Parthian would at least know how to use these men on the battlefield. Rhesus also stayed with them. I took Gallia and her company with me, stressing to Gafarn that he was to keep a close eye on them and keep them as a reserve. Behind the horse, marching six abreast along a dirt track and kicking up a large pall of dust, came the Germans, thousands of them dressed in mail shirts, big men with long hair, long beards, and carrying Roman shields and javelins. They had Roman swords in their scabbards and Roman helmets on their heads, but their long dark locks and bushy facial hair marked them out as enemies of Rome. I left Burebista in command of the main body of cavalry as I rode forward with Nergal to scout ahead.

We rode through rolling green hills, abundant vineyards and meadows filled with wild flowers. After two hours we ran into Byrd and his men coming from the opposite direction. He reported that the vanguard of the enemy's army was five miles to the south. It was now mid-morning and the day was getting warm. We had ridden into undulating country, through the centre of which snaked a river. The river itself was wide and its banks steep, though the level of water was low following the passing of the spring melt waters from the winter snows that had covered the slopes of the mountains many miles to the west. I told Byrd to ride north and instruct Castus to march with haste to this spot, for here, beside a river that one of Byrd's men had heard was called the Pisaurus, was where I would fight the Romans.

It took two hours for the Germans to arrive, and during that time I mapped out a battle plan in my head. A site that caught my eye was a level piece of ground between an outside bend of the river on my left and a large, gently rising hill on the right. The distance between the riverbank and the base of the hill was about a mile, perhaps more. While the men rested and sated their thirsts, watered their horses in the shallow river and ate a meagre meal of hard biscuit, myself, Nergal, Burebista, Castus and Cannicus gathered beneath one of the few trees that dotted the plain, an old chestnut with gnarled branches. I was conscious that I held command, but was careful not to assume a dictatorial tone.

'I believe that this piece of ground offers us the best opportunity for defeating the Romans,' I said.

'I am a gladiator, not a general,' observed Castus, 'so it is your words that should hold sway, Pacorus.'

'It is you and your Germans, my friend,' I smiled at him, 'who hold the key for us. But I fear the price in blood may be high.'

'We do not fear spilling our blood,' said Cannicus.

'That is true,' added Castus, 'so tell us your plan.'

I gestured ahead with my arm. 'Between that bend in the river, there, on the left, and the hill on the right, that is where we stand and fight. We anchor our left flank on the river and deploy in line between there and the base of the hill.

'It will be a thin line,' said Castus. He was right. The normal formation for a legion in battle formation was ten cohorts arranged in three lines, four cohorts in the first line, and three in the second and third lines. But to fill most of the gap between the river and the hill his two legions would have to deploy in two lines.

'On your right flank I will deploy five hundred horse,' I continued, 'with another two hundred on the other side of the river to protect against us being outflanked.'

'Where will the other two thousand horse be, highness?' asked Nergal.

'Hidden behind the hill. I'm relying on the Romans attacking what they see directly ahead as they deploy in front of your men, Castus. They always attack.'

'What if they don't?' asked Burebista.

'Their pride and arrogance won't allow them to fight a defensive battle, and remember that these are the legionaries that have destroyed Crixus. They will want to wipe out another group of slaves. That will work to our advantage.' I prayed to Shamash that it would be so.

Two hours later the first Roman soldiers appeared, small red figures fanning out over the plain in the distance. My two thousand horse were already hidden behind the hill, but I ordered Burebista to take his five hundred horse further forward and deploy into a long line the other side of the hill, to dissuade any curious Roman scouts. Burebista's men were mostly spearmen, for I wanted to keep our horse archers hidden until the trap was sprung. He wanted to charge at the Romans while they were deploying, for before very long the horizon was filled with legionaries, all advancing at a slow but steady pace, while on the wings were groups of horsemen. I told him to remain where he was, and to focus on preventing any Roman scouts from getting on the hill rather than meeting an early death at the hands of an enemy archer or slinger. There would be time enough for fighting.

It was now midday and still the Romans were deploying, while Castus had already drawn up his legions with his left flank anchored on the riverbank. The water may have been shallow, but at this particular bend the banks were steep where years of melt water surges had cut into the ground. I rode over to where he was overseeing the front rank of his men. His warriors were resting, their shields and helmets on the ground and nonchalantly talking to each other. I could see no apprehension in their faces. Why should there be? After all, many of these men had faced the Romans on the plateau last year and had won. Then again, so had Crixus' men. I put that thought out of my mind.

'Don't attack, let them attack you,' I said to Castus as I stood beside him looking at the Roman army, which was now being moved into battle position by officers on horses and centurions on foot. Cohorts were forming up into close order, with trumpets conveying instructions. The Roman cavalry was now grouping opposite our right flank as the Romans closed up on the riverbank. So far, so good.

'Take care, Pacorus,' said Castus, grinning at me. We embraced and he slapped me hard on the back.

'You too, my friend,' I replied, 'and remember, you have to hold them.'

He spat on he ground and hoisted up his shield with his left hand. 'We'll hold.'

I mounted Remus and rode over to where Burebista was slowly withdrawing his horsemen to fill the gap between the Germans and the base of the hill. His five hundred men were spread thin in two lines.

'Their horse will attack us soon enough, lord, and when they do they will cut through us. We are too few.'

'They will not bother with you once they have pushed you back,' I said. 'They will try to wheel into the Germans' right flank. Just pull back and stay alive and wait until I commit the rest of the horse.'

We shook hands and I rode back to where Nergal and two thousand cavalry were drawn up in two large blocks, each of ten companies standing side by side. Every company was three abreast and a hundred strong. Spear points glinted in the sun and quivers were weighed down with arrows. Gafarn was also present, his horse scraping at the ground with one of his front feet. I had sent Gallia, her women and another company of horse archers across the river, telling her that they were to cover the river and not let any enemy escape should they try to flee across the water. In reality I wanted to keep her out of harm's way as much as circumstances would allow.

'You are in charge of them, Gafarn,' I said. 'Just make sure they don't launch a mad charge or another act of insanity.'

'The Lady Gallia does not like to be told what to do.'

'Then persuade her instead, or ask her kindly.'

'Yes, highness,' he said unconvincingly. 'Keep safe, highness.'

'You too, Gafarn.' With that he was gone, galloping off behind the Germans and across the river. It was a relief that he was looking after Gallia. It was an odd turn of events that made me place so much trust in one who had once been my slave.

A strange silence descended over the battlefield as both sides dressed their lines before the initial clash. Then a crescendo of noise erupted from the Roman ranks as a host of trumpets signalled the advance. I walked Remus forward and up the slope of the hill. Within minutes I was at the top and looking down at an impressive sight – four Roman legions advancing in immaculate order towards Castus' Germans. Byrd must have missed one eagle, for he had told us that there were three. Sixteen cohorts made up their first line, with twelve following in the second, close to those cohorts in front. Following on behind, the gap almost twice as wide, was the third line of another twelve cohorts. The legionaries moved at a steady pace, a seemingly unstoppable tide of iron, steel and red-fronted shields heading towards our foot, which stood immobile. Keeping pace with the Roman front line, arrayed on their left wing, were two lines of horsemen. It was difficult to tell how many there were, but they slightly outnumbered Burebista's men who were still deployed forward of the Germans and in front of the hill. There appeared to be around six hundred of them. As the Romans advanced Burebista and his horsemen suddenly wheeled about and trotted back a couple of hundred yards, then faced their front again. As long as he made himself a target for the Roman cavalry they would not be thinking about the hill, and more importantly what was behind it. The two lines were now less than a hundred yards apart and the Romans halted for the last time as Burebista once again pulled his men back, to draw level with the right flank of the Germans.

A movement in the sky caught my eye. It was an eagle, which was flying south. I thought it a good omen as the emblem of the Roman legions was the eagle, and I said a silent prayer to Shamash to keep Gallia safe and not let my courage fail me on this day. Another blast of trumpets signalled the Roman attack. The whole of their front line raced forward, the distance between the Romans and the Germans being no more than fifty yards. The legionaries screamed their war cry as they ran forward and hurled their pila at our ranks. The air was thick with flying steel as the first ranks of the Romans charged the Germans, but not before those in the ranks behind had also thrown their pila. But the Germans, standing like a wall behind their Roman shields, responded in kind, the rear ranks of the first line launching their pila at the attacking Romans. Then the two lines collided, the sound akin to a piece of iron being scraped on a rock. And above the clash of arms rose a steady, guttural roar as thousands of men fought with sword and shield in a blood-soaked drama. Behind the Roman legions was deployed a line of archers, who were pouring volley after volley of arrows over the heads of their comrades and into the ranks of the Germans. But as I glanced at the battle for the last time before riding down the hill to join my men, I saw that Castus' men were standing firm, paying for the ground they defended with their lives.

I rode to the head of my horsemen and signalled the advance. Horns blew as I urged Remus forward, while to my left Nergal drew his sword and also led his men forward. Two thousand horse advanced at a trot as we moved out from behind the hill. Ahead I could see that the Roman cavalry had forced Burebista's men back to back behind the German line, and though he and his men had not broken and were still fighting with sword and spear against the enemy, some of the Roman cavalry had already broken off their fight with his men and were wheeling right to assault the right flank of the Germans. I moved into a canter as we cleared the hill and moved through the gap between the Germans and the base of the hill. The left flank of Nergal's column was already coming into contact with the Romans who were involved in a mêlée with Burebista's men, and would soon be fighting for their lives as they were engulfed in a wave of my horsemen. I rode on through the gap and then wheeled left to take my men behind the Roman line.

After a short period I was charging along the rear of the Roman army, followed by hundreds of my horsemen. At first the enemy did nothing, in fact they barely acknowledged our presence; they must have assumed we were their own cavalry. They were soon disabused of this notion as the first arrows began striking them. The first to die were the archers, who were so busy firing to their front that they only realised that the enemy was behind them when arrows began slamming into their backs. Some attempted to turn around and shoot at us, but our volume of arrows was such that they were cut down within minutes. Arrows were also pouring into the rear of the Roman third line of cohorts as we strung our bows, fired and then reached into our quivers for another arrow. I saw the Roman generals, a group of horsemen dressed in scarlet cloaks, red-crested helmets and surrounded by horsemen holding red standards. They were positioned immediately behind their third line, and they were suddenly being targeted by my archers. They wheeled about and several were frantically issuing orders, but their scarlet cloaks and steel cuirasses were no defence against our arrows, and soon almost all of them had been felled and were lying dead or injured on the ground, several crushed by their horses that had been pierced by arrows and had collapsed on the ground on top of them.

Now I was at the river, having ridden along the rear of the entire Roman army. My men were still firing arrows at the Romans, who had now turned about and were desperately organising a defence. I could see that the ground was now littered with dead legionaries, men who had been killed by our arrows as they faced their front. This was their third line, which instead of waiting to reinforce the other two was now fighting for its life. Nergal rode up as my officers were reorganising their companies into lines, ready to assault the Romans.

'Their horse has been scattered, highness.'

'Casualties?'

'Light, highness.'

'And Burebista?' I asked.

'He lives,' he smiled. 'He is eating his way into the Romans' flank.'

'Good, we need to hit them hard with a wedge. Bring those armed with spear and shield forward. We will aim at the centre of their line and try to break them in two. Archers immediately behind them. Go.'

He saluted and rode away. I rode back along the Roman line, away from the river, to a position roughly in the middle of their line. I threw a light screen of archers forward and told their commander to maintain a steady rate of fire along the whole of the line. I halted Remus as Nergal organised a wedge of horsemen behind me – three ranks of spear-armed horsemen who would hit the Romans like a giant arrow tip. Riding close behind them would be three ranks of horse archers, firing over the heads of those in front. To weaken the spot where the charge would hit, I ordered other companies to deploy in columns two across and commence riding towards the Roman lines, the men firing their bows and then wheeling left and right respectively, as those following on behind did the same, sending arrow after arrow into the Roman shields. The latter were wood covered with leather, but our arrows could pierce them and drive shafts of iron and bronze into arms and mail shirts. Not enough to kill, but enough to wound and shatter the morale of those who could only stand and be targets.

After ten minutes or so, Nergal signalled that the men were ready. I rode to the head of the wedge and he joined me.

'You will charge, highness?'

'Of course, I can't expect men to obey me if I skulk behind them. Shamash keep you, Nergal.' I drew my sword and dug my knees into Remus' flanks. My bow was in its case and so I grabbed his reins in my left hand as he began to move, Nergal followed at a canter. The air was thick with arrows hissing towards the Roman line as I screamed the charge and Remus broke into a gallop. The Roman line was approaching me fast and I could see that it was ragged. We were perhaps six hundred horsemen in three ranks charging at the Romans, with another six hundred horse archers tucked in behind them, while on our flanks more archers were firing at the spot where we would hit the enemy line. That line was now dissolving as legionaries were felled by arrows, others limped wounded to the rear, while a few threw down their shields and tried to run. For their courage had deserted them as I aimed Remus towards a small gap that had appeared either side of a dead Roman lying on the ground. Remus galloped through the gap and I slashed at the head of a legionary on my right as he did so, then started to hack left and right at a sea of Roman helmets that surrounded me. But I was not alone, and soon those helmets were falling left and right as lances thrust through shields and mail shirts. Men were crushed under the hooves of horses as they attempted to turn and flee, some were speared and others were killed by sword cuts. All semblance of order among the Roman ranks had now disappeared as hundreds of horsemen created a massive gap in their line, and then swept right and left behind them. What was left of what had been the Roman third line now dissolved into chaos. Some centurions, professional to the last, formed their centuries for all-round defence, but my archers merely halted their steeds out of pilum range and proceeded to shoot the shield blocks to pieces. The legionaries locked their shields over their heads and to the front, sides and rear, but there were still small gaps between shields held vertically and horizontally, and those gaps were an invitation to a skilled archer. Arrows hit eye sockets and necks, and soon those blocks were piles of dead and writhing legionaries, the centurions being sought-after targets, whose bodies were often hit by many arrows. Some Romans threw down their arms and tried to surrender, only to be killed on the spot. There was no mercy in the faces of my men on this day.

As the last of the third line was scattered and killed, I found a somewhat battered Nergal, his mail shirt torn and his helmet dented, and ordered him to form a new line.

'We have to aid Castus and his men, therefore assemble as many men as you can into a line and advance them to behind the Roman line ahead.'

He brought his sword up to his face in salute and rode away. His horse, like Remus, was tired and so he walked it to a group of my officers, who slowly began to form a new battle line. Ahead the sounds of men killing each other filled the air, and I wondered how Castus and his men were faring. It seemed to take an eternity, but eventually my men formed into a new line and walked their mounts towards the rear of what was the Roman second line. We halted and again we began to fire at the rear ranks of the enemy. We had halted about two hundred feet from the Romans, who had no missile weapons with which to reply. But they did not even bother to about-face and form a shield wall. Then I saw why – the Germans were pushing them back and every legionary was needed to steady the line. But that line was crumbling, aided to some extent by our arrows which were felling enemy soldiers along the whole line. Then the Germans were through, just the odd century or two here and there, but then a cohort and then two, and suddenly in front of us were hundreds of fleeing Romans throwing down their shields and weapons in an effort to escape German swords. But in their blind panic they were running straight at us, and soon the earth was carpeted with dead and dying Romans as we fired arrow after arrow into individuals running towards us until our quivers were empty. It was like some macabre competition to see who could shoot as many enemy soldiers in the quickest time. My instincts took over, pulling arrows from my quiver, stringing them and firing without thinking, always hitting a man and sending him spinning to the ground. This was murder, not war. My quiver was empty, so I drew my sword and began slashing at figures as they raced past me. Some Romans were running towards the riverbank, but they had to run a gauntlet of archers to reach the relative safety of the river a few hundred yards away, and hundreds were cut down before they saw any water.

I do not know how much time had elapsed, but I looked into the blue sky and saw that the sun was high in the sky. It must have been mid-afternoon now. The Roman army was no more. It had become a fleeing mob of terrified individuals, who were slowly and methodically being butchered by my horsemen and Castus' Germans. My officers kept their men under a tight leash, moving them about the battlefield in companies to reduce any remaining pockets of Roman resistance, which in truth were few. In front of me, German centuries were being marshalled by exhausted centurions into a new battle line. But there was no need, there was no Roman army left to fight. I walked a tired Remus towards the German lines and saw Castus striding towards me. I dismounted and we embraced. There was blood all over him. He saw my look of concern.

'Not mine, my friend. Are you hurt?'

I looked at my dust-covered tunic. 'Not a scratch.'

'You did it Pacorus,'

'We did it,' I said.

I suddenly realised that the air was no longer filled with screams and curses and that a hush had descended on this field of slaughter. Men were suddenly collapsing on the ground as their reserves of adrenalin and energy evaporated. I myself was suddenly gripped by a raging thirst, so I unhooked my water skin from Remus' saddle and drank with gusto. I passed it to a thankful Castus and then poured the remainder into Remus' mouth. He had a small gash on his right thigh but was otherwise unharmed.

As I stood with Castus among the dead and the dying, I saw to my right a slumped rider in the saddle of a grey horse that was riding towards the river. The man, a Roman officer by the look of his cloak and cuirass, was clearly wounded. Helmetless, his light hair seemed familiar, but perhaps my battle-drunk mind was playing tricks on me. Then I realised who it was. He was only a couple of hundred feet away, an easy target. I ran to Remus and pulled my bow from its case. Lucius Furius was about to die at my hand, finally. I reached into to my quiver. Empty! I turned and screamed at anyone who was listening.

'Stop that rider!' pointing frantically as Furius' horse slowed to a walk and then stopped. I was running towards it, gesturing to all and sundry that they should converge on the now stationary horse. I saw Nergal riding in my direction, followed by a score of his men, while behind me a panting Castus was trying to keep up as Lucius Furius dropped from his saddle onto the ground. I knelt beside him and felt at his neck for a pulse. He was still alive. Castus stood beside me, breathing heavily.

'Is he dead?'

'No,' I said, seeing that he had been wounded in the side of his belly, 'he lives.'

Nergal then appeared with his men.

'Keep him under guard. Get someone to look at his wound and

stitch him up if necessary. And see to it that he isn't harmed. If anyone is to kill him, it will be me.'

'Yes, highness.'

Castus looked perplexed. 'You know this man?'

I smiled. 'Indeed, he is an old friend.'

I walked back to Remus and rode him to the river. I sat gawping at the scene below me. Dozens of dead Roman soldiers were heaped at the foot of the riverbank and other bodies lay in the gently flowing river. On the opposite bank stood Gallia and her women, plus the company that I had sent to protect them. Behind the archers stood groups of horses being held by other soldiers. I recognised Gallia by her blonde hair showing beneath her helmet, standing proud with her bow. I waved at her and then rode downstream a few hundred feet to where the riverbank was not steep and crossed the river. Patrols of horsemen were also scouring each side of the river, looking for any legionaries that may have escaped. They saluted me as I encountered one patrol on the opposite side of the river, half a dozen riders led by a Dacian carrying a lance and shield, like his men.

'Have you found any?'

'One or two, sir. We speared them so they won't be giving us any more trouble. But some will have escaped and made it back to their camp. Do you want us to stay with you, sir, in case any of the bastards are lurking about?'

'No, carry on with your sweep.' They saluted and continued on their way east. I carried on upstream until I met Gafarn. I shook his hand.

'I see that my orders were disobeyed again,' I grinned.

'Yes, highness. The Lady Gallia thought it cowardly to stand idly by while you were fighting for your life.'

'I see, and you didn't think to order her to stay out of the fight?'

He thought for a moment. 'A hundred heavily armed women are not to be trifled with lightly, highness.'

'And the other hundred men who were with you?'

'They thought the same as I, highness.'

'I'm glad to see that you are unharmed, Gafarn.'

'You too, highness.'

I held Gallia in my arms for a long time as around us men and women cheered.

'You have won a great victory,' she whispered in my ear, which caused the hairs on the back of my neck to stand up. I wanted to hear more of her hero-worship of me. 'Remus is hurt.' She broke away from me and ran over to my horse, stroking his neck and telling him he was a beautiful boy. So much for me!

It turned out that Remus' wound was nothing more than a scratch, and once Gallia and Diana had seen this for themselves, everyone mounted up and we rode back downstream and across the river. I rode beside Gallia as we left the spot on the riverbank from where they had been shooting.

'Fine shooting,' I remarked.

'We nearly turned tail and ran when all these Romans started scrambling down the riverbank, until Gafarn pointed out that most had discarded their weapons and shields. Then we realised that they were fleeing, and all those hours spent on the training field were put to good use.'

'So it seems.'

'Afterwards, Praxima wanted to jump in the river and slit the throats of any survivors.'

I turned to see Nergal's woman riding behind us, her hair wild and her face lit up with excitement. A shudder went down my spine. 'I can imagine.'

It was early evening now but it was still light and warm, and so I moved the army two miles to the west, out of sight of the death and carnage of the battlefield and upstream where we could water the horses and refresh ourselves. We would burn the dead in the morning. We rode in silence, for men who have survived the cauldron of combat have much to reflect on – why they survived when others died, would death take them in the next battle and would they meet death with honour or, like they had witnessed today, with terror in their eyes and their bowels emptying without control? I sent Byrd and two of his riders north to take a message to Spartacus that we had defeated the Romans. I prayed to Shamash that he lived and that Byrd would not stumble upon a field of slaughter like the one we had just left, with a dead Spartacus staring with glazed eyes into the sky, or Claudia, or Godarz. I stopped myself entertaining such thoughts.

We pitched camp and ate our evening meal. Few fires were lit and the mood of the men was subdued. A veterinary attended to Remus and then I groomed and fed him. I instructed Nergal to post guards and relieve them every hour, though I doubted that there were any Romans within ten miles of us. Gallia came with Epona and I wrapped both of us in my cloak as we sat on the ground with our knees drawn up to our chins. It was dark now and the sky was cloudless, a myriad of stars flickering above us. There may have been nearly thirteen thousand soldiers and their animals camped all around us, but there was little sound and we could have been all alone in the world.

'They will keep coming back, you know.'

'Who?' I asked.

'The Romans. They will send another army, then another, until we are no more.'

'I know,' I looked at her, her perfect nose and high cheekbones highlighted in the moonlight. 'You know that I want us to be together, so come with me to Hatra and we can live our lives in peace.'

She turned to look at me. 'And what of Diana, and Praxima and the rest. I cannot abandon them.'

'They all have a place in my father's kingdom, if they so choose.'

She sighed. 'Do you think your mother and father will approve of me?'

I laughed. 'They will think that you are adorable, and they will love you, just as I do.'

She rested her head on my shoulder. 'Oh Pacorus, for a warrior you are such a dreamer.'

'All will be well, I promise. We will leave this accursed land and then head east back to Parthia. There we will be safe.'

'Can we ever be safe?' Tonight Gallia had a heavy heart, a consequence, no doubt, of the slaughter she had witnessed this day.

'Of course, the Parthian Empire is not some collection of stone huts. It is over a thousand miles across and stands unassailable like a rock in the face of its enemies. Do not think any more, rest my love.'

I held her close as she drifted off to sleep, and I stared at the night sky and prayed that my parents were safe and that I would see them again. And I prayed that I would also see my friend and lord, Spartacus, once more.

Chapter 12

The next day we went back to the corpse-strewn battlefield, to carry out the grisly task of stripping the dead of anything that might be of use to us. This included swords, javelins, bows, arrows, shields, helmets and mail shirts. I ordered more of my men to scour the battlefield and retrieve any undamaged arrows, for most of our quivers were empty. I sent Nergal with five hundred horsemen to find the Roman camp and take anything of use, and to burn what was left. The Germans and Dacians took great delight in hacking off Roman heads and mounting them on broken spear shafts and bent pilum and then planting them in the ground, until I ordered them to desist. Castus was taken aback, but I told him that we were there to take what would be useful and then march back north to Spartacus, not to indulge the worst aspects of our fantasies. He asked me what I was going to do with the captured Roman officer, who in truth I had forgotten about. As a vast pile of captured weapons and equipment grew by the side of the battlefield, Lucius Furius was brought before me. Despite his situation he still had that air of haughty arrogance that seemed endemic to all Roman officers. A small circle gathered round us as he faced me under a bright blue sky. Burebista stood behind him, Castus on my right, while a host of warriors gathered behind me. I had arranged for the captured legionary eagles to be held behind me as I spoke.

'Well, Lucius,' I said. 'You don't mind me calling you Lucius, do you? Only I've beaten you so often that I feel we are friends.'

A ripple of laughter came from behind me. Furius stood motionless, his eyes full of hate. Burebista kicked the back of his knee, causing him to fall to the ground.

'On your knees when you talk to a prince of Parthia,' my lieutenant sneered, drawing his sword and placing the point at the rear of the Roman's neck.

Furius was on his knees but still defiant. 'Kill me and have done with it,' he spat.

I gestured to Burebista to put away his sword and motioned for Lucius to stand again. 'I'm not a Roman, Lucius. I don't kill people for the pleasure of it. I'm not going to kill you.' There was a murmur of protest at this.

'Silence!' I shouted. 'I want you to take a message from me to the senate in Rome.'

'What message?'

'I want you to tell them that we desire free passage out of Italy, and that if they send more armies against us then we will destroy those, too. Tell the old men who rule Rome that we do not fear them, but if they antagonise us further then we will turn our wrath on Rome itself and burn it to the ground.' My men cheered wildly at this. I raised my arms to quiet them.

'Words are cheap,' he taunted me.

'Words are cheap but Roman lives are cheaper. Look around you, Lucius. It is not the bodies of slaves that are lying on the ground, but Romans. How many more times must you learn that we are soldiers, not a rabble? Your vanity does not permit you to believe that, does it? But let your eyes see the truth. Look at the captured eagles that are held before you. Be grateful that I let you live and deliver my message to your masters. Find him a mule.'

Moments later a rather sorry looking animal with not even a cloth over its back was brought before me. Lucius Furius was stripped naked, forced onto its back to face its hindquarters and then lashed out of camp. To the south a large column of black smoke was ascending into the sky. Nergal had obviously found the Roman camp. Burebista was very unhappy.

'You should have let me kill him, lord,' he said as Lucius Furius disappeared from view, heading east. 'A man like that despises all enemies of Rome.'

'You are probably right, but if I do kill him, it will be in battle with a sword in his hand.'

Castus shook his head. 'You talk too much sometimes, Pacorus. Burebista is right, you should have killed him. He would have killed you if the places were reversed.'

'You Germans are obsessed with killing,' I chided him, 'I find it hard to believe that there are any of you left.'

'We only kill Romans,' he looked at me and smiled. 'And any Parthians who are foolish enough to wander into our territory.'

It took us the rest of the day to loot the Roman dead and organise the collection of their equipment. By the time we had finished Nergal had returned with dozens of captured Roman carts and several hundred mules in tow. The Roman camp had been deserted, though he believed that those who had fled from the battle had visited it during their flight, as there was nothing of value remaining. However, perhaps more valuable were the standards that we had captured: four legionary eagles and a host of banners. There were small pieces of red cloth attached to a crossbar and carried on a pole. On each piece of cloth were gold Roman numerals and animals. There were other tall poles topped with various insignia, such as a silver hand, and many types of animals, with silver discs attached to the pole itself. Many of the standards carried the letters SPQR. I asked Castus what they meant and he told me it was Latin for Senatus populusque romanus, meaning the 'Senate and people of Rome'. I had them all dumped in a cart and gave it to Castus. His men had won the battle and it was only right that he should be rewarded.

I placed my hand on his shoulder. 'You are a good friend and a fierce enemy.'

'You and your men fought as well.'

'It is only right that your Germans receive the recognition they deserve. Carry them proudly back to Spartacus.'

Byrd rode into camp as Castus was trying on a Roman bronze muscled cuirass decorated with mythological designs. It was a beautiful piece of armour, though he complained that the arrow hole in its back spoiled the overall effect. Byrd dismounted and handed me a piece of folded paper. I opened it and read the scribbled message.

My friend

Byrd brought joyous news of your victory. I am pleased to report that we too were victorious against the Romans. I look forward to celebrating our joint triumphs when you return. Claudia sends her love.

Spartacus

I related the wonderful news to Nergal, Burebista and Castus, and soon the whole army knew that Spartacus had also vanquished the Romans. I rode off to inform Gallia, whom I had instructed to remain at our camp as I did not want her or any of her women on this field of carrion. I told her and the others about the note from Spartacus and they, like me, were delighted. It was a far happier camp that night, as everyone gathered round fires, drank, ate and talked of what they would do when they left Italy. Suddenly Rome seemed far away and insignificant. We allowed ourselves to dream, and in the intoxication of that warm summer's evening I asked Gallia to marry me. She was standing with Diana and Rubi next to a roaring log fire, her long hair turned orange by the glow of the flames, when I pulled her away and asked her to share my life with me. She whispered yes and we kissed long and tenderly.

The next day we broke up fifty of the Roman carts as the rest, loaded with supplies and equipment, were driven north to Spartacus. We used the wood to make a funeral pyre, and added to it those Roman shields that were beyond repair. Then we heaped the bodies of our dead upon the whole, doused them with oil and set it alight. We stood in ranks, both horse and foot, as the fire consumed the bodies. I prayed to Shamash that the spirits of our fallen be allowed into heaven, there to dwell for all eternity. We left the Roman corpses to the crows. Before we departed Castus brought me a fine leather cuirass that his men had taken off a Roman officer, a general he said, and by the look of the armour I did not doubt it. The man, whoever he was, had taken an arrow through his eye that had killed him instantly. The black two-piece cuirass was muscled in the Roman manner and was embossed with a splendid golden sun motif on the upper chest, with two golden winged lions immediately beneath it. It had fringed strips of black leather over the thighs and shoulders, which were adorned with golden bees. It was a beautiful piece of armour. He also presented me with the general's helmet, a fine steel piece that was padded inside, had large, hinged cheek plates and a polished brass crest. It had a large red plume, which I would replace with white goose feathers in due time.

'My men want you to have them, for giving us victory,' he said after he had fastened it over my white tunic.

'I accept, convey my thanks to your men.'

In my new finery I took my place at the head of the army as we marched north to rejoin Spartacus. Beside me rode Gallia on my right and Nergal on my left, with Gafarn, Diana and Praxima immediately behind us. The mad Rubi also rode with us, humming to herself in a world of her own.

It was a joyous occasion when we returned to the army and were reunited with our friends. Gallia and Diana hugged Claudia while I embraced Spartacus and Godarz. They were all unhurt, though Spartacus had taken a glance from a sword blade just above his right eye, which would have taken his sight if it had been two inches lower. 'I've had worse in the arena' was his only comment. There have been times in my life when I have experienced true happiness, and the meal that night, in Spartacus' tent, was one such occasion. Perhaps it was the fact that we all still lived after the battles, or more likely that Gallia had agreed to be my wife, but the wine was light and sweet and the food was the best I had ever tasted. It was no different to that we normally consumed, of course, but it was an occasion of sheer bliss. We sat round the large table, Spartacus at its head, with Claudia seated beside him. I sat next to Gallia, and all night we glanced at each other and swapped caresses and assumed no one noticed. Diana sat with Gafarn, and then there was Castus, Burebista, Nergal, Praxima, Rhesus, Akmon, Cannicus and Byrd, who had not wanted to attend, preferring the company of his rough scouts. But I insisted as I liked him and wanted him to share our joy. Even Rubi seemed to be in a happy mood.

The table was overloaded with bread, fruit and meat, which were heaped on great silver platters, which were refilled when one of us went outside and cut more strips off the whole pig and side of beef roasting over fires. A shrill chatter filled the large tent as we all swapped stories about the previous few days, wildly embellished as the wine flowed freely. Burebista regaled us with how he had, with but a handful of horse, defeated the entire cavalry wing of the Roman army, allowing me to 'sneak round the back' of the enemy and attack them from behind. Nergal said that the sky had been filled with so many of our arrows that they had blocked out the sun. Praxima boasted that she had killed as many Romans as any man, a claim that I doubted not. Eventually all of us fell silent and waited for Spartacus to tell us how he had defeated the Romans, despite their superior numbers. He sat with one leg over an arm of his chair and a cup of wine in one of his large hands.

'We fought them in a wide valley, between two great forests of trees that covered the hillsides. I knew that we had a chance if we didn't allow them to turn our flanks, so we formed a battle line across the whole of the valley, from one tree line to the next. But it was mighty thin. We drew up our cohorts in three lines, but the third line was held back and given strict orders not to attack until I gave the order. They came at us with banners flying and trumpets blaring, I counted four eagles but there may have been more. They tried to soften us up with archers and slingers, but the men locked shields and took their fire. Then they charged us, their whole front line, throwing their javelins and then running at us with their swords drawn. But all those hours spent on the training field paid off for us, for our men loosed their javelins and then used their own swords. And we stood and fought them, fought them long and hard for hours, fought them to a standstill. I know because I was there, listening to the screams and shouts, seeing the injured being hauled back, and shouting encouragement with the rest of the third line. For what seemed like hours thousands of men hacked and shoved and bled and died. But I knew that we were stronger and better, and I gave the order for the first two lines to fall back. And then the Romans thought that they had won, but as their exhausted lines stumbled forward we hit them with our third line, a screaming, frenzied mass of iron. We raced forward and stabbed like men possessed at their bellies and groins, disembowelling men where they stood. When we hit them they were still legions, but then they buckled, turned and fled. We followed them, snapping at their heels like wolves. Then their whole army dissolved and the

killing began. Romans trampled other Romans to death, many met death on the point of our swords, and others ran so fast that their insides ruptured, their mouths foamed blood and they died without a mark on them. Their horse made good their escape but thousands of legionaries never left that valley. Our own dead numbered less than two hundred, with another three hundred wounded, but Akmon reckons that six thousand Romans were killed that day.'
'It is true, lord,' said Akmon.
'The Romans have no armies left,' said Castus, raising his cup to Spartacus, 'you have destroyed them, lord.'
We all drained our cups and banged them on the table and cheered Spartacus. He raised his hands and gestured for us to desist.
'I fear, my friends, there are many more Romans left.'
'But there are none to stop us leaving Italy,' I said.
Claudia had been silent while Spartacus had been speaking, and had remained seated and downcast as we toasted him. Now she looked at us with her large brown eyes, which seemed to fix all of us with their cool stare.
'The talons of the eagle holds all of us still,' she hissed.
It was a strange comment, but then Claudia was given to making obtuse remarks and I merely put it down to the fact that she was not a man and did not understand war. Rome had had its talons well and truly clipped, on both feet! In any case, she cheered up later when she sauntered over to where Gallia and I were sitting and began probing us with questions.
'You two seem very happy.'
'Good company and fine wine, what more could a man want?' I beamed.
'A soul mate with whom to share his life,' she retorted, her eyes darting from me to Gallia.
I looked down and could feel my cheeks becoming hot.
'There is no need to be shy, Pacorus,' she continued, 'I'll wager that many men would jump at the chance of marrying Gallia.'
'Who said anything about marriage?' queried Gallia, grinning at Claudia.
'Is the thought disagreeable to you, my friend.'
'Not entirely disagreeable,' mused Gallia.
'And he is a handsome catch.' Claudia began to stroke my hair, 'and he does have a nice horse.'
'That's true. I'm very fond of Remus.'
'I'll fetch some wine.' I stood up, but in my eagerness to get away from being embarrassed further I tripped on a leg of my chair and was sent sprawling on the floor. All conversations stopped as I lay

on the wooden boards. Akmon frowned, as I scrambled to my feet, probably assuming that I was drunk. Spartacus observed me with a cool detachment while Gafarn and Burebista grinned to each other and Nergal looked concerned.

'Pacorus has an announcement,' said Claudia, pointing at me. Once again I felt my cheeks colour.

'I do?' All eyes were on me now as I stood in front of the table. I was suddenly transported back to my childhood, to when I was hauled before my father for taking a horse from the royal stables without his permission. It was an uncomfortable experience, and my present situation was beginning to resemble it. I had been given a good thrashing that day; I hoped that this evening would end happier.

Spartacus leaned forward, intrigued. 'Well?'

I glanced at Gallia, who seemed to be enjoying my discomfort.

'Good news should be shared, Pacorus,' remarked Claudia. 'To keep it to yourself is selfish, but as your tongue seems to have deserted you, shall I relate your news?'

This was too much. 'I have asked Gallia to be my wife,' I blurted out.

The room erupted in cheering and reverberated to the sound of dagger hilts being banged on the table. Spartacus left his chair and embraced me, while Akmon and Castus slapped me hard on the shoulder. Godarz and Rhesus offered me their hand and Diana and Praxima planted kisses on my cheek. Rubi jumped up and down like a cat on hot coals. All offered their congratulations to Gallia, and Nergal slightly embarrassed me by kneeling before me with his head bowed. I hauled him to his feet. 'We are not in Hatra now, Nergal.'

Gafarn embraced Gallia. 'Wedding feasts are lavish occasions in Hatra, lady. All the kings of the empire will be invited, I have no doubt. King Varaz is a generous host, not like his son. And all the people will love your blonde hair. Parthian women are all dark and plump, not slim and beautiful like you.'

'May I remind you, Gafarn, that my mother and sisters are all Parthian,' I said.

'Well, apart from your mother and sisters and a few others,' he corrected himself. 'Did I ever tell you that it was mooted that Prince Pacorus might marry the Princess Axsen. Now she is plump, well fat, really...'

'Shut up!' I ordered.

'You won't marry here, among your friends?' asked Spartacus.

'Well,' I stammered, 'I had thought that we would be leaving Italy soon.'

'It takes only an afternoon to be married,' he said.

'What do you say on this matter, Gallia?' asked Claudia.

'These people are my family, Pacorus, and I would like them to be witnesses to our betrothal.'

'Out-foxed yet again, highness,' beamed Gafarn. 'It's a good job you're a warrior and not a diplomat.'

'Leave him alone,' said Spartacus, putting his arm around my shoulder, 'all will be settled as they wish. So let us drink to their happiness, long life and good fortune.'

Later, when Burebista had been carried back to his tent by two guards after collapsing into a drunken slumber, I asked Claudia how she knew about Gallia and me.

'Was it a vision, like you saw at Thurri?'

She laughed and embraced me. 'No, my dashing young prince. Gallia told me, as she told Diana. She is so thrilled that she could not keep it a secret. You have made her very happy.'

'Really?'

She jabbed me in the stomach with a finger. 'Of course, you think a woman like Gallia gives her emotions lightly. She loves you body and soul, so you had better not let her down.'

'I won't,' I said, solemnly. 'By Shamash I swear it.'

She pulled a stern face. 'So serious. But I know you won't let her down.'

'Is that what Spartacus told you?'

'No, Pacorus, that is what a vision told me.' She filled her cup with wine and went back to her husband.

We spent two weeks in the province of Umbria, reorganising and commencing the training of new recruits, for many escaped slaves began to flock to our banner once more. They were men, mostly, lean individuals with faces made hard from living in the hills and mountains tending flocks, or living under the lash of the overseer in the fields. Women came also, mostly from the gangs who had worked in the fields, mostly in their teens or twenties, in rags and threadbare cloaks, but whose faces were alight when they walked into our camp and asked to see the slave leader Spartacus. They embraced him, shook his hand and some fell to their knees and wept, and to his credit Spartacus made every one of them feel as though he or she was a long-lost friend. To me he was a friend, but I think that all those who filled our centuries and cohorts also believed him to be one of them. It was that bond of comradeship that held the army together. I knew that now the strong bond of loyalty united us all behind him. To me he was always kind, but one does not become the commander of an army by being kind. He also possessed a streak of iron, a degree of ruthlessness that had enabled him to survive as a gladiator in the merciless arena. I saw this in the days following our two victories. Spartacus had captured a cohort of the enemy, men who had thrown down their weapons when they had been surrounded during the pursuit. They had begged for mercy and had seemingly been granted it. But it was not to be, for five days after he had defeated the Romans, Spartacus gave a great feast for the army. The plundered wine and food from far and wide was provided for those who had bled for him, tables stacked high with meats, fruit and bread. And afterwards, in a fenced-off area around which seating had been erected, the prisoners fought in matched pairs to the death.

Spartacus declared it to be the funeral games for Crixus and thousands stood by as pairs of fighters, some armed with gladius and shield, others with a trident and a net, fought each other to the death. The combat went on for hours, the audience, former slaves now turned masters, hooted and cheered in their drunken state, while all the time a stony-faced Spartacus sat on a wooden dais and observed the slaughter. Beside him, squat and rock-like, stood Akmon, with a black-haired and stern-faced Castus standing on his other side. Under a hot sun men sweated, bled and died, each death greeted with rapturous applause from those present. Some refused to fight and threw down their weapons, then stared in defiance at the dais. Spartacus merely nodded to one of the many guards who surrounded the temporary arena, who then speared the reluctant gladiator with his javelin. Claudia and Gallia had been present at the start of this gruesome spectacle, but had departed soon after the first blood had been spilt. I had been asked to attend, as had Rhesus, Nergal and Burebista, though I had little enthusiasm for this organised slaughter. Spartacus noted my discomfort.

'You do not approve, Pacorus?'

I shrugged. 'I see no point in it, lord.'

'Crixus was my comrade, so it is fitting that I should celebrate his life.'

'With death?'

'The first gladiatorial contests took place at the funerals of rich Romans,' he said. 'So I thought it right and proper that we should return to the old ways to give Crixus a proper send-off.'

In front of us two more men died, one screaming as his belly was sliced open by a gladius. Burebista smiled while Castus remained unmoved.

'That used to be us down there,' said Spartacus, 'spilling our guts for the amusement of the Romans. Now the roles are reversed.' He cast me a glance. 'You waste your pity on them, Pacorus, and pity will get you killed if you're not careful.'

'Tempted to try your hand, Spartacus?' Castus was being mischievous.

'It had occurred to me,' he replied.

'Then why don't you?'

Akmon look alarmed but said nothing. 'I would advise against it, lord.' I offered.

He turned to me and smiled, the first time he had done so that day. 'Why? Do you think they can beat me?'

Before I could answer he had stood up, drawn his sword and leapt from the dais and into the temporary arena. He walked calmly among the fighting pairs until he was about a hundred feet from where we stood. He raised his sword to me in salute, and then bellowed to those around him to attack him, shouting that whoever cut him down would win his freedom. Within seconds five Romans were circling him like ravenous wolves. They had swords and shields and wore helmets on their heads; Spartacus wore just a tunic and had only his sword. Any lesser man would have surely perished, but one did not become a champion of the arena by being ordinary. And whereas gladiators were trained to fight on their own, the Romans facing him had been trained to fight as a unit. On their own they were clumsy and uncoordinated. One, his shield tucked tight to his body, thrust at Spartacus but the slave general pounced to the man's right and stabbed the point of his sword into the man's upper arm. The Roman yelped in pain and dropped his sword, whereupon Spartacus pounced and thrust his sword through the man's neck. He used the Roman's body as a shield as a second attacker lunged at Spartacus' chest, only to become entangled in the corpse as he fell to the ground. He died with a gladius thrust through his back into his heart.

Spartacus was in his element now, his strong jaw thrust forward and his eyes alight with the thrill of the deadly drama he was involved in. He killed the third Roman at the end of a series of rapid sword strokes that his opponent could not parry, Spartacus driving his sword through the man's groin. The fourth died after Spartacus feinted a trip and the man, thinking his opponent would fall, rashly charged forward, only to be tripped himself and then have his belly sliced open as he fell. Thus the last Roman, a pathetic figure who clearly did not want to fight, threw down his sword and shield, fell to his knees begged for mercy. Spartacus walked up to the man, placed his left hand on his shoulder and then looked to where we were standing. He smiled at me, turned to look at the man before him and then rammed his gladius through his throat. He left the blade in place, his hand still on the Roman's shoulder, as the gladius was covered in a red froth. He then placed his foot against the dead man's chest and pushed the corpse onto the ground, extracting his sword as he did so. He then walked calmly back to the dais and retook his seat.

'Like I said,' he turned to me, 'pity is a weakness.'

I confessed that the gladiatorial contest was not to my liking and had seemed to me to be nothing more than sport.

'Of course it's sport,' remarked a surprised Gallia. 'Why are you so surprised?'

The two of us had ridden into the vine-clad hills surrounding our sprawling encampment, which was growing larger each day as new recruits joined us. The scenery we rode through was breathtaking, with deep gorges among the limestone peaks. The day was very warm, an intense sun beating down as we made our way upwards along an old goat track. The area teemed with wildlife and we saw deer, porcupine and a peregrine falcon fly overhead as our horses walked along the dirt track. Either side of us tall beech trees filled the landscape.

'I would have thought that having been forced to fight in the arena, he would have wanted to banish all traces of it from his mind.'

'It is not that simple.' She looked striking today, her hair flowing freely down the back of her blue white-edged tunic. She wore brown breeches and leather riding boots, her sword in its scabbard at her hip and her bow, like mine, tucked in its case and fixed to her saddle.

'He was a gladiator for a long time,' she continued, 'and that sort of experience leaves a permanent imprint on the mind. That's why he hates the Romans and that sort of hatred burns for a long time.'

'I hate the Romans, but I do not butcher defenceless ones.'

'You do not hate them, Pacorus.'

'I fight them, do I not?'

'Yes, but you fight for glory and because you are good at it. Spartacus is like a cornered animal. He is fighting to stay alive.'

'And I am not?'

She looked at me and smiled. 'Oh, Pacorus, your men say that you are a great warrior and leader, but you have a kingdom to go back to and an empire that will embrace you. Spartacus has nothing save the clothes he stands up in.'

'He has a homeland to go to.'

'Does he? Most of Thrace is under Roman rule. If he goes back there he will have to live the life of a hunted man. And that's true of the Spaniards and Gauls also.'

'Then where is he to go?' I asked.

She shrugged. 'Where indeed?'

We rode on in silence for a while, but then came to a small lake whose crystal clear waters were surrounded by trees. At the far end of the lake was a white rock face, over which teemed a small waterfall. It was an idyllic place, the birds singing in the trees and the scent of wildflowers filling the air. We tied up the horses in the shade of a beech tree, disrobed and plunged into the water, and afterwards we made love in the sun beside the waterfall. I lay face down on the warm, smooth rock gazing over the water, Gallia's lithe body lying beside me. She began tracing lines over my back with her finger.

'How did you get these marks on your back?' Her voices was low and sultry, her touch sensuous. The marks were the small scars bequeathed me when Centurion Cookus had whipped me.

'A present from a Roman.'

'They look rather striking, like scars earned in battle. What happened to the Roman who whipped you?'

'I cut his head off.'

She laughed and dived into the water.

'Well then, come and get your prize, lord prince.'

We were truly happy at that time, in that wonderful summer when we had destroyed Rome's armies and reached northern Italy. The world seemed to be at our feet, but perhaps it was because I was in love and I believed the impossible was possible.

We continued our march north, bringing us into a region called Cisalpine Gaul. Though it was a Roman province, it was populated by the Gauls, Gallia's people. They were ruled by a Roman governor who resided in the city of Mutina. The Gauls lived under their own rules and customs and were not Roman citizens. They paid tribute to Rome, but as long as they stayed loyal Rome left them alone. Spartacus was keen to enlist their help and so convened a council of war, to which he invited Gallia. She was not intimidated as she sat around the large table in the company of Spartacus' warlords. Claudia had made herself scarce.

'We move north in two days,' began Spartacus, a sudden storm outside shaking the sides of the tent and rattling its central supports. 'We will be moving through the land of the Gauls, your people, Gallia. I wish to know if they will help us.'

A thin smile crossed Gallia's face. 'They are a beaten people. They will not help you. You would be foolish to think otherwise.'

Nergal, Rhesus and Burebista were shocked by her words, while Akmon glanced at Spartacus and nodded.

'Nevertheless,' continued Spartacus, 'we must travel through their province. If they will not aid us, will they then fight us?'

Gallia snorted at the suggestion. 'They are a broken people. I doubt they will fight us, as even my company of women would be a match for a host of their warriors. But they will betray you to the Romans if they have a chance.'

I laid my hand on her arm. 'Yet there are still Gauls with courage.'

She snatched her arm away.

'You delude yourselves with thoughts of the Gauls helping you. They pay tribute to Rome. They would earn much esteem among the Romans if they delivered us up to them. Even now their scouts will have reported our position to the nearest garrison.' She bristled with anger.

'I have to ask you one more thing, Gallia'. Spartacus looked at her with a grave countenance. 'Byrd has reported that our army will march though the land of the Senones, your tribe, I believe. If your father is still their king, would you speak to him on our behalf?'

There was silence as Gallia stared at the table in front of her, her arms resting on the surface. I noticed that her fists were clenched and her knuckles were white. She stood up slowly and looked at Spartacus.

'No.'

She then turned and walked out.

'Sorry, lord,' I mumbled.

Spartacus rose. 'For what? If I had a thousand like her I could take Rome itself. We leave in two days. That is all.'

All my efforts to discuss the matter further with Gallia were to no avail. She did not want to talk about her father. Why should she? He was, after all, the man who had sold her into slavery.

The army moved along a splendid road called the Via Aemilia, which Godarz informed me had been built over a hundred years before. As with all the roads that I had seen, it was as straight as an arrow and had beautifully tended verges on either side. It would lead us to Mutina, the administrative centre of the province and the place that we would have to take if we were to reach the Alps and thereafter freedom. The morale of the troops was extremely high; indeed, the march started out resembling a carnival until a disgruntled Akmon issued orders for all cohort commanders to keep their men in check. I threw out a cavalry screen a few miles ahead of the army and on the flanks, while Burebista and his dragon was assigned to the army itself, under Akmon's command. He was most unhappy because he wanted to undertake scouting duties, fancying himself as fighting skirmishes with Roman horsemen rather than walking alongside bullocks and goats. However, I told him that I would rotate duties between me, Nergal and him, which kept him reasonably happy.

The first two days were uneventful as we advanced through the valley of the River Pagus, a fertile area crisscrossed by marshes, swamps and pine and oak forests. The area teemed with wildlife, chiefly among them wild boars which ignored us as they rummaged through the undergrowth searching for acorns. Near the road itself the Romans had established a number of settlements and farms, which Godarz informed me were populated by veteran soldiers and their families. They had also started the construction of dykes and canals to drain the area and turn it into farmland. How industrious these Romans were. All the farms and villages had been abandoned on our approach, however. We found only empty houses and fields.

Though she had made it clear that she wanted nothing to do with her people, I was still curious to find out more about these Gauls who lived as part of Rome, not free but not slave either. When the army camped I ordered Byrd to join me in my tent to discuss the Senones. My cavalry were spread across the area in a number of small encampments, none of which was fortified like the main camp.

'Senoni very dangerous, lord,' remarked Byrd, his unkempt appearance disguising the fine scout he had become. 'They all around, have eyes everywhere.'

I poured him some wine and we sat in two chairs outside my tent. The evening was warm and pleasant, with a slight breeze freshening the air. 'I have patrols out at all times, Byrd. They will not surprise us.'

He stretched out his legs. 'These Gauls not like Romans. They have lived here for hundreds of years. They move unseen. Killed one of my scouts yesterday.'

Now I was alarmed. 'Why?'

He shrugged. 'Do not know, lord. We found him tied to a tree with his throat slit. They had stripped him naked and blinded him first.'

'How do you know they put out his eyes first?'

He took a drink from his cup. 'No point in killing someone then blinding them. No sport in that.'

I shuddered. The thought of hundreds of men like Crixus prowling the forests all around us did not fill me with glee.

'Do you know where their main camp is?'

He finished his wine. 'Yes, lord, but would not advise you go unless you take many horsemen, but perhaps...' He turned away and looked at a group of mail-clad horsemen returning to camp, their mounts sweating after a hard patrol.

'Perhaps what?' I asked him.

'The Princess Gallia is the daughter of King Ambiorix. She could speak to her father, perhaps.'

'King Ambiorix?'

'Yes, lord. He is the master of the lands we march through.'

They came that night. How many I do not know, but they killed two sentries and two others who had the misfortune to be in their path. They cut open the side of the tent and stole inside, and after what must have been a brief but violent struggle they left as silently as they had arrived. I stood in her tent and stared at the lifeless body of a young Gaul lying face down on the floor, a wound in his side. A red-eyed Diana sat on the bed, likewise staring at the dead man, as if he would suddenly spring to life and give us answers. A cowered Rubi sat huddled in the corner, a look of terror on her face. I could hardly believe it. I felt as though a blade had been stuck into my belly and was being slowly twisted. Diana buried her head in her hands and wept again. I could not bear it so I waved a hand at a pale-faced Praxima to take her away. As she was gently lifted from the bed and shuffled past me, I laid a hand on her shoulder.

'We will get her back, I promise.' Was I assuring her or me? I did not know. All I knew that I would not rest until she was safely back by my side.

'I have sent our patrols in all directions, highness,' said Nergal.

'There were no horse tracks outside the camp,' added Rhesus.

'They would have left the horses in the trees,' I said, dejectedly, 'They will be miles away by now.'

Gallia slept among the women of her company. They had been in the main camp before we had defeated the Romans in Umbria, but after our triumphs I had grown too confident and had allowed them to stay with the cavalry. She would not countenance being away from them and said she would only share my bed as my wife. I respected her for that but did not like the idea of her being removed from me. So I had her company positioned in the centre of the camp every time we erected our tents. In this way, or so I thought, she would be safe. I was wrong. And now the woman that I loved had been snatched away and I was left helpless. I prayed to Shamash that she still lived, for life without her would have no meaning and death on the end of a Roman spear would be a blessing. They had taken her in the early hours, just before the dawn broke when men's senses are at their most confused. She must have fought them, though, because they left one of their number dead. I just hoped that her show of defiance would not go against her. But did she still live?

Spartacus and Claudia arrived at midday, both of them trying to offer solace. They failed. Nergal and Burebista returned shortly after to report they had found nothing. After a brief rest to drink and eat, they set out again on fresh horses. Gallia, and in truth all her women, had become very popular among my horsemen, many of whom regarded them as lucky mascots. Those who rode with me came to love her, with her blond locks, her riding skills and her prowess with a bow. And of course it is easy to become besotted with a beautiful woman. There was thus no shortage of volunteers to go looking for her, though none met with success.

'She is still alive,' said Spartacus, after inspecting the dead Gaul. 'If they had wanted her dead she would be lying there instead of him.'

'But why did they take her?' I was going frantic with worry.

He shrugged. 'They want something from us.'

'But what?'

'We will soon find out, I think,' added Rhesus.

An answer of sorts came at noon when a lone rider entered the camp, a young man stripped to the waist, his body covered in blue tattoos. He surrendered himself to the guards immediately and asked to be taken to see me. He was brought before Spartacus and me in my tent at spear point, though he seemed unconcerned at the malice that was being directed at him. One of the guards pushed him down on his knees. He was broad chested, with muscular arms and thick wrists. He had pale blue eyes and his hair had been drawn back and tied behind his neck, around which he wore a gold torque.

'What do you want?' He was smiling at me.

'You are the one they call Pacorus?' He spoke Latin with a guttural accent.

'You are to come with me.' Nergal and Burebista hissed in rage behind me, but I stilled them with a raised had.

'Why?'

'If you wish to see your woman again you will follow me, alone and unarmed.'

'And if I don't?' I knew the answer already.

'She will be killed.'

'Why shouldn't we kill you, also?' asked Spartacus.

The Gaul looked at Spartacus and then me. I guessed that he did not know the identity of the large warrior who stood next to me, though he must have detected the authority in his voice. The Gaul smiled.

'My father does not wish to kill anyone. He wants only to discuss – certain matters.'

'Your father?' I asked.

'King Ambiorix.'

I was surprised. 'Then you must be...'

'The brother of Gallia, yes.'

'What are these matters?' said Spartacus.

'Only my father knows. But if I do not return within four hours then he will assume I am dead. And...'

He did not have to finish his sentence. He was bundled outside as I gave orders for Remus to be saddled.

'Do not go, highness,' said Nergal. 'Give this man to me and I will make him reveal the location of his camp. Then we can rescue the Lady Gallia.'

'Thank you, Nergal, but no. This is their country and they are probably watching the camp now. If we harm this Gaul I might as well kill Gallia myself. I have no choice.'

'The fact that he sent his son means he attaches some importance to obtaining something from us,' mused Spartacus.

A few minutes later I was riding Remus out of the camp with my guide beside me. We rode through pastures, across shallow streams and followed dirt tracks though trees. He said nothing until we came to a great camp at the foot of the mountains, which stood in a vast clearing hewn from the forest we had been riding through. The camp was surrounded by a ditch and earth mound, on the top of which had been built a tall wooden fence. The track led across a wooden bridge over the ditch and through two large spiked gates. The gates were flanked by guard towers occupied by warriors armed with spears and shields. Before I rode through the gates my nostrils recoiled from the stench of animal dung and human sweat, and as I rode through the camp I saw pigs and goats in cramped pens living beside untidy huts. Naked children caked in filth ran between the huts, while everywhere stank of animal and human filth. Was this how the Gauls lived?

In the centre of the camp stood a large, squat building made from logs with a thatched roof. We tied the horses to a rail outside the main entrance, which was guarded by two long-haired warriors armed with spears, and went inside. It took a while for my eyes to adjust to the darkened interior, for the only light that entered was via small windows positioned high on each wall of what was a large hall. The roof was supported by thick pillars made from tree trunks, from which hung oil lamps. My guide strode confidently down the hall towards a dais that stood at the far end, upon which was seated a man in an oversized chair and next to him a thankfully unharmed Gallia. More warriors stood behind and on each side of the man seated in the chair, who I assumed was King Ambiorix. I stood a few paces from him and bowed my head, as is the custom when a prince meets a king. I also glanced at Gallia and smiled. She looked pale and tired but was not bound in any way. The man who had been my guide stepped onto the dais and took his place beside his father. The king was not like a typical Gaul. He had no facial hair and his face was lean, almost gaunt. He wore a gold torque around his neck and gold rings on his fingers, but his tunic and trousers were plain and his boots were also ordinary. His arms were not tattooed and, unlike those of his warriors, were not thick and hairy; rather, they were lithe and thin. His hair was fair and his eyes were blue, but unlike Gallia's they were full of cunning and malice. A young girl walked from the shadows holding a tray of silver goblets. She stopped before the king who took one, then offered me one. I took it and raised it to Gallia's father, who likewise raised his goblet and then drank. The atmosphere was unbearably tense. I sipped at the drink, which was crude mead that tasted of juniper berries and a hint of oak.

The king gestured to a warrior standing against one of the giant oak pillars, who brought me a chair to sit it.

'Sit.' King Ambiorix's voice was deep and severe.

'Thank you.' As I sat I noticed that the warrior who stood behind Gallia, thick set with high cheek bones, must be another of her brothers, as he had the same demeanour. He was slightly taller than she and he too was covered in tattoos. 'You have something that belongs to me, sire.'

He looked surprised. 'Do I? Please enlighten me.'

I looked at Gallia. 'My future wife sits in your throne room as a prisoner. I would ask why she was taken by your men against her will.'

He placed his goblet on the tray and I did likewise, and waved the girl away, then leaned forward.

'You speak of my daughter and yet I do not recall agreeing to her marrying you. In fact, your decision to marry her without my consent may be construed as gross insolence.'

'I do not mean to give offence, sire.' I think he liked me addressing him thus, but I had the feeling that we were only dancing around the real reason for this meeting.

'Prince Pacorus, I am sure that you do not mean to offend me. But you come into my land at the head of an army without my permission, you camp on my land, you take what livestock you want for food and lay waste great tracts of my territory. And not one emissary have I received from you.'

'Sire, I do not command the army.'

'Indeed you do not, for I know that the slave called Spartacus leads your band of ragtag murderers and thieves. You think that your activities have gone unnoticed in these parts? You loot all of southern Italy and then come north like a plague of rats, no doubt to carry out the same activities that you have perfected this past year.'

'We are merely attempting to leave Italy and reach our homes.'

He swiped the air with his right arm. 'What home does a slave have who was born to slaves in Italy? None. What homes did Crixus and his band of cutthroats have when they were camped on Mount Garganus and raided the surrounding area? None. Have you any idea of the trouble that I have had because fellow Gauls are running amok in Italy? Of course not, you are only concerned with your own desires and have no consideration for others.'

This was ridiculous, and I was rapidly losing patience. 'What do you want of me?'

His eyes narrowed. 'You do not ask the questions, prince of Parthia. This is my land, not yours. Imagine my surprise when I learned that a foreigner, a Parthian no less, on a white horse was leading a group of horsemen who were spreading fire and rapine throughout southern Italy. And imagine my horror when I further heard that his woman was a blonde-haired Gaul who rides and fights like a man.' He looked disapprovingly at Gallia. 'My daughter, who had escaped from her master, her murdered master, and was now shaming my good name.'

Gallia laughed at that.

'Silence!' Ambiorix rose from his chair and began pacing up and down on the dais and then pointed at me with a bony finger. 'You and your slave general have put me in a very delicate situation. She,' he jabbed a finger at Gallia, 'I once sold to a Roman for her refusal to marry the chief of another tribe. I will not tolerate insolence, you see.'

'He was old and fat, and it was more pleasurable being a slave.' Gallia's words were like javelins hurled at him.

Ambiorix was now seething with rage but kept it under control. He regained his seat and smiled at me. 'If you want your woman back you will have to buy her back.'

Now we were getting to the crux of the matter. 'Buy her back?'

He sat back in his chair. 'A somewhat delicious irony, is it not? I sold her once and now I will sell her once more.'

'I have no money, sire.'

His eyes flashed with rage. 'Do not take me for a fool, boy. I know that you paid the city of Thurri handsomely in silver and gold. I also know that every Roman legion has its own gold when it marches, gold that your slave general now possesses after destroying the Roman armies in Umbria.'

I looked at him contemptuously. 'How much gold will buy your daughter back?'

He smiled. 'Do not be so quick to judge me, young prince, for I have a kingdom to rule whereas you have no responsibilities save charging around like some tragic hero in a Greek play. You despise me? Why not, you have blazed a trail of infamy through this land and taken what you wanted. But I have to live in the real world. This was our land once, a long time ago when we came over the Alps south and made northern Italy our home. Rome was just a collection of villages then. Three hundred years ago a mighty army of Gauls sacked Rome and its citizens paid homage to us. But now Rome is like a hungry wolf and seeks to swallow us whole.'

'Then why don't you fight?' I asked, a question that drew murmurs of anger from those around him. Ambiorix silenced them with a raised hand.

'Fight? We are just one tribe. I am not so stupid to provoke a war that I cannot win. That road that your army has just marched up is like a spear though our hearts. Every year we are forced to pay tribute to the Romans, and every year they send more and more of their citizens to live on the land that they have cleared. Farms spring up where once there was forest, canals are dug to drain marshland and more roads are built across our land.

'The city of Mutina sits in our land like a nest of vipers, ready to strike at us at the slightest provocation. The governor is an individual named called Gaius Cassius Longinus. He has two legions under his command, but the mere whiff of trouble and he will squeal like a stuck boar and there'll be more legions flooding in to support him.'

'What of the other tribes?' I enquired.

'They are cowered by the Romans, but there are some among them who still dream of a Roman-free world. It was one such man, the chief of the Lingones, whom my errant daughter was going to marry. And if they join me then the other tribes, the Insubres, Cenomani, Boii and Salassi, will follow.'

I wave of naivety suddenly swept over me. 'Join with us, sire, and we can rid your homeland of the Romans.' There was silence, then Ambiorix began to chuckle.

'How many Roman armies have you defeated thus far, prince of Parthia?'

'Three,' I replied, proudly.

'And have you noticed that they when you defeat one army, another one takes its place, and another and another? Romans are like cockroaches – difficult to kill. There is only one way to defeat the Romans, and that is to destroy Rome itself. You and your slave general do not have the strength to take the city. As I said, the Gauls did that once, three hundred years ago. If the tribes were united then it could be done again. But to attempt such a thing requires a great deal of persuasion.'

Or gold. It suddenly became clear what his plan was. If he had enough gold then he could bribe enough tribes to unite against the Romans. Greed was the one vice that usually overcame common sense. His tribe was obviously poor judging by the conditions in which they lived, and presumably so were the other tribes. But gold could provide the spark that could ignite an insurrection that could destroy the power of Rome, and make him a king among kings, no doubt. Our coming into his country must have seemed like a gift from the gods to him.

'Twelve chests of legionary gold, delivered to me in two days at a time and place of my choosing.'

'That's a lot of gold.'

A thin smile crossed his lips. 'I assume you value your future bride highly. Look upon it as recompense to me for your stealing her from her master. And now I believe we are done. Iccius will escort you back to your camp.'

'What about Gallia?'

'What about her? She will remain here until our business is concluded to my satisfaction. If you attempt any sort of rescue, she will be killed.'

He must have seen the disgust in my face, for he leaned forward. 'You think I am cruel, you think that I am beyond contempt?'

I did, but said nothing.

'Go now, Prince Pacorus, and await my instructions. And do not disappoint me.'

I stood up and bowed my head. 'Sire, I request that I be allowed to speak to the Princes Gallia before I leave.'

'The time for talking is done. However, as a sign of my goodwill you may embrace her, in our presence.'

I moved forward as she walked towards me. She stepped off the dais and we embraced. As I wrapped my arms around her I suddenly felt totally helpless and desperate. 'I will not fail you,' I whispered into her ear.

'I know.'

'Sire,' I said, 'keep me hostage instead of your daughter. She can relay your demands to General Spartacus as easily as I.'

He laughed cruelly. 'Dear me, no. I think you value her life more than your own, and for that reason alone your request is denied. Be on your way now before you outstay your welcome.'

I rode back in silence, my escort, another greasy haired Gaul who stank of sweat, not attempting to engage me in conversation. The journey itself was a blur as I went over in my mind how I would get Gallia back. Her father would obviously have her throat cut without hesitation, and even if we supplied him with the gold there was no guarantee that he would keep his word. I rode back into camp thoroughly depressed, and in my tent sank disconsolately into a chair.

'Twelve chests is a lot of gold,' mused Spartacus as he handed me a cup of wine.

'He hopes to buy the loyalty of other tribes,' I said.

'For what purpose?' Spartacus sat himself down in a chair opposite me.

'He wants to overthrow Roman rule.'

'Then why doesn't he join with us?' queried Akmon, who had accompanied Spartacus.

'Because,' I replied, 'we are slaves and he would rather live under Roman rule than fight by our side.'

'I do not like blackmail,' remarked Spartacus, frowning. He must have seen the alarm in my face, as he quickly added. 'But on this occasion the price is worth paying to get a greater treasure back.'

'How do we know the Gauls will keep their word?' Gafarn was saying what I too was thinking.

'We don't,' said Spartacus, who stood up and pointed at Godarz. 'Have the gold loaded onto carts. Then all we can do is wait.'

We didn't have to wait for long, for the next morning a rider arrived from King Ambiorix with instructions for the delivery of the gold. He rode a grey horse with a blanket for a saddle, a shield strapped to his back and a long sword hanging from his belt. His large moustache hung down to his chest. He was shown into my tent. He stank of sweat and pigs. He stood proud and contemptuous before me.

'Follow the track that I have ridden along to get here. Five miles directly north of your camp there is a clearing in the forest. Through the middle of this clearing flows a brook. There is a wooden bridge over this brook. The exchange will take place there at noon tomorrow. You will bring carts only, no soldiers. Each cart will be driven by one man only, no weapons. If you attempt any treachery, the woman will be killed.'

I could have killed him there and then and was finding it difficult to control my temper, so I nodded curtly and waved him away. I turned to Godarz.

'You heard that? Prepare the wagons.'

I hardly slept that night and arose just before dawn to wash and shave. I would lead the group of twelve wagons, each one loaded with a chest of gold. Usually for such work heavy oak wagons would be used, each one pulled by four oxen, but today we would use four-wheeled wagons made of ash. These were lighter and thus faster – I did not want to be late for our meeting with the Gauls – and their wheels of twelve spokes banded with iron would be less uncomfortable while travelling along dirt tracks. Designed to haul heavy loads, today the wagons would be carrying a relatively light weight, as the chests were not large – though they were literally worth their weight in gold. Each wagon was therefore pulled by two horses instead of four mules or oxen. And on the return journey they would be carrying nothing at all. The chests were placed in the centre of the open cargo compartment behind the driver, so the Gauls could see that there were no hidden soldiers or other mischief.

As the sun began to climb in a clear blue sky, I and the eleven other drivers sat and ate a breakfast of porridge, bread and water. I looked at Godarz.

'All is ready?'

'Yes, lord.'

Spartacus and Claudia joined us, having spent the night in our camp, while Diana fussed around Gafarn, but ate nothing herself. Her black-rimmed eyes and pale face betrayed her distraught state and she said little to anyone. Trailing her every move was Rubi, like an obedient dog.

'Are you sure you do not want me to come with you?' said Spartacus.

I finished my porridge. 'No, lord, I must do this my way.'

Burebista was most upset. 'I should come with you, lord. I can kill many Gauls if need be.'

I placed my arm on his shoulder. 'I know that, but if anything happens to me and Nergal, who will command my cavalry? I need you here to take over should we not return.'

My answer did not satisfy him but it would have to suffice.

We left an hour later, twelve wagons ambling slowly in a northerly direction towards the thick woods that hugged the sides of the massive valley our army was camped in. The day was hot and airless and I sweated in my white tunic and straw hat, beads running down my face and neck and soaking the top of the cotton material. After half an hour we reached the trees and the relief of shade as we moved along the narrow track that was our route. The trees were oaks, many of them tall with thick trunks that had been standing there a long time. This was an ancient forest that existed even before the Gauls had come to this land. I wondered who had lived here when these mighty trees were saplings. Idle thoughts. Around us, great lumbering boars rooted through the undergrowth looking for food. Occasionally one would raise its massive head and stare at us, displaying its vicious tusks that could rip open a man's thigh with ease. I also saw deer, pigeons and ducks in this most abundant terrain. Of Gauls I saw none. But I suspected that they were there, watching us from the either side of the track among the trees and undergrowth.

Eventually we reached the clearing that I had been informed of, a wide expanse of meadow dotted with flowers and alive with insects. The track meandered through tall grass, eventually reaching a crude bridge of logs laid at right angles to the track and supported by upright logs driven into the water. The brook itself, a shallow course of water flanked by mud that flowed lazily across the meadow, was about forty feet wide. I led the line of wagons over the bridge and onto the far bank and there, just in front of the tree line ahead of us, was a group of Gauls. There were around fifty or sixty of them, most on foot carrying shields and large swords, though some had axes and spears. They were all bare headed with large moustaches and exposed chests. In the middle was Iccius mounted on a chestnut horse with a blanket for a saddle. Either side of him were half a dozen other warriors on horses, all carrying long spears and wearing winged helmets. And in the middle was Gallia, mounted on a grey horse whose reins were being held by one of the warriors. I brought my wagon to a halt and raised my hand at him. He kicked his horse forward accompanied by four of his horsemen. Behind me all the other drivers came to a stop. I stood up and raised my arms.

'I carry no weapons, as you requested.'

Iccius drew close to my wagon. He wore brown leggings and brown leather boots, and the sweat was dripping from him. At his waist he carried a sword in an ornate sheath, while on his head he wore a helmet of iron with a black horsehair crest. He looked from me to the chest in the back of the wagon.

'Show me the gold.'

'Show me Gallia.'

He jerked his hand over his shoulder. 'She is there, in plain view.'

'It looks like Gallia, but all Gaul women appear the same from a distance. I need to be sure.'

'You try my patience, Parthian.'

I jumped in the back of the wagon and opened the chest, which was filled with shiny gold coins. Iccius's eyes lit up, as did those of the men with him.

'A simple request, from one prince to another.'

He turned and gestured to the man holding Gallia's reins to come forward, and then directed each of the men with him to examine the contents of the other wagons. Within minutes they were beaming like children with new presents and shouting at their leader, obviously pleased with what they had found. I looked past Iccius to Gallia, who was about fifty feet away. Her wrists were still bound and her reins were still being held. Iccius turned away from me and signalled to the men standing by the trees for them to come forward.

The wagons were simple affairs, essentially rectangular wooden boxes with a tool chest at the front end, just behind the driver's seat. I now opened this box, removed my bow from inside, strung an arrow from the quiver that lay beside it and shot it at Gallia's guard. The shaft hit him squarely in the chest and knocked him from his horse. Fortunately he tumbled backwards and released Gallia's reins as he did so. I strung another arrow and saw it go through Iccius's neck. He remained on his horse, gurgling as blood poured from his neck and as he made feeble attempts to claw at the shaft. I leapt from the wagon and ran over to Gallia. I reached her and cut the rope around her wrists. Behind me, all the other Gaul horsemen had been killed by my men, who were now directing their fire at the other Gauls on foot. They had halted about two hundred feet away, having been dumfounded by what had happened to their prince. Now, eleven expert Parthian archers, the best shots I had, were standing on their wagons firing at stationary targets. There was no wind and so Gafarn, Rhesus, Nergal and the others were picking off Gauls with ease.

'Can you ride?' I said to Gallia.

'Yes.'

'Then follow the others back to camp. Go.'

I slapped her horse's hindquarters and the beast sprinted forward. I ran back to the horses tied to my wagon, cut the straps that bound them to the shaft and jumped onto the back of one. The horses that had been pulling the wagons were our cavalry mounts. I grabbed both sets of reins and kicked my mount forward. The others did the same while the surviving Gauls, maddened by our treachery, screamed their war cry and charged towards us. We galloped across the bridge, which was guarded by Gafarn and Nergal. I ensured that Gallia and the others were safely across before I ordered them to cross also, handing Gafarn the reins of my spare horse. They both picked off a couple of running Gauls before turning around and retreating like the others. I steadied my mount and strung an arrow in my bowstring. I saw a giant of a Gaul racing towards me, with a massive beard, a sword in one hand and shield in the other. He was ahead of the others, his long legs propelling him forward. He was heading straight for me, his face contorted in hate and bellowing something in his native tongue. I raised my bow and loosed the arrow, which travelled straight and true and hit him in the left shoulder. He staggered and fell and I laughed. But then my mirth disappeared as he got to his feet and continued on his way towards me, not as fast as before, but still walking determinedly in my direction. I put another arrow into him, this time in his stomach, causing him to roll forward. After a few seconds he rose to his feet again and roared his hate at me. Was he some sort of demon sent from the underworld? Behind him his companions were closing on me fast, so I strung another arrow and took careful aim, releasing the cord as the other Gauls sprinted past him. The arrow went into his right eye socket but he just stood there. I pulled on the reins and directed my horse back across the bridge. A spear flashed past me as I crouched low on the horse's back and screamed at him to move faster. I glanced back and saw the big Gaul topple onto the ground, though I never did find out if he sprang back to his feet a few seconds later. I galloped to the edge of the meadow where Gafarn and Nergal were waiting for me.

I was sweating and panting heavily. 'Is Gallia safe?'

'She rode ahead of us, highness.'

Behind us angry Gauls were still chasing me, but they were now some distance away and would not catch us.

'Time to go,' I said. I waited at the first trees until Nergal and Gafarn had ridden away, then followed them back down the track. Behind us we left twelve chests of gold and hopefully one dead Gaul prince and a slain bearded giant.

Our arrival back at camp was greeted with rapturous cheers. Gallia brought her horse to a halt before my tent, jumped to the ground and hugged a sobbing Diana and hopping Rubi. Next came Claudia, wrapping her arms around all of them, followed by a beaming Spartacus whose massive arms seemed to engulf all four of the woman. Burebista threw a screen of lance-carrying horsemen around the camp lest the Gauls tried to attack us, but none dared approach us. The area around my tent soon became a mass of people who wanted to convey their joy at seeing Gallia again. I didn't realise until that moment how popular she was and how many people must have also fallen in love with her. Then came Praxima and the rest of the women warriors, squealing with joy like a group banshees. Gafarn stood beside me as the din increased and a steady stream of individuals approached to pay their respects.

'It is good to have her back, highness.'

'It certainly is. That was good shooting back at the bridge, by the way. I am in your debt.'

'Of course, your skills with a bow are almost as good as mine.' He always had a knack of reminding me what a fine shot he was. 'Do you think the Gauls will attack us?'

I shrugged. 'They can try, but if they do I will personally burn the king's berg, and with him inside. Wretched man.'

Gafarn smiled slyly. 'You do know he will be your father-in-law?'

'I would prefer to celebrate him as a deceased father-in-law.'

'No invitation to the palace in Hatra for him, then?'

'No, Gafarn,' I replied irritably.

Gafarn did come in useful a while later when I asked him to prise Diana away from Gallia and also asked everyone else to leave us. Later, when Gallia had washed and changed her clothes, we had a meal alone in my tent. I sat next to her and put my arm around her shoulder as she tucked into a plate of roasted pork slices and vegetables.

'You can let go of me, Pacorus, I won't run away.'

'I'm never going to let go of you again. You and your women are to billet in the main camp, just in case your father decides he wants his daughter back.'

She laughed ironically. 'He never wanted me, and was glad enough to get rid of me when he could.'

'Why does he dislike you so?'

'Because I remind him of my mother.'

She saw the confused look on my face. 'Soon after I was born my mother died, I was told because the birth had been long and painful. With her died any feelings of affection my father may have had for me. He is a very unhappy man.'

'He will be unhappier now that one his sons has been killed.' I looked at her. 'For that I am sorry.'

She laid her hand on mine. 'Do not be sorry, my love, you came for me when I needed you most. But I fear you are right. Rage and my father are close companions. He hates the Romans, and for that I admired him. But he dreamed of a land free of them where he would be high king of all the tribes of Gaul this side of the Alps. But that dream gnawed away at him when he realised that it was just that, a dream. Like I told you before, they are a beaten people.'

Fat dripped onto my tunic as I picked up a slice of pork with my knife. 'Perhaps with the gold he now has he can unite the tribes.'

She looked at me with those piercing blue eyes that seemed capable of reading all my thoughts. 'Oh, Pacorus, you and my father would make good allies. You are both dreamers, but in his case his dreams are dangerous fantasies. The Gauls in Italy are slaves in all but name. Ever since I can remember, all I heard about was the Romans flooding into the valley of the Padus.'

'The Padus?'

'That is the name the mighty river that flows through the middle of the land between the Apennines and the Alps. You have seen for yourself how the Romans drain the land, cut down the trees and build roads and settlements. This is not a new thing; it has been going on for decades. But under the new governor of Mutina it has got worse. And all the time the Gauls, my people, are pushed into the hills and forests like hunted beasts, huddled in their villages dreaming of a time that is long gone.' She sighed. 'My father is eaten away with bitterness, like all people who want something they know they can never have.'

'I almost feel sorry for him.'

Her eyes flashed with anger. 'Don't. He is dangerous still and we are not yet out of his reach.'

I smiled. 'What can he do against the might of our army?'

We found out five days later. The army had struck camp and had moved directly north, through a land full of Roman villages, farms and neat, white-walled villas, a land divided into square fields and criss-crossed by irrigation ditches. Our route took us to within ten miles of the city of Mutina, but Spartacus saw no need to attack it as we could actually bypass it with ease. I had Byrd and his scouts riding on each flank and to our front, for we knew that the city's garrison comprised two legions, though not if it would attempt to intercept us. I myself doubted it, for our army now numbered fifty thousand men plus assorted women who had come with their husbands or who had run away from their masters on their own. I had no idea how many they totalled, but Godarz had complained to me that there were at least five thousand of them, 'all mouths we have to feed'. I told him that they kept the men happy, and a happy man is one who fights better. He was unconvinced by my argument, I think, but he was right about the food. Most days at least a third of my horse, a thousand men, undertook foraging duties, which in this fertile region was an easy task. We either looted Roman settlements for their grain or livestock, or helped ourselves to the abundant deer and boar that inhabited the forests. Indeed, I encouraged company commanders to hunt animals with their bows because it was good archery practice. Though we were always mindful not to stray too far into the trees as the Gauls still watched us.

'I can't see them,' I remarked to Gallia one day as we were riding five miles from the army's left flank along with three hundred of Burebista's men.

'They're there,' she replied, 'they watch us all the time.'

I glanced at the thick oaks that spread as far as the eye could see to our left and shuddered. No doubt King Ambiorix would pay a high price in gold for me being taken alive so he could extract a slow and terrible revenge.

It was just after dawn on the fifth day, as the army was breaking camp, when Byrd and two of his men galloped through its northern entrance and halted in front of my tent, for now all of us took shelter in the main camp. His men were the eyes and ears of the army, scruffy men on scraggy horses but individuals who were like the wild boars that populated these parts. They could smell trouble without seeing an enemy and were each worth a company of cavalry. Godarz was always complaining about their appearance, the condition of their horses and their insubordination towards him when he rebuked Byrd or any of his men.

'They are a law unto themselves, lord, and they should be under proper military discipline.'

'Ordinarily I would agree with you,' I replied. 'But they carry out an invaluable task and while they are undertaking that to my satisfaction I will overlook their more eccentric traits.'

And once again they had proved their worth. The sun was a yellow fireball in the east as Byrd drank greedily from a water skin and then gave the rest to his sweating horse.

'Romani army ten miles to the north, blocking our way.'

Thirty minutes later we were at a council of war, sitting on stools in the centre of Akmon's camp that was being steadily dismantled and packed away, a pall of dust hanging over the whole area as men packed tents into wagons, hauled their packs onto their backs, and sweated and cursed as their commanders got them into marching order. Trumpets sounded as centuries and cohorts were formed up and roll calls taken, while Spartacus drew patterns in the parched ground with the tip of his gladius.

He looked up at Byrd. 'How many?'

'My men count two eagles yesterday.'

'That's the garrison of Mutina, then,' said Rhesus.

Castus slapped me on the back. 'Two legions! Is that all that faces us. We will swallow them up.'

'Others with Romani,' added Byrd.

Akmon frowned. 'What others?'

'Gauls. They fill the land all around Romani camp with their warriors. Many thousands.'

A line of wagons pulled by mules trundled behind us, the muffled sound of their wheels mixing with the clanking of the pots and tools that hung from their sides, while their drivers shouted and cursed the animals to move more quickly. A pointless exercise when dealing with the most stubborn beasts in the world.

Spartacus stood up and sheathed his sword. 'So, it would appear that the Gauls have formed an alliance with their Roman overlords and intend to crush us. If we continue our march we will have to fight them on ground of their choosing. But if we do not fight them, we will have to find another way north, which will delay us many more days.'

'What are your orders, lord?' I asked.

He smiled. 'We fight them.'

Chapter 13

Three hours later we marched into a wide plain surrounded by gently undulating hills. Once it must have been filled with trees, but years of Romanisation had produced a landscape of neat fields and farmsteads as far as the eye could see. But one sight that dominated the horizon was a mass of men formed into a long line to our front. Earlier I had ridden in the vanguard of the army with Byrd and a hundred horsemen, and had seen at first hand the size of the army that barred our way. By mid-morning it was already forming into a long line across the horizon, mail-clad Romans in cohorts and armoured and bare-chested Gauls carrying shields, axes, spears and long swords. We had been spotted almost immediately and a group of Roman horsemen galloped out from the enemy lines, men carrying large red circular shields and armed with lances. They came at us in a column of three abreast and then formed into line some distance from us, lowering their lances in expectation of a fight at close quarters. But I gave the signal to retreat and we cantered away from them. I took up position at the rear of our group, and as the Romans got nearer I and a few other Parthians began firing at them over the hindquarters of our horses. This was a tactic they had obviously never encountered before, because when half a dozen of their saddles had been emptied they slowed their pace and then stopped as we carried on our retreat.

When we reached the army I immediately told Spartacus what I had seen.

'They obviously intend to fight us,' I reported. 'Byrd was right about the number of legions, but I've never seen so many Gauls gathered in one place.'

Spartacus, as usual, was marching on foot with Claudia and Akmon in the midst of his Thracians.

'Well, as they have been so kind as to gather all in one place, it would be rude not to accommodate them.' He grinned at me. 'Besides, killing them now will save us the effort of doing it later.'

'I'm sure they are thinking the same thing,' mused a grim-faced Akmon, whose mood always darkened before any battle.

It was noon when our army began to form up in their battle positions. I threw a screen of horsemen to the front of the foot to deter the enemy from interfering with our movements, but the Romans and their allies made no moves. Byrd reported that there was a large ditch that secured the enemy's right flank, and when I rode over to see it for myself I realised that it would stop any attempt by my cavalry to outflank the enemy from that direction. The ditch was wide – about thirty feet – and had sheer sides. It must have been at least ten feet deep and ran arrow-straight into the distance; obviously the commander of the Roman legions, the governor of Mutina (I assumed that no Gaul would have the intellect to think of such a thing) had a well-thought out battle plan. He had anchored his right flank on an obstacle that was impossible to cross, but what about his left flank? Byrd and I rode along the gap between the two armies, that piece of killing ground that belonged to no one but which would soon be full of dead and the wounded. We made sure that we were out of enemy bow range, though a group of their slingers tried their luck when we cantered past, loosing small lead pellets that fortunately whistled by us harmlessly. From the ditch to where the two Roman legions were forming up was a distance of around two miles and was filled wholly by Gauls, and in front of where they stood in groups or sat on the ground were wooden stakes over six feet in length that had been driven into the ground and angled towards our army, the ends of which appeared from a distance to have been sharpened to points. In fact, the whole of the Gaul battle line was protected by several rows of these stakes. In the centre of the enemy line stood the Roman legions, deployed side by side. They each presented a front line of four cohorts, so I assumed that each legion was deployed in a standard three-line formation. The Roman legions together covered around half a mile of front. As we rode past the Romans we discovered yet more Gauls, this time on the enemy's left wing, thousands of them in groups, again standing behind rows of sharpened wooden stakes, and again they covered a distance of around two miles. The enemy front thus measured nearly five miles. It was the largest army I had seen in Italy; indeed, it was the largest army I had seen in my life.

I told all this to the council of war who sat on stools in the shade beside a wagon filled with cooking utensils. While the army deployed, the wagons, mules, carts, oxen and non-combatants were being positioned in its rear. The wagons and carts were arranged in a square to form a sort of barrier, behind which the animals could be secured and the army's supplies and spare weapons could be stored. This makeshift camp was guarded by around five hundred soldiers, usually men who were too old to fight in a century but who still knew how to use a sword or a spear. If the army was defeated then the enemy would make short work of them, but it comforted us all to know that they were guarding our rear. I had wanted to use Gallia's women as camp guards as well, but she steadfastly refused, saying that she would rather die in battle than wait to be raped and then killed if we were beaten, so that was that.

Any walking wounded were also detailed to act as camp guards. The day was warm and getting warmer, and already the men in their centuries and cohorts were using up the contents of their water bottles. A steady stream of water carts were making their way to and from the river that we had crossed three miles to the rear to replenish our supplies on what would be a very thirsty day. The cavalry had its own carts, which were also making the trip to and from the watercourse, though two-thirds of my horsemen were still at the river watering their mounts. There would be plenty of time to bring them forward before the fighting started.

'They won't fight unless we attack them,' said Spartacus. 'They are inviting us to assault them while they sit behind their stakes.'

'My horse will be no use against those stakes, lord,' I added, somewhat dejectedly.

Akmon finished eating an apple and tossed the core aside. 'Whoever the Roman commander is, he knows his business. He's obviously heard of your cavalry, Pacorus, and at a stroke has neutralised it. Clever.'

'Put my men in the centre, lord, and we will cut through them like a sharp spear.' Afranius, the newly appointed commander of the two legions of Spaniards, looked like a young Akmon. He had olive skin, dark brown eyes and short-cropped hair. He was shorter then me by around six inches, but was far more muscular and thickset. He was also extremely aggressive, a consequence of fighting the Romans for five years in his native country before being captured and sold in the slave market. His fat old master thought that Afranius would make a good catamite, but instead found only death at the end of a knife that was thrust into his heart. He wanted nothing more than to butcher Romans, and only accepted the discipline of Spartacus because it was a means to the end of killing his foes. That said, he pushed himself and his men hard, and the three Spanish legions were reckoned to be among the best we had.

Spartacus shook his head. 'No, Afranius, that is what they want.'

'Then how do we beat them, lord?' asked Castus, his face and neck covered in sweat from the midday sun.

'We wear them down with arrows.'

'The only archers in the army belong to Pacorus' cavalry,' remarked Godarz.

Spartacus nodded. 'That's true, so we will place them on our wings, behind the second line of cohorts, to shoot arrows at the Gauls. The Gauls have no defence against arrows, they lack discipline and also cannot lock their shields together to form a roof of leather and wood as the Romans do. Hopefully we can goad them into attacking us, thereby rendering their wall of stakes useless.'

'How many archers do you need, lord?' I asked.

'A thousand on each flank, and make sure you have enough arrows.'

'I will issue extra bundles from our reserves,' said Godarz.

Spartacus stood and looked at each of us in turn. 'Just one more battle and we are out of this country, so remind your men of that. We've beaten them before and we can do so again. May the gods be with you all.'

We shook hands and returned to our posts, though I actually seemed to have little to do save form a reserve with the remainder of my horse. Spartacus had earlier decided on how our ten legions would deploy. He had the three legions of Spaniards under Afranius positioned on the extreme left, next to the ditch and facing the Gauls. Afranius was most unhappy about this, but Spartacus told him that if he was killed then he could do what he liked, but not until then. Next in line came the two legions of Castus' Germans, men who rivalled the Thracians for their calmness in battle and their dependability. Also put under Castus' command was another legion made up of those Gauls who had joined us after the defeat of Crixus, plus a large number Greeks, Dacians and Jews. On the Germans' right were Akmon's Thracians, twenty thousand men arranged in four legions, the first two of which faced the two Roman legions opposite them. The final two Thracian legions, our right flank, adopted a two-line formation in an attempt to match the frontage of the Gauls facing them, but failed. This meant that we were outflanked on our right wing by about half a mile, maybe more, and if the Gauls decided not to stand behind their forest of stakes, then they could easily envelop the whole of our right side.

It took two hours for our legions to form up and my remaining horsemen to arrive from the river. I told Nergal and Burebista of the battle plan and informed the former that he would take charge of one group of archers on the right flank and Godarz would command the other group on the left. The men's horses would be stationed well to the rear.

'In the unlikely event that the enemy breaks through our line, they are to run back to the horses and then ride to the river. That will be our rallying point.'

'Where will you be, highness?' asked Nergal.

'With Burebista's men guarding our right flank. And pray to

Shamash that the Gauls do not decide to attack that flank.'

Burebista's men were almost entirely armed with lances, with only a handful carrying bows. I joined him as his men were erecting canvas awnings supported by wooden poles to create shaded areas for the horses. Beasts offered even a modicum of shade would be fresher later for carrying men in battle. The Parthians had learned this long ago. He was his usual cheerful self, full of confidence and good humour, a confidence that had infected the men of his dragon.

'A fine day for killing Romans, lord,' he beamed.

At that moment Gallia and her company of women rode up. She was dressed in her full war gear of mail shirt, sword, dagger and helmet, with a full quiver of arrows over her shoulder and her bow in its case fixed to her saddle. She wore tight-fitting leggings and brown leather boots, as did all her women. They looked a fearsome spectacle, and with their closed cheek guards they could have passed for men. They rode in perfect formation, for Gallia was aware that many in the army thought that women could not drill and fight as well as men, so she ensured that her women drilled and practised twice as hard as anyone else. She halted, dismounted and strode over to me. She took off her helmet, her blonde hair in one long plait running down her back.

'Nergal told me that we cannot fight as archers with him. Is this so?'

I saw the look of disbelief on Burebista's face. He would not dream of talking to me thus. I took Gallia's arm and led her away.

'I would prefer, my love, that you and your women stay close to me during this battle. I have enough to worry about without wondering if you are safe.'

She yanked her arm free. 'You cannot stop us from fighting.'

I was in no mood to argue. 'You will stay here with Burebista until I return. These are my orders. Get your horses under cover, water them and eat something. It's going to be a long day.'

I mounted Remus and pointed at Burebista. 'Make sure they stay here, I hold you responsible.'

I rode to both wings of the army, first to the left flank where Godarz was giving instructions concerning the placement of spare quivers, each one holding thirty arrows. Like me he wore a cotton tunic only, though he at least had a silk vest underneath for extra protection. Though Spartacus had ordered a thousand archers to be positioned on each flank, in truth there were fewer. For a start, every tenth man was in the rear tending to ten horses, while others were charged with bringing water from the water carts to those who would be shooting. Those who were not archers did not realise that a bowman could not fire arrows all day. Even the most accomplished archer needed rest; it was impossible to maintain a firing rate of seven arrows a minute for long periods. Rather, short, intense bursts were the norm. I walked down the line as men attached their bowstrings and flexed their bows. Some I recognised as Parthians, their olive skin, long black hair and brown eyes giving them away. I slapped shoulders, shook hands and shared jokes. They were in high spirits. I wondered how many would still be alive in a few hours.

'Remember what I said, if the line breaks don't wait around. Get to the horses and get away as fast as you can. Men with bows on foot are no match for heavily armed legionaries.'

'Don't worry,' replied Godarz, 'I will outrun these youngsters if that happens.'

I embraced him and then rode across to the right flank where Nergal faced the Gauls. Because this wing was outflanked, I had positioned Burebista's dragon directly behind Nergal's men, around five hundreds yards to the south.

'We are there, Nergal, you see us? At the first sign of them attacking we will come to your aid.'

'Yes, highness, we will not let you down.'

He was a good man and I was thankful that he was fighting with me. 'Praxima is with Gallia and I will keep a close eye on them, so have no fear.'

He grinned and saluted. 'Thank you, highness.'

I rode back to Burebista's dragon with Rhesus.

'Clever, this father of Gallia,' he said. 'Obviously brains runs in the family.'

'The man is an animal,' I spat.

'True, but he certainly sees the bigger picture. Once he got our gold he obviously bribed all the other chiefs to join him, then went to the Romans and offered them the help of all the Gauls to crush us.'

'How does that help him?' I was not really interested in Gallia's father, but I could tell that Rhesus had been considering the matter, so I indulged him.

'He beats us, and afterwards he destroys the Romans as well. There must be sixty thousand Gauls here, more than a match for two legions, especially if he stabs them in the back. Clever, very clever.'

'You forgot one thing, Rhesus.'

'Highness?'

'He has to beat us first for his plan to work.'

Moments later I heard the blast of trumpets and bugles and then the roar of thousands of men cheering and shouting. Soon the air was filled with the low, thundering rumble of soldiers banging their spears against their shields. Spartacus told me later what had happened during the initial clash. Our legions had advanced, a great wall of steel, mail and leather, walking at a steady pace until they were within a hundred feet of the enemy, then the trumpets sounded the charge and the whole of the front line ran forward, the men hurling their javelins into the dense mass of the enemy. The Romans had locked their shields to their front and above their heads, so the javelin storm had a negligible effect, but on the wings it was a different matter. The rows of stakes made it impossible for our men to come to close quarters with their swords, but the ill-disciplined Gauls stood in open order, not in a solid mass of locked shields, and many fought bare headed, their hair washed in lime and combed into long spikes. Within seconds dozens had been felled by javelins, the thin points penetrating flesh and splitting heads. The Gauls threw spears and axes in return, but most slammed harmlessly into our shields. The Gauls also had some archers and slingers who kept up a withering fire against our line. The lead pellets of the slingers took a steady toll of our men for their accuracy was amazing, and they could put a shot into the small, arched-shaped gap between a shield held vertically by a soldier in the front rank and another held horizontally above his head by the man standing behind him. As all our men wore Roman helmets, the wounds were mostly serious but not lethal, though occasionally a pellet would kill a man and a gap would appear where he fell. It was filled instantly by the man behind. The Gauls kept up a steady volley of missiles against our men opposite, who were unable to pull down the stakes, as it would mean exposing their torsos to the enemy's fire. And once our line had steadied the Gauls retreated from their rows of stakes to keep just out of range of our javelins. So on the two wings the fighting became one of desultory missile fire as our men weathered a decreasing hail of spears, arrows and sling shots, for the Gauls quickly exhausted their ammunition.

In the centre the Thracians charged at the Romans with their swords and a vicious close-quarters mêlée ensued, men stabbing with the points of their swords at those opposite, trying to find exposed thighs, groins and bellies with their blades. A few men got careless and had their guts torn open, but the majority remembered their training and kept their shields close to their bodies. In this part of the line there was much pushing and shoving and stabbing but very few casualties, occasionally a wounded man being hauled to the rear by his comrades, his place being instantly filled by a replacement. After half an hour or more of this work both sides, as if by mutual consent, withdrew a few yards to rest and regroup. The day was hot and men wearing mail shirts and steel helmets were soaked in sweat and dehydrated. The centuries and cohorts of the second line moved forward to replace those of the first line, while the walking wounded limped to the rear to be treated and those more seriously injured were put on stretchers and carried back. Those who had been fighting and were now relieved drank greedily from water bottles that were passed to them by non-combatants, women and those too young to fight but fleet of foot.

On the left flank Afranius became impatient and ordered four centuries armed with axes, which he had organized before the battle, to charged forward through the front ranks and attempt to cut a path through the field of stakes. The result was that he lost two hundred men in two minutes, cut down by throwing axes, spears and a hail of arrows and lead pellets. He did not make a second attempt. My archers posted behind his second line moved forward and commenced a withering fire against the Gauls, which exacted a steady toll on their massed ranks. But they stayed stubbornly behind their stakes and we could make no impression upon them, save those we could pierce with arrows. And we did not have an inexhaustible supply of missiles, and so after an hour the archers were instructed to limit their rate of fire to two arrows every minute.

It was a similar story on the right flank where Castus was ever mindful of the Gauls who outflanked him by at least half a mile. He did not even attempt to close with the enemy but merely let my archers pour volleys of arrows into them, until they too were ordered to reduce their rate of fire. The Thracians in the centre, now with fresh soldiers in their front line, again attempted to break through the Romans opposite them, but it was the same story as before. The front ranks threw their javelins and charged with swords drawn, stabbing them into the legionaries to their front, grinding their way into the enemy's formations. At first it appeared that the enemy would break as dead and wounded men fell backwards and Thracians stepped forward into the gaps, stabbing left, right and to the front with their swords. The Roman line buckled, but then their accursed Scorpions opened fire and soon Thracians were being hit by iron darts that went through shields and mail with ease. Gaps appeared in our front ranks, but it was only when Spartacus diverted some of my archers from the wings and had them shoot at the crews of the Scorpions that the deadly storm of iron bolts was brought to an end, as the Romans withdrew their artillery to a safe distance. But they had succeeded in halting our attack, and once again both sides withdrew to lick their wounds and prepare for another struggle for possession of the churned-up, blood and piss-stained ground between the two armies, a strip of land that was now littered with dead.

Thousands of sandal-clad feet and tens of thousands of hooves had kicked up a great cloud of dust that choked man and beast alike. As the day wore on this cloud thickened over the whole battlefield.

The dust was just another thing to cope with on this day of slaughter. It was hot in my leather cuirass and helmet, and soon small streams of sweat were coursing down my face and neck and soaking my silk vest and tunic. It must have been an hour at least after the battle had commenced when Spartacus rode over to where my cavalry were positioned. Most of the men were lounging on the ground with their helmets lying beside them, though one in every five companies was mounted and deployed to our front and on our right flank, in case we were attacked. As the battle wore on, vigilance became more important as the wretched dust continued to reduce visibility.

'That proconsul in command of the Roman army is a clever bastard. We can't shift them.' Spartacus gulped down the contents of the water skin I had passed him.

I shrugged. 'We could break off the engagement. My horse can cover the retreat.'

'No. If we retreat the Romans will be back twice as strong. Besides, it will be bad for morale if we run away from two legions and a few Gauls.'

A short time later Castus ran up to inform me that he had shifted four cohorts to the extreme right of his line and deployed them so they were at right angles to the rest of his men who were facing the Gauls.

'Spartacus, forgive me, I did not realise that you were here. Are you hurt?'

'No. What has happened?'

'The Gauls are taking down their stakes where they outflank us. I think they are going to attack. Pacorus, we may need your cavalry to stiffen our line.'

I signalled for Burebista to attend me.

Spartacus gazed over to where Castus had ridden from. 'So, the Gauls have grown bored with standing idly by while their fellow warriors have all the glory.' He smiled. 'The gods may have just given us a sign. How many horse have you, Pacorus?'

'Fifteen hundred, lord.'

'Good.' He slapped Castus on the shoulder. 'Get back to your men and make sure they hold. Remember, the Gauls won't come at you like the Romans do. They will charge in a wild, screaming mass. But they will break on your wall of shields.'

Castus looked alarmed. 'But they may sweep around us and get behind the army.'

Spartacus shook his head. 'Extend your line by taking men from your second line. Use Pacorus' archers to shoot them down. There may be a lot of them but they are not disciplined, and it's discipline that wins battles. Now go.'

Castus saluted and departed in haste. Spartacus turned to me, his eyes wild with excitement. 'Pacorus, your horse is the key that will unlock their defence. Take your men and ride parallel to the enemy's left flank, then sweep around behind them. The dust should cover your movement.'

Riding along the enemy's front for more than half a mile would deprive the army of its reserve, and if the Gauls broke through our right flank then thousands of their warriors would be free to butcher the wounded and loot the baggage camp. That said, Castus could probably hold them, at least long enough for my horse to get behind them. It might just work.

'It is a gamble, lord.'

He grasped my shoulders. 'Your horse are the best trained and led cavalry outside Parthia.' He knew how to flatter. 'You have never let us down before, nor will you today.'

I felt a surge of pride go through me. I turned to Burebista. 'Get your men mounted, we are going to kill some Gauls.'

'Yes, lord,' he beamed, and began to order his company commanders to assemble their men. Soon the air was filled with horns calling men to assemble.

Spartacus jumped back on his horse. 'Get behind them, Pacorus, and do as much damage as you can. Good luck.'

Then he was gone. I walked to where Gafarn was holding Remus and his own horse. I took Remus' reins. Around us men and horses were forming into columns, lance points glinting in the dusty haze.

'Well, Gafarn, we are going to see how well Gauls fight.'

'With swords and spears, no doubt. They all seem to look like Crixus.'

'Don't remind me. Stay close to Gallia and Diana. They are to remain here to guard the baggage camp.' This was slightly

disingenuous as the wagon camp had its own guards, but no matter.
'Yes, highness.'
I mounted Remus. 'And take care of yourself, Gafarn.'
He nodded. 'You too, highness.'
No sooner had I ridden to the front of the column of horse that was now moving slowly to the right, fifteen hundred horsemen in companies arranged in three files each, than Gallia was at my side, her helmet's cheek guards open.
'Gafarn has passed on your suggestion. I considered it and rejected it. We fight today.'
'It was not a suggestion,' I said. 'It was an order.'
'No,' she said firmly. 'We have a right to fight. We will merely join the rear of the horse. Do you want a wolf as a wife or a lamb?'
There was no time to argue. 'Very well. But stay close.'
'Don't worry. I won't let any Gaul rape you.'
'Very well, I snapped, 'get your women behind my company. And stay close.'
She shouted with joy, closed her cheek guards and rode Epona away, and within minutes a hundred riders had slotted in behind the company of Dacians that I headed.
I was nervously peering to my left, in the direction of the Gauls who were massed on the left wing of the enemy's army. I could only see them with difficulty, the dust and the heat haze distorting the view. I prayed to Shamash that they were likewise handicapped.
To my right and riding at the head of the middle column was Burebista, lance in hand and shield tucked into his left side. To his right was another company, and behind us more columns riding three abreast and parallel to the enemy's wing.
Company commanders kept their men in check, for in battle there is a tendency, especially among inexperienced men, to quicken the pace and get the bloodletting over with as quickly as possible. But those who have been in a fight know that discipline and restraint are the keys to staying alive. There is no point in running a horse hard before a charge; all that happens is that he will be exhausted when you need his reserves of energy most. Similarly, a horse picks up on adrenalin careering through its rider and will become edgy and fretful, which is very undesirable when he is thrust into the maelstrom of the mêlée, he will most likely panic and become either uncontrollable or throw his rider in an attempt to flee to safety. So we rode at a steady pace, keeping our formation and reassuring our horses. Remus was feisty anyhow, so I continually said his name and comforting words to him. He would understand

the tone of my voice at least. I glanced behind me to ensure that Gallia and her women had done what they had been told, and sure enough they were moving in impeccable formation. We were kicking up a huge amount of dust, and it would not take a genius to work out that a large body of horse was on the move. I prayed that the Gauls were too busy attacking Castus and his men to notice.

We moved parallel to the Gauls until I estimated that we were well beyond their line, then I swung the column sharply to the left and led it forward about five hundred yards. Again the company commanders restrained the pace, and then I halted the men altogether. Ahead was empty space – we had moved beyond the enemy's left flank and were behind them. But to my left I could see a great mass of warriors moving slowly inwards towards our own right flank. So, they had indeed taken down their stakes and were attacking Castus' men. The Romans may have been disciplined, but the Gauls did not have the patience to stand and bide their time, thankfully for us. I felt a tingle of excitement go through me as I entertained the thought that we could charge them in the rear. I rode over to Burebista.

'All company commanders to deploy their men in line, three ranks only. Then we'll go straight at them. Wait for my signal'

He saluted and galloped back to his officers who had gathered in a group behind us. The next few minutes were a confusion of curses and shouts as fifteen hundred men on horseback cantered into position to form a thin line of horseflesh about two miles wide to face the enemy. As far as I could tell through the haze and dust, the Gauls were still wheeling inwards to attack Castus and his men, who I hoped were still holding their positions. I rode along the line, shouting encouragement and brandishing my sword at the men, who responded with hurrahs and cheers. Their morale was high and I knew that their training had been thorough. I rode back to the centre of the line where Rhesus and Burebista were sitting on their horses, fifty feet in front of the first rank. Either side of us, all along the line, company commanders were placed ahead of their men, ready to lead by example. I also saw Gallia, face enclosed in her helmet and bow in hand, in front of her women. I nodded at her, she nodded back. My mouth was dry and my heart pounding. I checked my helmet straps, sword belt and bow case. I patted Remus on the neck and lowered my sword, then gently nudged him forward with my knees.

Behind me horns sounded as Burebista's dragon followed my lead. I felt extremely isolated as the distance to the enemy decreased. I could see them now, small black figures moving slowly, though in what direction I could not tell. I could also hear them, a slowly increasing roar of thousands of men. I glanced behind me. The cavalry were maintaining perfect order. The companies were widely spaced, and the distance between each horseman was around twenty feet – if the Gauls managed to form a shield wall then each rider would at least have a chance to halt and turn around, for no horse would charge at a solid wall of the enemy. I held Remus back, for he wanted to be unleashed and gallop as fast as his powerful legs would carry him. But he would need all his reserves of stamina for the trial that lay ahead. We were nearing them now, and I could see that our presence had been detected, for groups of the enemy were clustering around their knights. Gallia had told me that each knight of a tribe had his own war band, and in battle these bands clustered around their leader. So it was now, and I felt a surge of elation as I saw gaps appearing in the enemy's ragged line. I kicked Remus into the charge as I directed him towards a space that had formed between two groups of Gauls who were hurriedly planting their long oblong shields on the ground and ramming the ends of their spear shafts into the ground to form a wall of iron points. I rode between the two groups and with my sword split the helmet of a Gaul who was unlucky enough to be in my path. I slashed at another figure who was vainly attempting to outrun me. My blade caught him on his helmet and spun him to the ground. Behind me hundreds of horsemen were spearing and cutting their way into the enemy's ranks, for there were ranks. No disciplined mass of Roman legionaries, just groups of warriors attempting to fight alongside their kinsmen and lords. Those who panicked and ran were killed easily; either speared by our lances or sliced open by sword cuts, or were simply trampled to death under horses' hooves.

After the initial clash the discipline of my cavalry and the ill discipline of the Gauls began to tell in our favour. Companies of horsemen not only cut down individuals, they also isolated groups that had clustered around knights and chiefs, slashing at them with their swords. Occasionally a rider fell from his saddle, either the victim of a spear thrust or with an arrow through his chest. But the Gauls had few archers and my men knew how to stop their horses getting too close to the spears of the Gauls. As my horsemen regrouped after the initial clash, the ground was littered with dead Gauls. It was a good start.

We redressed our lines and charged again, this time the companies in wedge formation three ranks deep. We drove deep into the enemy, slashing to the right and left with our swords, Burebista's men protecting themselves with their shields. Once more we cut down many warriors, who were now mostly a mass of disorganised individuals. But the depth of the enemy was too great and we could not force our way through them to reach Castus' men. I prayed they held still.

Those who have never fought in battle talk of cavalry being able to roll up an enemy flank, but armies are not carpets and thousands of soldiers cannot simply be rolled up and put away like some scroll on a library shelf. It is impossible to control, much less direct, hundreds of horsemen across a two-mile front. All one can hope for is that their officers and those they lead stay calm and remember their training, that they try to put aside their fear and bloodlust and keep to their task. But it is hard, so very hard. Gauls were running in all directions and we were cutting them down, but in front of us, haphazard and disjointed, a new line was steadily forming as knights and chiefs frantically herded their men into place, forming a thin shield wall that was slowly thickening. Between that line and the groups of Gauls who we had isolated during our first charge, lay a corpse-strewn ground that stretched for nearly two miles. We pulled back to a point just in front of the Gauls' new line. But not all of the cavalry was reforming. I glanced behind me and saw Gallia shouting and gesticulating as her women formed a cordon around a large group of Gauls. Burebista had ridden to join me. He had a nasty gash on his right arm that was bleeding heavily.

'Get that seen to.' I pointed to the thickening Gaul line to our front. 'Keep an eye on them but don't attack them, not yet. Wait for me here.'

I rode back to Gallia, who was stringing an arrow in her bow. In front of me her riders were shooting the enemy to pieces. She had ordered all her women to remove their helmets, thus revealing their sex to the enemy. The Gauls took the bait, jeering and throwing their shields to the ground, and then thrusting their hips obscenely at them. Most of the Gauls were stripped from the waist up, some were naked altogether and smeared in war paint. They thought it hilarious that their opponents included a group of women. Some were still laughing and exposing their genitals when the first volley of arrows cut through flesh, sinew and bone. One hundred bows shooting three arrows a minute soon reduced the Gauls to a mound of dead and dying men.

Gallia next ordered her women, who had now put their helmets back on, to reform around the next group, about a hundred men mustered around a banner of a bull's skull draped with what appeared to be strips of flesh, human I assumed. They truly revolted me.

'You think my women are a waste of equipment now, Pacorus?' Gallia's eyes were aflame with fury. I was suitably put in my place.

'No, lady,' I replied. 'I thank Shamash that you are here.'

She kicked Epona and rode away. Her women now surrounded the bull's skull standard. Praxima galloped up and saluted her. Was this a dream?

'They are ready, lady.'

Gallia walked Epona to within fifty feet of the Gauls and removed her helmet. I rode over to be beside her. She spoke in Latin, not in her native tongue.

'Warriors of the Senones. I am one of you but fight against you. You are beaten, the price you have paid for fighting alongside the Romans. Put down your weapons and prostrate yourselves before me and you shall be spared. Refuse this and you will die.'

The Gauls whooped and jeered in response, some turning around, bending over and exposing their backsides, others laughing and inviting Gallia to come down from her horse and play with their manhoods. She merely smiled at them then shouted. 'Fire'. The arrows made a hissing noise as they cut though the air followed by a dull thud as each one found its target. Their shooting was impeccable, almost beautiful.

The first volley cut down scores of Gauls, as the others desperately grabbed their shields and attempted to form some sort of defence, but Gallia's archers were firing from a stationary position and were taking careful aim. The second volley produced another heap of dead, this time arrows striking eye sockets and necks as only the knights among them wore helmets. The rest were bare headed, with their long hair washed in lime and combed into points. There was nowhere for them to hide, and some threw down their shields and spears and held up their arms to signal their surrender, but their tormentors were in no mood for mercy, and so a third volley felled what was left of the men who only a short time before had been hurling insults and taunts. From the circle of dead and dying came pitiful moans and cries of pain, and I saw a few figures writhing in agony on the ground with arrows sticking in them. Others were attempting to crawl, using their arms to drag their pierced bodies to seek safety. It was a forlorn hope, for Gallia nodded to Praxima who slipped her bow back in its case and jumped from her saddle. She was joined by every fifth woman, while the rest covered their comrades with their bows. Praxima drew her sword and then calmly walked among the Gauls, killing any she came across. The others did likewise. I watched in horror as this went on, but I knew that if the roles had been reversed we would have received a similar fate. Gafarn sat next to Diana, who I noticed took no part in the killing, and a glance at her quiver revealed she had fired no arrows. She was not of the disposition to be a slayer, but Gallia liked to keep her close and Gafarn watched over her like a hawk.

Praxima had sheathed her sword and had drawn her dagger, with which she used to cut off the genitals of a dead Gaul. Grinning, she held up her bloody trophy for me to admire. I heard squeals and yelps as the last Gauls were finished off. Gallia was studying me intently. 'When your women have finished their sport, rejoin the line.' I wheeled Remus away and returned to where my companies were reforming. Burebista was riding along the line shouting encouragement and telling the men that it would take only one more charge, and they would break. Only one more charge. But I knew we could not make that charge. We had done well and killed hundreds, perhaps thousands, of Gauls, but several hundred feet in front of us was a new line of them, those we would not be able to break. For one thing our horses were tired, and for another they would not run at a solid wall of shields and spears. We had failed.

I spurred Remus forward to take a closer look at the new Gaul line, halting him about two hundred feet from them. There was much shouting coming from their ranks, directed towards me no doubt. Suddenly an arrow slammed into my saddle. I quickly moved Remus back to rejoin the rest of the horsemen. I had been lucky; if it had struck six inches to the right it would have hit me in the groin. A lucky escape, but as I looked at the three-sided head of the arrow I realised that it was one of our own. How could this be?

I peered towards where the Gauls were grouped and could just make out small black slivers dropping from the sky into their ranks. Now I understood. Castus' men must be grinding their way into the Gauls, who were no longer protected by their rows of stakes. And behind Castus and his centuries were Nergal and his archers. This was confirmed when I edged Remus forward and began to see arrows fall just in front of the ragged enemy line that was facing us. These were missiles that were overshooting their intended target. I gestured for Burebista to join me. When he arrived I saw that his injured arm was now heavily bandaged. I pointed towards the enemy.

'Those are our arrows that are falling among them. See how some have hoisted their shields above their heads. Castus and his men must be cutting through them. And see how their line doesn't move. If they were still advancing against our men they would be moving away from us. They are going to break. Pass the word and tell your men to be ready.'

He looked at me in amazement. 'Are you certain, lord?'

'Of course I am,' I snapped irritably. 'Now go!'

I wasn't absolutely certain, but my instincts told me that soon the Gauls would be running for their lives. I glanced behind me to my left and right, and saw men drawing their swords as word passed along the line of what was going to happen. Gallia halted Epona beside me, followed by Gafarn and Rhesus on my other side, as her women formed up behind me. She had her helmet back on and its cheek guards closed, but I could still see that her eyes were alight with excitement.

'They are going to break, and when they do they will be running in every direction. It will be like hunting a heard of lambs.' I looked at her quiver. 'You are nearly out of arrows.'

'I have my sword and dagger,' she growled, and then looked at my quiver, which was full.

'Is your bow broken, Pacorus?'

Gafarn laughed. 'Perhaps Gallia should lead, highness, if you are not up to the task.'

'Perhaps you should shut up,' I snapped.

'Eyes front, lord,' barked Rhesus.

And then it happened.

At first it was just a few individuals who started to abandon their ranks. They were followed by more and more until any semblance of order among the Gauls had disappeared. They had either forgotten all about us, or their terror was such that they considered facing us less of a danger than what was happening behind them. And that was surely terrifying enough, for the centuries of Castus, thrusting and stabbing with their short swords, were hacking a path of death and carnage through the mass of Gauls who stood in their way. And so those who could ran. They fled towards us and ran across our front left and right. Perhaps they believed that because we had halted and now were just sitting on our horses we were exhausted, or that our horses were blown and incapable of carrying out another charge. More likely men thought only of their own survival and fled to save their skins, for panic is infectious and once it is unleashed it is like a virulent plague that sweeps through a city.

I wrapped the reins around my wrist, drew my bow from its case and made sure I could reach my quiver, and then dug my knees into Remus' flanks. He lurched forward and began to gather momentum. I didn't bother to look behind me for I knew that the companies would follow, keeping in tight formation as they approached the enemy. The sound of thousands of hooves hitting the hard earth sounded like a low rumble of thunder as we neared the fear-gripped Gauls. Then I heard the wild cheering of hundreds of horsemen as we crashed into them, riding through them like the wind goes through ripened corn. And then the killing began. I shot the first Gaul in the chest, a brute wielding a large two-headed axe. He crouched with his weapon ready to disembowel Remus, but instead was felled by an arrow. It didn't kill him but did stun him. As I rode past him he dropped his axe and I swivelled in the saddle and put another shaft into his back. To my left Rhesus was leading his company, which was three ranks deep, in a wedge formation. Like a spear blade it cut deep into the enemy, Gauls being trampled under hooves or cut down with sword strokes. Then as one the men wheeled left and then left again, cutting their way back through and then out of the enemy, keeping moving until they were not surrounded by opponents, for the bellies of standing horses are a tempting target for enemy spears, axes and swords, even if that enemy is fleeing. When they had retreated and reformed, each company charged again, almost like a gladius made of horseflesh, thrusting into the enemy's guts and then withdrawing quickly, and stabbing again and again.

I saw horses bolt from the mêlée, their saddles empty, while some riders had become separated from their companies or had allowed themselves to believe that they were invincible. Most were either surrounded and pulled from their saddles, to be hacked to death by a frenzied mob of Gauls, or were mortally wounded as they tried to escape the battlefield. But for every rider who died a score of Gauls or more were cut down. One group tried to form a circle of shields to fight us off, rallying around a few bloodied and battered knights who still retained some cohesion. It was not enough.

'Gallia,' I shouted at the top of my voice, and seconds later she was at my side. I had made sure that I stayed close to her when we had charged, and now I had need of her arrows.

'How many arrows have you got left?'

'No more than half a dozen,' she replied.

'Cover me, then, my dear. If you can keep up.'

I galloped forward to where the Gauls were standing. As I thundered past them I shot one man holding a spear and a giant oblong shield painted blue. The arrow hit him in the neck and he squealed before he toppled backwards. Gallia was following hard on my heels and dropped another warrior as I wheeled left and left again, then galloped back on the opposite side of the enemy circle, dropping another warrior as I swept past. Gallia did likewise, and then Gafarn, Praxima and the rest began felling the remaining Gauls with their arrows. The last warrior, a tall fat man with a large moustache that hung down to his waist, screamed with rage and frustration as he surveyed his men lying dead and dying at his feet. He joined them when Gallia put an arrow through his right eye socket and into his brain. It was an exceptional shot.

The whole left wing of the enemy army had by now disintegrated, ground into nothing by my horsemen and the foot soldiers of Castus, who were now finishing off the last remnants of the Gauls and were wheeling inwards to assault the exposed flank of the Romans. Burebista rode over to me. He looked exhausted and in pain, and I could see blood seeping through his bandage.

I pointed at him. 'Gather the companies here, dismount those who are injured or whose horses are blown.'

'Where are you going?' asked Gallia, removing her helmet and still looking amazingly fresh after all these hours.

'To find Castus.'

I nudged Remus forward. He was tired now and I could feel his heightened body warmth next to my lower legs, so I kept him at a walk as we threaded our way across a churned-up ground that resembled an open-air slaughterhouse. The dead lay still, but around them dozens, hundreds, of the wounded writhed and crawled in agony, while some of them, their bodies speared and lacerated, lay for death to take them, their lifeblood oozing out of them onto the earth. I saw a Gaul on all fours coughing blood, another sitting on the ground and trying to hold his guts in place inside a belly that had been sliced wide open. Men whimpered clutching at stumps that had once been their arms. Interspersed between the dead Gauls were slain horses, while others lay fatally wounded on the ground. In places there were heaps of dead clustered around a slain knight or chief, faithful to their lord to the end. It seemed to take an age for me to traverse this stretch of horror, but eventually I saw blocks of red shields marching across my front, century after century being marshalled left to assault the Romans' flank. I smiled as I saw the telltale long black hair jutting from beneath steel helmets. Their discipline was excellent, but Castus' Germans still looked like barbarians dressed up as Romans. Those who had been selected as centurions had spotted me early but did nothing; they had seen me often enough in their camp to know who I was, or at least they knew my white horse.

I found Castus sitting on a stool with a surgeon stood over him applying a bandage around his head. At his feet lay a helmet that had a large dent in it. A concerned Cannicus was observing the surgeon, a small thin man wearing a simple grey tunic with a large canvas bag hanging from his left shoulder. He tied off the bandage, then examined Castus' eyes and announced, 'You'll live.' Then he walked away to attend to others. Castus saw me and stood up as I dismounted and led Remus over to him. We embraced; I also took the hand offered by Cannicus.

'Glad to see you are nearly in one piece, my friend,' I grinned.

He winced. 'Gaul bastard with an axe nearly took my head off. Managed to rip open his belly, though. Where are your cavalry?'

'About half a mile away. They're no use now, the horses are blown.'

'It doesn't matter, lord,' said Cannicus, 'you helped to halt them and then they gave way when we attacked them. Then it was just a matter of pushing forward and killing as many as we could.'

Castus nodded. 'That's about right. They should have kept behind their stakes. Once we had stopped their charge we got nice and cosy with them, and sliced them to pieces. It wasn't a pretty sight, and I should know, I was in the front rank at the time.'

I took a drink from a water bottle Cannicus offered me. 'I can imagine. Where's Nergal?'

'Spartacus rode over and ordered him and all your archers over to the other wing when he realised that we were winning here.' Castus looked behind him as rank upon rank of his men marched forward, javelins in their right hands and their shields tight to their left sides. 'It won't be long now.'

He picked up his helmet and grimaced as he forced it back on his head over the bandage. He clasped my arm. 'I will see you later, my friend.'

'Keep safe, Castus, and you too Cannicus.'

They both grinned at me and then strode away to rejoin their men. In the distance the muffled sound of shouts mingled with weapons clashing indicated that the battle was still raging.

The battle was now entering its final, bloody stages, as Castus' legions were not only cutting their way into the Romans' left flank, they were moving into the rear of the enemy army. And that army was now on the verge of defeat. Our men were tired, but the destruction of the Gauls on our right wing had given them a second wind and now they could taste victory. One German legion, the one nearest the Romans, was wheeled sharply left into the flank of the Roman formation that had fought the Thracians to a standstill. But now it was being assaulted in the front and on its flank, and could do nothing to prevent Castus' other legions, those who had been facing the Gauls, from advancing forward and then swinging left to get behind the Romans. The latter were being herded steadily to the left, towards their right wing where the Gauls were positioned opposite Afranius. And those Gauls still standing as they were behind their stakes presenting an easy target were being shot to pieces by my archers. They could withstand short, intense volleys, but a steady, withering fire that went on and on was more than they could bear. Afranius had pulled his men back where they locked shields to the front and overhead – he had made more charges – where they were mostly safe from the enemy's projectiles: axes, spears, sling shots and the occasional arrow. Our archers were brought forward to stand directly behind the first line of Spanish cohorts, from where they shot at the enemy.

After I had given the contents of my water skin to Remus, I rode him back to Burebista's men. When I reached them many were lying on the ground with their saddles beside them. A screen of riders had been placed around them to warn of any impending attack, but there was no Roman cavalry to be seen anywhere; indeed, I had seen few mounted enemy this day. Rhesus, Burebista, Gafarn and Gallia were stood in a circle of officers on the edge of the group. It was apparent that the men accepted her presence without protest. Her prowess in battle had obviously won them over.

'All company commanders to assemble their men,' I shouted as I neared them.

Burebista spoke to his officers, who sprinted away, as did Gallia.

'What news, lord?'

'The battle goes well,' I replied. 'We need to make one last effort to help our comrades fighting on foot.'

A worried look crossed his face. 'The horses are tired, lord, and so are the men.'

'I know, but we will not be making any more charges. It will be more a case of casting a large net so that the little fishes will not escape.'

'Lord?'

'All will become clear, Burebista.'

I rode at the head of a thousand riders, for we had lost two hundred killed and another three hundred wounded, plus dozens of horses slain and hurt. The wounded were left behind and told to make their way back to the wagons, where they would be treated. The injured horses were likewise left to receive treatment. It was well past mid-afternoon now, and the heat of the day was slowly abating, though it was still warm. We were all covered in grime and soaked with sweat, for it had been a long day.

We rode in one great column, five companies riding side-by-side, and each one in two files, with another five behind them. The pace was a slow canter to preserve the horses' last reserves of strength, but when we rode behind the diminishing enemy army I saw that Castus' men were doing likewise and were filling the ground in front of us. So we rode on, towards the irrigation ditch that the enemy had used to anchor their right flank. Here there were no troops of our army, but as we deployed into line several hundred feet behind the Gauls, I could hear a terrible tumult coming from their ranks. I could not discern what was happening, and my view was partly obscured by clouds of dust, but I surmised that there was some fighting going on. I gave the signal for the line to advance and we walked towards the Gauls. As we got nearer I could see many figures lying on the ground directly ahead, with others being carried on stretchers or limping to the rear – the wounded. There were hundreds of them, perhaps thousands, and when they spotted us a pathetic cry came from their lips. I rode back to Burebista and signalled Gallia to join us. Then I gave the order to charge.

Our attack failed.

The horses, already tired from hours of exertion, were not pushed by their riders, and in truth I realised that Remus was sweating heavily and I was unwilling to risk his health for the sake of glory. So we cantered up to where the Gauls had actually formed a makeshift line of shields and spears in front of their wounded. My cavalry slowed and then stopped around a hundred feet from that line of steel and wood. We did some damage, though, as Gallia and her women used up their last reserves of arrows and I did the same, so that after a few minutes there was yet more enemy dead heaped in front of their wall of shields. There was nothing else left to do. I signalled the withdrawal and we walked our horses back beyond the range of any archers or slingers who might be lurking among their ranks. There we waited.

We didn't have to wait long, for the Roman legions, still fighting with discipline, were still being pushed towards their right flank and the irrigation ditch. Through the clouds of dust that were constantly being kicked up I could see Gauls slowly shuffling to our right. And on the left I could make out fresh cohorts – Castus' men – moving in their blocks of centuries and gradually overlapping the Gauls. The two Roman legions were now surrounded on three sides, front, left and rear, and I wondered how

many legionaries were still alive. It was now late afternoon and the sun was slowly sinking in the west, but it was still warm and there was no breeze. My mouth was terribly dry and my tongue felt as though it was too large for my mouth. My eyes stung from the sweat that had run into them. I pulled off my helmet. The leather lining inside was soaked and my hair was pasted to my skull. Burebista appeared beside me.
'Are you hurt, lord?'
'No. Tell the men to dismount and give what water they have to their horses. There's nothing we can do now.'
He looked sheepish. 'I am sorry we failed, lord.'
I reached over and laid my hand on his shoulder. 'The fault was mine entirely.'
Our part in the battle was now over, yet I did not realise that the battle itself would soon be over as well. Our army was now herding the enemy towards the ditch, though order was now breaking down among the Gauls as the grim realisation that they had been overwhelmed dawned on them. The Romans, to give them credit, fought and died in their ranks, though one or two centuries broke and tried to escape. It availed them little, for they merely joined the press of men who sought sanctuary across the ditch. But that ditch had been chosen to anchor their flank because it was wide and its sides were sheer, and it was bone dry for it was summer. Men jumped and tumbled over the sides and broke legs and arms when they hit the hard surface. Hundreds hurled themselves in, falling on those who had jumped seconds before, and soon there was a writhing mass of tangled and twisted bodies crammed into the ditch. Some, the lucky ones, managed to escape by freeing themselves from the mound of humanity and then walk, run or limp along the ditch northwards. I did not know how long they would have to travel for the ditch stretched for miles into the distance.
The remaining Romans in their centuries threw down their weapons and held their hands up to beg for mercy. Our troops, mostly Thracians and Germans who had fought them all day long, were exhausted and were probably glad to stop hacking and thrusting. The Romans were marched to the rear, to await Spartacus' decision as to their fate. Afranius was not so merciful. When the Gauls facing him, who had been subjected to a withering hailstorm of arrows all day, broke and fled, he ordered his men to pull down the stakes between him and his adversaries. And when it was done he threw them forward. The only resistance they faced was a thin line of Gauls who were trying to cover the retreat of

their comrades. They died in a matter of minutes as all the cohorts of Spaniards raced forward and butchered everything in their path. Within fifteen minutes they had linked up with Castus' men and the battle was over. But not the slaughter.

I ordered my cavalry to mount their horses once more and form into companies, and then we rode forward to lend what assistance we could. I found Cannicus, bloody and tired, holding an impromptu conference with some of his cohort commanders. He raised a hand when he saw me.

'You live, Cannicus. Where is Castus?'

He slapped one of his officers on the back and then ordered them away. 'He also lives. He is with Spartacus escorting the prisoners.'

'We have prisoners?'

'Once we had broken their left wing and surrounded them, the fight went out of them, especially as their commander was cut down. We cut his head off and threw it into their ranks. I reckon there must be about four or five thousand of them, all Roman.'

So the governor of Mutina was dead. I hoped that King Ambiorix also lay dead on the battlefield.

The sounds of battle were still coming from the direction of the ditch, about half a mile away. Cannicus took off his helmet and wiped his brow with a rag. 'There's still some fighting going on over there. Some of the Gauls must have been cornered.'

'I will see if we can be of assistance. Take care of yourself, Cannicus.'

He smiled wearily. 'You too, Pacorus.'

I rode at the head of my horse to where the last remnants of the Gauls were being destroyed by the soldiers of Afranius. A great group of Gallic warriors had been surrounded by his men about three hundred yards from the ditch. They stood now, packed shoulder to shoulder with their shields locked together and their spears pointing outwards. They had formed into a large square, within which there was no room, just a mass of mostly bare-headed warriors standing in mute defiance. On each side of the square, a cohort of Afranius' men faced the Gauls, while behind these cohorts were companies of my archers. I saw Godarz and rode over to where he was standing. I dismounted and embraced him, while his archers cheered when they saw their fellow cavalrymen ride into view.

'Good to see you, highness.'

I released him. 'You too, Godarz. It has been a hard day.'

'It has indeed.'

'Where is Nergal?'

Godarz gestured to the north. 'Afranius sent him and his men along the ditch. It is full of fleeing Gauls. Dead Gauls by now, I should imagine.'

I looked towards the square of Gauls. 'What's going on here?'

Godarz spat on the ground. 'We managed to trap this lot and now Afranius is deciding what to do with them. Look's like there's around three or four thousand.'

Afranius suddenly appeared, smiling when he saw me. 'A great victory, Pacorus.' He bowed his head to me. 'I dispatched Nergal north to kill as many Gauls as he could who were in the ditch. Your men are fine archers.'

'Of course,' I said, 'they have been taught by Parthians.' I jerked my head towards the Gauls. 'Are you trying to persuade them to give themselves up?'

Afranius looked horrified. 'No. We sent an emissary under a banner of truce but they cut him down. They stood behind those wretched stakes all day. It was only when the rest of their army had been surrounded that they beat a retreat. And then we were knocking down those posts as fast as we could. They thought that we would be delayed long enough to make their escape. But they were wrong.'

I looked towards the Gauls. Indeed they were. Did you see a king among them?'

'A king?'

'It doesn't matter. He pays others to do his handiwork.'

'As soon as my men are in position we will kill them all,' said Afranius.

I turned to Godarz. 'How many arrows do your men have left.'

He shrugged. 'Down to our last ten each, or thereabouts. We did a lot of shooting today.'

I looked at Afranius. 'Let Godarz soften them up first.'

'Use all the arrows you have left,' I said to Godarz, 'we can always make new ones.'

I put a hand on Afranius' shoulder. 'Well done.'

He beamed with delight as I remounted Remus. 'Godarz, when it's over stay here. I am going to find Nergal.' I looked up at the sky; it was early evening by now. 'I should be back before nightfall.'

We rode north parallel to the ditch, while behind me I heard the hiss of hundreds of arrows slicing through the air, followed by shouts and screams as their metal heads hit flesh and bone. There was no hurry now, so we adopted a gentle trot as we followed the route of the ditch. Like most things the Romans built, it was perfectly straight. I rode a few feet from the edge of it, with Gallia beside me and her women, Gafarn and Burebista behind us, followed by his companies. The ditch itself was filled with dead Gauls, the victims of Nergal's archers. We travelled for at least a mile before we came across the first group of his men, a company of his dragon riding back towards the battlefield. They cheered as we approached. I spoke to their leader, a tall Parthian with a dark-skinned face and long arms.

'Where is Commander Nergal?'

'Half a mile ahead, highness. We have no more arrows left, so he sent us back.'

I looked at him. 'Where are you from?'

'Hatra, highness, ten years in your father's army.'

'Excellent. You and I will see Hatra again. You have done well today.'

He bowed his head. 'Thank you, highness.'

We at last found Nergal a mile further north, marching back on foot at the head of his companies and leading his horse. He looked tired and was covered in dust, but he beamed with delight when he saw us and halted his column. He bowed his head to me and then we embraced. It was good to see him. When we separated Praxima raced up and threw her arms around him, which brought a mighty cheer from his men.

'Are you too out of arrows?' I asked him.

He held up his empty quiver. 'Not one left among us, highness.'

'I have arrows left, my love,' said Praxima. 'We can go back and kill some more.'

Nergal and those men within earshot laughed. 'I think there has been enough killing today, my sweet.'

And so there had been, for the stretch of ground that some call the field of honour had today been seeded with the dead. They lay in heaps where the fighting had been the fiercest and where men had been unable to escape the rain of arrows that had been showered upon them. Dead Gauls lay piled around their knights, while scores surrounded their dead chiefs, cut down trying to protect their lords. The ditch was filled with a great mound of dead and dying Gauls where they had thrown themselves in, while along its bottom for a distance of at least three miles lay a carpet of corpses.

'A great victory, highness, my congratulations,' said Rhesus.

'Thank you, Rhesus.'

I looked at him and suddenly realised that he was very pale. Then he tumbled from his saddle onto the ground. I leaped down from Remus and crouched by his side, as others also dismounted and crowded round.

'Give us some room,' I shouted. 'Fetch some water.'
Diana gave me her water skin and knelt beside Rhesus, then gently lifted his head so he could take a sip. A spasm of pain shot through his body and I saw that his right side was soaked with blood. Diana cradled his head as the pain swept though him.
'A Gaul spear, highness,' he said to me weakly.
'Don't talk. We'll soon have you patched up.'
Diana looked at him with brown eyes filled with kindness and understanding, smiling and giving him another mouthful of water.
'Thank you, lady.' He looked at her. 'Do you believe in heaven?'
'Of course,' she replied.
'I lost my wife and child to the plague a few years ago. I have always hoped that they would be waiting for me.'
She smiled at him. 'They are waiting for you, Rhesus, they are waiting for you in a place where there is no sickness and pain, only happiness and love. Go to them.'
Diana held his hand as Rhesus, a brave soldier from Thrace, slipped away from this life and joined his family in heaven. Diana closed his eyes and then kissed his forehead as those around knelt and bowed their heads. I nodded to Diana in thanks as tears began to run down my cheeks.
Thus ended the Battle of Mutina. We were now free to march north and out of Italy. Spartacus had kept his promise.

Chapter 14

After spending a night fitfully sleeping on the ground, we awoke on a mist-filled dawn with aching limbs, dry mouths and unshaven faces. I stood, bleary eyed, amid a group of similarly dishevelled and unwashed horsemen and their mounts. The air stank of sweat, leather and horse dung. An hour after dawn I held an impromptu meeting with Burebista and his senior officers. We chewed on hard biscuits and drank lukewarm water from our water skins, those who had any. Gallia also attended, her eyes puffy from lack of sleep and her hair tied in a plait. My hands were filthy and my tunic was smeared with blood, though none of it my own. The edge of my sword had been blunted somewhat in the previous day's fighting. I had four arrows left in my quiver, most had less or none at all. Burebista was downcast, as ten of his men had died of their wounds during the night.

'We will take them back and their bodies will be consigned to the balefire with all the others, including Rhesus,' I told him.

I glanced at Gallia, for Gafarn had informed me that eight of her women had also been killed in the battle and a further thirty wounded, but she said nothing, looking ahead with a face as hard as stone. The battle must have been a sobering experience for her and her comrades, but she and they had fought well. She could take comfort from that at least.

'We will walk the horses back to camp, but two companies will serve as flank guards at all times. I don't want to be surprised by a war party of Gauls.

'The Gauls in this region will never again carry their weapons to war,' said Gallia, curtly. She looked at me. 'The best of them lie dead upon this ground. The rest are now broken in spirit. They will trouble us no more.'

On the way back to camp we skirted the battlefield to avoid the piles of carrion that were even now providing a feast for the mass of crows who had come to add to the horror that stretched for miles around. Their squeals and squawks got on our nerves and made our horses jittery, and made us even glummer. We had won a great victory, though all I wanted to do was eat a good meal, wash my filthy clothes and body and rest, above all, rest. I walked beside Gallia as she led Epona, her stare fixedly ahead. The mist had been burned away by the sun now; it was going to be another warm day. I broke the silence first.

'I am sorry.'

'For what?'

'For the deaths of so many of your warriors, the Gauls I mean.'

She smiled wryly. 'The Romans used them and now they have paid the price. You think I would weep for such wretches?'
'But they are your people.'
'My people? What does that mean?'
'Well,' I replied rather meekly. 'Gauls.'
'How big is Parthia?' she asked me.
'Thousands of square miles,' I replied, proudly.
She continued to look ahead. 'And in that territory you class all the people that live there as your brothers and sisters? Do you feel an affinity with them above all others.'
'No.'
'Then why should I have any bonds to a people who yesterday were trying to kill me, much less to a king, my father, who sold me into slavery and then enslaved me himself and again tried to profit from me? I feel nothing for these people except contempt.'
I persisted. 'But...'
'Enough, Pacorus,' she snapped. 'Your talk is giving me a headache.'
Her mood improved when Spartacus and Claudia arrived escorted by Nergal and two companies of his horse archers. The reunion between Claudia, Diana and Gallia was an emotional one, and all three wept as they embraced. The battle had obviously been harder on Gallia than I had imagined, and Diana must have been terrified and horrified in equal measure. It was good to see Spartacus again, and he looked as though there was not a scratch on him. He embraced me and slapped me on the shoulder.
'Still alive, then,' he beamed.
'Still alive, lord.'
'Let us walk together back to camp.'
After I had greeted and embraced Claudia, I walked beside him as we headed south towards the camp of wagons.
'It was a hard fight, Pacorus, but you did well. Once you had broken their wing it was just a matter of rolling them up.'
I smiled. 'Like a carpet.'
'Carpet?'
'It matters not, lord.'
He shrugged. 'Anyway, we are making a rough count of the enemy dead and it looks as though thousands of them have perished. And I've also got a couple of thousand Roman prisoners that I don't know what to do with.' He looked at me mischievously. 'Perhaps I should kill them, what do you think?'
I had to admit I was appalled at the idea, but said nothing. 'It is your decision, lord.'

He laughed aloud. 'Do not worry, my young friend, I promise I won't kill them. In any case they are proving useful at the moment. Godarz has them prising arrows out of their dead comrades and Gauls. He was complaining earlier that your men shot too many arrows during the battle. He's a typical quartermaster. When I served in the Roman Army they were often worse than the enemy, as they were most unwilling to surrender their carefully hoarded stores.'

'You have done it, lord,' I said. 'We are free to leave Italy and leave the Romans behind us.'

'Yes, we are finally free, though not quite yet. The army will need a few days to recover, and afterwards I have a small task to perform.'

'Small task?'

A thin smile spread across his lips. 'All will be revealed, my friend. But first we bind our wounds, bury our dead, rest and take stock of our losses.'

The next few days were occupied with the task of recovering from the effects of battle. Men and horses were tired, many were wounded and some were dead. The fact that we had Roman prisoners was fortuitous, as they dug great pits into which the dead were thrown. Normally we would have left the enemy dead to rot. But because we were staying in the area rather than immediately marching north, the dead had to be dealt with lest disease broke out. At the very least we would be rid of the crows and their incessant cackling. Under the watchful eyes of our guards the prisoners stripped the Roman dead of their mail shirts, sandals and anything else that our army could use. It was a grisly business, though Spartacus had no qualms about using what fell into our laps. The haul meant that all of his foot now had shields, mail shirts, helmets and swords. Many were still armed with spears, but each legion now had enough javelins to equip their first line cohorts, though Godarz still grumbled that the men had been wasteful during the battle when I found him directing a group of prisoners to search among the bodies of the dead Gauls and extract any arrows that were still usable. The blood-encrusted shafts were thrown into the back of a cart, one of many that dotted the carrion-filled ground. The stench of dead flesh was nauseating, and the area was alive with large black flies and the accursed crows.

Godarz, his nose covered by a cloth veil, was yelling instructions at guards and prisoners alike. 'Once you have taken anything useful, get the bodies over to the pit and throw them in.'

He was referring to a large rectangular hole that had been dug by the prisoners and which was now rapidly being filled with the dead. Our own dead we had burned on massive balefires made from the thousands of stakes that had kindly been fashioned by the Gauls. We had lost nearly three hundred horsemen killed, most from Burebista's dragon. The army as a whole had suffered an additional two thousand killed but the enemy had suffered more grievous losses. No one counted the enemy dead, but Godarz and his team of quartermasters estimated that each pit that was dug was filled with around three thousand corpses.

'This one's the sixth we've dug and I think we will have to dig at least three more.'

'Lucky you had these prisoners to help.'

He sniffed. 'If we hadn't we would not have bothered. But it gives me a chance to salvage some iron and steel.' He shot me a glance. 'The foundries will be busy replacing all the arrows your men fired.'

'You can never have enough arrows, Godarz.'

'So it seems.'

He looked at two Romans, their faces dirty and their tunics drenched with sweat, hauling a dead Gaul towards the death pit.

'Any idea what Spartacus intends to do with them?'

I shrugged. 'No.'

'For some reason he wants to stay in this area, otherwise we'd have left the corpses to rot where they fell. But seeing as we are apparently staying a while, we have to get them buried as quickly as possible.'

The reason Spartacus wanted to remain in the area was revealed to me a few days later. Castus and Cannicus had both recovered from their wounds, while Akmon and Afranius had survived the battle unscathed. Spartacus' expression was one of stone when I entered his tent.

'We must punish the Gauls for their treachery,' he said. 'Pacorus, your scout, Byrd, will lead us to the berg of Gallia's father.'

'To what end, lord?' I asked.

'To burn it, of course, and all those within it.'

The others banged their fists on the table in agreement. 'First they kidnap one of our own, then they steal our gold and finally they take up arms against us,' raged Akmon. 'I say let them reap the whirlwind they have sown.'

Spartacus held up a hand to silence the din. 'Our retaliation will be swift and merciless.'

And so it was. We formed four flying columns of horse, each numbering three hundred men and composed of my best horse archers. We burned everything – homes, villages and farms. The dwellings of the Gauls were made out of wood with thatched roofs, and they burned beautifully. It took only a single torch or firebrand to ignite them, and once alight the dry timbers were soon consumed by fire. The larger settlements, the villages surrounded by palisades made from sharpened logs that mounted fighting platforms, we first surrounded. Then flame arrows were used to set the wooden houses inside them alight. It was so easy. We wrapped straw soaked in pitch in pieces of cloth and tied them to arrows, lit them and shot the arrows into the village. The straw roofs were bone dry, and soon flames and smoke were billowing from inside the palisade. Then the screaming began as those inside realised that they would die in the flames. The Gauls barricaded the gates so we could not batter them down, but when the flames erupted they desperately tried to escape from the settlement. And we were waiting. Spartacus had thought of everything, and afterwards I realised why he was such a capable commander. He weighed up all the options available to him and then chose the one that suited his purpose. So when the villagers, in their desperation to escape the flames, managed to open the gates, they ran straight onto our swords. In return for their freedom, the Roman prisoners were forced to cut down the Gauls as they fled their settlements. Each Roman was given a sword, nothing else, and told that he would be cut down instantly if he tried to use it against any of us. They were told that they were going to be killing Gauls. Only by shedding blood could they buy their freedom. Spartacus told them this when they had been gathered in one place after they had buried all the dead. And when asked what would happen if they refused, he ran the man through who had asked the question with his sword and then hacked off his head. One sword, nothing else. And so at village after village the Roman prisoners were the ones who did the killing, as we exacted revenge on the Senones and their allies.

Most of the tribes' warriors had been slaughtered at Mutina, or were hiding in the forests, so those who were left were the very young and the old. But many still summoned a courage born of desperation, and in the brief fighting before the raping and the slaughter began, some Romans were killed. And Spartacus watched impassively as Gauls and Romans, former allies against him, killed each other. I also realised then that Spartacus possessed another quality that contributed towards his skill as a general: utter ruthlessness.

The final part of Spartacus' retribution against the Gauls was an attack against the residence of King Ambiorix himself. Gallia's father had been conspicuous by his absence during the battle, no doubt preferring to pay others to shed their blood on his behalf. Spartacus led the attack, which he announced would be on foot and would comprise a thousand Thracians personally commanded by Akmon. He asked me to accompany him with a hundred of my best archers. I asked Gafarn to be one of them but forbade Gallia or any of her women to attend. I knew that we were going to kill and burn and it was not appropriate that she should witness the death of her father, even though she despised him. She did not protest and I was glad and so, on a warm summer's day under a blue sky littered with white, puffy clouds, we entered the forest that shielded the king's fortress. We walked in a long column along the same track that I had ridden on after Gallia had been kidnapped, and had then driven a cart along when we had bought her freedom with gold and I had killed her brother. And now I came a third time, this time to extract vengeance. Spartacus and his Thracians were dressed in Roman attire – sandals, tunics, mail shirts, helmets and shields painted red with yellow lightning bolts emanating from their central steel bosses. The Thracians all had short swords at their waists and hoisted javelins, though Spartacus and Akmon carried only swords and shields. I walked next to Spartacus at the head of the column, with Akmon on his other side. Behind us marched Domitus, who had risen to be first spear centurion in one of the Thracian legions, a rank of some importance and prestige I was informed. Out of sight, Byrd and his scouts rode ahead and on our flanks to ensure we were not surprised. I had my spatha at my waist with a full quiver slung over my right shoulder. I wore my white tunic, trousers, boots and my silk vest next to my skin. I left my cuirass in camp.

'Good to see you, sir,' said Domitus.

'You too, Domitus. I'm glad that you survived the battle.'

'Not much to it, sir,' he replied. 'Just a case of keeping your shield tight to your body, your head tucked down and stabbing with your sword. Easy enough. Easier than fighting on horseback.'

'Fighting on foot is a new experience for Pacorus,' said Spartacus. 'But he still could not leave his bow behind.'

'You and your men need not have brought their weapons with them,' I chided him. 'We will kill all the enemy before they get near us.'

Akmon was in his usual irritable mood. 'Horses are all very well, but once you lock shields they're done for.'

'But once that happens,' I said, 'then you are like a statue, and my horse can assault you on every side and nibble away at you.'

Spartacus slapped Akmon on the shoulder. 'Can't imagine any horse wanting to nibble Akmon.'

Domitus laughed. 'They're fine horsemen, I'll say that for you. Are all Parthian soldiers horsemen?'

'Mostly, yes,' I replied. 'At Hatra we have a garrison that defends the city. They are foot soldiers. But aside from them my father's army consists of horse archers and cataphracts.'

'What's a cataphract?' asked Domitus.

'A man in armour that covers his arms, legs and body who sits on a horse that is also encased in armour, and who carries a heavy spear that takes two hands to hold.'

'I would like to see one of those,' he said.

'You would be welcome to come back to Hatra with me, Domitus, should you so desire.'

He seemed delighted. 'Truly?'

'Of course. Parthia has need of good soldiers.'

Spartacus finished the apple he was eating and threw away the core. 'Are we all welcome in your father's kingdom, Pacorus?'

'You, especially, lord,' I said.

He laughed. 'He might not take kindly to a band of former slaves invading his lands.'

'He would welcome all those who fight the Romans, and especially one who saved his son's life.'

'Well, Akmon,' he said, 'looks like we are going to Hatra.'

'If we don't get killed first,' he sniffed.

'Death is a constant companion of the soldier,' I said casually.

'And the gladiator,' added Spartacus. 'Would you have liked to have been a gladiator, Pacorus?'

I was aware that both he and Akmon were veterans of the arena and was careful in my answer.

'I do not think so, lord.'

'Why not?'

'Because I have no appetite for killing for sport.'

'Ah, I see, so you do not regard war as sport?'

'Of course not, lord.'

'Then what is it?'

I thought for a moment. 'The highest expression of honour,' I answered.

Spartacus and Akmon burst into laughter.

'I've never heard it called that before,' said Spartacus. 'So you wouldn't kill just for the sake of it.'

'No, lord.'

'But what about that merchant in Thurii whose throat you slit,

wasn't that killing for sport?'
I was indignant. 'Of course not. He broke his word and tried to have me killed. He did get some of my men killed. He deserved no mercy. I gave him my word, but he broke his.'
Spartacus continued with his questioning, clearly enjoying himself. 'But you were just a slave to him, and lying to a slave is nothing to a Roman.'
'I am not a slave,' I insisted.
'No, you are far worse,' chipped in Akmon. 'You are a runaway slave.'
'I am not a slave,' I said again.
'You are to the Romans,' said Spartacus.
'They have no honour,' I said, 'no offence, Domitus.'
'But they do have half the world,' retorted Spartacus. 'You see, Domitus, that once you are born into royalty you have a view of the world that is unique from that of all others.'
'It has nothing to do with that,' I snapped.
'It has everything to do with that,' insisted Spartacus. 'You fight for honour and glory, Pacorus, which is a dangerous game.' He slapped Akmon on the shoulder. 'Akmon and I fight to stay alive, nothing more. Same here, same as in the arena.'
'But today you fight to avenge treachery,' I remarked.
'Not so,' he shot back. 'We are going to kill Gauls because they are our enemy. You of all people should be able to relate to that. They did, after all, kidnap Gallia.'
'But we defeated the Gauls in battle.'
'True,' said Spartacus, 'but their commander is still alive and while that is so we are under threat of attack. Besides, fire and sword is a useful method of intimidating the enemy. We can't all fight just to please the gods Pacorus, some of us must bear in the mind the practicalities.'
We tramped through woodland teaming with life. I saw boar, wildcats, deer and heard the tap-tap-tap of a woodpecker, which ceased abruptly as we neared him. Above us, through the trees, I saw sparrow hawks, falcons, redshanks and ducks. White butterflies with grey spots on their wings fluttered around us, and at one time a huge brown bear lumbered out of the undergrowth and stared at us with its small black eyes set in a massive head. Then he grunted and disappeared back into the bushes. The sun-dappled forest was a beautiful place, so different from the sun-bleached land of Hatra, and I could understand why people would want to live within it.
After three hours at a steady pace, two horses galloped up to the

head of the column. It was a dust-covered Byrd and one of his scouts, a man with a sallow complexion and sunken cheeks who looked as thin and haggard as the horse he rode. Byrd looked concerned.

'Gauls coming this way.'

'How many?' asked Spartacus.

Byrd shrugged as he looked at the soldiers behind us. 'More than you.'

'How far away?' said Akmon.

'Mile and a half, maybe less,' he replied. 'You turn around and go back?'

'No, Byrd, we advance to meet them,' said Spartacus, determinedly.

Byrd exhaled loudly. 'Best place is here. Track narrows further on, no room to spread out.'

I looked around. Though there were around fifty yards or so of clear ground either side of the track until the trees began, it was hardly the best place to fight.

'They could flank us by moving through the trees, lord,' I remarked. 'And they know this country better then we do.'

Spartacus stared at the track ahead, which narrowed considerably three or four hundred yards from where we had halted. Akmon was scraping the earth with his foot while Domitus had drawn his sword and was examining the blade. Spartacus turned to me.

'Pacorus, I want you and your archers to run ahead and find a good place to hide. Spring an ambush and then get back here as fast as you can. If we annoy them enough they might forget about flanking us and come straight at us in a rage, like most Gauls like to fight.'

'Yes, lord.'

I went to where my archers had been marching as Domitus began getting his two cohorts into line to span the clearing. Gafarn was at the head of the column.

'Gather round,' I shouted.

The men shuffled into a semi-circle around me. They were a mixture of Parthians, Dacians, Thracians and Spaniards, all of them excellent archers.

'We are going to run ahead and ambush a war band of Gauls that is heading towards us. The plan is that we hide, we shoot as many as we can, and then we get back here as fast as our legs will carry us. No heroics, just make your arrows count.'

Five minutes later, sweating and out of breath, we melted into the oak trees either side of the track, fifty archers on one side and the other fifty on the other. We had barely concealed ourselves when I heard the crump of feet upon the ground and peered round the thick trunk I was using as cover, to see a mass of Gauls marching towards us. I was nearest to them, with my men spread among the trees behind me. I glanced across to Gafarn who was behind a tree and stringing an arrow in his bowstring. He nodded at me, his face calm and hard. I glanced back at the Gauls, a dense but disorganised column of men with long moustaches and hair drawn into points. Some wore helmets and carried brightly coloured shields, none had armour save one or two who were mounted. They were about five hundred feet away, moving slowly, shields by their sides and spears resting on their shoulders.

I shot from slightly behind and to the side of the oak tree, aiming at a bare-chested Gaul who carried an axe in his right hand and wore red, baggy trousers. There was no wind and the distance was around three hundred feet; it was an easy shot. The arrow hit his belly and he slumped forward onto the ground. Seconds later several dozen arrows began to hiss through the air, each archer waiting until he had a clear shot. The Gauls were not marching in ranks; those at the front of the column, six or seven men, were all felled by arrows, then those immediately behind them were likewise hit, and another ten or twelve were struck before the enemy halted. For a few seconds they were stunned, like a man who has taken a heavy blow on the head. I shot another four arrows before they rallied, a burly warrior with a spear and shield, his face a mass of swirling blue tattoos, pushing through the mound of dead and wounded in front of him and charging forward with his spear levelled. He screamed as he ran towards us, and in an instant hundreds of warriors were racing down the track.

'Back,' I shouted, 'back.'

We broke cover and ran as fast as we could from an enemy bent on revenge. The Gauls were big men, obviously the most fearsome of King Ambiorix's warriors, but they could not outrun us and so we were able to keep a safe distance between them and us. I saw two arrows planted each side of the track ahead of me and ran past them, then stopped and turned. The others also stopped and turned around, then began jeering at the Gauls pursuing us. The warriors must have thought we were dead meat, for they slowed and licked their lips in anticipation of slaughtering us. The tattooed warrior pointed his spear at me and smiled, revealing a mouth full of brown teeth. He hardly flinched when the first arrow hit his chest, just looked slightly bemused as he glanced down to see the shaft buried in his body. The two arrows had denoted the position of the rest of my archers, who now began cutting down the Gauls with fearsome efficiency from either side of the track, which was soon littered with dead. The enemy checked their advance and locked their shields to the front to form a wall against our arrows.

'Fall back,' I shouted, and again we ran back towards the clearing. The Gauls watched us go and then charged after us, urged on by their leaders on horseback, richly attired warriors in mail shirts, silver horned helmets and blue leggings.

We raced back to the edge of the clearing where the Thracians were massed in their centuries. Behind us were the Gauls, screaming their fury and yelling their blood-curdling war cries. Whether they saw the wall of shields in front of them I did not know, but I did know that they wanted to kill me and the rest of my archers, reduce us to pieces of offal for what we had done to them. Then I tripped, I don't know what tripped me, a tussock of grass or a large stone, but whatever it was it sent me sprawling to the ground, scattering the arrows I had left over the hated earth and spilling my bow from my hand. Ahead of me my archers were streaming through two paths that had appeared in the Thracian ranks; behind me the yells and screams got louder. Time seemed to slow as I rolled over on my back, to see a fat, ugly brute with a huge double-headed axe slow to a walk as he neared me. Then he was standing over me and grinning. I could smell his pungent odour of sweat and age-old dirt and lay transfixed as he raised his mighty axe above his head. This was where I was going to die, in a forest clearing in northern Italy at the hands of a rancid Gaul.

The Gaul was screaming in triumph, his mouth wide open, when the arrow went through it and lodged in the back of his throat. Then Gafarn was standing over me and roughly yanking me to my feet. I quickly regained my wits, gathered up my bow and ran as fast as I could for the sanctuary of the Thracian ranks. We made it with seconds to spare, and as I rushed past the first two ranks I heard a sword blade clattering on the rim of a shield, missing me by inches. Because we had been between the Thracians and the Gauls, Spartacus' men had been unable to throw their javelins, but as I and my men collapsed on the ground gulping for air, safely behind the Thracian line, the last two ranks in each century turned around, marched back a few paces, then ran forward and hurled their pila over the ranks of those in front and into the Gauls who were now hacking and jabbing against the Thracian shields.

As Spartacus had predicted, the Gauls attacked in a mad, disorganised rush of feral rage, hoping that the fury of their charge would carry all before it. But their assault broke like a wave against a seawall. For a few seconds the Thracian line buckled but did not break, then the front rank went to work with their swords, stabbing them at exposed thighs, legs, bellies and groins. Very few of the Gauls wore armour, some were naked, and though they hacked and jabbed with their swords, spears and axes, they could not find a way through the disciplined ranks of their opponents. The first rank held their shields in front of them, the second rank held their shields above the heads of those in front, and all the while the front rankers stabbed with their swords. Three inches of steel, Spartacus had once told me, was all it takes to kill a man. And how the Thracians were killing now, grinding their way forward one pace at a time. The Gauls in the rear were pushing those in front forward, hoping to create enough momentum to push through our ranks, but all they did was push their comrades onto Thracian swords. Death in battle is seldom instantaneous; rather, it is a long drawn-out process. A few, the lucky ones, are pierced through the heart or have their throat slit, but most are run though the belly by a spear, slashed by the edge of a sword or stabbed by its point, or hit by an arrow or slingshot. They die bleeding from the resulting hideous wounds, screaming or weeping as they watch their lifeblood gushing from shattered limbs and sliced bellies. If they stumble and fall in the mêlée they are crushed to death by their comrades or the enemy in the ebb and flow of the battle line, or are suffocated by a press of the dead and dying piled on top of them. In their terror they foul their leggings and piss themselves, the stinking effusion mixing with blood and churned-up earth to create a disgusting manure of death. And so it was today as the Gauls were slaughtered. The terrible din of battle resounded across the clearing and reached a crescendo as the Thracians gave a mighty cheer and then began to advance. They stepped on and over their dead enemies, ramming their feet down hard on faces, necks and arms, shattering bones as they did so.

'They are breaking,' I said to Gafarn.

'Yes, highness, they are.'

I turned to him and offered my hand to him. 'You saved my life, I am in your debt.'

He grinned. 'I had no choice, Gallia would never have forgiven me.'

In front of us the rear rank of the Thracians threw another volley of pila, the shafts angling through the air to pierce flesh and strike shield. If they hit a shield the soft iron of their shaft immediately bent, making it impossible for it to be freed from the shield and thus rendering it useless to its owner. I saw a riderless horse bolt in terror into the trees, and saw another horse carrying a man wearing a green cloak, steel cuirass and helmet, and armed with a long sword in his right hand and a round shield on his left side painted with some sort of animal symbol. He was riding up and down behind his men, waving his sword, urging his men on. He gestured to and instructed other mounted warriors, who rode away to do his bidding. I recognised him. It was King Ambiorix, who by his frantic activity was obviously seeing any hopes of victory rapidly disappearing. The Thracians were still pushing forward, grunting like pigs as they cut through the wall of flesh in front of them.

I turned to Gafarn. 'An arrow, quick.'

He passed me a shaft and I placed it in my bowstring. I could see Ambiorix, waving his sword in the air and shouting, though he was several hundred feet away but I could not discern his voice amid the general tumult of the battle.

'You'll never hit him from here.' Gafarn had guessed my intention and his archer's instinct told him that the shot was too long against a target that only fleetingly showed itself. I took aim but realised that Gafarn was right. Ambiorix was riding up and down the line, shouting encouragement, and he frequently disappeared behind other riders.

'You're right,' I said to Gafarn. 'I need to get a clear shot.'

I called my men to gather round me.

'We need to get into the trees and behind the Gauls. Share out the arrows you have remaining.'

A quick count revealed that there were only enough arrows for each man to have two each, thus I picked ten men at random, including Gafarn, told the rest to surrender their arrows to us, and led them towards the right flank and into the thick oaks that surrounded the clearing. We slowed as we moved through the trees, fanning out in a line with bows at the ready. I was at the far left of the line, and out of the corner of my eye I could see the two sides hacking and stabbing at each other. We kept moving forward until we were well behind the Gaul battle line. I raised my right arm and gestured to the rest to close up on me. I knelt on the ground and they huddled round me.

'That man on the horse, with the green cloak, steel cuirass and shiny helmet, that is their king. Kill him and it's all over.'

I looked at each of them to make sure they understood. They all nodded solemnly. One of them suddenly looked wild-eyed at me and lurched forward onto the ground. In his back was a spear, and then there were shouts and cheers as the Gauls came at us. There were around a dozen of them, all carrying square shields and

spears, their half-naked bodies covered in tattoos and filth. They must have been sent into the woods to scout, and now they had found an easy prey. I raised my bow and shot the man who had thrown the spear, while the rest of my men likewise returned fire. We cut down another five but then they were on us. I threw my bow aside and drew my sword, just in time to deflect a spear that was aimed at my belly. The Gaul's momentum carried him past me and I hacked down hard on the back of his neck as he did so, sending him sprawling to the ground with blood oozing from the wound. He did not get up. A wild man, naked aside from a silver torque around his neck, came yelling at me with a long sword held above his head clasped with both hands. I jumped aside and rolled on the ground to avoid the blow, then sprang up as he turned and came at me again with great scything sweeps of his blade. They were easy enough to avoid, but his attack was relentless. I could smell his sweat and foul breath as he threw insults at me. His bloodshot eyes were bulging in their sockets. He swung his blade again, he was amazingly quick for a big man, but it swept past me I lunged with my own sword and stuck the point into his upper arm, just below the shoulder. He screamed in pain. He came at me once more, raising his sword above his head and then bringing it down where he thought my head would be, but once again I leapt aside and he cut only air. Blood was pouring from his wound, and every time he raised his sword he winced in pain. He attacked once again, but this time his strikes were slower and more predictable. He cut down at my left shoulder, missed and as his blade swept towards the ground I lunged and stabbed him in the belly. He gasped with surprise, stood for a moment and then sank to his knees. I screamed and aimed a downward cut against the side of his neck. The steel blade cut deep into his flesh, sending a fountain of blood into the air as he collapsed on the ground. I glanced around me. I could see three of my men lying lifeless on the ground, but the others had fought off the Gauls and were now firing arrows at the last three who were alive. They felled two but the third escaped. I retrieved my bow and ran up to Gafarn.
'Are you hurt?'
'No, highness, but we have few arrows left.'
There were seven of us left and each clutched his remaining arrows in his right hand. Not one had more than two, three had none at all. I took all the arrows, gave half to Gafarn and told the men to get back to the others. They could do nothing here. They saluted and departed, while Gafarn and I went to kill a king.

We ran forward through the trees and then swung left into the clearing, where we emerged well behind the enemy's position. In front of us hundreds of men were still fighting each other.

'You see him?'

'I see him, highness.'

'Then let's kill him.'

We both fired but it was Gafarn who hit him. It was a masterful shot, a once-in-a-lifetime shot, for as my arrow went though the air and disappeared into the mass of fighting men, Gafarn's arrow hit Ambiorix in the face at the moment he was turning his horse. He immediately fell from his saddle onto the ground, dead. Gafarn whooped with joy and I slapped him on the shoulder, but within seconds men on horseback were coming at us, for we had been spotted. We ran as though a demon was snapping at our heels, back into the trees and then raced through the oaks until we reached the safety of our own lines. Gafarn and I were like excited children as we jumped, embraced and laughed with delight, for he had given us victory because the Gauls, seeing their king killed, lost heart and began to flee the battle. Their chiefs and knights tried to stop them but they had had enough. Soon their retreat turned into a rout and Spartacus and his Thracians stood triumphant on the battlefield.

I went to search him out and found him in the front rank of his men, who were drinking greedily from their water bottles. Beside him Akmon was nursing a nasty wound to his shoulder, his mail shirt having been ripped open.

He spat blood on he ground. 'These Gauls love their axes.'

I was concerned. 'Are you badly hurt?'

He grinned. 'Nothing that won't heal. I've suffered worse as a gladiator.'

Spartacus embraced me and I told him about King Ambiorix. 'So, the bastard's dead. I wondered why they gave way so suddenly.' He looked around at his men sitting on the ground and taking off their helmets. 'Akmon, get them back on their feet. We are going to march on.'

'They are tired, Spartacus.'

'They can sleep tonight. We are near to their royal headquarters, and I want it to be a pile of ashes before we turn back.'

And so, after only half an hour to gather ourselves, we continued on towards Ambiorix's berg. We had suffered fifty dead and a hundred more wounded but the clearing was littered with slain Gauls, most lying in a long strip from tree line to tree line where the battle had been fought, hundreds of them. We found the body of Ambiorix with an arrow through its right eye socket. Spartacus cut the head off, rammed a spear into the earth and stuck the bloody head on top of it.

We left the wounded and a hundred uninjured Thracians to escort them back to camp as we tramped onwards. Our pace was slower now for battles are tiring affairs, but we ate hard biscuit and drank and refreshed our water bottles from the stream that cut through the meadow on the route that led to the berg. It was here that I had killed Gallia's brother when we had delivered the gold, and now we were back. How unnecessary it had all been, really. If only Ambiorix had left us alone. But his cunning and ambition had led him to believe that he could use us to free himself of Rome's rule and become the king of kings of the Gauls. And now he was dead, his warriors slaughtered and his people emasculated. Like Gallia told me, they were a beaten people.

The berg fell without a fight. When we arrived the gates were open and the walls and platforms unmanned. The people, no doubt having learned of the death of their king, had fled. Byrd reckoned they had gone into the mountains, though Spartacus suspected that some still watched us from the forest. It didn't matter. We took firebrands and threw them into the royal hall, which was soon a raging inferno as the flames devoured the Senones' centre of government. Here, generations of their kings and princes would have sat and carried out their duties, and now it was being turned into ash. The rest of the buildings were also set alight, the loud roar of the fires at our backs as we marched away.

In the evening, after we had reached camp and I had washed and changed, I told Gallia that her father was dead. She looked into my eyes, then put her arms around me and kissed me.

'I am glad you are safe.'

'I am sorry for your loss.'

She shook her head. 'I was nothing to my father, so why should I weep for him? You and the people that I am close to here are my family. I have no other.'

In the next few days the army moved north to the River Pagus, a great, winding river that flowed east to the Adriatic Sea. Here, we made camp and enjoyed, for the first time since we had left Thurri, a period of rest. We pitched our tents on the south side of the great river, which was a thousand feet wide at this point, with Thracians in the centre and the other contingents either side in a great but organised sprawl that extended for miles. My horsemen were established on the right flank of the army, occupying a spit of land half a mile across on a great bend in the river. The grassland either side of the river was lush and the river itself full of fish. Very soon, a host of men were fishing along the banks and reaping a rich haul of rainbow trout, lake trout, brown trout, grayling, whitefish, barbel, catfish, pike, perch, tench, carp, chub, dace, bream and roach. Immediately west of our camp was a stretch of open ground on the concave bend of the river. Here, the riverbank was almost flat and we could take the horses up to the river and walk them into the water. The river itself, though deep, flowed gently so it was possible to coax a horse into the water up his shoulders quite safely. I did this with Remus, and though at first he was slightly reticent, he soon got to enjoy the experience.

The wounded were tended to and began their recovery, weapons were mended in the forges that were set up and Godarz organised the making of thousands of new arrows. As usual, Byrd established his camp on the perimeter of the army and sent his scouts out each day to watch for the enemy. But no enemy came. Indeed, his men found scarce evidence of anybody. Clearly our fearsome reputation had spread far and wide and had terrified all and sundry.

We had been at the Pagus two weeks when I rode with Gallia, Diana and Gafarn to find Spartacus after receiving an invitation to attend him. Byrd had just returned from one of his scouting missions and had informed me that a great trail of people were fleeing towards Mutina, but that he and his men had seen nothing to the north, which meant that our route to the Alps and freedom was open. We found Spartacus in the river, stripped to the waist, standing up to his thighs in the water with a javelin in his hand. Beside him stood Domitus, likewise stripped to the waist, both of them looking at the water intently. On the bank sat Claudia and Akmon, with two wicker baskets between them. We halted and dismounted, tying the horses to a wagon lying nearby. Claudia raised her hand to us then put a finger to her lips to indicate that we should not make any noise. Suddenly Domitus jabbed his pilum down and extracted an impaled wriggling trout from the water. He grabbed the fish and threw it onto the bank, then Akmon put it in one of the baskets.

'Ha,' exclaimed Akmon, 'that's three to nothing, Spartacus. Looks like you and Claudia will be going hungry tonight.'

Spartacus drew back his javelin so the tip was near his waist and then thrust it down as hard as he could. He missed.

Domitus shook his head. 'No, no, no. You're not trying to kill a man, just tickling a trout. Let them swim near the tip, then strike.' And just to prove his point, he flicked his wrist and speared yet another fish.

Spartacus threw the javelin onto the bank in frustration and then waded ashore. The sun glinted on his thick, muscular arms, huge shoulders and broad chest, the left side of which carried a long white scar that coursed down from his shoulder blade. He saw me looking at it.

'A gift from a big Nubian in the arena at Capua. Occupational hazard when you are a gladiator.' Claudia passed him a tunic and he then embraced Diana and Gallia, both of them now sitting beside Claudia on the riverbank.

Spartacus frowned when he heard a splash and an exultant yell from Domitus, then saw another fish being tossed onto the ground beside him. 'Enough fishing for one day, Domitus. We have other things to attend to.'

At that moment Castus and Cannicus appeared, dressed in tunics and sandals, swords at their waists. Following behind came the stocky shape of Afranius, who had shaved his head so that he appeared fiercer than ever. He nodded curtly to all assembled and stood bolt upright with his arms by his side.

'Sit, Afranius,' said Spartacus, gesturing to some stools placed in front of a table that was loaded with bread, fruit, jugs of wine and plates of meat that had been cooked earlier. 'Have something to eat and drink. All of you, please, refresh yourselves.'

As we were eating and indulging in idle chat, Godarz and Byrd arrived, which was the signal for Spartacus to reveal the reason he had summoned us all.

'Friends,' he began, 'we have travelled a long way together and have won many victories.'

I, Domitus, Castus and Cannicus cheered. Spartacus held up a hand to still us.

'But now we have reached the end of our journey. Tomorrow I will assemble the army and release every man and woman from my service. They will be free to march north and cross the Alps, thence to travel to their homelands or wherever they will. I can ask no more of them, or you. Thus today I wished to share the company of my friends one last time, before we all go to fulfil our destinies.'

He walked over to me and placed his hand on my shoulder. 'For Pacorus, this means going back to his father's kingdom.' He smiled at Gallia. 'And he will take with him a great prize that he has won, perhaps the greatest prize in the whole of Italy and Gaul.'

I blushed and Castus slapped me on the back. Spartacus looked at Godarz and Domitus in turn. 'I know that others will join our young prince in Parthia, and it fills me with joy that they will do so, for I know that they will be safe there.'

'And you, lord?' I said.

He looked at Claudia. 'I fear that for us there may not be a happy ending. Rome will hunt us down wherever we go.'

'You will always be welcome in Hatra, lord,' I said. 'Roman reach does not extend to Parthia.'

He smiled. 'Thank you, but no, Claudia and I have our own plans. We think it best if we slip into the mists of anonymity and disappear from history.'

'You're too big to be anonymous,' grumbled Akmon.

'What about you, Afranius?' said Castus.

'I will stay in Italy. I have not finished with Rome.' He reminded me of Crixus, bursting with hate.

Yet it was a happy day, full of laughter and good company, and as the sun began to set in the west we toasted our friendship and our freedom, for what I had always taken for granted had become a precious thing for me, though the most precious of all was seated beside me and I was taking her back to Hatra. But freedom was the idea that bound us all to each other, the invisible sinew that tied the whole army together. And on that day I made a vow that I would never own a slave again, for I had been one and knew what misery they had to endure. And on a warm summer's evening in northern Italy, by a mighty meandering river, I fell asleep in the midst of my friends and in the arms of the woman I loved.

Two days later the army was assembled by noon, nearly sixty thousand troops and another five thousand women and children we had somehow collected on our travels through Italy. We looked magnificent that day. We still had much Roman gold and silver that we had taken from the enemy, and I had earlier sent Byrd into Mutina to purchase the finest black leather bridle, breast girth and saddle straps money could buy for Remus, Roman money that is. To the Romans Byrd was just another trader with a wagon, albeit one with a strange accent. When he returned I had the leather inlaid with silver coins that were pierced through the centre and then sewn onto the leather. I cleaned my black cuirass and hung alternating strips of thin steel and silver from its base so that they shimmered in the sun. Byrd also purchased a new thick woollen cloak for me that was pure white with a silver clasp. Remus' mane was tied in place with black leather strips and his tail was wrapped with a black cotton guard that was also decorated with silver strips. He looked like a steed of the gods, as befitting a prince of Hatra. On my head I wore my Roman helmet with a thick white crest of goose feathers and at my waist I wore the sword that Spartacus had given me many months before.

During the time we had spent by the Pagus I had asked a number of women, who had been weavers for their Roman masters, to make me a standard. The review of the army was the first time it was displayed, and I had to fight back tears when I first saw it. It was a six foot square of heavy cotton, coloured scarlet with a white horse's head stitched on each side. When we rode onto the parade field it was carried behind me by a large Parthian named Vardanes, who had served with me since Cappadocia. The slight easterly breeze that blew that day caused it to flap in the wind and everyone could see the white horse on a scarlet background. And behind the standard rode just over three thousand horsemen, two thousand horse archers, Burebista's thousand mounted spearmen and Gallia's one hundred female horse archers. Every quiver was full of arrows, and at camp more wagons were full of replacements, for Godarz and his quartermasters had worked tirelessly to replenish our stocks. The surrounding countryside, made up of thick forests, had been plundered ruthlessly for wood for shafts and great tracts had been cleared.

We formed up in our dragons on the right flank of the army, each one composed of ten companies of one hundred horsemen. The sun glinted off whetted spear points and burnished helmets, while every man in Burebista's command wore a mail shirt, carried a shield and a sword at his waist. As we were moving into position, to our left the legions of Spartacus were forming into line. Beside us were the three legions of Germans under Castus, which included the remnants of those Gauls who had fought under Crixus but who had managed to escape north after the Romans had defeated him. Occupying the centre of the line were Akmon's four legions of Thracians, with another legion filled with Greeks, Jews, Dacians, Illyrians and even a few Egyptians and Berbers attached to the Thracians. On the left flank stood the three Spanish legions of Afranius, who Akmon now reckoned to be the best trained in the army, and also the most unpredictable, like their leader. They were, nevertheless, a credit to the angry young Spaniard who led them. In front of the army, mounted on a line of wagons, were the standards we had taken from the enemy – silver eagles, red pennants, poles with silver discs fastened to them, and cavalry flags – dozens of them, testimony to the generalship of Spartacus, one time gladiator and lowly auxiliary, now master of all Italy.

The orders had been issued the night before. Word had been passed to all commanders of cohorts and centuries that the army would parade on the morrow for one last time. And then those assembled would be dismissed from their service at the sound of one hundred trumpets being blown, after which the men would make their way back to their respective camps where they would be issued with one month's food ration and then they would be free to go. They were to take their weapons and clothing with them, and those who were determined to make their way in groups would be issued with one tent per eight men. All remaining coin was to be distributed evenly, and Godarz and his assistants had worked out how much gold and silver was to be issued to each century, after which each centurion would divide the amount among his men accordingly. Byrd had sent parties of his men to the foot of the Alps themselves, and they reported that there were no Roman garrisons along the route, or indeed any Roman soldiers anywhere. To all intents and purposes they had fallen off the edge of the world.

Before the trumpets were sounded Spartacus rode to every cohort assembled, speaking to their commanders and thanking the men for their valour and loyalty. It took him over two hours before he had completed this task, and at the end there were many with tears in their eyes. I rode over to where he and Claudia sat on their horses. That day Claudia looked the beauty she was, her long black hair flowing freely around her shoulders. She wore a simple white tunic edged with green, with light brown leggings and red leather boots. Spartacus, as usual, was dressed in his plain tunic and mail shirt, with an ordinary legionary's helmet on his head. He never pretended to be anything more than a common man and soldier, and that was why thousands were devoted to him. I halted Remus beside him. He looked at my horse and smiled.

'Remus has certainly put on his best attire today, Pacorus.'

'Yes, lord. I thought it fitting that today he, and the rest of your horsemen, should look their best. It was the least we could do.'

'Well, my friend,' he said, 'it has been an interesting journey that has led us to this place. But now it is time for all of us to start a new adventure.'

'You know,' I said, 'you can both come to Parthia with Gallia and me.'

'We know that, Pacorus,' answered Claudia, 'but to do so would only bring war and destruction to your people and we think too much of you to let that happen.'

Domitus walked up dressed in his war finery. He had once been a centurion and he was now dressed as one, with steel greaves, red tunic, mail shirt adorned with silver discs and a transverse red crest on his helmet. He looked a different man from the poor wretch we had rescued at the silver mine at Thurri, and I liked to think that he was happy to be with us. He acknowledged me and then spoke to Spartacus.

'We wait on your signal, sir.'

Spartacus looked around him and sighed. At that moment there was a deathly silence. It seemed that even the birds had stopped flying. The only thing that stirred was the wind, which made my scarlet standard flutter, revealing glimpses of the white horse's head that it sported. Remus chomped at his bit and scraped at the ground with his right front foot. I leaned forward and stroked his neck. I felt a trickle of sweat roll down the right side of my face, for the sun was at its height, the sky was cloudless and it was warm.

Domitus turned smartly and signalled to the trumpeters, whose piercing sound blasted across the assembled massed ranks. Remus shifted nervously at the sudden noise, as did a number of other horses among the cavalry's ranks. So this was the moment when the army that was undefeated would simply melt away. The trumpets ceased blowing and I watched to see the ranks break as the troops made their way back to camp. Nergal and Burebista had relayed my orders to their company commanders, who had in turn informed their men that they were free to leave when the signal was given. As they had no food or water with them whilst on parade, this would necessitate them also riding back to camp and being issued with food for both horse and man, enough to take them over the Alps at least.

As the seconds passed I realised that nothing had happened. Nothing. No one had moved, not one. Had they not heard the trumpet blast? Of course they had. Then what? Then a new sound began to be heard, this time from the ranks, barely audible at first, but then gaining in strength and volume until the whole plain was filled with the mighty din of thousands of voices shouting as loud as they could. Troops were raising their javelins in the air in salute as they shouted, while those on horses were holding their spears and bows aloft. And into the air they shouted the same word over and over again, tens of thousand in unison acclaiming their general.

'Spartacus. Spartacus. Spartacus.'

The chanting was getting louder and men on horses were having difficulty controlling their mounts as I glanced over to the man whose name they were hailing. He sat rock-like on his horse, staring straight ahead and seemingly oblivious to what was going on in front of him, but as I looked more closely I saw that there was a thin smile on his face. I looked across at Claudia who had tears running down her cheeks. Spartacus suddenly snapped out of his daze and turned to me.

'It would appear that my troops are disobeying me.'

'It seems so, lord.'

Across from us strode Castus, Akmon and Afranius, who all stopped in front of Spartacus' horse. Akmon spat on the ground.

'What are you going to do now?'

'Well,' replied Spartacus, 'it would seem that no one wants to go over the Alps.'

'The south, then. Sicily, perhaps?' said Akmon.

Spartacus nodded. 'Sicily would offer us hope, though how we get across the sea I do not know.'

And so it was that the army of the slave general Spartacus stayed in Italy. I often looked back on that moment, how absurd it appeared at the time but how it actually made perfect sense. The ranks of the army were made up of individuals who had nothing, had been condemned to a life of back-breaking servitude, many born to slave mothers and fathers. To Rome they were mere beasts of burden to be used and abused. But Spartacus had given them hope, and what's more he had given them victory over the hated Romans. Not just one, but a string of triumphs. Those men who had fought in those victories, and who had formed bonds of friendship with those they stood beside in battle, had no wish to meekly lay down their arms and crawl away like whipped dogs. I should have thought of it myself. Gallia herself had told me the same when she had announced that her family was here, with me, with Spartacus, with the army. In each legion, in each cohort and in each century men felt the same bonds to their friends and comrades. They wished to remain with the family that was the army of Spartacus.

Spartacus had never told them that they could topple Rome itself, but many must have dreamed so. They had, after all, smashed every Roman army that had been sent against them. Did Rome have any more armies left? Victory was intoxicating, addictive, especially to those who had only experienced the bitter taste of slavery. Even if many of them suspected that their adventure would eventually end in defeat, every one of them knew that it was indeed better to die on one's feet than live on their knees.

Chapter 15

I often thought of that summer's day, the day when we had seemed invincible. We would march south, attack Rome itself perhaps, cower our enemies into submission and treat Italy as if she were our plaything. Everything seemed possible. Even my fellow Parthians had become intoxicated by victory and believed themselves to be immortal. Nergal, loyal Nergal, forgot about Hatra and could think only of sweeping Romans before him with the wild-haired Praxima riding beside him. He and his company commanders drank and boasted of how they had destroyed the armies of Rome. Burebista dreamed of leading his Dacians into Rome and torching the city, and thereafter laying a host of captured legionary eagles in the great forum itself. How the Romans diminished in size at the end of that summer; whereas our legions stood as titans astride the Roman world, and the mightiest titan of all was Spartacus, our general. Our undefeated leader who had become like a god to many of our troops. And in the intoxication of victory all thoughts of crossing the Alps disappeared. The truth was that in our desire to reach northern Italy no one had thought of how we would actually cross the mountains, and once over them what route we would travel. It mattered not now, for the undefeated army was not dissolving but was going to inflict further torments on the enemy.

We marched south in high spirits, wanting the Romans to fight us again so we could defeat them once more. The battles that we had fought, brutal bouts that had been long, bloody affairs, in the minds of many became easy routs that were over in a matter of minutes. How the memory quickly erases reality and blocks out unpleasantness. We marched west and then south, sweeping down the east coast of Italy, making use once more of well-engineered Roman roads. I got restless marching with the army, which for the cavalry involved guarding the flanks, covering the rear and scouting ahead for any signs of the enemy. All very important tasks, but ones that could be done by a handful of horsemen and not hundreds. Trudging along on foot, amidst a constant cloud of fine dust thrown up by thousands of people and animals, with our horses beside us, was both boring and irritating. The army, strung out over many miles, barely covered ten miles a day, and my mood darkened considerably when Godarz informed me that Sicily was around four hundred miles away. He was in his element, of course, organising columns of march, being kept informed daily of food supplies, the quantity of spare horse shoes, the number of sick animals, allocating teams to drive and repair carts and wagons, and all the other myriad of duties that were essential to keep the army functioning. His staff of clerks and quartermasters grew.

'Organisation is a necessary evil, Pacorus,' he reminded me.

It was early, just after dawn, and he had barely finished briefing his subordinates on the coming day's march, which would begin in three hours following the dismantling of the massive camp in which everyone slept during the night, even my cavalry. I was visiting him because Nergal had complained to me that he had commandeered two of his companies of horse archers to hunt down wild boar for food, and another company to plunder the countryside of any cattle they came upon.

'That may be, but my men are not farmers, Godarz, to be set gathering the harvest.'

He handed me a piece of bread and cheese. The cheese was strong and firm, the bread appeared freshly baked.

'No, they are not, but at the moment they and their horses do nothing but eat rations. Might as well have them doing something useful to earn their keep.'

'You should have asked me first.'

'And what would you have said?'

'I would have agreed with you.'

He grinned. 'Excellent! Please inform Nergal of your decision.'

'I would prefer that you speak to me first before you send my cavalry out on food-gathering expeditions.'

'This may come as a surprise to you,' he remarked, stiffly, 'but men and horses eat a lot of food, as do princes and their betrothed. It is quite amazing how much Gallia and her women consume. Looking at their frames you would never think so.'

'That may also be, but get my permission first.'

But he was right, of course, and during the next few days I agreed that more horsemen should be sent out to undertake foraging duties. Byrd and his men were riding far and wide, and I only saw him occasionally. I decided that I too would partake of a little scouting, and selected a hundred men from my dragon. I told Spartacus that I was going to spread a little terror among the Romans. He was walking as usual, like a common soldier, with Claudia beside him. It always struck me as strange that they did not ride, but then he said that he preferred to fight on his two feet as he had done in the Roman Army, in the arena and now as a free man.

'You should try it some time.'

'I did try it, when we killed Gallia's father. I found it limiting. In any case, Parthians prefer to fight on horseback, lord.'

'That's because if things turn badly they can flee faster than everyone else,' quipped Akmon, mischievously.

'Only the enemies of Parthia flee,' I reminded him.

'Ha. You hear that Spartacus. There speaks a man whose homeland has never been touched by the enemy's sword.' Akmon looked at me. 'I used to think that, but the Romans taught me otherwise.'

'That's very glum, Akmon,' said Claudia, 'and it's such a nice day.'

Akmon spat, looked at the sky and shrugged. It was a pleasant day, true enough, though Claudia appeared exceptionally happy today. Gallia and Diana had joined me and they were walking either side of her, the mad Rubi, in a world of her own, trailing in their wake. I noticed that she kept glancing at Spartacus, who smiled back at her like a naughty boy. Most strange.

'Why don't you tell them?' he said. 'They are our friends, after all.'

Claudia blushed, and then linked arms with Gallia and Diana. 'I'm pregnant.'

They kissed and embraced her, while I offered my hand to Spartacus. 'That is truly wondrous news, lord. My congratulations.' Rubi jumped up and down in delight, though she knew not why.

He slapped me hard on the shoulder, almost knocking me over. 'Thank you, Pacorus.'

'When is the birth?' asked Gallia.

'Spring next year,' replied Claudia, embracing Diana who had tears in her eyes.

The news of Claudia's pregnancy spread like wildfire throughout the army and its morale soared accordingly. It was reckoned a good omen, for the son of Spartacus would be an even mightier warrior than his father, and would surely be blessed by the gods. Whether that was true or not, that autumn the whole army seemed to be blessed. We raided far and wide, often reaping a rich haul, for this was harvest time when vineyards yielded grapes for central Italy's crop of red wines, and olive groves heaved with fruit. The country estates teemed with slaves who were stripping grapes from their vines, carrying them in baskets to the end of each row of trees and then heaving them into carts. I took Gallia with me as part of my company. She had wanted to lead her women to make up another party but I forbade her. I had visions of her and her women being ambushed, raped and then crucified and the thought terrified me. So I said she could accompany me but that her women must stay with the army. I even increased the number of men who rode with me to two hundred to ensure her safety, and also made sure that they were the best archers and swordsmen in my dragon.

The countryside of central Italy was beautiful that autumn, with misty olive groves interwoven with rows of cypresses and vineyards covering gently undulating hills. And always in the background were the mountains with their lush alpine meadows, streams and tracts of savage wilderness. Nearer the coast were thick forests and marshland, the woodlands filled with wild boar and wolves. We camped hidden in the trees at night, and in the dawn light visited fire and sword upon unsuspecting towns and villages. It was easy enough. Two of Byrd's scouts accompanied us, and on their mangy horses they would ride to a habitation the previous day, taking note of any walls or barriers that might impede our assault. Frequently there were none; indeed, often there was no official Roman presence at all. The cities and big towns had their walls and garrisons, but we weren't interested in those. We killed any overseers we came across when we raided the large agricultural estates and freed the slaves, giving them directions to the army. Whether any made the journey or merely fled to the hills and woods and became bandits, I do not know. When we attacked we came out of the pre-dawn mist, my huge scarlet banner with its white horse's head billowing behind me. We carried flaming torches that we tossed into carts, barns and haystacks. We killed only those who offered resistance. Most fled for their lives, clutching a few possessions with some mothers holding infants at their breasts. These we let live. Occasionally a group of men, perhaps veterans who had been granted land by a grateful Roman senate, made a stand against us – a ragged line of men with cracked shields, no helmets and rusty swords and old spears for weapons. They remembered their legionary training well enough, but had no answer to our speed and arrows. We rode round and behind them and shot them to pieces. We torched villas, farms and staging posts for the Roman mail system, always scouring for gold and silver before we did so. We collected a tidy sum of both. But I got bored of striking easy targets and so we ventured towards towns, raiding Luna, Faesulae, Ad Fines, Ad Novas, Vepete and Sahate. I often sent half a dozen riders to the main gates and had them hurl insults at the guards. Then the gates would open and a detachment of riders would gallop out to apprehend them. But my men were merely the bait, and over the crest of a hill or hidden among trees we would be waiting, and the Romans would fall into the trap and would be slaughtered to a man. Or we would burn a large villa, then conceal ourselves and wait for the nearest garrison, who would see the tall columns of black smoke billowing into the sky, to send troops to investigate. And when they arrived we would cut them down from our hiding place with arrows, or charge them on horseback, screaming and yelling. The shock momentarily froze them to the spot, giving us just enough time to reach them and hack them down with our swords before they had chance to organise themselves into formation.

One of the scouts reported that the city of Arretium, located on a steep hill beside the floodplain of the River Arno, had walls that were half demolished. A local had told him that they had been destroyed during a civil war and had not been repaired. There were four gates into the city, located at the four points of the compass, but on the southern side the walls had been torn down after an army had stormed and sacked it. They had not been repaired. Instead, the masonry had been plundered to erect new dwellings that now stood outside of the original circuit. A rampart of earth had been erected around these new homes with the purpose of building a new wall to encompass the city's overspill, but the rampart stood neglected. The city authorities had grown lax; but then, they were in the centre of Italy and what threat was nearby?

We camped around five miles from Arretium, in a wooded gully through which ran a stream of fast-flowing, ice-cool water. We lay up during the day and rested. Two hours before dusk, after we had eaten a meal of biscuit and fruit, I gathered everyone in a semi-circle.

'We ride tonight and attack before dawn.' I looked at the scout who had visited Arretium, a tall, wiry man in his late twenties with black eyes and an evil grin. His name was Diaolus and he was a Greek. No one knew anything about him except that he had been a slave, but had lived as a bandit before he had joined Byrd's men. He spoke Latin well and had not been branded, as far as I could tell. I believed he had some sort of an education, but he resisted all attempts to extract information from him.

'The gates have guards, but they are not always closed at night. The soldiers are fat and lazy and are only interested in bribes.' He cast a glance at Gallia. 'And women.'

'How large is the garrison?' I asked.

He threw up his hands. 'Maybe one cohort.'

'That is more than we are,' said one of my officers.

Diaolus smiled. 'But they are lazy cowards and you are warriors.'

'And you are sure about the earth rampart?' I said.

He nodded. 'It is nothing more than a large tussock. It is no barrier at all'

'Very well,' I said, 'that will be our way in. We ride in fast, hit them hard and get out quickly. No bravado, no loitering and no getting into fights. We burn, we kill, we leave.'

Before we left we checked and re-checked weapons, straps on the horses and then the animals themselves, especially their iron shoes. After night had fallen we walked for the first three miles of the journey, moving through waist-high grass, along dirt tracks and through trees. There was no moon and at first it was difficult to follow Diaolus. After a while, though, our eyes grew more accustomed to the night and three hours later we reached the paved road that led to Arretium. The smooth, perfectly dressed flagstones seemed to exude a ghostly glow in the dark, showing us the way to our target. We mounted our horses and rode them on the verge, for the horse shoes on the paving stones would make a racket loud enough to raise the dead. We rode in silence to the city, swinging away from the road half a mile from its walls. Moving parallel to the stone defences, we were soon at the gap in the masonry that Diaolus had spoken of. He had not exaggerated. The wall was missing for at least half a mile, the glow from the night lamps and from buildings within providing an illuminated backdrop. I saw the mound, a gently rising heap of earth, in front of which stood a motley collection of poorly constructed dwellings, hovels in truth. In the east the first rays of dawn were emerging over the high Apennines in the distance, making the clouds glow red and yellow. Soon the city folk would be stirring. It was time to wake them up.

Arretium burned fiercely that morning. Firebrands soaked in pitch were tossed into homes and shops as we rode through the city's streets. Like all Roman towns it was arranged in the form of a grid system, with streets laid out at right angles to each other. The two main streets ran north-to-south and east-to-west, and where they met was where the Romans placed the forum, around which were clustered shops and other businesses. They may have been made of stone, but the buildings had wooden balconies and the shops wooden shutters, and all these things burned brightly once we had fired them. And then the panic and screaming began. Once fires are raging fear grips people, and soon they were blindly running around seeking sanctuary. They instinctively flocked to the temples that fronted one side of the forum. I never reached into my quiver once when we were inside the city, for all I saw were unarmed civilians. And they were already dying, from smoke, from flames, from being trampled to death in the panic. Dogs with broken legs limped into view whimpering, mules ran around in a frenzied state with their sides seared by flames, and all the time the fires spread.

Gallia halted beside me on a main street just off the forum, and pulled off her helmet as terror-stricken individuals raced past us to reach the temples. Two of my men were on the other side of the street, firing arrows at anyone unlucky enough to be within range. Gallia looked on in horror as one of their arrows struck a woman in the back. She was carrying a baby in her arms. She pitched forward onto the ground as the arrow struck her, the baby disappearing under the feet of the desperate mob.

'Enough!' I screamed at them, but in the din they did not even hear me.

Others among my men, scenting an easy kill akin to a wolf slaughtering a lamb, were gripped by blood lust and began riding in groups into the forum and hacking around them with their swords.

'Stay close, and put your helmet back on,' I shouted to Gallia and rode into the forum.

I had seen enough. I ordered the trumpeter to sound withdrawal, and as he did so I rode to each group of horsemen and gestured with my sword that we were departing.

We formed into a line at the end of the forum opposite a great temple that had now become the citizens' sanctuary. Rising high into the sky, it had stone steps on all sides and was fronted by fluted columns, with a large frieze on its architrave. The pediment was topped with sculptures. The forum was now littered with corpses, men and women who had either been trampled to death in the rush to avoid us, or, I am ashamed to say, killed by my own men. But now, in front of the temple steps, was gathering the town garrison. They had been conspicuous by their absence up to now, but I saw them flooding into the square, beginning to assemble into their ranks. I glanced right and left and raised my bow; my men answered by raising theirs. We were ready. I had been fighting in Italy for two years now, or at least two campaigning seasons, and I had come to recognise the tell-tell signs as to whether a unit was battle hardened or full of inexperienced recruits. Those who faced us were nervous. It took their centurions an age to get them into formation, the men being struck by vine canes as they were thrown into place and hit across the back. Their officers were also screaming orders at them, though no one seemed to be taking any notice. But I did notice that said officers, three of them mounted on horses, kept glancing at us nervously. The whole scene was illuminated by an eerie red glow as the fires that raged around the forum provided light. Then, from within the temple, there came a dirge as the citizens prayed and sang to their gods that their lives would be spared.

I had thought of withdrawing and leaving for whence we had come, but the sight of the enemy forming in front of me persuaded me otherwise. It would be dishonourable to retreat in the face of the enemy, and my men would think ill of me, if they thought of me at all at that moment. The Romans were in position now, two hundred paces from us, about four hundred of them in five centuries. They outnumbered us two to one, but numbers are only one part of the equation in war. Behind them the awful sound coming from the temple must have unnerved them, for it seemed to have turned into a drawn-out lament.

I gave the signal for the whole line to advance and we moved forward a few paces, then halted. My men had their bows at the ready.

The Romans could have advanced against us, but I suspected that because they were only garrison troops it would take a mighty effort to move them from behind their shields. I also noticed that they were armed with spears not javelins, and they had no archers or slingers.

I looked at their uneven, ragged line and could almost smell their fear from where I was sitting on Remus. They presented their wall of shields to us, but I knew that it would be as effective as paper when the killing began. Their officers were still screaming at them, no doubt in an effort to fill their own hearts with courage. Hours before they had been officials in some forgotten backwater in Italy, and now they were fighting for their lives. What thoughts were filling their minds I did not know, but I knew that I could magnify their terror.

I placed my bow in its case and nudged Remus forward a few steps. I spread my arms wide as I faced the Roman line, being careful to keep out of spear range.

'Soldiers of Rome, I give you this opportunity to lay down your weapons and save your lives.'

The Roman officers and their centurions stopped yelling and looked at me.

'Do you not know who I am, Roman filth? I am Prince Pacorus whom you call "The Parthian". I demand once more that you lay down your weapons and prostrate yourselves before me. Only then will your lives be saved.'

At that moment a centurion stepped from the ranks to throw his javelin. He was dead before the shaft left his right hand, an arrow in the middle of his chest.

I laughed at the enemy. 'Did you not hear me, Romans, for I speak in your own language, the language of the gutter. Behold my might.'

I lowered my arms and my men instantly killed the Roman officers on horseback.

'If Roman armies cannot defeat me, how much less are the chances of a tiny, ill-trained garrison? I give you this one last chance. Throw yourselves on my mercy and you will live. Resist and you will die. Archers!'

As one my men pointed arrows at the enemy, ready to fire. Then a Roman soldier at the end of the line threw down his shield and darted from the square, followed by another next to him. A centurion cut down a third man attempting to flee with his sword, but was himself killed by one of my men. And then the whole Roman line dissolved into a disorganised mass of frightened individuals attempting to save themselves. A few, a tiny minority, tried to throw their spears at us, but a hail of arrows cut them down along with those trying to run away. It was all over in less than a minute. I had not shot one arrow. Before me, enemy shields, helmets and spears lay scattered on the tiles of the forum.

Gallia rode up beside me.

'It seems that you can defeat the Romans with mere words now.'

'I knew they wouldn't stand. Terror can often be deadlier than the sharpest sword.'

'Are you starting to believe your own legend?'

I shot her a glance. 'What do you mean?'

'All this nonsense about "the Parthian" and the like. Pride often comes before a fall.'

I smiled at her. 'You of all people should know, beautiful one that Parthians never fall off their horses.'

We had suffered no casualties. But now the smoke was beginning to swirl around the forum, grey clouds that stung the back of the throat and made us cough. The sound continued from the temple, seemingly reaching a dreadful crescendo of wailing. One of my men rode up and saluted.

'Do you want us to fire the temple, lord?'

'No, we do not want to anger their gods. Besides, the flames might do it for us.'

The shops around the forum were beginning to catch alight now and I could feel the heat increasing all around us. It was time to leave. We rode back down the main road and left the way we had come. Behind us, the flames consumed Arretium.

I do not know if the people in the temple survived, though I liked to think so.

'You are a fool, Pacorus,' said Spartacus with Claudia beside him. Both were reclining on cushions on the floor of his tent. The floor was covered with a large red carpet.

It was now over a month since I had raided the city, and the army had moved south through Latium and was now in Campania. My cavalry had raided far and wide with impunity, there being no opposition to stop us.

'Leave him alone, Spartacus.' Claudia smiled at me.

'There is no honour in killing civilians, lord,' I said, picking another rib from one of the platters on the table.

'You hear that Spartacus?' added Akmon. 'He's talking about honour again.'

Spartacus drank wine from his cup. 'You are a fine soldier, Pacorus, and a great leader of horse.' I winked at Gallia beside me, who rolled her eyes. 'But all this talk of honour will get you killed if you're not careful. The Romans have no honour, remember that.'

'A man without honour is a man without a soul,' mused Gafarn.

'Are you a poet, or just drunk?' asked Spartacus.

Gafarn looked at him, then me. 'No, lord, but that is what King Varaz has always told his son. Is that not right, highness?'

'That is right, Gafarn,' I said proudly.

Spartacus proffered a jug of wine and filled my cup. 'You are a lost cause, my friend.'

The tent flap opened, a guard walked in and saluted Spartacus. 'There is a man outside, sir, a Roman.'

Spartacus stood up, as did we all. 'A Roman? Is he mad, or perhaps he has a wish to end his life?'

'He says he has a letter, sir.'

'For me?' Spartacus spread his arms wide. 'Perhaps the Romans want to surrender.' We all laughed.

'No, sir,' replied the guard. 'The letter is for Prince Pacorus.'

All eyes were on me. I was stunned.

'It must be a mistake,' I said. 'Who knows me aside from those in this army.'

'Who indeed?' said Spartacus. He pointed at the guard. 'Bring the letter.'

'And the Roman?'

'Kill him,' said Akmon, his teeth battling a rib. The rib was winning.

'No. Let him go,' said Spartacus, 'but see he doesn't loiter. No doubt he is also a spy.'

'All the more reason to kill him,' grunted Akmon.
'He says he has to obtain a reply before he leaves.'
'You can't kill everyone,' I said.
'Why not?' he mumbled.
The guard brought in the letter and handed it to me. It was a scroll with a wax seal. Claudia and Gallia sat back down on the cushions as I handed it to Spartacus.
'You read it, lord.'
'Me? But it is addressed to you.'
'I have a feeling that it also concerns you.'
I sat down beside Gallia as Spartacus cut the seal, flopped down beside his wife and read the letter out loud.

To Prince Pacorus, son of King Varaz of Hatra.
Greetings.
My name is Marcus Licinius Crassus. Having been appointed by the People and Senate of Rome to safeguard their freedom and lives, I have vowed in the temple of my ancestors to bring to an end the murderous uprising of the slaves under the criminal Spartacus. But I know that you are not a slave and that you are the son of a noble line whose blood flows from the ancient Arsacid dynasty. By what curious fate you find yourself among slaves and criminals I know not, but I do know that the kings of the Parthian Empire are men of honour, and therefore knowing that there is nobility in Parthia, I have no hesitation in assuming that you too are a person of quality and importance.
This being the case, I invite you to meet with me at my house in Rome so that we can discuss more fully the sad present state of affairs you find yourself in, and perhaps reach an understanding that is beneficial to us both. Know that this invitation is given freely without any preconditions or expectations, and be assured that your person will be esteemed inviolable should you grant me the honour of meeting with you in person. This letter shall grant you safe conduct to and from my house in the city of Rome.
I eagerly await your reply. I remain your friend.
Marcus Licinius Crassus, General and Senator of Rome.

'Who is this Crassus?' asked Claudia.
I shrugged. 'Never heard of him.'
Spartacus rolled up the scroll and handed it back to me. 'Well, he has obviously heard of you. What are you going to do?'
'Ignore it, I suppose. What is this Crassus to me?'
Spartacus gestured at the guard. 'Bring in the messenger.'

The man, in his forties, dressed in a tunic of quality with a thick cloak around his shoulders, was shorter than Spartacus and had a full head of hair. His countenance was one of wisdom and maturity.

'What is your name?'

'Ajax, sir.' I noticed that the man did not look directly at Spartacus but stared at the floor in front of him.

'You are a slave.'

'Yes, sir.'

'Who is your master?'

'Marcus Licinius Crassus.'

'How long have you been a slave?'

'Many years, sir, in the house of my master.'

Spartacus poured a cup of wine and handed it to Ajax. 'Would you like a drink?'

Ajax took the cup and drank, aware that everyone was watching him.

'Would you like to join us, Ajax? To be a free man?'

Ajax drained the cup and handed it back to Spartacus, still looking at the floor.

'That is a most generous offer, sir. But my master has been very kind to me and treats me very well. I must, therefore, decline your magnanimous offer.'

'You see, Pacorus,' Spartacus looked at me, 'how making the leap from slave to free man is a chasm too wide for many.'

'I must beg an answer from Prince Pacorus,' Ajax said.

'You are walking into a trap,' snorted Akmon, finishing his wine and then pouring himself some more.

'My master has vouchsafed the life of Prince Pacorus,' replied Ajax, still staring at the floor, 'and no harm will come to him.'

'Do you trust your master, Ajax?' asked Spartacus.

'With my life, sir.'

Spartacus laughed. 'That much is obvious, for he has sent you into the wolf's lair sure enough. Well, Pacorus, it is your decision.'

I looked around me. Akmon was shaking his head at me, Claudia was glancing at me and then Spartacus, while Diana looked very worried and Gafarn bemused. I turned to Gallia.

'I would like to see Rome, I must confess.'

'It is your choice, my love. But the Romans have put you in chains once; can you be sure they will not do so again, or worse?'

I could not, of course, but I must confess that the chance to see Rome itself was too much to resist. Rubi began hissing at Ajax, until Gallia told her to be silent.

'I will go with you, Ajax.'

Akmon sighed with disgust, Diana grabbed Gafarn's arm while Claudia cast her eyes to the floor.

'It is decided, then,' said Spartacus.

'I hope you are not disappointed, lord,' I said.

'Of course not. You are free to make your own choices. That is why this army exists, and why the Romans hate us so much.'

While I waited for Remus to be brought to me, I said my farewells. They were more tearful than I expected, though strange to say the quiet presence of Ajax was reassuring. He fervently believed in the word of his master. I hoped he was right. I embraced Gallia and promised that I would take care of myself. As we were walking from the tent Spartacus called after us.

'Ajax, if anything happens to Pacorus, tell your master that I will kill ten thousand Romans in retaliation.'

Our army was around fifty miles from Rome, and for the first thirty of those a company of men led by Nergal trailed us. In the end I halted and rode to meet them. I sent them back to camp, telling Nergal that their presence would only provoke the Romans into attacking them. Nergal was most unhappy, but he reluctantly obeyed and so I was alone with Ajax. We rode at a leisurely pace, he on a brown mare with his cloak wrapped around him, me on Remus dressed in my armour, white crested helmet and white cloak.

'He's a fine horse, sir.'

'His name is Remus.'

'Ah, named after one of the founders of Rome. A fitting name.'

I patted Remus' neck. 'He is a trusty horse, though wilful. Which land do you come from, Ajax?'

'Greece, sir.'

'Have you always been...' I hesitated to finish the sentence.

'A slave? Since I was five, sir.'

'Were you captured in war?'

'No, sir, sold by my parents.'

'Sold by your parents?'

'It is a common practice. The Romans like Greek slaves to work in their households. They believe we are more intelligent than other races, on account of the great philosophers and writers being in Greece in the time when Rome was but a small village. The Romans wish to be better than the Greeks, you see, and one way they can do that is to learn everything about Greece and the Greeks. Since my first arrival in Rome I was taught languages, the law and financial accounts. And now I help run my master's household in Rome.'

'Have you no wish to see your homeland again?'

'I have seen it, sir, three times. My master owns property in Greece as well as in Italy, and his business interests have taken me to Athens twice and Corinth once. But I have no wish to live there. I find the people irksome, with their continual complaints about living under foreign rule and their longing for the Golden Age.'

'What is that?'

'Supposedly when every Greek was free and lived in prosperity. In reality, it was a time of constant war when cities were burned and people enslaved. One only has to read their histories to discover that this was so. At least Greece is peaceful now.'

'But under a Roman yoke.'

He laughed. 'All men live under some sort of yoke, sir, even kings and princes. The burden of wanting to be a great or just king, or the continual lust for glory. For the poor man, the yoke of filling the bellies of his wife and children with food can grind him into nothing. The yoke of Roman rule can be worn lightly enough.'

I thought about the thousands of slaves toiling under the lash in the fields or in the mines. No doubt they would have a different view.

We stopped for the night in a well-appointed inn by the side of the road, which had good stables, clean albeit sparse rooms and served simple food in large portions. Ajax paid for our rooms in advance, with an extra amount for the horses to be watered and fed and then groomed. He paid the innkeeper in gold coins from a large purse that was full of money. He spoke to the man, a portly middle-aged gentleman with ruddy cheeks and a bushy beard, as an equal, and to the man's servants as a master.

We set off at mid-morning under an overcast sky. Remus had been cared for well, and I had to admit that it was nice to sleep in a bed again. Ajax informed me that we would be in Rome by the afternoon, and I felt a tingle of excitement in my stomach. As we got nearer the city the amount of traffic on the road increased. Carts overfilled with wares to sell in the markets, herds of cattle and goats being marshalled for sale and then slaughter, and groups of travellers on foot heading both east and west. Most paid us no heed as we rode on the verge by the side of the road, for Ajax's horse had no iron shoes on its feet. We were just two more among the throng that was heading for the city. I rode bare headed that day, fastening my helmet to the saddle. Amid the bustle and chatter of a thousand voices, war and killing seemed far away.

We had travelled along a road that Ajax informed me was called the Via Salaria, which like all Roman roads was a masterpiece of engineering. As we neared the city itself I began to see more and more gateways either side of the road, each one set in an immaculate high, white stone wall and leading to a grand villa. Ajax told me that they were called pars urbana, where rich citizens sought quiet and refuge from the bustle and smells of Rome. He informed me that his master did not have such a residence, being content to have one house only, in Rome itself.

We entered the city through the Porta Collina, the so-called 'hill gate', a massive structure with two three-storey gatehouses flanking the two wooden gates, which were studded with great iron spikes. The walls either side of the gates were thirty feet high and patrolled by legionaries. There were also soldiers at the gates, who cast a watchful eye over all who were entering and leaving the city. A centurion watched us as we ambled up to the gates and then passed by him, but though he frowned at my long hair he did not stop us. Ajax must have noticed my unease.

'Have no fear, sir. Many different races come to Rome. For all they know, you might be a foreign merchant coming to the city to seal a deal.'

I carried only my sword for protection, no bow, and those who looked at me at all must have assumed that I was a foreign soldier of some sort. By the different skin colours on display and the languages I had heard on the road, I realised that Rome must contain a host of different races. There were dark-skinned Africans, Arabs in their flowing robes, Jews with straggly beards, and fair-skinned men and women who must have originated from north of the Alps. One thing was certain, a solitary Parthian would not stand out among this collection of various peoples.

'Do they close the gates at night?'

'They do, sir, though the city has grown considerably since the walls were first built, and now large sections of Rome lie outside of the walls. And now, sir, if you please, we must wait for our escort.'

'Escort?'

'Oh yes. Otherwise it would take forever to get to my master's house.'

We waited for around ten minutes, and then a detachment of legionaries appeared. There were twenty of them, commanded by a burly centurion with a red crest atop his helmet and the ubiquitous vine cane in his right hand. He saluted Ajax stiffly, noted me and then barked orders at his men, who formed up either side and in front of us, with the centurion at the head.

'We must be at my master's house by noon, centurion. Our business is most important.'

We travelled through streets teeming with people and crammed full of shops, taverns and eating places. Most of the buildings were whitewashed multi-storey affairs, with shops and eating places on the ground floor and lodgings above them. The level of activity was frenetic, with thousands of citizens shouting, arguing, laughing and haggling at the tops of their voices. The soldiers pushed anyone in their way rudely aside, and the centurion would occasionally shout. 'Make way, by order of General Marcus Licinius Crassus.' This Crassus was a man of some importance, given that people did indeed move out of the way at the mere mention of his name. Our journey took us to a flat-topped hill with two separate peaks called, so Ajax informed me, the Palatium and the Ceramulus. The hill itself was called the Palatine and was home to General Crassus, and judging by the magnificent villas that adorned it was also home to Rome's richest residents. Here there were no crowds or shops, just walled villas, immaculately kept roads and quiet. We halted in front of a pair of wooden gates set in a high stone wall at which the road we were on ended. Ajax dismissed the centurion, who marched away with his legionaries. We dismounted and Ajax knocked at one of the gates. A pair of eyes appeared at a peephole and seconds later the gates opened. We rode through them and into a large landscaped garden filled with exotic shrubs, trees and brightly coloured flowers. Gardeners were tending to flower beds while other slaves were feeding huge carp that swam in ornate ponds. It was truly a magnificent place, heavy with sweet scents, and would certainly rival our own royal gardens in Hatra. Two slaves took our horses (Ajax assured me that Remus would be well cared for – I did not doubt him), and then we walked along a path flanked by cypresses to the villa itself, which had a peristyle of white stone columns enclosing the interior of the building itself. A slave approached and bowed to Ajax.

'The master wonders if our guest would like to bathe and change his clothes before he eats.'

'Perhaps a bath and massage before dining, Prince Pacorus?' Ajax said.

'Thank you, that would be most welcome,' I replied.

The massive villa had its own baths, a beautiful tiled structure with a steam room and an adjacent pool of cool water. After washing and steaming the dust and grime of the journey from my limbs, a small, muscular Numibian massaged my body, his strong, bony fingers reaching deep into my joints and sinews. I emerged from his hour-long session feeling refreshed and invigorated; indeed, not since I had left Hatra had I felt so relaxed. I was then led to my room, a large, sumptuous area with a white stone balcony with an intricate stone balustrade that had an impressive view of the city of Rome. The city was huge, its buildings sprawling into the distance. In truth I had never seen such a large city, and at that moment I feared for Spartacus and his army. I also remembered the words of King Ambiorix that Rome never seemed to run out of armies. I understood this now, for you could fit ten cities the size of Hatra inside Rome.

Fresh clothes had been laid out on the bed, a white silk tunic, sandals and a belt of black leather. After I had changed into them a slave came and took my old clothes away to be cleaned, while Ajax also appeared to escort me to dinner. We walked along corridors adorned with marble busts on columns of stern-looking Roman gentlemen and walls painted with beautiful frescos depicting mythical scenes from Rome's ancient history. Ajax ushered me into a medium-sized room that was occupied by a number of large sofas piled with cushions, upon which reclined a man dressed in a white toga, who upon my entering rose and walked towards me.

Ajax stood stiffly to attention. 'Prince Pacorus, may I present to you my master, Marcus Licinius Crassus, senator and general of Rome.'

The man who stood before me was perhaps forty years old, of average height with a full head of neatly cut brown hair. He had a broad forehead, long nose and large ears. His visage was rather severe, accentuated by his rather thin lips. I bowed my head to him, as befitting his rank.

'An honour, sir.'

'The honour is mine, Prince Pacorus.' His voice was deep, his tone serious. He gestured with his right hand towards the sofas. 'Please, be seated so that we may eat.'

I knew that rich Romans liked to eat whilst reclining on sofas, a habit that I found curious but not unpleasant. I reclined on my left side whilst Crassus, his sofa at right angles to mine, reclined on his right side. Ajax clapped his hands and a procession of servants served us a variety of exotic dishes. First we were served salad with asparagus and salted fish. Then followed combinations of game and poultry. The wine we were served was truly wonderful, no doubt made from the finest grapes. I was aware all the time that

Crassus was observing me as I was eating, and noted with surprise that I thanked each slave who offered me a tray of food.

'You find the food to your satisfaction, Prince Pacorus?'

'Very much so, sir.'

'And your room is comfortable?'

'A most impressive view of the city.'

He nodded and sat up on his couch. 'Good. You must be wondering why I asked you here.'

'I assume it was not just for the pleasure of my company.'

'Mm. Let us then get to the matter in hand. I have been entrusted by the Senate and people of Rome with the task of destroying the slave army led by the criminal Spartacus. This being the case, I thought it prudent to meet the man who is responsible for that army being able to vanquish so many of Rome's legions.'

'You flatter me, sir. But I am just a small part of that army.'

'Indeed. Your cavalry is but a small part of the whole, but it is like the keystone in the structure of a bridge. Small, but essential. Take that stone out and the whole edifice collapses.'

The thought suddenly crossed my mind that he intended to have me killed here, today. 'My death will avail you not, for my commanders are all competent and will lead the cavalry without me.'

He was hurt by my suggestion. 'Roman senators are not assassins. If I had wanted you dead I would not have invited you to my house.'

'My apologies. But why did you ask me here?'

He clicked his fingers and held out his silver goblet, which was filled by a slave holding a jug of wine. 'To make you an offer, Prince Pacorus. I am willing to pass over your campaign of rapine in Italy, on condition that you leave this land. Should you agree, I will arrange for your passage and safe conduct back to Hatra. I will even organise a safe passage for your woman.'

'My woman?' He seemed to be well informed.

He sighed, as though disappointed by my underestimation of him. 'I have in my study reports from the provinces of Bruttium, Lucania, Campania, Apulia, Samnium, Picenum and Umbria of a long-haired warrior riding a white horse with a blonde-haired woman riding with him, who with their band of mounted archers have cut a trail of destruction throughout Italy. They call him, that is to say you, "the Parthian", and your woman "blonde everto", the blonde demon. Were you a mere brigand leading a band of raiders you could be easily dealt with, but this Spartacus has trained his slaves well, and you are the instrument that gives him victory.'

'I think you overestimate me…'

He rose from his couch and waved his right hand at me. 'Do not insult me, young prince. I have studied the battles that you have won and the methods you use. Your cavalry is his eyes and ears and the thing that makes this villain victorious.'

I was immensely proud. He noticed my pleasure. 'That this is a source of pride to you is understandable, though I wonder what your father would say if he knew that his son was in an army of cutthroats and criminals, a highborn prince cavorting with lowly slaves.'

'My father? What do you know of my father?'

He regained his seat and his composure. 'I know that King Varaz is a mighty warrior who over two years ago led a great raid into Syria, attacking the towns of Hierapolis, Boroea and Chalcis. He reached the sea at Antioch before returning to Hatra. He too left a trail of destruction; unlike you he did not get captured. It seems that laying waste a country runs in your family.'

'That expedition was in retaliation for a Roman invasion of my father's kingdom.'

A wry smile crossed his face. 'That is a moot point, but let us put it aside for the moment. Surely you wish to see your father and homeland again?'

More than he could ever imagine. 'I do, but to abandon my men would be dishonourable.'

He laughed. 'Honour, you speak of honour? Was there honour when Spartacus burned and looted Forum Anii or Metapontum? Would you speak of honour to the relatives of those who were butchered in those and other places by his soldiers and your horsemen? This man you follow, this Spartacus, is nothing more than a deserter from the Roman Army, a man who took to banditry who, after he was captured, was given a second chance. Instead of being condemned to be a galley slave or to work in the mines, he was given the chance to atone for his misdeeds by becoming a gladiator. But what does he do? Spits in the face of Rome a second time and instigates a rebellion.'

'Spartacus saved my life,' I said coolly. 'And I count him as a friend.'

'Then you should be more careful in the choice of your friends. Be that as it may. As I said earlier, I have been tasked with suppressing this slave revolt, and I intend to do so. I am first and foremost a businessman. I own silver mines in Spain, landed estates in Italy and Greece, some of which you and your compatriots have burned and liberated, so-called, the slaves who worked on them, as well as a number of properties in Rome itself. Spartacus and his slaves have thus directly harmed my interests, therefore the coming campaign is both personal as well as being in the service of the state.'

'How do you know that you will not suffer the same fate as the previous Roman commanders who were sent against us?' I asked.

'A fair question. I will tell you why. Firstly, the legions I will lead will be financed from my own pocket, and I am not the sort of man to waste money on ill-advised ventures. You will find them of sterner stuff than those you have previously encountered. Secondly, another army is on the way and will presently land at the port of Brundisium. You will, in fact, be trapped between two armies and vastly outnumbered. Finally, as we speak a third army is marching from Spain and will be in Italy in the new year. So you see, Prince Pacorus, whatever you do the end result will be the same. I merely wish to expedite the sequence of events.'

He was probably bluffing, and yet there was no hint of gloating in his voice or exaggeration, just a calm recounting of facts.

He clicked his fingers and a slave appeared with a bowl of water, in which Crassus washed his hands. Another slave offered him a towel to dry them. Two slaves performed the same duty for me.

'An excellent meal.' I said. 'Your hospitality is most generous.'

'Then take advantage of it some more. Accept my offer and go home, because I can assure you that once I take the field I will not rest until this slave uprising has been crushed and all those who have taken part in it have been destroyed. That is the promise that I have made in the temple of my ancestors, and that is the promise I give to you.'

'It is a fair offer, sir, and one that only a fool would refuse.'

He smiled at me, the first time he had done so. 'And you are going to be a fool.' He raised his hands and let them fall by his side. 'I understand. Honour, that invisible thing that holds so many individuals and families in its grip. But in this instance, I fear that your honour will also be your executioner.'

I laughed out loud and he looked at me quizzically. 'Sorry, sir. It's just that someone else told me that not so long ago.'

'He is obviously a man of some sense, you should listen to him. But it is late. Please sleep on the matter and give me your answer in the morning.'

Despite being in the house of my enemy I slept well that night, the gentle sound of fountains underneath my balcony soothing my senses. One thing was certain, this Crassus was a very wealthy individual and obviously a man of some power. I had no way of knowing if what he had told me about the army landing at Brundisium and the other marching from Spain was true, but why would he lie? If it were true, then Spartacus would indeed be in a perilous position. And yet we had beaten Roman armies before, and I comforted myself with that fact before I slipped into a deep sleep.

The next morning I rose early, just after dawn, and took breakfast in my room. I asked to be taken to the stables where I found Remus being groomed by two young stable hands. I then went to pay my respects to my host, and was escorted to his study, a well-appointed office with a large desk in the centre flanked by two marble busts on chest-high stone columns. One of the busts resembled Crassus, who was seated at his desk pouring over a number of scrolls.

'Good morning. Have you eaten?'

'Yes, sir, thank you.'

He caught me looking at his marble likeness. 'My father, Publius Licinius Crassus, and the other one is my brother, Publius.'

'Do they also live in Rome?'

'Both dead, killed during one of our civil wars that happen from time to time.'

'Killed in battle?'

He rolled up the scroll he had been reading and looked at me. 'Alas, no. They were killed when the side that they were fighting against captured Rome and executed all those of the opposing faction. I escaped the slaughter because I happened to be outside the city inspecting a family estate at the time. I managed to flee to Spain before the enemy's troops could get hold of me.'

'The gods must have protected you that day, much like Shamash has looked over me thus far.'

'Shamash?'

'A Parthian god, and a powerful one.'

He looked at me with a bemused expression.

'The gods, young prince, are invented so that the masses, miserable as their existences invariably are, believe that there is a better life waiting for them after they have toiled through this one. But they endure this misery in the belief that the gods will reserve for them a place in heaven, where they will reside for all eternity in eternal bliss and free from pain, disease and the other afflictions that made their lives miserable in this life.'

I was shocked. 'You do not believe in the gods?'

'Of course not. Important men have better things to do with their time than prostrate themselves before stone idols.'

'I believe that Shamash protects me when I ride into battle.'
'Of course, you have the youthful belief in invulnerability and immortality. And it suits your purpose to believe that you have a mighty warrior god fighting beside you. I imagine that you believe him to look like you as well. This woman of yours, for example, is she beautiful? Does she eclipse the sun with her perfection and dazzle you when she smiles?'
'Yes, she is like a goddess, sir.'
He clapped his hands. 'Of course. Have you noticed that all the statues and paintings of gods and goddesses depict them as being all young and beautiful. No deformed bodies, twisted limbs or ugly faces among the immortals. The poor believe in the gods, while princes and kings seek to become them.'
'I try to live my life so that Shamash will be pleased with me, so that He will smile on Hatra and the Parthian Empire.'
'Alas, much as I would like to argue religion with you, I have much to do today and regret that I cannot spend any more time talking with you.' He leaned back in his chair. 'Have you changed your mind?'
'No, sir.'
'That is unfortunate. You will go back to the slave army?'
'Yes, sir, for to do otherwise would bring shame and dishonour upon myself and my father.'
'Very well. I can see that more words would be wasted. But remember my promise, Prince Pacorus. When you leave my house you will be my enemy once again, and one that I intend to hunt down and destroy. If we should meet again, you will find that I will be acting on the orders of the Senate and people of Rome, and they will expect retribution for what you have done.'
'I understand, sir.'
He rose from his chair and walked round his desk to face me. He nodded in approval, I like to think, and then offered me his hand. I took it.
'Farewell, Prince Pacorus. It was a pleasure meeting with you.'
'You too, sir.'
After I had left his study, Remus was brought to me and I rode from the villa accompanied once again by Ajax. This time we did not have an escort and it took us some time to descend the Palatine. Once again the streets heaved with a mass of humanity speaking many tongues aside from Latin. Today was if anything even busier than yesterday, as attested to by Ajax, who informed me that it was a market day when all the farmers who lived outside Rome brought their produce into the city to sell. Indeed, we had to take a detour

as several streets had been closed to traffic to allow the farmers to set up their stalls along designated 'market streets'. The smells that came from these streets confirmed that goods on sale included goats, sheep, fish, cured meats, spices and cheese. I asked Ajax if it would be possible to visit the Forum, the site that was the very centre of the Roman Empire itself.

'Of course, sir. My master instructed that you were to be shown whatever sites you wished to visit before you left. He asks only that you do not proclaim your identity to all and sundry.'

I smiled. 'That would be most sensible, I think.'

We left our horses at one of the properties owned by Crassus, an apartment block that had a shop selling leather goods on the ground floor and stables around a courtyard immediately behind it. Ajax gave orders that the horses were to be groomed and fed (Remus had never been groomed so many times in so short a space of time), and that we would return for them later. It was mid-morning when we walked to the valley between the Palatine, Quirinal and Viminal hills, the location of the Forum. Unfortunately, the entire Roman Empire seemed to have had the same idea, for the paved open space was a seething press of people. But they were dwarfed by the magnificent buildings that enclosed the area, white colonnaded structures with red-tiled roofs. The senate house itself, though having impressive bronze doors, was actually the least impressive building in the Forum. The grandest were the temples: tall, imposing structures built to pay homage to deities called Saturn, Vulcan, Concordia, Vesta and Castor. I noticed a large group of young men gathered at the doors of the senate house and asked Ajax who they were.

'The sons of senators who are currently sitting inside, sir. They listen to the debates so that one day they will be familiar with its procedures, and will thus be able to take their place as senators when their time comes.'

'Is your master debating today.'

'No, sir, he has more pressing matters to attend to.'

'Such as planning to crush the slave rebellion.'

He looked sheepish and uncomfortable. 'Yes, sir.'

I also noticed a large wooden platform in front of the senate house, on which a speaker was addressing a crowd. I also noticed that there were spikes mounted on either side of it. Ajax told me that the platform was called a rostra and was used by speakers to harangue the crowds. The heads of notable Romans who were on the losing side in Rome's seemingly frequent civil wars were mounted on the spikes. I wondered if the heads of the father and brother of General Crassus had ended up here. After an hour we left the Forum and retraced our steps back to where our horses were stabled. After a meal of bread and cheese we began our journey out of the city. We left via the Porta Collina and rode east. After ten miles I halted and bade Ajax farewell. He told me that the latest news he had heard was that the slave army had moved further south, towards Campania. I shook his hand and asked whether he would reconsider his decision about joining us. He said no, and who could blame him? He may have been a slave, but he enjoyed a position of power serving a powerful Roman senator.

I rode hard and camped for the night at a miserable place called a hospitium, a wretched hovel where I had to share a large, draughty room with around a dozen stinking fellow travellers. In the morning I had to hunt down and kill the lice that had migrated from them to me, but from talking with them I did learn that Spartacus had camped fifty miles southeast of Rome. It took another day to reach the army, the diminishing number of travellers on the road a sure sign that I was getting close to its camp. On a drizzly autumn morning, with my cloak wrapped around me in a futile attempt to keep dry, I ran into a patrol of cavalry armed with spears and shields. I recognised them at once as being part of Burebista's dragon. Fortunately, they also recognised me and told me that the army was five miles away.

'Any sign of the enemy?' I asked their commander.

'No, lord.'

I dismissed them and carried on with my journey. An hour later I was in the arms of Gallia , brushing away the tears of joy as I told her that I loved her and would never leave her side again. It was so good to see her, as well as Godarz, Gafarn, Nergal, Burebista and Diana, even the wild Rubi gave me a sort of smile. Godarz informed me that we would be moving south into Campania within two days, and Nergal said that he had patrols operating up to fifty miles away from the army.

'So far, highness, they have not encountered any Romans.'

Later that day I rode with Gallia to see Spartacus, and found him on the training ground practising his swordsmanship. He stopped when he saw me and we embraced.

'Not tempted to become a Roman, then?'

'No, lord. But I must speak with you about a matter of some importance.'

We walked back to his tent where we found a blooming Claudia darning one of his tunics. We hugged each other and I told her that pregnancy suited her.

'And having you back suits Gallia,' she smiled. 'Don't go away again.'

'No, lady.'

Spartacus told me to wait in his tent and then went to fetch the other members of the war council, leaving me alone with Gallia and Claudia.

'What did you think of Rome, Pacorus?' Claudia asked me.

'It was unlike any city I have ever seen, huge and imposing.'

'Is Hatra not large?' said Gallia.

I took her hand. 'It is, but in truth it could fit inside Rome many times.'

Half an hour later Spartacus returned, along with Akmon, Castus, Cannicus and Afranius. Castus gave me a bear hug.

'There was a rumour that you had joined the Vestal Virgins, but I said you were too ugly for them.'

'And certainly not a virgin' said Akmon, at which Gallia blushed.

When we had all settled into chairs and wetted our lips with wine, I told them of the meeting I had had with Crassus.

'He is rich, that much is true. His reputation for greed is known throughout Italy,' said Spartacus. 'I talked with Godarz while you were away, and he had certainly heard of Marcus Licinius Crassus, of his reputation anyway.'

'He told me that in addition to the army he was raising, another army was going to land at Brundisium and a third was on its way from Spain.'

Akmon looked at me. 'Do you think he was trying to awe you with his power?'

'That was part of it, but he was also sending a message to you, lord.'

Spartacus nodded to himself. 'That the only outcome of this war would be our slaughter.'

'Yes. How did you know?'

'Because that's the only fate for slaves who rebel. Death. And that's why he would only speak to you. You are a royal prince whereas we are lower than animals. Their pride forbids any Roman to talk to a slave as an equal.'

'There is one thing more,' I said.

All eyes were on me. I took another gulp of wine. 'He offered me safe passage out of Italy, back to Hatra.' I glanced at Gallia. 'Along with Gallia.'

Spartacus' expression did not change. 'So why are you still here?'

'Because all of you are my friends and I will not abandon you. And I could not go back to Hatra having abandoned my friends. This I told Crassus.'

'And your honour forbids you from deserting this army, doesn't it?' Akmon's tone was one of mockery but I also detected a hint of admiration in his voice.

'That too.'

'Well, then,' said Spartacus, 'it would appear that Hatra will have to do without you awhile yet.'

Chapter 16

Crassus was as good as his word. It took us three months to reach Rhegium in the toe of Italy, marching down the Via Annia. The journey was straightforward enough, but the army that Crassus had raised in Rome snapped at our heels like a dog and we were forced on a number of occasions to halt and form a battle line. We beat off their probing attacks with ease, but we could not shake them, and Spartacus was unwilling to risk a battle with the threat of other Roman legions coming from Brundisium. He did not realise it, but the movements of Crassus were dictating his strategy.

'We don't know if any enemy troops will even land at Brundisium, lord,' I said.

It was a cloudy day but humid. Spartacus was marching on foot as usual, though he had insisted that Claudia, now she was pregnant, should ride on a cart. A bad-tempered mule pulled the two-wheeled contraption and Spartacus had a firm grip on its bridle.

'I know that, but if we can stay ahead of Crassus then there is no need to fight him, at least not yet. In any case, I hope to move the army across to Sicily within a month, and then we won't have to fight anyone. And once in Sicily it will be extremely difficult for the Romans to attack us.'

'We can't swim across the Strait of Messina,' muttered Akmon, whose mood had an uncanny knack of matching the overcast weather.

'Two miles?' said Spartacus. 'I think I could swim that. What about you Pacorus?'

I was shocked. 'Swim? Across the sea, you are not serious?'

Spartacus smiled. 'Well, I might make Akmon swim. But the rest of us will be using boats.'

'Boats?' Akmon was unconvinced. 'Where are you going to get boats from?'

'The Cilician pirates, my friend. They have plenty of boats and we have lots of Roman gold and silver. If we pay them, they will transport us.'

'They might also betray us,' I said. 'We should not put our trust in such people.'

'Unfortunately,' replied Spartacus, 'we don't have much choice. When the army decided it did not want to leave Italy, Sicily was the only practical option, and to get there we have to get across the Strait of Messina. The pirates are the only ones who have the means to get us there. The alternative is to stay in Italy, and I believe Crassus when he says that the Romans will not tolerate that.'

'The Cilicians it is, then,' said Akmon.

The army marched at a slow pace, for it took three hours each day to take down our palisaded camp and another three at the end of the day to put it up again. But with the Romans so close it was unwise to risk camping without defences. So every day over fifty thousand troops, their equipment, the non-combatants and thousands more animals were herded into an area surrounded by a freshly dug earth mounds surmounted by wooden stakes. Even my horsemen were in camp and so we also became expert with the spade and pick.

The geography of Bruttium is mostly mountainous, with lush green forests on the lower slopes. Most of the people lived on or near the rocky coast, and the small villages dotted along the coastline seemed to literally hang from the rock face next to the sea. The sea was always a deep blue or turquoise, and the land was often draped in a clammy mist. The forests themselves, vast stretches of oak, ash, maple and chestnut trees, were full of red deer, roe deer, brown bears, wolves and eagles. Eventually we reached the port of Rhegium, a bustling centre of naval activity whose harbour was crammed with vessels of every description. The city was situated on the lower slopes of a long, craggy mountain range. The mountains were steep-sided and formed of overlapping terraces. Around the port, along the coastal strip, citrus fruits, vines and olives grew in abundance.

The city's walls were decayed and neglected, and as we rode through the large though crumbling gatehouse, I could tell that this was a place that had seen better days. Godarz had told me that it had more than once sided with Rome's enemies and had paid the price when Rome had invariably triumphed. There appeared to be no garrison, or none that would face us. The forum and basilica were insignificant compared to those in Rome, the basilica being a long, rectangular covered hall with a nave, aisles and an apse at both ends. But the roof was missing. Many tiles and the plaster on the exterior walls were crumbling. Nevertheless, the port was obviously thriving and as we rode towards the harbour area the traffic on the road increased so much that we were forced to dismount and walk through the throng. There were half a dozen of us: myself, Spartacus, Godarz, Akmon, Nergal and Domitus. It occurred to me that a few Roman archers could have destroyed the leadership of our army, and probably the whole rebellion, with only a handful of arrows.

We eventually arrived at the docks where Spartacus pointed out a warship with a bronze ram and two banks of oars each side. The vessel was tied to the main quay and was guarded by a group of muscled sailors with skin darkened by the sun and long black hair around their shoulders. They each wore earrings and carried scimitars at their waists. None wore anything on their feet but all had gold rings on their fingers. Their baggy knee-length trousers and dirty vests completed their appearance. They did indeed look like pirates. They lounged around the gangplank that led onto the vessel, though when Spartacus approached them all four picked up short spears and barred the way.

Spartacus halted a few feet from the man standing in front of the rest, a nasty looking individual with a scar that ran from the right side of his forehead down to his jaw. He had black eyes that narrowed as Spartacus neared him.

'Greetings, friend. I am looking for a representative of the Cilician pirates.'

Their leader said nothing but stood his ground. I moved my right hand to the hilt of my sword.

'Who wants to know?'

Spartacus smiled. 'A man who could make him very rich.'

Their leader shrugged and relaxed his stance. 'You're lucky. Our local representative is about to ship out with us in a couple of days. He thinks it will be safer to go back to Crete for a while. Most of the ships you see in the harbour are leaving, too. The Roman boats cleared out days ago, apart from those who are too brave or foolish to do otherwise.'

'Really?' said Spartacus. 'Why is that?'

The leader laughed. 'Where have you been? Don't you know that there is a huge slave army on its way? Led by a gladiator called Spartacus, so they say. He's got the Romans running scared, I can tell you. He'll squash this place like a fist flattens a fly when he gets here.'

'So will you take me to see your representative?'

The leader said something to the other men, who put down their spears and began to talk among themselves. 'Follow me.'

We trailed after him along the quay and into an alleyway beside two huge warehouses that by the smell of them were used to hold pigs, then along a paved road for two hundred yards, before arriving at the gates of a white-walled villa. Two guards, dressed in similar attire to the sailors we had met earlier, stood sentry at the gates. Our guide waved them aside and we entered the villa's grounds, which comprised flower beds bisected by a wide curving path that led to the two-story villa itself. Two more guards stood at the entrance to the villa, but they too let us pass when they saw our guide. Inside, slaves were hurrying from room to room, carrying chests, papers and clothes. Our guide told us to wait while he went to find the master of the house.

'Looks like they are leaving in a hurry,' I said.

'Obviously your infamy has preceded you,' said Akmon to Spartacus.

After a couple of minutes our guide returned with a gaudily dressed man beside him. His skin was dark brown, as were his eyes, and his teeth flashed brilliant white when he saw us. His clothes were a bright ensemble of greens and reds, while on his feet he wore expensive red leather shoes that curled up at the toes. On his head he wore a white turban that had a red ruby sewn into its front. He wore gold on his fingers and I could have sworn that he was also wearing perfume.

'Welcome, welcome. Salcia has told me that you wish to hire our services.'

The man called Salcia whispered into his ear and the pirate chief bowed his head to Spartacus.

'My name is Sherash Patelli, representative of the Cilician pirates in the Ionian and Tyrrhenian seas. Whom do I have the honour of addressing?'

Spartacus stood erect and proud, his massive shoulders and chest extended. 'I am Spartacus, general of the slave army, and these are my lieutenants.'

Patelli blinked and then tried to say something, but though his mouth opened no words came out. Salcia gazed wide-eyed at us, while around us the servants stopped their activity to stare. Where there had been bustle and noise, there was now silence.

'Perhaps it would be better if we could discuss matters more privately,' suggested Spartacus.

'Of course, of course,' said Patelli, quickly regaining his composure and clapping his hands at his servants. 'Stop what you are doing and bring us wine and sweet meats to my office. Hurry, hurry!'

His office was a large room that had marble tiles on the floor, a massive wooden desk, richly adorned bronze seats and couches around the walls. Patelli sat behind his expansive desk and invited us to sit. Spartacus did so directly opposite him. The rest of us sat behind Spartacus on the bronze seats that were first put in place by servants.

Patelli had recovered from his shock and now the slippery businessman in him took over. I noticed that he frequently brought his hands together in front of him as he talked, then placed them on the table, before once again bringing them together. A clerk stood on his right side taking notes as the negotiations got under way.

'Your coming is fortuitous, general,' said Patelli, 'for it means that we no longer have to leave. I take it that you do not mean to burn the town.'

'I have not decided, but when I do you shall be the first to know. Where is the garrison and governor.'

Patelli raised his hands in exclamation. 'He and his soldiers left yesterday, leaving the town at, er, your mercy. But to business. How may I be of assistance to you?'

'I intend to move my army to Sicily. For this I will need to hire your ships.'

Patelli nodded gravely. 'I see. And what sort of figures are we talking about?'

Spartacus turned and looked at Godarz, while behind us a host of slaves came into the room carrying platters filled with sweat meats, pastries, fresh fruit and nuts, while others brought jugs of wine.

Godarz reeled off the figures. 'Nearly sixty thousand people, four thousand horses and around ten thousand other livestock, plus wagons, carts and supplies for the army.'

Patelli's eyes lit up when he was told this, for such an immense load of people and animals would mean a lot of ships, and a lot of ships would mean much gold flowing into Cilician coffers. As we drank his superb wine and ate his exquisite morsels, he sat back in his chair and placed his hands on his portly belly. He smiled.

'My friends, this is truly a great day. For Sandon, our god of war, has smiled upon you all. Only the Cilicians can fulfil such a mighty task, and I want you to know that subject to an equitable price being agreed, you can look forward to being in Sicily within three months.'

'Three months?' Spartacus was surprised at this. 'Why so long?'

'Unfortunately, my friends, we are fulfilling a previously agreed and paid for contract with the Romans.'

'I thought you were at war with the Romans?' spat Akmon, wine running down his tunic.

'Rome rules the land, we rule the sea. Whatever the Romans say, they need our ships to supply them with,' he looked sheepish, 'slaves, and sometimes to transport their troops.'

'What troops?' I asked.

Patelli looked alarmed. 'So many questions, and yet I do not know all your names.'

I stood and pointed at Akmon. 'This man is second to General Spartacus. His name is Akmon and he is a Thracian like my lord.

Godarz,' I looked at my fellow Parthian, 'is the quartermaster general of the army. While this man, named Domitus, is a Roman and our loyal comrade.' Domitus tipped his silver goblet at me.
'And you?' queried Patelli.
'My name is Prince Pacorus, and I command the army's horseman.'
Patelli nodded. 'You are the Parthian, the one who rides a white horse.'
I sat back down. 'Yes.'
'Your fame precedes you, and I thank you for the introductions. But the fact is that my hands are tied until we transport the army of General Lucullus from Macedonia to the port of Brundisium, for we have been paid in advance for our services.'
My heart sank and I felt sick to my stomach. So Crassus had been telling the truth and a new army was indeed coming to southern Italy. We were at the end of a peninsula with no way of escaping. We had one Roman army directly to the north and another would soon be marching west to join it. We were truly trapped, and to make matters worse we were at the mercy of this greedy pirate who sat opposite us.
To his credit, Spartacus betrayed no emotion as he stood and nodded his head to Patelli. 'Thank you for your time. I await your decision as to the price of renting your ships and a date when you can transport us to Sicily. My camp will be north of Rhegium.'
Later that day, at a meeting of the war council, Spartacus was in a subdued mood, no doubt reflecting on how he had allowed himself to be boxed in by the legions of Crassus, which were hovering to the north. Too far away to be of immediate danger, but casting a dark shadow over us all.
'There is nothing to stop us attacking Crassus while we wait for these pirates to assemble their ships,' said Akmon.
'That would certainly give us the advantage,' I added. 'At the very least my horse could harry him and keep him on the defensive.'
'What do your scouts report at the moment?' asked Spartacus.
I shrugged. 'Nothing. They are sitting in their camp doing nothing. And when they send out cavalry patrols they retreat as soon as they see any of my men.'
'He's waiting for reinforcements to arrive from Brundisium, that's why he's quiet,' said Akmon. 'And that's why we should attack.'
Spartacus drummed his fingers on the table, while outside the wind lashed the outside of the tent. Winter in Bruttium was mostly mild I was told, but was prone to frequent and violent storms, one of which was now blasting our living quarters with high winds and a

heavy downpour. Godarz had organised the building of temporary stables for the horses, made from the logs and wicker panels, as I suspected that Spartacus would not budge from this place of his own volition. I was proved right.

He made a fist and slammed it on the table. 'No! We stay here as long as the Romans remain where they are. If we advance north and defeat Crassus, what then? If we destroy him, we will still have to come back here if we want to get to Sicily. We will be shedding blood for nothing.'

'And once those reinforcements arrive we will be shedding a lot more blood,' added Akmon, grimly.

'It's three hundred miles between here and Brundisium,' snapped Spartacus. 'We shall have plenty of time to decide what to do.'

'Do you trust that pirate, Spartacus?' asked Castus.

'Not really, but I can see that he is a greedy little bastard and he knows that we have a lot of gold. That's why he will do business with us. In the meantime, we stay here and keep our swords sharp.'

The enforced stay meant we could devote more time to training and drills, and as an added bonus we practised on the seashore, the long, narrow beaches of mainly sand with a sprinkling of pebbles being ideal for the horses to stretch their legs. We planted targets in the sea, ran our mounts along the wet sand at the water's edge and loosed arrows at circles of tightly packed straw strung between two poles standing in the water, while on other beaches Burebista's dragon fought mock battles with their lances tipped with bundles of cloth and used small, long sacks crammed full of leaves instead of swords for close-quarter combat. It was great fun and all the horsemen and women wanted to take part in the 'sack battles'. On one occasion a thousand horsemen on a ten-mile stretch of beach fought a mock battle, though what started out as a serious drill aimed at perfecting company level manoeuvres descending into hilarity as companies tried to outflank each other and ended up riding their horses into the sea until the water lapped around the beasts' shoulders, with men hitting each other with sacks soaked in seawater. Gallia's women took part and hit their opponents with gusto, until the sacks burst and the whole beach was covered with leaves. Afterwards we groomed and tended the horses, collected driftwood and had a giant feast after I gave orders that several bulls were to be slaughtered. As we watched the sun go down in the western sky, over a calm and smooth sea, I held Gallia close and wrapped her in my cloak.

'Well, soon we will be on this island of Sicily and then we can think about getting back to Hatra.'

She turned and looked at me, the gentle wind ruffling her hair ever so slightly. 'Do you truly believe that?'

'Of course, we have only to wait a few more weeks and then we will be out of Italy.'

She laid her head on my shoulder. 'The Romans will follow us wherever we go. Of that I am certain.'

But the Romans seemed far away as the weeks rolled by, and as the new year dawned we almost forgot that they existed. I sent out patrols to alert us of any movements by Crassus' legions, but they merely stayed behind their palisades and waited. But while we trained, sharpened our weapons and kept our bowstrings taught, a new enemy emerged.

'We are running short of supplies' said Godarz, pacing up and down Spartacus' tent. He pointed at me. 'Each horse eats around twenty pounds in weight of fodder a day and there are nearly four thousand of them.'

'We can confiscate all the hay and grain from this area,' I replied.

Godarz stopped pacing and put his hands on his hips in frustration. 'I've already done that, and we are still running out of food. This is a poor area for hay. Pasture and grain are also not in abundance.'

'How long before you run out of food for the horses?' asked Spartacus, drawing the point of his dagger across his desk.

'A month,' replied Godarz, 'perhaps less.'

'Then we shall have to go north and replenish our supplies,' I said. 'Lucania should be able to fulfil our needs.'

'There's a Roman army between here and there,' mused Akmon.

I did not think it much of a threat. 'I'll swing east and go around it. Crassus won't budge while the main army remains here.'

'No, he won't,' said Spartacus, idly. He jumped out of his chair. 'And we will use that to our advantage.'

'How? asked Castus.

'It's simple.'

'It is?' I was confused.

'Pacorus, you are right when you say that you will have to go north, but instead of Lucania I think it would be best if you went to Brundisium.'

Akmon laughed. 'So you solve the problem of feeding the cavalry by getting them all killed. It was a pleasure knowing you, Pacorus, and I hope you have a good death.'

I stared at Spartacus in disbelief.

'Don't look at me like that. Listen. Take your cavalry and raid Brundisium while the Romans are disembarking their army. Surprise them and hit them hard. They won't be expecting an assault, because as far as they know we are all nicely boxed in at Rhegium. Hit them hard and then get back here as fast as you can. When you return I will attack Crassus while you assault him from the rear. And then hopefully our pirate friends will have their ships ready to take us to Sicily.'

Akmon was shaking his head. 'It's a risky plan, Spartacus. If Pacorus loses then we lose his cavalry, and his horsemen have been the difference between victory and defeat on more than one occasion.'

'Akmon,' I said. 'you flatter me, but you shouldn't, really.'

He snarled at me. 'I only want you to live so you can provide a screen while we embark on the ships for Sicily. Then we'll leave you to the tender mercy of Crassus. You can wave at me from your cross as I sail across the Strait of Messina.'

'Crassus will have scouts out like us, Spartacus,' said Castus. 'It will not be easy slipping three thousand cavalry past him.'

Spartacus sat back down in his chair and grinned. He was in a good mood at the prospect of doing something at last. 'Don't worry about that, we will undertake a little diversion to get friend Crassus' attention.'

'An attack on his camp?' asked Akmon.

'A small diversion, nothing more. I will send Afranius and his Spaniards. Who knows, perhaps he will destroy Crassus all on his own.'

'More likely get himself killed,' sniffed Akmon.

'When do I leave, lord?' I asked.

'In two days, Pacorus.'

Godarz nodded approvingly. 'That will certainly alleviate the supply situation.'

The day before we left was a rain-lashed affair that drenched the ground and reduced the avenues in our camp to rivers of glutinous mud. I sat with Gallia in my tent as the wind made great indentations in its side. Though it was not normally cold, today the wind and the rain had reduced the temperature to such an extent that we sat in chairs with our cloaks wrapped around one another, and held our hands to the coals of a brazier. Her hair was tied into a plait and her eyes appeared icily blue. As soon as she had heard of the great raid she was determined to accompany me, she and her group of women. I knew that the men would not object, as they had come to view her women archers as good luck charms. I was far from happy, though.

'That is your final word, then?'

She flashed a stern look at me. 'It is.'

'I don't suppose I could appeal to your better nature.'

'No.'

'I can't guarantee your safety.'

Her face melted into an expression of affection and sympathy. 'Oh, Pacorus, ever the valiant knight. Do you think that I am safer sitting here than riding with you to Brundisium? Of course not. But if I am to die I would prefer to do so killing Romans, and so would my women. And if I am to die I want to do so fighting beside you.'

I shuddered. 'So be it, though I think it would be better to leave Diana behind. I fear she has no heart for being a soldier.'

Gallia laughed. 'Yes, she is not an Amazon.'

'A what?'

'The Amazons were a race of women warriors who lived on the island of Lemnos in the Aegean Sea. That is what we call ourselves, the Amazons.'

'A truly terrifying idea, my love. Perhaps I should stay here while you and your women burn Brundisium, and I can wait for the pirate ships to arrive.'

She looked at me with amusement. 'You think that the pirates will honour their agreement?'

'Why not? We have already paid their representative, Patelli, a deposit in gold. Besides, they will make a lot of money from dealing with us.'

'Do you know that the Cilician pirates make most of their money from the slave trade? Their main slave market is on an island called Delos, north of Crete. They capture Roman trade vessels and enslave their crews, then sell the same crews back to the Romans as slaves. They raid all over the Mediterranean and take who and what they want. Greed is their only motivation. Spartacus is a fool to think they will do his bidding.'

'I thought you liked him,' I said.

'I do. He is like a brother to me. But what's that to do with anything? He is still a fool to trust anyone save those that are around him. Even the lowliest soldier in his army knows that we can only look to ourselves for our safety. These pirates are, if we are to believe them, at this very moment working for the Romans. Do you think the Romans will want them being our mules afterwards?'

I leaned back in my chair. 'If, as you say, the pirates are only interested in profit, then why shouldn't they work for us?'

Her blue eyes narrowed. 'Because the Romans have the money to persuade them to do otherwise.'

'I would have thought that the Romans would be glad to see the back of us.'

She raised her eyes to the ceiling in exasperation. 'The Romans will not rest until we are wiped out. You know so little about them. They are ruled by pride and vanity, and the existence of this army is a gross insult to both of those vices. They can't parade themselves as masters of the world with an army of slaves roaming at will throughout Italy.'

'The Romans are not the masters of the world, my sweet. They cannot fight everybody.'

She shrugged and then grinned. 'Do the Parthians believe that they are better than the Romans?'

'Of course not,' I said. 'We know we are better. After all, no Roman army has ever stepped foot on Parthian soil and survived, and yet here am I leading horsemen in the Romans' backyard.'

She threw a cushion at me. 'Is that why you stay? To prove that you are better than the Romans; is that not vanity?'

'You know why I stay. To be with you.'

'Ah, so if I said I wanted to leave tomorrow would you accompany me?'

'To where?'

'What does it matter? Would you leave with me, leave the army, leave Spartacus and your horsemen?'

'Yes.'

She studied me for a moment. 'Are you giving that answer because you know I would never ask that of you?'

'No, it is the truth. If you asked me to leave with you then I would go, because I could not live without you.'

My answer obviously delighted her, because she rose from her chair and wrapped her arms around my shoulders. 'You must love me if you are willing to sacrifice your honour for me.'

'I love you more than life itself, Gallia.'

She kissed me tenderly on the cheek. 'I promise that I will never ask anything of you that would compromise your honour.'

At that moment the flap of the tent was thrown open and a sodden Claudia stood at the entrance, the wind flapping her sodden dress that clung to her body, emphasising her large belly. Gallia and I were momentarily stunned by the apparition that was before us, before Gallia leapt from her chair and wrapped Claudia in her cloak. She ushered her into the tent while I secured the flap. Before I did so I shouted to one of the guards huddled in an eight-man tent feet away that he should take the horses that had been pulling Claudia's cart to the temporary stables made from wood and canvas. It was raining so hard that I could see barely fifty feet in front of me. Why had Claudia made a journey in such inclement weather? Inside the tent Gallia was drying Claudia's hair by the brazier with a towel and ordered me to fetch some hot broth. So outside I went again and commanded another guard to fetch us a pot of hot broth from the field kitchens. I returned and was told by Gallia to wait outside until Claudia had changed into one of my tunics and leggings. This was ridiculous! I was kept waiting just long enough for the wind and rain to soak me to the skin, before being summoned back inside, though I did relieve a thoroughly sodden and unhappy spearman who was struggling with his spear and shield while carrying an earthenware pot containing food.

'Are you ill, lady?' I asked, handing Claudia a plate of steaming thick broth.

'Of course she isn't,' snapped Gallia, glaring at me and placing another dry towel around Claudia's neck.

'Thank you,' Claudia said, rather weakly, 'you are very kind. I needed to see you both.'

'You should have waited until this storm passed, lady. You don't want to make yourself ill in your condition.'

'I needed to see you both today, before you left.' She put down her wooden plate and looked at Gallia, welling tears coming to her eyes. 'You two are my only hope.'

Gallia embraced her and tried to comfort her as Claudia sobbed, about what I did not know, and feared to ask a simple question lest my head was bitten off once more. Eventually Claudia composed herself and gobbled up all her broth. Then we all sat in silence for what seemed like an eternity, the only sound being the wind toying with the sides and roof of the tent. Gallia was content to sit while Claudia decided to reveal her mystery, while I drummed my fingers on one of the tent poles, until Gallia froze me with a look that told me to desist. I was putting on a new tunic when Claudia began to speak, in a low monotone voice that made her sound as though she was in a trance.

'Last night I had a dream in which I saw the whole of this army destroyed and the earth soaked in its blood. I was walking barefoot among the broken, lifeless bodies, pierced by arrow, sword and spear. Black eyes stared up at me and gore engulfed me on all sides, but as I walked among the fallen I felt no sensation in my feet. Though I glided through horror no mark was made on the pure white dress I wore. And then I realised that I too was dead, and was but a wraith moving unseen among the dead.

'I wandered for a great length of time, and still the ground was covered with dead, both Roman and slave, but as I moved I saw ahead a warrior on a mighty black horse. It was the Thracian Horseman. As I got near to him I saw that the warrior was dressed wholly in black, black boots, leggings, tunic and helmet. And though his helmet was open I could not see his face, only hear his deep, commanding voice. I asked him where I was and he said that I was near to heaven, but he told me that I could not enter until I had asked the rider on the white horse to take my most precious gift to the land of the sun. I asked the horseman where my husband was, and he replied that he was waiting for me under a tree, around which was coiled a serpent. I knew this was Spartacus and that he was also dead, for when he was an infant a snake had coiled itself around his head while he slept, but had caused the babe no harm. This he told me many years ago. I also knew that I was no longer pregnant and that my most precious possession was my newly born child.'

Claudia turned and looked deep into my eyes, her intense stare unnerving me.

'Are you my friend, Pacorus?'

'You know that I am, lady.'

'Then if I asked you to do something for me, would you respect my wish?'

'I would always strive to do your bidding, lady.'

She paused for a moment, seemingly looking into my soul for the answer. But then she spoke. 'Then I ask you this. When my child is born, I want you to promise that you will take the infant with you back to Parthia, for you are surely the rider on the white horse of which the Thracian Horseman spoke. Will you do this for me?'

I was confused, and thought her words the ramblings of a pregnant woman, for I had heard that when females are with child they are prone to bouts of lunacy.

'But, lady,' I said. 'Spartacus will take care of you and your child.'

At this she grew angry. 'Have you not heard my words, do you think I am some sort of imbecile? Do you hold me in such low esteem that you treat me with such contempt?'

I took her hand to calm her. 'Lady, I would lay down my life for you, surely you know that.'

She snatched back her hand. 'Then accede to my wish, young Parthian.'

Once more she held me with her gaze, only this time her eyes flared with anger, daring me to refuse her. I did not. 'If that is your wish, then it is my command and I will do so. I swear it.'

At once the rage within her disappeared and a wave of relief swept through her. She grabbed my hand, then Gallia's.

'Thank you, thank you, my friends.'

When the storm had abated I had Claudia taken back to the tent of Spartacus under escort, for I was sure that her mind was still unbalanced and that she might harm herself if left to her own devices. But when she embraced me before her departure and kissed me, she seemed truly happy and carefree, almost like a child. Gallia stayed behind, for she and her women had to prepare for the following morning. She examined me closely as we drank a cup of warm wine together in the early evening. The wind had dropped by now and the rain was but a light drizzle. The air was still cool and fresh.

'Well?' she said.

'Well what?'

'You gave your word; are you going to keep it?'

I laughed. 'It won't come to that.'

'Will it not?'

'She had a bad dream, the storm upset her and...'

'And you choose to ignore the truth.'

I drained my cup. 'I'm sure Spartacus would be most unhappy if he knew what Claudia had said.'

Gallia rose and made for the entrance. 'I need to ensure my women are prepared.'

'We leave an hour before dawn.'

'I know. And I also know that Spartacus had heard Claudia's words before we did. Goodnight, Pacorus.'

We moved out of camp in the pre-dawn gloom of a winter's morning, the mist hanging over the land and sea, clinging to the earth and our bodies. Even though I wrapped my cloak around me I still felt cold, though maybe it was fear. For Claudia's words had unnerved me and I had slept but little. I tried to dismiss what she had said, but she had been right about my coming to the army and about the ambush on the beach at Thurii. So why not now? I dismissed the thought from my mind. The night before, after Gallia had left me, I had ridden over to the see Afranius, where I found his men busy with preparations for the attack on Crassus. The air reeked with the smell of leather and the grating sound of blades being sharpened on stones. I found Afranius in his tent surrounded by his officers, most Spaniards like himself, all of them young and eager to get at the Romans. He was immensely proud of his three legions, and rightly so. He had trained them hard over the last year, though I feared that his desire to prove that they were the best in the army, better even than Akmon's Thracians, would lead him to an early grave.

'Remember,' I told him after he had dismissed his officers. 'You are making merely a diversion. Don't get yourself killed.'

'It may be just a diversion, but we can make an impression on this Crassus that he is unlikely to forget in a hurry.' He cast me a sidelong glance. 'Besides, why should the cavalry grab all the glory?'

'You think I lust only for glory.'

'Of course, what else is there?'

I suspected that he was talking about himself rather than me. 'Are we not fighting to win our freedom?'

'I thought we were fighting Romans, but I accept that for some freedom is enough.'

'But not for you.'

He displayed an uninterested expression. 'My homeland is under the heel of the Romans, or most of it. So there is little appeal in going back to scratch a living on some sun-blasted mountain and existing like a bandit. Here, we make the Romans dance to the tune we play. War is work I like.'

'We cannot remain an army in Rome's breast forever.'

He sat back in his chair and filled a cup from a jug. He offered to me while he filled another. To my surprise it was water. 'Why can't we? Have you heard of Hannibal?'

'He was an enemy of Rome, I believe.'

'He and his army roamed Italy for twenty years. Twenty years! Can you imagine?'

I shook my head. 'I do not want to remain in Italy for twenty years.'

'Of course not. You are a prince with a kingdom to go back to. But you are not like the thousands who fight in this army. They have no homes, or if they do they are either under Roman rule or so miserable that they are not worth going back to. That's why no one wanted to go over the Alps last year. Spartacus has shown us another path that we can stand tall and be someone.' He stared at his cup. 'I shall stay with Spartacus when we get to Sicily, so will my Spaniards. We have all discussed it and it is agreed. And your horsemen, what will they do?'

'They are free to follow their own conscience.'

He looked up at me. 'And you? Will you go back to Parthia?'

'Of course, I have a duty to my father and to my people. But not before this army is safely on Sicily.'

'If it were up to me I would stay on the mainland and destroy the Romans, all of them.'

I decided that it was time to leave, for Afranius' head was full of notions of great victories. 'Keep safe Afranius, and remember that your attack is only a diversion.'

'Ride well, Pacorus, and don't be disappointed if we Spaniards steal a little of your glory.'

The sound of three thousand horses moving out of camp produced a low rumble, like distant thunder. In addition, accompanying us on our journey were a hundred and fifty four-wheeled carts, each one pulled by horses that were the mounts of cavalrymen, their riders sitting on the carts. And each cart was piled high with either fodder for the horses or spare arrows, tools and clothing. Each man carried a month's rations in a bag tied to the rear of his saddle, and we would take what we could find along the way, either by hunting or looting. Each company had five carts, and I ordered that the horses pulling them should be changed every day. This meant that at any one time there were ten men not riding with their company but sitting on the carts, but it was a necessity. Each company of one hundred horses consumed a ton of fodder a day, and it was three hundred miles to Brundisium. It would take us fifteen days to reach our destination, averaging twenty miles a day. Burebista wanted us to go faster.

'We could move at least thirty miles a day, lord, maybe more. We could be roasting the backsides of Brundisium's citizens within nine days, maybe less. We waste time hauling these carts.'

'They hold food for the horses,'

He was riding beside me at the head of the column. In front of us, Byrd and his scouts were as usual making sure we would not be surprised by any enemy forces along the route. Burebista himself had just returned from a flank patrol that we deployed every day. Our column was strung out over many miles and was extremely vulnerable to any sort of assault.

'We can feed the horses along the way. There are plenty of Roman farms with fat owners in these parts.'

'Are there, Burebista? The harvest would have been collected in the autumn of last year, and any grain and hay can easily be hidden or destroyed before we get to it. I want the horses and their riders fresh for the attack on Brundisium.'

Gallia was riding the other side of me and was taking a keen interest in what was being discussed, though she kept her counsel. Her Amazons also undertook scouting duties, and sometimes I and the rest of the men forgot that they were women. This was one such occasion.

Burebista was unconvinced. 'There are no Romans in these parts, lord, and my dragon can take any town or village before the inhabitants have risen from their beds.'

He had obviously caught the same fever that infected Afranius, the one that banishes reason and replaces it with delusions of glory.

'Let me tell you an old Parthian tale, Burebista. Two bulls atop a hill are looking down on a valley filled with cows. One of the bulls, young and bursting with lust, says to the older bull, his father. "Let's run down the hill and ravish a couple of them." The older bull then says: "Son, why don't we walk down and ravish them all?" You understand what I am telling you?'

'That Parthian bulls are in desperate need of being castrated,' said Gallia dryly.

Burebista leaned forward and looked at her in confusion. 'Is that what the story means, lady?'

I shook my head. 'It doesn't matter. But we will maintain this rate of march until we reach Brundisium. Just make sure we don't have any nasty surprises along the way.'

He saluted. 'Yes, lord.' Then he was gone, no doubt to join the scouts and try to find some deer or boar he could hunt for amusement. I had given strict orders that villages and towns were to be avoided if possible. I wanted us to be like ghosts moving unseen through the countryside, if thirty companies of horsemen could do such a thing.

'An interesting story,' remarked Gallia, irony in her voice. 'I hope all Parthian fairy tales don't involve amorous bulls. Actually Burebista reminds me of a bull, short-sighted, all brute force and stupid.'

'He is a good fighter, though.'

'Have you told him that there is a home for him in Parthia should he so desire?'

'Of course,' I replied, proudly.

'I'm sure the cows of your father's herds will be delighted to hear that.'

We kept away from the coast and settlements as we moved north, skirting Caulonia, Scolacium Croton and Thurii. How long ago it seemed when we were last at the latter place, when I had nearly been killed by Roman treachery and had been saved by Gallia's skill with a bow. From Thurii we quickly crossed the land to the burnt-out shell that was Metapontum. A few poor wretches were still living among its blood-stained and charred buildings, but they squealed in terror and fled for their lives when a patrol of Byrd's men entered the city. They were looking for food or anything else that might assist our journey, but found nothing but the bones of the dead, still unburied from when the Gauls had attacked, and the stench of death that hung over the empty husks of buildings. I rode into the city and saw for myself and smelt the nauseous odour of decay and human waste. I saw the small harbour choked with smashed and tangled boats. There was nothing for us there.

We left Metapontum and advanced to north of Tarentum, crossed the Appian Way and then made a dash across country towards the coastline a few miles south of Gnatia. Sixteen days after we had left Rhegium, I stood on a long sandy beach looking at the gently lapping waves of the Adriatic. The cavalry was five miles inland, setting up camp for the night, and only Nergal and I had ridden to the shore. The afternoon was giving way to early evening and a light sea breeze blew in our faces. I pointed out to sea.

'In that direction, many miles away, is Hatra, beautiful, majestic Hatra.'

'We will see it again, highness.'

'You really think that?'

'Of course, highness. Why would Shamash save our lives and give us all the great victories we have won without some purpose.'

I looked at him. Brave and loyal Nergal. He never complained or doubted that we were on the right course. I placed a hand on his shoulder. 'When we get back to Hatra, I would like you to be an officer in my father's royal bodyguard.'

He flashed a smile. 'I would be honoured, highness.'

'No, Nergal, it is I who am honoured to have such an able commander by my side.'

But first we had to kill more Romans.

That night Byrd and his scouts returned from their reconnaissance of Brundisium. They had ridden right into the port and even to its harbour. But then, a group of scruffy individuals on untidy horses and carrying no weapons, dressed in dirty clothes and unshaven, would elicit more pity than concern. Now Byrd drew Brundisium's layout on the earth using his dagger. I had gathered all the company commanders to attend his briefing, which he gave beside a wagon, as I had given orders that no tents were to be erected this night.

'Port lies on one side of large bay. But before sea reaches port it goes through a narrow channel where land on either side is close, before widening at Brundisium. This means that Romani cannot send many ships in and out because channel is only wide enough for one ship.'

'Are there pirate ships in the harbour?' asked Burebista.
Byrd nodded. 'Many ships lie out to sea as well.'
'What about the city's defences?' I asked.
Byrd stood up and replaced his dagger in its scabbard. 'Walls enclose port on all sides except where there is water. Big city, walls are all manned. You will not be able to storm it. But no need for Romani are unloading troops on beaches north of the city. On way back we saw many ships anchored off beach, with troops camped on sand. No walls there.'
'Are you sure?' I said.
'Of course. Romani think slave army is far away. Why should they worry?'
'Why indeed?' I replied.
We rested for three hours, during which time we fed and watered the horses, removed their saddles and checked the straps and fittings, and then groomed them. The veterinaries checked horseshoes and then we examined our weapons. It was dark by the time I once again assembled the company commanders and gave them their orders.
'We ride in quick, hit them hard and then get out as fast as we can. Use flame arrows on any ships that are close enough to the shore, but don't let your men wade into the water, tempting though it may be. They will merely make themselves slow-moving targets for any archers or slingers the enemy may have.'
'What about the port, lord?' asked one.
'We leave it. We're here to kill Roman soldiers, not capture cities.'
The full moon illuminated our route well enough as two and a half thousand cavalry trotted in column towards the stretch of sandy beach where the Romans were landing. In many ways it made perfect sense. Why use a port that would quickly get congested when they could also take advantage of long beaches where the sea was shallow for at least a hundred yards out from the shore? Byrd led us, the redoubtable guide who had once been a seller of pots. How strange was fate!
The carts and the remaining five hundred men I had ordered south to just north of a small town called Caelia. Once we had made our assault, the carts would slow us down and I wasn't sure how many horsemen the Romans had. Byrd and his men had seen no horses being unloaded from the ships, but that did not mean that Brundisium's garrison did not have any. The landscape we moved through was largely flat, very dry and was punctuated by dry riverbeds, and the whole area was filled with olive groves and vineyards. We scattered flocks of sheep, the animals parting before

us like a giant white blanket being torn in two. Fortunately the sheep outnumbered humans by around a thousand to one, for Calabria appeared to have few villages and villas. Aside from the towns, this was a sparsely populated region, and for that I was glad. Gallia rode beside me, her Amazons behind, followed by my dragon, then Nergal's and finally Burebista's. We had ridden for two hours when Byrd and one of his scouts galloped up to me and halted. By now our eyes had become accustomed to the moonlight and I could see the terrain around us with ease. I could also smell the salty air of the sea, and Byrd confirmed that we were less than a mile away from the beach.

I dismounted and gave the order for everyone else to do likewise, each man (and woman) conveying the command with a hushed voice. There was no sound and I was worried that the Romans would become aware of our presence, though as the wind was blowing off the sea, at least any noise we made would not be carried towards them. I knelt on the ground, one hand holding Remus' reins. Byrd knelt opposite me. Nergal and Burebista joined us while Gallia and Praxima stood over us.

'Romani guards every twenty paces just off the beach,' said Byrd.

I stood up and looked ahead. I could not see the beach because the ground rose up slightly around four hundred yards in front of me, beyond which it sloped down to the beach. Byrd had told us that the beach itself was about three miles in length and that ships were anchored along its whole length.

'Many ships anchored both at the shore and in sea. Dozens of ships.'

It was about an hour to dawn. Nothing stirred.

'Very well,' I told them. 'Nergal and Burebista, get your men deployed into line, but keep them on foot for the moment. I will take the centre. Nergal, you will form the right wing and Burebista, you will be our left wing. Once we are in position, we will walk the horses to the top of that small rise ahead, and then we will mount up and attack. Ride straight through any screen of guards and onto the beach. And order everyone to be as quiet as the dead. Surprise must be total.'

It took half an hour, maybe more, for hundreds of men and their horses to move from column into line, and every minute that passed shredded my nerves a little more. I kept looking in the direction of the beach, straining my eyes for any sign of the enemy. My imagination taunted me, and any minute I expected to see the massed ranks of several Roman legions cresting the ground ahead of us. Gallia touched my arm and I jumped. She passed me a water skin.

'Are you unwell?'

I drank the lukewarm water. 'No, just jumpy.' It was curious how the burden of command bore down on me like a colossal weight just before battle.

Finally we were ready. I glanced left and right to see men holding their horses stretching into the distance. Each dragon was formed into two lines, and as I raised my hand and led Remus forward, twenty-five hundred others did likewise. It took us another fifteen minutes to traverse those four hundred yards to the crest, each rider carefully picking his way through wild grass, tussocks and rabbit holes. Some stumbled and fell, cursing as they did so, their noise increasing the thumping in my chest. I looked up and saw that the sky had changed, the eastern horizon was now turning a dark orange – dawn was breaking. We reached the crest at last and I vaulted onto Remus' back, behind me my dragon did the same. For a few seconds Remus stood and I looked ahead. I could see the orange sky and the yellow ball of the sun just creeping above the sea. In front of me the beach was littered with groups of Roman soldiers sleeping on the sand, their shields and javelins neatly stacked beside them. The sea, smooth as a mirror, was filled with ships, their sails stashed and their oars at rest. It was an impressive display of Roman might, but they were as vulnerable as a newborn lamb.

I pulled my bow from its case, then strung an arrow in the bowstring and dug my knees into Remus' flanks. He snorted and raced forward. Ahead I saw a guard, his shield on the ground resting against his leg, staring at us. He was only a couple of hundred feet away. He peered, realised that the wall of horseflesh galloping towards him was not a dream or phantoms, then shouted and grabbed the handle of his shield, just as my arrow hit him in the chest, the rhomboid head piercing his mail shirt sending him spinning backwards. I rode past him, screaming a war cry as Remus thundered onto the sand.

Each company worked as a team, either riding over men who were still lying on the ground or sweeping around others who had managed to wake themselves and were attempting to form into some sort of unit. The beach itself was approximately three hundred yards wide, and those Roman legionaries who were sleeping the furthest from the water suffered the most. They slept in eight-man tents grouped into centuries – even in slumber the Romans retained their formation – and our first line rode through and over them. Those who hadn't been trampled, speared or shot were then assaulted in quick succession by our second line, who hacked at bleary eyed individuals with their swords. As I rode Remus to the water's edge and then wheeled him right, the beach was suddenly engulfed in noise: screams, shouts, curses and whoops. Cavalry horns blasted as company commanders isolated groups of Romans and began reducing them with arrow fire, while Roman trumpets sounded assembly.

All along the beach the battle assumed a predictable pattern, as horse companies sought to isolate and then destroy Roman units. The Roman Army's strength was its discipline and belief in its formations, the century, cohort and legion. But today, while the sky turned from orange to yellow as the sun rose in the east, that very same strength began to work against the Romans as legionaries rallied into their centuries. However, instead of other centuries and cohorts being to their right and left, groups of fast-moving horsemen were between them, searching for weak points and unleashing a hail of arrow against them. Century after century was shot to pieces in this way. Other centuries, to their credit, managed to form an all-round defence, the front ranks kneeling and forming a shield wall, and the second and third ranks also kneeling and hauling their shields above their heads to form a sloping roof against which our arrows could not penetrate. Occasionally a legionary would lose his nerve, or goaded beyond his limit, would break formation and charge out to attack a horseman, only to be felled by an arrow before he had run ten paces. As so it went on, a myriad of isolated battles all along the beach. Some centuries withdrew to the water and then attempted to wade to the safety of the ships, but my archers merely followed them, keeping out of javelin range, and then shot at them when their cohesion fell to pieces in the water as the Romans tried to reach the boats. Soon the sea was dyed red with the blood of dead Romans.

Now flame arrows were arching into the sky and landing on the anchored ships, whose crews had awakened to discover what was happening on the beach. Captains screamed at their crews to cut anchor ropes and man their oars. But it takes time to move a ship, and in those precious few minutes a torrent of flame arrows was launched against those boats nearest to the shore. We had not come to burn boats, but soon a dozen or more were aflame before the rest had managed to row beyond the range of our bows.

Gallia, her Amazons tight around her, ripped off her helmet when faced by the locked shields of over a hundred legionaries. She tossed her blonde hair back and laughed at them.

'Soldiers of Rome, are you afraid of a woman, where is your courage?'
Behind her the Amazons, cheek guards fastened hiding their sex, closed in upon the Romans. The front rank of the later, taunted beyond endurance by this woman on a horse in front of them, shouted and charged forward, javelins poised to be thrown. Gallia did nothing as the hiss of arrows flashed past her and struck the legionaries. Then another volley was loosed and yet more Romans fell, and then Gallia dug her knees into Epona and screamed a blood-curdling cry. The Amazons charged into the disorganised and demoralised Romans, riding straight into their midst and destroying any semblance of formation that had existed. I saw Praxima hacking left and right with her sword, Gallia shooting a hapless Roman in the back at a range of about ten feet and the others turning mail-clad soldiers into a mound of offal. It was terrible, exhilarating and glorious at the same time. I gave the order to sound retreat, the horns blasting their shrill sound. I rode over to Gallia, her women reforming around her.
'Put your helmet back on, we are withdrawing.'
There was fire in her eyes and adrenalin was clearly pumping through her veins.
'Why? We should stay and kill more Romans.'
Around me horsemen were turning their mounts around and heading off the beach, as more and more horns were sounding withdrawal.
'No,' I said. 'Get your women off the beach. The Romans are recovering and to stay any longer would be to invite death.'
And so it would, for at the far end of the beach, in the direction of Brundisium, a solid wall of red Roman shields was approaching, their right flank anchored on the water's edge and their left flank protected by slingers. The later were finding their range and were bringing down horses and riders with their deadly lead pellets. If any cavalry tried to charge them they sought sanctuary behind Roman shields, and then emerged again to unleash another deadly accurate volley of pellets.
Nergal rode up with two companies who stayed on the outer edge of the beach as a covering force. I stayed with them. I watched Gallia and her women trot past me in sullen silence, no doubt aggrieved that I had interrupted their glory. Looking at the beach from right to left, I saw the fresh cohort approaching at a steady pace, while before them lay their dead and wounded comrades, most lying in groups where they had been surprised while sleeping. A few ragged clusters of still-living legionaries stood all along the

sand, many bare headed and wounded by arrows or sword and lance thrusts. In the water I counted fifteen ships alight, many blazing fiercely as the flames had taken hold of dry timbers and sails. At the water's edge was a grim flotsam of Roman dead, men who had tried to escape us by wading into the water, but who had only presented their backs to our arrows as they tried to reach the ships lying offshore. We had not destroyed the Romans, but we had given them a bloody nose and would hopefully slow down their preparations to march south to join Crassus. Nergal told me that a preliminary count had revealed that we had lost only two hundred and fifty men and their horses. Before I rode away I looked one last time at the beach. There must have been ten times that number of Romans lying dead upon the sand. It had been a triumphant morning, but in the south disaster had befallen the slave army.

Chapter 17

The ride to the rendezvous point was uneventful, and after a brief muster, roll call and rest, we moved southwest from Caelia to skirt Tarentum and then head south to the empty husk of Metapontum. The men's spirits were high, and they told and retold each other their stories of the battle on the beach until all vestiges of the truth and rationality had departed.

'We must have slaughtered their whole army,' proclaimed Burebista, his left arm in a sling where a javelin had sliced into his forearm. 'I killed so many that after a while my sword arm became a dead weight that I could no longer lift.'

'We fired so many arrows,' added Nergal, 'that they blocked out the sun.

'Godarz will be most annoyed by our profligacy,' I reminded them. But nothing could shake their delight at giving the Romans a bloody nose, the more so because we had surprised them utterly. We caught up with the wagons after two days, which allowed us to replenish our arrows with the supplies. After three more days of marching we made camp thirty miles south of Siris, along a long curved shingle beach in the Gulf of Tarentum. There we tended those horses that had received wounds and patched up soldiers who had been hurt. The surgeons, formerly slaves who had been trained by their masters to treat wounds, went to work with their tourniquets, ligatures and arterial clamps. Unfortunately, those who had abdominal wounds where the intestines had been pierced were beyond help, and they died despite being treated. Nothing could be done for them. I came across one doctor, a wiry individual with dark skin and a shock of thick black hair who was treating a nasty gash to the right leg of one my horseman. He had cleaned the wound and was about to apply the dressing.

'What is that on the bandage?' I asked him out of curiosity.

'A few spiders' webs, sir.'

I was horrified. 'You are going to put spiders' webs onto his wounds?'

The doctor regarded me with amusement. 'Of course, it will stop the bleeding and bind the flesh together more quickly.'

He applied the dressing, tied off the bandage then smiled at his patient, who limped back to his company.

'The cure has been known in Greece for hundred of years, before the Romans stole it, like they do with most things.'

'Will you ever go back to Greece?'

He motioned to another soldier in line to sit on the stool set before him. The man was holding his left arm, which appeared to be out of its socket, and he told the surgeon that it had happened during a fall from his horse. The surgeon examined the man's shoulder. He then bent the patient's elbow at a ninety-degree angle and rotated the arm inwards to make a letter 'L'. He then slowly and steadily rotated the entire arm and shoulder outwards, keeping the upper portion of the arm as stationary as possible. He made a fist with his hand on his patient's injured arm, and then held on to his wrist and began to push slowly. Just when the bottom of his arm was past ninety degrees from his chest, the shoulder fell back into its joint. The patient's face was contorted with pain as the doctor was manipulating his arm, but after a few seconds a look of relief and gratitude came over his visage. He thanked the doctor profusely before leaving.

The doctor turned to me. 'I am from Corinth and that city is now under Roman rule. I have no wish to go back there.'

'What is your name?'

'Alcaeus.'

'Parthia can always find a use for skilled surgeons.'

'Thank you, sir. If I am still alive I will consider it, though I have to confess that the chances of that are lengthening the longer we stay in Italy.'

'You think we are doomed?'

He gestured to another man to sit on the stool. This individual had a bloody bandage wrapped around his leg, no doubt the result of a javelin wound.

'I think that if we get out of Italy we have a chance, otherwise not.'

He began to gently unwrap the bandage.

'Then why do you stay with the army?'

'Simple, sir. The air tastes sweeter when you are free. Better to be a free man for a while than a slave forever. And now, sir, if you don't mind, I have work to do.'

We remained in camp for three days before continuing our march south. But on the second day Byrd returned to us, accompanied by a column of horsemen led by Godarz and Gafarn. To say I was surprised was an understatement, and in the pit of my stomach I felt a knot tighten, for I feared that something was wrong. My fears were confirmed when I was informed what had happened. Though Gallia was delighted to see Diana and the deranged Rubi, as were the rest of her Amazons, the faces of Gafarn and Godarz told their own stories. After a brief pause the column continued its journey south, albeit at a leisurely pace as I absorbed what they told me.

'Afranius' attack was a disaster,' said Godarz. 'He thought that he could wipe out the entire Roman camp, but all he achieved was getting two thousand of his men killed.'

I was stunned. 'Two thousand?'

'And many more wounded,' added Gafarn. 'Spartacus was furious.'

'There's worse,' said Godarz grimly.

'The Romans haven't attacked our army?' I was becoming alarmed.

Godarz continued to stare fixedly ahead as he spoke. 'Not yet. But Crassus has built a line of wooden fortifications across the whole peninsula, effectively trapping the army in a giant prison camp.'

'Impossible,' snapped Nergal.

Godarz smiled wryly. 'I assure you that it is very possible and has been done.'

'It's true, said Gafarn, 'and to make things worse that pirate representative...'

'Patelli?' I asked.

'That's him. Well, he's gone, absconded in the middle of the night along with his staff and all his ships in the harbour. And to rub salt in the wounds, he took the gold that Spartacus had given him as well.'

'I knew that slippery bastard was not to be trusted,' I said, recalling the pirate's insincere smile, his shifty eyes and easy way with words.

'Well,' continued Godarz, 'he's gone and with him our only chance of getting to Sicily. The only alternative now is to break through Crassus' fortifications. If we don't the army will starve, simple as that.'

'How long before the food runs out?' I asked.

'Three weeks, maybe less. And this weather isn't helping. Men starve more quickly when it's cold.'

I had noticed that over the last few days the temperature had dropped markedly, with a cool northerly wind blowing most of the time during the day, and the mountains in the distance on our right flank were no longer grey mounds, but were now covered in snow.

Godarz continued. 'Spartacus ordered us out before it was too late. You are his best hope now, Pacorus.'

That night we camped a few miles north of Sybaris, a city once mighty when occupied by the ancient Greeks, but now a poor relation of Thurii located further south. We built no palisaded camp, but I had patrols riding out to ten miles in all directions to ensure that we were not attacked. We had brought only eight-man

Roman tents for our journey, and I now sat huddled in one of these, wrapped in my cloak, as a single oil lamp sat upon the ground and lit the faces of my companions: Godarz, Nergal, Burebista and Gafarn. It was Godarz who did most of the talking, thoroughly briefed as he had been by Spartacus.

He unrolled a parchment map and laid it out before us, securing each corner with small stones he had collected from outside. The map was old and cracked, but I could make out that it showed southern Italy and Sicily, the island we would now never visit. 'You will have to march south, then swing west across country towards Caprasia where we can march down the Popilian Way. Crassus has built his line of defences about ten miles north of Rhegium, from one shore, then across country to the Ionian coast, on the opposite shore.'

'What sort of defences?' I asked.

'Spartacus mounted a raid when it became apparent what the Romans were doing. It was a failure, but he did capture a centurion who gave a detailed description of what they were building. First, the Romans dug a ditch about twenty feet wide with vertical sides. Then, four hundred or so paces back from the ditch, they dug two more ditches, each about fifteen feet wide. Behind these ditches the legionaries built an earth rampart some twelve feet tall, on the top of which they put a parapet and battlements. And to top it all, every hundred feet or so they have constructed a watch tower.'

'What happened to the centurion?' I asked.

'Spartacus had him crucified in front of the Romans as they were erecting their fortifications.'

'Horses can't charge through wooden walls,' I said.

'The best we can do is to create a diversion and hope to draw off some of the Roman troops, so as to weaken one part of their line,' suggested Nergal.

Godarz shook his head. 'No, that won't do. For one thing the line must be at least twelve miles long. It is no use us attacking at one point and Spartacus attacking at another five miles away. We must attack at the same point as he does, only then will he stand a chance of breaking out.'

'That's all very well,' I said. 'But each attack must be coordinated to strike the same spot at the same time. That means we, or rather I, have to speak to Spartacus before anything happens.'

'And there are eight legions between you and him,' mused Gafarn.

'The only way in is by boat to Rhegium,' I said. 'In the meantime, we must stay hidden until the plans are finalised. Crassus doesn't realise that we are here, and so we must indulge his ignorance for as long as possible.'

I had nothing else to add and so dismissed them all, leaving me alone to reflect on the nightmare position we were now in. I sought the company of Gallia and found her with her women sharpening their swords and daggers and flighting new arrows.

'You look troubled.' Gallia was familiar with my moods and expressions by now, as I was with hers, and as we walked among the horses of her company tethered among linen wind breaks, I could not hide my anxiety. I told her about what had happened at Rhegium.

'I know, Diana told us.'

'She should have kept her mouth shut.'

Gallia was stung by my criticism of her friend. 'Why? Do we not have a right to know what has become of our friends? Some of us have been with Spartacus longer then you.'

I ignored the jibe. 'It will not be easy to break through those Roman defences. And even if we do, what then? Where will the army go? We will be back where we started all those months ago, and in a far worse position. We should have gone over the Alps when we had the chance.'

'But we didn't, so there is no point in wasting words on the matter.'

'I knew it would end like this,' I continued. 'We were so close to freedom and instead of seizing it we allowed ourselves to become deluded that we could roam through Italy at will. And this is how it turns out.'

'Why don't you take out your frustrations on the Romans instead of my ears,' she said.

'You think this is a subject for levity? It's my cavalry that has to shed blood to save the situation.'

'I thought it was Spartacus' cavalry. You serve him, do you not?'

'What? Of course, but I resent having to waste men's lives in getting the army out of a predicament that it should never have got itself into in the first place. That stupid imbecile Afranius should be held to account for his incompetence.'

'There is no point in all this, Pacorus.'

'There is every point,' I shot back. 'You don't understand. I have raised this cavalry and now I have to throw them against fortifications. It's not right.'

She laughed. 'Not right? Is that your sense of honour talking again? Would it be right to leave them where they are, to starve or to be killed by the Romans?'

'Of course not, I was only saying that a night attack against fortifications is unsuitable for horsemen. Skulking around in the dark like a bunch of assassins.'

'That's it, isn't it?'

'That's what?' I asked.

'You prefer the idea of fighting in daylight when everyone can see your great banner and your men on their horses, cloaks flying behind them as they charge to glory.'

'Don't be absurd,' I retorted.

'It's still all a game, isn't it? One giant exercise in honour and glory. Until now you have been the shining star of the army. Pacorus the bringer of victory, the man known throughout the enemy's lands as "the Parthian", perhaps even more famous than Spartacus himself. Except that now your honour demands that you must carry out something that you have no interest in.'

'Spartacus was a fool for getting himself trapped.'

She walked up to me until our faces were but inches apart. 'You are a fool, Pacorus. He is a great man whose force of personality has united thousands behind him. He has given you all that you desire. He even said to me that you were a fine man, even though I thought otherwise. Do not make me change my mind about you.'

I was horrified at even the thought of losing her. I looked into her eyes. 'My words were hasty. Forgive me. Of course I will not abandon Spartacus. The cold has obviously addled my brain.'

Her expression, formerly hard and unyielding, now softened somewhat. 'I know that you will do the right thing. And do not be angry with Afranius. He does, after all, only want to be like you.'

I laughed. 'I suspect he dislikes me.'

'Perhaps, but he so wants to be a victorious general like you, to be known as a great warrior.'

I shrugged. 'I'm not a great warrior.'

Her head tilted slightly as she regarded me. 'Spartacus regards you so, and so do Castus and Akmon, and the last one is a particularly hard judge. So I hope you will not prove them wrong.'

I felt elated. 'They really said that?'

'Perhaps, for a great warrior, leading horses against wooden walls is not such a difficult task.'

I smiled, for she had out-foxed me. I conceded defeat. 'Perhaps not.'

Like me she too was wrapped in a cloak, with a felt cap on her head, her hair tied into a thick blonde plait. 'It's cool, isn't it?'

'The wind is blowing from the north and it will bring snow soon.'

'More misery,' I remarked.

It always amazed me that, however grave the situation, there could always be found someone to undertake the most hazardous of tasks, as long as the price was right. This proved to be the case now, as Godarz found me the means to get to Rhegium. In a dirt-poor fishing village on the Ionian coastline, where the hovels clung to the rocky outcrops that fronted the sea like limpets, he located a boat owner named Cunobarrus who, for a handful of gold pieces, would take me down the coast to Rhegium, as well as bring me back. Godarz had visited the village alone and got chatting to the inhabitants. His passed himself off as a distraught tradesman from Sicily whose terminally ill brother was trapped in Rhegium, his only wish being that his young nephew, me, should see his father before he died. The two score of people who listened to his story were mostly disinterested until he revealed the leather pouch he was carrying and its gold contents. Thus it came about that I sat in a stinking fishing boat as it bobbed among the white-flecked waves whipped up by the cool northerly wind, which filled the dirty grey single sail. Cunobarrus sat at the stern, holding the tiller, while a youth about eighteen years of age, his son I assumed, busied himself bailing seawater out of the boat's bottom and casting glances at me. Cunobarrus was a filthy, lice-ridden individual who had obviously spent many years on the sea. His hands were calloused and his nails black, he spat frequently and his teeth were rotten. His boat was around fifteen feet in length, five feet at the beam and four feet in depth. It was held together by mortise and tenon joinery and was constructed mainly of cedar planks and oak frames, though by their varying colours I suspected that some of the wood had been used in other, older vessels before this one.

We had set off just after dawn when the sea was calm, but an hour into our voyage the wind had picked up, increasing both our speed and my misery as the boat rose and pitched on the choppy sea. Cunobarrus was delighted.

'Good wind, this. We'll have you in Rhegium in no time.' He brought up phlegm loudly and then spat it over the side. 'Mind you, don't know what you're going to do when we get there. The place has been taken over by a load of slaves.'

'I know,' I replied. 'Perhaps they will let a son who only wants to see his ailing father alone.'

'Maybe.' He spat over the side again. 'If he ain't dead already. Hosidius, you worthless sewer rat, tighten that sail or it'll rip. And get us something to eat.'

Hosidius, scampering around the boat like a tame monkey, whipped out a sack bag from under a bench, fished around inside it and brought out a loaf of bread and a jug, which turned out to contain vinegar. The bread was mouldy and the vinegar tasted disgusting, but Cunobarrus tucked into it with gusto. He grinned at me frequently, no doubt seeing me as his route to a better life. For security, Godarz had given him half the price before the journey, the rest to be collected upon my safe delivery back at his village. After two hours I began to feel decidedly nauseous, made worse by the increasing wind that tossed the boat around alarmingly, though Cunobarrus assured me that it was perfectly safe. As I watched Hosidius bale out the boat faster and faster, thoughts of drowning began to enter my mind.

But we didn't drown, and five hours after setting sail our miserable vessel edged its way into the harbour at Rhegium, the entrance to which was between two breakwaters made of rocks that extended into the sea like the claws of a giant crab. The harbour itself was fairly voluminous and could accommodate perhaps two-dozen large ships, though today only two wide-beamed cargo vessels were moored to the quay. Large warehouses fronted the harbour but their shutters were all closed, and the only activity was a score of soldiers who were patrolling the quay itself. As our boat neared the stone steps of the harbour wall, a burly centurion in the distinctive helmet of his rank appeared at the top of the steps. He was joined by half a dozen legionaries in full war gear. The centurion pointed at Cunobarrus.

'You, up here quick!'

I recognised the voice. 'Have you rejoined the Roman Army, Domitus?'

Domitus squinted at the boat and then smiled. 'Prince Pacorus. Have you lost all your horsemen?'

I left Cunobarrus and Hosidius filling their bellies with warm porridge as I walked with Domitus into the town, which appeared to be deserted. He told me that Spartacus had made him governor of Rhegium, and his first order was to evacuate the inhabitants.

'We threw them out some time ago, sent them packing towards the north. Then we put our soldiers into the houses. I have the governor's house, which is quite agreeable.'

'Is Spartacus in the town?'

He laughed. 'No, he's still living in his tent with Claudia. Said he would never sleep under a Roman roof again.'

'How are things?'

He shrugged. 'Spartacus is like a boar with a toothache since that pirate deceived him. Then the Romans built their fortifications and we are stuck here like pigs in a pen. I hope you fared better at Brundisium.'

'We did. They weren't expecting us, and when we attacked we killed many on the shore, but we have merely slowed them down, not stopped them.'

We walked through the town and then north into the army's camp. The wind had if anything increased and it was becoming even colder as I drew my cloak around me. When we reached Spartacus' tent my fingers were numb and I was glad to get inside and warm myself by a brazier. The tent was empty and so Domitus went off to search for Spartacus while feeling returned to my fingers. Moments later he was back with Spartacus at his side. He looked older and more haggard, with dark rings round his eyes. Physically he was still the impressive, muscled figure that I had seen all those months ago at Vesuvius, but he had a haunted look, as though he was weighed down by unbearable responsibilities. His eyes lit up when he saw me, though, and he locked me in an iron embrace.

'Welcome, my friend. Domitus has told me how you savaged the army at Brundisium. A piece of good news at last, I shall have it spread throughout the army. It is good to see you.'

He released me from his bear-like hold. 'You too, lord. How is Claudia?'

'Pregnant and tetchy,' he replied, 'but well. She is sleeping at the moment.'

As cooks brought us warm wine, hot porridge and freshly made bread, I relayed to Spartacus what had happened at Brundisium. As he listened to how we had slaughtered many enemy soldiers on that Ionian beach, his mood brightened. It increased still more when a bleary eyed Claudia appeared from an adjoining part of the tent. She looked as beautiful and sultry as ever, her belly now heavily swollen with her unborn child. We embraced and she kissed me on the cheek. She asked after Gallia and me before reclining next to her husband on his couch.

'You smell of fish,' she remarked, screwing up her nose.

'Alas, my mode of transport here left a lot to be desired.'

Half an hour later we were joined by Akmon and Castus, the latter his usual cheerful self and the Thracian as dour as ever.

'At least we got the rest of your horses away,' he said, 'before the Romans penned us in. Where are they now?'

'Not too far north, all safely away from Roman eyes.'

'Three thousand cavalry won't stay unnoticed for long,' he sniffed.

'True enough,' added Spartacus. 'That is why we must act fast.'

He motioned to Akmon, who walked over to the table and spread across its top a map similar to the one possessed by Godarz. We gathered round it to look at southern Italy. I pointed to the map.
'We are near Scolacium, camped in the hills.'
Akmon nodded approvingly. 'Good, that means you can go through the valley of the Lametus River to reach the western coast.'
Spartacus traced his finger on the map from Rhegium northwards. 'You need to get your horse down the Popilian Way to attack Crassus from the north. At the same time we will attack from the south and break through. Then your horse will screen the army as it moves north.'
'To where?' I asked.
I saw Castus glance at Akmon. 'To Rome,' replied Spartacus.
'Rome?' I was staggered.
'We have no choice, Pacorus,' said Spartacus. 'When that pirate took off, our last chance of getting out of Italy went with him. I have a Roman army in front of me, one coming from Brundisium and probably another marching from Spain. But if we can break out of here and strike north, then we may be able to take the city.'
'It's a big city, Spartacus,' I said.
'I know, but Crassus must have denuded it of troops to raise his army, and that's the last thing he will be expecting. If we take Rome then we free hundreds of thousands of slaves in the city. If we do that then our blow will reverberate throughout the Roman Empire, and may just deal it a mortal blow.'
I wondered if he was trying to convince himself or me. I said nothing. So that was it; we would smash through Crassus' defences, march north and then capture Rome itself. My initial thought was that it was an insane plan, but then Spartacus had thus far never been defeated, and had beaten every army that had been sent against him. Why shouldn't he be victorious again? With these thoughts swirling in my mind I walked with him, Akmon and Castus to see these Roman fortifications for myself. They were located ten miles north of Rhegium. They were just as Godarz had described, with an earth bank surmounted by a wooden palisade of sharpened logs, with sharpened stakes planted in the earth bank that faced us. And at intervals of a hundred feet were wooden watchtowers, each one about twenty feet higher than the palisade, and each one having three fighting platforms. Two sentries stood on the highest platform of every tower. In front of the ramparts were two parallel ditches and in front of the ditches were two rows of stakes driven the ground. Out of the corner of my eye I saw a

solitary cross in front of the Roman lines, on which was nailed the Roman centurion who had been captured. A single crow picked at the corpse. I shuddered and said a silent prayer to Shamash that I would be spared such a death. The wind was still blowing, its icy blast coming from the north and carrying flecks of snow that blew past us as we stood looking at the Roman lines.

'It will be bloody getting through their defences,' said Spartacus. 'Before we get to the stakes their catapults mounted on top of the towers will open fire, and as we cut through the stakes they will be firing arrows at us from the towers and from firing steps on the other side of the palisade. Then we have to get across the ditches, which we will fill with bundles of brushwood. And all the time we will be under their fire. They will also put slingers on the watchtowers who will exact a fearsome price. Then we will charge their ramparts and try to smash our way through the wooden wall, by which time a hail of javelins will be raining down on us.

'But you, Pacorus, you hold the key to our success. The Romans will not be expecting an assault from behind, much less one conducted by cavalry. Their eyes will be looking south, and when your horsemen appear in their rear there will be panic, and when fear and uncertainty grips them, we will break through. If we don't, we die, it's as simple as that.'

I thought of those who would be in the front ranks of the attackers, who must approach the Roman defences and try to get through stakes and across ditches before they even reached the earth rampart with its palisade on top. They would suffer fearful losses.

'Who will lead your attack, lord?'

'I will, of course, and alongside me will be that young idiot Afranius and his Spaniards. After all, it is only right than the person responsible for these defences being built should be the first one to take them down.'

'Where is our Spanish friend?' I asked.

'I sent him to the east coast to make a lot of noise in front of the Roman lines. Make them think that we will be attacking there rather than here, north of Rhegium.'

'You'll get yourself killed,' said Akmon. 'It will be suicide attacking that lot.'

Spartacus looked into the sky, which was still filled with tiny swirling flecks of snow. 'Maybe not. We will attack at night and hopefully the weather will aid us.'

'The weather?' Akmon laughed grimly. 'For all you know it will be still and cloudless and the entire area will be flooded by moonlight.'

'When do we attack, Spartacus?' asked Castus.

'In three days. That should give Pacorus time to get his cavalry into position.'

That night I ate with Spartacus and Claudia, after taking a relaxing bath in the governor's house in the town and ensuring that Cunobarrus was still in port. He was, enjoying the hospitality of a dingy inn near the harbour that had been requisitioned by a group of Thracians. Though Rhegium had been taken over by the army, its discipline was still impeccable and there had been no looting or wanton destruction. It was a testament to Spartacus that, despite its precarious situation, the army's cohesion remained intact.

'Every man still knows that his best chance of staying alive is to stay with this army. I was at fault for trusting that pirate, but there was little choice, and now that option has gone our only hope is to take Rome itself.'

Claudia sat in silence, her eyes avoiding mine. Did she think that our whole venture was now doomed? Spartacus caught me looking at her.

'Claudia thinks I am mad for wanting to march north once again. What do you think, Pacorus? Speak freely.'

'You have never failed us, lord,' I said.

'A diplomat's answer,' said Claudia, looking up and smiling at me. 'But no answer at all.'

I blushed. 'We have never been defeated yet, so why should the future be any different?'

'Why indeed?' she retorted. 'Except that armies are flooding into Italy and eventually they will trap us and destroy us.'

'Are you now general of the army, my love?' said Spartacus irritably. 'What would you have me do?'

'What you should have done weeks ago when we were near the Alps.'

'We've discussed that,' he snapped. I was feeling distinctly uncomfortable. 'I could not leave the army; they wanted me to stay.'

'No,' she corrected him, 'your vanity, the thing you most despise in the Romans, dangled the prospect of glory in front of your nose, and like a spoilt child bribed with a toy you could not refuse. And now we are holed up like pigs in a pen.'

Spartacus jumped to his feet and threw his cup across the tent. 'Enough! I will not be spoken to thus. I know what I am doing.'

Claudia, her eyes aflame, remained cool and aloof, but her words were like darts aimed at her husband. 'That is debatable, but it is plain to see that we are no longer free but are dancing to the Romans' tune, like a tame bear in the market place.'

Spartacus threw up his hands in despair and sat back down on the couch. 'Then, I say again, what would you have me do? We cannot sprout wings and fly to Sicily.'

Claudia rose and crossed the floor to sit beside him and took his hand. 'I know, but your mission from now on must be to get this army out of Italy. The longer we stay the less likely the chances of us seeing our homes again. Forget Rome, for the only members of this army who will see Rome will be condemned men.'

'First we have to get through those Roman defences,' said Spartacus.

Claudia looked at me and smiled. 'I think our salvation sits a few feet from us, my dear, for surely the gods have sent Pacorus for just such a purpose.'

Spartacus laughed and went to retrieve his cup. 'You know, Pacorus, when you first came to us Crixus said that you were just a boy with long hair who would prove as useful as a one-legged man in an arse-kicking competition.'

'He was ever the poet,' I said.

'I was inclined to agree with him,' he looked at Claudia, 'but someone told me that a man on a white horse would come and be our salvation. And so it has proved to be. I am honoured to call you a friend, Pacorus.'

'And I you, lord.'

Claudia yawned and it was clear that she was tired. I made my excuses and left them alone together, embracing Spartacus and kissing Claudia on the cheek. As I was about to exit the tent, Claudia called after me.

'You remember your promise to me, Pacorus?'

'Of course, lady,' I replied.

As I walked back to the town, past rows of tents and groups of soldiers clustered around braziers, I drew my cloak around me. The wind had abated somewhat and the night sky was clear, though if anything it was colder than when the wind had been blowing. In the distance, overlooking the port, the Roman fortifications and our army, stood the brooding Sila Mountains, great granite mounds covered with vast forests that teemed with game. I stopped and listened intently. Coming from the mountains I thought I heard the howl of a wolf. I hoped it was a good omen.

The trip back to the fishing village was a nightmare – hours of tacking to and fro in a stinking fishing vessel that was being tossed around on a rough sea. There were no snowflakes; rather, icy sleet that the wind threw into our faces and which stung like small needles being driven into my flesh. Cunobarrus spent the entire journey either hurling abuse at Hosidius or taking pleasure at my discomfort. The sea was a cold, ominous grey, occasionally flecked with white when the wind ruffled the top of a wave. Cunobarrus wrapped himself in a disgusting oilskin cape when the sleet increased in intensity. He fished one out from under his bench at the tiller and threw it to me.

'Better put this on, don't want you freezing to death, your majesty.' He grinned to reveal teeth black and infected gums. He was obviously intrigued as to my identity but did not enquire further.

Halfway through the journey the sleet ceased and the wind dropped, and suddenly the boat was pitching and rolling less. My stomach returned to something like normal, and I told Hosidius to serve the food that I had brought with us. Cunobarrus' eyes lit up as the youth unbuckled the leather bag I had brought aboard, to reveal fresh bread, cheese, fruit, roasted pork and strips of salted beef. Cunobarrus rested his left hand on the tiller as he shoved a piece of pork into his mouth and began gnawing at the meat, stopping occasionally to drink some of the wine that I had also brought aboard.

'You important, then?'

'Important?' I asked.

'By the way those soldiers treated you back at Rhegium, I'd say you are some sort of leader of theirs.'

'Idle speculation is such an amusing pastime, is it not?' I remarked.

He looked at me with narrowed eyes. 'I reckon the Romans would pay a handsome price for you, your lordship.'

I reached down to check that my dagger was still tucked into my boot. It was. 'You are getting paid well for being a ferryman.'

'Reckon I could get more from the Romans and keep the gold I've already got.'

'Don't get greedy, my fisherman friend, it is not an attractive quality.'

He spat some gristle over the side. 'When you're poor it is.'

'How long have you lived in your village?' I asked him.

'All my life.'

'And you have family there?'

'A wife and two sprats,' he beamed, 'and another on the way. Should be here by the summer.'

The thought that any woman could lie with this odious wretch filled me with horror, but I managed to keep down my food.

'If I fail to return, my men will burn your village and impale every one of its residents. Have you seen anyone being impaled?'
He shook his head.
'It's like crucifixion,' I said, 'only it's done with a sharpened stake driven up your arse.' I took a swig of wine. 'I'm sure you wouldn't like your family to die a death like that, would you?'
At that moment Hosidius came at me then with lightening speed. For a scrawny little wretch he was quick, lunging at me with a fishhook in his right hand, but I had seen him grab the weapon out of the corner of my eye, and as he lunged I jumped up and grabbed his right arm, then kicked him in the groin. He collapsed in the bottom of the boat where the seawater collected, spluttering face down in the fish guts and water. I drew my dagger and placed the blade next to his throat, grabbing his hair and yanking his head back with my left hand.
'Please, please,' said Cunobarrus. 'He's not a bad lad, just a bit simple and protective. I didn't mean anything. It's just the wine talking. I will get you back, no bother. Please.'
I flicked my right wrist and gave Hosidius a small cut next to his windpipe. Not deep, just enough to draw blood and cause him pain. Then I threw the fishhook overboard and shoved him back down in the filth. I went and sat near the bows. 'You two sit at the stern where I can see you. And don't say another word until we have finished our journey.'
Two hours later we pitched up on the beach near to the miserable collection of huts that Cunobarrus called home. There to meet us was Godarz, Burebista and a company of the latter's horsemen. The cavalry filed onto the beach as I marched towards them.
'Good trip?' asked Godarz as he handed me the reins of Remus.
'I'll tell you later,' I replied, accepting my sword from Burebista and buckling it around my waist. Cunobarrus scuttled up to us.
'My fee, lord,' he grovelled. Around us the inhabitants of the village began to gather, the men aged beyond their years by their hard toil, the women ugly and in rags and the children naked and covered in grime. I mounted Remus and ordered Godarz to give me his bag of gold for Cunobarrus.
'Come and receive your payment, fisherman.'
Cunobarrus grinned to an over-sized woman who had a swollen belly, his wife I assumed, and walked over to me. I held out the bag and he took it, and then I reached down and struck him hard across the face, sending him sprawling on the sand. His wife screamed and waddled over to him.

'That is for trying to betray me.' I motioned to Burebista. 'Make sure all the dwellings are empty and then burn them. Then burn the boats as well.'

There were shouts of protests from the inhabitants, but I was in no mood to debate the issue and my horsemen were armed and menacing.

'This man,' I shouted at them, pointing at Cunobarrus, 'tried to betray me. You are paying the price for his attempted treachery. If you have any protests take them up with him. He has enough gold to rebuild your village and purchase new boats. If you have any sense, you will hang him and his assistant from the nearest tree.'

I watched as Burebista's men fired the homes and then the boats on the shore, while an angry crowd closed around a wildly gesticulating Cunobarrus.

'You have ill tidings?' Godarz was on his horse next to me.

It was good to be seated once more upon the muscled frame of Remus. I stroked his neck as the flames consumed the village. 'Spartacus is going to attempt a breakout and we must attack the Roman lines at the moment he does so.'

'Makes sense. He can't stay there forever. And after he has broken out?'

The first of the boats was now aflame on the shore. 'We are to march on Rome, Godarz, to capture the greatest prize in Italy, perhaps the world.'

The vast pine forests of the Sila Mountains provided ample space and security for the cavalry, with each dragon establishing its own camp in a wide arc whose southern flank was anchored on the Helleporus River. Most of the inhabitants of the region had fled before us, the majority north to Croton and a few poor unfortunates south towards the Roman defence lines. No doubt they would inform the Romans of the great number of strange-looking horsemen who had raided their homes and villages for food, and would thus know of our presence. That is why we had to act fast. Byrd and his trusty scouts were patrolling both north and south and reported no enemy activity thus far, but their inactivity would not last long. On the morning of our departure, I assembled all the company commanders to my temporary command post that consisted of a canvas sheet ceiling fastened between two carts with sides of linen sheets for wind breaks. It was still cold but at least the sun was shining and there was no snow. A round, flat shield resting on boxes sufficed for a table, upon which was spread Godarz's map. Cooks brought warm wine and hot porridge for those who tramped in, all wearing boots, leggings, tunics and cloaks, with most also sporting fur or felt caps. Godarz stood beside me as I gave my briefing, while across from me Gallia stared intently at the map, her lithe figure wrapped in a blue cloak and her hair cascading around her shoulders. Gafarn stood next to her, but I noticed that the others stood a little apart around her, clearly out of respect. Everyone knew that she was my woman, but they also knew that she was an excellent archer and a good fighter. Word had also spread of her unyielding nature; she had earned her right to be here.

I looked at their faces. They were Parthians, Spaniards, Thracians, Dacians, Greeks and Germans, all of them young aside from Godarz, and all of them brimming with confidence. It tore at my guts to think that I now had to hurl them against Roman defences. A part of me, I had to admit, wanted to order them to ride north with me, ride beyond the Alps back to my beloved Hatra. But what would posterity think of such an action, and of the man who ordered it?

'Listen closely,' I said. 'We are going to go through the valley of the Lametus west to the Tyrrhenian coast, then ride south to attack the Romans from behind while our comrades at Rhegium will attack at the same spot from the south. The attack will take place during the hours of darkness to increase our chances of surprise, and hopefully add to the Romans' confusion. The carts and two companies will remain in the hills of the Lametus until we have freed the army. We will join them once we have escorted the army from Rhegium. Godarz, you will command the force that stays with the carts, and Gafarn, you will keep Godarz company.'

'I would prefer to ride with you, highness,' he said.

'And I would prefer if you obeyed orders, just this once.'

The others laughed.

'It is twenty miles through the pass,' I continued, 'and another forty to the Roman lines. We leave at midday, rest tonight and then ride south to arrive at the Roman lines at midnight. That is when Spartacus will attack. He cannot break through without our aid; so tell your men to ensure their horses are fed and watered, their bowstrings tight and their quivers full.

'Burebista, your dragon will assault the Roman camp that Godarz informs me will be in our path.'

'That's right,' said Godarz, pointing at the map. 'If Crassus has eight legions and his lines are about thirty miles in length, then each legionary camp will be two miles apart. We will move down the Popilian Way and ride right past the first camp, whose men will be manning the first two-mile section of the palisade, or thereabouts.'

'So,' I interrupted, 'Burebista, your dragon will detach and deploy to our left flank to cover the camp while the rest of us concentrate on killing as many as we can on the watchtowers and ramparts.'

'How far back from the defences will be the camp?' asked Burebista.

'About half a mile,' replied Godarz.

'But remember, Burebista, you and your men are to keep them penned into the camp, nothing more.'

'Like shepherds.'

'Yes,' I said. 'And take care to keep out of range of any catapults or archers they may have. Don't give them any easy victories.'

'It is our victories that are easy, lord,' said Burebista, and the rest of my officers growled their approval. A few slapped him on the back. They were such good men.

'Very well, then,' I said. 'Go back to your men and make your preparations. We leave in three hours.'

The Lametus River begins its journey high in the Sila massif before winding its way to the Tyrrhenian Sea. The valley through which we travelled bisected the Sila Mountains and made our task easier. Byrd had sent six of his men out before the main column struck camp, and he himself decided to ride with me as hundreds of horsemen, the cavalry of the army of Spartacus, began their journey to save their general. The air turned cooler as we rode up into the high valley, with thick pine forests either side of us, and higher up snow covered the tops and slopes of the mountains. A hundred yards ahead rode a dozen of Burebista's spearman, while Gallia was beside me and her Amazons behind us. Gafarn, Godarz and Diana rode with us, while Nergal was commanding the rearguard.

'No Romani in these parts, lord,' said Byrd, 'too cold. My men have seen nothing since we arrived.'

His horse was a shaggy brown mare with broad shoulders and a matted mane, the appearance of which never ceased to irritate Godarz.

'Your horse needs a good groom,' he said disdainfully. So could Byrd, but I said nothing.

Byrd shrugged. 'Horse draws no attention to itself when we are sniffing out Romani. She blend into surroundings.'

'Parthians like to have their horses immaculate,' I said.

'I not Parthian, lord,' he said.

'Where are you from, Byrd?' asked Diana.

'Cappadocia, lady.'

'Will you go back there?'
'No, lady. My country is under Romani rule.'
'Byrd is coming back to Parthia,' I said to Diana. 'Aren't you, Byrd?'
'Yes, lord.'
'You will be a royal scout?' asked Gallia.
'No, lady. I sell pots.'
'Pots?'
'I no soldier, but can read terrain well enough, and I have a debt to pay the Romani.'
'What debt?' Gallia asked.
Byrd did not answer, but instead kicked the sides of his horse and rode forward.
Gallia was perplexed. 'What did I say?'
'Nothing,' I said. 'His family was killed by the Romans.'
As we climbed higher into the valley we dismounted and led our horses over ground littered with stones and tufts of grass. The uneven ground slowed the carts and Nergal had to allocate men to push and pull them over obstacles, which slowed the rate of advance. The afternoon sun waned as the sky began to fill with grey clouds, and after two hours snowflakes began to appear all around us, settling on our cloaks and horses. A light breeze began, creating swirling clouds of flakes that blew into our eyes. We were no longer climbing, and after a further hour leading our horses through the snowflakes we came to the cold, fast-flowing waters of the Lametus thundering towards the western sea. The flakes were getting larger as we followed the course of the river and began our descent. I looked behind me to see the first few ranks of the Amazons, and after that nothing save white. It was snowing heavily now, and as I led Remus he frequently tossed his head to clear the flakes from his eyes. Gallia was beside me, leading Epona who was now covered in white.
Two hours later we camped among the trees of the lower Lametus valley, putting the carts under the trees and erecting canvas sheets between the branches to make covers for the horses. Once we had ensured that the beasts had been rubbed down, fed and watered, we put up our tents and ate a sparse meal of biscuit and wine.
'What do you think about the night before a battle?'
Gallia and her women had camped near to me in a clearing in the woods, which was now deathly quiet as darkness and the cold gripped the land. The snow had stopped falling, but enough had descended from the heavens to blanket the whole valley. She sat on the floor in my small tent with her knees drawn up to her chin, and

looked at me with those enticing blue eyes. Even in the freezing conditions she still looked beautiful.

I was combing my hair, a practice that the non-Parthians among us found hilarious, especially the Germans whom I doubted had ever clapped eyes on a comb, never mind use one.

'How I will conduct myself in combat. Will I be a credit to my family and my city?'

'Do you worry about your men?'

I thought for a moment. 'Not really. If I have done my job properly, then they don't need my thoughts. My old mentor had a phrase, "train hard, fight easy". I know that my men, and indeed your women, are well trained and know their task on the battlefield. That being the case, I have every confidence in them.'

A sentry pulled back the flap of the tent and handed me a cup of warm wine, then passed one to Gallia.

'All is well?' I asked him.

'Yes, highness, even the owls are sleeping tonight.'

'What is your name?'

'Vagharsh, lord.' It was a Parthian name, and his long black hair and olive skin also revealed his place of origin.

'What dragon are you in?'

'Your own, lord.'

'How long have you been riding horses?'

'Since just after I could walk, lord.'

'And using a bow, lance and sword?'

He thought for a moment. 'I was given my first bow when I turned five.'

'And what do you think about before you go into battle, Vagharsh?'

He did not have to think about a reply. 'To acquit myself well, lord, and also that I be granted a good death.'

'Thank you, Vagharsh.' I looked at Gallia as he left. 'You see, I need not concern myself while I have men such as him riding beside me. And what about you, my love, what do you think of?'

'Killing Romans.'

I laughed. 'You should never hate your enemies, it clouds your judgment.'

'Easy for you to say, you enjoyed their hospitality for but a blink of an eye.'

'I was a slave,' I said indignantly.

'But only for a short time. Some in this army were slaves for decades and they would rather die than go back to that existence. That is why they fight so well for Spartacus, because they have no fears about dying to stay free. I myself was sold and then displayed in the slave market like an animal, where fat, ugly men drooled over me. Then they bid for me so I could become their plaything and they could indulge their degenerate fantasies. I loathe them all, and if they all had but one throat I would slit it without hesitation.'

I was clearly not going to win this argument, so I executed a tactical withdrawal.

'There is something else that I think of before battle,' I said.

'What?' she snapped.

'You, of course.'

She rolled her eyes and shook her head in despair. 'Like I said before, Pacorus, you are a hopeless dreamer.' She pulled out her dagger. 'I will kill myself before I let another Roman touch me.'

'Don't worry,' I said. 'Only Parthian blood flows in my veins.'

She laughed, and suddenly the hatred in her eyes disappeared and her beauty was restored. It may be cold outside, but I always had a warm glow inside me when I was with her.

We moved out at midday, leaving the carts and their escorts to make their way to the rendezvous point. As we descended to the coastal plain between the Sila Mountains and the Tyrrhenian Sea, the amount of snow on the ground lessened, until there was none at all as we joined the Popilian Way and headed south. We formed three great columns, Burebista's dragon on the left wing, mine in the centre and Nergal's on the right. The road was heavy with traffic, mostly people on foot who scattered on our approach, though also a good number of wagons carrying supplies to Crassus' army. I did think about sending them north to Godarz, but that would have required detaching riders as escorts, and I knew that we would need every man in the coming clash. So we killed the drivers and any accompanying guards, and burned their contents. After four hours of riding we were within twenty miles of the Roman lines. I sent Byrd ahead with his scouts to ensure that there were no enemy troops coming from the south, and then gave orders for the column to rest.

There was little talk as each man checked his horse, its straps, saddle and bridle, and then his weapons. Everyone carried a spare bowstring and I was no different, mine being carried in the case that housed my bow. I checked the string that was already attached to the bow for taughtness. It was fine. I drew my sword from its scabbard and spent a few moments sharpening both its edges on a stone, then examined my dagger. I checked my quiver to see that it was still full and then replaced its cover in case it snowed again. Nergal rode up.

'All is ready, highness.'

I put on my helmet and mounted Remus. 'Very well. No horns. Pass the word to move out, and tell everyone to keep their eyes open. We may run straight into a legion.'

He saluted and rode off, and moments later hundreds of men began to gain their saddles. I walked Remus over to where Gallia sat at the head of her Amazons.

'Keep close,' I told her.

'Don't worry, I will keep you safe.'

I smiled and then took my position at the head of the three columns. I glanced right and left and waited until the lead companies, each in three files, formed up, and then nudged Remus forward south. As we moved the air was once more filling with snowflakes.

Two hours later, having encountered no traffic on the road, it was almost dark, the sky heavy with dark-grey clouds that were spewing snow onto the earth in ever-greater quantities. The road had almost disappeared under a white blanket, and we necessarily slowed to reduce the chances of our horses losing their footing. Ahead I could barely make out the coastal plain, while the mountains to our left were obliterated by the snowfall. Up to now there had been silence save for the snorting of Remus and the muffled thud of his hooves on the ground, but now I heard a new sound, like the wind whistling through a ravine. As we rode on the sound changed to one of thousands of voices cheering, but then ahead I saw the orange glow produced by hundreds of camp fires and realised that the noise was the sound of men dying, for Spartacus' soldiers were trying to break through the palisade.

They wore Roman mail shirts and helmets, carried Roman shields and were armed with long Roman spears, and as far as the centurions, officers and legionaries who were pouring out of their camp and frantically getting into formation in the dead space between their tents and the palisade, the horsemen galloping past were but reinforcements to prevent the slave army from escaping. As the companies of Burebista trotted past, some of the Romans even cheered their comrades on horseback, cheered until the shrill horns of the horsemen blasted the signal to wheel left, and then sounded the charge. As one the horsemen lowered their spears and galloped into and around the disorganised centuries of startled Romans, spearing the first ranks and then slashing with their swords at necks, arms and torsos of those behind. Those centuries struck first by Burebista's men stood no chance; they just crumbled like an earthen jug being stamped on. The wild shrieks of the cavalry proclaimed their triumph as they literally cut deep into the Roman ranks. It was the easiest victory my men had tasted.

Nergal's and my own dragon rode on, forward towards the palisade, which reared up in front of us, framed by patterns of swirling snowflakes and illuminated by braziers standing on each platform of the watchtowers and torches planted at regular intervals in the ground from the legion's camp to the palisade. Each watchtower, a hundred feet apart, had three fighting platforms, from which archers and slingers were raining death upon our comrades on the other side of the palisade. I strained my eyes and saw that the occasional javelin was being launched at the two watchtowers immediately in front of me, while all along the palisade itself legionaries were hurling down javelins from a firing step.

'Clear the firing platforms,' I screamed at my men behind.

The horsemen behind me swept into line each side of me. They halted and then began shooting ahead. The legionaries standing on the firing step behind the palisade, looking away from us, were easy targets notwithstanding the poor light and swirling snow. In no time they were felled by arrows, most of them being killed before they had time to turn and see their assailants. It was another easy victory, like brushing snow off a window ledge.

I turned to the men behind me. 'Dismount, we need to get on the towers.' Gallia was beside me. 'When we've cleared the two towers ahead, get your women to the fence and use your horses to pull it down.'

I led two companies forward to the towers, with each fourth man staying behind to hold the horses. Around us the sounds of battle filled the air as I shouted to one company to take the tower on the left while I led the other towards the right-hand tower. Missiles flew through the air – arrows, slingshots and javelins – and something hissed past my ear as I reached the ladder leading to the first firing platform. Dead Romans lay on the ground, pierced by our arrows, but others were still alive above me and were now firing their projectiles towards the horsemen. I slung my bow over my shoulder and began to climb the ladder, which led to a square space in the centre of the first platform. I hoped my Roman helmet would fool those on the platform into thinking that I was a friend; otherwise a quick-thinking Roman could lop my head off my shoulders as it popped up among them. Behind me my men followed.

I raced up the ladder and through the trapdoor to gain entrance to the platform, which had wicker screens on three sides. Behind these screens archers and legionaries were launching javelins and arrows down upon the army of Spartacus. They were all facing away from me as the others scrambled up the ladder, all that is until one turned to take a javelin from one of the racks that was stacked on the platform. He froze in terror when he saw us, then died as one of my men shot him through the chest with an arrow. Instinctively we strung arrows and loosed them at our targets. Most of the Romans never even knew we were there before we killed them. I pulled a second arrow from my quiver and shouted at those men appearing through the trapdoor.

'Up, keep going, we have to clear the tower.'

They duly carried on up the second ladder that was just behind where I stood. The last Roman on this platform was killed when one of my men raced up to him and thrust his sword into his groin, and then he grabbed his collapsed form and hurled it through the wicker barrier. I ran to the edge of the platform and stared ahead, transfixed by the sight that greeted my eyes.

In front of the tower, stretching left and right and into the distance as far as I could see in the darkness, were thousands of soldiers, their shields hoisted horizontally above their heads for protection against the deluge of missiles that was being hurled against them. Dotted among their ranks were burning bundles, which were being fired from the top platforms of the towers. I recognised the smell of sulphur and realised that the Romans were firing incendiary projectiles at the attackers from their catapults, no doubt sulphur mixed with tar, rosin and bitumen.

I raced up the ladder to the second platform, which had also been cleared, but looked up to discover that the trapdoor leading to the one above had been shut.

'Oil, oil,' I shouted down at those below. 'Get lots of oil. Move.'

The lamps that lit the platforms were quickly collected and their contents poured over the wicker screens. More lamps were passed up from below, plus anything wooden that could be broken up and used as firewood. This was heaped in the centre of the platform and then also covered in oil. Then we lit the screens and the woodpile and retreated back down the ladders. When we had reached the bottom the second platform had flared up in flames, which licked the thick corner supports and then lit the wicker screens of the top platform. Soon, frantic Romans were looking for ways to escape the platform, but the only way was to jump, which meant death. I looked, both fascinated and horrified, as some of the Romans did jump while others waited to be roasted alive.

'Back, back to the horses,' I shouted as the flames engulfed the tower and its wooden supports began to fracture and disintegrate. A few minutes later it collapsed with a mighty crash. We hauled our frightened horses forward and secured ropes to the sharpened logs of the palisade, then tied the other end to our saddles, mounted our horses and then screamed our encouragement as they used their strength to pull each log down. I looked across at the watchtower to my right, which was now in the hands of my men – they had succeeded in taking it with surprise. The tower on my left was also intact and no longer firing at Spartacus' men. I heard a mighty cheer, and suddenly hordes of men were flooding through the breach made in the palisade, a breach that was widening by the second as more of the palisade was torn down. We had done it, we had beaten the Romans once again. Perhaps we would always achieve easy victories; perhaps we were blessed by the gods. As thousands of troops swept through the breach and headed north, cheering my horsemen as they did so, I began to believe that we were invincible.

But even in that moment of triumph disaster was unfolding on our left, for the gods can be cruel as well as kind.

Burebista's companies had charged with fury into the Romans forming up in front of their camp, and his men had cut deep into their ranks, killing and routing century after century. He and his men had never seen so many Romans flee in terror, and so they rode them down, speared them, hacked them with their swords, and the Romans kept on running. The horsemen swept into the camp and began firing the tents, until it was aflame. And while this was going on, Burebista was leading the charge with wild abandon, taking him further and further away from the coast road. But not every Roman was running; indeed, the second legion's camp two miles to the west was stirring, having been alerted by the sounds of battle and then the red glow of the fires that signalled that the palisade and first legionary camp were under assault. And in the half-light and with heavy snow falling, fresh cohorts formed up to face Burebista and his horsemen. The Dacian, flushed with victory, instead of withdrawing steadily in the face of a wall of locked shields, led a glorious, insane charge against the Romans. I heard later that he was the first to fall, pierced by a javelin that went through his chest. Amazingly, with the enemy spear still through him, he carried on advancing until both horse and rider were cut down by a hail of javelins. At first the horsemen actually stopped the Romans, but they could make no impression upon the locked shields and saddles began to empty under volleys of javelins. Leaderless and taking heavy losses, the horsemen fell back, leaving scores of dead on the snow-covered ground.

While this tragedy was being played out, I was marshalling my dragon to provide a protective screen to allow the army to escape north. As I sent two companies to the west to find Burebista's men and keep a watch for the enemy, behind me the cohorts of the army marched into the darkness and safety. First came the Thracians and Spaniards, the men who had traversed the obstacles in front of the rampart and palisade, and who must have taken heavy casualties. I was dismounted, instructing one of my company commanders to man the two watchtowers directly to our front with more archers, with Gallia's women grouped around me, who had become my sort of personal bodyguard. I heard Gallia shout and then saw her vault from her saddle and race away. I turned and saw her embrace Spartacus.

I bowed my head to him. 'Still alive, then,' he grinned.

'Still alive, lord.'

'Where is Claudia?' asked Gallia.

'She's with Akmon and the carts. They are in the rear of the column.'

'How long will it take to get everyone out?'

'Two hours, maybe longer,' said Spartacus. 'Can you cover our retreat?'

I nodded. 'Good. I am going to fetch my wife. Keep watch for the Romans. They'll know something's up by now.'

'Did you lose many, lord?'

A pained expression suddenly crossed his face. 'Too many. But at least we're out of the pig pen. Keep safe, Pacorus.'

Then he disappeared into the darkness.

I moved my dragon further to the left, past the burning Roman camp, each man straining to see what was happening ahead. It was perhaps half an hour before the first rider's of Burebista's dragon came into view, half companies and individual horsemen, tired and demoralised, the heads of their horses cast down. Many bore wounds to their bodies. I ordered them to go north with the army. I stopped one rider, a Dacian with no helmet whose mail shirt was torn and with blood running down a gashed cheek.

'Where is Burebista?'

'Dead, lord. Killed in the first charge.'

I sent him on his way and sat in silence, remembering the brave Dacian who had shared in my victories for the past two years. Now he was a corpse covered in snow. It was with a heavy heart that I covered the retreat of the army, as the first light of a grey dawn signalled the beginning of a new day.

We had escaped the Roman noose, but for how much longer I did not know.

Chapter 18

We marched all that day, and the next and the day after that, travelling north along the Popilian Way. We tramped through Bruttium and into Lucania, Spartacus pushing the army hard to get us to safety.

'If the Romans are moving west from Brundisium, and with Crassus pursuing us from the south, we will be caught in a trap and all our efforts will have been for nothing.'

'My scouts report nothing on the road to the south, lord.'

'Keep as many out as possible and as far as possible. The Romans know that they have us on the run and they will scent blood.'

It took us two weeks to reach the River Silarus, the barrier between the provinces of Lucania and Campania. There we found a spot near the upper reaches of the river and made our camp. We at last were able to take stock of our situation. At least the cold weather had abated and the snow had disappeared, leaving a landscape of undulating hills covered in vegetation. The Silarus Valley was known locally as the 'land of a hundred springs', and it lived up to its name, with clear, ice-cold water flowing down from the high peaks. Dotted with meadows and woods, the Silarus itself teemed with fish and otters. Spartacus established his camp on the slower, tree-covered slopes of the mountains. I thought it a good position, as no army could approach us from the north as in that direction stood the high peaks of the Apennines, while the east and west were also barred by rocky barriers.

'It's a bad position,' growled Akmon, his usual dour expression made worse by the sword wound to his left shoulder, which he suffered during the breakout from Rhegium. 'There's no way out of this valley and we'll be trapped again.'

'I have riders out in all directions,' I said. 'If the Romans approach to within fifty miles of us we will have plenty of notice.'

'We need time to rest and reorganise,' said Castus, who though unwounded looked gaunt and ill, no doubt as a result of half rations during the time at Rhegium.

'That's true enough,' offered Godarz. 'Our supplies are in a woeful state.'

'We should be attacking the Romans, not running from them.' Afranius was his usual arrogant self, and totally oblivious to the position that we were in.

Spartacus had been strangely withdrawn since the breakout. Worried about Claudia, no doubt, but also seemingly weighed down by a great burden. I wondered if it was the realisation that our options were fast disappearing. He looked at Afranius.

'You'd like that, wouldn't you? A final, heroic battle in which you can throw the rest of your men's lives away in a fruitless display of idiocy.'

Afranius stood up. He may have been headstrong, but he did not lack for courage. 'My men and I have shed blood for this army. It was not I who led it into a trap at Rhegium. Perhaps it is time for a new leader.'

There were gasps around the table at his words. Spartacus merely sighed and slowly rose to his feet. Afranius stood his ground, the two men facing each other across the table. One small and stocky, the other tall and muscular and immovable like a rock. Spartacus drew his sword and threw it on the table.

'If you want to lead this army you will have to kill me, Afranius. There is my sword. Use it or your own, but do it quickly. Otherwise, take your seat.'

Our general stared intently at Afranius, not blinking once, his face expressionless like stone, as the younger man crumbled before Spartacus' presence, first licking his lips, then looking round at each of us nervously, before regaining his seat. Spartacus retrieved his sword and did the same, then nodded at Godarz.

'Pay attention, Afranius, you might learn something,' he said, sliding his sword back into its scabbard.

Godarz then gave us a summary of the army's current state. 'We lost five thousand men at Rhegium and during the breakout, many succumbing to the cold and disease as well as to Roman weapons, with another two thousand seriously wounded. And not forgetting those lost when the Spaniards attacked Crassus by way of a diversion.' I glanced at Afranius, who was actually blushing, his eyes downcast. 'Of the wounded, less than half will be able to carry a weapon in the next two months. Prince Pacorus,' he nodded at me, 'lost a further eight hundred horsemen and a similar number of horses during the breakout. He has an additional three hundred men recovering from wounds of varying severity.

'We consumed all our cattle, pigs and goats at Rhegium, and are therefore relying on our supplies of grain, which will last three weeks, plus any food we can take from the surrounding country. Prince Pacorus has his own supplies for the horses, which are enough to last for a month.'

'We are raiding into Campania,' I added, 'gathering any food we can.'

Spartacus stretched back in his chair. 'So you see, Afranius, if we don't find enough food the Romans won't have to kill us, as starvation will do that for them.'

After the meeting I walked with Akmon, as Afranius strode past us, heading for where his Spaniards were located.

'That little bastard's on thin ice,' said Akmon.

'I fear we all are.'

'You do not trust Spartacus?'

'With my life,' I replied, 'but there are still three Roman armies converging on us, and I don't think we are in any position to fight even one at the moment.'

Our position over the next two weeks improved somewhat, however, as I sent parties of horse into Campania, towards Picentoni, Salernum, Paestum and Pompeii. They reaped a rich haul of foodstuffs, and effectively emptied the area of cattle and goats, which they herded back to our camp in the hills. There was still no news of the army of Crassus.

A month had passed when Byrd rode into camp on a beautiful spring afternoon. We had established the cavalry camp in the hills on the opposite side of the River Silarus from the main camp, in a pleasant area between the trees of the slopes and the river itself. The plain through which the river ran was wide and was bisected by a number of small streams, which provided fresh water for both horses and riders. We had set up a shooting range plus workshops for repairing bows and making fresh arrows, and I was practising with Gafarn and Gallia when my chief scout appeared, dressed in a shabby tunic and with a threadbare cloak around his shoulders. His horse as usual looked dreadful, with a matted mane and hooves that needed filing. He dismounted and bowed his head as Gafarn put an arrow through the middle of mine in the centre of the target.

'We are trying to preserve arrows,' I said to him.

'I have news, lord. Many Romani cavalry riding south down Popilian Way.'

'When?'

'Two days ago.'

'How many, Byrd.'

He shrugged. 'Maybe fifteen hundred, riding hard. Led by a man with angry face and red hair.'

'Thank you, Byrd. Go and get some food and take your horse to the veterinaries. Get him groomed and seen to.'

As Byrd rode towards the makeshift stables we had constructed from felled trees, I unstrung my bow. Gafarn noticed my concern.

'His news troubles you?'

'Roman cavalry riding south means that they are going to link up with Crassus, which means that once that happens he will be at our

throats like a wolf with a newborn lamb. And to rub salt into the wound, I can guess the commander of those horsemen.'
'Who?'
'My old adversary, Lucius Furious.'
Gafarn put another arrow into the centre of the target.
'You should have killed him when you had the chance.'
'You know, Gafarn, for once you are absolutely right.'
Worse news came three days later. Two of Byrd's scouts who had been sent into the west to keep watch on the Roman forces at Brundisium had ridden through the mountains, pulling their horses through snow-blocked paths to reach us. They sat in my tent, looking wet, bedraggled and filthy, as they recounted what they had seen on the Appian Way just west of Tarentum.
'The Romans are on the march, lord.'
'How many?' I asked, my heart sinking.
'We counted five eagles, lord, plus auxiliaries,' said the other man, who had told me that he had been a shepherd in the hills of Lucania for ten years, and who knew all the high passes in the area. I relayed this information immediately to Spartacus, who convened a council of war. As yet there was no news of the army of Crassus.
'But that force poses the greatest threat,' said Spartacus, 'pointing at the map that lay on the table, around which I, Castus, Cannicus, Godarz, Akmon and Afranius were assembled.
'They'll march along the Appian Way to Capua, then swing south and either reinforce Crassus or, if he hasn't got here by then, perhaps assault us themselves.' Spartacus looked up at us.
'That's thirty thousand men,' said Akmon, his shoulder no longer bandaged, 'plus whatever Crassus has.'
'Another thirty thousand,' said Castus, whose colour had mostly returned to his cheeks.
'And we have?' Spartacus looked at Godarz.
'No more than fifty thousand, probably less, and five thousand of those are only half-fit for duty.'
'They can still stand and carry a sword,' remarked Spartacus. He looked at me. 'Those scouts of yours.'
'The shepherds?'
'Yes. They came through the mountains, you say.'
'Yes, lord.'
He peered at the map. I looked at Akmon, who shrugged unknowingly.
'If we could stop one of those armies, then we might stand a chance of defeating the other. We could send some of your cavalry through the mountains to attack the Romans on the Appian Way.

Nothing big, maybe a thousand horse, and they would only try to slow the Romans down.' He was talking more to himself now, speaking aloud his thoughts. 'They won't be expecting that. They don't have any cavalry so they won't have any patrols out, and in any case their guard will be down because they are on home ground and as far as they know we are bottled up here. So, what do you think?'

'In theory it sounds as though it might work, though if something goes wrong then we lose half our cavalry,' said Akmon. 'Why can't we hit Crassus before the others arrive?'

'Because this is a good defensive position,' replied Spartacus. 'It can't be outflanked, we have plenty of water and we can make the enemy fight on a ground of our choosing, not his.'

'I will lead this raid, lord,' I said.

'No, Pacorus,' said Spartacus, 'I need you here. Let Nergal lead it. With any luck he will be back within a week.'

I thought of a thousand men and their horses going through the high passes, which may still be full of snowdrifts and lashed by high winds. It was not an inspiring vision. And it might take more than a week.

'A thousand horse cannot stop thirty thousand troops, lord,' I remarked.

'I know that,' snapped Spartacus. 'But their task will be to interrupt and disrupt, not defeat.'

'I doubt they will be able to do even that,' added Afranius.

He sat with his right leg dangling over the arm of the chair, with a stupid grin across his face, and was displaying that annoying arrogance that had always been his trademark. Ordinarily I would have ignored it, but today was different. Maybe it was because I was annoyed that nearly half my cavalry, which I had recruited, trained and led in battle, was being taken away from me, or more likely was the realisation that the army was living on borrowed time and I would never see my home again. But whatever the reason, I sprang from my chair and lunged at Afranius, knocking him to the ground. I grabbed his tunic with my left hand and hit him hard across the face with the back of my right hand, then clenched my hand into a fist and smashed it into his nose, which began to bleed. I threw him to the floor.

'I have heard enough of your voice to last a lifetime.'

Enraged, he sprang to his feet and drew his sword, and I retaliated by drawing my spatha and faced him. His eyes burned with rage and his face was contorted in a mask of fury. He stood five inches shorter than me and blood was trickling from the corner of his mouth, but like an angry dog he stood his ground. I welcomed the opportunity to fight him. I found him irritating and my frustration at the position we were in needed an outlet. I smiled at him, willing him to attack. It would be a joy to kill him. No doubt he thought the same about me.

'Whoever wins this little schoolboy scrap,' said Spartacus calmly, 'I will kill. Put down your weapons or you will both die. Decide!'

Afranius still glared at me but did not move. I glanced at Spartacus who stood with his muscled arms crossed in front of his chest. He had a look of contempt on his face. His friendship meant a lot to me; after all, he was the reason I was with this army. But I also remembered that he was also my commander. I replaced my sword in its scabbard. Afranius smiled in triumph.

'Put it away, Afranius,' growled Spartacus, 'otherwise I will cut off your right hand and have it nailed to your head.'

Akmon rose and pushed the point of his dagger into the small of Afranius' back.

'You heard your commander, put it away. You don't want you to cut yourself, boy.'

Afranius sheathed his sword and sat in sullen silence.

'Idiots,' said Spartacus. 'Sixty thousand Romans marching against us and you want to fight each other. Perhaps we could build an amphitheatre and then the Romans could watch you both fight to the death. A matched pair, just like the old days.'

'They wouldn't last ten minutes,' said Akmon.

'Perhaps even less,' added Castus.

'This is what is going to happen,' continued Spartacus, regaining his seat. 'Nergal will take a thousand horse through the passes and interrupt the march of the Romans on the Appian Way. We will stay here and fight Crassus lower down the valley when he returns. Once we have destroyed Crassus, we will make a lunge for Rome and win the war. Questions?'

What could anyone say? It was an insane plan born of desperation. But who was I to assume that it would fail? After all, this was Spartacus, the man who for two years had defeated army after army that Rome had sent against him. The more I thought about it, the more I believed that it might just succeed.

'You really believe that?' Gafarn offered me a plate full of freshly roasted venison, one of the brace of deer that he had killed that afternoon and which was now roasting over a log fire.

'Why not?' I replied, biting off a great chunk of meat, whose juices ran down my cheek.

'You don't think the Romans might have thought of that, also?' He sat down next to Diana, handing her a plate of meat.

'Better to fight one Roman army at a time than both combined.' I replied.

I had arranged the feast to bid Nergal farewell and god-speed, for he and half the horse would be leaving tomorrow, guided though the mountain passes by Byrd's scouts. Byrd was present, as were Diana, Gallia, Castus, Nergal himself, Godarz and Praxima. The insane Rubi sat behind Gallia and Diana, eating her meat and occasionally looking up and snarling at one of the men folk who caught her eye. The evening was cool, still being early spring, and made worse by our location in the uplands, so we sat wrapped in our cloaks around the fire that was cooking our venison.

Byrd jabbed a finger at Gafarn. 'That one is right, the Romani could attack us here from every direction. My men know of many passes and tracks through these mountains. Fortunately, Romani legions do not know of them.'

I was alarmed. 'Does Spartacus know this?'

Byrd shrugged. 'Does not matter, I have posted men all around who will warn us of any attack. Besides, it would take long time for Romani army to move through the mountains. And Romani legion doesn't like to leave its carts behind. Prefer to use roads.'

'And what about my horse?' enquired Nergal.

'My men show you quick way through mountains, have no fear.'

Praxima, sitting next to her love, looked at me. 'I would go with Nergal tomorrow, lord.'

She certainly did not lack for boldness, nor courage come to that. I nodded.

'You may accompany him, and take some of your Amazons with you. I'm sure Gallia will not object.'

'I sanction it willingly,' she said.

'Good, that's settled, then.'

I hoped that they would both return, though if they did not then they would die together. I could grant them that privilege at least.

'Perhaps we should all go with Nergal over the mountains,' remarked Castus, his face illuminated by the red glow of the fire. He threw a piece of gristle into the flames.

'Tired of killing Romans, my friend?' I asked

'Tired of living in their backyard, more like. We should get our arses over those hills and then march north as fast as we can.' He took a large swig of wine. 'Then we can get over the Alps because it will be summer, and then...'

'And then?' I queried.

He sighed loudly. 'It doesn't matter now. We are set upon a new road. To be masters of Rome.'

'You think Spartacus' plan is ill-advised?' asked Godarz.

'I think,' replied Castus, 'that Spartacus is a greater general than any that Rome possesses, but he loves this army too much and that will be his downfall.'

'And you, Castus?' I asked.

'I love Spartacus like a brother, as do you, and so our fate is sealed my friend.' He refilled his cup and drained it. 'So let us drink and not torment ourselves with what might have been.'

'Everyone loves this army,' remarked Diana, staring into the flames, 'and I love all of you, and that is why no one will leave as long as Spartacus lives. For of all the thousands who stand beside us, it is him that we love above all. That is why we are here. And despite the dangers we face, we are all happy.'

I had never heard Diana talk so much.

'Because we are free?' I asked.

She smiled at me. 'Yes, Pacorus, because we are free. I was but a kitchen slave, destined to live my life no better than an animal.' She looked at Gallia. 'But then the gods sent a guardian angel to watch over me and I became free. And I realised that freedom was the greatest gift that a man or woman could receive, greater than any wealth or titles or fame. And I think that it is better to die free than live a lifetime in chains. That is why we are here, and that is why we have no fear.'

The next morning Nergal left an hour after dawn. I watched the horsemen file out of camp and ride north into the forest that blanketed the hills all around us. Led by Byrd and two of his scouts, they would travel on horseback for around an hour, then dismount for the long, slow trek through the mountains. Each rider carried two weeks' supply of horse fodder, plus two weeks' rations, though they would supplement their food with whatever they could catch on the way. Nergal said he had never tasted bear and was determined to shoot one. As ever he was in high spirits, especially with Praxima riding with him, but as I watched them diminish in size and then disappear altogether, I suddenly felt a great loss. I did not know why.

In the subsequent days the valley was, as usual, filled with the sounds of workshops and forges mending weapons, fixing mail armour and shoeing horses. Hammers shaped metal on anvils, forges cast new arrowheads and farriers attended to the hooves of our horses. Swords were sharpened, drill filled the lengthening days and patrols ranged far and wide into Campania. I knew that it was only a matter of time before Crassus' army would be upon us, and so it was, six days after Nergal had taken his men into the west, that a patrol galloped into camp in the late afternoon with news that a large number of Roman troops were leaving Lucania heading towards us. Like so many times before, a council of war was summoned, and then abruptly cancelled. I asked the messenger who brought the news why. He told me that Claudia had gone into labour. As I rode with Gallia, Gafarn and Diana to Spartacus' tent, the sun disappeared behind grey clouds and the low rumble of thunder came from high up in the valley. The sky continued to darken as black clouds began to gather above us, and then our faces were being assailed by rain, a hard, pelting deluge that appeared as if by magic. The air was rent with loud, violent claps of thunder that startled the horses and caused Remus to rear up in fright. It took all of my skill to regain control of him. As we trotted through the shallow Silarus the rain increased in intensity, striking us like hundreds of tiny darts and soaking us to the skin. A mighty clap of thunder roared overhead and I was thrown from the saddle as Remus reared in terror. He bolted away.

'Let him go,' I shouted at the others.

'Are you hurt?' asked Gallia.

I shook my head. 'Only my pride.'

Epona was less frightened, and so Gallia galloped after Remus, grabbed his reins, and then led him back to me. He was still alarmed, his eyes wide with terror, so I took his reins and walked beside him towards the camp, talking to him in a futile attempt to sooth his fears. The others did the same, four rain-lashed figures pulling frightened horses as overhead thunder and now lightning filled the sky. We arrived at Spartacus' tent looking like drowned rats. We put the horses in the stable block nearby and I ordered the attendants to stay with them. The rain was still lashing the earth as we entered, and after Gallia and Diana had dried themselves and changed into some of Claudia's clothes, they went into the bedchamber to see their friend. Already attending Claudia was the Greek doctor Alcaeus, who ushered Gallia and Diana out after a few minutes. Akmon arrived dripping wet and complaining, while overhead the cracks of thunder grew louder. Guards brought hot porridge and wine from the kitchens positioned just behind the tent. I could hear low groans coming from the bedchamber, and I caught the worried look in Spartacus' eyes.

'She will be fine, lord. I shall pray for her.'

'Is your god strong in this land, Pacorus?'

'He is lord of the sun. He rules everywhere.'

At that moment a loud crack of thunder filled our ears, while driving rain battered the side of the tent and rattled the centre poles. Alcaeus appeared and beckoned me.

'She wants to speak to you.'

'Me?'

'Yes. And hurry, we are not here for your benefit.'

I looked at Spartacus in confusion. 'Go, Pacorus, go.'

I walked briskly into the bedchamber where Claudia lay on a cot, covered in a blanket and with beads of sweat on her forehead. She smiled weakly when she saw me, offering me her hand. I knelt by the side of the bed, bowed my head and kissed her hand. She laughed weakly.

'Oh, Pacorus, I meant for you to hold my hand.' I did so.

'We are all praying for you, lady.'

'Thank you, I…' a spasm of pain wracked her body. She looked at me.

'You remember your promise?'

'I remember.'

'You still hold to it?'

'On my life, lady.'

She smiled again. 'Good. And Pacorus.'

'Lady?'

'Take care of my girls for me.'

She looked very pale, her eyes no longer full of fire but pools of hurt and fatigue. Her grip was weak and her breathing fast. I felt tears welling in my eyes and so I averted my gaze lest she saw my weakness. I was ashamed of myself. I forced myself to be strong.

'Every person in this army is praying for your safe deliverance, lady, and the gods will surely hear their voices.'

The doctor laid a hand on my shoulder.

'It is time to leave now.'

I lent over the bed and kissed Claudia on the cheek.

'I will stay with Spartacus, lady.'

'Thank you, Pacorus.' Another wave of pain shot through her body and she grimaced as she fought it. I left the bedchamber as Diana passed me with a bowl of water.

The hours passed and I sat staring at the floor, as in the next chamber the strength drained from Claudia as the baby refused to come. Spartacus paced up and down incessantly, occasionally stopping to peer at the curtain that was drawn across the entrance to the bedchamber. Claudia never screamed during her ordeal, but her moans of pain grew fainter and fainter as the evening ebbed. Eventually Spartacus could stand it no more and strode into the bedchamber. I looked at Gallia, whose face had drained of colour, who just stared at me with a blank expression. Akmon, sat in the corner of the tent and drinking from a large jug of wine, looked at me and shook his head. He suddenly looked old and tired. Then I suddenly became afraid, the emotion coursing through me like a tidal surge. And still we waited, and still the groans of Claudia grew fainter and fainter. I don't know how long we sat there as the rain battered the outside of the tent with unremitting fury, but it suddenly became very cold, signalling that dawn was about to break. And from within the bedchamber came a loud wailing shout from Claudia. Then there was silence. I stared at Gallia in bewilderment. My throat was bone dry and it felt as though a massive weight was bearing down on my shoulders. Then we heard the cries of a baby and for a moment I was elated. Then the pale, drawn figure of the doctor came out of the bedchamber and looked at me. He didn't have to say anything; the pained look in his eyes told me that Claudia was dead.

Gallia ran into the bedchamber and screamed in anguish as the doctor poured water into a bowl on the table and splashed it on his face. Akmon buried his head in his hands and began to weep silently. I walked slowly into the bedchamber where Diana held the newborn babe. Spartacus stood beside the bed looking down at his dead wife who lay still covered with a blanket. Gallia, kneeling beside the bed, was rocking to and fro and sobbing. It was the first time I had seen her cry. I knelt beside her and placed my arm round her shoulders but she was inconsolable, tears coursing down her cheeks. I looked at the face of Claudia, now serene with its beauty restored. Spartacus was like a statue, his face displaying no emotion as he looked at the lifeless body of his wife. Behind him, Diana held the babe wrapped in its swaddling clothes.

'Do you wish to hold your son, lord,' she said, offering the boy to Spartacus. There were no tears in her eyes, just a face that was a mask of determination.

He turned slowly to look at his son, who looked at his father with blue eyes. Spartacus slowly extended his right hand so the baby could grasp one of his thick fingers. He kissed the boy gently on his head, cupped Diana's face with his palm and then walked from the chamber. As the tears welled in my eyes I looked at Diana.

'What happened?'

'She haemorrhaged badly after she gave birth. Her life just drained away and there was nothing the doctor could do.'

I wiped the tears from my eyes and gently lifted Gallia to her feet.

'We must be strong for Spartacus' sake,' I whispered to her. 'Come, let us attend to his son.'
I led Gallia out of the bedchamber as Diana followed with the baby. I went outside the tent and told the guards to spread the word that a wet nurse was needed urgently. Hopefully one could be found among the hundreds of women who were still with the army. The valley was filled with pale early morning light, though everywhere was grey, cold and wet and it was still raining, though not with the intensity of the previous night's violent storm, but a steady, heavy drizzle that was soaking everything. The river, which the day before had been a shallow, gently flowing watercourse, was now a raging torrent of brown water that separated me from my cavalry which was camped on the other side. Then I saw Spartacus walking slowly down the central avenue of the camp, away from his tent. I went inside the tent and retrieved my sword and fastened it to my belt. I walked after him, the going slow on the ground made soft with rainwater. I caught up with him after a hundred paces or so. He was bare headed, a shield held on his left and a sword in his right hand.
'Where are you going, lord?'
'To join my wife.'
'Why don't you come back to the tent, lord. Your son needs you.'
He stopped and looked at me, his eyes full of despair.
'Without Claudia I am nothing and do not wish to go through this life without her by my side. You made her a promise. Do you keep to it, Pacorus?'
'You know that I do, lord.'
He began walking again. 'Then keep your word.'
With horror I realised that he was going to fight the Romans on his own. I ran back to the tent, shouting at anyone within earshot to sound assembly. Trumpets began sounding.
'Akmon, assemble the army. Spartacus intends to fight the Romans on his own. He wishes to die.'
Akmon at first did not realise what I was saying, he was still gripped by grief, but then sprang to his feet as my words sunk in. I grabbed Gafarn by the shoulder.
'Stay here and look after Gallia and Diana. The river is swollen, you won't be able to get back across it. If the worst happens, get to the hills. I will find you.'
I kissed Gallia and then raced outside. All around me disorientated and tired men were forming up into their centuries. I saw Domitus hitting a man with his vine cane.
'Get your helmet on, and look sharp.'

I walked over to him. 'What is happening, sir?'
I pulled him to one side. 'Claudia died giving birth. I believe Spartacus wants to get himself killed.'
'Ill tidings indeed, sir. I am truly sorry'
Around us centuries were forming up to form a cohort in column formation.
'Follow me, Domitus. We have to protect Spartacus.'
I paced away south, to follow my lord and no doubt die by his side. Behind me Domitus barked his orders and his cohort followed at double pace. Akmon joined me, shield in hand.
'It will take hours to get the army assembled,' he said. 'You keep Spartacus alive in the meantime.'
Around me hundreds of men were donning mail shirts and helmets and falling in, while centurions, hungry and wet, were screaming orders and taking out their misery and frustration on those they commanded. In every army it was ever thus. Akmon paced away to speak to a knot of officers, while in front of me the solitary figure of Spartacus walked steadily towards the enemy.
The Romans had built two camps, one on each side of the river, and they were located around a mile south of where our army was positioned. My scouts had kept a close eye on them since they had arrived, but thus far they had made little attempt to interfere with us. Today, however, as I ran after Spartacus in an attempt to catch him up before he reached the Roman lines, I saw that there were parties of legionaries digging some sort of ditch several hundred feet in front of their camp. They obviously intended to repeat the tactics they had used at Rhegium. They were wrapped in their red cloaks in the rain as they hacked at the mud with entrenching tools.
I caught up with Spartacus and walked beside him.
'I think this is ill-advised, lord.'
'Then go back,' he said, cutting the air right to left with his sword.
'I cannot let you fight them alone, lord. Why should you have all the glory?'
He laughed grimly. 'It doesn't matter now. Everyone dies, but I would prefer to do so at a time and in a manner of my own choosing.'
The Roman party to our front, about a dozen legionaries, had spotted us walking towards them and had dropped their entrenching tools, and were picking up their shields and drawing their swords. We were now about two hundred yards from them.
'Last chance to save yourself, Pacorus.'
'I will not desert you, lord.'

'Then I who am about to die salute you, Pacorus, Prince of Parthia.'

I quickly looked behind me and saw the cohort of Domitus marching towards us, though too far away to reach us before we ran into the party of Romans to our front. I said a silent prayer to Shamash for a good death as Spartacus suddenly sprang forward, screaming at the top of his voice. I pulled my dagger from my boot with my left hand, then drew my spatha and raced after him as the Roman soldiers likewise charged, no doubt in anticipation of an easy victory. Spartacus literally hurled himself at the first Roman, smashing his shield boss into the man's chest and thrusting his sword deep into his neck. He extracted the blade as the second legionary came at Spartacus with his sword low, ready to delivery a mortal upwards thrust into his groin or chest, but my lord and former gladiator was too quick for him, and merely leapt aside as the Roman stabbed air, then died as he passed Spartacus who reversed his sword and ran it hard into the man's back. A third Roman came at me and tried to kill me using an overhead stabbing action. I deflected the blow with my spatha and then thrust my dagger around the edge of his shield and into his right armpit. He screamed and dropped his sword, then collapsed on the ground, clutching at the wound. I left him there as another Roman swung wildly at me with his sword, missed and then tripped over his wounded comrade and sprawled face down on the ground. I put the heel of my boot on the back of his neck and rammed my spatha through his spine. He never got up.

Spartacus killed the last Roman of the party, who, seeing his comrades being slain, lost heart and attempted to run away, but was killed when Spartacus caught up with him, tripped him, ripped off his helmet and then caved in his skull with the pommel of his sword.

Another party of Romans, who had been digging the ditch nearer the river, were approaching us, as was a third group from the opposite direction. At least a score of legionaries were now bearing down on us and we would now certainly die. Spartacus was a man possessed, though, shouting curses at the Romans, calling them women and maggots and spitting on the corpses of their dead comrades. Then he lifted his tunic and pissed on one of them, which served to enrage the others who were running at us. I stood beside him as the first group, four Romans in a line with shields to their front and swords in their right hands, came at us with hatred on their faces. Spartacus laughed like a demented man, picked up a gladius lying on the ground and then threw it with all his strength. I stared in disbelief as the blade whirled through the air and went straight through the throat of one of the Romans, who collapsed in a heap on the ground. The others stopped in disbelief as Spartacus charged them, screaming again like a wildcat. He killed a second legionary who simply stood, like a rabbit hypnotised by a cobra, waiting to die. He offered no resistance as Spartacus thrust his sword through his heart. Spartacus killed the other two in blur of sword strikes that cut down the Romans as a farmer scythes corn. Spartacus threw down his shield and raised his sword at the second group of Romans, numbering at least a dozen soldiers, formed into line and shuffled towards us. They were more hesitant than the others, having seen their compatriots killed by only two men.

'I am Spartacus, general of slaves, and I piss on the people and senate of Rome, on its senators, its gods and its maggot-ridden army.'

Then the Romans came at us running, shouting their rage and hatred. Spartacus picked up a gladius and waded into them, a blade in each hand, slashing and hacking in wild abandon. I raced after him and thrust my sword into the face of a legionary, whom Spartacus had wounded with a deep cut on his sword arm, which now hung limp by his side. The man died easily on my sword. I leapt at another who was behind Spartacus and about to run my lord through, but he did not see me and so was skewered on my spatha, its point going through his mail shirt and into his spine. I managed to wrench the blade free just in time to deflect the gladius of a legionary who came at me from my right. His blade met mine, but the momentum of his charge carried his shield into my body and bowled me onto the ground. He sprang to his feet and drew back his sword to plunge it into my chest. A split-second later a javelin pierced his chest and he collapsed onto his knees. The next moment Domitus was hauling me to my feet and his men were making short work of the Romans who surrounded Spartacus. Amazingly, he was unhurt.

'Get your men into line,' Spartacus barked at Domitus.

'Thank you, Domitus,' I said.

'A pleasure, sir, looks like we arrived just in time.' He motioned towards the Roman camp where a great column of legionaries was filing out and deploying on the flat ground in front of their defences.

'Time to retreat,' I said.

Spartacus swung round and glared at me. 'No! We advance.'

With that he began striding towards the Romans who were deploying into line half a mile or so in front of us. Akmon raced up, panting heavily.

'Where's he going?'

'To get himself killed, I fear,' I replied.

Akmon cleared his throat and spat out the phlegm. 'Him and the rest of us, I reckon. Well, let's get on with it.'

He signalled to one of his officers who stood in front of the Thracian cohorts who were flooding the valley to the left and right of where we stood, while behind us cohort after cohort was marching from our camp as reinforcements. And in front of us the Romans were doing likewise.

Thus began the last battle of the slave army of Spartacus.

I looked over to our left flank, which was anchored on the flooded river, and across the fast-flowing brown water to where more Roman soldiers were marching from their second camp to form into battle formation. On that side of the river their only obstacle was my cavalry, of which there was no sign. It had stopped raining now, and slivers of sunlight were appearing through the clouds as the slight breeze began to clear the rain clouds away to reveal small patches of blue sky. Around us trumpets blared, signalling the advance, while a similar sound emanated from the Roman ranks. Domitus moved his cohort forward at a trot until it and we caught up with Spartacus. I took my place beside him with Domitus on his other side as we approached the first Roman formation – two cohorts drawn up in line. Domitus had found me a shield and a Roman helmet that was smeared with blood, though I had no javelin. I replaced my dagger in my boot.

Spartacus dashed out of front and raised his sword. 'Straight through them. Follow me!'

There was no pause, no opportunity to dress our lines, just five hundred soldiers in a mad rush at the Romans. These were among the best troops that Spartacus possessed and they did not let him down, throwing their javelins and then charging into the enemy, stabbing at thighs and bellies with their swords. We carved our way into the Romans, who then broke and ran headlong towards the safety of the cohorts standing behind them. We halted to redress our lines. I looked over to the right, to where Akmon's Thracians were coming to blows with the Romans. Spartacus was wounded. He clutched his right side and I could see blood appearing on his torn mail shirt.

'You are wounded, lord,' I shouted at him.

'It's nothing. Form ranks,' he shouted. 'Follow me.'

This was madness. We had broken two cohorts of the enemy, but now whole legions were deploying in front of us and still Spartacus wanted to attack. I saw bolts flying from Scorpion catapults tearing holes in the front ranks of Akmon's Thracians. On our left Castus' Germans were moving forward to engage two legions that were likewise advancing. The clash, when it came, sounded like a loud grating noise, and then came the shrieks and screams of hundreds of men fighting for their lives.

A fresh line of Roman soldiers appeared to our front, advancing at a steady pace with a long wall of red shields facing us. The battle that was developing was haphazard and disorganised, a collection of separate actions in which cohorts and legions tried to destroy those enemy formations in front of them. But there was no overall control. We charged again, Spartacus wearing a grimace of pain on his face as he did so. Again we cut our way into the Roman ranks, literally scything down their first five ranks and then grinding to a halt as more and more Romans reinforced the cohort we had assaulted, the legionaries forming new lines behind their comrades in front. Then the Romans surged forward, stepping over their dead comrades to get at us. The mud, blood and dead flesh at our feet made keeping our footing very difficult, and several times I slipped and stumbled as I hacked, thrust and parried with my spatha. Myself and Domitus flanked Spartacus as he fought bare headed and with wild abandon. A giant centurion attempted to decapitate him but was too slow and had his sword arm severed at the elbow. He screamed and clutched his shortened arm as blood gushed from the wound, and then died as I swung my sword and buried its blade deep in his chest. The Roman tide was unending, though, and as the time passed my strength began to ebb. I don't know how long we fought in that mêlée, but it seemed to last for hours. Eventually sheer fatigue brought a temporary halt to the fighting. Both sides, battered and bloody, retired a hundred paces or so and stood facing each other, men bloody, sweating and panting profusely. A raging thirst gripped me, and I drank greedily from a water bottle that was shoved into my hand. Runners were despatched to the river, heavily laden with empty water bottles, while I rested on my blood-splattered sword. I wore no mail shirt and had, miraculously, sustained no wounds but my limbs felt like lead.

The sounds of battle still raged around us as Castus's men fought the Romans on our left and the Thracians battled the enemy on our right. But eventually those conflicts too died down and a strange quiet descended over the battlefield. An orderly wrapped a bandage around Spartacus' midriff, and then he put his mail shirt back on. Akmon demanded that Spartacus withdraw to the rear to consult with him, though he had to make do with standing behind our depleted cohort as Spartacus drank water and chewed on a loaf of bread. Castus joined us, limping slightly from a leg wound.

I was concerned. 'You should get that seen to.'

'It's not serious,' he shrugged.

Akmon was angry. 'We need to pull back now, Spartacus. We are too close to the Roman camp and they are tearing holes in us with those damned catapults.

'Then advance and destroy them,' replied Spartacus.

Akmon threw up his arms in despair. 'The Romans are also deploying on the other side of the river, and I don't see any of our troops standing in their way. Where are your horses, Pacorus?'

'I know not. But they won't let us down.'

'Forget about the other side of the river,' said Spartacus. 'If we win on this side, we win the day.'

'We should pull back and let the Romans attack us,' spat Akmon.

Spartacus smiled grimly and laid a hand on Akmon's shoulder. 'It's too late now, my friend, it's all too late.'

The conversation ended there, for a great blast of trumpets signalled that the Romans were now advancing all along the front and the focus of their attack was our position. This time a legion was directed against us, its centuries packed tight in a solid mass to our front. I could see a group of Roman officers mounted on horses immediately behind their first line. One was bare headed and I recognised him. At first he was too far away to identify, but as the enemy slowly drew closer, I saw that the man was Marcus Licinius Crassus.

'That's Crassus,' I shouted, pointing my sword at the man in the silver cuirass with a red cloak around his shoulders.

Spartacus looked at me. 'What did you say?'

'That is Crassus, lord. The bare-headed man with the silver armour mounted on the horse.'

Spartacus laughed and then raced forward to stand in front of our line. He turned to face all of us.

'That man wearing the fancy silver armour sitting on a horse is Crassus, general of their army. Kill him and we win this war. Your orders are: kill Crassus.'

Our men cheered and began chanting 'kill Crassus, kill Crassus', and then suddenly we were running as fast as our legs could carry us at the Romans. One under strength cohort against a legion. Their volley of javelins cut down many in our front ranks but then we were among them, hacking and thrusting. Crassus had told me that his legions would be made of stern stuff, but on that mad, glory filled morning the troops that we fought were always second best to us. They may have been well trained and equipped, but we were veterans, undefeated, and we were quicker, more ruthless and possessed by a contempt for death. Against these qualities the Romans had no answer.

Spartacus was screaming like a demon as he sliced, stabbed and carved a path of dead Romans as he made a superhuman attempt to reach Crassus. Did he get close to his prey? I do not know, but I do know that I saw the death of my lord, killed when he tried to fight three centurions at once. He killed one, wounded another as I desperately tried to reach him, but the third plunged his sword into his heart. Spartacus died instantly, his body slumping to the ground as I, screaming like a madman, swung my sword with both hands and lopped the centurion's head off. I grabbed the body of Spartacus and hauled it back as Domitus shouted 'back, back,' as what was left of our cohort gave ground.

The Romans inched forward warily. They had been badly shaken by our mad charge and were reluctant to counterattack. Their dead and wounded lay in heaps on the ground. As we pulled back, two fresh cohorts of Thracians closed ranks in front of us to form a new battle line. A stretcher was brought forward and the body of Spartacus placed upon it. I wiped away the tears as I covered it with a filthy cloak that I found on the ground so no one would see who it was. Domitus stood opposite me with a gash on his neck and his mail shirt ripped.

'Have him taken back to camp,' I ordered.

It was past midday now and the sun was high in a clear blue sky, for the rain had ceased and the clouds had dissipated. Steam rose from the sodden ground while the river on our left still frothed with dirty brown water, though less so now than earlier. Though wide at this point, some one hundred yards, it was shallow, no more than three feet, though now bloated with fast-flowing water running down from the mountains after the storm. There was a blast of trumpets to our front – the Romans were attacking again. This time we stood on the defensive, the Thracian front ranks locking shields to form a wall facing the Romans, while those in the rear ranks hoisted their shields overhead to protect themselves from the deluge of javelins that would surely come. Domitus reformed the cohort, now down to around two hundred men, into two centuries, each one ten across and ten deep. At that moment a panting and sweating Cannicus ran up.

'Pacorus, where is Spartacus?'

My expression gave him his answer.
'No!' he wailed. 'We are finished.'
I grabbed him by the shoulders. 'Not yet. We fight on, Cannicus, that's what he would have wanted. Why are you here?'
'We are holding the Romans but more are forming up on the other side of the river, and they are going to wade across to hit us in the flank. If they do, they will sweep in behind us. Castus asks if you can spare any men.'
The sounds of battle had erupted once more to our front as the whole Roman line surged forward against the Thracian legions. Behind us there were no more troops coming from the camp. There were none left. The whole of the army, save my cavalry, was now fighting.
'Only these men with me.'
Cannicus looked at the paltry and grubby soldiers grouped behind me in close order.
'They will have to do.'
We followed Cannicus at a fast pace to where the Germans were located beside the river. Two legions arrayed side-by-side were battling the Romans to their front, with a Thracian legion kept in reserve half a mile behind them, ready to reinforce any part of the line under threat of giving way. The third German legion was deployed at the extreme left of the line, but was facing the river at right angles to the others. I found this curious, for if the Romans to our front broke through they would smash into the right flank of this legion and roll it up like a carpet. I laughed out loud as I remembered that legions were not carpets. We found a battered and unhappy Castus berating a group of officers. He sent them away when he saw us. We embraced and I told him about Spartacus. He closed his eyes for a few seconds.
'We will grieve later.'
'I do not understand your dispositions,' I said, pointing to the German legion facing the river.
'Do you not? Then follow me.'
He led us through the legion's ranks that were facing the river. We walked through the gaps between the centuries grouped in close order to emerge two hundred paces from the river, which was flowing less speedily now. Across the water were massed three Roman legions; their silver eagles glinting in the sun, while between them were massed groups of slingers and archers. Other Romans were hauling forward Scorpion catapults. Centurions were barking orders and shoving men into position.

'They are getting ready to cross,' said Castus, 'and when they do I have only one legion against their three. They will outflank me and get in behind us, then slaughter us. You see those catapults. They will open fire first, tearing great gaps in our ranks. Then the slingers and archers will open fire and drop more of my men, and all the time their legionaries will be wading across. And when the Scorpion bolts, slingshots and arrows have finished flying, fifteen thousand Roman soldiers will hit us like a thunderbolt from the gods. How many men did you bring with you.'

'Two hundred.'

He laughed aloud and placed his hand on my shoulder. 'Then die well, my friend. For surely we are doomed.'

And it was as Castus had said. Dozens of trumpets sounded across the river and then the Scorpions opened fire, their bolts streaking across the water to cut through mail, shields and flesh. Then the slingers and archers joined them, lead pellets and steel-tipped arrows slamming into shields, helmets and mail shirts. The discipline and courage of Castus' Germans was magnificent as they stood defiantly, despite their front ranks being methodically mown down under the hail of enemy missiles. And then the Romans began to cross the river – three legions, a total of twelve cohorts in the first line marching in perfect step to the river and then slowly wading through the water. And we were powerless to stop them.

Soon the whole of the Roman front line of cohorts was in the water, with their second following close behind, when a high-pitched sound echoed across the battlefield, and not since that day have I heard a sweeter noise, which was soon joined by others of a similar note. And then the ground started to shake and the air was filled with the low rumble of thunder. But there were no clouds in the sky and this thunder was not made by the gods but by the hooves of hundreds of horse. And as I looked across the river to where there had been a flat, empty plain, I saw that it was now filled with a dark mass. And the victory that the gods had seemingly granted the Romans, which dangled tantalisingly in front of their eyes, was suddenly snatched away. The slaughter would go on, for the gods had sent a new instrument with which to torture the eagles.

For my horsemen had come.

They swept across the plain as they galloped forward to assault the Roman legion situated on the enemy's right wing. Its first line of legionaries was already in the water as the first companies swept around its flank and behind its rear-most cohorts, firing arrows into the packed ranks of the Romans. Other companies charged forward between the troops in the water and the legion's second line of cohorts waiting to cross the river. The result was chaos, as those in the water were struck from behind by arrows and their comrades on the bank momentarily panicked. But moments were all it took for centuries to collapse in panic and attempt to flee. Some ran back into the third line and broke the latter's formation, others tried to withdraw south towards their camp, but only succeeded in crashing into and disrupting other units deployed on their left. Soon, what had been an impeccably disciplined Roman legion became a disorganised rabble assailed on all sides by horsemen shooting arrows and hacking at individuals with their swords. My company commanders kept their men under tight control, working their way in and around isolated groups of Romans and then killing them with arrows, then withdrawing and reforming, before once again seeking out easy targets and destroying them.

Castus led his legion forward to the river to allow his men to hurl their javelins at the men still in the water. The Scorpions were still firing, those whose crews had not been killed by my horsemen, but they soon stopped as hordes of fleeing Romans turned tail and tried to escape back out of the water. Those were the lucky ones. Hundreds were speared in the river as the Germans hurled every javelin they had at the men in the river, whose waters were soon turned red by the butchery.

The three Roman legions, what was left of them, now withdrew badly shaken, so assured of victory and now demoralised and disorganised. My horsemen kept them under attack as they shuffled back to the safety of their camp, leaving the field littered with their dead and dying and most of the Scorpions, whose crews had abandoned them. Two cohorts disintegrated and ran towards the trees that covered the slopes of the valley. None made it, being ridden down and slaughtered to a man by horsemen. The Roman legions on that side of the river would take no further part in the battle.

A company rode across the river and headed towards us. The Germans cheered them loudly and the horsemen raised their bows in acknowledgement. They were led by Nergal. Gallia was behind him leading Remus, and behind her Vardanes carried my banner. He dismounted and I shook his hand.

'We did not know where you were, highness.'

Gallia jumped down from Epona and we embraced. She looked at my tunic splattered with mud and blood.

'Are you hurt?'

'No. Where are Diana and the child?' I asked.

'Safe with Gafarn and Godarz,' she replied. 'Where is Spartacus?'

I told them what had happened but Gallia did not cry; she had used up all her tears.

'When did you get back?' I asked Nergal.

'Yesterday, highness. We sheltered among the trees in the hills while the storm was raging, and then came down this morning. Godarz told me what had happened. I moved the cavalry down the valley but kept it hidden among the trees. The Romans were so busy preparing to cross the river that they didn't think to put scouts out. We waited until they began to cross and then hit them.'

'You did well, Nergal.' I turned to Domitus. 'I must rejoin my men. Stay here and inform Castus where I have gone.'

To our front, the sounds of battle had once again died down as the Romans withdraw once more, the failure of their river crossing having dented their morale somewhat. Gallia rode beside me.

'I thought I told you to stay in camp.'

'My place is with my women,' she replied.

My horsemen were reforming in their dragons on the plain across the river. Their ranks looked somewhat depleted.

'What happened on the Appian Way?'

'We lost three hundred men, highness,' said Nergal. 'We achieved surprise at first and killed many Romans, but those troops we fought are veteran soldiers. We were too few and they too many.'

'Do you think you slowed their march?'

He shrugged. 'Maybe for a day or two, but no longer.'

It was a poor reward for losing three hundred men but I said nothing. It was my orders that had sent them to their deaths. I pulled my bow from its case and fixed its bowstring in place. I checked my quiver. It was full.

'Has anyone got anything to eat?' I enquired, 'I'm starving.'

Gallia passed me some bread and cheese, which I devoured greedily, then washed it down with lukewarm water from my water skin. Around me horsemen lay on the ground resting while their mounts chewed at the lush grass that filled the valley. I was weighing up in my mind my next course of action when a scout thundered up and halted in front of me. One of Byrd's men, no doubt, by the threadbare state of his attire and unshaven face.

'Roman cavalry are forming up two miles or so to the south.'

'How many?' I asked.

'Twelve hundred, maybe more, deploying into line and heading this way.'

I turned to Nergal. 'It appears that our old friend, Lucius Furius, has arrived.'

'What do you intend to do, highness?'

'We must fight him, otherwise he will cross the river and charge our forces in the flank. Pass the word: all archers in the front rank to shoot at their horses first.'

Nergal rode away to take command of his dragon while horns blared and men remounted their horses. My standard was held behind me.

The large scarlet banner barely fluttered in the light breeze, but would billow as our speed increased. The sky was cloudless and the sun was beating down, drying out the ground nicely – perfect for cavalry. I wondered why the enemy's horse had not appeared earlier. I could only surmise that they had been camped some miles away and had received a desperate summons when Crassus' army had been assaulted.

Gallia and her women formed line immediately behind. I motioned for her to take her place beside me. It was useless to try to persuade her to ride back to camp, so I didn't bother. Her face was a mask of stern concentration. I nodded to her; she did likewise, then replaced her helmet and closed the cheek guards. I nudged Remus forward then turned him to face my horsemen. I raised my bow over my head; two thousand others did the same. Then I returned to face the front and urged Remus forward.

We began at a steady trot, covering thirteen feet a second. I reached into my quiver, pulled an arrow then placed its nock in the bowstring. I could see the Roman cavalry now, a great black mass growing larger by the second. Men in steel helmets and mail coats carrying long spears and green shields. Some carried standards of square pieces of cloth mounted atop a pole. In front of them rode a rider on a black horse, his red cloak fluttering behind him and his helmet crested with red. His outstretched right arm held a sword that was pointing directly at us. Furius himself.

We were nearing them; perhaps a mile now separated the two groups. I urged Remus to increase his speed and he moved into an easy gallop, his mighty hooves traversing nineteen feet of ground a second. I could hear the Romans cheering and see their spears levelled to ram their points through our bodies. I screamed and Remus increased his speed, charging at a full gallop of over thirty feet a second. If the Romans had reached us unbroken they would have hit us like a steel blade being rammed though a wicker shield, but once more they underestimated us and our tactics, for in their arrogant eyes we were but slaves fit only to be slaughtered.

They were already thinking of victory and glory when the first volley of arrows hit their mounts and riders, sending both crashing to the ground. We opened fire seven hundred paces from them and kept stringing and loosing arrows. In ten seconds each horse archer had fired at least three arrows. For the Romans it was like riding into a steel rain. Their front rank went down and their second crashed into the wounded and flaying horses in front of them, throwing many to the ground and causing others to rear up in panic. At once their charge disintegrated and then we were among them. I galloped past one rider and swung around in the saddle to shoot him in the back, then shot another rider who was bearing down on me with his long spear, the arrow piercing his chest and throwing him from his mount. We had broken the Roman formation as each of our companies kept its arrowhead formation, thirty or so riders in each of its three ranks. We charged straight through the Romans and out the other side, leaving the ground strewn with dead and dying men and horses. Horns blasted and we halted and turned. We had also suffered losses, many horses running around with empty saddles. I glanced to my left; Gallia was still with me.

We charged back into the Romans, this time not galloping but moved our mounts forward at a gentle trot. The Romans were disorganised and stationary, and so presented easy targets. We emptied our quivers, each rider firing up to seven arrows a minute. We didn't fire wild, we made each arrow count, creating a swathe of death in front of us as we neared the enemy. Some Romans attempted to charge but died before they got close to us. The Romans were being slaughtered. As one rider ran out of arrows another behind him moved forward to take his place and began to shoot at a diminishing number of Roman cavalry. I heard a man shouting and screaming wildly and saw Lucius Furius riding up and down the line, frantically trying to restore some order. He failed. The surviving Romans broke and galloped away, this time north, in the direction of our camp. We charged after them.

I had no arrows left now, so I drew my sword and rode level to an enemy rider. His shield covered his left side so I swung my sword to strike the side of his helmet. He squealed like a stuck pig and toppled from his saddle. During the next half hour or so we methodically hunted down and killed most of the Roman horsemen, who had become nothing more than a host of desperate fugitives. Some were still dangerous, though, and one group of around fifty led by Furius turned and charged straight at me, killing a number of Gallia's women before we surrounded and then fought them in a desperate mêlée. I reached Furius and tried to run him through, but he blocked my thrust with his shield and then swung his sword to try and decapitate me. I ducked and hacked at him, but again his shield saved him, though his horse became frightened and reared up in alarm. Furius fell from his saddle and sprawled on the ground. I jumped down from Remus as he staggered to his feet and I thrust the point of my spatha into his right shoulder. He screamed in pain and fell to his knees. I drew back the blade to send him to hell when I heard Gallia's shout of 'Pacorus', and turned to see a Roman horseman bearing down on me with his spear aimed at my chest. Gallia shot his horse with an arrow and the beast collapsed to the earth, spilling its rider onto the ground. I stood over him, rammed my foot down on the base of his spine, grasped the handle of my spatha with both hands and then rammed it down as hard I could through his back. I nodded at Gallia and turned to see the wounded Furius being hauled onto a horse by one of his men, who rode away with my nemesis laid flat across his horse's back. I ran to Remus but my quiver was empty. Lucius Furius lived again. How many lives did this man have?

I ordered recall to be sounded and over the next hour or so horsemen regrouped around my standard. We were now at least a mile south of where the battle was being fought on the other side of the river, and I was eager to get back to offer support. The news was not good. We had lost five hundred riders in the fighting with the Roman cavalry, though they must have lost perhaps three times that number. Gallia had lost forty of her women killed and now her company numbered a mere thirty riders. I sent them back to camp in case any Roman cavalry had found their way there, and told them to remain there until I returned. Then, as the sun began its descent into the western sky, we rode south again.

The battle had ended. Both sides were exhausted after hours of close-quarter fighting in which thousands had been killed. Among the dead was Castus, who had died while leading a desperate charge against a Roman assault that had threatened to split his line. His attack succeeded in driving back the Romans, but he himself was killed under a plethora of sword blows. Cannicus now led the Germans, what was left of them, but he himself was also wounded.

'It's not too bad, Pacorus,' he said, holding his right side that was soaked in his blood.

'I am sorry about Castus.'

'He was a good man and my friend. But still, at least we beat the bastards.' He grimaced and coughed, spitting blood onto the ground.

The Romans, what was left of them, were leaving the field now, crawling back to the safety of their camp, many of them limping and others being loaded onto stretchers. They left thousands of their comrades dead on the field. There would be no more fighting today.

I left Cannicus and rode over to the centre of the line where Akmon's Thracians were located. I had to navigate Remus around mounds of dead Romans and Thracians; their corpses intermingled in a ghastly embrace of death. Most of the Thracians still alive were either sprawled on the ground or resting on their shields. They barely looked up as we rode past them. I found Akmon lying on the ground surrounded by his officers, one of whom was Domitus. His face was white and his eyes were closed. He had joined Spartacus. I knelt beside his lifeless body and bowed my head in respect.

'You had better get your men back to camp,' I said Domitus. 'You lead the Thracians now.'

'I will, sir, when they have the energy to walk.'

He looked numb, as though he had seen a vision of hell. Looking round, he probably had. How strange fate was. Here was a Roman leading the Thracian warriors of Spartacus, and I for one was glad for he was a brave and loyal soldier. We rode over to the right flank where Afranius and his Spaniards had fought. There were barely any of them left, while in front of them the ground was carpeted with dead Romans as far as the eye could see, Afranius himself stood alone among the dead, far in front of his still living troops. He sneered when he saw me.

'Where were you, Parthian?' he shouted. 'Where were you?'

It was useless to try to talk to him. He was obviously still possessed of blood lust. We rode through the remnants of his command back to our camp with his words ringing in my ears.

'Where were you, Parthian?'

We still lived, but the army of Spartacus was no more.

Chapter 19

We built a massive funeral pyre that night on a knoll near to the entrance to the camp and burned the bodies of Spartacus and Claudia upon it, laying them side-by-side so that they were together in death as they were in life. Diana stood next to Gallia holding the infant as the flames consumed the bodies in a huge fireball that hissed and crackled with fury. We stood in silence, thousands of us, and watched our lord and general and his wife depart from this world to take their place in heaven. I said a prayer to Shamash and hoped that He would be kinder to them in the afterlife than the Romans had been in this life. I looked around at the ocean of faces that stood illuminated by the red and yellow flames, a myriad of different races – Thracians, Spaniards, Dacians, Gauls, Germans, Jews, Illyrians, Greeks and Parthians – all of whom had been forged into an army by a former gladiator, a man who had nothing and yet one who had commanded the respect, love and loyalty of thousands. But then what were positions, titles and possessions? I was a prince by an accident of birth, called highness by those who did so not by choice but because they had to. I who had lived in palaces and been given the best things not because I had earned them, but because of who I was. I was proud to be a prince of Hatra, but I was prouder to have fought for Spartacus and my pride burned as bright as the flames before me when I considered that I had also been his friend. And as his friend I would carry out his and Claudia's wish to take their son back to Parthia. But what about the rest of the army, what would those who had fought for Spartacus these past years do now? The answer came in the days following.

I had stood and watched the fire diminish and die, until in the dawn light it was only a large mound of smoking black ash, the bodies of Spartacus and Claudia seemingly whisked away by invisible phantoms that had born them to heaven. Or so I liked to believe. The camp was full of those who had fought the day before, the dying, the badly injured, those like myself who had been in the foremost ranks and never suffered even a scratch, and those whose bodies were untouched but whose minds had been turned to mush by what they had seen and experienced. The morning and afternoon were filled with screams and groans as doctors sawed through mangled limbs and probed wounds for fragments of arrowheads and splinters of steel and iron.

I sent out cavalry patrols to determine if the Romans were going to attack us, but they returned to report that the enemy was shut up in their two camps and showed no signs of movement. I was not surprised. Thousands of them lay rotting on the battlefield and many more must have been wounded. They were probably in a worse state than us.

'Exactly,' said Afranius, 'and now is the time to strike and finish them off.'

Godarz laughed. I had convened a meeting to determine what course of action should be followed now that Spartacus was dead. Amazingly, Cannicus still lived, but he was pale and weak and I feared that it was only a matter of time before he succumbed to his wounds. His entire belly and chest had been wrapped in bandages, but the blood was still seeping through. Two of his men had carried him to the meeting in a chair and had wrapped him in a cloak to keep him warm, for the morning air was cool. Nergal was present, as was Gafarn.

'We are going home, Pacorus,' said Cannicus, breathing heavily with the effort of talking.

'You speak for all the Germans?' asked Afranius.

'I do, what's left of us. We will go north through the mountains and then head for the Alps. We wish to see the great forests of Germania once more before we die.'

'And you, Afranius, what will you do?' I asked.

He looked at me with contempt. 'I have spoken to others in this camp who do not want to flee when victory is within our grasp. We will attack the Romans and destroy them.'

'Did a Roman hammer strike you on the head yesterday and knock out any little sense you may have had?' said Godarz incredulously. 'They are down in their camps waiting for another thirty thousand troops to join them, and once they do, they will march up this valley and slaughter anyone foolish enough to remain here.'

'What Godarz says is true,' said Nergal. 'I fought them on the Appian Way and you will not prevail against those soldiers.'

But Afranius was living in a fool's paradise and our words had no effect on him. If anything they made him more contemptuous of our opinions.

'I will lead an army against the Romans,' he said. 'And when we have destroyed them, I will fulfil the dream of Spartacus and march on Rome itself.'

'It was the dream of Spartacus that we should be free, not lying dead on a battlefield,' said Cannicus.

'There is no more fight left in this army,' added Godarz.

'Will you make yourself emperor, Afranius?' I asked.

He said nothing, only snorted dismissively, then rose and walked from the tent. I never saw him again.

During the next few days the main camp and my cavalry camp across the river were hives of activity as the various contingents made provision for their journeys.

I held a final parade of the cavalry. Now reduced to seven hundred riders, such had been the scale of our losses at Brundisium, Rhegium, on the Appian Way and here, on the Silarus. Companies reduced to mere shadows of their former selves, but still the men sat proudly on their horses, even Byrd's ragged band of scouts, and Vardanes held my banner as I addressed those assembled.

'Friends, today we depart this valley and embark on many journeys. Some of you have elected to come with me to Parthia, others have decided to march south to Bruttium, and there are those who will head north to the Alps and over the mountains.

'We have fought many battles and won great victories over the Romans, and in all the time that we have been together we have not been defeated. We are undefeated still.' They gave a mighty cheer at this, which startled some of the horses.

'So I say to you all, wherever you go, each of you can take pride in your achievements and know that you were once part of a great army under the command of one of the greatest generals in history, Spartacus, whose name will live on long after we have departed this world. Go with pride, my friends, and let us look forward to the day when we are done with this world and shall once again be reunited.' I drew my sword and held it aloft.

'Spartacus.'

They shouted his name long and hard on that spring day. On the other side of the river those who had elected to follow Afranius mustered into their centuries and cohorts under a brilliant blue sky. It was a decent showing, and I was tempted to join them. Godarz, who had been working with his quartermasters to ensure that what supplies left were distributed fairly, must have read my thoughts.

'They are fools and you know it,' he said dismissively.

'For wanting to stay free?'

'No, for refusing to face facts, and the plain truth is that we cannot win now. A year, six months ago, perhaps, but the gods have turned against us and nothing we can do can change that.'

Byrd arrived on his scruffy horse, much to my surprise. He nodded at Godarz, who nodded back.

'We have more important matters to attend to,' said Godarz.

I was bemused. 'We do?'

'It is time to plan for the future, highness. And for that I must have your trust.'

'I trust you, Godarz.'

'Very well.' He was obviously possessed of a great purpose, though what it was I could not discern.

Byrd dismounted and ambled up to us. Godarz frowned at the state of his horse and his appearance.

'You remember the spot, Byrd?'

'I remember, of course. Can find easily.'

Godarz smiled contentedly. 'Good.'

'Would one of you care to explain what this is about?' I asked.

'Our way out of Italy, highness,' replied Godarz. 'I believe that I can get us passage out of this accursed land and back to Parthia if you are in agreement.'

In truth I had no plan to get us through the next day, let alone get us out of Italy. 'Our fate is your hands, Godarz.'

It took us most of the day to get organised, to load mules with food for men and horses, and to burden others with spare weapons and arrows. Godarz insisted that the only shelters we should take were papilios, the eight-man oiled leather tents of the Roman Army that we had captured. There were to be no command tents, ovens, braziers, kitchens or field forges. Weapons and food were the priorities. One of Byrd's scouts, a local man named Minucius, would lead us into the Apennines and through to the other side. He had lived all his life in these hills and knew every track, gully and valley. He had joined Spartacus because his master had refused to purchase a new cloak to see him through the winter, and I privately thanked his master for his parsimony.

And so it was, on a warm spring afternoon in the upper Silarus Valley, that I began my final journey through Italy. We were a motley collection of different races, all bound together by loyalty to Spartacus and Claudia and their living child, whom we had sworn to protect and lead to safety. It was a strange fate that a swaddled babe could command the lives of those who took him into the mountains. We were but a handful, but not since that day have I travelled with such cherished companions. Accompanying me were Gallia, Gafarn, Diana, Byrd, the scout Minucius, Godarz, Nergal, Praxima, Domitus, Alcaeus, fifty Parthians, twenty Amazons, a score of Thracians, thirty Dacians and five Greeks. All my Parthians and Gallia's Amazons were mounted, the rest walked. As they set off in a long line pulling a host of ill-tempered and heavily laden mules, I rode Remus over to where the Germans were about to strike northwest into the hills. They had placed the deathly pale Cannicus on a sled, which they fastened to a horse, though that was the only one they took. There were five thousand of them, all that remained of Castus' legions. I tried to shake the hands of as many as I could before they departed. They wore their hair long and their language was coarse, but they had met and bested the finest that Rome could throw at them.

I knelt beside Cannicus. 'So, my friend, you go back to the great forests of Germany.'

He looked at me with eyes filled with resignation. 'To hunt boar and bear, and spread my seed among the young women.'

'Your fame will make you a king among your people, or the young women at least.'

'I feel that we let him down, Pacorus.'

He was talking of Spartacus. I felt the same. 'I know, but he will forgive us.'

'The child?'

'Is safe.'

'Promise me that you will tell him about us all and what we did, Pacorus.'

I took his hand. The grip was weak. 'I promise, my friend. He shall hear of his father and mother and all those who were their friends and who fought beside them. And especially he shall hear of the fierce and wild Germans led by Castus and Cannicus.'

He smiled and let go of my hand. A giant man with a shaggy beard and thick black hair stood beside me.

'We have to be going now, sir.'

I shook Cannicus by the hand once more. 'We will meet again, my friend, but not in this life.'

I watched as he and his men began their ascent. I stayed there until the last group had disappeared into the trees and then there was silence. Remus chomped on his bit and scraped the earth with his hoof. I rode into the camp that had been the home of my lord. That was now deserted. The tent of Spartacus, the smaller tents of his troops, arranged in neat lines, the captured Roman standards planted in the earth for everyone to see, mute testimony to the brilliance of the man I had followed. I halted Remus in front of his tent and sat in silence. For a brief moment I thought I saw Spartacus and Claudia both standing arm-in-arm at the tent's entrance, both smiling at me, her head resting on his muscled shoulder. But then the wind blew and the vision was gone and I rode away to rejoin my comrades, and the tears ran down my cheeks.

The rest of that day we walked on foot and led our horses, all except Diana who rode carrying the infant in her arms. We maintained a brisk pace, lest the Romans sent patrols after us. I doubted that they would, though. For one thing many groups, both large and small, had scattered in all directions that morning, some heading south to the wild hills of mountainous Bruttium, others going north to find sanctuary among the Gauls living on the other side of the Alps. Others had a desire to seek a glorious death under Afranius. Ironically, most of the surviving Thracians had elected to join him, though I suspected that it was their desire to die fighting rather than serve under the young Spaniard.

Soon we were moving along a narrow track through a dense forest of fir trees, occasionally coming across grassy clearings and lightly wooded ridges filled with wild pear and apple trees. After two hours we came to a saddle in the mountains and descended out of the trees to skirt a hillside filled with scented broom, and then down still further to travel beneath a ceiling of cypress trees. It was a beautiful and peaceful country and I almost forgot about the Romans, though I was mindful to always have at least a dozen men as a rearguard, just in case we had unwelcome visitors. The dense woodlands masked our group, though Godarz prohibited the lighting of any fires for the first five days of our journey, which was a pity because we saw brown bears, deer and boar, and I would have loved to have killed some game so we cold eat some hot meat. But we were in Godarz's hands so we ate bread and hard biscuit instead. After ten days he relented, though, and so Gafarn and I left the party camped in the lee of a cliff face near to a fast-running stream and took our bows to find some prey. We rode through broom and juniper brushes and then woodland until we came to a group of old oaks, through which ran a well-used animal track. There was no wind to carry our scent and betray us to the keen senses of any prey, so we tied the horses behind a tree, crouched in the undergrowth and waited. After half an hour five red deer ambled into view, two stags, their antlers beginning to show, and three hinds. The stags were big, standing at least seven foot high and weighing around four hundred pounds, I guessed. They could not see us but stopped and stared all the same, their noses twitching. We were about two hundred feet from them.

'You take the stag on the right and I'll drop the one on the left,' I whispered to Gafarn.

Seconds later the two stags were dead and the rest had bolted away, as Gafarn and I walked our horses over to the carcasses and tied them to our mounts' saddles.

'You and Diana should look after the child,' I said to him as we rode back to camp hauling our prizes behind us.

'Did not Spartacus and Claudia wish for you to take him?'

'I vowed I would take him back to Hatra, but when I do, I don't think my father would look favourably on me raising the child of a slave general.'

'I suppose not. You think it better that two slaves should look after him?'

I halted Remus and looked at him. 'You stopped being a slave long ago, Gafarn. And Diana I class as a friend. You and Diana shall live like royalty when we get back, that I promise you. And,' I hesitated, 'I would like to be considered your friend.'

'I would like that too, highness. Of course all this depends on us getting back to Hatra.'

Gafarn, ever the realist.

Seven days later we were in the Sila Mountains, having escaped the notice of the Romans thus far. Godarz and Byrd took me into the thick forests that blanketed this region and led me to small clearing surrounded by chestnut trees. The day was still and warm and the forest was filled with the sweet scent of wild herbs and flowers.

'This is the spot?' Godarz said to Byrd.

'This is the spot, yes. I cut notch in that tree.' He jerked his hand towards one of the chestnuts, which had a diagonal gash across its truck.

They dismounted and walked over to the tree, before disappearing behind it.

'Bring the spades from my saddle bag,' shouted Godarz. I pulled the shovels from the leather bag and took them to where they were standing, ten paces into the forest from the chestnut. I passed one of the two spades to Godarz who handed it to Byrd. He pointed to a spot directly in front of him.

'You two can dig. I'm too old and my back is too weak for such youthful labour.'

I was confused. 'Dig for what?'

'The sooner you get started, the sooner you will find out.' Byrd and I dug for the next hour, creating a hole five foot square as we cut into the dark earth. It was hard work, and soon I was stripped to the waist and sweating profusely, while Godarz stood and watched us.

'I didn't realise we buried it so deep,' he remarked.

Then Byrd's spade hit something solid and he stopped digging and fell on his knees, scraping away at the earth with his hand. Then I saw that he had uncovered some sort of box. I helped him clear away the soil from its top and saw that it was a solid wooden chest with iron fittings. Though its top measured only nine foot square, when we tried to lift it I realised that it must have been filled with lead.

'Not lead,' said Godarz, who disappeared and then returned with his horse. He tied a rope to its saddle and then threw the other end at us. We tied it around the chest and together with the horse we managed to haul it out of the hole and onto the ground. Byrd and I stood with our hands on our knees, panting and dripping with sweat. We looked like a pair of miners, covered in dirt and with grime on our faces. Godarz smashed the lock on the chest with a hammer and then opened the lid. I stood speechless as I saw that it was filled with silver denarii. There must have been thousands of them.

'Enough money to pay around two thousand Roman soldiers for a year,' said Godarz. 'And, more importantly, enough money to get us all back to Parthia.'

He must have caught my puzzled expression.

'It's quite simple. A year ago we were awash with money, the result of a string of victories. But what did Spartacus want with money? Nothing. But I had lived among the Romans for too long to be fooled by the fantasies of a dreamer. And, for all his gifts as a general and leader of men, and the fact that I like him, that was what Spartacus was. And dreamers always wake up and face cold reality, eventually. So I enlisted the help of Byrd and I invested in what you might call some insurance.'

'You did not believe that we could win?' I asked him.

He thought for a few seconds. 'When we stood in northern Italy with the road to the Alps open, I dared to believe the unbelievable, but when we turned back south I knew it was over. This is Italy, Pacorus, not a desert. You can beat the Romans over and over again, but in their homeland they always win the last battle.'

'You think we can just buy our way out of Italy?' I asked.

'Actually, yes.'

And that is what happened. Domitus and Godarz rode into Thurri and made contact with Athineos, the Cretan sea captain whom I had dealt with all those months ago. And so it was, on a spring day on a deserted shore south of Thurii, that we boarded ten ships to take us across the eastern Mediterranean. The ships were commanded by Athineos, who embraced me with a great bear hug when he saw me.

'Good job you've got a man like Godarz with you, young prince,' he said as we both watched some of the horses being loaded onto the boats, their legs dangling beneath great canvas sheets that were slung under their bellies. They whinnied in alarm as they were lowered into the hold, where they would be tethered in place for the next fifteen days. It was not ideal for them, though they would be groomed, fed and watered, their dung would be tossed overboard and their quarters kept as clean as possible during the voyage.

Athineos frowned. 'You sure you don't want to leave the horses behind? I could get a good price for them.'

'A Parthian never leaves his horse,' I told him. 'Are your men trustworthy? I mean, can they be relied upon to keep their mouths shut?'

He threw his head back and roared with laughter. 'This lot will slit your throat as much as look at you. But I've already given them a hefty load of money upfront for the trip, so you have no worries. I've told them you're a bunch of rich pilgrims on the way to the Orient to worship some strange god. I've also told them that they will each make more money on this little jaunt than they would normally make in year, so they are quite content. In any case, we all learned long ago that as long as a client pays his money, what he's up to is his business.'

'That's a very Roman way of looking at things.'

'I suppose it is, but money is money.'

Godarz had paid him half of the monies before we set off, the rest to be paid when we arrived near Antioch, a prosperous trading city where a group of travellers would pass unnoticed. It was not part of the Roman Empire, but the Romans had many agents in and around the city and I did not want to take any chances.

'No doubt there is a price on my head.'

'Probably is,' he said, 'but the Romans have got their hands full rounding up the rest of Spartacus' army. They are vindictive bastards, though. I heard Crassus had six thousand slaves crucified all along the Appian Way, all the way to the gates of Rome itself, to make an example of them, you see.'

So Afranius had made it to Rome after all, though not in the manner he would have hoped.

'They are savages,' I said.

He cocked me a wry smile. 'I heard that you yourself killed a few Romans on your travels up and down Italy.'

'That was war, it was entirely different.'

'Not to the people of Metapontum or Forum Annii it wasn't.'

The last of the horses were being loaded onto a large, wide-beamed cargo boat and the remaining guards I had posted along the beach were wading through the water to the boats.

'That Crassus must be rich,' mused Athineos.

'Why do you say that?'

'Well, see, normally when there is a slave revolt they make an example of the ringleaders and the like, but return the rest of the captives to their masters. But six thousand is a big number to nail to crosses, and he must have paid a lot of Roman slave owners a lot of money in compensation, otherwise they'll be chasing him through the courts for years.'

We sailed on that evening's tide, the wind filling the sails as the sun went down on the western horizon like a huge red fireball. I stood on the deck with Gallia and watched it disappear. I, Godarz, Gallia, Diana, Gafarn, Byrd, the infant and ten others travelled on Athineos' vessel, the rest being divided between the other nine boats. I had been worried about Cilician pirates, but Athineos assured me that these waters were clear of them, as they had moved all their ships north to convey Roman troops from Greece to Brundisium, the same troops that I had attacked on the shore several weeks previously. I had asked Athineos for writing paper and then sat down to compose a letter to my father, explaining what had happened during the past three years.

'Do you mention me in this letter?' asked Gallia.

'Of course.'

'And what do you say of me?'

I smiled at her. 'That I never knew how empty my life was until you filled it.'

She shook her head. 'Tell me the truth.'

I pulled her close and kissed her. 'That is the truth. I am nothing without you and I do not wish to live in a world that does have you in it.'

'Still the dreamer, Pacorus. You should have been a poet rather than a warrior.'

'Perhaps I will be now that the fighting is done,' I slapped her behind. 'That and siring children, of course.'

She suddenly looked serious. 'You think the Romans will forget you?'

'I think the Romans will not dare to come to Parthia. If but a handful of Parthians can rampage through their homeland for three years, think of what a whole army and empire could do to them.'

She smiled. 'Perhaps.'

The voyage east was uneventful and even pleasurable. It was certainly infinitely more enjoyable than my journey to Italy. We were blessed with fine weather and good winds, though several of my Parthians were seasick and several of the horses suffered diarrhoea, which caused the crews to complain bitterly. It was cured when Godarz realised that the beasts were being fed twice their daily intake of hay by sailors wishing to be kind. This was soon stopped and the unpleasant side-effects disappeared. Of the Romans or Cilicians we saw none. When we reached Syria it took us a whole day to offload the horses and acclimatise them to movement once more. The days spent in a stationary position had weakened the muscles and joints in their legs, so once they were hoisted out of the holds and into the sea; each rider spent two hours walking them in the water. That night we camped on the shore and slept on the sand, with the ships anchored in the water.

The next day we said goodbye to Athineos and his crews. Godarz paid the balance owed him and he put one of his massive arms around my shoulders.

'If you want my advice, young prince, you will stay in Parthia from now on. You've brought back a beauty, that's for sure, so concentrate on keeping her happy and you'll be fine.' He suddenly looked serious. 'Remember, the Romans are like a bad-tempered cobra. You don't want to antagonise them.'

'I'll try to remember that, captain.' But in truth all I was thinking about was Hatra and my parents.

As we watched the ships disappear over the horizon, I inhaled the air into my lungs. It smelt and tasted like my homeland, and I swore I could smell the spices of the Orient on the eastern breeze. I sent Gafarn and Godarz into Antioch to purchase camels, tents, food and fodder for the horses. Six Parthians went with them for protection. While we waited for them to return, we camped just off the beach beneath a cluster of apricot trees. The day was hot and dry, but we pitched our Roman tents in the shade of the trees and the gentle eastern breeze made our location pleasant enough. Diana, had the infant in her care, and the rest of the Amazons grouped around in their tents, while the various races also stayed together. I posted a screen of guards two hundred yards inland from our camp, but we saw no one that day. Antioch was at least ten miles away and Athineos had disembarked us on a stretch of coast that had no villages nearby. Nevertheless, I was worried that his ships had been seen, and I had bad memories of being once before surprised on a beach.

In the early evening Godarz and Gafarn returned, bringing two dozen spitting and ill-tempered camels with them, each one loaded with supplies. Many of our party, including Gallia, had never seen a camel before and she was filled with joy, patting their long necks and faces. She found them amusing, but camels take themselves very seriously and do not like to be mocked, and a particularly angry looking one spat in her face, which mortified my love but prompted many of the Parthians to smile. We had learned long ago to treat these beasts of the desert with respect.

'They are disgusting creatures,' she said, wiping her face with a towel.

'Welcome to the East, my sweet.'

We no longer needed the Roman shelters, for that night we slept in tents that were far removed from the Roman variety. Each one was made from strips of cloth woven from goat or camel hair and vegetable fibres, sewn together and dyed black. They were large enough to provide a place to sleep, to entertain guests, and also a place to prepare and eat food. And that night we ate roasted goat, bread, cheese, figs and drank local wine, which was surprisingly palatable. We sat round a giant fire with the tents arranged in a large circle at our backs. After we had all eaten I addressed the assembly.

'Friends, this is our first night free from the shadow of tyranny, the first occasion when we will all sleep together on ground that is not part of the Roman Empire. And while we live, the memory and legacy of Spartacus and Claudia still live.' They banged their wooden platters on the ground in acknowledgement of this. I raised my hands to still them.

'We are less than one hundred miles from my homeland, and so in a week you will all be free citizens of the Parthian Empire, each one of you at liberty to decide how you will live your lives. No longer will you be the property of a fat, idle Roman landowner, chained and whipped like a dog. You have shed blood and lost friends to earn that freedom, and I know that each one of you is worth ten Romans. All of you are welcome to come and live with me and my future wife in Hatra.' I smiled at Gallia.

'The son of Spartacus and Claudia will be raised in the royal palace at Hatra by Gafarn and Diana, but I would like to think that we are all, in our own way, parents to the boy. And so let us drink to our lord and general, Spartacus, and to his wife Claudia, that we promise to keep their memory alive and tell the truth about his life and fight for freedom. And let each of us swear loyalty to his son, who shall be brought up to learn about his parents and who is, and forever shall be, free.'

I knelt and raised my cup of wine to the sleeping child in Diana's arms, while around me everyone did likewise. Then the child opened his eyes and began wailing.

The next day we struck camp and headed east. Before we set off I summoned two volunteers chosen by Nergal to convey my letter to my father at Hatra. They were both olive-skinned and slight of frame, in their early twenties with long black hair about their shoulders.

'Ride fast and true,' I told them, 'and with Shamash's blessing we will meet again at Hatra.'

I and the other horsemen rode in full war gear, those who had them wearing their mail shirts and I my sculptured black leather cuirass. I also wore my Roman helmet with its white crest. I instructed all riders to wear their white cloaks, though I kept my standard furled for the moment, as I did not want to offend the authorities in Antioch. The city had formally been a part of the Seleucid Empire, but had risen in revolt and was now ruled by Tigranes the Great, so called. An enemy of Parthia, he had, fortunately for us, become embroiled in a war against Rome that was sapping his empire and his authority. Nevertheless, with our camels I hoped that we would pass as yet another caravan that had hired its own guards to protect its goods. I ordered all the women to wear their helmets so as not to draw attention to themselves.

On foot, marching at the head of his makeshift century, strode Domitus in his centurion's helmet, his trusty cane in his right hand. He led seventy-five men, made up of Dacians, Thracians and a handful of Greeks, and they marched in perfect formation along the dusty track that was taking us east. The presence of a solid block of soldiers wearing mail shirts, Roman helmets and carrying javelins and Roman shields made somewhat a mockery of our attempt to pass ourselves off as a trade caravan, but I could not deny these men their right to march as soldiers.

'You never learned to ride, then, Domitus?'

'No, sir, never saw the point, truth be told.'

'It doesn't matter now. Hatra has need of all good soldiers such as you, even if they cannot ride.'

I dismounted Remus and walked beside him. 'I fear you may never see Italy again, Domitus.'

He shrugged. 'Rome was quick enough to discard me. Reckon I can do the same to it easy enough.'

'Once we are back in Parthia, perhaps we could raise a legion for you to command.'

He looked at me, then jerked his head towards those he was leading. 'This lot are good soldiers, because they've been taught to fight like Romans. Not sure if Eastern types are suited to be legionaries. No offence, sir.'

I laughed. 'None taken. But surely any man can be taught to fight in a certain way if he has the right instructors.'

Domitus shrugged. 'Maybe, sir, though it takes the Romans five years to train a legion. That's a lot of time and I'm only one man.'

'But the men behind us could help you, could they not?'

'Again, maybe,' he cast me a glance. 'I would have thought that you would have been sick of the Romans and all things Roman by now.'

'Parthia's horsemen are the best in the world, Domitus, but an army that combines them with Roman legionaries is truly a powerful thing.'

'Like Spartacus did, you mean.'

'Exactly. I do not intend to let the knowledge I have gained in Italy go to waste. I would like you to think about it, at least.'

He suddenly shouted at the top of his voice, causing Remus to jerk his head in alarm. 'Pick up those feet you miserable worms, we're not on a pleasure trip.'

He looked at me. 'I will certainly consider it, sir, but I thought you would be thinking of a more quiet life, not planning more wars.'

I mounted Remus. 'I have a feeling that war will be coming to Parthia soon, and I want Hatra to be ready. I fear that only the dead have seen the end of war.'

We crossed the River Orontes and travelled into the vast fertile region between that river and the Euphrates, the western border of the Parthian Empire. The first five days of our journey were uneventful, but on the sixth day our outriders galloped back to the column in alarm, bring their horses to a halt feet from Nergal and myself.

'Cavalry approaching, highness.'

'How many?' I asked.

'Unknown highness,' replied the other, 'but we spotted them on the horizon. They are kicking up a lot of dust, there must be many of them.'

'Yes, I can see that,' said Nergal, pointing to the east and the sky that was filled with a light brown cloud.

'Armenians?' I mused.

We were on a track that was in the middle of a wide expanse of semi-arid desert, though there were a few hillocks dotted either side of the road and stretching into the distance. One on our left, around a quarter of a mile away, was slightly higher and larger, and I decided that it was as good a spot as any. We marched over to the hillock and deployed into line, sixty riders, seventy-five soldiers and two dozen camels about to face a multitude. At that moment a rage welled up inside me. To have come so far and with the border of Hatra within touching distance, only to die in this miserable stretch of Syria made me mad beyond description.

Godarz must have been reading my thoughts. 'We could try to outrun whoever they are.'

I shook my head. 'They are too close and will catch us, especially those on foot.'

'Perhaps they are Romans,' said Nergal.

An unpleasant thought entered my mind. Surely Lucius Furius could not have crossed the sea to track me down? But the riders approaching were coming from the east, not the west.

'Perhaps they are not interested in us at all,' suggested Gafarn. 'After all, we are just another caravan on the road.'

He may have been right, but my instincts told me that something was wrong.

'Nergal,' I snapped. 'We will form an all-round defence on this hillock. Put the horses and camels in the centre. Domitus.'

He ran up to me and saluted. 'Yes, sire.'

'I fear that our line will be thin. I will place archers behind your men. Hopefully we can shoot their horsemen before they get near us. Go.'

He raced away and began organizing our defence.

'Each archer has only thirty arrows, highness,' said Godarz.

'They might disorganise our line, highness.'

I looked at him and burst into laughter. The absurdity of it all. He looked at me as though I had gone mad.

'Do not worry, Godarz, I fear that whatever tactics we use this day will avail us little.'

The dust cloud was getting closer as Domitus formed a line of his men around us and my horsemen dismounted and took up position behind the foot soldiers, and if I squinted my eyes I could make out tiny black shapes on the horizon. Whoever they were, they were in a hurry to get to us.

'Gafarn,' I said.

My former slave and trusted companion was at my side.

'Gafarn, you and Diana will ride south and then swing east where you will be able to cross the Euphrates. There are bridges there you can use.'

'I would rather stay with you, highness.'

'And I would rather you, Diana and the child live. This is my final request to you as a friend. If you all live, then it will have all been worthwhile.'

For once in his life he appeared speechless.

'I'll take that as a yes, then.' I shouted along the line again. 'Godarz and Alcaeus, please attend me.'

They arrived half a minute later.

'I would ask a favour of you both, and that is to accompany Gafarn and Diana to Hatra.'

Godarz began to speak. 'I would rather...'

'I know what you would rather do, but I am making this request. It is not an order, but one friend asking a favour of another. Let me die knowing that our quest was not in vain.'

'Please get some supplies and go,' I told them, for the enemy horsemen were fast approaching, a great line of men on big horses filling the horizon. Whoever they were, their riding skills were impeccable, for their frontage was unbroken and arrow straight. There appeared to be thousands of them. I dug my knees into Remus and rode to stand in front of our ragged, sparse line. I faced those I led, Parthians, Gallia's Amazons, Thracians, Dacians, Gauls and Greeks and one Spaniard.

I raised my bow. Vardanes, it is time to unfurl the banner.'

I felt a shot of pride as the breeze caught the large standard and I saw the white horse's head flutter in the breeze.

'We are many races, but we are also one. We are united by one thing, something so strong that death itself cannot defeat it. We are free and we shall die free. Sons and daughters of Spartacus. Freedom!'

They screamed and shouted the cry back at me, the noise loud and piercing enough to wake the gods. I put on my helmet. I would die beside my woman this day, that much was certain, but afterwards we would be together in heaven for all eternity, she and all these present whom I had come to love. I nudged Remus forward to take my place in the front rank and then dismounted. They were about three miles away now, still maintaining their formation and discipline. Suddenly Nergal was beside me.

'They are riding white horses.'

'What?'

'They are riding white horses, highness.'

I peered into the distance. The main body of horsemen, who indeed did seem to be on white horses, was now being overtaken by a host of other riders on each flank who were filling the valley.

'I see a white horse's head on their banner!' Nergal was pointing frantically at the large banner being carried by a rider in the centre of the line. Behind me cheering erupted and some of my men began chanting 'Hatra, Hatra'. They were two miles away now and

I saw before me not an enemy but the Royal Bodyguard of my father, King Varaz.

I turned around. 'Hatra has come! Hatra has come!' and jumped on Remus and kicked him forward. Many of those behind me followed, which panicked the camels, who either stood still or bolted in the opposite direction. I thundered down the slope of the hillock and raced across the plain, my cloak billowing behind me. I could see my father now, a gold crown atop his shining helmet, flanked by his bodyguard, among them the bony faced Vistaspa. I pulled Remus up sharply when I had closed to within five hundred paces of my father and vaulted from the saddle, then went down on one knee and bowed my head to my king. My father's horsemen slowed and then halted. I heard footsteps on the parched ground and then two hands grabbed my shoulders and hauled me up. Then my father and I were locked in an embrace, as all around us cheers filled the air. I could barely see through the tears that filled my eyes and ran down my cheeks. The day that I had dreamt about for so long had finally arrived, and for several minutes I was unable to speak, so great was my joy. I saw Vistaspa greet Godarz and embrace him, and I thought I saw tears in those dark eyes as he met again a man who had ridden by his side so many years ago, but perhaps it was only my own tears that clouded my view.

'You look older, my son.'

'You look the same, father. How is mother?'

'When your letter arrived, it was like magic had suddenly restored her to me, for she had been grieving terribly these past three years.'

'And my sisters, Aliyeh and Adeleh?'

'Older, perhaps wiser, certainly more beautiful, but eager to see their brother again.'

The rest of that day was a blur of emotions, though I remember vividly the moment when I introduced Gallia to my father. She rode up on Epona, dismounted and then walked up to him. She was in her full war gear of boots, leggings, mail shirt, sword at her hip and helmet on her head, the cheek guards closed. My father's bodyguard was mounted behind him as he stood before her; what happened next I would remember forever. She unstrapped the cheek guards and then removed her helmet, her long blonde hair tumbling around her shoulders. The men of my father's bodyguard gasped in admiration at this beauty before them as she bowed her head to my father. I felt ten feet tall, for they had never seen such a woman before, one who stood proud and strong but whose looks could melt the hardest heart. My father took her hands and kissed them, and then she smiled that dazzling and disarming smile, and in that instant I knew that she had conquered the kingdom of Hatra. Six days later we rode into the city on a crystal clear day under a vivid blue sky. The whole of the garrison lined the road to the western gates, and it seemed the entire population had turned out to welcome us back. I don't know how long it took to wind our way through the city's streets, but it must have been hours. Eventually I gave up trying to steer Remus through the throng and dismounted and made my way to the palace on foot. Men shook my hand, women kissed me and mothers held out their babies for me to kiss, or at least I think they wanted me to kiss them. I kissed them anyway. Every one of those who had come with me from Italy was treated like a hero, and I think many of the young warriors stayed in the city that night with whatever young woman took their fancy.

Gallia walked beside me. She wore a plain blue tunic now, no mail tunic or helmet, though she still wore her sword. Many of Hatra's citizens gaped open mouthed at her as she passed. Her pale skin, blue eyes and long blonde hair contrasted sharply with their own dark complexions and black hair. Some believed that she was a goddess and fell to their knees as we passed them, and I heard them say that only an immortal could have delivered their prince from the Romans. Others tried to touch her hair, and still more bowed their heads to this beautiful foreign woman who was among them. Eventually we reached the royal palace where the crowds were kept out and where the nobility of the city were gathered in their finery. But my eyes only saw my mother, Queen Mihri, and my sisters, Aliyeh and Adeleh. The latter had indeed turned into striking young women. I fell to my knees in front of my mother and our reunion was long and emotional, with my sisters wrapping their arms around the both of us. And then my mother greeted Gallia, who also bowed before her.

We walked to the grand temple, on the steps of which stood the grim-faced High Priest Assur and his subordinates, all of them with long black beards, hair tied in plaits behind their backs and dressed in pure white robes. We all filed into the temple where Assur conducted a rather long and tedious ceremony in which he gave thanks to Shamash for the safe return of Hatra's heir and his companions. Halfway through, Spartacus' son started to cry and continued to wail until the ceremony had ended.

A banquet was held several days later in our honour. It was lavish and enjoyable, mostly because I sat beside Gallia and my parents on the top table, while all those who had come with me from Italy were arranged either side of a long central table set before us.

Gafarn, now the adopted son of my father and made a prince, left early with Diana to attend to the son of Spartacus.
They lived in the palace with me and Gallia, as did the others. Nergal and Praxima had married as soon as we had arrived back at Hatra, and it would have been a double wedding except that my father insisted that my joining with Gallia should take place several weeks hence to allow invitations to be sent to all four corners of the empire. Indeed, Sinatruces himself at Ctesiphon had requested our presence at his palace. My father said it was because I had returned from the dead and he wanted to congratulate me in person, though mother insisted that the real reason was that he wanted to see Gallia. The fact that he had requested my attendance only and not my father's could be construed as an insult, but my parents were so filled with joy at my return that they gladly consented. Only Assur grumbled that it was not proper protocol.
He told me so when I had been sitting in silence in the empty temple, staring at the Roman eagle that I had taken so long ago. It was lying at the foot of the altar to Shamash, a tribute to the god that I worshipped. I heard footsteps behind me and turned to see the stern figure of Assur looking down at me.
'Do I disturb you, prince?' His voice was serious and deep, and he still unnerved me as he did when I was a child.
'Not at all, sir. I was just thinking how strange is the fate of man, and how life hangs by a thin thread that can be severed at any time.'
He sat his bony frame down beside me. 'All the things that you have done, and the long journey that you have made. How can all that have been possible without Shamash looking over you?'
'But why me and not the dozens of others, thousands of others, that died around me during my time away?'
He smiled; one of the few occasions I had seen him do so. 'We cannot and must not question the will of god, but I believe that He has some great purpose for you yet. That is why He returned you to us.'
I nodded at the Roman eagle lying prostrate at the altar of the god I worshipped. 'The man I followed in Italy took many of those, and yet he died, cut down in battle while I lived. One day I will have to tell his son that I saw his father die and could not save him.'
Assur laid a hand on my shoulder. 'When the time comes you will find the words. I have heard that you fulfilled your vow to this man called Spartacus to safeguard his son. You have no reason to reproach yourself.' And yet I did reproach myself, for I lived and Spartacus died.

We had been in Hatra for ten days when I asked my father's permission to ride to Nisibus to see my old friend Vata.

'Gladly, Pacorus. Take Gallia with you, he could do with some brightness in his life. When news reached us that Bozan's column had been destroyed he became very morose. He had, after all, lost his father and best friend at the same time.'

'I can't imagine Vata being morose.'

My father and I were at the royal stables to take our horses out for a morning ride. It was the first time I had done so, for the celebrations and thanksgivings had filled our days since our arrival. Gallia was given rooms in the palace near mine, though my parents' strict protocol meant that Gallia's door was firmly locked at night. In any case, my future wife informed me that even if we were not in a royal palace we would not be sharing a bed until we were man and wife.

'What about a rock ledge next to a waterfall?' I asked mischievously, which earned me a slap on the arm.

'We are not in Italy now.'

'No,' I replied, 'more's the pity.'

Afterwards the whole of Hatra's nobility had visited the palace to pay their respects to me, though I suspected that the real reason was to meet Gallia. The story of the return of Prince Pacorus with his warrior princess by his side began to travel far and wide, made more intriguing when it became known that her coming had been foretold by the sorceress of King Sinatruces himself.

The stables were a hive of activity as a small army of squires, farriers and veterinaries went about their business. The stable area was huge, with each horse having a well-appointed stall in an airy and clean stable.

'So,' said my father as he stroked Remus' neck, 'this is the horse that carried you in Italy and brought you back to us. He is a magnificent specimen.'

I threw the saddlecloth onto his back and then the saddle.

'His name is Remus,' I said. 'Named after one of the founders of Rome. I was told that Remus had a twin called Romulus, and they were both reared by a she-wolf.'

'A strange tale, Pacorus, though no stranger than your own story.' He laid a hand on my shoulder. 'I cannot begin to tell you how joyous your return is to your mother and me. Truly a gift from god.'

'Thank, you father. It is good to be back.'

I looked into the next stall where Epona was housed, to see that it was empty and being cleaned out by a young stable hand.

'Where is Epona?'

'The Princess Gallia took her out earlier, highness.'

'Alone?' I was slightly concerned.

'No, highness. The princess and her, er, her women warriors rode out to the training fields.'

'Who else was with them?'

'Prince Gafarn accompanied them, highness.'

'Well,' said my father, 'looks like they have stolen a march on us.'

I secured my quiver to the saddle and then mounted Remus. My father's horse, a seven-year-old mare named Azat, was brought to him and he likewise saddled her and then we rode from the stables. The morning was getting warm and the sky cloudless as we travelled west out of the city. As usual, there was heavy traffic on the road coming from the east, long caravans of camels loaded with spices, silk and other materials, donkeys piled high with fruit for the markets, and individuals on foot weighed down with heavy sacks on their backs. The training fields were located five miles west of the city, a wide expanse of ground divided into archery ranges and drill areas. It was mid-morning by the time we left the city, the traffic on the road making way for the royal party of the king, me and a dozen members of his bodyguard. After a short while the officer in charge rode up to us and saluted.

'Trouble ahead, majesty.'

'What trouble?' asked my father.

The man cast me a nervous glance. 'The Princess Gallia, majesty…'

Before he had finished his sentence I dug my knees into Remus and galloped ahead. After a couple of minutes I came across a large crowd gathered round a richly attired plump man standing next to a donkey in the middle of the road. The beast had a large load of hides on its back and had clearly collapsed through exhaustion. The man had a stick in his hand and beside him, resplendent in her mail shirt, tight leggings and steel helmet, stood Gallia, a dagger at the man's throat. The man, a merchant I assumed, was obviously an individual of some wealth as he had a personal escort of a dozen guards, all wearing mail armour, helmets and carrying heavy spears. The guards would normally have protected their master, but twenty women pointing loaded bows at them made them think twice. Gafarn was beside Gallia, no doubt translating for her. The crowd around them was both amused and nervous, for anyone could see that this fierce woman and her riders meant business.

I pushed my way through the crowd and dismounted.

'What is this, my sweet?' I asked, taking my place by Gallia's side.
'Trouble, Pacorus,' said Gafarn.
'I can see that. My love, why don't you put the dagger down.'
Gallia held the point firmly at the man's neck.
I looked behind me to see Praxima with her bow pointed at the merchant, while the other Amazons covered his guards.
'Will someone tell me what is going on?'
'Ask this fat bully,' growled Gallia.
'Allow me to illuminate further,' offered Gafarn. 'We were riding back from archery practice when we came across this individual beating this poor beast with his stick, whereupon the Lady Gallia took exception and tried to persuade said gentlemen to desist.'
'I threatened to slit his throat unless he stopped,' said Gallia.
The merchant, sweating and alarmed, obviously believed me to be his salvation, for he had heard Gafarn speak my name and he must have known that I was the heir to Hatra's throne.
'Highness, this is an outrage. This woman, this demon from the underworld, has dared to threaten me for nothing more than attending to my own business. This beast is my property and I will treat it as I see fit.'
The miserable, half-starved donkey was still sitting on the ground, no doubt glad of the opportunity to snatch some rest.
I could tell by the look on her face that Gallia would not yield, and neither would the merchant. I had visions of dead bodies and the road soaked in blood when I heard shouts of 'make way for the king' behind me.
All noise died away as my father dismounted and walked to where Gallia stood.
'What is going on here?'
Gafarn spoke to him in whispers and then my father spoke to Gallia.
'If I purchased the donkey for you, would you grant me a favour and lower your weapon, daughter?'
Gallia looked at my father and lowered her dagger. 'As your majesty commands.'
'Thank the gods,' said the merchant. 'Your majesty, I really must protest...'
'Silence!' bellowed my father, making me for one jump. 'I did not ride out of the city today to bandy words with a lowly merchant. I could have you executed for daring to raise your voice to my son's future wife, but as I don't want to pollute the ground with your blood, I will purchases this sad creature that you have abused so foully. Pay the man, Pacorus.'

With that my father turned and went back to his horse. I reach into the purse hanging from my belt and threw some gold coins on the ground, which the merchant gladly accepted. With such a sum I could have purchased a dozen donkeys. He bowed his head and then gestured to his guards that they should be on their way. Gallia signalled for her Amazons to lower their bows and the crowd dispersed. She walked over to the donkey and cut the straps to free it of its load. The merchant gestured to one of his guides to collect the hides that were now lying on the ground.

'The gold includes the baggage it was carrying,' I shouted, daring anyone to question me.

The merchant's guard stopped and looked nervously at his master, who clapped his hands and smiled.

'Of course, of course, highness. As you wish.'

After a couple of minutes the donkey got back on its feet. Gallia handed it to Gafarn and walked over to my father. She bowed her head to him.

'You are most generous, majesty; I did not mean to cause offence. But I cannot stand by when I see cruelty.'

My father smiled at her. 'You are indeed a rare beauty, Gallia. Are you riding back to the city?'

'Yes, majesty, we have been attending to our archery skills.'

My father looked at the Amazons drawn up by the side of the road. 'Do your women shoot well, Gallia?'

She smiled. 'Yes, majesty, like me. they always hit what they aim at.'

My father nudged Azat forward. 'I don't doubt it. Have a good day, Gallia.'

I embraced Gallia and kissed her on the cheek. 'My father and I are going to the training fields. Try not to kill anyone between here and the city.'

She jabbed me in the ribs. 'Thank you for the gift.'

The story of Gallia and the merchant only added more to the myth that surrounded her, as well as to that of her 'wild women'.

She left the Amazons at Hatra when we rode north to Nisibus to see Vata, though I did take Nergal and the fifty Parthians who had come with me from Italy. He met us ten miles south of the town with a handful of the garrison. I recognized his round face and stocky frame as he jumped down from his horse and ran towards me, and then we embraced. He was nearly thirty years of age now and his face had a slightly haggard look. In truth, the years had not been kind to him.

'It is good to see you, my friend,' I said.

Gallia had dismounted and stood several feet behind me, though when he saw her he let go of me and went down on one knee before her.

'Your servant, lady.'

She lifted him up and kissed him on the cheek.

'I am glad to meet you, Vata. I have heard a lot about you.'

'Not all bad, I hope,' he winked at me.

As we rode to Nisibus together, Vata gave me a brief summary of events in the empire.

'Our friend King Darius still wants to be a Roman, but we have placed forces on our northern border to try and pre-empt any Roman invasion. For the moment things are quiet.'

'And what of King Sinatruces?' I asked.

'He still lives, just.'

'Who is King Sinatruces?' asked Gallia.

'The king of kings,' said Vata, 'he's over eighty years old, and when he dies there will be civil war.'

'Surely not,' I was surprised.

'The empire has become a more fractious place since you left us, Pacorus. There are rumours that the title will not pass to his son, Phraates, but will be challenged by other kings of the empire.'

'And if that happens?' Gallia was inquisitive about the workings of the empire.

Vata smiled. 'Then, lady, there will be war.'

Nisibus was in truth a dismal place, which suited Vata's mood. That night he gave a lavish feast in our honour, though I could tell that his father's death had cast a dark shadow over him. He was the town's governor and his loss and his duties weighed heavily on him. I saw little of the carefree young man whom I remembered. He had changed; but then, so had we all.

'It's good that you are back, my friend,' he said as we relaxed after our meal in his governor's palace, a large, rather austere limestone building in the city's northern district. 'Your father will have need of all the great warriors he can lay his hands on.'

'Really, why?'

'Because many in the empire are jealous of Hatra and its wealth. They will be even more so now that you have returned.'

I took another sip of wine. 'I doubt that anyone has noticed.'

He laid a hand on my arm. 'You are wrong, my friend. Your story spreads like a wildfire to all parts of the empire.' He looked past me to where Gallia was talking to Nergal.

'It's true what they say about her. She is a stunning beauty, my congratulations.'

'What about you, my friend. Is there a woman in your life?'
He laughed, and for a brief second the old Vata returned. 'Many, though none that I would want to introduce to my mother.'
'I am sorry about your father.'
He looked and me and shrugged. 'It is a soldier's fate to die in battle. And my father was a soldier.'
'The best,' I said.
He leaned in closer. 'Tell me, is it true what they say about Gallia?'
'What?'
'That she fought beside you in battle.'
I finished my wine. 'It's true. She has fought in many battles. What's more, she saved my life once when a Roman was about to run his sword through me.'
'Hard to believe that one so gorgeous is capable of fighting. I've heard it said that her coming was predicted by the old hag that Sinatruces keeps at his palace.'
'That is also true.'
He slapped me hard on the shoulder.
'We live in strange times, my friend.'
Once we had said our farewells to Vata, Gallia and I returned to Hatra and then set off on the journey across my father's kingdom to visit King Sinatruces, taking a leisurely trip down the west bank of the River Tigris. My retinue numbered over two hundred and included most of those who had travelled from Italy, though Gafarn and Diana remained at the palace along with Alcaeus, Byrd and Godarz. The latter had been appointed to be Prince Vistaspa's personal envoy, and when I asked what that meant exactly, he had smiled and replied, 'it mostly involves talking for hours about the old times when we ride together. Obviously I am too old to fight, but my old lord is kind and we are planning a trip to Arabia to source new breeding stock for the king's stables.'
Godarz was a welcome addition to my father's household, not least because his presence had made Vistaspa less severe than I remembered him. Nergal had become the commander of my personal bodyguard, which was made up of those who had come from Italy. Many of my father's bodyguard had wanted to join, as well as others who came to Hatra having heard of my adventures, but I refused them all. I had a close bond with those I had fought beside in Italy, and I only wanted their swords and bows to protect me. My father had raised an eyebrow when I told him that Gallia's Amazons should be included, but at that time he could refuse me

nothing and so twenty fierce female horsemen led by the wild Praxima rode behind my scarlet banner.

How fine we looked during that journey, those on horses dressed in white tunics, white cloaks, mail shirts, silver helmets with white horsehair crests, red-brown leggings and leather boots. Our saddlecloths were red edged with white, while our horses wore black leather bridles decorated with silver strips. Domitus and his cohort were also equipped with white tunics, and their shields were no longer painted red but white, with their bosses burnished bright. With his white crest atop his helmet, he still looked liked a Roman centurion, even down to his short-cropped hair.

'Long hair is for women. No offence, sir.'

I was walking beside him, holding Remus by his reins. 'None taken, but most of your men have long hair.'

'That's different. Normally I would insist that they all trim their manes, but they fought for three years under Spartacus and travelled halfway across the world to stay with you, and they are among the best soldiers I have seen in battle, so I make an exception for them. But only for them.' He cast me a glance. 'If you are serious about raising a legion...'

'Never more so,' I replied.

'Then those who join it will have to look, dress and drill the way I want them to. There can be no argument about that.'

'I would not have it any other way, Domitus.'

'Thank you, sir. By the way, I've enlisted a lot of those who came to your city to volunteer their services. Their training will begin when we return.'

'But I told them that I didn't want them.'

'No, sir. You told them that you didn't want them in your bodyguard. But I took a look at them and I reckon that they could be useful, and so told them they could stay if they were prepared to fight on foot.'

'But why, Domitus? Frankly, most of them seemed to be adventurers, dreamers and the like.'

He laughed. 'That they are, but men who fight for ideals are often better than those who do so just for pay. Besides, I reckon that a man who has tramped from god knows where to enlist in your service can be turned into a loyal soldier. You can't buy that sort of enthusiasm. And loyalty is priceless. Hope you don't mind.'

He had obviously been thinking far into the future. 'Not at all, Domitus. I leave the matter in your capable hands.'

We rose at dawn and rode during the morning, then rested in large tents during the blistering heat of the middle of the day. The horses and camels were secured under large canvas awnings that also protected them from the heat.

I relaxed with Gallia at the entrance to my tent, watching farmers in the distance tending to their fields. This part of Hatra was lush, with irrigation canals running off the Tigris, watering the fields up to two miles from the river itself.

'So, what do you think of my father's kingdom?'

She looked at me with those piercing blue eyes and smiled. 'I like it, and I like its people.'

'And they like you. I think you have conquered them already.'

'This king we are going to see, this Sinatruces. Is he higher than your father?'

I thought for a moment. 'Yes and no. He is the King of Kings, appointed to rule over all the other kings in the empire, but those kings are rulers in their own right. It is more like a collection of equals who are happy to elect one of their number to take charge of the empire.'

'What if one king decides he wants to be king of kings instead of the one already appointed?'

'Such a thing has happened only once or twice in our history. We recognise that there is strength in unity, and while we are united, we are invincible.'

It took us five days to reach Ctesiphon, and on the final morning of our journey we were met by five hundred cataphracts sent by Sinatruces to escort us to his palace. Their commander was a thickset man in his forties named Enius. He and his men were encased in scale armour that covered their torsos, arms, legs and feet. On their heads they wore open-faced helmets with blue plumes, and rich yellow cloaks draped around their shoulders. Their horses also wore armour, which covered their bodies, necks and heads. The armour of both man and horse was composed of both iron and bronze scales. I saw that some of the scales were also silver strips, which made both man and horse shimmer and glisten in the sunlight. Enius carried a shield on his left side but no spear, whereas his men were armed with long spears that had blue cloth strips fluttering from beneath their whetted points. The cataphracts looked both magnificent and intimidating, a nice touch by Sinatruces, I thought. They gave just the right balance between a demonstration of power and an impressive reception party. Gallia's eyes lit up when she saw them; the first time in her life that she saw Parthian cataphracts in all their glory. Enius, who rode beside me on my left, was eager to ingratiate himself with my beloved. She was, like all of us, not wearing her helmet as the day was getting hot, and her hair was flowing freely down her back and over her breasts. I could see that Enius and his men wanted to see this warrior woman from the west, as most of his cataphracts rode not behind us but in two large blocks on our flanks. I smiled when I saw their heads turn to catch a glimpse of her and some pointed at her. She was certainly dazzling their commander.

She flashed him a smile. 'Your men and their horses are beautiful, Lord Enius.'

'They pale beside you, lady,' he replied.

'I have never seen horses wearing armour.'

'We have cataphracts in Hatra, my sweet,' I said.

'Then why have I not seen them?'

'Because they are only used on the battlefield or to honour a special guest,' said Enius.

'Or to impress a beautiful woman,' I added. Enius ignored my jibe.

In truth, though, Sinatruces did honour us, for when we reached Ctesiphon two hours later, the walls of the city were lined with soldiers and the route through the streets was also lined with guards of the imperial household. Enius led us under the gatehouse of the palace walls to the marble palace steps, where the chancellor welcomed us and where a host of attendants took our horses and camels to the stables.

'Welcome, Prince Pacorus,' announced the chancellor, who had a high-pitched voice and whose face was covered in rouge. His soft, feminine hands which he held in front of him like a pious man of religion were adorned with gold rings. Gallia looked at him and began to laugh, before controlling herself. The chancellor frowned at her most severely. Obviously he was an observer of strict court etiquette.

'Please follow me,' he said, before turning abruptly and marching up the steps.

'He's a eunuch,' I whispered to her as we followed him, which caused her to laugh even louder. I glanced apologetically to Enius, who had a broad grin on his face as he trailed after us.

The palace was larger and more lavish than the one at Hatra, with walls made of blue and yellow bricks and columns adorned with mythical paintings. It was as impressive as I remembered it from my first visit, which now seemed to me to have be in a different age. We were informed that after we had bathed, dressed and eaten, Sinatruces would grant us an audience. We were also informed that King Phraates, his son, would not be present at the audience as he was on a diplomatic mission to Armenia. Gallia and I were shown to separate rooms where slaves had prepared baths of scented water. After I had soaked away the grime of the journey, a big muscular Nubian slave massaged my shoulders and back. Then two waif-like girls who giggled continuously filed the nails on my hands and feet, massaged my head and combed my hair. Gallia was shown into my room where a table had been heaped with sweet meats, fruit, bread and olives. Servants poured us wine from silver jugs into gold and silver cups.

Gallia looked like a goddess. She had swapped her mail shirt and leggings for a long white silk gown that left her arms bare. She wore gold anklets and bracelets. Her gown was inlaid with gold that ran under her breasts and around her neck. She also wore a gold waist chain, while on her head was a gold diadem inlaid with red and green jewels. Her hair shone like it had been polished for hours, the locks tumbling around her neck and shoulders. Even her white sandals had golden buckles. I just stood and stared at her.

'Has someone cut out your tongue?'

'You look like a goddess,' was all I could utter.

She smiled and took my hand and led me to large couch where we were served food and wine. Afterwards the chancellor came and led us to the throne room, though not the one where I had first met Sinatruces. This one was a medium-sized square room with a high ceiling and a grey marble floor. The large white stone dais stood at the opposite end to where we entered, through two large doors painted white and inlaid with gold. Marble columns lined the walls of the throne room, each one surmounted by a gold mythical beast – chamrosh, hadhayosh, huma, karkadann, zahhak, roc, manticore, simurgh and shahbaz. In front of each column stood a guard dressed in a yellow tunic, baggy white trousers, and holding a short spear with a long, broad blade. We walked across the floor towards the dais, where Sinatruces was sitting on his throne dressed in a simple yellow robe covering his whole body. There was a vacant chair on his left side. Light streamed into the room via square windows positioned high up on the walls. Incense burned either side of the dais where four fierce-looking Scythian axe men, huge Asiatic thugs, stood with their hands on their large and keenly sharpened two-headed axes. Gallia and I halted in front of the dais and bowed at Sinatruces. He looked every bit his eighty years, with his thin bony face, narrow nose and wispy white hair on each side of his bald head. But his eyes were like a hawk's and were fixed on Gallia.

'So, young prince, this is the beauty who has set my empire alight with gossip, speculation and rumour.' He spoke Latin so Gallia could comprehend, for as yet she had only a basic understanding of our language.

'Yes, highness,' I said. 'This is the Princess Gallia.'

His fingers rapped on the arms of his golden throne. 'A princess? From what race are you from, child?'

She stood proudly in front of him and her voice did not falter when she answered. 'From a land called Gaul, your majesty, a land far from here that is green and mountainous.'

Sinatruces leaned forward, resting his pointed chin on his right hand. 'Come and sit beside me child, so that I may hear more of your land.'

Gallia took her place beside him, leaving me standing on my own and feeling somewhat ignored.

'Ha! The young lion burns with jealousy, Sinatruces. I would have a care if I were you. His sword is sharp and his reflexes quick. I doubt that even your axe men would be able to save you should he decide to water the ground with your blood.'

The Scythians hoisted up their weapons and fixed me with their black eyes after a voice I recognised had uttered these words. Out of the shadow in the corner of the room behind the dais shuffled the old crone Dobbai. She looked as dishevelled and unwashed as I remembered her, her hair lank with grease and her black robe filthy. She shuffled into the room and walked onto the dais, ignored Sinatruces and stood before Gallia. She took my love's hand, who for once was lost for words. Dobbai then looked at me.

'So, you have fulfilled the prophecy young prince. You intend to marry her?'

'I do.'

'You hear that, Sinatruces. And you had a design to make her one of your harem. If you imprison her here, this son of Hatra will tear your empire apart.' She cackled at Gallia. 'Have no fear, child. The only part of the king's body that works at all is his tongue.'

Dobbai pointed a finger at Sinatruces. 'The fantasies of tired old men are pathetic to behold. Do you think that this woman, this beauty whom Prince Pacorus has crossed oceans and vanquished armies to be with, could be traded like a cheap trinket?

'You may cut down this young man where he stands, but to do so would cause a storm to descend upon you such as the world has never seen. Do you know, Sinatruces, that even as you sit on your throne men flock to Hatra to serve under Prince Pacorus? They have heard of the manner of his return, and from all lands the brave, the fanatics and the pious flock to Hatra to serve him. Some say he is a god, while others say that this young girl is a goddess who has been sent from the heavens to protect him. To touch even one hair on his head would be enough to conjure up a mighty army under King Varaz that would destroy you and reduce your city to dust. To dust, Sinatruces.

'All this will come to pass if you seek to possess her, for many are saying that he, and she are beloved of the gods.'

Sinatruces, clearly alarmed, shook his head and professed his innocence.

'I did not think to imprison her,' protested the king. 'I merely wanted to see her. I meant no harm.'

'Well,' snapped Dobbai, 'you've seen her.'

Dobbai took Gallia's hand and led her from the dais, then placed her hand in mine. Sinatruces sat back looking crestfallen.

Dobbai then stared at the king. 'And if you are thinking of retracting your gift to Pacorus, the price that your devious mind had settled upon for her, then think again.' She jabbed a bony finger at him. 'The gods are watching us at this very moment, watching your every move. And for one whose time on this earth is coming to an end, and who will be standing before them soon enough, I would choose your words carefully.'

The king looked at Dobbai then to me, then at Gallia. He sighed and looked down at his feet, and appeared like a man who had let a great prize slip through his fingers.

'Of course, we are glad to see you. Both of you. It is a miracle that you have returned safely to Parthia. My wedding gift to you, Pacorus, is this.'

He clapped his hands and the eunuch chancellor came from behind us to stand beside the dais. He unrolled a scroll and began to speak in his high-pitched voice.

'Sinatruces, king of kings, lord of Parthia from the banks....'

'Get to the meat of it,' snapped the king.

The eunuch frowned. He was not having a good day. 'Pacorus, Prince of Hatra, is hereby created King of Dura Europus, said position to be held by him and his offspring for all eternity. This is the word of Sinatruces, and is the law.'

I was stunned. Dura Europus was a city on the left bank of the Euphrates positioned on cliffs high above the river, looking west across the Syrian plain towards the city of Palmyra. It was a large, bustling place protected by a curtain wall and towers. And it was just across the river from my father's kingdom. It had always been the domain of the king of kings of the empire.

I was lost for words, for this was indeed a great gift.

'I do not know what to say, majesty,' I stammered.

'Then say nothing,' replied the king, in no mood to indulge me, 'it is often better to stay silent.'

Dobbai sat in the chair next to Sinatruces and looked at us both. 'They will make a fine couple, Sinatruces, and he will be a great general for Parthia. Better a friend than a terrible foe, I think. You have made a wise decision. And the gods will be pleased with that decision.'

Sinatruces had had enough of our company and waved us away. We bowed and walked from the room.

'I am a king and you will be my queen,' I whispered to Gallia as I enclosed her hand in mine.

She suddenly stopped, turned and walked back to the dais. She bent down and kissed Sinatruces in the cheek, then asked one of the Scythians for his dagger. The man suspected foul play but Sinatruces was enraptured and waved his hand to get the fellow to acquiesce. Gallia took the blade and cut a lock of her hair, then placed it in the reptile-like hand of the king. Dobbai was delighted and clapped her hands. Gallia then walked back to me.

Dobbai called after us. 'Keep your sword blade sharp, young prince, for the eagles will come looking for you.'

'What does that mean?' asked Gallia.

'I have no idea, my love, but the words of that filthy old woman have a nasty habit of coming true.'

But in truth I did not care about the utterances of the old crone, for I had my beloved by my side and my own kingdom to rule. And I would have my own army to lead, and I would make that army the greatest in the whole of the Parthian Empire.

The next day we made preparations to leave Ctesiphon, for I felt that we had out-stayed our welcome. In any case I had no wish to see Sinatruces, who had lured us here on false pretences. Enius had come to see me earlier and had asked if we required an escort from the city, but I dismissed him curtly as I was strapping my saddle onto Remus back in front of the stables. Gallia and the others were likewise preparing for the journey back to Hatra, and she looked at me as the figure of Enius ambled away with hunched shoulders.

'That was rude.'

Remus was in a fidgety mood and wouldn't let me buckle up the last strap. 'Stay still.'

Gallia frowned. 'There's no need to take it out on your horse.'

'Take what out?'

'You're in a sulk, though I do not know why?'

'Do you not?'

'No. I was the one whom he wanted to imprison here and make one of his wives, not you.'

I gave up trying to fasten the strap and walked over to her. 'I would never have let that happen. Disgusting old man. He's eighty years old.'

Gallia put her arms round me and kissed my cheek. 'My gallant knight. Even if he had locked me up here I would have escaped back to you; no walls can keep me from you. But I'm not a prisoner, so there's no need to rebuke poor Remus for an old man's lust.'

She began stroking his neck, and after a couple of minutes had fastened his strap.

'A fine horse, young prince.'

I felt the cold rush of fear run down my spine as Dobbai spoke her words. I turned to see her walk from one of the stables. She grinned at Gallia and then once again took my love's hand.

'You are not going to say farewell to Sinatruces before you leave?'

'No,' I snapped.

'He is old and may not live to see you again.'

'Well,' said Gallia, 'I don't suppose it would hurt.'

'No!' I was insistent. 'I am a king now and not a boy to be ordered about. And this is my future wife, a princess in her own right and my future queen.'

Dobbia threw her head back and cackled loudly. Then she looked at Gallia. 'You see, my child, how quickly they are seduced by titles and positions. It is the doom of men. Well, let us talk no more of Sinatruces, for he is but a feeble old man.'

'He is also the king of kings,' remarked Gallia.

Dobbai cupped Gallia's cheek with her right hand. 'Yes, princess, he is, and he desired to make you his queen of queens, to rule as such when he had left this life. You hear that, son of Hatra? Had it been so, you would have been kneeling before her err long. But, my child, your destiny lies elsewhere. And now we come to it, for I have a message for you both.'

I had had enough. 'If it's from Sinatruces, then you can tell him…'

Dobbia let go of Gallia's hand, turned and glared at me, her eyes suddenly filled with rage and her face a visage of cold fury. 'Do not bandy words with me, boy. I have not come here to be lectured to, but to convey a message. So you will be quiet!'

I stood frozen to the spot, slightly alarmed that a frail old women had suddenly turned into a fierce demon. Then the anger in her eyes abated somewhat.

'Stand before me, both of you.'

Gallia moved to be beside me and I held her hand. Suddenly it felt as though we were the only two people left in the whole world, for our attention was fixed wholly on Dobbai, who now spoke to us in a calm, authoritative voice.

'She came to me last night in a dream. She said that she is pleased with you both, especially you, Pacorus. She told me that she is happy and you are not to worry about her, and that you must tell all your friends that this is so. She watched over you during your voyage to Parthia, and now that you are both safe she can go and join her husband with a happy heart.'

I felt Gallia's grip on my hand tighten.

'Her husband?' I enquired.

Dobbai smiled. 'Yes, son of Hatra, her husband; your lord and friend. For Claudia told me that you had fulfilled your oath to her by bringing her son to this land.'

I saw that Gallia had tears running down her cheeks. 'And she is happy, lady?'

'Yes, child,' replied Dobbai, 'for now she does not have to linger but can join her husband. You know his name, don't you, son of Hatra?'

I nodded and felt my mouth speak the name of my lord, my general and my friend.

'Spartacus.'

Epilogue

The villa of Marcus Licinius Crassus was bathed in autumn sunlight as Lucius Furius made his way up the Palatine Hill and entered the abode of his lord. Crassus had risen high since he had crushed the slave rebellion. He had come to Rome's aid when others had failed her, and had raised armies from his own pocket that had crushed Spartacus. The common people did grumble, though, about the smell caused by the crucified slaves, whose bodies along the Appian Way had been left to fester and rot for weeks, on the express orders of Crassus himself. Most had been picked clean by fat crows, but the sight and smell were unpleasant and there were frequent protests. In recognition of his achievements Crassus had been made consul, a post he shared with his rival General Pompey. The two men disliked each other intensely, but had seen fit to enter into an alliance to keep an eye on each other, as well as to ensure that Rome would not be weakened by civil strife. During the triumphs that had followed the crushing of the slave rebellion, Crassus had paid for ten thousand tables for the common people to feast off, and had also given them each a free gift of three months' supply of corn to fill their bellies. Such largesse made him very popular among the masses.

Lucius was shown into Crassus' study where he was seated opposite the consul and served wine. Crassus smiled at his young protégé, who still walked with a limp.

'How are you, Lucius?'

'Well, thank you consul.'

Crassus picked up a scroll that had been lying on his desk and passed it to the younger man.

'I thought you might be interested to see this. It arrived early today.'

Lucius took the parchment and unrolled it. The words were Latin.

'To Marcus Licinius Crassus.
Greetings.
It has been some time since our last meeting, and I thought out of politeness that I would update you on the state of affairs since I left Italy. The son of Spartacus is a fine young boy and continues to thrive in Parthia, where those who journeyed with me also enjoy a life of freedom and prosperity. I have heard that you have also prospered since our game of cat-and-mouse that we played in Italy. I am pleased for you and salute your fame. I trust that your high position among the people of Rome will satisfy your ambition and not tempt you to cast your eyes to the east, where a mighty

army stands ready to defend the Parthian Empire. Should this not be the case, I cannot promise that the same courtesy you extended me in allowing me to depart Italy unmolested will be extended to you and your legions should you be tempted to cross the Euphrates.
I wish you long life and happiness. May Shamash smile on you.
Your friend.
King Pacorus of Dura Europus.'

Lucius Furius threw the letter on the table. 'This is an outrage. What is Parthia but a collection of mud huts, bandits and renegades? They must be punished. He especially must be punished.'

Crassus sat back in his chair and observed Furius. He was fond of the young tribune; after all, his father had been a loyal supporter in the Senate. But his son had cost him a lot of money, not least the hundreds of horsemen he had lost during the slave rebellion.

'Lucius, your bravery and valour are undoubted. But a wise head is called for at this moment. It took us three years to crush Spartacus and his army, and in the last battle I lost nearly ten thousand dead and you lost all of your cavalry, if my memory serves me right. And now Pacorus, King Pacorus, has returned to his homeland where there are tens of thousands of horsemen who fight like him.'

Furius looked aghast. 'Then we do nothing?'

Crassus stood up and walked over to his balcony that overlooked the Tiber. 'No, Lucius. We take our time and make thorough preparations for our campaign to conquer the Parthian Empire.'

'And Pacorus?'

Crassus smiled to himself. 'I will bring him back to Rome in an iron cage.'

Printed in Great Britain
by Amazon